On *The Buckskin Line*

"Wonderfully satisfying, sophisticated, unsentimental, superbly crafted, and full of a whopping good humor out of Twain. Hard to beat."

—*Kirkus Reviews*

"Elmer Kelton has surely established himself as one of the grand masters of Western literature. A preeminent storyteller, Kelton has been blessed with the ability to create a cast of fictional characters which bring history to life with such honesty and believability that the reader himself literally becomes part of the story. And so it is with the author's latest offering, *The Buckskin Line*. . . . It is Kelton's understanding of human weaknesses and strengths that makes his writings so captivating. From this perspective, the reader is able to understand both sides of a conflict, thus gaining a quiet empathy with the challenges each character must face. *The Buckskin Line* is a fascinating new direction for Kelton's work, and one that is certain to have a sequel."

—*The El Paso Scene*

"Carefully researched and realistically presented. This picture of 1860s Texas, with its strong people, tells yet another good story about our state and our ancestors."

—*Austin American-Statesman*

On *Badger Boy*

"Award-winning writer Elmer Kelton—a star in the shrinking Western genre—totes you effortlessly to the post–Civil War Texas frontier, where white settlers were just learning to live with freed slaves, Comanches, and each other. . . . His characters, like Shannon, make mistakes, arc far from perfect, and take life in stride."

—*New York Post*

"In 1995, the Western Writers of America voted San Angelo's Elmer Kelton the best all-time crafter of Western-themed fiction. *Badger Boy* reinforces its author's already glittering reputation. . . . Kelton himself would disavow any pretension to literary greatness. What he does here, as always, is tell an entertaining story about the West. Longtime fans will be pleased, and newcomers to Kelton's work will realize what they've been missing."

—The San Jose Mercury News

"Kelton is a master of both plot and character development, and his Rusty Shannon is a down-to-earth, dusty cowboy whose exploits always thrill Kelton's fans."

—Publishers Weekly (starred review)

On *The Way of the Coyote*

"*The Way of the Coyote* stands as a testament to Elmer Kelton's consistently honest treatment of the times and people that he so obviously loves. Kelton demonstrates not only grasp of historical events but also an unerring sense of how these events affected the daily lives of ordinary people."

—Review of Texas Books

"As gratifying as a McMurtry side plot and with more gritty excitement than just about any Hollywood cowboy flick . . . Kelton covers a wide swath of history with aplomb . . . in this rough-riding adventure tale."

—Publishers Weekly (starred review)

"Elmer Kelton is a splendid writer. If you've somehow missed this master of the Western, try his new *Way of the Coyote*."

—The Dallas Morning News

"Kelton again lives up to his reputation as one of the finest and most prolific of today's Western authors."

—Abilene Reporter-News

Forge Books by Elmer Kelton

Badger Boy
Bitter Trail
The Buckskin Line
Buffalo Wagons
Cloudy in the West
Hot Iron
Jericho's Road
The Pumpkin Rollers
Ranger's Trail
The Smiling Country
The Texas Rifles
Texas Vendetta
The Way of the Coyote

Lone Star Rising
(comprising *The Buckskin Line*, *Badger Boy*, and *The Way of the Coyote*)

For Phyllis Travis —

three Texas Ranger stories —

Elmer Kelton

5/28/05

LONE
STAR
RISING

THE
TEXAS RANGERS
TRILOGY

ELMER
KELTON

 FORGE® A Tom Doherty
Associates Book
New York

LONE STAR RISING: THE TEXAS RANGERS TRILOGY

Copyright © 2003 by Elmer Kelton

The Buckskin Line copyright © 1999 by Elmer Kelton
Badger Boy copyright © 2001 by Elmer Kelton
The Way of the Coyote copyright © 2001 by Elmer Kelton

Book design by Milenda Nan Ok Lee

A Forge Book
Published by Tom Doherty Associates, LLC
175 Fifth Avenue
New York, NY 10010

www.tor.com

Forge® is a registered trademark of Tom Doherty Associates, LLC.

Library of Congress Cataloging-in-Publication Data

Kelton, Elmer.
    Lone star rising : the Texas Rangers trilogy / Elmer Kelton.
        p. cm.
    "A Forge book"—T.p. verso
    Contents: The buckskin line—Badger Boy—The way of the coyote.
    ISBN 0-765-31230-1
    EAN 978-0765-31230-3
    1. Texas Rangers—Fiction. 2. Texas—Fiction. 3. Historical fiction,
American. 4. Western stories. I. Title.

PS3561.E3975L64 2003
813'.54—dc21   2003046852

Printed in the United States of America

0 9 8 7 6 5 4 3 2

CONTENTS

THE
BUCKSKIN
Line

FOREWORD

The Alamo, the cowboy on horseback, the towering oil derrick are powerful Texas icons. Another, just as universally recognized, is the Texas Ranger. In the public imagination he is a mythic figure seven feet tall, unflinching in the face of danger, sticking to the trail through hell and high water until he gets his man. Folklore is replete with stories such as one about a single ranger being sent to quell a riot. One riot, one ranger.

In reality, of course, the ranger historically has been a common man with virtues and faults reflecting his time and the environment in which he lived. He has had courage and endurance when the need arose, but he has known frustration and uncertainty as well. Just the fact of his being a ranger has given him a moral advantage in confrontations, inspiring awe and fear in those who opposed him. On the other hand he has not been immune to mistakes in judgment. In reflecting the views and mores of his time he has sometimes been intolerant. He has sometimes been arbitrary.

In short, he was and is a human being.

He was not the first ranger in American history. Others came before him, such as Rogers's Rangers during the time of the revolution. The word *ranger* has implied someone who ranges widely and freely. Usually the term has been applied to keepers of the peace, though in Australia the "bush ranger" was an outlaw on the loose.

Texas's first rangers were a horseback force organized by colonizer Stephen F. Austin in 1823, when Texas still belonged to Mexico and Americans there were scarce. The rangers' primary duty was to protect colonists from Indian raiders, though they were instrumental in putting down the ill-conceived Fredonian rebellion of 1825, a less-than-honorable prelude to Texas's revolution against Mexico.

A small ranger force existed during the revolution, primarily serving as scouts for Sam Houston's army. They helped refugees escape into Louisiana during the so-called runaway scrape when it appeared that Mexican General Santa Anna's troops would overrun all of Texas and repeat the wholesale slaughter already demonstrated at the Alamo and Goliad.

Texas won its freedom from Mexico in the Battle of San Jacinto and the capture of Santa Anna. During the ten years that it was an independent republic it faced not only a constant threat of Indian raids but also Mexico's attempts to reinvade and regain possession of its former province. The rangers remained in service, their fortunes rising and falling with the ups and downs of the new nation's meager treasury and the vagaries of its politicians.

Though authorized by the Texas Congress, the rangers during that time were more like a loose local militia than the centralized professional force they would eventually become. There was no uniform, not even an official badge to demonstrate their authority. Pay was low and often deferred, sometimes not delivered at all. Enlistments were limited to comparatively short periods, usually in response to a specific Indian raid or prospect of hostilities. Ranger turnover was high.

From the time of the republic until the chaos of the Civil War, ranger energy was largely devoted to Indian fighting. The larger tribes were considered hostile, especially Comanches and Kiowas, in the western and central part of the state, and Apaches, in the southwestern and extreme western part. They frequently raided the settlements of Texas and northern Mexico, running off with horses and mules, taking scalps when and wherever they could. Reckless was the frontier farmer who went to his fields unarmed.

The rangers set up outposts beyond the settlements, constantly guarding against Indian incursions. This buckskin line was Texas's first line of defense. When the line was breached, the rangers often led local volunteers in pursuit of the invaders, occasionally following them far into Indian strongholds.

In 1840, a peace conference between Comanche chiefs and Texans turned ugly. The Council House Fight burst out into the streets of San Antonio and caused heavy casualties on both sides. A thirst for vengeance led to a huge and unprecedented Comanche raid all the way to the Gulf of Mexico. In the port town of Linnville, white survivors of the surprise attack jumped into rowboats and fled out into the surf, pursued by Indians on horseback. The devastated town never recovered. However, rangers and area volunteers followed the retreating raiders. Though badly outnumbered, they surprised and routed the invaders in a reckless counterattack at Plum Creek.

That is where this story begins.

PROLOGUE

The Texas Rangers had their beginnings in 1823, when land impresario Steven F. Austin raised a volunteer company of ten men to act in defense of his colony in Mexican Texas. Rangers served during the decade of the Texas Republic and rode alongside the United States Army in the war against Mexico. Later in the years before and during the Civil War, volunteers manned a ragged picket line along the western frontier, guarding against Indian incursions. They had no official title but were commonly called rangers or ranging companies, minutemen, or spies.

During Reconstruction they were disbanded and replaced by a state police force, which did some good work but was badly stained by internal corruption and unwarranted cruelties. When the Confederate Texans finally regained the right to vote they dissolved the hated state police.

The reorganized state legislature created two battalions of Texas Rangers in 1874, giving them for the first time their official name and the famous star-in-a-circle badge, which was to become the stuff of legend.

This is a story of the early days, when small companies of poorly paid, poorly fed volunteers in homespun cloth and buckskin rode an unmarked frontier line for a primitive Texas that had only a toenail hold on survival. They had no uniform, no badge, not even an official name.

But they had a job to do, and against all odds they managed to do it.

The story begins with one of the most unlikely events in early Texas history, the great Comanche raid that led to the sacking of Linnville town on the shores of the Gulf of Mexico.

CHAPTER
ONE

He was Comanche, and he was known among The People as Buffalo Caller. Once in a time of hunger, when he was a fledgling on one of his first hunts, the older and more experienced men had ridden their horses to exhaustion without scaring up so much as one lone, lame bull. But Buffalo Caller, riding alone, had heard a faint and distant bellow. He had responded in the voice of a buffalo, and the buffalo had answered him. The calls led him to a small herd in a hidden canyon.

It was not buffalo he hunted now. He scouted as a wolf for the largest assembly of raiders the Penateka band had ever put together, moving to strike the land-greedy, hair-faced American settlers of Texas. Beside him against the Texans rode Swift as the Antelope, so named for his fleetness of foot.

Buffalo Caller tingled with excitement over the sights he was about to behold. He had never seen an ocean or even a boat, so it strained his imagination to visualize what old men had described around their campfires. If the veterans had not let fanciful dreams overcome the realities of memory, those wonders lay no more than half a day's horseback journey ahead of him. It was claimed that the great water stretched so far one could not see all the way across. None of The People had ever ventured out upon it to determine how far it extended, for they were of the land, not of the sea. It was said that white men's boats might travel for many days without touching shore and that fish larger than horses lived in the dark and frightening depths.

Buffalo Caller doubted much of what he had heard. It sounded typical of the white *teibos'* lies. He had forded many rivers, and he had visited lakes wider than the rivers, but none were so wide that he could not see the opposite side.

Where he rode now was far to the south and east of the short-grass prairie and the limestone hill hunting grounds he was accustomed to roaming. A journey of many days had brought the massive Comanche war column into a gently rolling land of sandy soil and tall, summer-cured grass much different from the higher, drier land the Penatekas claimed as home. The hot, humid wind carried a smell foreign to his experience and left a faint suggestion of salt upon his lips. Summer heat sent sweat rolling down from beneath his buffalo-horn headdress and into his paint-streaked face, burning his eyes.

The foreignness of this land made him uneasy despite the persistent gnawing of curiosity. Though he wanted to see the great water for himself, he would be relieved when they finished what they came to do so they could return to country more suited to his experience.

What they were about was vengeance, blood for blood. In the early spring many tribal leaders and warriors had met with white chiefs in San Antonio de Béjar's council house to discuss an earlier agreement by the Comanches to free all their captives. Some had reconsidered the promise and balked, holding out for stronger terms. Talk had led to quarrel, and quarrel to the loosing of arrows and an explosion of gunfire. When the smoke drifted away, more than thirty Indians lay dead and dying in the council house and in the foul dirt of San Antonio's narrow streets.

In retaliation The People had killed most of the remaining white captives, but those had not bled enough to wash away the stain of the San Antonio disaster. The indignant Penatekas had undertaken this huge punitive expedition, carrying them far beyond their normal range, all the way eastward to the Gulf of Mexico. He did not know how many of The People were on this grand adventure. He had attempted to count them on his fingers and thumbs, but the task overwhelmed him. They were so many that they defied his understanding of numbers. Their horses left the grass beaten down and the ground scarred in their wake like the slow passage of a large buffalo herd. Though the object was war, many women and children had come along to watch and cheer as their warriors carried calamity to the white enemy.

Mexican allies guided them, for they knew the route. They knew how to pick their way through the sparsely settled region and avoid detection until time for the great force to loose its thunder and lightning. Buffalo caller understood that the Americans had won this land from the Mexicans in a fierce war. Mexico wanted to take it back and had sent emissaries to the tribes, promising many good things in return for their aid. Buffalo Caller cared nothing for Mexico, for the first raid in which he had ridden had been against Mexicans. He had fought them often and had killed many. But he welcomed any chance to strike the Texans. A temporary alliance with a former adversary was justifiable if it promised victory over an enemy hated even more.

Antelope pulled up on his rawhide reins. "The wind brings the smell of smoke." He raised his head, sniffing, testing.

Antelope was notoriously subject to quick judgments and quick action without considering where they might lead. Buffalo Caller smelled only dust, for the ground was so dry it had cracked open in places. The soil would all be up and moving on the wind were it not bound by a heavy stand of brittle grass, the result of last spring's rains. He drew the skin taut at the edge of his right eye, trying to sharpen his vision. He decided Antelope was right, this time. "I think I see a house. It is beyond the timber, there."

His companion thumped the heels of his moccasins against his mount's ribs, putting him into a trot. "If they have horses, we shall take them."

Buffalo Caller feared that Antelope's zeal would make him forget their real mission. "Taking horses is not what you and I have been sent to do."

The principal concern so far had been to avoid premature detection as the army of warriors moved along. The wolves were to overtake and kill any whites who might observe their passage before the trap was sprung. That precaution seemed less important now because scouts had reported that the town of Victoria lay only a short distance ahead. The Americans would soon know of the column's coming. One Mexican guide had lived in Victoria until the Texans drove him out, and he itched for retribution. Victoria had been chosen as the first target.

Buffalo Caller recognized Antelope's determination. He relented, knowing Antelope would do whatever he wanted, regardless of advice to the contrary. "If we find horses, there is no reason they should not be ours." He set his dun horse into a trot that matched Antelope's pace.

Antelope grunted. "If we find any *teibos*, we will take their scalps as well as their horses." His taste for vengeance was strong. A brother's blood had soaked into the floor of the San Antonio council house.

"So long as we do not leave our own."

Emerging from a small patch of timber, they saw a man afoot in a cornfield, wielding a curved knife to cut heads from the stalks, tossing them into the bed of a wagon drawn by two horses. His back turned, he did not see the warriors' approach.

Antelope said, "You take the horses. I will take the man."

Not until he heard the hooves did the farmer turn. He wasted a long moment frozen in startled disbelief as the two Comanches rushed down upon him; then he ran for the rail fence. Antelope's arrow struck him in the middle of his back. He fell forward onto his face. The warrior leaped from his horse, vaulted over the low fence, and knelt beside the dying man, slicing a patch of scalp with his knife. Buffalo Caller saw no need for undue haste. He climbed over the fence and cut the two horses loose from the wagon. They were docile. What human beings did to one another concerned them little.

Antelope raised the bloody trophy for Buffalo Caller to observe, then looked toward the log cabin. "There may be others."

Whoever was at the house might have a rifle or shotgun. Buffalo Caller saw none here. This was far from normal Comanche range, and the once-formidable Karankawas native to this region had been reduced to a pitiable scattered few. The farmer probably had seen no reason to burden himself with a weapon in the field. "We have the horses. That is what we came for."

Antelope insisted, "If you leave one wasp, it will rebuild the nest."

"But if they fire upon us, we must leave. We can do no good for anyone if we are dead." It was not that he feared death. A warrior who died in battle was promised a happy afterlife. But the life he was living here gave him pleasure, for he was yet young, and so were his two wives. He would enjoy this life as long as he could. The next would endure forever, so he was in no hurry to begin it.

They approached by way of the barn, larger than the cabin and built of rough boards instead of logs. His gaze was focused on the house, for if there was to be trouble it would come from there. Antelope touched his arm and pointed in silence. Beneath a roof that extended beyond the barn, a woman sat on a stool, milking a cow. Like the man, she faced away from the Indians and was unaware of them.

The two warriors slipped down from their horses and moved toward a log fence that separated them from the barn. Buffalo Caller climbed to the top and swung his legs over. A log cracked beneath his weight. Startled, the woman looked around, saw him, and jumped to her feet, spilling the bucket of milk. With a cry of fear, she ran to the barn door and turned, a pitchfork in her hands.

Buffalo Caller had never seen a pitchfork and did not know what use it was meant for, but he recognized that the sharp steel tines could pierce like a lance. She made a threatening gesture, thrusting the fork toward him. She shouted, but her words meant nothing. White people's talk was like the grunting of their stinking pigs.

He entertained the thought of taking her along, for his wives would welcome a slave woman to lift some of labor's weight from their shoulders. Too, he had never taken a *teibo* woman into his blankets, and he wondered how different one might be. But she came at him with the pitchfork, and he had no choice. He fitted an arrow to the bowstring and drove it into her heart. She died quickly, with little sound and little struggle.

He had noticed from the first that her hair was reddish, like the hair of a buffalo calf. He knelt over her and lifted a strand of it, wondering if she might have colored it somehow. But none of the color came off on his fingers, so he decided it was natural. It would be a great curiosity when he showed it to his friends. He made a wide circle with the keen blade of his knife, wanting to keep as much of the hair as he could. He placed his foot on her back and pulled on the scalp. It tore free with a sucking sound.

He heard a movement in the barn and turned quickly, bringing another arrow out of the quiver. He stopped, for in the doorway stood a small boy with hair redder than his mother's. Buffalo Caller could only stare.

Antelope spoke from behind him. "Are you frightened of a baby? I will kill him for you if you are afraid."

"I am not afraid, but I have never seen hair of such a color, not on a human being." He recognized that the Americans were humans, though of a lesser order. The Comanches were the real people, the True Human Beings.

Antelope said, "The Texans have hair of all colors." He brought out his knife and moved toward the child.

Buffalo Caller blocked his path. "My wives have given me only girl babies so far. I will take this boy for a son."

"And carry him into the fight? He will be a burden."

"But I can teach him to be a good hunter. He could keep us from hunger when we are old."

"A white-skinned Penateka with hair like fire? Who ever saw such a thing?"

"The buffalo will not care about the color of his hair."

The People had often taken Mexican children and raised them as their own. Captives helped offset the death rate caused by war and by accidents during the hunt. Since Americans had begun moving into Penateka lands, a sprinkling of lighter-skinned children had also appeared in the lodges. Most who survived the trauma of the first weeks would assimilate into the tribe. In time a majority would forget their past lives and become as Comanche-born.

Antelope argued, "We should kill him. The color of his hair is like blood. It could sour our medicine."

"What has hair to do with medicine?"

The boy looked in bewilderment at his mother's body. He whimpered as Buffalo Caller picked him up and tucked him under his right arm.

Antelope said, "I cannot tolerate a squalling child." He touched the handle of his bloodstained knife. "If he cries, I will cut his throat."

Buffalo Caller shifted the boy to his left arm and drew his own knife. "You will have to cut mine first." It was unthinkable that one of The People might kill another, but he would inflict grievous pain with the blade if Antelope made it necessary.

His companion backed off. "Then do not let him cry."

"This one is too brave to cry. Now let us go. We do not want to miss the big fight."

"First I will burn the house." Antelope's eyes pinched in warning. "If you are wise, you will kill that red-haired boy."

Buffalo Caller tightened his hold on the youngster. "Go on. Set your fire."

Buffalo Caller had seen white-man towns before. He had visited San Antonio in his early youth, riding boldly up and down its streets, challenging any and all to come out and fight him. It was a way of demonstrating his bravery to other young men in the event any might have doubted it. No townsman had accepted the challenge face-to-face, but Buffalo Caller proudly bore the scar of a bullet wound inflicted by some coward who hid inside a doorway to shoot him. When he painted himself for ceremony or battle he always made a black circle around the scar so everyone would see and know that bullets did not easily kill him. For a fighter, scars were marks of honor.

The column crossed a creek north of Victoria and paused while warriors took time to paint themselves and their mounts for battle. The paint carried strong medicine and helped ward off bullets. Buffalo Caller had turned his small captive over to the care of his younger wife, Whippoorwill. While women and children waited, the warriors split to make a circle around the town. Buffalo Caller saw no sign that the raiders' approach had aroused alarm. That surprised him. He could only surmise that the column had been mistaken for something other than what it was. It was known that members of the Lipan tribe sometimes visited the town for friendly barter, and Mexican horse traders came occasionally with large *caballadas* to barter or sell.

A shout from one of the chiefs traveled quickly around the circle, picked up and relayed by other voices. The charge began with high-pitched yelling and a thunder of hoofbeats as warriors urged their horses into a run. Not until then did the town's citizens begin to realize they were under attack. The first resistance was a scattering of gunfire from buildings on the outskirts. That resistance soon mushroomed into desperate firing from the more central part of town. Warriors and horses began to falter and fall. Despite the Texans' slowness to recognize their danger, they put up a strong and costly defense.

Buffalo Caller brought his horse to a quick stop after a bullet passed his ear, singing like a locust, then whining off the stone wall of a house. He saw his companions beginning to pull back. It seemed prudent to follow. Only someone who had yet to prove his valor or who valued glory above life would willingly plunge into a hailstorm of bullets fired by determined men hidden behind walls that arrows could not penetrate.

He did not have to prove his courage anew. This was not a day he would choose to die. There was yet much he had not seen.

Someone shouted that horses had been found just outside of town. Buffalo Caller withdrew from the siege. Though he had come for blood vengeance on the Americans, he would also be pleased to take their horses.

He was amazed at the number. Mexicans had been loose-herding several hundred on the prairie before recognizing their danger and fleeing into the protection of the town. Buffalo Caller guessed they had brought the horses to trade or sell. He would not have expected this welcome bonanza. With enthusiasm he pitched into the rounding up of these horses and many others from nearby farms. By the time the gathering was done, the horse and mule herd had grown to tremendous proportions. Moving, it raised a towering cloud of dust, like an early-spring windstorm out of the west.

Even if the invaders were to turn back now, this had been a most profitable venture.

Others in the band had killed several men unfortunate enough to fall into their path and had stolen a white woman and her baby. After camping along a creek that night, they continued on their way, driving the great band of captured horses and mules. They came upon two men in a wagon, killing one but somehow losing the other despite a diligent search.

The white woman's baby began to cry. The impatient Antelope wrested it from its mother's arms and impaled it on a spear. The baby quivered and died while the woman screamed.

Buffalo Caller thought that a regrettable waste. The child might have grown up to be useful. He did not feel pity for mother or child, however. Both were Texan, and pity on an enemy was a dangerous indulgence for a warrior. An enemy spared was an enemy who might have to be faced again another day.

Linnville was a small but prosperous seaport, its several warehouses holding goods brought in by ship for wagon and cart transport to such inland towns as San Antonio and Nacogdoches.

As had been the case at Victoria, the townspeople took little notice of the approaching warriors. Buffalo Caller guessed the huge horse and mule herd had misled them into assuming the visitors were traders like the Mexicans at Victoria, bringing animals to barter or sell.

Citizens of the town began to shout and scream as they belatedly recognized the disaster thundering down upon them. They were too late to mount a defense the way those in Victoria had done. By dozens they scrambled toward the shore. Men, women, and children ran in desperation. They piled into small boats tied to the wooden pier and frantically rowed away into the sea.

Farther out, Buffalo Caller saw what appeared to be a large house floating, a curl of black smoke rising from its tall chimney. Beyond the steamship, he could see nothing but water and more water, endless to the horizon, reflecting the sunlight and burning his eyes. He stared in wonder. People had told him of such strange things, wooden houses that sat atop the water, but he had never quite believed them.

He saw warriors kill a white man and drag two struggling women out of a boat, one white and one whose skin was black. They also captured a child.

Antelope shouted, "Too many are getting away." He forced his horse out into the surf, trying to catch one of the boats and its shrieking passengers. Buffalo Caller followed so far that the water rose up and soaked his moccasins, chilling his feet. He loosed a couple of arrows, but the boats bobbed like fallen leaves on the waves, and the stone-tipped shafts fell harmlessly into the gulf. He chose to waste no more, though Antelope kept trying. Buffalo Caller turned back, for the town lay open and defenseless, awaiting the raiders' pleasure. Several townspeople lay dead in the streets, caught and killed before they could reach the boats.

Buffalo Caller moved toward a large building a short distance from the docks. The Mexican guides had promised that the warehouses would be full of goods wondrous beyond imagination. The People could take whatever they wanted and be welcome to it. There was no shame in stealing from Texans, the biggest thieves of all.

Some of the boats went all the way out to the ship that lay offshore. Others stopped and simply floated along out of range, their passengers watching helplessly while the town fell to the invaders like wild plums dropping from a tree.

Warriors who had followed them into the surf turned back to begin a joyous plundering of homes and warehouses. Buffalo Caller entered a store and marveled at the variety of treasures it offered. He had tasted apples in San Antonio, and he found a barrelful here. He bit eagerly into one while he searched the store for other delights. On the shelves he found rolls of cloth, some plain, others in bright colors. Antelope joined him, shouting in glee as he yanked down a bolt of red material and began to unfold it, wrapping it around his shoulders and waist. He picked up a stovepipe hat and jammed it onto his head, bending the feather he wore tied into his braided black hair.

Buffalo Caller thought Antelope looked ridiculous. He would not trade his buffalo headdress for all the hats in the store. But he carried out an armload of cloth he was sure would please his wives. A long string of red ribbon stretched behind him.

He began smelling smoke. Other warriors were setting fire to houses as they finished their looting.

The Comanches celebrated high carnival, sacking and burning while frustrated townspeople witnessed the destruction from sanctuary far out on the water. Late in the afternoon, wearying warriors began to draw away. They had packed many of the captured horses and mules with goods taken from Linnville homes, stores, and warehouses. Buffalo Caller laughed at the sight of a mule with ribbons tied in its tail, kicking at a bolt of blue cloth that dragged in the dust behind. Many of the men wore white-man clothes and hats of various descriptions. The wind tugged at several open umbrellas.

Antelope had placed a hat on his horse's head after cutting slits so it would fit over the ears. It was proper that the horse wear a Texan hat, he said, for it had been taken from a Texan corral west of San Antonio.

Hardly a building remained intact. Most not already burned to the ground were ablaze now as the raiders retreated. A heavy pall of dark smoke hung over the town. Linnville would be little but ashes and ruin when its citizens mustered courage to row back from the sea. Then they would know the true price of Texan treachery.

It mattered not that the people here probably had nothing to do with what happened in the San Antonio council house. They were white. In the eyes of The People, vengeance against one enemy was vengeance against all. They had no patience with individual responsibility, separating the guilty from the innocent. All their enemies were guilty.

Buffalo Caller noted that the head of the column was moving in a northwesterly direction. That pleased him. In a few days he would be back in the familiar and pleasant surroundings of his own country. He had gazed upon the big water once, had felt its wetness and tasted its salt. His own eyes had witnessed a great house that floated upon the sea. He had not seen the fish as large as horses, but he had seen enough. His curiosity was satisfied.

He thought of the boy he had taken and the pleasure a son would bring to his lodge, even one whose hair was red. It was time now to go home, to enjoy the fruits of conquest. It was time for dancing and celebration, for the proud telling of great and daring deeds.

CHAPTER

TWO

Warren Webb enjoyed riding alongside Michael Shannon on the wagon road to Linnville. The jovial farmer was pleasant company, never short of stories to tell. It mattered not whether they were totally true or were partly a construction of an imagination enriched by Shannon's thirty years or so of drifting from Tennessee across Arkansas and Louisiana and finally down the Texas coast. He had entered into every conflict he could reach, however far it might have been out of his way. Mike Shannon had never seen a fight he did not want to mix into, bringing all the gusto other men put into games and horse races.

Though summer heat made each mile seem like two, conversation helped relieve the weight of fatigue. And if Shannon's speech easily lapsed into the profane, that too afforded its guilty pleasures. For Webb to use such language would be unseemly if not actually forbidden by the Scriptures. He was a circuit-riding minister whose small farm was sadly neglected because of the travel requirements of his higher calling. Coming from someone else, a little profanity offered a tantalizing hint of wickedness, a minor and harmless rebellion he found refreshing. Shannon seemed little inhibited by the fact that his riding companion was a man of the cloth who carried the Word far past the forks of the creek where settlers could not afford a live-there preacher.

He said, "'y God, Preacher Webb, this country is gettin' so choked up with people, they'll pretty soon be stumblin' all over one another. I'm studyin' on movin' west, out on the Colorado River. There's land to be had there, not half so dear as this on the coast."

Shannon did not own the tract he plowed. He simply squatted on unclaimed land, using it until he tired of it or a rightful owner came along to take possession from him and his wife. In such a way had generations of poor farmers progressed slowly westward from the Alleghenies to the Ohio Valley and across the Mississippi into Texas, amassing little of the world's goods but incurring little in the way of debt and obligation. They could plant and harvest a crop, then leave when the spirit moved them or a real owner came along with the deed. Shannon had already done that more than once, though he was little if any older than Webb, and Webb would be thirty come October.

For many, squatting was a means of survival in a country where cash was a stranger to most men's pockets. Now and then a farmer might roll up his sleeves and fight when someone came to move him, but most accepted their lot and looked to the west, confident that they would soon find a better place. It was a melancholy fact of life that trailblazers rarely profited like those who followed in their tracks. One sowed. Another reaped.

Webb would miss having Shannon around. "Surely you'd not depart our midst before you've harvested your crop."

"And leave the fruits of my labor for somebody who never broke a sweat? Old Mother Shannon never raised no halfwit sons, 'y God. I figure we'll leave in the fall and locate us a place. I'll break the land this winter and have her ready to seed in the spring."

Webb understood the pioneer wanderlust, for he harbored a liberal case of it himself. It had caused him to leave his boyhood home in Alabama and had brought him by fits and starts to the Republic of Texas after the revolution against Mexico. "I'd not mind followin' after you, Mike. I've an itch to be seein' new country."

"Come with us, then. There's fever in this low ground, and I've noted that you've got an unhealthy cough. There's others movin' out yonder. Where there's people there's a need for somebody to teach the ways of the Lord, lest they go heathen."

Shannon was right. Webb's lungs sometimes ached, and often he felt himself short of strength. He was tall of frame but so thin he sometimes wondered how he managed to cast a decent shadow. He attributed his condition to the humidity and smothering heat of this region near the Gulf of Mexico. A higher elevation should be better for his health.

Shannon said, "It ain't good to stay in one place too long—dulls a man. You wear out one farm, you move on to another. That's what the Lord put the land here for."

"I don't know that He meant for us to wear it out."

"He must've, 'y God, because He gave us so much. There ain't no end to it." Shannon made a broad sweep with his arm toward a horizon flat and endless.

For a while Webb had been aware of a tan cloud hovering low in the northeast. He had first thought it might be a dust storm, because the weather had turned dry of late, but it occurred to him that the wind did not seem strong enough to raise that much dust. Besides, the cloud appeared localized, moving slowly westward.

Shannon thought along similar lines. "Kind of odd doin's yonder, don't you think?"

Webb had seen large horse herds stir dust like that, but this seemed an out-of-the-way place for traders to be taking a remuda, away from the major settlements. "Might be a group of immigrants, strayed off of the main trail to look for grass."

"If so, maybe they're in the mood to hear the Word, and might be me and you could get us a woman-cooked meal."

"You had a woman-cooked breakfast this mornin'. Your Dora is as good a cook as ever I ate after."

"But I can't remember the last time I had a cup of real coffee that wasn't stretched out with parched grain. Maybe them folks have got some."

Webb had intended to be at the Linnville settlement by dark, but he supposed tomorrow would be soon enough. If these people were in need of preaching, it was his obligation to offer it. "Let's go see about that coffee."

First sight of the horses aroused a strange sense of foreboding, a queasy feeling of finding himself in the wrong place. "Did you ever see so many in one bunch, Mike?"

Shannon hauled up on the leather reins. Ordinarily given to shrugging off life's everyday aggravations with an easy "Aw, what the hell?" he appeared suddenly alarmed. "Somethin' queer-lookin' about this. They ain't no traders, and they ain't no movers. What they are is Indians, 'y God!"

Webb could not believe this at first. The only Indians he had seen this near the coast had been small gatherings of Tonkawas, the poorest, raggedest people he had ever encountered, come to barter or beg. Folks said they could be ferocious as hungry wolves against their enemies the Comanches, and that they even had cannibalistic tendencies. To him they had appeared harmless except for a little sticky-fingered thievery.

These were not Tonkawas.

Shannon said, "I hope you have favor in the eyes of your Maker. He'd better not let them see us before we get into that timber yonder."

Webb thought it prudent to be running while he consulted the Lord. He applied his spurs and drew his rifle from its long scabbard beneath his leg.

It seemed impossible that they were not discovered, but the passing Indians gave no sign they had noticed.

Shannon said, "They think we're part of their bunch."

"Our clothes and hats ought to tell them different."

Shannon turned for another squint-eyed look. "A lot of them are wearin' hats, too. The store-bought kind, and I'd bet you a U.S. dollar they didn't buy them."

A few wore coats as well, despite the summer heat. A couple had them on backward, buttons in the rear. Many horses and mules were laden with blankets and bolts of cloth.

Trophies of war, proudly displayed.

Shannon tried to make a rough count but gave it up. "Looks to me like there's a couple thousand horses and mules, and maybe a thousand Indians. Odd thing is, they've got squaws and children with them."

"But who are they? Where'd they come from?"

"Comanches, and I'd guess they're fresh from lootin' the hell out of some place. Headin' back to their own country now, most likely."

"God pity any poor souls they happen upon along their way."

Shannon frowned, mulling on that thought. "There's some farms out yonder, the direction they're travelin'. They'll gobble up them folks like wolves gobble a rabbit."

"We could circle around ahead of them and give warnin'. How's your faith?"

"Strong enough, long as I'm ridin' with a preacher. The Lord ain't goin' to let nothin' happen to you."

The column inched along, the animals traveling in a walk. Webb could see women and children. Were it not for the evidence of loot being carried away, he might take this for a tribe peacefully moving from one hunting ground to another. He saw no outriders, though it stood to reason there must be some somewhere. "They don't seem to be in a hurry or worried about anybody jumpin' them."

Shannon said, "I'd feel safe too, if I was them. It'd take an army to jump a bunch the size of that."

Riding at an angle away from the Indian column, the two remained within the cover of the timber to its southern edge. Webb looked back. "We ought to be far enough now." He set his horse into a long trot, paralleling the Comanches.

Shannon spurred alongside him, glancing warily in one direction, then the other. "They didn't pick all them doodads and all them horses and mules off of the trees. I'd wager they've left a string of dead folks behind them."

"First we need to look after the ones still alive. I'll pray for the others when I have the time."

At the first farm they found a man and his wife working in a garden just south of a log cabin. The farmer listened to their report with suspicion. "A bunch of Indians that size don't seem likely. You sure you don't just see them in a bottle?"

The farmer's wife seemed to believe right off. She brought her hands to her mouth to stifle a cry.

Shannon was not inclined toward patience when calamity bore down. "I been known to sip a little whiskey now and again; but Brother Webb don't drink, nor is he given to lyin'. Take a look at that dust comin' yonder. It ain't no sea breeze, 'y God."

The urgency in Shannon's voice began to temper the farmer's skepticism. "But Comanches, this close to the coast? Must be a bunch of Tonks, or maybe Karankawas."

"There ain't that many Karankawas in the whole nation. Wouldn't make no difference anyway. One'll kill you as dead as the other. You've got to get out of here."

The farmer at last believed, and with belief he reached a state bordering on panic. "Martha! Get the young'uns ready. I'll hitch up the team."

The woman rushed screaming into the cabin. Webb and Shannon helped the farmer harness his mules and saddle his horse. Webb boosted the woman up onto the seat while Shannon lifted three frightened children into the bed of the wagon.

The farmer pointed. "You'll find the Johnson family over that-away where you see that stand of trees. Old Man Blessing and his boys are a mile or so further on. They're the last ones I know of in that direction." He put his horse into a run, trying to catch up to the fast-moving wagon. The woman was applying the whip, and the children clung desperately to the wagon's sideboards to keep from being bounced out.

The Johnsons required no persuasion. Webb had known the young family at camp meeting, and they accepted his word. Their only question was which direction they should run. They wasted little time gathering up a few possessions and quitting their place.

Shannon watched them with regret. "Ain't apt to be much left here when they come back."

"There'll be the land."

Abner Blessing was a towering, rawboned farmer whose broad shoulders appeared to sag under their own weight. Webb had once heard him declare that he had "fit Injuns all over hell and half of Georgia" before coming to Texas. He was ready to take these on. The Blessings had built their cabin of stone, befitting a family of great strength. He pointed to his three grown sons, all rough-cut out of raw oak, in his image. "Me and my boys ain't givin' up our place. We'll take our stand behind them stone walls."

Webb argued, "You'd just as well try to wipe out a hornet's nest with a sharp stick. I don't doubt your fightin' spirit, Mr. Blessing, but you know what happened at the Alamo."

"Them fellers killed a heap of Mexicans."

"But they lost the battle."

"Me and the boys, we've worked hard to build what we've got here." Reluctantly Blessing turned to his sons. "Tom, Bert, Jim . . . go gather the horses and mules. Them varmints may burn the house, but be damned if they'll add our stock to their string." The young men hastened to comply. Shannon moved to help them. Blessing said, "I hate to leave here without a fight. Where you reckon them red devils've been?"

Webb could only shrug. "They were comin' from the direction of Linnville when we saw them."

"Linnville." The farmer clenched his fists, his knuckles bulging like pine knots. "I've got a sister there, and her family. You don't reckon . . ."

"I don't know."

Misery came into the man's blue eyes, followed by a building anger. "Everybody can't just up and run. There's bound to be somebody with the guts to stand and fight."

"Maybe, if the Comanches didn't leave everybody dead behind them."

"Maybe me and the boys can put some fightin' men together. There's four of us to start."

"Six. Mike and me, we'll go with you." Webb looked to Shannon for silent confirmation.

They struck southward, driving the family's extra horses and mules several miles before they came upon a brush-lined creek. Blessing told his sons, "Scatter the stock down in there. I doubt the redskins'll come this far off of their line of march."

That done, he said, "Let's be headin' for Linnville." He led off without waiting for argument. Webb offered none, and Shannon seemed as eager as Blessing for a fight.

They pushed their horses into a lope for short distances, then slowed to a trot to conserve the mounts' strength. Webb could see the cloud of dust to the north, marking the location of the Comanche column.

The oldest of the Blessing boys, Tom, drew up on the reins. "Listen. I think I hear shootin'."

Webb first thought the Indians might have caught one of the families he and Shannon had warned. But he decided that was not the case; the sound indicated many guns.

The elder Blessing said, "Somebody's done lit into them. Come on, boys, or we're liable to miss the fight." He spurred off toward the dust. His sons struggled to catch up.

Webb gave Shannon a questioning glance. Shannon said, "Hell, Preacher, who wants to live to get old and decrepit?"

They never managed to close the distance between themselves and the Blessings, but presently through the dust they could see a back-and-forth surging of men and horses. Rifles and pistols snapped in a desultory manner. Webb reined up, for he wanted to grasp the full situation before riding into the middle of it. He saw a large company of white men dismounted, shooting at horseback Indians who circled them. Farther ahead, the main column of Comanches hurried away with their women and children, their horse and mule herd, while this detached set of warriors fought a delaying action.

Blessing and his sons had halted, watching the fight from two hundred yards. Uncertainty held the big farmer back, though he chafed to ride headlong into the scrap. "We'd probably all get killed if we was to try to break through. Maybe we can do them fellers more good from out here."

Shannon said, "At least, 'y God, we can give them devils somethin' else to be worryin' about."

The men dismounted. Webb tied a knot in the end of his split leather reins and slipped them over his arm so the horse could not easily jerk away. He dropped to one knee and aimed his rifle as he heard shots fired on either side of him. After the flash, a white cloud of smoke blossomed around the barrel. He could not see if he had hit anything.

Some of the Indians immediately split off and charged toward the six men. Anticipating this, two of the Blessing boys had held their fire. While four reloaded, the pair took their time in firing. A horse went down, and the charge broke up. The Indians zig-zagged in a rough circle, reconsidering. By the time they decided to rush again, the reloaded guns blazed a second volley. One of the Indians fell from his horse. The others halted, two grabbing him between them, carrying him back toward the main group.

Soon the larger column had moved well beyond the skirmish. The nearby Indians broke their circle and began to travel slowly in a westerly direction. Those who had firearms kept shooting back in the direction of their adversaries. The company of white men continued firing toward them. The range became too great for accuracy by either side.

Shannon said, "Looks like they've had enough entertainment for a while. Let's go see how the boys yonder made out."

A rough count told Webb that the company was made up of more than a hundred men. Most had managed to hang on to their horses through the fight, though a few animals were wounded and at least a couple lay dead.

A horseman rode out to meet the six incoming riders. "Welcome, men. You almost missed the skirmish."

Webb thought he knew the face. "Seems to me I've seen you at camp meetin'."

The man nodded. "You're a preacher, as I recollect. We're volunteers out of Victoria. We've followed this bunch all the way from Linnville."

Blessing pressed, "Linnville? What happened there?"

"They took the town by surprise. Killed several folks, burned down just about everything. Ain't much left but ashes."

Blessing swore, mostly under his breath. "I have a sister in Linnville."

"Most of the people got away in boats. Like as not she did, too. The dead were mostly menfolks, I think. They tarried too long, fightin' a losin' battle."

Blessing swallowed and looked at his sons, then back to the man from Victoria. "You-all ain't givin' up the fight, are you?"

"We haven't even started yet. We'll nip at their rear 'til more outfits catch up to us."

Webb said, "There's more on the way?"

"The alarm's been sent out in all directions. There'll be some rangin' companies along, I expect."   ·

Several Victoria men stood in a circle, heads bowed, staring down at a man on the ground. It was evident that he was dead.

Shannon said, "Since we've got a preacher with us, I expect you-all would like some words spoke."

One of the bystanders said, "We'd appreciate it mightily."

Webb removed his hat, and the others followed suit. He said a brief prayer for the stranger who lay before him. One of the Victoria men said, "Pray that before we get through, we send most of them bloody-handed Comanches after him."

Webb doubted the propriety of such a prayer, but at the moment, standing in the presence of death, he could think of no reply. Most of the Victoria men took solace in the fact that they appeared to have killed or wounded several Indians. It crossed Webb's mind that he might pray for those too, but he dismissed the thought. The devil had sent them; the devil could have them.

The captain of the volunteers came forward. "I'd be pleased to have you men join us if you have no company of your own."

Blessing was torn. "I ought to be seein' about my sister."

His son Tom placed a large hand on his father's shoulder. "You go find Aunt Bess. Me and Bert and Jim'll do the family's share of the fightin'."

The two brothers signaled agreement. Blessing cleared his throat and shook hands with his sons, each in turn. "I've always been proud of you boys. A man couldn't've asked for better." Shortly he rode away, toward whatever was left of Linnville.

Tom Blessing told the captain of the volunteers, "We got cousins in Gonzales. They'd be mighty put out if they was to miss the main fight. Reckon we've got time to go and fetch them?"

"You might run into Indians along the way."

"It'll be their own fault if they mess with us Blessings."

The captain glanced toward the dust left by the departing Comanches. "'Til the ranger companies show up, there aren't enough of us here to do more than pester their rear guard a little. If you can gather up some more help, go with my blessings."

Shannon said, "Me and the preacher'll go with you, Tom. Just in case you do run into some Indians." He glanced at Webb. "All right, Preacher?"

"You said it yourself: Who wants to get old and decrepit?"

CHAPTER
THREE

Riding at the rear of the long column, Buffalo Caller looked back toward the white men who trailed behind like wolves following a buffalo herd. Their pursuit had become something of a game—parry and thrust, feint and retreat—in an effort to draw warriors into a trap. After a couple of these episodes resulted in a few casualties, the Comanches had become slow about rising to the bait.

Buffalo Caller saw no reason such a superior force should play the white man's game. The People had all the advantage. It appeared to him that the whites were trying to delay the Indian retreat by pecking at its edges. They probably hoped for reinforcements. He doubted that they could muster enough fighting men to mount any serious challenge against a force this strong. Should they try, it would only mean more scalps dangling from war lances, more celebration when The People were back on their home ground. Buffalo Caller would welcome a stiff fight. Linnville had been so easy he almost felt cheated.

Swift as the Antelope kept looking back, sweat running from beneath the band of the white-man stovepipe hat he had worn since they had sacked the coastal town. Because of the heat he no longer wore red cloth wrapped around his body, but he had not abandoned it. He had it loosely rolled and tied behind his rawhide-covered saddle. It was for his wife, he claimed.

Antelope was impatient, as usual. "We should strike them like the lightning. We could kill them all before they have time to catch a breath."

They had tried that already, though with only a small portion of their fighting force, expecting the Texans to flee in terror. Instead, the hair-faces had surprised them with a stiff resistance. Several warriors had had to be carried away after the skirmish.

"There is time enough," Buffalo Caller said. "Let them become tired and hungry. Sooner or later they will begin to straggle. Then we can cut them to pieces."

"But they are growing stronger. More *teibos* keep joining them."

"All the more of them to die."

He had noticed small groups joining the pursuers periodically, but the Texans remained relatively small in number. Buffalo Caller was confident that they were much too weak to make any meaningful dent in the Comanche column, strung out so far now that he could not see the head of it. If the enemy should have the poor judgment to try, their blood and bones would enrich this prairie ground, and the grass would grow stronger for years.

Antelope opened his hands, showing all his fingers. "With this many men I could run them all the way back to the water."

He had always been prone to overstate his accomplishments and sometimes took personal credit for deeds performed by others as long as he did not expect to be challenged by someone who had been there.

"Go, then. I will marry your widow and give her many sons."

"You have two wives already, and your seed produces only girls. You have no son except that Texan boy."

Buffalo Caller saw danger in Antelope's eyes. Antelope had repeatedly made veiled threats against the child since they had taken him from his dead mother's side.

"The boy is not your concern."

"I tell you again, that hair is an ill omen. It looks like blood. I had a dream last night. The boy will bring evil. If you do not have the stomach to do what must be done, let me." He clasped the deer-horn handle of his knife.

Buffalo Caller stiffened. "You will not touch him!"

Antelope roughly pulled his horse away and joined other warriors, but a dark scowl said the question was not settled. Buffalo Caller knew their friendship, though of long standing, would not be enough to protect the boy. Antelope believed strongly in medicine and omens. He had a remarkable ability to sense the presence of dark spirits when no one else was aware of them.

Buffalo Caller believed in medicine as strongly as anyone, but his guardian spirits often disagreed with Antelope's. Antelope claimed to carry the power of the badger, and certainly he possessed that animal's belligerent temperament. Still, Buffalo Caller sometimes wondered if Antelope was not misled by Coyote, the trickster. Coyote was always up to mischief. He liked to play with men's minds and lead them into folly.

Antelope's implied threat began to play upon the mind of Buffalo Caller. To reassure himself that the boy was all right he put his mount into a long trot, passing the rear guard and going around the massive herd of stolen horses and mules. The women and children rode near the head of the column, where they were considered safest from attack by the trailing Texans. He sought out Whippoorwill, the younger and prettier of his two wives, the one he had chosen to accompany him on this long journey. She carried the boy in front of her on a high-stepping sorrel mare taken from the Mexican traders at Victoria.

"Is he all right?" he asked, though he could see no evidence to the contrary. The boy still wore his homespun clothes, now dirty and beginning to ravel from the stresses of traveling. He did not look Comanche, but the shirt and trousers would have to last until the band made its way back to the homeland. Then he could be put into something more suitable.

"He does not understand anything I tell him," Whippoorwill said. "At times he talks, but they are not words I know."

"He will learn soon enough to speak like a Comanche. Has Antelope said anything to you about him?"

"This morning, as we broke camp. He said the spirits came to him in a dream and told us we should kill the red-hair before he brings death to us."

"Watch out for him. Do not let him get close to the boy."

"What if he is right? What if the red-hair is bad medicine?"

"My spirits have told me no such thing. Antelope makes wind and thinks it is spirits speaking to him."

Satisfied for the time being, he dismounted and let his horse graze the dry grass while he waited for the column to pass. Its movement was slow as a turtle's, he thought. He remembered his doubts when the council first decided to allow women and children to accompany this grand punitive excursion. Ordinarily it would be considered too dangerous, but so many warriors had massed together that the expedition seemed secure enough to allow such luxury. It was argued that the outnumbered whites would fall like dry leaves in an autumn wind. Though resistance had proven strong enough to turn the raiders back from the heart of Victoria, Linnville had been crushed like a beetle beneath a warrior's moccasin. The spoils had been extraordinary. Those who had chosen to remain behind in the home-land would soon be ashamed for their timidity.

The rear guard came along after a time, and Buffalo Caller grasped his horse's mane, pulling himself up. His eyes met those of Antelope for a moment before Antelope looked away. What he saw there convinced him that once they reached home he would have to remove his family from Antelope's reach.

A warrior known as Feared by His Enemies pulled up beside him. "More white men have joined their brothers back there." He pointed his chin toward the horsemen, who trailed at a respectful distance.

The number had increased; that was evident. "There are still far more of us than of them."

Feared by His Enemies held up three fingers. "It has been three days, and they have not given up."

"They will, or we will destroy them when we get back into our own country."

Before camping that night, Buffalo Caller noted where Antelope located himself and found a place far away for Whippoorwill and the red-haired boy.

The next morning was the fourth since they had chased the boats into the big water. The column had been traveling on gradually rising ground. The air was drier and less oppressive than at the coast, though the summer sun began spreading its heat soon after its rising. He could not yet see them, but Buffalo Caller could visualize the limestone hills not far ahead. Soon The People would be back in their own environment. The raid had been more than satisfactory, especially in terms of the wealth they had taken, but it would be good to breathe the familiar air of home.

The unexpected approach of four Texan horsemen seemed more an affront than a threat. Surely they would turn back when they saw the full strength of the Comanche force. But they did not. Antelope gave a shout and led several rear-guard warriors in a charge. One of the Texans fired, and a warrior fell. The charge broke up in the face of unexpectedly fierce gun-fire. The warriors turned back, rejoining the rest of the rear guard.

The Texans kept coming.

From a flank, a second group of Texans broke out of a fringe of live-oak timber and quickly halted, seeming surprised by the number of Indians they faced. They turned back into the trees. This time Buffalo Caller joined other warriors in pursuit. Yelling for blood, they charged into the timber. The Texans retreated, though one somehow lost his horse and ran after his companions afoot. In their haste to get away they appeared unaware of his predicament.

He turned with terror in his eyes to meet death as the warriors rode him down. They celebrated over his scalp, but the celebration was short-lived. Gunfire erupted farther ahead. A larger Texan force plunged into the exposed flank of the main column. Buffalo Caller heard shooting, loud shouting, cries of dismay.

The herd panicked, breaking into a wild stampede. Thousands of hooves drummed against the prairie sod. Some of the pack animals lost their loads, the contents bouncing as they struck the ground. Long bolts of colored cloth came unfolded, dragging along behind them in the dust and the grass.

Unbelievable! There could not possibly be that many Texans. Buffalo Caller looked around with wide eyes, confusion giving way to fear. His wife and the red-haired boy were up there where the Texans were on the attack.

It was his place to stand his ground and fight, but he could not. He had to see to Whippoorwill's safety, and the boy's. He put his horse into a hard run, passing the rear-guard warriors, flinging an arrow at a Texan who popped up ahead of him. He missed and had no time for a second try.

Though the whites had trailed for four days, their sudden bold attack had taken the column by surprise. Some warriors were trying without success to stop the stampede of the loose horses and mules. Very quickly they had to give up that attempt and fight for their own survival against the yelling, fighting *teibos* who seemed now to be everywhere.

Just ahead, the women and children were fleeing, surrounded by a thin guard of warriors. Some were already falling behind and being swallowed up by the rapidly advancing Texans.

The Comanches' supreme confidence seemed to have evaporated. They were caught up now in a wild rout, no longer an organized force but a thousand individuals running for their lives.

Antelope appeared like a vengeful specter out of the choking dust. His stovepipe hat was gone, his face twisted in fury. "I told you!" he shouted. "That red-hair has brought this calamity down on us."

His intention was clear. "No!" Buffalo Caller protested. He fitted an arrow to the bowstring. He could not kill Antelope. For one Comanche to kill another was unthinkable. But he could kill Antelope's horse.

He heard the thud of a bullet. His own horse faltered, missed a stride, then went down. Buffalo Caller rolled away from him in the dry grass. He pushed to his feet, the dust burning his eyes, choking him. He felt around desperately for the fallen bow and found it. He looked up but saw Antelope nowhere. The warrior had disappeared in the brown cloud raised by all those pounding hooves.

He tried to catch a riderless horse but was bumped hard and flung aside, falling to his knees. Another loose horse leaped over him, a sharp hoof striking his head. Buffalo Caller fell on his face, stunned, spitting out dirt and dry grass. He tried to push to his feet but could not. His scalp burned like fire.

He heard a shout and saw a Texan bearing down upon him, a pistol extended at arm's length. Buffalo Caller tried to roll out of the way. He saw the flash and felt the hard shock as a bullet drove into his ribs.

A blanket of darkness descended over him, but not before he gave way to despair. He was powerless to save the red-haired boy from Antelope's vengeance.

Warren Webb could only guess at the number of volunteers and ranging companies who had gathered to challenge the Comanche invaders, but he feared they were not enough. The new Republic of Texas had little in its national treasury except hope, and it could ill afford to pay the number of rangers it needed to patrol its broad frontier. Webb and Michael Shannon had once answered a call to enlist in a minuteman company during an Indian scare but had never received the promised wage. Even those officially enlisted as full-time members of ranging companies were sometimes obliged to pay their own way. They had little advantage over civilian volunteers except their official-sounding titles.

Webb had never been this far inland, so the country was new to him. The word had been spread that all available Texas forces—organized ranging companies as well as volunteers—would gather at Plum Creek, which lay ahead. There, win or lose, they would stage the confrontation before the Indians could reach their hill-country sanctuaries.

Shortly after dawn, scouts had come into camp to report the Indians were just a few miles away. Webb and Shannon had attached themselves to a group of volunteers headed by Captain Matthew Caldwell, known as "Old Paint" for the white splotches in his beard. Caldwell gathered his company around him and made a rousing speech. They knew him as a battle-seasoned veteran of the revolution against Mexico, a man always cocked and primed for a fight.

"Boys," he declared, "there are a thousand Indians. They have our women and children captives. But we are eighty-seven strong, and I believe we can whip hell out of them!"

An approving murmur arose from the men.

Caldwell shouted, "What shall we do, boys? Shall we fight?"

Loud cheers gave him the answer.

A biblical phrase came to Webb's mind: *the faith of the mustard seed*. He thought it more likely that the Texans would be the ones who got hell whipped out of them, but the infectious enthusiasm among the settler congregation convinced him that to voice a contrary opinion would be to cry out in the wilderness, a voice lost in the wind.

Mike Shannon said, "Better cinch your saddle up tight, Preacher. We're fixin' to have ourselves a run, 'y God."

But in which direction? Webb wondered. He took some comfort in the knowledge that Caldwell's eighty-seven were only part of the force converging for the fight. It had been reported that Colonel Ed Burleson was on his way up from the Colorado with a large company including Chief Placido and several Tonkawa Indians, blood enemies of the Comanche. But even so, the invaders would still be greatly superior in number.

Though most of the men favored Caldwell, Old Paint acceded command to Felix Huston, a major general of the Texas army. Under Huston's orders the Texans moved into concealment to await Burleson's arrival. The Indians appeared first, a long, thin column stretching for several miles across the prairie, people and animals moving in and out of the dust like spectral figures, seen a moment, then disappearing.

Shannon said, "They have to know we're somewhere about because they've been trailed the whole way. Talk about arrogant . . . they must figure they can swat us away like so many horseflies."

Maybe they can, Webb thought. But he began to take hope. It occurred to him that the Comanches did not seem to know much about large-scale military tactics. They should realize their strung-out column was vulnerable to being flanked, cut, and diced into sections. They must regard themselves as invulnerable because of their number.

Pride goeth before a fall.

He tried to make a rough count of the horses and mules but found it impossible. There might have been two thousand, even three. A considerable number carried plunder the Comanches had acquired in Victoria and Linnville.

Burleson arrived with his men. What caught Webb's attention most was the contingent of Tonkawas, all afoot and stripped to no more than breech-cloths and moccasins, their bodies painted for war. They wore white cloths tied on their arms so the Texans would not mistake them for Comanches in the excitement of battle. Most did not know one Indian from another.

Distant firing indicated that the fight had opened, though Webb could not see the action and had no idea which way the contest might be going. A contingent of Comanches charged upon Webb's group, yelling, firing what rifles they had, loosing arrows that made a peculiar singing sound as they flew. Their initial strategy was clear: to pin down the Texans while the main body escaped with the women and children, the booty-laden horses and mules.

Webb had never seen a more splendid spectacle, savage though it was. One Indian cast aside an umbrella he had carried to shade himself from the sun. He came in a run, waving a war club. On his head was a beaver hat with red ribbon tied around the crown. A ribbon of the same color streamed from his horse's tail. Webb found himself so fascinated, watching, that he did not take aim. The Indian was within twenty yards when someone's rifle brought him down. The beaver hat rolled on the ground. The Indian reached for it, but the wind carried it away. His fingers clawed the ground, and he died.

Shannon shouted, "If you ain't goin' to use that rifle, give it to me."

"I'll tote my load." Webb bore down on a warrior who wore antelope-horn headdress. Hit, the Indian twisted and laid forward on his horse's neck but managed to hold on as the horse galloped away from the fight.

Webb lost sight of the overall battle, for he was concentrating upon his own small part of it. He could hear firing all around him, the exuberant yelling of the Texans sensing victory, the war cries of the Comanches. The Tonkawas, though on foot, charged into the fray with a fury like hell un-leashed, slashing, clubbing, scalping their enemies while they still breathed. It was enough to turn Webb's stomach had he not been too busy to let the horror of it soak in.

Soon the confrontation was less a battle than a runaway. Unaccount-ably, the Comanches seemed to have been caught off balance and unpre-pared. Any semblance of unity was lost. The big *caballada* of horses and mules was scattering to the winds, many losing their packs, littering the open prairie with all manner of white-man store goods.

Comanches, dead and dying, lay along the trail. Webb had to spur to keep up with the race.

Ahead of him he saw an Indian woman on a sorrel mare, holding a small boy in front of her. A Comanche warrior rushed to overtake her. A husband bound on protecting wife and child, Webb thought. He brought his rifle up, though it was next to useless from the back of a running horse. He felt a pang of conscience for having even considered leaving woman and child without a husband and father.

He realized suddenly that the man was swinging a war club, and the woman was trying to avoid him. She leaned over the boy, holding her arm out to deflect the blow. He heard her scream.

Webb could not believe what he saw. The man was trying to kill the youngster.

The mare stumbled, pitching woman and child out into the grass. The warrior's speed carried him past them. He wheeled his horse about and started back. She screamed again, trying to shield the boy with her body. She brought up a knife, brandishing it at the man.

Webb had no time to consider options. He drove his horse forward to intercept the warrior, who seemed so intent on the boy that he did not see the larger enemy until it was too late. The Comanche's eyes met Webb's, and he raised the club.

Momentum slammed the two horses together. Webb felt himself catapulted out of the saddle. He rolled in the dry grass and grabbed frantically at the rifle. He brought it up and pulled the trigger, but impact had spilled powder from the pan.

The Indian had managed to stay on his horse. He reined it around and came back, holding the club high. Webb instinctively raised the rifle, trying to let it take the blow. The club came down hard against his left arm. A sharp stab of pain told him the bone was broken.

Mike Shannon appeared suddenly, coming up behind the Comanche. Wild-eyed and shouting, he jammed the muzzle of his rifle against the painted body and fired. Blood spurted from the Indian's stomach as the bullet tore through him and exited. He tumbled from his horse and writhed on the ground, pressing his hands against a huge hole that gushed red. He struggled, then lapsed into a quiet quivering as life drained away.

Broken arm throbbing, Webb turned quickly to look for the woman. He saw her on hands and knees, gasping for breath lost in the fall. The knife lay on the ground beside her right hand. The boy stood beside her, bewildered.

Only then did Webb notice that the child's hair was red, his frightened eyes blue. He wore the homespun clothing typical in poor farm families. A white captive, Webb realized, probably taken in Victoria or Linnville. He looked as if he might be two years old, perhaps three.

"Come to me, lad," Webb said.

The boy hesitated. The Indian woman cried something and reached toward him. Webb knew Comanches often killed their captives when they were under pressure, so he kicked the knife away. He placed himself between the child and the woman, lifted the boy with his right arm and turned to catch his horse. The youngster clung tightly to his neck.

Shannon rode in close, drawing a pistol because he had not had time to reload the rifle. He gave the woman a hard look. Webb feared for a moment that he might shoot her.

"Spare her," Webb said.

"Less'n she makes a move toward you." He frowned. "Got your arm busted, looks like. Better let me carry the boy. White, ain't he?" He leaned down and drew the lad up in front of him in the saddle.

The woman pleaded in words Webb did not comprehend, though her expression told him she did not want to give up the child. Knowing she would not understand, he felt compelled nevertheless to try to explain. "The lad has people somewhere. He needs to be back with his own kind."

The mare had risen to her feet and was walking shakily. Webb motioned toward the woman, then toward the mare. "You'd best be slippin' away while you can."

She understood his motions if not his words. She hopped upon the mare's back. Crying, she made one last plea, holding out her arms. Shannon turned the boy away from her. She gave up and moved westward in the direction of the general runaway, though she kept looking back at the boy in Shannon's arms.

A volunteer rode up, eyes ablaze with excitement, sweat running down his face into a stubble of beard. His hands were bloody, but the blood did not appear to be his own. He pointed toward the fleeing woman. "Ain't you goin' to shoot her?"

Shannon said, "I never shoot women without I have to."

"Indian women make babies, and babies grow up to do murder. If you ain't goin' to shoot her, I will."

Shannon set the boy down upon the ground and eased the muzzle of his rifle in the horseman's direction. "Do and you'll answer to me."

The man's face went scarlet. "You wouldn't shoot me over a Comanche squaw."

Shannon's voice was crisp. "I might. And then again, 'y God, I might just whip the hell out of you."

The man lowered his weapon. "One day her sons'll come to take your scalp, and you'll wish you'd killed her before she bore them."

"They've got plenty of fightin' men left up yonder if you're bound on more killin'. Go get *them*."

The fight, what was still left of it, had swept on past. "I figure to." The volunteer looked down at the boy on the ground. "You takin' Indian boys to raise, are you?"

"Look closer. He ain't an Indian."

The rider's eyes reflected surprise. "Good thing he ain't, because I'd be of a mind to kill him before he has a chance to grow up and kill me and mine." He rode on.

Shannon watched until the man was swallowed up in the dust. He turned back to Webb. "Yonder's a bunch of men gathered. Maybe there's a doctor amongst them. Your arm needs lookin' after."

Webb carried a medical book in his saddlebags with his Bible and administered limited physical aid along his circuit because real doctors were scarce in settlements beyond the main towns like San Antonio and Houston. But he doubted he had the fortitude to set his own broken bone. He mounted, careful not to use the left arm.

Shannon rode up to the small group of Texans. "Anybody recognize this young'un?"

No one did.

"What's your name, lad?" Webb asked.

The boy did not reply. Webb repeated the question. "What do your folks call you, your daddy and mama?"

The boy murmured, "Davy. Me Davy."

"What do they call your mama? And your daddy?"

"Mama. Daddy."

He saw that further questions would yield nothing. The boy was too young to know his family name.

Shannon inquired about a doctor but found there was none, at least not in this group. A young man with an upturned moustache and a German accent said, "Is best we bind that arm anyway, so it will not stay always crooked."

Webb came near fainting as the German pulled the arm straight, then tore a long strip of blue cloth off a bolt that had fallen from a pack animal. He bound it around a temporary splint, a rough piece of live-oak limb. Webb broke out in a cold sweat, his body trembling. But he managed to keep his head as the young man hurried the task.

"August Burmeister is not doctor, but the arm will not crooked be."

Shannon was impressed. "Where'd you learn to do up a broken arm like that?"

"In the old country, in Westphalia. I was a soldier in the army."

"How come you to be in Texas?"

"I did not like to be a soldier in the army. In the old country they tell of Texas. When they do not watch, I walk out to the *niederland* and the sea. On a boat I come to Galveston, to look for myself."

"Hell of a sight you're seein' here." The sounds of battle trailed away to distant spotty firing. Shannon said, "We gave them a royal whippin', 'y God. There'll be a trail of Comanche bones all the way to the mountains. They'll study long before they ever come this far again."

Evening fell. The arm throbbed, and Webb knew he was running a fever. He and Shannon shared a camp with the Blessing brothers and a small gathering of volunteer rangers in the service of the republic. Nearby, another group sang and shouted. The Tonkawa scouts who had accompanied the white men on their punitive strike were celebrating victory. Webb wondered how one tribe could be induced to aid the Texans in their fight against other Indians. The only answer he could see was that they did not consider themselves to be of the same people despite the fact that white men regarded them that way. The Tonkawas, a small and vulnerable tribe, saw the Texans as allies in their long struggle against domination by the stronger and far more numerous Comanches.

Shannon went over to watch but did not remain long. He came back, looking a little pale. "They're roastin' meat over yonder."

Webb was aware of that, for it smelled good. He assumed the Tonkawas had cut up one of the horses or mules killed in the fight.

Shannon asked, "Did you notice that some of them dead Comanches had their limbs chopped off?"

Webb had not. His broken arm had taken precedence over other considerations.

Shannon said, "Right now them Tonks are feastin' on the haunch off of a Comanche. They've got a couple of hands and a foot roastin' on the coals."

Webb thought at first that Shannon was joshing him, but his friend's expression was serious. Shannon said, "They invited me to join them. I said I was already full."

The Tonkawas had a reputation as cannibals, eating flesh from their enemies in ceremonial rites. This trait they shared with another coastal tribe, the Karankawas, who had been implacably hostile to the first settlers and by now had been hunted almost to extinction. It was said other tribes held Tonkawas and Karankawas in contempt for their consumption of human flesh and gladly killed them on sight.

Webb shuddered. He wished he had not smelled the roast on the Tonkawa fire. "Praise God they're our friends and not our enemies."

"Me and you wouldn't suit them much as enemies. We'd be too tough and stringy to eat." Shannon turned his attention to the rescued boy with the reddish hair. "What we goin' to do with him, Preacher?"

"Nothin' we *can* do except ride back over the trail the Indians left and ask if anybody knows him."

"Chances are that the Comanches killed his folks when they stole him."

Webb felt his throat pinch with pity. He had considered that probability. "If we can't turn up his family we'll have to find somebody who'll give him a good home."

Shannon seated himself on the fallen trunk of a lightning-struck live oak and lifted the youngster up into his lap. "Davy, is it? Nice name. He'll be a good-lookin' young'un when he gets his face washed. That rusty-colored hair means he'll be a fighter someday. Reckon he's Irish?"

Webb was pleased that Shannon was warming to the boy. "All I know is that he's not Comanche."

"He'll be needin' a woman's care. My Dora'd be right pleased to keep him 'til we find his own folks."

"And if we don't find them?"

A fly buzzed around the boy's face. Shannon brushed it away. "Dora always wanted a big family, but as you know, she ain't been able to bear. She'd take this young'un as her own and be glad for the chance."

"I'd keep him myself, only I've got no wife to see after him. I couldn't take him on the circuit with me, and I couldn't leave him."

"Then it's settled. This boy'll be good company for Dora. We'll treat him like he was born to us and give him a good Christian raisin'. That's a promise, 'y God."

Exhausted, the red-haired youngster drifted off to sleep in Shannon's arms. The Irishman smiled.

Webb tried to smile too, but his arm hurt too much.

CHAPTER

FOUR

COLORADO RIVER, 1859

Rusty Shannon realized the morning was off to a bad beginning when he stepped out onto the open dog run of the double log cabin and saw that the mule team was not in the corral. He had personally penned them last night so he could get a daylight start in the field. They had included a big gray mule named Old Zach, one of a pair Daddy Mike Shannon had brought home from the Mexican War. The mule was smart as paint, but it had never learned to untie a knot in a rawhide string or push open a heavy gate that always dragged the ground and strained a man's muscles to lift and move it.

Rusty trotted out to the pen and saw the gate slumped half open, dead weight against its leather hinges. Leaning down to pick up the rawhide strip, he saw that it had been cut. He became aware of moccasin tracks, and his heartbeat quickened. Instinct made him look up, his gaze sweeping the open ground between the cabin and the river. His stomach, warm and full from a breakfast of coffee and cornbread, honey and venison, seemed to do a quick turnover.

"Daddy! Daddy Mike!"

He had taken to calling his foster father *Dad*; it sounded more mature.

But in a moment of excitement he reverted to the name he had used since boyhood.

He started back toward the cabin in a hard run. Mike Shannon limped out of the kitchen onto the open dog run, one arthritis-knotted hand raised to shield his eyes from the rising sun. His graying whiskers had not felt a razor in a week or more. His thick gray hair was disheveled, for he had not taken time to use a comb. He combed his hair only for company, and he had no reason to expect any.

"What's all the noise, young'un? Fox been amongst the chickens again?"

Rusty was too old to be called *young'un*, but he supposed Mike would hold to the habit as long as he lived. No one knew Rusty's age, exactly. The best guess was that he should be a year or so on the far side of twenty.

"Indians, Dad. Indians got the mules."

Mike Shannon snorted. "Ain't seen an Indian here since . . ." He did not finish the sentence. He had seen a lot of Indians in his time, most of them over the sights of a rifle. He had been in so many skirmishes that they tended to run together. When he began telling about them, one incident often became mixed with another. He contended that the fine details did not matter so much as the innate truth and spirit of the story. Even a village idiot could cite dry facts.

Michael Shannon hobbled out to meet Rusty and accompany him back to the corral. He had come home from the Mexican War a dozen years ago with two mules and a sense of duty fulfilled. But he had gone off on an Indian campaign a year or so ago and came home with a wounded leg that still pained him every day. He had had to lean heavily upon Rusty to work this farm that the state of Texas had awarded him for service. Texas had little cash to pay its volunteers, so they often went unpaid despite the best intentions of governor and legislature. But it had land aplenty. It sometimes settled its debts with real estate.

Mother Dora came out onto the dog run, arms folded as if they were cold, thin shoulders slumped. She had been ill of late for no specific reason that met the eye. Preacher Webb was the nearest thing to a doctor within a day's ride, when he was not off to some distant point carrying the Scriptures to the farthermost settlers. Webb knew a lot about poultices and potions, but he could not fathom what was wrong with her. Country women tended to age rapidly on the frontier. An old saying declared that Texas was heaven for men and horses but hell for women and dogs. She had simply worn herself out, for a woman's work began before daylight and did not end until she crawled into bed, exhausted.

Rusty asked no foolish questions. He preferred to figure things out for himself or leave them alone. He handed Mike the cut string. "Look at the moccasin tracks."

Mike said, "Them thievin' rascals." A hint of admiration crept into his voice. "Snuck up here in the night, 'y God, and got off with them mules without us hearin' a thing." He squinted at Rusty. "You *didn't* hear anything, did you?"

"No, sir. I'd've raised a holler." For a fleeting moment Rusty wondered if Mike might think he heard but was scared to do anything about it. Mike should know him better than that. Rusty never went looking for a fight but did not run from one if it came looking for him. He had learned from Mike that skinned knuckles heal, but wounded pride just festers.

It struck Rusty that the family's brown dog should have raised a ruckus. It never let so much as a raccoon approach the place at night without sounding an alarm. Sometimes, lacking anything else to bark at, it just barked at the moon. He found the dog lying in the grass, an arrow driven deeply into its body. It might have barked a little before it was struck, but no one in the cabin would have paid attention if the racket stopped quickly.

Mike tugged at the arrow. It was too deeply embedded to be pulled out easily. He examined the shaft. "Comanche."

Comanche was a word that sent a chill up a man's back. It traveled up Rusty's and down again.

Mike grumbled, "A fool dog he was, but good company." He wasted but a moment in regret. "We're not rich enough that we can afford to furnish work stock to the Comanche nation. Ain't but one thing to do, and that's go after them, 'y God."

"Afoot?" Rusty asked.

"I saw our horses grazin' down by the river just at sundown. Maybe them redskin thieves missed them in the dark. You go see."

Rusty had trotted a hundred yards before it dawned on him that he was not armed. But it was unlikely the Indians still lingered. On a horse-stealing raid they tended to strike hard and get away fast.

He thought the chance of getting the mules back was about the same as finding a pot of gold down by the river. But he would not tell Mike so. He was as conservative with words as he was with the little bit of money that ever came into his hands. Visitors had spent the night at the Shannon farm and left the next day believing Rusty was deaf and dumb.

People not well acquainted with the family often assumed that Rusty had been born to it. Many did not know that Mike Shannon and Preacher Webb had taken him from the Comanches on the battlefield at Plum Creek. The minister had ridden many long miles and made a lot of inquiries before abandoning hope of identifying the boy. Mike and Mother Dora had regarded him as their own and gave him their family name, for he had none of his own.

The only thing markedly different about Rusty was his reddish hair, which had gained him his nickname. Mike always said red hair went with a name like Shannon anyway; it was the Irish coming out.

Hardly anyone except Mother Dora ever called him by the only name he had brought with him: David. She clung stubbornly to it, though everyone else had long since called him Rusty.

At times, when he lay half asleep at night, Rusty could almost remember his true mother—not so much what she looked like, for he could never quite conjure up her face, but something vague about the way she felt cradling him in her arms and the sound of her voice talking and singing to him. He remembered the warm and comforting feeling of love. It was not much, but it was enough to make him wonder, to give him a sense of loss, of something missed that he would never recover. It saddened him at times, even as he remained grateful for the Shannons. Had he been able to choose his parents, he would have wanted them in the Shannon image.

Still, he often wondered who he really was.

Though he made no claim to being a tracker, the broad trail led him to guess that the Comanches must have been riding or driving seventy-five to a hundred horses and mules. A lot of people besides the Shannons had been set afoot. But he found the two Shannon horses grazing calmly a hundred yards from the river. As Mike had said, the Indians had probably overlooked them in the dark.

Rusty walked up to the gentler of the pair, a black much favored by Mike. "Easy, Alamo, easy." He spoke softly until he could rub the animal's shoulder; then he grabbed a handful of glossy mane and swung up bareback. He guided the horse with his knees and gentle pats on the neck. "Come on, Alamo. You too, Goliad."

Mike Shannon was pleased as Rusty brought the two horses to the cabin and put them in the pen from which the mules had been stolen. "I was afraid we'd have to go afoot."

That would have been futile sure enough, Rusty thought, though he did not say so. The federal army's foot soldiers had never been able to catch up to any Indians, though they had worn out a lot of shoe leather trying.

Mother Dora left the dog run and came out, her steps careful and slow as if she were unsure of her footing. She did not often criticize her husband, however much she might deplore his fighting nature. But this time she said, "You're goin' off on a fool's errand, Michael. Even if you catch up to them, what'll you do? Get yourself killed, more than likely, and David with you."

Mike Shannon had never admitted defeat in his life, even if it faced him nose to nose. When his time came to die, he meant to go down fighting. "We'll come up with somethin'."

She asked, "How far do you think you can ride? What about that bad leg?"

"It's a long way from the heart. Saddle up, Rusty, then let's go get our guns."

In the cabin, Rusty fetched down from its pegs a flintlock rifle Mike had brought home from the war with Mexico. It was the only one the family owned. He handed it to Mike.

From a corner he took an old shotgun Mike had carried to Texas in 1836 in hope of using it on Mexican general Santa Anna, or *Santy Anna*, as Mike called him. He was just in time to be on hand when Sam Houston took that fancy gentleman's measure on the battleground at San Jacinto. Mike had felt cheated, getting to participate in only a single engagement, so one-sided that it was over almost before it began. He had to wait ten years for another full-blown war to break out. Mother Dora had reluctantly given her blessings and sent him off with a company of ranger volunteers to fight Mexico as his forebears had fought the British in two earlier wars.

Scouting for the United States Army, Mike and other Texans under command of Colonel Jack Hays had harried the enemy all the way to Veracruz and Mexico City. Rusty had heard him tell many a rousing tale, most of them more or less true, allowing for a little enthusiastic stretching of minor parts that otherwise would not have been so interesting. A faded and battle-worn U.S. flag hung in a place of honor on the kitchen wall.

A muzzle-loading horse pistol usually rested on a set of pegs beneath the rifle, but it was missing. A greasy-whiskered neighbor named Fowler Gaskin had borrowed it weeks ago. Gaskin was notorious for borrowing first one thing and then another, sometimes asking, sometimes just coming and getting. He was also notorious for not bringing anything back. If the owner wanted it, he had to go and get it . . . if Gaskin hadn't misplaced it somewhere or sold it to somebody. A couple of weeks ago he had borrowed Mike

Shannon's best mule, Chapultepec. He hadn't asked but had chosen a time when the menfolk were elsewhere. He led the animal out of the corral and told Mother Dora, "I need the borry of your mule," then had shouted "Thankee!" back over his shoulder as he rode away bareback. The bridle had been Mike's, too.

It might just be that the Indians had missed the Gaskin place, Rusty thought. If so, the Shannons still had one plow mule after all. They could team him with Alamo if they had to, though it would hurt Mike's conscience to hitch the black to a wagon or plow. Especially alongside a mule.

Indian raids were no longer commonplace along this section of the Colorado, though they still occurred with regularity farther west. Texas had been a state in the Union for more than ten years now. Federal troops guarded the frontier, but most were infantry, restricted to guard and garrison duty and ill equipped for pursuit of the Comanches' light cavalry. Several times Mike had enlisted in the state's volunteer ranging companies for limited periods. Horseback, they moved faster than the federals, were burdened with less equipage, and did not have to answer to every pip-squeak bureaucrat misled into an overappraisal of his own importance.

Rusty had no clear recollection of ever having seen a Comanche close up, though faint and confusing fragments of memory sometimes came to him unbidden, so elusive he could never grab hold of them. He knew Indians had carried him away from his original home, and he was aware that he had stayed with them a short while. Mostly he remembered being bewildered and frightened, not able to understand.

Mike checked the rifle and the shot pouch that went with it. "Mother, we'll drag that dog off before we leave. He'll be stinkin' before long."

The dark circles beneath her eyes seemed heavier this morning, and her hair had never looked quite so gray. "I wish you wouldn't go. You're not as young as you think you are. How far do you think you can travel?"

"I rode many a mile and crossed many a river durin' the war."

"That was ten years ago, before a Comanche bullet ruined your leg. There are lots of things you used to do that you can't anymore."

Fearing the two were about to plunge into a full-blown argument, Rusty stepped out onto the dog run to avoid being a witness. He saw riders approaching and shouted, "Company comin'."

Mike hobbled out with the rifle cradled in his arms, ready for use. "Hard to believe they'd come back for more. They already took more than enough."

"It's white men," Rusty said. "Looks like Tom Blessing in the lead."

Mike squinted, uncertain. His eyesight was not as keen as it used to be.

Blessing had often served as a captain when the state treasury got a few dollars ahead and the governor called ranger companies into service. Several times Rusty had watched Mike ride away with Blessing and others in search of Indians or bandits or to put down one of the foolish but bloody feuds that seemed always brewing in the older settlements of Texas. A year ago Mike had gone off under command of Captain John S. "Rip" Ford on an expedition against hostiles. The rangers and federal troops had been aided by friendly Indians to whom the Comanches were longtime enemies. They had devastated a large village, but Mike had come home with a wounded leg that would have been amputated had he not resisted with his shotgun and threatened to shoot anyone who touched him.

Rusty was aware, from stories he had heard, that Blessing had been present when he was recovered from the Comanches at Plum Creek. He had always felt that he owed his life to Tom Blessing, Mike Shannon, and Preacher Webb. He was pleased to see Preacher Webb riding just behind Blessing. Every man was armed. It was plain that they were trailing the Indians.

Blessing's pale blue eyes were a major contrast to his fierce black beard speckled with gray. He had a deep, booming voice that bespoke authority. "Mike, I judge by the tracks that you-all had visitors last night."

"We sure enough did. Tried to clean us out of horse and mule flesh, 'y God. Me and Rusty was fixin' to take up their trail."

Blessing seemed more amused than surprised. "Just the two of you?"

"Didn't figure on Dora goin'."

"Mind if we join you?"

"Me and Rusty'd be tickled for the company, long as you don't get in our way."

Rusty's heart leaped with excitement at the thought of riding with the volunteer rangers. He had long wanted to, but Mike had always said he was too young. Mike easily forgot how young *he* had been when he set out for Texas on his own.

Preacher Webb moved forward, looking relieved. "Thank the Lord that the Indians were after stock more than scalps."

Blessing said, "They took some scalps to the east of here, though. Killed most of a family, stole a woman and a boy."

"A boy?" Mike Shannon said. He glanced at Rusty. Rusty guessed he was remembering Plum Creek.

Blessing said, "Last time I saw you, Mike, that leg was still in bad shape. You sure you're ready for a long ride?"

" 'y God I'm always ready. You never seen me lag behind like some people." He directed his gaze to Fowler Gaskin, sitting on Mike's mule Chapultepec.

Gaskin held a hand behind his right ear, trying to hear better. He was thin as a slab of bacon, his face ruddy with tiny red veins threaded across it, his ragged old vest spotted with tobacco juice and remnants of past meals. He took more sustenance from a jug than from a plate.

Rusty said, "Dad, there's Chapultepec. They didn't get him."

Gaskin growled, "I wish they had. He's the roughest-trottin' mule I ever rode. Looks like you-all could keep a better one around for your neighbors to borry."

Ordinarily Rusty was careful to speak respectfully to his elders, but he had no respect for Fowler Gaskin. Neither did anyone else around here that he knew of. "You didn't ask, you just came and took him. We could've told you he's a plow mule, not a ridin' mule."

He figured Gaskin would have no stomach for a close view of the Indians. At the first sign of a feather he would probably find out just how fast Chapultepec could run, in the opposite direction.

Blessing seemed to figure that way too, for he gave Gaskin a chance to turn back. He managed deference, but it was clearly a strain. "It's apt to be a hard ride, Fowler. At your age I'm sure you'd rather be at home watchin' over your family."

Gaskin did not watch over his family very well under the best of circumstances. He and his wife and daughter Florey barely tolerated one another, and Gaskin did not even like his two sons much. Neither did Rusty. Eph and Luke Gaskin used to lie in ambush, waiting to chunk rocks at him when he came into range. Usually they scampered as soon as Rusty began hurling the same rocks back at them. His aim was better. The Gaskin boys were too lazy to practice, but Rusty was not. Lately the brothers had outgrown rock-throwing but still baited him and threw insults.

The whole family was a lean and hungry lot, looking to reap where others had sown.

Gaskin seemed torn. Rusty suspected he had come this far only because someone had shamed him into it.

A tall, angry-looking man named Isaac York pushed his horse against the mule Gaskin rode. "Go back, Fowler, and leave the fightin' to people who know how to kill Indians! You'd just be in the way."

Though Gaskin was a man of little pride, and for good reason, that little made him stubborn enough to refuse. "I've come this far. I'll go the whole hog." He spat on the ground and gave York a look of defiance. Rusty was surprised that he could rouse up that much gumption.

Mother Dora said, "I wish you wouldn't take David. He's just a boy."

Blessing gave Rusty a quick study. "Maybe you haven't looked at him close, Miz Shannon. Rusty's a man."

Rusty warmed at Blessing's acceptance. He had waited a long time for it.

Blessing said, "We're goin' on, Mike. When you're ready, you can lope up and catch us."

Pulse racing, Rusty watched the men ride away, Gaskin trailing behind on the mule. The faces were known to him, and most of the names. They were neighbors, friends of Mike's, farmers and tradesmen from the settlement five miles downriver. Each had his own life and his own interests, but in times of challenge the community pulled together. In that way it had survived the poverty of the early years, the pressure from Indians and from Mexico.

Though that country had relinquished formal claim on Texas after the Mexican War, many people on both sides of the border had never acknowledged the treaty. They regarded Texas as Mexican territory and sometimes raided north of the Rio Grande to bolster their point. This, in turn, invited retaliation by Texans, who felt no compunctions about raiding into Mexico, often less from patriotism as from expectation of personal gain. Even up here on the Colorado River, far north of the Rio Grande, settlers could not feel secure against the border troubles. Only a few years ago a Mexican army had invaded all the way to San Antonio, capturing the district court in session and taking Texan prisoners back to Mexico. There had been hell to pay over that incident and the retaliations that followed. Always ready for a scrap, Mike Shannon had ridden off on a punitive expedition. Wisely, he had stopped at the Rio Grande. Some who crossed the river had paid with their lives.

Preacher Webb said, "I'll wait and ride with you-all." He dismounted and stepped up to Mother Dora. His voice was full of concern. "How do you feel, Dora? Any improvement?"

She attempted a faint smile that never quite came to life. "I know better than to lie to a preacher."

Webb turned to Mike. "I wish you'd stay and watch over Dora. It's time you left the fightin' to younger men."

"I ain't any older than you are."

"I've got no sick wife at home."

Dora said, "He's set his mind to go, Preacher Webb, so let him be. I can take care of myself. Always have." She turned toward the cabin's kitchen door. "I'll sack up some vittles. And you-all had best take blankets. The nights can get chilly out in the open."

Mike nodded. "Go fetch them, Rusty."

Rusty was so excited at riding with the volunteers, at calling himself a ranger if only for a few days, that a small thing like blankets would not have crossed his mind. But he rolled up a blanket apiece for himself and his foster father.

Dora Shannon came out of the kitchen and handed Rusty a bulging cloth sack. "There's coffee and some bacon and salt. And the biscuits from breakfast. You be real careful, son." She hugged him, and he felt the wetness of her tears when their cheeks came together. Many a time she had bid Mike good-bye this way.

Mike said, "The young'un'll do his duty."

"Duty." She spoke the word with irony. "Duty'll be the death of you someday." She put her thin arms around her husband. "Don't take any chances tryin' to get our stock back. We can buy more somehow. Just bring yourself back in one piece, and make sure nothin' happens to David. He's the only son we'll ever have."

Mike tried to dismiss her concerns. "We probably won't catch up to them anyway." He turned. "We'd best be movin', Preacher."

Webb gave Dora Shannon one more worried look. "God bless this house, and all who live in it." He swung into the saddle and spurred his brown horse into a trot.

Rusty waved his floppy old felt hat and shouted back over his shoulder to his foster mother, "Don't you worry. We'll be comin' back."

If she answered, he could not hear her for the wind.

"We *will* be comin' back," he repeated, softer now, and more to himself than to Mike or Preacher Webb.

For years he had worked the farm without anything exciting happening to him. Following the plow and the mules day after day, year after year, he had dreamed of joining a minuteman ranging company as Mike had so often done. He had seen himself riding boldly into action, making Mike and Mother Dora proud of the raising they had given him. Now his backside prickled with anticipation.

The three did not press their animals to catch up quickly. Mike said they had plenty of time because they were unlikely to overtake the Indians before tomorrow or next day at the earliest. They moved along in a stiff trot, gradually closing the distance between them and the other volunteers without breaking into a run that would tire their horses. The hooves of the stolen animals had beaten down the grass and left a wide band of tracks that anyone could have followed.

Most members of Blessing's little band had fought Indians, and several had seen action in the Mexican War and border skirmishes.

It felt natural to Rusty that he ride alongside Preacher Webb. Several times he had accompanied Webb on his preaching circuit when he had no pressing responsibilities at home. The minister had always been pleasant company and a good teacher without blatantly appearing to try. He was widely read and could talk at length on subjects totally foreign but fascinating to Rusty. Moreover, he withheld his sermons for the pulpit. His best preaching was done by example, living the kind of life he urged upon others. If the man had any vices beyond a little affinity for horse races and a bachelor's way of staring wistfully at good-looking ladies, Rusty had not seen it.

He had long marveled at the man's stamina. The minister would sometimes ride until fatigue dulled his eyes and he could barely stay in the saddle. Yet once Webb reached his destination and found a crowd waiting to hear him, his shoulders straightened and his weak voice took on the power of the Word.

"The Lord never gives us a job to do without He gives us the strength to carry it out," Webb often said.

His left arm was crooked, having healed that way after being broken by an Indian club at Plum Creek, so Rusty had been told. The arm was always subject to the miseries when weather changed, but the minister never let it handicap him if work needed to be done.

He and Mike and Rusty caught up when Blessing's men stopped for a noon rest. The trail was still plain. Rusty thought, though he did not say so, that it was a mistake to pause while the Indians rode on. But the pursuers' mounts could only be pushed so far and so fast. The Indians could switch to fresh horses from among those they had taken. Blessing's men had to make do with what they had. If a mount gave out or went lame, its rider was out of the chase.

The ranger captain walked out to meet the three incoming horsemen.

"Better get down and let your mounts blow a little." He waited for Rusty to dismount. "Your daddy has been sworn in so many times there don't seem any point to it. But I'll swear you in if you want me to. You'll not likely see a dime of state money, but at least you can put in a claim . . . for whatever that's worth."

Rusty had not even considered that he might be paid. Mike had always told him that a man owed it to his neighbors and to his country to serve when duty called, and he should never ask about reward. "You just ask what they want you to do. It's your way to pay for the privilege of livin' in Texas and the United States of America."

Rusty had been no more than seven or eight years old at the time, but he remembered how joyfully his foster father had celebrated when Texas gave up its status as a free republic and became a state in the union. Mike had declared, "If it hadn't been for my daddy comin' over from the old country when he did, we'd still be in Ireland today, workin' a shriveled-up potato patch and starvin' to death, 'y God."

Indeed, the Shannons had come near starving a time or two when they first broke out their present farm. But determination and helpful neighbors had allowed them to survive.

Rusty told Blessing, "I don't worry about pay, but I'd take it kindly if you made me a ranger, even for a few days. So would Daddy Mike, I think." His foster father had always been proud of the times—some short, some long—he had served in a ranging company.

Blessing administered a brief oath that officially made Rusty a member of his company for whatever time his service might be deemed necessary. He stated that Rusty was obliged to furnish his own firearm and horse and was to be paid a daily allowance from the state treasury should such monies be available. "The state insists on the first part," Blessing said. "It's a lot more flexible as to the last. I'm sorry I can't give you a badge to wear, but I don't have one myself. Badges wouldn't impress a Comanche much anyhow."

From Mike's stories, Rusty knew the rangers did not stand on ceremony. They had no official uniform, no official badge, not even an official title. They were most often called simply rangers or ranging companies, minutemen, and sometimes spies. Their rules were mostly made up as they went along, based on common sense and the realities of the moment. The main requirement was that they do the job or bust themselves trying. Sometimes they did indeed bust themselves, but more often they did whatever they thought it took to get the job done. If they happened to maim or kill a few more people than was really necessary . . . well, that was just too damned bad. It was ranger logic that such casualties resulted from folks being in the wrong place at the wrong time, and they were probably guilty of something anyway.

Blessing did not call a halt until dusk faded into darkness. He stopped where the steep banks of a near-dry creek bed would hide their meager campfire from view should the Indians send scouts to survey their back trail.

The men needed rest, especially Mike and Preacher Webb. Mike rubbed his bad leg and winced with pain when he thought nobody was looking. The minister seemed wrung out like a freshly washed shirt. He gripped his crooked arm as if the miseries had set in deep.

Blessing offered, "Oscar Petrie had the foresight to bring a bottle of whiskey if that would help you, Mike."

Mike accepted with gratitude. "Oscar Petrie is the smartest man I know."

Blessing turned to Webb. "How about you, Preacher?"

"After I have made whiskey the subject of a hundred sermons?"

"It has medicinal properties."

Rusty remembered that Mother Dora had put coffee in the sack of grub she had given him. "I'll boil you some coffee, Preacher. I never heard you sermonize against that."

"And you never will. When the Christians drove the Turks from the gates of Vienna, the Turks left their stores of coffee behind. I feel sure that was the Lord's notion of a proper gift to His faithful."

Rusty had no idea where Vienna was. Probably not in Texas, or he would have heard about it.

He noticed that Isaac York kept pacing back and forth atop the creek bank, staring toward the north. Blessing called, "Isaac, you'd better get some rest while you can."

York's voice was harsh. "I doubt that woman and boy they stole are gettin' any rest."

"You can't do them any good if you're too worn out to keep up."

"Moon's risin'. Plain as the tracks are, we ought to be able to follow them pretty soon."

"We'll never catch up on dead horses. Come on down." Blessing poured a tin cup almost to the brim with steaming coffee and held it high as enticement. York descended from the bank. A black man who always accompanied him took the coffee Blessing offered and handed it to him as if it were his place, and his only, to serve York.

York said, "Go get you some sleep, Shanty." He squatted near the fire, a towering man with a slight hunch to his broad shoulders. Rusty studied the brooding face, made bloodred and fearsome by the flickering reflection of the coals. He knew the man mostly by reputation. He was said to be a ferocious fighter in any scrap with Indians. Mike had fought side by side with him in the Mexican War. He said York seemed to take that conflict as a personal crusade and killing as many enemies as possible a personal obligation. Back home, York was known as a heavy drinker and dramshop brawler always looking for a new war to fight.

Though Mike Shannon was a good scrapper himself, he gave York room except when duty called them together.

Rusty was intrigued by the man's intensity. He eased himself down at Preacher Webb's side and asked, "What do you think of Isaac York?"

Webb considered the question gravely. "He's been to the edge of the pit and looked down into the fires of hell. He's a good man to have at your side in a fight, but some dark day the fire will draw him in. You'd not want to be at his side then."

Rusty stared at the troubled face and shivered.

It seemed he had barely gone to sleep when Mike shook his shoulder. "Time to saddle up and go, young'un. Tom Blessing's given the word."

Rusty's body resisted at first. He was painfully stiff from lying on the ground, and his stomach was uneasy because of the need for more sleep. But he felt a renewal of yesterday's excitement at riding with these men. Moreover, he was ashamed to lag when he saw that the minister, much older than he, was up and moving. So was Mike, limping heavily as he saddled his horse. Looking to the east, Rusty saw no sign of sunrise.

Webb seemed to read his thoughts. "Moon's still up. The Lord has given us light enough that we should be able to follow the trail, plain as it is."

The sun was three hours high when they came upon the place where the Comanches had spent the night. Buzzards had already found what remained of a horse they had slaughtered and roasted. They led the pursuers to something else as well.

Rusty took one look at the naked, bloody corpse of the woman and quickly turned away. The exhilarating sense of adventure vanished. He almost lost his quick breakfast of coffee and cold biscuits. He leaned far out of the saddle in case it all came up.

Isaac York went into a frenzy, spurring toward the buzzards, firing his pistol at them, cursing them and all the Indians that ever lived. The birds rose sluggishly into the air. One of York's bullets struck home, and black feathers exploded. The buzzard fell to the ground and flapped one wing, futilely trying to rise again.

Fowler Gaskin stared at the body with bold curiosity as if he had never seen a woman naked before.

Preacher Webb's voice had a sting. "Have you no decency in you, Fowler?" He dismounted and untied the blanket from behind the cantle of his saddle. He shook it out and covered the woman with it, removed his hat and began a quiet prayer. The other men bared and bowed their heads. Rusty sensed a quiet fury rising among the group, though no one spoke while Webb prayed. Even York managed to contain himself, but barely.

The prayer finished, York faced Blessing and took an accusatory stance. "They probably done this to her while we was takin' our rest last night."

Blessing seemed stunned by the sight of the dead woman. That surprised Rusty, because he had always regarded Blessing as a man who could not be shaken. Blessing said, "We couldn't have gotten here in time to stop it if we had ridden straight through." He turned to the other men. "Look around. The boy may be here somewhere, too."

No trace was found. The boy evidently was still with the Indians.

"Damn them!" York's eyes were wild. "The only way to stop them is to kill them all—every last redskinned heathen for a thousand miles!"

"You know we can't."

"Why not? Who'd stop us?"

"The United States Army. They'd stop us at the reserve."

Rusty was aware that a reservation had been set up on the Brazos River in North Central Texas for those Indians who would come to council and formally agree to peace. He knew from what he had heard around the settlement that even some southern Comanche bands were there. Other Comanches remained unfettered, ranging at will across their accustomed hunting grounds and beyond, occasionally raiding southward all the way into Mexico. Most Texas residents would not have minded—might even have cheered—if the attacks had been confined to Mexico, but of course they were not.

The settlers were distrustful, even hostile to the concept of reserve Indians. It was common belief that raiding parties ventured out from the reservation, then fled back to the army's protection once they had committed their depredations. This was accepted as fact, though some of the warriors now on the reserve had sided with the whites as scouts and fighting allies in two recent major campaigns against hostile Comanches.

Comanches preyed upon other Indians as well as upon the white settlements. They saw everyone around them as either friend or enemy. They had few friends.

York cried, "The federals! They don't do a damned thing to protect white people, but they'd shoot us all to save their Indian pets."

Blessing did not argue. Rusty had a strong feeling that he agreed even if he did not say so. The captain said, "Preacher, we never thought to bring a shovel, but there's a plenty of rocks here. Reckon you and Rusty can cover her decent and then try to catch up to us? We'll move on as fast as we can without killin' the horses."

"We'll do our best by her."

Blessing sought out Gaskin. "Fowler, why don't you stay and help?"

Gaskin was quick to dismount. "If you say so, Tom, but you know I'm ready and rarin' to go on."

York looked down a last time at the blanket-covered body. "We ought to kill them all and send them back to hell where they came from!"

The black man called Shanty rode beside him, talking quietly, trying to calm him. "You liable to bust a blood vessel, Mr. Isaac. You know what happened to you the last time."

Rusty had heard that York got into a violent argument at the settlement and went into some kind of fit. Witnesses had feared for a few minutes that he might die.

As the men rode away, Rusty asked, "Was this lady maybe some kin of York's?"

Webb shook his head. "I doubt he even knew her. But out here we're so few that in one sense we're all kin."

"I just thought from the way he acted . . ."

"A few years ago, down on the Brazos, he and Shanty went to help a neighbor raise a cabin. When they got back he found his own cabin burned and his wife dead. The Comanches did to her what they did to this poor woman, and killed his two little girls besides. Such a thing has driven stronger men than Isaac York out of their minds."

Rusty and Webb wrapped the blanket around the body and began picking up rocks. Fowler Gaskin made a halfhearted effort but contributed only a few stones to the mound. He kept mumbling about the likelihood that the rangers would run into an ambush. "Tom Blessing don't know what he may be gettin' into."

"He knows what he's doin'," Webb said. "He always does."

When the minister decided the body was covered with enough stones to discourage wolves and coyotes, Gaskin declared, "This sorry mule is about give out."

Webb suggested, "Then the best thing for you to do is go on home. You wouldn't be of much use on a worn-out mule."

Gaskin tried to look disappointed, but the relief in his eyes made him a liar. "You tell Tom Blessing how bad I hate to have to drop out."

Webb was much kinder than Rusty thought the situation warranted. "He'll understand. We all do."

Gaskin rode away, putting the mule into a stiff trot. The animal was not too tired for that.

Rusty wasted little time brooding about Gaskin's desertion. He stared regretfully at the grave. "It don't seem right—no fitten grave, not even a marker, no kinfolks to say good-bye."

"What's here is just the clay, not the soul. The Lord's takin' care of her now."

Bitterness crept into Rusty's voice. "Where was He last night when she really *needed* takin' care of? He could've struck them butchers down."

"It's not given to us to know His reasons. He tests the strength of our faith."

"I'm not real sure about mine right now. I don't think He's even lookin' in our direction."

"Lad, this is no time to yield to blasphemy."

"You think He's liable to strike *me* down?"

"You're young. You have but little notion how cruel man can be to man. You'll learn, though, and you'll need a strong faith to get you through it."

"I'd have a stronger faith if I could see a dozen Comanches layin' here dead."

"You might not like it once you saw it. Be careful what you pray for, lest it be given unto you."

CHAPTER

FIVE

uffalo Caller, stripped down to breechcloth and moccasins and a
few streaks of paint, allowed the horses and mules to be driven past
him in a generally northward direction. He held tightly to the
rawhide rein of the bay horse he rode and looked southward along
the trail they had just made. He saw no one, but he sensed that the
Texans were back there somewhere. He had seen them in a dream last
night. He could feel them in his bones. A blind man could follow these
tracks, and the Texans were hardly blind.

Ordinarily this would trouble him. On most horse raids he took every
precaution to make the trail difficult or impossible to follow. But this time
was different. This time he had a purpose.

A young brave drew up beside him and studied the tracks. "If we
divide the horses it will be much harder for the Texans to follow."

Buffalo Caller felt the prickling of impatience. He was the leader of
this raid. The young men's fighting ability was as yet unproven. It was not
for them to question his judgment. But he put down the flare of resentment, for this was Black Horse, son of an old friend who had died at Texan
hands long ago, after the big raid on Linnville. Buffalo Caller avoided ever
saying Antelope's name, though it crossed his mind from time to time. It
was not good to speak the names of the dead lest one summon their ghosts.
Ghosts were often known to be unfriendly, though in life they had been

family and friends. Antelope might feel he had ample cause to be unfriendly because Buffalo Caller had drawn a knife on him to defend the Texan boy of the red hair.

Buffalo Caller thought occasionally of the boy, wondering if he yet lived. Whippoorwill had said he was alive when the Texans took him from her, but only because a Texan bullet had struck down Antelope as he tried to kill the youngster. Buffalo Caller knew that dark spirits could summon all manner of ill fortune to fall upon child and adult alike. Diseases once unknown to the Comanche had spread among them with a vengeance after the white man's coming. The spotted sickness was the worst, snuffing out the lives not only of children but of their elders as well, leaving many lodges in mourning.

The white man had much to answer for.

He had often thought upon Antelope's warning that the boy's red hair was bad medicine and could bring misfortune upon them all. True, the big fight had been a disaster for the Comanches. Buffalo Caller had almost died of a bullet wound and later had had to make his way afoot all the way from the battlefield to the encampment on the plains. Many a long and sleepless night, he had pondered Antelope's warning and wondered if it might have been correct.

In the fight, Buffalo Caller had lost the scalp of the red-haired woman who had been the boy's mother. He wished he could have burned it, for at times he felt its evil had followed him. He had encountered a few white people with red hair in the years since. He had drawn away from them as if they carried the spotted sickness. He had not considered killing them, for he feared the possibility that evil spirits dwelling within them might transfer themselves to him at the moment of their deaths. Shamans had said this could come to pass. A wise man did not risk the displeasure of malevolent spirits.

Blinking against the bite of dust, he looked toward the herd of horses and mules. He could not see the white boy they had taken. He had feared all along that one of the young warriors might take it in his head to kill the youngster as Antelope had tried to kill the other one long ago. That would be contrary to Buffalo Caller's order, but the young men were not bound to obey if they chose otherwise. A war leader could not compel; he could only use his powers of persuasion and hope they were strong enough. He had given his approval for the young men to violate and then butcher the white woman in hope that spilling her blood would cool the fire in their own. She had been a burden anyway weeping all the time. How could white men expect to raise strong sons if the mothers were weak?

It had long been a Comanche observation that captive children should be separated from their mothers as soon as possible if they were to make a successful conversion to the ways of The People. Texan and Mexican mothers tended to exert an adverse influence. This boy, who appeared to be three or four summers old, had the chance to become a good warrior once his mettle had been tested. The young men had been quirting him at intervals and jabbing the points of their arrows into his skin to determine if he was of strong spirit. So far he seemed to be. He had cried a bit at first, then had grown sullen. This morning he had lashed out at a couple of his tormenters. Buffalo Caller took that as a good omen.

He put the bay into a lope to catch up and pass the herd. He noted with satisfaction that the captive boy appeared sound enough, riding in front of a young warrior who had suggested that he might take the lad as his brother. Buffalo Caller said, "He has borne up well. Do not let them torment him anymore."

He rode beyond the herd to where Wolf That Limps was scouting out in front. He said, "We have entered the reserve. We must be watchful and not fall into the hands of the soldiers."

It was well known that horseback troops of the White Father in Washington patrolled the perimeter of the Indian reserve, as much to protect their wards inside from hostile whites as to prevent those wards from slipping away and committing depredations. Buffalo Caller had only contempt for Indians who gave up their freedom and allowed themselves to be penned like cattle, accepting whatever paltry gifts the White Father deigned to give them. A real man would choose to range free, hunting buffalo, raiding his enemies, and living from the land, or he would die fighting, as wild horses sometimes died rather than submit to the rope. Moreover, Buffalo Caller was resentful because some of the reserve Indians had aided soldiers and rangers against those Comanches who still chose to remain outside, living in the old ways. Many a weeping widow had mutilated herself in mourning for husbands who died at the hands of these pet dogs from the reservation.

Most Texans could not distinguish between tribes. Reserve Indians who rode with them against the Comanches had to tie white cloths to their arms so the whites would not kill them by mistake. Buffalo Caller knew that most settlers believed the reserve Indians were taking advantage of their protected status to commit theft and murder in the settlements, then flee back to safety under the soldiers' guardianship. The Texans were chafing at a chance for vengeance.

So was Buffalo Caller. He thought it a delicious irony that the whites themselves might give him that revenge.

Wolf That Limps said, "Would it not be much safer to go around the reserve? The soldiers do not range far. They would never see us."

"If we are careful they will not see us anyway. But the Texans will follow the tracks. They will believe those who live on the reservation have made this raid. Sooner or later they will fall upon them with gun and knife. The ones who helped them against us will pay for what they did."

"Are the whites so easily fooled?"

"They are bad-hearted people who do not know Comanche from Waco or Caddo or Kiowa. They will kill our enemies for us and believe they have done a great thing."

The sun had not traveled much farther overhead when a warrior approached from the south in an easy lope. Buffalo Caller had sent him to watch the back trail.

"The Texans are coming," Black Wing said, turning and pointing. "They follow the trail just as you wanted."

"Onto the reserve?"

"Yes. But the horse soldiers will stop them soon. They also are coming."

Buffalo Caller had not counted on the soldiers, but after a moment's consideration he decided benevolent spirits were indeed riding with him today. It might be even better than he had planned if the soldiers and the Texans confronted one another. Perhaps some would be killed. Even if not, this would only anger the Texans more against the traitorous people who lived on the reserve. One day soon the Texans would rise in fury, and the Comanches would have vengeance upon those who had brought the rangers and the soldiers against them.

He caught up to the others and signaled for them to stop the herd. "Now," he said, "the trap is sprung. It is time we divide and disappear like smoke."

The horses and mules were split into small groups whose tracks would be difficult to follow. If the Texans managed to get past the soldiers and penetrate this far, they would be confounded by loss of the trail. It would seem obvious to them that the reserve Indians were the authors of their trouble.

Black Wing said, "You are clever, elder brother."

"I have studied the Trickster. Coyote is a good teacher."

Isaac York was livid. "See there, Tom, what I been tellin' you? These tracks have led us straight onto the reserve."

Blessing appeared torn, believing even as he wished he did not. "Don't you think I can see for myself?"

"You didn't want to, but there's the evidence right before your eyes. How much longer we got to put up with this before we do what we ought to've done before they ever moved them red heathens in here?"

"The agents've said all along that they're keepin' the reserve Indians under control. I can't say I trusted them all, but I trusted Robert Neighbors." Neighbors was the chief agent, approved by both the federal government and the governor of Texas.

"That dead woman back yonder tells you he lied. She tells you they all lied. We'd just as well have a rattlesnake den in our backyard as to have this reserve here."

"I don't know what we can do about it."

"We're fixin' to get a chance. Yonder come the yellow-legged soldiers."

Rusty turned to look in the direction York pointed. A small federal patrol—he counted seven men—moved rapidly up from their right flank. The officer in the lead waved his hand as a signal for the Texans to halt.

York said, "There's twice as many of us as there is of them. We ain't stoppin' for them, are we?"

Blessing raised his hand. "Let's see what they say about these horse tracks."

Mike drew his horse up beside Rusty. "If any trouble starts, young'un, you get out of the way. Your mother would never forgive me if I let you get shot. Especially by a United States soldier."

So far as Rusty knew, Mike had never retreated in his life. "If you don't run, I don't run."

The officer reined up and glanced first at York, then at Blessing, trying to decide which was the leader. Both had a formidable look, as if they were ready for the war to start. Blessing did not leave him wondering long. "Do you have business with us, sir? If not, we have business of our own."

The officer took on an imperious tone. "Are you aware that you are trespassing? You crossed over the reserve boundary some miles back."

"With good reason. Some of your wards butchered a woman back yonder, and they kidnapped a boy. Besides that, they've stolen a big bunch of horses and mules. We intend to get them back."

"None of our Indians are out. We have been making certain of that."

"Look at the tracks. They speak for themselves."

The officer gave the trail only a moment's attention. "If any of our Indians have a captive, we shall see that he is freed. If livestock has been stolen from you, it is the responsibility of federal troops to recover them. Now, gentlemen, you will turn around and leave!"

York leaned forward in the saddle and pointed a finger straight at the officer's nose. "We've come to free that boy and get our property back. And we intend to make some of your red pets pay. If you think you can stop us, you'd best count your soldiers and then count us."

The officer's face reddened, but he yielded no ground. "This is a federal reserve. You have no right to be here."

Blessing said, "It may be a federal reserve, but it's in Texas, and we are officers of the state of Texas, duly sworn. If your reserve Indians are not guilty, who is?"

"That must be determined. By us, not by you."

"You'll have to shoot us to stop us. It'll look bad in Washington, federal troops shootin' citizens who only want to get back what's rightfully theirs."

The officer did not answer. Rusty could see doubt in his eyes.

Blessing took silence as a positive sign. "All right, boys, let's go ahead." He turned his back on the officer and touched his heels to his horse. The rest of the volunteers followed. Rusty's mouth went dry as he saw the soldiers draw rifles. Blessing saw, but if he had misgivings he did not betray them. He kept riding, his back straight and stiff. After a few tense moments the officer shouted an order and the soldiers put the rifles back into their scabbards. He signaled for his troopers to follow the ranger volunteers. He spurred forward, pulling up abreast of Blessing.

"You are all under arrest, you know."

"The hell you say." Rusty knew both Blessing and the officer had been bluffing, and Blessing had made his bluff stick, at least for the moment. He could see how ludicrous the situation was, seven troopers trying to arrest a group of armed and determined Texans more than double their number. But he could not laugh.

Neither could Mike or Preacher Webb. Mike kept his voice low. "Stay close to me, young'un. Right now it wouldn't take but one fool on either side to spark a small war."

"What'll we do?"

"One thing we *won't* do is fire on federal soldiers. I fought beside them in Mexico. I won't fight against them."

Webb said, "Wise words, well put."

The passing of miles gradually drained away the tension. Rusty decided that neither Texans nor soldiers wanted a fight, except perhaps Isaac York. The officer calmed enough to begin a conversation with Tom Blessing, who explained to him the settlers' fears and frustrations.

The officer said, "I assure you we are not uncaring. We are doing our best to keep the reservation Indians contained. But at the same time we have a responsibility to protect them against harm from outside."

"You've already shown that you can't protect *us*. All we're after now is justice, and to get back that boy and our stock. We'd rather have you with us than against us, but we'll do what we have to no matter which way you go."

Blessing stopped his horse and looked at the ground. He rode a little farther and stopped again. "They've split off into several bunches. We can't follow them all."

Mike frowned at Rusty and Preacher Webb. "Ain't no way to tell what bunch took the boy."

Webb nodded. "It won't matter. Whichever trail we follow, it will soon disappear. I'm surprised they've let us track them this far."

The officer overheard. "They did it because they wanted you to follow. It's a Comanche trick to make you believe our reservation Indians were responsible."

Isaac York argued, "Ignorant savages, they're not smart enough to figure out a scheme such as that."

"You've not seen them from my vantage point. Just because they cannot read books does not mean they lack native intelligence. They are as smart as any of us."

"You sayin' it don't make it so," York retorted. "Ain't no two of them got the brains of a white man."

Exasperated, the officer went silent.

Blessing chose a trail that seemed the largest. "We'll follow this one and see where it takes us."

It did not take them far. It led to a stream that the officer said was a tributary to the Clear Fork of the Brazos. There it vanished. Tracks were visible to the edge of the water, but none appeared on the other side. Blessing divided the detail, sending half upstream and half down. The soldiers also split, half following one group of Texans, half the other. The officer remained with Blessing.

The search was futile. The point of exit could not be found.

Isaac York fumed. "Crafty bastards. Let's go back and follow one of the other trails."

Blessing shook his head. "Wouldn't be of no use. It'd end up just like this one. When they want to, Indians can disappear like dust after a whirlwind."

"We can't just up and quit. Let's search every village on the reservation 'til we find them."

"We're out of grub, and we've just about rode our horses down. Besides, do you think seven soldiers are all there is? The lieutenant can go and fetch however many he needs to stop us. And he will."

The officer's eyes were fierce. "You can count on it."

For a moment Rusty feared he was about to see York go into a fit like the one they talked about at the settlement. York said, "I'll go by myself if I have to. Just me and Shanty."

The little black man pulled in beside him as if to give weight to the threat.

The officer said grittily, "I'd have you in irons before the sun is down."

Blessing turned to look grimly over his men. "That won't be necessary. We're goin' home . . . unless you've still got a foolish notion that we're under arrest."

"I bow to reality. But I warn you once more: This reserve is protected ground. Trespass again and you will face the full might of the United States Army."

Blessing looked up the stream in the direction the trail had led. "Damned little might you've ever shown against hostile Indians."

The officer promised, "We'll search the reserve for the boy and for your stock. But I believe they are beyond the reserve now, bound for Comanche country."

Blessing's voice was bitter. "Believe what you want to, but you'd better find that boy. Otherwise we'll be back, and you and your army can go to hell!"

Rusty expected the soldiers to accompany the Texans across the reserve boundary, but they did not. The officer said, "I'll get reinforcements and some Indian trackers. We'll follow up on the trails." He led his troopers away.

York watched them. His voice was sour. "Ain't nothin'll come of it. Them soldiers couldn't find an elephant in a hog pen."

Rusty had a gut feeling that the captive boy would never be found. "What'll they do to him?"

Mike Shannon stared to the north, where the Indians had probably gone. "They'll make a Comanche out of him or they'll kill him."

"That's what they'd've done to me, isn't it? But you and Preacher Webb got in their way."

Mike's face showed despair. "I'm afraid there ain't nobody goin' to get in their way this time."

The volunteers had ridden north like a military unit, heads high, driven by a stern determination. Retreating southward now, they straggled without order, shoulders hunched in an attitude of failure. The mood was contagious. Rusty felt an emptiness that went beyond hunger. He had eaten nothing since yesterday noon.

"We didn't accomplish a thing," he lamented to Mike.

Mike only grunted. "It ends up this way more often than not. Many a time I've ridden a hundred miles after Indians and never seen a feather. But we've got to try or we'd just as well pack up our wagon and go back to wherever we came from."

Preacher Webb added, "There's no shame in losin', provided you made an honest effort. There's shame only when you give up before you start."

Rusty heard Isaac York raise his voice. "Yonder's a pair of tepees."

They stood three hundred yards away, within easy water-carrying distance of the stream.

Blessing said, "Probably just a family or two out huntin' for meat. The ones we're after wouldn't camp where they're so easy found."

"They're Indians, ain't they?" York put spurs to his horse and set him into a run. Behind him the black man Shanty tried vainly to catch up. He had no spurs. He did not even have shoes.

Blessing called in vain for York to stop.

Mike said, "We'd better go after him. Ain't no tellin' what he's crazy enough to do." He put his black horse Alamo into a lope. Rusty and Blessing and the others followed.

Rusty saw two women scraping flesh from the hide of a deer. Three children played nearby until they heard the horses and saw the oncoming riders. They fled into scrub timber alongside the stream. The two women screamed. An elderly man stooped to come out through the open flap of a tepee. He motioned for the women to run, then pushed himself as erect as his age would allow and waited for the horsemen.

York shot him.

One of the women turned back and hurried to the fallen man. She knelt at his side, then pushed to her feet and rushed at York, screaming at him and shaking her fists.

He shot her, too.

By then the rest of the Texans arrived. Blessing shouted in a rage, "Goddamn you, Isaac York, put up that pistol!"

York said, "I ain't through yet. There's still more of them."

Mike Shannon drew the old pistol he had brought home from the Mexican War. "Put it away, or 'y God I'll shoot you!"

York gave Mike a look of pure hatred. "They're gettin' away. I saw a boy amongst them young'uns."

Blessing said, "I saw him, too. He was an Indian boy. Put up the gun, Isaac."

York resisted. He looked down at the dead man. "There's one good Comanche. He'll never kill another white woman or steal a white boy."

Mike said, "These're not Comanches. Take another look."

York shrugged, unmoved. "Makes no difference. They're Indians. One or another, they're all alike." He started to ride after the others.

To Rusty's surprise, Mike Shannon spurred up beside York and pulled him from his horse. The two men landed together in the grass and began to fight. Blessing stepped in to separate them. "That's enough. Both of you, back away."

Shanty placed himself protectively in front of York. York was shaking and shouting incoherently. Rusty quickly dismounted and gripped Mike's arms. "No more, Dad. It's over with."

Preacher Webb stood between the dead man and the wounded woman. He removed his hat and began a prayer in a voice almost too low for Rusty to hear. "Lord God, forgive us all."

Blessing's face was scarlet. Rusty thought he looked as if *he* were about to go into a spasm. "Isaac, there's no tellin' how much trouble you may have got us into. Bad enough killin' the old man, but shootin' a woman, too?"

York trembled in the aftermath of rage. "They killed a white woman. I hope this one dies. She won't be birthin' no more babies to grow up and kill white folks."

Blessing saw the futility of argument with York. "If the troops heard the shots they'll be comin' to see what happened. We'd better put the reservation behind us as quick as we can." He waved his hand and set off southward in the lead, putting his horse into a long trot.

When the Texans departed, the other woman and the children emerged from the timber and set in to wailing. Rusty felt a chill.

Darkness lingered in his foster father's face. Mike Shannon said, "Young'un, we did accomplish somethin' after all. We killed a defenseless old man and maybe a woman. Ain't that somethin' for a ranger to be proud of?"

As Mike and Rusty turned off toward the farm, leaving the rest of the volunteers, Tom Blessing said, "You-all consider yourselves still sworn in. If things go the way they're pointed right now, I'll be needin' you."

Mike did not wait for Rusty to react. "Just holler any time. But next time leave Isaac York to home."

Rusty was not sure he would want to go again, not if the next mission turned out as this one had.

Preacher Webb brought the call. He rode up to the cabin one morning, his grim expression indicating he carried a message of importance. He delayed its delivery until he had inquired about Mother Dora's health.

Mike's worried eyes reflected the burden he had carried lately. "I'm afraid the medicine ain't helpin' her. Most days it's all she can do to get out of bed. Me and Rusty been doin' the cookin' and all."

Webb entered the cabin. He returned in a few minutes with a deep frown. "I wish we had a sure-enough doctor to see after her. Isn't much I can do that I haven't already done."

"You've done your best, Preacher." Mike grimaced. "The rest is up to the Almighty."

Rusty feared the Almighty was looking somewhere else. But he would not say so where the minister could hear.

Webb said, "These are dark days. I suppose you've heard the talk that Texas may pull out of the Union?"

Mike grunted. "I have, and it's damned foolishness."

"A lot of people are dead serious about it. And there's been more trouble up on the reserve. A bunch of white men rode in there and started a fight. When it was over there were dead on both sides. So the army has been ordered to move all tribes off of the reserve . . . take them north of the Red River into Indian Teritory."

Mike scowled. "Even the ones that helped us fight the Comanches?"

"That's what we're told. I'm afraid most Texans don't put much faith in Indian loyalties."

"Damned poor piece of business. What ever became of gratitude?"

"Tom wants to take some of us up there and help see that the move stays peaceful."

Mike observed, "Then he'd best not take Isaac York."

"Isaac's not goin'. And neither are you, Mike. You'd best stay here and watch over Dora."

Rusty expected Mike to roar in angry protest because he had always welcomed any opportunity for adventure. Instead, he seemed almost relieved at not going. His easy acceptance brought home to Rusty—though he needed no reminding—that his foster mother was failing.

Mike gripped Rusty's shoulder. His legs might be weak now, but his hands were strong as steel. "You'll have to serve for both of us, young'un. It won't be a happy sight to watch. Gather up what stuff you need. I'll go saddle my black horse for you."

Rusty remembered the bitter ending of the last trip and did not want to go. But Mike had drilled the notion of duty into him too deeply for him to voice his reluctance. He rolled a blanket, collected a little grub and the rifle, and went in to say a hasty good-bye to Mother Dora. She clutched his hand as if she feared she would not see him again. She whispered, "Hurry back as soon as you can."

"Just a week or ten days, Preacher Webb says. It won't be forever."

"Not for you, but maybe for me."

Rusty blinked back the threat of tears and tried to make light of the turbulence he felt. "I'll be back before you know I'm gone."

Mike led the saddled horse out of the corral and watched Rusty tie the blanket behind the cantle. "Tom Blessing is a good man, so listen to what he says. But don't put all your faith in other people, because sometimes they can be wrong. Do your own thinkin'. In the long run every man has got to answer to himself, and *for* himself." He looked up at Webb, in the saddle and waiting. "Keep an eye on him, won't you, Preacher?"

"Don't you worry about Rusty. You take care of Dora."

Rusty and Webb cut across the river and put their horses into a trot. They intercepted Blessing and six others after a couple of hours. Webb explained about Mike's remaining behind. Blessing took the news with regret. "I always felt that everything would turn out all right when I could see Mike Shannon at my side. You've got a big pair of boots to fill, Rusty."

Rusty did not know how to reply. Webb smiled. "He'll fill them. He's still gettin' his growth."

Rusty glanced quickly over the men and was pleased to see that Isaac York was not among them. He had lain awake many nights, his mind's eye seeing York shoot the old man and the Indian woman over and over again. The memory usually brought him to a cold sweat. He would seek a balance by remembering the white woman so cruelly butchered, but that made him feel no easier about York. The man had a streak of madness in him, Rusty thought. Given provocation, there was no telling what he might do.

It took the rangers two days to reach the boundary of the reserve. There they met a couple of similar volunteer companies gathered to keep the peace. Looking at their determined faces, Rusty suspected that a few might welcome any excuse to break the peace instead, to kill a few more Indians before they were moved out of the state and, in theory at least, out of reach. Besides the rangers, a number of civilians came straggling along, well-armed and talking loudly. It was apparent that they were not burdened with the weight of good intentions.

Rusty was relieved to see a large contingent of U.S. Army troops on hand to accompany the march out of Texas. Without their protection, he suspected, many of the Indians would not live to see the Red River.

Major Robert Neighbors, the Indian agent, accompanied the final group of refugees that started the long northward trek. Rusty heard him mutter something about Philistines and the exodus from Egypt.

Rusty saw grown men weeping. He saw an Indian woman throw her arms around a tree and refuse to move until two soldiers forcibly pulled her away. He saw a travois with a woman lying on it, her shoulder heavily bandaged. He could not be sure, but he thought she was probably the one York had shot. If so, she had survived the wound. He hoped she would survive the long trip, the travois bumping along on rough ground and jarring her mercilessly.

The rangers followed at a respectable distance. It was plain to Rusty that the Indians were bitterly opposed to the move, forced upon them so suddenly that they had not had time to gather most of their livestock. He could imagine what would happen to the animals. As soon as the troops were out of sight, opportunists would drive off all the horses and cattle they could find. Even if the government permitted a delegation of Indians to come back for a roundup, they would find that most of their property was gone.

Finally watching the long, sad column cross the river into the territory, Tom Blessing said, "We'll all breathe easier with them gone."

Preacher Webb replied, "No matter how we may want to justify it, this is a damned poor reward for the help they gave us against the Comanches."

Rusty had never heard the minister use the word *damned*, at least not in that manner. It showed the depth of his feelings.

Blessing said, "You've got too busy a conscience, Preacher. There's times a man has to lock it away and do what needs to be done. The white man and the Indian are too different to live side by side. We tried it, and it didn't work. Somebody has to give way. There's a lot more of us than there is of them."

Rusty listened in a quandary, swinging at first to Blessing's view, then back to Preacher Webb's, and finally hanging uncertainly somewhere in the middle. Daddy Mike had talked a great deal about the recent campaign against the Comanches who shunned the reservation. He claimed that had it not been for help from the reserve Indians, the expedition would have had no chance. Still, correctly or not, most people believed the reserve Indians were responsible for much of the raiding.

It was hard to know what was right. Watching the last of the Indians trail off into the distance, he was glad the decision had not been his to make.

North of the Red River, a satisfied Buffalo Caller sat on his horse at the edge of a stand of timber and watched the straggling column making its way toward a new homeland the federal government had staked out. This was what he had hoped for, why he had made false trails into the reserve. He felt no pity for the distress he saw among the evacuees. They had aided the *teibos* against the Comanches. They deserved whatever misfortune the dark spirits might visit upon them.

Now perhaps they would understand what the Comanches had known all along, that the whites were a treacherous and grasping lot, stealing everything they saw. Given their way, they would drive the Indian to the edge of the Mother Earth and push him over into the great emptiness.

Up to now the reserve tribes had regarded the Comanches as their enemy. Perhaps this would show them who their true enemy was.

CHAPTER

SIX

Rusty watched with misgivings as Mike Shannon threw his saddle up over his horse's back and buckled the girth. "Don't you think I ought to go with you?"

Mike adjusted his coat, for the wind carried a chill. "Ain't no need. I'm just goin' to the settlement to have a drink or two and visit what friends I've still got left."

Lately there had been much less talk about Indians than about a proposed Texas referendum on secession from the Union. Most people along the river seemed to favor joining the new Confederacy. Mike vigorously opposed it, so longtime friends had been falling away from him.

Rusty said, "At least, don't be talkin' politics. It'll just get you into another fight."

"Why shouldn't a man say what he thinks when he knows he's right? Them boys've got no idea what they're talkin' about. Wantin' to take Texas out of the Union . . . they've forgot how hard we fought to get *in*."

"It won't make a particle of difference what you or anybody else says in a little cotton-gin settlement most people never heard of. It'll be decided in places like Austin and San Antonio. That's where the big votes are."

"Just the same, if a man don't exercise his right to say what he thinks, pretty soon they won't let him say anything."

"Even Tom Blessing has given up on the Union, and he used to be as strong for it as anybody. He says a little bunch of Yankees up north are tryin' to boss everybody. Says it's time to rise up and tell them to go to hell before we lose all our rights."

Face reddening, Mike shook his finger at Rusty. "Don't you ever let me hear talk like that comin' out of your mouth. I was born American. I've fought under the United States flag. I'll not stand idle while anybody talks against it . . . not you, not anybody." He swung up onto the horse. "Not anybody, 'y God!"

Watching Mike ride off eastward on the wagon road, Rusty felt chastened by the harshness of his foster father's voice. He should be getting used to it, he thought. Always one to speak his mind and opinions with his fists, Mike had been increasingly argumentative since the secession talk became serious. Moreover, he had taken to drinking considerably more since they had buried Mother Dora at the edge of the oak grove west of the cabin. Nobody had ever quite decided what her ailment was. She had simply faded before their eyes, becoming grayer and thinner, losing strength until one day Mike and Rusty had come home from the field and found her dying.

In a voice so low he could barely hear it, she had asked Rusty to look after his father. He had promised he would, but he feared he had done poorly at living up to the promise. Mike Shannon was too old to take orders from Rusty and too headstrong to accept advice. He had come home from the settlement more than once with his face bruised, his knuckles skinned and swollen.

Some of it was patriotism, Rusty reasoned, but some was simply a result of grief and restlessness, a combination too much for Mike to bear with grace.

Rusty was wrestling with his own feelings about the secession question. On one hand, he could see his father's side of it. The fiercely partisan Mike had drummed patriotism and duty into him from the time Rusty was old enough to understand the words. On the other, he could understand why Tom Blessing had joined so many in disillusionment with the federal government. It had long promised to protect settlers but had not delivered. The troops it sent to the frontier were limited in number and too often foot soldiers, incapable of anything more than holding a defensive position. Cavalrymen were so few that they were unable to keep Indians from stealing army horses out of the military's own corrals.

Yet the same Washington officials responsible for such unwise decisions felt obliged to exert increasing control over the daily lives of the faraway folk they served so poorly.

Some people were saying the whole problem was over slavery, but Rusty did not accept that. Tom Blessing owned no slaves, yet he staunchly defended secession on the grounds that the federals were becoming dictatorial. The only slave Rusty knew in these parts was Isaac York's man Shanty. Whatever York's faults, and he had many, he treated Shanty more like a friend and partner than a piece of property.

Maybe the whole notion would run its course and blow over like a whirlwind that raises a lot of dust, then falls away. Rusty did not relish the prospect of having to make a choice.

He harnessed old Chapultepec. The mule had recently caused a fist-fight between Rusty and the Gaskin brothers. Twice Mike had asked Fowler Gaskin to return the animal he had borrowed without a by-your-leave. Gaskin always had an excuse for keeping it a little longer. Seeing Mike's growing impatience and afraid he was on the verge of getting into a serious quarrel with Gaskin, Rusty rode to the neighboring farm alone, determined to fetch the mule home whether the Gaskins liked it or not.

They had not liked it. Fowler Gaskin had a way of looking pathetic as a beggar on a village square when he wanted something, and he usually wanted something. "Boy, you don't know how it is to be poor folks. We can't afford to buy a good strong mule for ourselves. We'd be obliged if you-all'd let us keep the use of this'un just a few more days."

Rusty acted as if he hadn't heard. "Where's he at?"

"He ain't real handy right now. Tell you what, I'll have one of the boys take him home the first of next week."

Suspiciously Rusty demanded again, "Where you got him?"

Gaskin backed away, half a step at a time. "Truth of the matter is, he ain't here. He's over at the Joneses."

By this time the two Gaskin brothers had come up to stand on either side of their father. Rusty could see fight in their eyes.

Anger rising, Rusty was in a mood to accommodate them. He balled his fists. "How come he's at the Joneses? Thought you borrowed him for your own use."

"Old Man Jones offered me fifty cents a day to hire him, and me and the family sure do need the money."

Rusty could feel heat rising in his face. He prepared to remount. "I'll go over to the Jones place and fetch him."

Gaskin took hold of Rusty's bridle reins. "You can't do that. Old Man Jones paid me for ten days, and he ain't used them up yet."

Rusty trembled with anger. "Then I reckon you'll have to give him his money back."

"But it's done spent, and I don't know how I'll go about gettin' any more."

"You might try sendin' your boys out to work."

"You act awful high and mighty, Rusty Shannon, because you-all have got a bigger farm and a lot more money."

"You've got just as much land, but you're all too lazy to work it proper. As for money, I can't remember the last time we had twenty dollars cash."

He lifted his foot toward the stirrup, but Eph Gaskin grabbed the back of his coat. "You ain't goin' noplace."

Rusty whirled and swung a knot-hard fist at him. Gaskin's head snapped back under the impact. The other brother rushed in, and Rusty found himself entertaining two at the same time. The scrap lasted only a minute or so. When it was over, both younger Gaskins were sitting on the ground with bruises and contusions, showing no inclination to get up.

Fowler Gaskin shook his fist but dropped it quickly when Rusty took a step toward him. "I'm a crippled-up old man. The law wouldn't like it, you hittin' a crippled-up old man."

Eph Gaskin did not arise, but he growled, "We'll get you, Rusty Shannon. You just wait, we'll pay you back."

Rusty said grittily, "You'd better worry about how you're goin' to pay back Old Man Jones for the loss of the mule."

Riding away, he could hear Fowler Gaskin railing at his sons for letting "that redheaded son of a bitch" whip both of them. Rusty rubbed his skinned knuckles in satisfaction. It had been the best day's work he had done all winter.

It had been three days since the fight. Now Rusty hitched Chapultepec alongside a young mule Mike had traded for. The young one had a double portion of stubbornness and only a small portion of the older mule's intelligence. It was constantly testing the limits of Rusty's patience, but at least it helped keep his mind occupied so he did not dwell on grief over Mother Dora or brood too much on the troubles brewing between North and South. These seemed far away except when Mike went to the settlement. Then they came close to home.

Rusty had the wagon half full of deadfall timber when he stopped to drink from a jug he had brought beneath the seat. His attention was caught by movement on the road from the east. Preacher Webb approached on a bay horse. The minister altered his course when he spotted Rusty down by the river. Rusty held the jug high so he would see it. "Water, Preacher? It ain't coffee, but it's wet."

"Much obliged." Webb dismounted and tipped up the jug for a long drink. "I never could understand why so many people insist on whiskey. Water is better by far." He wiped his mouth on the frayed sleeve of his coat and glanced toward the cabin. "Is Mike anywhere around?"

"He's gone to the settlement."

Webb's face looked pinched. "I must have missed him somewhere on the way. Wish I'd gotten here in time to head him off. Things are commencin' to get ugly."

"How ugly?"

"Ugly enough. There's been a lot of agitation stirred up against those who oppose secession. I'm afraid it's gettin' dangerous."

Rusty suspected Webb had heard about the fights Mike had had over the question. "He's always taken care of himself."

"He's never seen old friends turn into enemies before. It's been bitter enough to cause a few killin's."

The minister's apprehension was infectious. Rusty began to feel it, too. "It might do some good if you'd talk to him. He doesn't listen to me much. Still figures I'm just a kid."

"I'll go back to the settlement and look for him."

Rusty watched Webb ride off. His stomach had been uneasy since Mike had left, and it was worse now. Politics had brought on this trouble. This could be a happier world if it weren't for politics and politicians, he thought. He wondered if Indians had them, too. He decided they probably did. They fought among themselves just like white folks, sometimes with even deadlier results.

If he ever found himself in a position to rule the country, he would pass a law against politics.

Rusty waited for supper until almost dark, hoping Mike would come home. The work and the cold had made him hungry, however, so he finally fried up some smokehouse ham and made corn bread. He had almost finished eating when he heard voices outside. Stepping onto the dog run without taking time to put on a coat, he saw Preacher Webb and Mike dismounting from their horses. Mike had to hold to the saddle a minute to steady himself. His face was dark with bruises, his shirt torn and bloody.

Rusty hurried out to help. Mike waved him and Webb away. He said curtly, "I can get into the house by myself." Rusty guessed that he and the minister had argued. It was evident that Mike had been drinking, for no other way would he have said a cross word to his old friend. Rusty stepped aside and let him alone.

Mike stumbled getting up on the dog run but caught himself on a post. "Come on in where it's warm, Preacher. Me and Rusty'll fix you some supper." He weaved his way into the kitchen side of the double cabin and bumped into a chair. He promptly slumped in it.

Rusty remained outside, shivering from the night's chill. "Who did he fight with this time?"

"Isaac York. Isaac's strong for secession. Shanty managed to get hold of him after a few blows were struck. I took Mike out of there."

"I'll bet he wasn't happy about leavin'."

"He wanted to finish the fight, but I was afraid I might have to bring him home dead. Isaac was mad enough to kill him."

Rusty looked toward the door. "I'm obliged. Come on in, Preacher. Dad ought to be in a better humor after he gets some supper in his belly to soak up that whiskey."

Mike's eyes defied Rusty to offer criticism. Rusty held silent as he fried more ham. Preacher Webb tried to smooth Mike's ruffled feathers by talking of other matters such as the promise of ground moisture for next spring's crops, a new baby he had christened for the Mather family, the rumors about building a railroad into Texas.

None of them distracted Mike. "I ain't finished my discussion with Isaac."

Webb argued, "You know he has a crazy streak in him. He's dangerous."

"I'm an American, born free and raised to stay that way. Nobody can tell me what to say or think."

"A man doesn't have to go around *tellin'* everybody what he thinks. He can keep it to himself and stay out of fights that might get him killed."

"Isaac York ain't seen the day he could kill me, not in a fair fight."

Rusty thought of the old Indian and the woman. "What promise have you got that it'd be fair?"

Mike soon began to yawn. Rusty saw him to bed, then returned to the kitchen and the minister. "I wish we could get him away from here for a while. Ain't there Indian trouble someplace, or maybe somethin' stirrin' down on the border?"

"Not anything serious that I know about. I'll talk to Tom Blessing. He might cook up an excuse to get Mike away."

"Tom's strong for secession, too."

"But he's too decent a man to put politics ahead of an old friendship."

Tom Blessing showed up one frosty morning as Rusty prepared breakfast. Mike, still stiff and sore from his fight with York, was having difficulty getting out of bed. Rusty had not been eager to push him, for Mike's mood was not forgiving. He had been pulled away from a fight before it was finished, and it rankled.

"Come on in this house," Rusty called to Blessing. "Coffee's ready, and the rest will be in a few minutes."

Blessing paused at the kitchen door, then glanced back toward the room where Mike grumbled to himself, trying to get his clothes on. "Is he all right?"

"He's movin' kind of slow. I guess Preacher Webb talked to you?"

"He did. I'd already heard about Mike's set-to with Isaac. Preacher's right. Tempers bein' the way they are, it'd be smart to get Mike away from here 'til the secession election's over with and things quiet down."

"I'm afraid he doesn't realize how serious things have got. Preacher says there's been killin'."

"Other places. Not here . . . yet."

"Even Sam Houston talks against secession. Why shouldn't Mike?"

"Nobody's goin' to kill Sam Houston. He's a Texas hero. But he's old now, and not many people listen to him anymore."

Mike struggled through the door about the time Blessing finished his first cup of coffee. His shirt was buttoned wrong. The left side of his face was swollen and colored a patchwork of blue and red. He groped for a chair to steady himself and winced in pain as Blessing shook his hand. "You're out mighty early. Sun ain't made it all the way up yet."

"I've come lookin' for a good man. Got a little job of work for him."

"I don't feel like much of a man this mornin'. Almost everything hurts, and what don't hurt ain't workin'."

"You'll be all right soon as I get you on horseback and you work the kinks out of your system."

"Where we goin'?"

"Not we, just you. I've had word from a volunteer company up close to the Red River. They've got some green boys ridin' patrol to keep raiders from sneakin' down out of the territory. They need guidance from an experienced old-timer who won't turn tail and run from the first Indian he sees."

"I reckon I'm your man. What about Rusty?"

Blessing frowned. "I figured you'd want him to stay here and take care of the farm."

Rusty handed Mike a cup of coffee. Mike seated himself and poured the coffee into a saucer. He blew across it and poured it back into the cup but set it down without drinking. His eyes clouded with suspicion. "You sure they asked you to send them a man? Or is this just somethin' you cooked up to get me away from here?"

Blessing hesitated. "They need all the help they can get."

Anger roughened Mike's voice. "So you're fixin' to move old Mike Shannon out of sight because you're afraid Isaac York is liable to hurt him."

"Those boys up there really need you."

"No they don't. As for Isaac, I'd made a good start toward whippin' him when I was dragged off against my will. I'm stayin' here to be at his service if he wants some more of the same."

Blessing set his cup down half full of coffee. "We've all got your best interests at heart."

"You can serve my best interests by leavin' me the hell alone. Mike Shannon ain't ever run from a fight."

Rusty could think of several strong arguments, but he knew they would be futile. When Mike's eyes took on that defiant look, a four-up team of mules couldn't pull him loose.

Blessing said, "I thank you for the coffee." He pushed his chair back from the table.

Mike's voice softened a little. "You've come a long ways. You'd just as well have breakfast with us."

"Somehow I don't seem to have any appetite." Blessing shook Rusty's hand, then paused at the door to look back at Mike. "I'd give you some advice if I thought you'd take it."

"I won't seek Isaac out, if that's what worries you. But if he comes lookin' for me, I won't be hard to find."

Discouraged, Rusty followed Blessing out onto the dog run. "I thank you for tryin'."

"Isaac's as stubborn as Mike is, but I'll go talk to him. And you keep an eye on your daddy. Tie him up if you have to."

Rusty walked back into the kitchen. Mike looked up from his breakfast. "I think I can see Preacher Webb's fine hand in this. And yours too, like as not."

"None of us want to see you get hurt."

"What hurts the worst is knowin' you don't think I can take care of myself anymore. You figure I'm too old?"

"No, but this is a new situation. Preacher Webb says a lot of people are talkin' war."

"I've been to war before. I'm still here."

Rusty gave in to frustration. "Maybe I ought to go up to the Red River and quit worryin' about you."

"Maybe you ought to."

Rusty knew he would keep worrying if he went halfway around the world. "What am I goin' to do with you, Dad?"

"Nothin'. Just admit that I'm a grown man and let me do things my own way."

You always did, Rusty thought, but he held his tongue.

Walking out to the barn, he began to wonder about his real father. If he were living today, would he react to the current situation the same way as Daddy Mike? Would he be for secession or for the union, and would he be willing to fight for whichever he believed in?

I wish I'd known you, Rusty thought. *Maybe if I knew which way you'd have gone, I'd know which way to go myself.*

A young heifer heavy with calf had not been seen in a couple of days, then showed up with her udder swollen and her sides flatter than they had been. Rusty could tell that she had calved. She probably had hidden the baby somewhere in the timber along the river, where it would be fair game should a wolf or a coyote come prowling about. He saddled Mike's black horse, Alamo, and followed the heifer at a distance, hoping to find the calf and bring it into the pens, where it would be safe until it was stronger and better able to survive.

As he expected, the heifer led him to her new offspring. The calf lay in some heavy undergrowth where she had left it. The heifer tossed her head belligerently as Rusty dismounted and led the horse toward the hiding spot. Warily, for a new mother could be dangerous if anything threatened her baby, he eased close to the calf. It eyed him without fear until the heifer snorted and began to paw. It arose on shaky legs. Rusty caught and lifted it up, stretching it belly-down across the saddle. Its umbilical cord was dried but not yet lost.

He tried to soothe the heifer's anxiety with a calm voice. "Sook now.

Sook." Holding the wriggling calf, he swung up behind the saddle and put the horse into a slow walk. The heifer slung her head, offering fight, then began to follow, bawling.

He was halfway back to the cabin when he heard a shot. In the crisp air the echo reverberated through timber along the river. He thought at first that Mike had fired at a varmint, but the report had not sounded like Mike's rifle.

He shivered with a sudden cold fear and put the black horse into a long trot, then into a lope. He came near losing the calf as it struggled and kicked. The heifer fell behind but kept coming. At the pens, Rusty slid to the ground and lifted the calf down, then looked fearfully toward the wood-pile, where he had last seen Mike chopping fuel for the cabin.

"Dad! Dad, where are you?"

He heard no answer. He trotted toward the tall stack of dead timber and called again.

Hearing a muffled voice, he checked his stride, trying to determine from where the sound had come. He heard it again, a rasping "Rusty!"

Mike lay on his stomach near the chopping log. He tried to arise, but he could do no more than push up on one elbow, then slump back. Rusty saw blood spreading across the back of Mike's old shirt and staining the wood chips upon which he lay. The ax was beside him where he had dropped it as he fell.

Rusty fought to keep from crying. "I'll get you to the house." Mike cried out in pain as Rusty tried to lift him. Rusty eased him onto his back, placing Mike's hat beneath his head.

"Don't move me no more. Don't move me."

"You'll bleed to death if I don't get this blood stopped."

"Won't do no good. Son of a bitch, he's a better shot than I thought." Mike coughed up blood.

"It was Isaac York, wasn't it?"

"Didn't see." Mike's voice dropped to a whisper. "If he'd only made it a fair fight . . ." He reached out. Rusty took his hand. Mike gasped, trying to speak.

Whatever he wanted to say, it died with him.

Eyes afire, Rusty bent over his foster father and cried as he had when Mother Dora died.

A cold realization gradually crept over him while he knelt, gripping Mike's lifeless hand. It staggered him as he absorbed its full import. So far as he knew, he had no blood kin, not anywhere. He did not even know who he really was, and it was improbable that he ever would. Now the couple who had given him a name and a home and the security of their love had been taken from him.

For the second time in his life, he was alone.

Rusty was disappointed at the small number of neighbors who came to pay their final respects to Mike. He had not fully realized the deep feelings many people held about secession, or how much they had resented Mike's firm stance against it. For some, his record as a ranger and the many times he had volunteered his strong arms for service to the community were not enough to erase the stain of his political leanings.

Rusty told Preacher Webb, "Now I can see who his true friends were."

"Don't blame them too much. We may be lookin' at a war, and war takes a hard toll on friendships. If this one comes to pass, it may even break up families. The Mike we knew couldn't deny his true convictions. You wouldn't have wanted him to."

"I would if it could've saved his life."

"You'd have lost respect for him, and he'd have lost respect for himself."

"Nothin' is worth somebody murderin' him." Rusty cast a dark look toward the sheriff, who stood at the edge of the small gathering, gesturing broadly as he expressed his opinion that Texas should cut loose as soon as possible. "*He* don't seem any too concerned over catchin' Isaac York and bringin' him in."

"There isn't any proof that Isaac did it."

"Who else would've? You were there. You helped break up the fight between him and Dad. And he's not here for the funeral. He's afraid to come because he knows I know he's guilty. So do lots of folks, whether they'll admit it or not."

"Several other neighbors aren't here either, but that doesn't mean they murdered Mike."

The sheriff caught enough of the conversation to arouse his interest. He walked up to Rusty, his face burdened by a deep frown. "Son, you've got a right to be upset, but you've got no right to accuse anybody without you can show proof. You got that proof?"

"I didn't see him, but I know. I think you know, too."

"If I'd always really known half as much as I thought I did, I'd be the smartest man in Texas. We're here to bury your daddy, not to set off another killin'. And that's what it'll lead to if you keep makin' accusations. It'll come down to you or him, and I'd have to lay my bet on him."

Rusty knew his resentment showed, and he didn't care. Mike wouldn't have, either. But he said no more, and the sheriff turned away to resume his lecture on politics. He had a receptive audience. Just about everybody here was ready to cut ties with the union.

Despite their political feelings, a few friends like Tom Blessing from around the settlement had come to be with Rusty when word spread about Mike's death. Blessing and a couple of others had dug the grave while Rusty and Preacher Webb fashioned a coffin out of rough-cut pine torn from the side of the cow barn. There had been no extra lumber lying around. It cost too much to waste.

Rusty stood numb at the graveside, unable to absorb all of Webb's eulogy, the recounting of Mike's brave deeds and exploits, of his and Dora's devotion to one another, of their unselfishness in taking an orphaned boy to raise as their own. Rusty's mind ranged back to the earliest events he could remember with any clarity. Always, it seemed, Daddy Mike and Mother Dora had been there to pick him up when he fell, to encourage him when he faltered, to cheer him when he did something well. Blood kin could have done no more.

Carried back in time by his memories, he did not hear the minister call for a closing prayer. He did not bow his head until he blinked his eyes clear of tears and saw that the others were all looking downward.

A strong arm fell upon his shoulder. Tom Blessing stood beside him, sorrow in his light blue eyes. "Son, it'd do you good to get away from this place for a while. I've got a job for you."

Rusty coughed his throat clear. Blessing had tried to send Daddy Mike away to keep him from harm until the secession fever subsided. Now he had the same idea, except this time it was to put distance between Rusty and Isaac York. "What'd become of this place?"

"It does a field good to lie fallow a year or two and rest, same as it helps a man to pause in his labor now and again to give thanks for the Lord's bounty. The place won't go anywhere. It'll still be here when you come back."

"I've got a thing or two that needs doin' first."

"You're thinkin' of Isaac York. I can tell by the look in your eyes. Forget that. Come to my house, and come prepared to travel."

While the grave was being filled in, the visitors began to drift away. Preacher Webb waited. He talked quietly to first one and then another but did not take his eyes from Rusty for long.

Fowler Gaskin had surprised Rusty by coming to the funeral though without his two sons. He hung back until almost the last, then approached Rusty, his voice tentative. "Boy, I hate to be askin' you at a time such as this, but I know Mike's clothes won't fit you. I was wonderin' if you was of a mind to give some of them away? I sure could use a good winter coat."

The audacity of the man caught Rusty standing on his left foot. "The dirt hasn't even settled over his grave and you've already come scavengin'. Get the hell out of my sight, Fowler!"

Gaskin backed off. "Just felt like I ought to ask before somebody else comes along and carries everything away. After all, me and your daddy been neighbors a long time."

"A lot too long."

Gaskin gave Rusty a hard look while he mounted his slab-sided old mule. He kicked the mule vigorously and rode off, mumbling.

Rusty noticed Webb watching closely. The minister said, "First time the Gaskins catch you gone, they'll help themselves to whatever they want of Mike's stuff."

Rusty had not thought of that. "We'll head them off. You probably know some poor folks who could use Dad's clothes."

"They'll be grateful to you." Webb's expression darkened. "I heard you tell Tom Blessing you have somethin' to do before you leave. I don't like the sound of that."

"Would you have me turn my back on what happened to Dad?"

"Better than to do somethin' you might be sorry for the rest of your life."

"I won't be sorry."

The Isaac York place lay north and a bit west of the cotton gin and general store that were the nucleus of the settlement. Rusty had been there just once, when Mike was trying to trade mules. York had been half drunk, and the black man Shanty had done most of the dickering for him. It had struck Rusty odd, seeing a man supposed to be a slave assuming that kind of responsibility for his owner. Mike had not been one to take advantage of a drunk, but even if he had, Shanty had been too sharp a trader to let him get away with it.

Rusty had hardly slept last night, trying to decide what his course should be. By rights he should shoot York down like a dog, but he would not shoot him in the back. He would prefer that York be looking at him, knowing what was coming and why.

As he rode he kept turning over the options in his mind. Maybe he would not shoot York at all but instead force him to confess, then stand back and let the law hang him. Hanging was a more fitting death under the circumstances. A bullet ended things too quickly. Still, there was always the chance that the law would not mete out the punishment York deserved. After all, Mike had been a union sympathizer, and the community was strongly pro-Confederacy.

The longer Rusty pondered, the less sure he was about what he would do. But he felt that when he got there he would know. Mike had always said that when the time came to act, most men knew instinctively what to do.

"Trust me," he had advised, "and if I ain't there, trust yourself. You'll know what's right."

Rusty went suddenly short of breath as he rounded the winter-bared cotton field and saw the cabin ahead. Trembling, he reined up and drew Mike's old pistol from its scabbard to recheck the load. He had never fired the pistol much and did not fully trust it. He liked a rifle, for he could hit anything he saw over its sights. A pistol, extended at arm's length, seemed unwieldy and felt heavier than a rifle, though it was not.

He started for the cabin but changed course when he saw York seated on a wooden stool beside the door of a log shed, soaking up the meager winter sunshine. York raised a jug on the crook of his arm and drank.

Drunk, like as not, Rusty thought, disappointed. He had hoped to find York sober and able to understand fully what was happening. On the other hand, if he was drunk he might not have his guard up. It might be easier to draw a confession out of him.

Rusty dismounted twenty feet from York and drew the pistol. York blinked, trying to clear his eyes. "Who are you?"

"You know me. I'm Rusty Shannon."

"I can't quite make you out." York kept blinking. He was too drunk to see straight.

Rusty seethed. "You were seein' all right when you shot Mike Shannon. I'm here to make you pay for it."

The slave Shanty stepped out of the shed, staring with wide eyes at the pistol. "Please, boy, put that thing away."

York pushed to his feet but swayed and braced one hand against the shed wall. "You sayin' I shot Mike? How could I? I been drunk for three, four days."

"Not too drunk to shoot him in the back. And you'll admit it, or I'll shoot you where you stand."

A firm voice said, "No you won't."

Rusty turned quickly. Preacher Webb and Tom Blessing stood behind him. Webb reached out. "Give me the pistol. You're too young to get yourself in this kind of trouble."

Rusty was too surprised to move. Webb quickly gripped the pistol and pushed the muzzle down, then gave it a twist that wrested the weapon from Rusty's hand. "I was afraid you'd take a notion to do this."

Rusty choked from frustration. "He's got it comin'."

Blessing said, "You have no proof. He says he's been too drunk to leave the place. Shanty yonder backs him up."

The black man nodded, relieved that the pistol had not been fired.

"What else could Shanty say? Isaac owns him."

Blessing said, "I'll admit that from the looks of things you could be right. Isaac and Mike both left mad after their fight broke up. But these are bitter times, and there's other people around who didn't like Mike's politics. You can't kill a man on suspicion."

"That's more than he killed Mike for." Shaking with anger, Rusty reached for the pistol. Webb turned, keeping it from him.

Blessing said, "Settle down, son. I promise you we'll look into Mike's killin'. If we find proof that Isaac did it, he'll pay. But that's not for you to do, it's for the law."

"I talked to the law yesterday. The sheriff won't do a damned thing. He as much as told me so."

Webb said, "Have faith, lad. The Lord finds His own way to punish the evildoer. If it was Isaac, he'll settle accounts with the Almighty. If it wasn't . . . you wouldn't want an innocent man to burden your conscience as long as you live."

"I've got no faith in the law, and not a hell of a lot in the Almighty. How come He wasn't watchin' over Daddy Mike?"

"It's not for us to understand His ways."

"*I* sure don't. If he really punishes the evildoers, how do we know he didn't send me here to strike Isaac down?"

"He wouldn't have let us stop you."

Blessing laid his heavy arm on Rusty's shoulder, as he had yesterday. "I told you before, you need to get away for a while. Let things here take their own course. That job I tried to give Mike . . . it's still waitin'."

"Job?" Rusty was too upset to remember. "What job?"

"South of the Red, in a minuteman company scoutin' for Indian sign. Turnin' them back if they cross into Texas. The boys are shorthanded up there."

Rusty glared at Isaac. "What about *him?*"

"He won't be goin' anywhere. If it's proved that he killed Mike, he'll still be here when you come back. Or hung."

It wasn't enough. Rusty wanted him to pay now. But he could see that it was not to be. Even if York went on trial, chances were strong that a secessionist jury would acquit him. "You're tryin' to protect him. That's why you want me gone."

"We're tryin' to protect you from yourself, and maybe from some others. There was hard feelin' against Mike. Some of that feelin' is bound to be laid over onto you. It's best for you and everybody else if you're not seen around here 'til this secession business quiets down."

Rusty could not take his gaze away from York. Shanty stepped protectively in front of his owner.

Reluctantly Rusty shrugged. "All right, I'll go. Do I get my pistol back?"

A flicker of a smile crossed Webb's face. "I'll ride along part of the way with you and give your pistol back when I feel like it's safe."

"Isaac York won't be safe 'til he's dead."

CHAPTER
SEVEN

Paper was scarce, so Tom Blessing sketched a map on the back of an old order he had received from the governor's office in Austin during one of his limited terms in volunteer ranger ranks. "You'll remember the Fort Belknap country from when we went up north to attend the Indian removal. You oughtn't to have much trouble findin' the company camp. When Texas secedes, there won't be anybody but our own volunteers watchin' the frontier. Just a buckskin line, and a thin one. That's why they need you up there."

Rusty studied the map. "There's several rivers to cross between here and there."

"You'll cross a lot more if you stay with the rangers. You just mind what goes on around you and be careful. Some Indian would be tickled to hang your red hair on his lance."

Preacher Webb handed Rusty a book. "Put this in your saddlebag. It'll be good readin' for you of a night."

Rusty saw what the book was. "I'll be carryin' Dad's old pistol in there. You think it and the Bible fit together?"

"Samson prayed, then slew his enemies with the jawbone of an ass. Lord knows it sometimes takes violence to bring peace."

Blessing said, "I've known many a man who carried a Bible in his pocket and a pistol on his belt. I'd rather ride with that kind than them who just carry the gun."

Rusty reasoned that it could do him no harm to make room for the book. Whether he read much from it or not was another matter. Though Mother Dora had read from hers every day, it had not saved her from the wasting illness that carried her away. Mike Shannon had been a strong believer, after his fashion, yet a bullet had found his back.

He wanted Preacher Webb to feel contented. With the Shannons gone, the minister was the only real link Rusty had to his past. "Thanks for the book, Preacher. Don't you reckon it's time we got started?"

Webb said, "I'm ready."

Rusty stepped past the sagging door of Blessing's cabin and turned to where he had tied Mike's favorite horse, Alamo. The mule Chapultepec stood patiently waiting, a pack on his back. Rusty told Blessing, "I'd appreciate it if you'd keep an eye on Fowler Gaskin. Soon as he knows I'm gone, he's liable to carry off everything that's not rooted down." He had already let Webb give Mike's and Mother Dora's clothes to families who needed them.

Blessing shook Rusty's hand. "You're doin' the right thing, goin' away for a while."

"I'm not forgettin' Isaac York."

Blessing said, "But forget about takin' your own vengeance. Leave it to the law." He looked at Webb. "And to the Lord."

"For now." Rusty turned his eyes toward the Colorado River. Beyond it lay the Llano and San Saba, the Brazos . . . and how many more?

He said to the horse and mule, "I hope you-all can swim."

Following a faint wagon road that led in a northwesterly direction, Rusty and Webb made a dry camp the first night. They ate a meager meal of cold cornbread and pork Tom Blessing's wife had sacked for them. In his lingering grief, Rusty had not felt like eating much since Mike's death, so he took his supper mostly in boiled coffee stretched with parched grain.

Webb studied him a long time in the faint light of a modest campfire that barely held back the night's chill. "I don't like the look in your face. I'm afraid you still have murder in your heart."

"Won't matter how far we go. Whatever's inside, I'll carry along with me."

"You'll have other things to think about besides revenge. Distance will give time a chance to cool the passion."

"I don't want it to cool. If the law doesn't settle with Isaac, I will. Won't make any difference how long it takes . . . a month, a year, ten years."

Webb's eyes held pity. "That book I gave you . . . I could cite you some passages. It might help you to read them."

"I don't see you readin' out of yours."

"I don't have to. I know it by heart."

Toward noon the third day Webb turned off the wagon road and bore northeastward.

Rusty looked back to be sure the pack mule was following. "Aren't we goin' out of our way?"

"Some people I know have a farm off yonder. They'll make us welcome, and the womenfolks are fine cooks."

Though Rusty still had little appetite, he perceived that Webb was eager to make the stop. The minister enjoyed being among friends, and given any chance, he made friends of almost everyone he met. "I don't reckon there's any big hurry about me gettin' to Belknap. The main thing was to get me away from home."

"These people's name is Monahan. Lon Monahan is a good farmer and a good man. You'll like him. You'll like the whole family."

Rusty was not keen on making new acquaintances right now. They would try their best to make him feel good, and he didn't really want to feel good. Mike's death hung over him like a dark cloud. He was not yet ready for the sunshine.

Webb added, "They've got a daughter about sixteen or seventeen. Her name is Geneva. Pretty as a china doll."

That's an old bachelor for you, Rusty thought. *Go miles out of his way to keep from missing a pretty woman.* He suspected Webb's definition of pretty was undemanding.

Rusty found the Monahan farm larger and neater in appearance than the Shannon place. It bespoke prosperity, at least by the modest standards of a Texas still in its settling-down stage. The main house was built of sawmill lumber rather than logs, though an older double log cabin still appeared to be in use. He suspected it had been the Monahans' first home and had been set aside for older family members or the boys of the family, a fairly common usage in such cases. Like the main house, the newest, largest barn was of lumber, the smaller barn and sheds older and of logs. A low rock fence surrounded a large garden. Out past the big barn, two men were building a new corral, stacking trimmed oak branches between double oak posts to form a fence. It was typical wintertime work for a farmer who had nothing to do in the fields.

Webb said, "There's Lon Monahan, out yonder with one of his sons. We'll stop and say howdy before we go up to the house."

Monahan's sun-bronzed features, droopy-brimmed felt hat, and brogan shoes would mark him anywhere as a farmer no matter how far he might stray from the plow. He wiped a huge hand on the bib of his faded overalls before reaching out to shake with Webb. "I swear to God, Preacher, it's damned good to see you."

Webb said, "You remember Mike Shannon? This is his boy Rusty."

Monahan's grip was strong enough to crush bones. His broad, easy smile added to the creases of middle age but made Rusty feel at ease with the farmer. He did not always meet strangers well. "Pleased to make your acquaintance, Mr. Monahan. Preacher has told me a right smart about you." He hadn't, really, except to warn that Monahan's language tended to be salty.

"I knew your daddy in the Mexican War. Hell of a good feller. I hope he's well."

Rusty looked at the ground. "No, sir, he's dead."

"I'm sorry. How . . ." Monahan broke off as Webb gave him a quick negative signal. "We'll say a prayer for him tonight at meetin'. You *are* goin' to stay and conduct meetin' for us, ain't you, Preacher? I'll send the boys out with word to the neighbors."

Rusty suspected Webb had anticipated Monahan's request. In any case he appeared pleased by it. Webb said, "Sure enough. I've always got time to share the Word."

Wherever he went, people expected him to conduct prayer meetings. Many who lived far from sizable settlements rarely had an opportunity to attend church. For them, circuit-riding ministers met a deeply felt spiritual need.

The other fence builder finished wedging a branch tightly into place and joined his father in greeting the visitors. He was a strapping youth near Rusty's own age. Monahan introduced him as his oldest son, James. "You-all tie your horses and go on up to the house. Clemmie'll have dinner ready directly. Been awhile since we've had a real soul-cleansin' around here, so she'll be damned tickled to see you, Preacher."

Rusty sensed that the welcome was genuine, not put on for appearance's sake. He found it easy to like Monahan. The sunburned James seemed cut from the same cloth. Rough hands and muscular shoulders bore the stamp of hard work.

James asked Rusty, "You like to hunt?"

"When I've got time."

"Maybe after supper we'll go up the river a ways and see what we can find."

Lon Monahan said, "Not tonight. We're goin' to have meetin'. Maybe Rusty can stay around a few days."

"Can't. I'm supposed to report to the ranger camp up north of here."

James shrugged. "Rangers don't range all the time. Maybe when you get a little time off."

Walking toward the house, Webb said to Rusty, "I baptized all the Monahan children. I baptized you too, remember?"

"I remember. I thought you were fixin' to drown me."

"Just tried to wash away all your sins."

"I was maybe six years old. How many sins could I have had?"

"The Lord and me looked to the future. I think we headed the sins off pretty well, up to now."

"And now?"

"You're a grown man. From here on it's up to you."

Rusty doubted that Clemmie Monahan weighed ninety pounds. When she first stepped out onto the porch he took her for a half-grown girl. Closer, he saw her lined face, her graying hair, her work-hardened hands. Building this farm had left the marks of wear and worry on both her and her husband. Her face lighted up as she recognized Webb.

"Preacher!" she shouted. "Come on in this house."

Quietly, so only Rusty could hear, Webb said, "Now, lad, there is a handsome woman."

"Handsome? Maybe she was once."

"She still is. Beauty is not what you see on the outside but the spirit you know is within."

Webb bowed to the woman in a courtly manner so ingrained that Rusty doubted he realized he was doing it. Rusty self-consciously tried to emulate him but knew his was a poor imitation. Webb introduced him. Mrs. Monahan's expression turned sad for a moment when the minister told her Rusty's father was dead. He did not state the cause, and she had the good manners not to ask.

"He'll be missed, your father," she said. "Well, you-all come on in and rest a spell." She called to a boy working at the barn. "Billy, take care of the horses. And watch that mule. He's liable to kick."

The boy, about fifteen years old, shouted back, "Yes, ma'am." He led the two horses and Chapultepec into a corral.

Clemmie Monahan said, "I expect you'll want to wash off some of the road dust. There's a wash pan on the back gallery. Geneva, see that there's water in the bucket out there."

A girl appeared in the doorway. She was almost a duplicate of her mother except for being a generation younger. To call her slender would have been charitable, Rusty thought. Skinny was more like it. But she had a pleasant face, eyes filling with curiosity as she looked at him. In the room's poor light, he could not tell what color they were.

He blushed as he realized he was staring and that she was staring back.

She said, "I already did, Mama, soon as I saw Preacher Webb comin'. Brought in fresh drinkin' water from the cistern, too. Figured he'd be thirsty."

Webb accepted the hospitality with easy grace. "Such a fine welcome from such handsome young ladies reminds an old bachelor what he has missed in his life." He glanced back at Rusty. "And should be a lesson to a young one."

The girl smiled. Rusty felt his cheeks warm. He wanted to say something to cover his discomfort, but he conjured up no words that seemed appropriate. He was conscious that his clothes were dusty and trail-worn. He touched a hand to his face and felt several days' growth of stubble. Mother Dora would have pointed to Mike's razor and suggested that he use it.

The girl Geneva kept looking at him. "Does he ever talk?"

Webb grinned. "I've seem him go for days without sayin' a word except 'Please pass the corn bread.'"

Defensively Rusty said, "I don't talk just to hear myself." Feeling slightly wicked and trusting that Webb would take it with good humor, he added, "I'm not a preacher."

Clemmie Monahan said, "Leave the gentlemen be, Geneva, so they can wash for dinner. We've both got work enough to do in the kitchen."

Webb was first at the washbasin. Drying himself on a square of homespun cotton cloth, he smiled. "You've not been away from home enough, lad. You need to work on the social graces."

"You have them, but they never got you married."

Webb's smile faded. "The ladies I fancied always seemed to fancy someone else."

Rusty had long suspected Mother Dora was one. It could be that Clemmie Monahan was another.

Webb emptied the wash pan so Rusty could pour fresh water into it. "Besides, I've been on the journey too much to have any normal life at home. My circuit, and the times I've ridden away with the volunteers . . . I could not ask a good woman to sit in a lonely cabin and wait for me."

"I'll bet there's some would've been willin'."

"Perhaps, but it would've been unfair to ask it of them."

"Haven't you wanted to?"

"Once or twice. I always managed to think better of it. I hope you never have to look at yourself in a mirror and face a decision between your needs and your duty."

"I don't expect I'll ever be a preacher."

"There are other duties that demand all one has to give. If you should ever hear the call, you'll understand."

The family was large and the table long, with benches on either side, chairs at each end for Lon Monahan and his wife. Clemmie was on her feet much of the time, bringing food to the table, pouring coffee. Geneva sat opposite Rusty, where he could steal glances at her. Two younger sisters and the youngest brother, Billy, sat beside her. On the bench with Rusty and Webb were the oldest brother, James, and Clemmie Monahan's father, a small, thin man named Vince Purdy. He squinted as if he had a hard time seeing. Rusty suspected his sight was slowly failing. His knuckles were knotted with arthritis.

Lon Monahan asked, "Been much talk down you-all's way about this secession foolishness?"

More than just talk, Rusty thought darkly, but he let Preacher Webb answer.

"There has. There are bitter feelin's on both sides."

"Same here, I'm sorry to say. Serious enough that I'm afraid it could lead to bloodlettin'."

Clemmie protested, "Lon, don't be scarin' the children."

"It's the truth. I ain't seen folks get so worked up since the war against Mexico. This may be worse, because it has neighbor buttin' heads with neighbor. Damndest notion I ever heard of, wantin' to pull out of the union! Don't you agree, Preacher?"

Webb looked about the table before he answered. "Every argument sounds good while you listen to it. Then you hear an answer from the other side, and it sounds good, too. As a minister I think I'd best stay out of it."

"The way it looks, everybody's goin' to have to choose a side, like it or not."

"I'm on God's side, and God wants us to live in peace."

Monahan's eyes were fierce. "There won't be peace if Texas pulls out. We'll find ourselves in the damnedest war this country ever saw."

Clemmie broke in. "This is no fit subject for the dinner table. James, pass your daddy the gravy."

In deference to her, the conversation turned to subjects that sparked no controversy, such as speculation that a railroad might be built to haul farm produce from the interior to a gulf port, and the need for a soaking rain.

Rusty only half listened to most of it. He did not know enough about railroads to voice an opinion, and all the talk in the world would not bring rain so long as the wind was out of the west. He kept his chin down as if he were concentrating on eating, but he lifted his gaze to Geneva, across the table. Somehow she didn't seem quite so skinny as he had first thought. The longer he looked at her, the more he wanted to look. He did not have a lot to judge her by. Girls of her age were scarce down on his section of the Colorado River. He had gone to school with Fowler Gaskin's daughter, Florey, but she looked too much like her brothers to arouse any interest. The only person he knew uglier than the Gaskin brothers was their father.

After dinner James saddled a horse and set out eastward to notify neighbors that Preacher Webb would conduct services that evening at the Monahans'. Billy Monahan rode north and west.

Lon Monahan shouted after James, "You tell them to be sure and come! Ain't a one of them but what can stand a damned good dose of salvation!"

Rusty thought it might not have been necessary for the boys to ride out. Monahan could have stood on the porch and hollered loudly enough to reach everyone within four or five miles.

Clemmie admonished, "Lon, is it necessary to use that kind of language in front of the preacher?"

"Hell, he's heard it all before. A little honest swearin' wipeth away anger and bringeth peace to the soul." He winked at Rusty.

Rusty was reminded that Mike Shannon had looked at it that way too, and the thought brought sadness. Mike had had much in common with Lon Monahan besides their political leanings.

Clemmie noticed Rusty's expression. She said, "You re lookin' kind of down, son. Not feelin' good?"

Rusty did not want to get into a discussion about what had happened to Mike. He replied, "Just thinkin' over what Mr. Monahan said about war."

Clemmie turned on her husband. "See what you done, talkin' so free? Some things you'd ought to keep to yourself."

Monahan said, "Ain't no dodgin' what's true." Once the boys were gone, he suggested, "We'd just as well forget about fence buildin' today. Preacher, I'd like to show you my horses. Traded for a nice little set of mares and a sorrel stud since you were here last."

"As I recall, the Comanches cleaned you out last year."

"I'm hopin' the volunteers can keep them crafty devils from comin' south." He looked at Rusty as if for verification.

Rusty found Geneva looking at him too, and felt compelled to make some kind of answer, even if it meant nothing. "I'll just be followin' orders, but I expect we'll do the best we can."

Monahan said, "The country you've got to cover is big, and there won't be many of you. Seein' how poor Texas is now, I can't understand how anybody thinks it'd be better off by quittin' the union. Everything the union's been doin' for us, we'll have to do for ourselves."

Rusty could see the other side of the argument. "A lot of folks don't think it *has* done much for us."

"A lot of folks are wrong. I'm afraid they're fixin' to find that out."

Rusty was not overly interested in seeing Monahan's mares. He would rather have stayed and gotten acquainted with Monahan's daughter, but he felt it his obligation as a guest to act pleased and accept in good grace whatever courtesy the host extended. He rode out with Monahan and Webb.

Monahan said, "If it hadn't taken us so long to borrow horses to ride, we'd've caught up to them Indians and got our own back. As it was, we trailed them all the way to the Red River, me and James and Billy."

Webb was incredulous. "The three of you? What would you have done if you'd caught up to the Indians?"

"Like I said, we'd've took back our horses. By the tracks there wasn't but six or seven hostiles. Me and the boys could've whipped up on them easy."

The stallion made a threatening rush at the three horsemen, but Monahan put him to flight by waving his hat and shouting at the top of his voice. Rusty thought he might have flushed birds out of the trees half a mile away.

By the time they returned to the house, the first neighbors had begun arriving a-horseback, in wagons and buggies. Most brought food in baskets or sacks to help the Monahans feed the expected crowd. Rusty was introduced to so many that he had no chance of remembering the names. It had always been that way when he had accompanied Preacher Webb on his circuit. Prayer meeting was more than a religious event. It provided a rare excuse for a social gathering where the men could swap yarns, horses, and dogs. Women could exchange news about weddings and births and discuss whatever they had been able to learn about fashion in faraway places like St. Louis and New Orleans.

This gathering also provided a forum for extended discussions on secession. Rusty noted that the preponderance of opinion favored pulling out. Monahan's was definitely a minority view. In another setting the debate might have sparked violent quarreling, but here the visitors respected the host's views even as most disagreed with them.

Clemmie Monahan walked out onto the porch, drying wet hands on an apron. She told her husband, "Appears to me that just about everybody's here and lookin' hungry."

Her father said, "I sure am."

Lon Monahan asked Webb, "You want to eat first or do it after the preachin'?"

"Minister first to the body, then the soul will be ready for the Word."

Old Vince Purdy said, "Amen."

Preacher Webb broke up the scattered conversations by calling for the visitors to bow their heads. He beseeched the Lord to heal divisions and restore peace to troubled hearts.

He had barely reached the "Amen" when a large man of commanding presence rode up on a big white horse, trailed by three riders whose subservient manner indicated they were in his pay or in his debt. The man wore a long black coat, open so that no one could miss seeing the pistol he carried in his broad waistband.

Lon Monahan was obviously displeased about the late-arriving guests, but he showed himself a good host by walking out to meet them. "You're late, Colonel, but we're just fixin' to eat supper. There's plenty for all of you. And Preacher Webb ain't delivered his sermon yet."

Rusty heard Vince Purdy mutter, "Colonel Caleb Dawkins. I'd rather be bit by a hydrophoby dog."

Dawkins did not dismount. He seemed seven feet tall in the saddle, a huge man with shoulders that looked wide enough to bump a doorway on both sides and hands big enough to choke a mule. "We have not come to eat or listen to platitudes." His voice was deep and resonant, like Mona-han's, and chillingly calm. "We have come to see how many choose to align themselves with traitors."

Stung, Monahan struggled to recover his composure. "You'll find no traitors here, Colonel Dawkins. There is scarcely a man in this crowd who has not answered the call against Mexico or against the savage."

"We've a different enemy this time. You and your family have openly allied yourself with the northern union. I must assume that those who break bread with you support you in your sedition."

The accusation aroused angry shouts from among the visitors. Half a dozen men surged forward in protest. The three with Dawkins dropped their hands to their weapons, and the threat cooled. Dawkins remained unmoved, showing no emotion. He seemed to be above anger or fear.

Monahan's face colored. "Damn you, Colonel, you've just abused the hell out of my hospitality." He moved toward the man, but Preacher Webb stepped in front of him.

Webb said, "You are wrong, Colonel Dawkins. A vote here tonight would probably be ninety percent for secession. These people have come for a prayer meeting, not a political fight. I would invite you to join us in fellowship and worship."

Dawkins looked at Webb as if he were a beggar on the street. "You call yourself a man of God, yet you sup with one flagrantly disloyal to his state. The devil rules here tonight, not God." His chilling gaze swept over the crowd. "I warn all of you, judgment day is coming. When the vote is taken and Texas secedes, a swift and just punishment will be visited upon all who are not on God's side." He leaned forward, piercing eyes fixed on Lon Monahan. "Be warned. You will be the first."

Rusty was reminded of Isaac York. This man could have been York's close kin except that York was highly excitable, where Dawkins was stolid and cold. Rusty could not help shivering.

James Monahan, trembling with anger, reached down to pick up a rock. "Git off of this place, Dawkins, before I chunk you off."

Lon Monahan caught his oldest son's throwing arm and held it. "This is for your daddy to take care of." He looked up at Dawkins. "James said it as good as I could: Git! Else I'll be forced to stomp hell out of you in front of the Lord and everybody."

Old Vince Purdy joined his son-in-law. "And damned if me and James don't whip the other three."

Caleb Dawkins could have been leaving church for all the emotion he showed in departing. The men with him followed without speaking, though they kept looking back over their shoulders as if expecting trouble to run and catch up.

James hurled the rock, missing Dawkins by only a couple of feet. "We could've beaten him, Pa. Him and that hired trash with him."

"He ain't worth skinnin' our knuckles over. He talks strong because it's the only way he can get anybody to listen to him."

Webb said, "*I* listened to him, and he scared me."

"God save us from zealots." Monahan turned his back on the retreating Dawkins. "He'll keep. Right now we've got company."

They did not have it for long. Caleb Dawkins's appearance sapped all the pleasure from the gathering. Conversation was subdued as the people ate. Preacher Webb sensed the crowd's distraction and trimmed his sermon short. Guests thanked the Monahans for their hospitality and Webb for his message, of which most had probably heard little. They saddled horses and climbed into wagons and buggies, then headed off in several directions.

"I'm sorry, Preacher," Monahan apologized. "Everything kind of went to hell after the colonel got here."

"It wasn't your fault."

"He's been itchin' for a killin' ever since he came into this country. Everybody knows he's a little crazy."

"That makes him all the more dangerous."

Rusty asked, "Who is he, and how come you-all call him colonel?"

Monahan said, "He was one once, in the war against Mexico. Hung a couple of men for cowardice because they retreated without orders when the Mexicans was fixin' to overrun them. Got cashiered out of the army. He never could see where he'd done anything wrong. He's hated the federal government ever since."

Rusty saw worry in Geneva Monahan's eyes, and for the first time he was certain of their color: blue, like his own. He felt an urge to put a protective arm around her, but he did not know just what he could protect her from or how he would do it.

Clemmie jerked her head to beckon her daughters. "Come on, Geneva, you and the other girls. We've got some cleanin' up to do."

Lon Monahan looked glumly toward the last departing guests, three hundred yards down the wagon road. He said to his sons, "We'd best be gettin' the stock fed. The horses probably think we've forgotten them."

James grumbled, "I still say we could've whipped them. I was cocked and primed to do it."

Lon replied, "You're too eager to fight, son. Time you've been in as many scraps as me and your granddaddy and the preacher, you won't be so anxious for another one."

Rusty and Webb trailed behind, prepared to help. Rusty said, "If I was Lon Monahan, I'd never be more than a step away from a gun. Dawkins sounds a lot like Isaac York, and everybody knows what Isaac did to Daddy Mike."

"We don't know that for sure."

"I'm as certain as if I'd been there and seen it. And one of these days he'll pay."

"Vengeance is best left to the Lord."

"When the day comes, I'll give the Lord some help."

The next morning Rusty went out before breakfast to saddle Alamo and pack Chapultepec for an early start. Preacher Webb walked with him but remained outside of the corral. Rusty said, "I thought we were leavin' today."

"*You* are, but I'm not goin' the rest of the way with you. Looks like I'm needed here."

Rusty suspected the quarrel between Monahan and Dawkins weighed heavily on the minister's mind. "Maybe I'd better stay with you."

"You're obliged to obey orders and go on. I feel my obligation is to try to pour oil on troubled waters. I smell blood in the air."

Rusty paused, his hand on the rope that tied the mule's pack. "You don't reckon Dawkins would do somethin' to the family . . . to the women-folks and all?"

"I doubt he's crazy enough to hurt the women. People around here would turn against him in a minute." Webb seemed to see through Rusty's eyes and into his mind. "You're worried about the girl."

"Her and all of them. They're good folks."

Webb nodded. "Good people, caught up in bad times. I'm afraid that's been the way of the world since the first days. We won't see the end of it in our short span upon the earth."

The family filed into place at the table. Rusty waited until everyone else was seated, then took the position he had been given at the end of a bench across from Geneva and the younger girls. Lon Monahan's eyes were tired, his shoulders sagging. After Webb said grace, Monahan gulped half a cup of coffee. He tore a biscuit in half, started to eat it, then laid it on his plate. His face was grim.

"I didn't sleep none last night," he said. "Caleb Dawkins kept runnin' through my mind. Ain't there somethin' in the Scriptures, Preacher, about handwritin' on the wall?"

"It foretells things to come."

"The handwritin' is on the wall here. Texas is about to pull out of the union. When it does, all hell is liable to bust loose. Fanatics like Dawkins will run wild and free, for a while at least. They'll be comin' after folks who've talked against Texas pullin' out."

Clemmie protested, "Everybody around here is your friend, Lon, even if they don't agree with you. They wouldn't let him—"

"He won't ask them. He'll just go ahead and do it, or try to."

James's voice was confident. "You've always been able to take care of yourself, Pa. And we'll be with you, all of us."

"I couldn't ask for a better family. But anything that puts me in danger puts you-all in danger, too. The way I see it, we've got two choices. We can stay and tough it out, or we can leave here before the trouble starts."

Geneva cried, "Leave? But where would we go?"

"I hear that a few folks've already gone south to Mexico. Or we could move west out to Arizona or California. Maybe even to Oregon, where there ain't no north nor south, where there won't be no war."

Clemmie demanded, "What about the farm? We've worked so long and so hard—"

"The Vanderfords've been after me a long time to let them buy it. We could be halfway to Arizona before Dawkins and his crowd even know we're gone."

James stood up, fists clenched. "Turn tail and run? That ain't like you, Pa. It ain't like *us*."

"You're way too young to remember the runaway scrape, when Santy Anna marched across Texas, bent on wipin' us all out. A lot of brave folks packed up and ran because they didn't see any other way to survive." He looked at Webb. "You know what I'm talkin' about, Preacher?"

Webb nodded sadly. "I'm afraid I read the handwritin' on the wall the same way you do."

Rusty saw anguish in Geneva's eyes and wished he could do something to ease it. He said, "There ought to be somebody who could do somethin'. The rangers, maybe. There's more to the rangers than fightin' Indians. Aren't we supposed to keep the peace?"

Webb said, "When Texas secedes there won't be any peace to keep.

Not likely to be much of a government, not for a while. May not even be any rangers."

James declared, "To hell with Caleb Dawkins. We'll fight him. We'll kill him if we have to."

Webb cautioned, "You shouldn't speak of killin'. Don't even think of it."

Rusty imagined he could hear Clemmie's teeth grinding. She declared, "This place is ours. We built it from nothin'. We're not goin' to Mexico or Oregon or anywhere else. We're stayin' right here."

Lon Monahan's gaze moved to the other members of the family—Billy, Geneva and her sisters, Clemmie's father. "You-all say the same? Even knowin' the risk, you're bound to stay?"

Geneva looked at Webb. "There'd be risk on the trail too, wouldn't there, Preacher Webb?"

Webb's eyes were sad. "Indians. Sickness. Outlaws. No tellin' what-all."

Geneva said, "Then we'd just be tradin' one risk for another. Maybe a bunch of them."

Clemmie folded her arms, her eyes stern. "Here at least we know what the danger is. It's got a face, and that face looks like old Caleb Dawkins. There never was a time, on the sickest day of your life, that you couldn't beat the whey out of that son of a bitch. Pardon me, Preacher."

Monahan's eyes brightened. "I just wanted everybody to know what we're up against and to let you have your say." He turned back to Webb. "I've told you before, and I'll say it again. I've got the best damned family of anybody I know."

Webb still looked sad. "I envy you your family, but I do not envy the position you're in."

Monahan shrugged as if his worries had largely evaporated. "Long as we stick together, ain't nothin' can whip us." He turned to his breakfast.

Webb ate little. Monahan's renewed cheer had not transferred itself to him. Rusty finished his eggs and biscuits and pushed to his feet. "I wish I could stay longer, but I've still got a ways to travel." He shook hands with Monahan and with each member of the family, including the smallest of the girls.

Geneva said, "You'll be comin' back this way sometime, won't you?"

"That is my intention." He lingered a moment, held by the sparkle in her eyes.

Webb said, "I'll walk out to the barn with you."

They strode in silence to where the horse and the mule were tied. Rusty asked, "You sure you can do anything here?"

"There is no certainty in this life. I'll do what I can to keep the peace. The rest is up to a greater power than ourselves." He grasped Rusty's hand. "Be careful. The Indians have been given a bad bargain, and they're mad. You had nothing to do with it, but you're white. That makes you fair game."

"I'll watch out."

"I'm proud of you, Rusty. You were a good boy, and you've grown up to be a good man. Now go and be a good ranger."

Riding away, Rusty looked back. He already missed the comforting presence of Preacher Webb. Except for the farm itself, Webb was the only remaining strong tie to his life with Mike and Dora Shannon. He saw the Monahans scattering, each to his or her own chores, and regret was a wrenching pain. For a while he had warmed himself in the glow of this closely knit family. Now he mourned anew the loss of his own, for he was alone again, rootless and adrift.

CHAPTER
EIGHT

I t was not a lot farther to Fort Belknap, and Rusty did not push hard. He did not want to wear down his animals. Tom Blessing had not indicated there was any particular hurry. His main concern had been to put distance between Rusty and Isaac York until feelings cooled down. Rusty stopped occasionally to allow the horse and mule to graze and to give himself an opportunity to study the land. He had counted the rivers and streams he had crossed and knew there were more than Blessing's rough map had indicated. But good water made for a good country.

From time to time he came upon scattered small gatherings of buffalo, their winter hair rough and matted. He was tempted to shoot one just for the hell of it, but Daddy Mike had taught him long ago to kill only for meat, not for pleasure. If he shot one of these shaggy animals he would have to leave most of the carcass to spoil. Mike would say that was wasteful of Nature's gifts, and not pleasing in the sight of the Lord.

Despite his edgy feeling of aloneness and vulnerability, he found pleasure in traversing the rolling plains after breaking out of the cross timbers and its scrub-oak country. They were different in many ways, both in terrain and in vegetation, from the Colorado River region of his upbringing. It was not entirely new to him. He had seen the area before, going and coming back from following the Brazos reserve Indians on their reluctant march to new and less desirable country north of the Red.

It required no stretch of his imagination to understand why they so hated leaving after having set down roots near the Clear Fork of the Brazos on land pledged to be theirs forever. Forever had proven to be painfully short. Though most had no cultural inclination toward being farmers, many had put forth an honest effort to learn, to break out fields and plant crops the way the white agents showed them. Then they had been hurried away under military escort, obliged to leave most of their livestock for the whites who moved in behind them.

Yet Rusty understood the other side of the argument. Warfare was an integral part of Indian life—at least for the horseback Indians who roamed the plains. Warrior status was coveted by every ambitious young male. Only through war and the hunt could he prove himself worthy of being regarded a man. A life without war would be idle and pointless, too dreary to contemplate. Sometimes war was fought against nearby tribes. More often the targets were American settlers and Mexicans, whoever came handy.

To these people of European extraction and vastly different culture, it was intolerable to live in constant fear of potentially hostile neighbors. Most could recall violent deaths of kin and acquaintances at Indian hands. In many a home, chilling family stories were told and retold about depredations against forebears in the Alleghenies, the Mohawk and Ohio Valleys, the Southeast, or down in Mexico. A rumor of Indians could panic a community or arouse it to arms.

Coming into the region that had been the reservation before removal, Rusty saw a few new cabins. Some structures built by or for the Indians were occupied. Settlers had not wasted time moving into the vacuum after the former residents were dispossessed. He knew there had been political string-pulling well ahead of the removal and that hunger for land had been at least as potent a motive as fear in breaking up the Brazos reserve.

His opinion about these new settlers was immaterial, whether favorable or otherwise. As a ranger, paid or not, he would have to defend them against reinvasion by the displaced Indians. Since removal, any Indian found inside the borders of Texas was assumed to be hostile and subject to being shot on sight unless accompanied by federal or state officials. Even then he would be regarded with suspicion and kept under watch lest he try to take back by force that which he regarded as having been his.

Rusty came to a creek he thought too narrow to be the Clear Fork. He was sure it was not on Blessing's crude map. Nearby stood a new picket cabin built of upright oak logs and covered by a sod roof that he doubted would keep all the rain out. The sod was thick enough and heavy enough to pose a hazard if it became saturated with water. Its weight could collapse the cabin into a heap of ruin and bury anyone unlucky enough to have sought shelter inside. But perhaps its owner was better at farming than at carpentry.

A man was stacking stones, building a rock fence around a garden plot. He was so intent on his work or whatever else was on his mind that he remained unaware until Rusty was almost close enough to reach across the fence and touch him.

"Howdy," Rusty said.

The man jumped backward, bringing a large rock up defensively as if to brain Rusty with it. A trickle of brown down his chin showed he had been chewing tobacco. He swallowed most of it. "My God!" he exclaimed after a moment's startled silence. "You could've been an Indian. Why don't you make a little noise before you slip up on a feller?" He dropped the stone and spat out what remained of the tobacco, coughing in an effort to bring up some that had lodged in his throat.

Rusty said, "This old mule sloshes like a water barrel on a wagon. You must've been studyin' hard not to've heard us."

It took the farmer a minute to get rid of the tobacco and calm down. "Maybe I was. I need to pay more attention if I'm to keep livin' in this country. Just because they've moved the Indians out don't mean they might not come back."

"Could you blame them? They were given this land, and then it was taken away from them."

"It wasn't me that gave them the reservation, and it wasn't me that told them they had to leave. Damned government never did ask my opinion about anything. If I hadn't took up this place, somebody else would've. Can't blame me for that, can you?"

Rusty shook his head. "Seems like it doesn't do much good to blame anybody. It's a mess, and we have to live with it the best we can. Mind if I water my stock at your creek?"

"The creek ain't mine, just the land that runs up to it. If you and your animals drink it all up, them fellers downstream will just have to take care of theirselves." The farmer had recovered from his momentary fright, though Rusty suspected it would take longer to get over the tobacco he had swallowed.

"I'm on my way up to Fort Belknap. I've been through here before, but I'm a little hazy about the distance."

The farmer studied the horse and mule, satisfying himself of their soundness. "You'll make it in another day easy enough. Less if you lope up a little. What kind of business draws you to Belknap?"

"I'm reportin' for duty there."

The farmer's eyebrows went up. "You look kind of young to be one of them minuteman rangers."

"Captain Blessing thinks I'm old enough."

"You're liable to age in a hurry. Some hard old boys hang around in the brush outside of Fort Belknap. They don't take kindly to the law messin' with their business."

"What kind of business?"

"Some peddle whiskey up north of the Red River, on the Indian reservation. Others go up there and steal Indian horses. When the Indians get mad enough or drunk enough to start raisin' hell, it's always somebody innocent that gets hurt. They don't try to find the ones that's actually caused their trouble. Anybody white will do."

Rusty decided the farmer was not going to invite him to break bread with him or to spend the night. It was early in the afternoon anyway. He could make several more miles before time to camp.

The farmer said, "I don't ordinarily give advice where it ain't been asked for, but you look like some mother's nice young son. If I was you I wouldn't advertise too high about bein' a ranger. Some of them rough boys might decide to leave you layin' out on the prairie and pretend like the Indians done it."

"Once I join the company I'm assigned to, there won't be any secret about who I am."

"Rangers up in this country generally travel in packs, or at least in pairs so one can watch the front while the other watches the rear. Indians ain't the only danger around here, not by a long ways. You heard about agent Neighbors gettin' murdered in Belknap? Just because he tried to help the reserve Indians."

Rusty had heard. He had also heard that the ranger company caught the murderer and made short work of him. "I suppose some of those rough boys pass this way from time to time?"

"I try to see very little and tell even less. If I was to peach to a ranger, somebody might come by here some dark night and blow my light out. If any of them was to ride up here now and see me talkin' to you, and they found out you're a ranger, they might get the same idea. So I'd take it kindly if you'd water your stock and move on."

Rusty pulled the mule's lead rope. "I'm obliged to you for the water and the words of wisdom."

"They never cost me nothin'. Watch out for yourself. I'd hate for your mother to have to grieve for you."

Rusty saw no point in saying that he had no mother, no father, no kin that he knew of. The farmer had his own problems.

He tried to be watchful, for he knew this could be dangerous country, but he missed seeing the band of horses until they came boiling over a hill and swept down toward him. A rider galloped along in front, pointing the way. Several others rode alongside and behind, keeping the animals moving at a fast clip. Rusty felt a wild jolt of apprehension, thinking the horsemen were Comanches. His fear eased as he saw they were white. He realized that Comanches were in the habit of taking horses north, not south.

He pulled to the left to be out of the way. The driven horses began spilling past him, though the man who rode point reined around and came directly toward Rusty. He was followed quickly by two men who had been riding swing alongside the remuda.

The point rider gave Rusty a close scrutiny without speaking. His hard gaze brought back Rusty's uneasiness.

Rusty offered a tentative "Howdy."

"I don't know you. Who are you?" The man was young enough that his several days' growth of whiskers looked soft and uneven.

Not much older than me, Rusty thought. But he saw hardness in the eyes and the set of the jaw. "My name's Rusty Shannon. What's yours?" He extended his hand.

The rider did not answer the question or accept Rusty's hand. "Where you headed?"

"Up the country a ways." Rusty remembered the farmer's admonition about not revealing his mission.

"What for?"

"Lookin' for kin." That was not quite a lie. He always harbored a faint hope that he might run into kin somewhere, though he would have no way of recognizing them if he did. It was frustrating not to know what his real name had been.

The suspicious gray eyes had a piercing quality that compounded Rusty's discomfort. The other two horsemen had pulled up on either side of the point rider. Rusty sensed threat in all three. Whatever they were up to, it was not good.

The point rider asked, "You sure your kin ain't in the federal army? Or maybe the ranger spy company up there?"

"I don't know anybody in the army, or in any spy company either." It was true that Rusty didn't know anyone in the ranger company *yet*.

He strongly suspected these were Indian horses, stolen off the reservation. The threat of war had raised the price of horses enough to tempt even an honest man, much less one already inclined to be a thief. Rusty's life might not be worth a brass peso if these men knew his true business. He made an effort to keep his hand still, not to let it move down toward the stock of his rifle. He doubted he would live to bring the weapon clear of leather.

"I don't mean to hold you fellers up. You look like you're in a hurry."

The three men glanced at one another, indecisive. The last of the loose horses trotted past, two riders following. Another rider spurred up from far behind, his face flushed with excitement. "What the hell have you stopped for? They're right behind us!" He pointed in the direction from which he had come.

That threw the others into a similar state of excitement. The point rider drew a pistol from his hip. He brought it up as if to aim it at Rusty, then changed his mind.

The man who had come up last shouted, "Shoot him, damn it, and let's get out of here!"

The point rider hesitated. The other drew his pistol to do the chore for him. The point rider pushed between him and Rusty. He said, "They *might* hang us for horse stealin', Pete. They'd sure as hell hang us for a killin'." He stared hard at Rusty. "Reckon you can forget what we look like?"

The muzzle of the pistol was leveled on Rusty's stomach. "I've already forgotten."

He had not, however. The images of the man with the pistol and the one named Pete had burned themselves indelibly into his memory.

Pete looked back, his voice desperate. "We'd better let the horses go. We can't save them and our scalps, too."

Reluctantly the point man said, "All right, there'll be more horses another time." He turned back to Rusty. "I wouldn't stay here if I was you. You're fixin' to meet up with a bunch of real mad Indians."

Rusty's anxiety over the horsemen was replaced by anxiety over what was coming next. He saw a thicket a couple of hundred yards away. "Don't let me hold you back."

The horsemen put spurs to their mounts and quartered south-eastward in a hard run. They motioned for two men who still rode on the near side of the remuda to quit the bunch and join them. The stolen horses at the rear realized they were no longer being pushed and slowed down. A few stopped and nickered for their running mates. Rusty touched his heels to Alamo's sides and put him into a long trot. Chapultepec lagged so that Rusty had to turn loose of the lead rope to prevent being pulled from the saddle. He circled back to recover the animal.

"Damned mule, you're liable to get me killed."

The delay prevented him from reaching the thicket in time. More than a dozen riders appeared on the hill where he had first seen the stolen horses. As they galloped down the slope, several split off and came after Rusty while the others continued pursuit of the remuda. There was no doubt this time. These were Indians. Rusty saw that he had no chance to reach the thicket. He pulled hard on the reins and slipped the rifle from its scabbard, then stepped quickly to the ground.

Even as he did so, he knew he had no chance. He might shoot one, but the others would cut him down before he could reload. He held his breath until his lungs ached, then sucked in enough air to fill them and stood with the rifle at arm's length in a posture of surrender.

Daddy Mike had always said the worst thing a man could do was to give himself up to Indians, but the only other option he saw was to go down fighting. It seemed futile to kill just one when he could see half a dozen coming at him. He waited, his heart pounding and his mouth dry as old leather.

He wished Preacher Webb were with him. Preacher could charm his way into or out of almost any situation. Rusty whispered, "Lord, if You're really up there and payin' any attention, You'd better do somethin' quick."

The first Indian to reach him shouted furiously and pointed toward the horses still moving southward. Rusty did not understand the words, but the tone was unmistakable. The rest surrounded him in a hostile manner. He knew they assumed he was one of the thieves.

He pointed in the direction the real thieves had taken. They were still in sight but fading rapidly into the distance. "Yonder go the ones that stole your horses. It wasn't me."

He realized they probably did not understand what he was saying. He hoped they understood his gestures. He pointed again. "Yonder they go."

A voice came from behind him. "How come you didn't go with them, bub?"

He had not noticed that one of the men was white. *Lord*, he thought, *maybe You were paying attention after all.* "Because I wasn't with them in the first place."

Being white did not mean the man was friendly. He had a hangman's look about him, darkly suspicious eyes peering from beneath the drooping brim of a weather-beaten felt hat, his mouth a flat line barely visible through heavy brown whiskers. "You tryin' to make us believe you just happened into them?"

"Yes, sir, or they just happened into me. I was headed the other direction, to Fort Belknap."

Several sets of dark and glittering eyes stared accusingly at him. He suspected some of the Indians understood enough English to get the gist of what he had said. They argued among themselves. One pointed to the mule. Rusty feared he was claiming the animal, which would mean they had made up their minds he was a thief. He shivered, wondering how it felt to take an arrow in the chest or to have a war club smash his skull.

The white man listened intently to the Indians' conversation, which he seemed to understand. Rusty assumed he was some kind of scout or interpreter. When the talk dwindled away, the man told Rusty, "Walkin' Eagle says there wasn't no mules among the bunch that was stolen."

Rusty began to hope. "Not this one, for sure. I brought Chapultepec with me all the way up from the Colorado River. Alamo, too." He pointed to the black horse's brand. "That's the Shannon brand, an *S* with a bar under it. I'm Rusty Shannon."

The name meant nothing. The man pointed to the brand and said something to the Indians, part in spoken words and part in sign. They argued, but when the argument quieted down, Rusty was fairly sure none of them was claiming the brand. He breathed easier.

The white man demanded, "What's your business at Belknap?"

Rusty pondered his answer. Given what had been done to them in recent times, it was unlikely these Indians had any good feeling toward the rangers. He repeated the evasion he had offered to the horse thief. "I'm lookin' for some kin."

"Who are they? Maybe I know them."

"Our family's the Shannons." That was not a lie.

"I don't recall any Shannons up that way. You sure they're there?"

"I'm not sure of anything. But I thought I'd look."

Rusty could see that several Indians who had followed the thieves had abandoned that chase and were helping run down the loose horses. He saw a couple of army uniforms as well.

The interpreter said, "I don't like to call anybody a liar 'til I know for sure, but let's just say I ain't done wonderin'. Soon's the Tonkawas finish roundin' up their horses, we'll all head back toward Fort Belknap together. We'll see if we can find any Shannons."

Rusty was mildly surprised. "Tonkawas? I figured these were Comanches."

The man seemed short of patience. "That's one big trouble with you people in Texas. You never could tell one Indian from another. It's caused you no end of grief, and them, too. The Comanches are as wild as deer."

"These looked pretty wild too, comin' at me like they did."

"If they was the killin' kind of Indian, you'd already be halfway to hell and smellin' the smoke. The Tonkawas don't mean harm to anybody, except Comanches. They used to give you Texans a lot of help against the wild Indians. The reward you gave them was to kick them across the river."

Rusty remembered the sad exodus, but under present circumstances he had no intention of letting them know he had been there.

The Indians had turned back the leaders of the stolen horse herd and were pushing the bunch in Rusty's direction. The two army men rode ahead, reining up as they reached Rusty and the interpreter. One of the pair bore himself with exaggerated dignity, which led Rusty to assume he was an officer of some kind. *Probably a lieutenant,* he thought. Daddy Mike had always said lieutenants tended to have an inflated view of their importance. By the time they made captain, most had had their egos punctured often enough to let the excess air out of them.

The officer gave Rusty a study of the most negative sort. "I see you captured one of them, Harrison."

The interpreter had not introduced himself. Now, at least, Rusty knew his name.

Harrison replied, "We're inclined to believe he's not one of them. He says he was on his way north and just happened to run into the thieves. None of the Tonks claim his horse or mule."

The officer continued his hard scrutiny. "Perhaps. Not all have seen them yet." To Rusty he said, "If you are what you claim to be, I must say that I find fault with your choice of company."

"They weren't any company of mine. It looked for a minute like they were fixin' to shoot me." He considered showing the note Tom Blessing had written for the captain of rangers but decided it might be well to wait until they reached Belknap. He did not know the army's opinion of the rangers. If it was like the rangers' opinion of the army, he had better keep his mouth shut.

The officer said, "What matters most is that the Indians recovered their horses. To be on the safe side, we'll turn you over to the authorities as we pass Belknap. If they find no fault with you, they'll free you quickly enough." He scowled. "They do not seem to find much fault with people who steal from the Indians."

Rusty decided against continuing to proclaim his innocence. He had already said more than usual, and the lieutenant would keep doubting him anyway.

The officer asked, "Should the occasion arise, do you think you could identify the thieves?"

"One or two, maybe. Most of them were too far away." Under duress Rusty had implied a promise of silence to the thieves' point rider, though he did not feel honor bound to respect it. With luck he might never be called upon to face that moral decision.

Though technically not a prisoner, Rusty felt like one. Should he try to escape his mixed escort he suspected he would be run down or shot. He decided to make the best of the present situation inasmuch as he was being taken where he had intended to go in the first place.

The lieutenant rode on one side of him, Harrison on the other. The lieutenant had little to say. Rusty suspected he did not like talking to inferiors more than necessary, and it was clear enough that he saw Rusty as an inferior.

Harrison interested Rusty the most. "Where'd you learn how to talk to Indians?"

"Tonkawas, mainly. The only talkin' I ever done with the Comanches was with the business end of a gun. I ain't no Texan, but I lived there awhile, near the Tonks. They're good people if you overlook their eatin' habits."

"Like what?"

"Ain't nothin' pleases them more than a little barbecued Comanche. Eatin' their enemy gives them some of his strength, the way they figure it. Of course that makes other Indians hate them. Now you Texans have moved them up into the territory and put them smack-dab in the middle of their enemies. It'll be a wonder if the other tribes don't kill them all."

The lieutenant said, "They have the army's protection."

Rusty blurted, "Like the army's always protected Texas?"

The lieutenant's pained expression showed that the barb had bitten into the flesh. "I suppose you are one of those who plans to vote for secession?"

"I doubt I'll get a chance to vote one way or the other. If I did, I'm not sure which way I'd choose."

"Perhaps you have not heard. The vote is to be taken this coming Saturday. There are a few counties in the northern section still strongly pro-federal, and the German colonies near San Antonio. The rest of Texas seems bound and determined to charge up Fool's Hill."

Rusty had not realized the voting day was imminent. The news shook him a little. Daddy Mike had predicted bad trouble once the vote was taken. So had Lon Monahan. "What happens to the federal army if Texas pulls out?" he asked.

Harrison said, "The soldiers may find theirselves fightin' Texans instead of Comanches."

The lieutenant frowned. "No, more than likely the army will simply be ordered to withdraw all troops from the state."

Rusty knew many Texans would welcome that result, but he feared they had not thought the implications through. Despite the army's many shortcomings, it had provided the frontier at least a little protection. If it withdrew, Texas would have to fall back entirely upon its own resources: the local militia and rangers or minutemen. During the ten years it had been a republic Texas had never put together enough money to wad a shotgun. It had fared but little better as a state. He saw no reason to expect its positions to improve once it was no longer part of the United States.

He remarked, "Looks to me like we're fixin' to cook our own goose."

The officer suggested, "You could vote against secession."

"That wouldn't change anything. I'd about as well try to dam up the Brazos River with a pitchfork."

Rusty kept watching in fascination the Indians who pushed the recovered horses along. Most had changed to fresh mounts, having worn down their original ones in the pursuit. The stolen animals had been driven hard but had not carried the burden of men on their backs. The Tonkawas' winter clothing was a mixture of long breechcloths, tanned leathers, and whiteman castoffs. For protection against the cold, some covered their shoulders and torsos with buffalo robes, others with woolen blankets. Some wore earrings and necklaces of animal teeth or shells.

Harrison told him, "You'd best take a good look at them. The Tonkawas are dyin' out."

"These look pretty strong to me."

"As Indians go, there ain't many left. White man's diseases . . . hostile tribes . . . Pretty soon they'll all be gone."

"I expect a lot of people would be glad to dance at the last one's funeral."

"Just you Texans who can't tell Indians apart. If you ever got to know them, you'd see that there's a world of difference between Tonkawas and Comanches."

"The Comanches stole me once when I was little. I can't remember much except bein' scared."

"It's lucky your folks got you back."

"They evidently killed my folks. Other people took and raised me."

"You Texans think because some Indians are bad, they all are. I guess your experience made you hate all Indians."

"I don't hate anybody." Rusty reconsidered. "Except maybe one man, and he's white."

"Indians have got ways of their own. That don't make them good or bad, it just makes them different. These Tonkawas were ready to've killed the horse thieves if they'd caught them, and you'd've heard weepin' and wailin' about an Indian massacre. But do you think white men would've been different? If it was their horses they'd've been hell-bent to hang everybody they caught."

"Texans aren't all alike, either. Because some are bad, you think they all are."

Harrison almost smiled. "There may be an exception here and there."

They were a few miles short of Fort Belknap when a dozen horsemen suddenly appeared three hundred yards in front of them, fanned out as if to offer battle. One prematurely fired a shot, which took no effect that Rusty could see. A soldier who had been riding point ahead of the remuda spurred toward them, his right arm raised, so the riders could see that the Indians had a military escort. One of the newcomers, evidently their leader, waved his hat and signaled for those on the flanks to rejoin the main group. As they pulled together, he motioned for them to hold their position while he rode forward. He swung out to one side and slowed to let the driven horses pass. He gave the Indians a critical study before proceeding to meet the lieutenant. He wore no uniform but carried himself in a military manner. He brought his hand up in a sharp salute, touching the brim of a well-worn felt hat. His back was arrow-straight, his black-and-gray moustache smartly trimmed and turned up at the ends.

In a stiffly formal manner he said, "We were sent a report of Indians passing through the country. It was our fear that they were Comanche or Kiowa."

The words were clipped. Rusty detected a trace of accent similar to that of Germans he knew on the Colorado.

The lieutenant's tone was condescending. "As even a Texan can see, they are Tonkawas."

"Often I have ridden with the Tonkawas. But even they are forbidden now south of the Red River. From where obtained they so many horses?"

The lieutenant plainly was not used to being questioned by civilians who did not show proper deference to their betters. "These horses belong to them. They were stolen off the reservation. And who are you to be asking questions of a military officer?"

"I am August Burmeister, a captain of the state rangers."

The lieutenant was not impressed. "If you Texans were as diligent in going after white thieves as red ones, these Indians might not have found it necessary to come south of the river. But as you can see, they are under federal military escort."

"Ah yes, the federals." Burmeister was not impressed either. He pointed his chin northward. "You are on your way to Belknap, I assume?"

"No. Do you think I would give the trigger-happy citizens of that illbegotten community an excuse for killing more peaceful Indians? However, we have a man here to turn over to the proper persons." He jerked a thumb in Rusty's direction.

Burmeister tugged at one end of his moustache while giving Rusty an intense scrutiny. "And what is it this man has done?"

"We found him with the horse thieves. He claims he was traveling north and encountered them by chance. We'll leave it to you to determine the truth of the matter. I trust if he is guilty of stealing Indian horses, you will deal with him in an appropriate manner?"

The question was offered in an ironic voice that said the officer had no such expectation.

Rusty saw no harm in revealing his mission now. He took from his coat pocket the map and a note Tom Blessing had written. "I was on my way to Fort Belknap to report to you," he told the ranger.

As the captain read the note, his expression lost its severity. A smile lifted the moustache. "Tom Blessing. A good man he is. I was with him when we battled Comanches at Plum Creek."

"I was there, too," Rusty said.

"How could that be? Twenty years ago, it was."

"Do you remember a little boy there, rescued from the Indians?"

"I do. He was red-haired." The captain gave Rusty a closer study. "It would seem he is still red-haired."

"The name's Rusty Shannon. In the letter, Tom Blessing calls me *David*."

The captain shook his hand. "Shannon. The name seems *bekannt*. Was there not someone called Shannon at Plum Creek?"

"Mike Shannon, my father. Foster father, anyway. They never found out who my real folks were, so he took me to raise, him and Mother Dora."

"A man of the cloth rode with him, I believe. His arm was broken in the fight."

"That'd be Preacher Webb. Him and Daddy Mike were always close."

"They are both well, I hope."

"Preacher Webb still carries the Word to the folks of the creek." Rusty's throat tightened. "Daddy Mike is dead."

"That I regret. They fought a good fight. We all fought a good fight." Burmeister looked back to the lieutenant. "This young man need concern you no longer, Captain."

"Lieutenant."

"Lieutenant. Yes, I should have known." Burmeister's look showed his opinion of lieutenants.

The officer rebuked Rusty with his eyes. "You should have told us you belonged to this company."

"I was afraid you might have less use for Texas rangers than you do for Texas horse thieves."

"I find them similar in many respects. Come along, Harrison. The Tonkawas are getting ahead of us."

The scout Harrison gave Rusty a wink and put his horse into a long trot to catch up with the departing officer.

Burmeister watched the two ride away. "I agree not with this talk of breaking away from the Union. But such officers could do much to change my mind."

With a nod he bade Rusty to follow him to where the rest of his ranger contingent waited. One of the men, rangy and hungry-looking, leaned forward, bracing his hands on the horn of his saddle. He wore a tattered buckskin jacket, crudely patched. His face was heavily freckled, and his eyes laughed. "Couldn't you talk us into a fight with them Yankee boys and their Indians, Dutch? We need the practice."

"I have ridden with the Tonkawas as allies. You would not want them for an enemy." Burmeister's moustache lifted at both ends. "Besides, Tanner, you are too skinny to interest them. Not even good soup would you make."

The man named Tanner turned his attention to Rusty. "Looks like they rejected this one, too. He ain't got much more meat on him than I have."

Burmeister introduced Rusty to the group. "David Shannon. Tom Blessing has sent him to join our little company."

Tanner shook Rusty's hand. "Welcome, David."

"Call me Rusty."

"Hope you brought money enough to run us awhile, Rusty, because pay don't come often around here and don't amount to much when it does."

Rusty had only four dollars but saw no reason to admit to poverty. Many in this group had a ragged appearance, which indicated they could not show even that much.

Tanner pointed at Chapultepec. "Worst come to worst, we can always eat the mule."

Somebody shouted, "Ain't that cannibalism, Tanner, eatin' your own kind?"

Rusty decided he was going to like this bunch.

CHAPTER
NINE

Before they reached the tent camp, two men passed them, racing horses at breakneck speed across the open prairie and shouting in glee. It looked like fun to Rusty, but Burmeister frowned. "They have not enough to do when they do not ride the line. They will break a horse's leg one day, or a man's neck. But I cannot forbid them. Two months' pay they are owed."

The camp crowded against a clump of timber a short distance from Fort Belknap. The military post that had lent the small settlement its name had been vacated by the army a few years earlier. Rusty suspected the rangers had been placed away from the town so they would be less exposed to urban temptations. However, lack of spending money accomplished that purpose. The state required each man to furnish his own horse and firearms, and it was to supply the other necessities. The spartan nature of the camp indicated to Rusty that the state's definition of *necessities* was poor and lean. Texas was rich only in ambition and spirit. Its leaders had nothing in their pockets except their hands, but they gave voice to extravagant dreams. Texas was a great *someday* land.

Burmeister watched Rusty remove the pack from Chapultepec. "I wish I could say the state will pay you for use of the mule. Promises I can give you. Money I cannot."

"Wasn't money that I came for."

"For what *did* you come?"

The primary reason was that Tom Blessing had told him to, but he doubted that was what Burmeister would want to hear. "Duty. Daddy Mike always preached that we owe it to our neighbors to serve wherever we can."

"A wise man, your father. I hope he taught you well in other things."

"He taught me to plow a straight furrow. He taught me to hit what I aim at."

"Did he teach you to know what you should aim at and what you should not?"

Rusty frowned. "I'm not sure what you mean."

"Never mind. When it is important, I think you will know."

Burmeister queried Rusty at length about the horse thieves he had encountered and jotted a few notes in a small book. Rusty doubted that he had told enough to be useful.

Burmeister frowned. "If you see some of them again, it would surprise me none. There are in this vicinity those who have little regard for property other than their own."

As the captain moved away, the lanky Tanner edged closer, observing Rusty's saddle and other accoutrements. Rusty thought about counting the freckles on the ranger's face but decided that would take until dark, even if Tanner held still.

Tanner said, "You ain't long off of the farm."

"How can you tell?"

"Your hands are set in the shape of a plow handle, and ain't nobody but a dry-dirt farmer would be ridin' a saddle as old as that."

Rusty felt defensive. "It keeps me on the horse."

"What you want to do is catch you a lawbreaker that's got a good saddle. Shoot him and confiscate the saddle as contraband. If a man is a sure-enough shot, he can put a good outfit together in almost no time atall."

Rusty was momentarily taken aback until a twinkle in Tanner's eyes told him the ranger was trying to run a sandy on a newcomer.

Tanner said, "That's how I got my saddle. Only it turned out he was innocent. The joke was on me."

"I'll bet you both got a laugh out of it."

Tanner grinned. "You've got to kill a high class of criminal to get ahead. Poor folks never carry anything worth confiscatin'."

He pointed to a nearby tent, the canvas old and badly stained. Rusty suspected it leaked like fishing net, should rain ever chance to fall.

Tanner offered, "I'll help you carry your stuff."

There was not much of it, but Rusty accepted the offer, grateful for the welcoming manner. "What all does the company do?"

"Mainly just patrol, watchin' for sign of Indians comin' into the country. Most of the time it's dull and tiresome. Now and then we get a little excitement, like today when we thought we was about to do battle with a bunch of Comanche horse thieves. That one flickered out like a candle in the wind. Most of them do."

"What about Captain Burmeister? You get along with him all right?"

"Dutch? Sure. Don't let his way of talkin' fool you. He can't help it if he don't talk good like me and you. He came from someplace over in Europe . . . Westphalia, he calls it. I don't know just where that is; I ain't been further than San Antonio myself. I just know that he was a soldier over there a long time ago, and he took French leave—snuck off and left them."

"I don't suppose he's ever snuck off and left this outfit."

"Never. A man smart as he is could be set real pretty by now if he'd put his mind to it. He's spent too much of his life volunteerin' and not enough takin' care of his own interests. Acts and thinks a little too much like a Yankee for some people's tastes, but he'd charge hell with a bucket of water. And most every man in this outfit would follow him into the fire."

Inside the tent Rusty saw several bedrolls spread on the ground. Tanner pointed to an open spot. "There's your bed."

"My bed?"

"You wasn't lookin' for a cot, was you? This ain't exactly the Menger Hotel. The rangers get bed and board from the state. It gives them ground to roll out their bed, and it lets them eat all the game they can shoot for theirselves."

"Mighty generous."

"Ain't as bad as it sounds. We get a payday now and again when the politicians in Austin don't spend it all first. Ain't much to waste it on anyway . . . bad whiskey, slow horses, loose women ugly as mud."

"But you're makin' it a better country to live in."

"Ask your Tonkawa friends about that. The way we've treated them, they might not agree."

Two rangers came riding in from patrol, one carrying a deer carcass tied behind his saddle. Tanner hailed them. "Looks like fresh venison again tonight. I'd give a month's pay for a bait of good salt pork."

Rusty had left some hanging in the smokehouse back home. The Gaskin family had probably sneaked over and stolen it all by now.

Tanner introduced him to Jim and Johnny Morris, brothers who had brought in the deer. They had the same ragged appearance as Tanner, though Jim wore a new buckskin shirt that seemed out of place with his frayed and patched woolen trousers. Tanner raked charred bits of wood from a shallow pit and coaxed a few sparks into blazing life amid a small pile of shavings.

He hung a coffeepot from a steel bar over the fire and melted deer fat in a skillet, preparatory to frying the meat. "I'm no more than a fair to middlin' shot, but I'm a pretty decent cook when I've got somethin' to work with."

Jim Morris commented, "He fixes a pretty fair possum."

Not all the rangers Rusty had seen around camp were as lank as Tanner, but none ran much to fat. He could easily see why.

As they finished the fried venison, Captain Burmeister walked over from his tent. He carried a notebook and pencil. "I must have information for Austin so you will be paid. Perhaps."

He ran his finger down a short list of questions, beginning with name and birth date. Rusty explained that he did not know his birth date or even his birth name, reminding Burmeister that he had been picked up on the battlefield at Plum Creek.

Burmeister said, "It makes no difference. A few men in this company know their true name but use another. I am at peace with it. Now I must ask—"

Tanner interrupted. "Pardon, Dutch, but look what's comin'."

Rusty turned as he heard horses approaching camp. Burmeister squinted, then uttered a few words of German that by their tone suggested profanity. Rusty quick-counted ten horsemen. He knew the man at the center and thought he recognized a couple of others.

"Caleb Dawkins," he said.

Burmeister gave Rusty a surprised look. "You know the colonel?"

"Met him. He spoiled a good supper a few nights ago."

"For me he has spoiled several. But he is a citizen. We must show respect." Burmeister walked out to receive Dawkins. His voice was edged with irony. "To what, Colonel, owe we this pleasure?"

"It's no pleasure for me, Burmeister. I have with me my son and several other men who just lost a large number of horses to raiding Indians. They barely escaped with their lives."

Rusty was certain now. At least one of the riders had been with Dawkins when he had threatened Lon Monahan. He turned his attention to two more who moved up almost even with the colonel. They had been among the thieves who had stolen horses from the Tonkawas. One was the young man called Pete, who had urged the point rider to kill Rusty and move on. The other was the point rider himself, who could have shot Rusty but chose not to. The point rider's eyes met Rusty's and locked on them. Recognition was immediate, and so was sudden fear. The young thief surreptitiously shook his head, silently pleading that Rusty not give him away.

Burmeister said, "We saw but one band. They were Tonkawas with federal escort. They had just recovered horses stolen by white renegades."

Rusty studied Dawkins, wondering if the colonel knew the truth or if the thieves had duped him. Nothing in the man's expression gave a solid indication either way.

Dawkins said, "Did you have anything more than their word that the horses they took had been stolen?"

"The word of a federal officer."

"Federal officer!" Dawkins spoke the words like a curse. "I had rather trust a gypsy horse trader." He turned to the young man beside him, the one called Pete. "That wouldn't be the same Indians you told me about, would it, son?"

The reply was so quick it overlapped the question. "No sir, Papa, the ones that chased us was sure as hell Comanches. And the horses they took was mine, bought and paid for over east. We wouldn't lie to you."

The young point rider looked again at Rusty, silently begging. The one called Pete carefully avoided Rusty's gaze. That he had recognized Rusty was almost certain.

Dawkins said firmly, "I assume you intend to pursue the matter, Burmeister?"

"Patrols are out. They will find the trail if one there is, and we will pursue. Tell me where it happened."

Pete proceeded to offer an ambitious lie. He placed the raid well to the east of the point where Rusty had encountered first the outlaws, then the Tonkawas. He was vague and uncertain when Burmeister asked him to describe the horses, their number and their brands. His excuse was that he had just recently bought them from a number of farmers and had not yet had time to become familiar with the individual animals.

The ranger had to maintain appearances, though the sarcasm in his questions made it clear that he saw through the hoax. He said, "Whoever took the horses, they are by now across the river. There it is forbidden for my men to go. Your friends can go to the federal officers and make a complaint."

Rusty knew that was a polite way of closing the matter, for going to federal authorities was the last thing either Dawkins or the horse thieves would want to do.

Dawkins seemed vindicated by the rejection. "I told my son you would give him no satisfaction. You so-called lawmen helped the federals protect Washington's pets while they were on the Brazos reserve, and you have no stomach for facing them now."

Burmeister's ire began to rise. "Always the rangers are in the middle. The settlers said it was the Indians we protected. The federals said we were with the settlers against the Indians. You are free to complain to Austin or to the federal authorities. I stand not in your way."

"I will not talk to any federals, and I can see I'm wasting my time talking to you. You're a foreigner anyhow."

"How long is it you have been in Texas, Colonel Dawkins?"

"Twelve years. I'm proud to say I came from Mississippi."

"More than twenty years I have been here. So who is the foreigner?"

"At least I can speak proper English. There'll be changes after the election. When Texas is free of the Yankee yoke, you and your whole damned command will have questions to answer. I suspect it is infested with unionists."

Burmeister took an angry step toward Dawkins, then stopped, his feet planted apart in a challenging stance. "We have no more to say, Colonel. You are free to go."

"Hell yes, I'm free, and I intend to stay that way. I don't have to ask your permission to come or to go. But you'll wish you'd never seen me."

"That is my wish already."

Dawkins made a point of being slow to turn away, as if allowing the full weight of his disdain to settle upon Burmeister and the men around him. Pete remained beside him, and the young point rider was quick to follow, as if afraid Rusty might be about to turn the rangers loose on him.

Rusty wondered why he hadn't. It would have been easy to have pointed a finger. His hunch was that Dawkins did not know what his son had been up to. It would have shut him up in a hurry if Rusty had told. But Rusty had been dissuaded by the desperation in the young point rider's eyes. He remembered that the thief could easily have killed him but had not.

We're even now, he thought. *Next time I catch you in the wrong, I don't owe you a thing.*

Tanner stood slouched and looking like a scarecrow with hands in his pockets, his ragged buckskin jacket open and flapping in the wind. He said, "That Dawkins is a peculiar son of a bitch, ain't he?"

When the riders had pulled away, Burmeister faced Rusty. "I believe among those men were the very thieves the Tonkawas chased. Did you not recognize them?"

Rusty did not want to lie, but neither did he want to betray the point rider. "I never saw most of them very close. I didn't care to accuse somebody and turn out to be wrong."

"Next time, accuse. If a man is innocent, we can turn him loose. If he is guilty . . ." He left it at that.

If Rusty had hoped distance would lessen the pain of Mike Shannon's death, his first night in the ranger camp proved the hope to be futile. Long before dawn he awakened out of a violent dream in which he saw Daddy Mike lying dead beside the woodpile. Standing over him was a drunken, laughing Isaac York, a smoking rifle in his hand. Though in his dream Rusty held a pistol, he was unable to raise it. His arm hung stiff and useless at his side. Crying in frustration, he struggled but was unable to move. Isaac York drifted away like a wisp of smoke stolen by the wind. The opportunity to kill him was gone.

The rest of the night Rusty lay with his eyes open, listening to the snoring of fellow rangers. Moonlight filtered through the thin canvas so that he could see the forms of the others sleeping on the ground. He turned onto his right side, then his left, his stomach and his back, trying in vain to be comfortable. The ground was hard and unyielding. After a long time he began hearing a rooster crow somewhere in the distance. He turned back his blanket and found his hat, then his trousers. He had slept in his shirt because his shoulders were cold. He pulled on his boots after shaking them to be certain no unwelcome tiny visitor had crawled into them during the night.

Tanner sat up and stretched, yawning and blinking his eyes. "I ain't heard the call yet."

"Me neither, except for a rooster. Go back to sleep."

"Too late now. You've done woke me up." Tanner had stripped down to long underwear. He hobbled to the front of the tent and peered through the flap. His thin legs reminded Rusty of a spider. "It'll be daylight directly anyhow. You want to start the coffee?"

"Just as well. I've got nothin' better to do."

"We'll be headin' out to ride the line this mornin'. I hope you've rested enough to make a long sashay."

"I wasn't sent here to rest."

"What *was* you sent here for? You kill somebody or somethin'?"

"I was sent here so I *wouldn't*."

Tanner's jaw dropped. "You want to tell me?"

"It's not somethin' I like to talk about." He thought about it, though, whenever his mind was not occupied with the urgencies of the moment.

Tanner sat on his bedroll and tugged at his bootstraps until his feet found bottom. "You'll not likely kill anybody up here unless it's Indians, and probably not even them. I'll bet I've been up and down that line a hundred times, and damned few trips did I see as much as a feather."

"That's all right with me. I've got no grudge against any of them except maybe the Comanches."

"I heard what you told Captain Burmeister about them stealin' you when you was little. You'd be a Comanche yourself today if somebody hadn't rescued you. A redheaded Comanche. Now wouldn't that be a sight to behold?"

Burmeister's long-ago service as a soldier made him try to maintain some semblance of military order in the ranger company, though Rusty quickly saw that the men did not consider themselves soldiers. They submitted to morning formation and roll call, but their notion of standing at attention was decidedly informal. Some chewed and spat tobacco. A couple smoked black and odorous cigars. Company sergeant Whitfield, chunkily built but muscular as a blacksmith, impatiently read the roll as if he considered it a waste of time better spent on more fruitful activity. Some of the men talked among themselves or looked at the sky as if appraising the chance for rain or snow. The roll call was indeed unnecessary except as a faint stab at military routine because the sergeant and the captain both knew who was here and who was out on the line.

The sergeant said, "All present and accounted for except one, Dutch." He frowned as if he had bitten into a sour apple. "Private Haskins is absent without leave again. But I already told you that." Whitfield's tobacco-stained moustache, heavy and unkempt, lifted and fell with each word he spoke. It was in sharp contrast to the captain's moustache, neatly trimmed, its ends upturned.

Burmeister shrugged. "How long must it be before he learns he cannot dry up Fort Belknap? Always, freight wagons bring fresh whiskey. And where does he get the money to buy?"

"There's people in town who buy it for him. I think they get him drunk so he'll tell them what we're doin' out here and what we're fixin' to do. There's many that don't want rangers interferin' in their business."

"Detail someone to bring him. Handcuff him to a tree until the whiskey has gone from him."

"Was it left to me, I'd give him a lick or two with a quirt and send him packin'."

"Sober, he is a good man."

"Drunk, he's useless to himself and to this company. But you're the captain, Dutch. If you want to keep him on the payroll, that's your business."

"On the payroll? I think you make the joke. How long is it since we have been paid?"

"Money is one thing I don't joke about. I've never had enough that it ever got funny."

Burmeister's gaze sought out Rusty. "Haskins was to be on patrol today. David Shannon, you will take his place."

Rusty was not certain of the proper response, so he made an effort at a salute. He said, "You bet."

Burmeister winced.

Rusty whispered to Tanner, "Did I do somethin' wrong?"

"I think you're supposed to say, 'You bet, *sir*.'"

The patrol moved northward toward the Red River. At first Alamo looked back, wanting to travel southward toward home. But after a half mile or so he reconciled with reality and plodded along, keeping good pace with the other horses. Rusty studied the riders around him. They had little of a military look about them. Their clothing was a rainbow of colors and a random mix of homespun cotton, wool, and buckskin, most of it showing the effects of rough use.

He remembered what Tom Blessing had called the volunteer patrols along the frontier: the buckskin line.

Tanner asked Rusty, "You any good at followin' tracks?"

"I've trailed deer. Followed a wolf one time for two miles 'til I found its den."

"This ought not to be too tough, then. We'll be watchin' for horse tracks that don't belong."

"How do you know which ones don't belong?"

"When the hair raises up on the back of your neck."

Sergeant Whitfield was in charge of the patrol. He seemed a man not given to smiling easily, for Rusty had seen no sign of levity about him. Nor did he have much to say beyond the orders necessary to get the patrol under way. Despite his considerable size, Whitfield seemed to sit easy in the saddle. He set the pace, an easy trot the horses could maintain for long stretches of time.

Rusty soon saw that the sergeant had a way of watching the ground without missing anything that happened around him. Once, seeing distant dark objects that aroused his suspicion, he detailed Rusty and Tanner to ride out and investigate. "Don't get too close 'til you're sure it's not Indians. I don't want to explain to the captain why I let a couple of chuckleheaded boys get themselves killed."

Tanner assured him, "I've already laid out my plans for the day, and gettin' killed ain't on the list." He made a halfhearted attempt to laugh but dropped it when he received no response from Whitfield. The sergeant was all business.

Rusty noted that though Tanner seemed on the surface to shrug off the notion of danger, he was cautious in his approach to the dark specks Whitfield had seen in the tall grass. Tanner carried his rifle across the pommel of his saddle, his right hand nervously rubbing the wooden stock.

Two buffalo bulls jumped up, snorted, and loped away in an awkward rocking gait, grumbling at the disturbance. Relieved, Tanner expelled a long breath. Rusty realized he had been holding it.

Tanner said, "At least it'll give the sergeant somethin' to write in his report. 'Jumped two buffalo. Found no Indians.'"

"The day's a long way from done. How do you know we won't find any Indians?"

"If there'd been any around, they'd've already killed them two bulls for meat."

Tanner's professed confidence did not lessen Rusty's watchfulness. He found himself looking to the horizon more than to the ground where any horse tracks might be. But he reasoned that sergeant Whitfield was watchful enough for both of them.

They camped on the south bank of the Red River. Whitfield detailed Tanner to make bread and Rusty to brew the coffee. Rusty dipped the pot into the river to fill it. Somehow the water looked a bit less muddy in the pot than it did out in the channel, though it still retained some of the red clay color.

Tanner saw Rusty's uncertainty. "A little mud makes for stronger coffee. They say our bodies are made of clay anyhow. But if it bothers you, grow yourself a moustache like the sergeant's. Then you can strain your coffee."

Whitfield had started a fire. Rusty hung the pot on a short steel bar and looked at Tanner. "Did you ever have a serious thought in your life?"

"Sure. I've tried cryin' and I've tried laughin'. I like laughin' better."

Sergeant Whitfield looked reproachfully at Tanner. "I want to hear you laugh someday when the Comanches swarm down on us like a bunch of hornets."

Tanner turned to kneading dough, which had a faint reddish tinge from the river water he mixed with the flour. "You'll be way too busy to listen to me."

The meager supper of bread and salt pork and coffee left Rusty wondering how much Red River mud he had ingested and whether it might leave any lasting damage to his digestive system. He had been too hungry to notice if it had any distinctive flavor.

Sergeant Whitfield beckoned him a little distance away from the rest of the men. Whitfield seemed reluctant to broach his subject. "Ordinarily, I don't ask a man about his politics. Who he votes for is his own business. But you know the people of Texas are votin' right now as to whether or not they want to stay in the union."

"So I've been told."

"We won't get a chance to vote out here, but just the same, we'll be in the stew when the pot comes to a boil. You heard Colonel Dawkins. He's just one of a great many that's ready to breathe fire and brimstone after the vote is counted. It's goin' to be almighty important where every man stands."

"My daddy was strong for stayin' in the union. A lot of good friends are for pullin' out. If I could vote, I don't know which way I'd swing."

"I don't know if you'll be able to sit on the fence. They're apt to tear it down, and you'll be forced to take a stand."

"Then I'll stand with Texas. Not the union, not the confederacy, but Texas."

Whitfield's mouth was grim. "That suits me, but there's lots of people it won't. You may be in for hell."

Rusty thought back to the pursuit of the Comanches, to the finding of the butchered woman. He thought back to the murder of Daddy Mike. He said, "I've already had a taste of hell."

Good news travels afoot. Bad news rides a fast horse. The election results were quick to reach the frontier, and they held no surprises. By a strong majority, Texas voters had supported secession. The report brought cheers in Fort Belknap but found a mixed reception in the ranger camp. Though a rumor had spread quickly among the men, Captain Burmeister called them into formation to make the announcement official.

His face was solemn, his voice so subdued that Rusty could barely hear it. "Men, the news is come. The vote was as we have thought, for secession. Very soon the Texas legislature will meet. No longer will we stand under the flag of the United States."

The men waited in silence, contemplating their individual futures, until Tanner asked, "If we ain't Americans anymore, what are we?"

Burmeister stared at the ground. Rusty thought he saw tears in the captain's eyes. "That, you must each decide. Almost thirty years now, I have been an American. An American I will remain."

He turned and walked back to his tent without dismissing the formation. Sergeant Whitfield gravely watched him go. "All right," he said finally, "dismissed."

The following morning Burmeister called the company into formation and turned the command over to Whitfield. "Until they send someone, you will be in charge. Perhaps they will send no one. Then the company is yours if you want it."

Uncertainty creased Whitfield's face. His heavy moustache seemed to droop. "The whole country's fixin' to turn upside down. They may not want any rangers at all. Where'll you go, Dutch?"

"Across the river. I will offer myself to the federal army. If they do not want me . . . perhaps to Colorado. Texas under a different flag cannot be my home."

"It won't be the same without you."

"With or without me, it will not be the same again." Burmeister shook Whitfield's hand, then turned to the men who stood in loose formation. "May God be with us all."

Rusty felt a catch in his throat. He had not been here long enough to know the captain beyond a modest surface acquaintance, yet in a strange way he felt he had known him always. He lent his voice to those of the men, who all shouted their individual good-byes.

As Burmeister rode away, leading a pack mule, Rusty heard a man behind him say, "The captain was a foreigner when he came here, and he was still a foreigner when he left. He never was a real Texan."

Angrily Whitfield turned on him. "He's a hell of a good man, and as good a Texan as you'll ever see. I'll not have you or anybody else speak ill of him."

The man's voice indicated no backing down. "What about you, Whitfield? You for the union or the Confederacy?"

Whitfield looked at Rusty before he answered. "I stand with Texas."

CHAPTER
TEN

RED RIVER, FALL 1862

Buffalo Caller had left his horse and the rest of his raiding party in the cover of timber while he walked to the edge of the muddy river for a careful look at the other side. To his right, the sun had descended almost to the horizon and was reflected in brilliant colors against a few flat clouds barren of rain. It had been a dry summer and fall. The horses had not fattened as he would have liked for the journey, but a full moon was near. If the enterprise was to be undertaken at all, it must be done now. Shorter days promised that winter's bitter breath would soon blow across the land. No Comanche liked to travel when snow lay heavy on the ground and ice crusted the edges of every stream. That was a time to hover near the lodge center's fire and recount the glory deeds of olden days.

Buffalo Caller paused at the edge of the brush that lined the upper bank. His gaze searched the far side. He had no reason to fear the bluecoat soldiers, for most had gone away to fight a white man's war somewhere to the east. He knew that on the Texas side of the river, the bluecoats were regarded as an enemy just as the Comanches themselves were.

He did not understand why white men had gone to war against one another, but the reasons were of no importance. What mattered was that the *teibos* were distracted by their own fight. Many white men had left the Texas settlements to join the war, leaving the countryside thinly defended. It had become easier for raiding parties to reenter their old hunting grounds and escape with whatever spoils they were able to garner along the way. Many settler families had abandoned homes on the leading edge of the frontier, retreating eastward to the relative safety of the older settlements. Others had gathered into makeshift forts for mutual protection, venturing out only in numbers sufficient for a meaningful defense.

Buffalo Caller hoped the white men's war would go on forever. Perhaps The People might regain the lost portions of Comanchéria. It was theirs by the sacred right of conquest. They had won it the honorable way, in war, wresting it from the hated Apaches and other claimants. They had not stolen it piecemeal like the white man, but boldly and swiftly at a high cost in blood. They had held it with lance, arrow, and club until the Americans had come swarming in, numerous as the ants and greedy as the fat hogs they brought with them.

He watched until the sun disappeared beyond the source of the broad, shallow river, for they would wait until darkness before crossing. Not once did he see any sign of white men. Lacking the bluecoat soldiers anymore, the Texans had only scattered roving groups belonging to a warrior society known as rangers. They could be ferocious when encountered, but with help from benevolent guardian spirits a raiding party could usually go around them. Buffalo Caller had always been careful to observe the requirements of his spirits and avoid their displeasure. Rarely had his medicine proven weak.

When darkness had swallowed the shadows and before the moon rose to magnify its brilliance in the water, he decided it was time to cross over. He felt no need to voice orders, for The People's way was fully democratic. It was each warrior's right either to follow the leader or to head off in his own direction. Buffalo Caller had never lacked for warriors eager to accompany him, however. Seldom did one of his raids fail to reward them with horses, and more often than not, their victories yielded a few scalps as well. It was always good to make the white men bleed for their perfidy.

He grasped his pony's mane and pulled himself up onto its back. Of late he had become aware that his knees no longer had the spring he remembered from his youth. Exertion that never used to bother him would set his heart to pounding. But though the body had slowed and gray was invading his once-black hair, the mind had gained in wisdom. Among the

People, age was accorded respect. Lessons taught by experience offset the weight of years. He paused at the riverbank to take a final look, then put the pony into the water. He did not have to look back to know that his warriors followed. He could hear their horses splashing.

They were good men—young, of course, except for his friend Broken Leg, who was perhaps becoming too old for the kind of fast travel that would be expected of him the next few days and nights. Buffalo Caller had been hesitant about allowing him to come along, but Broken Leg had pointed out that they were the same age, born the same winter in a tribal encampment sheltered by high walls of the caprock. Buffalo Caller had reluctantly accepted him, though he feared his friend might handicap the party in an emergency. He hoped some young warrior would not die because of the old one.

Especially his own son Jackrabbit, still unseasoned but eager to learn. Whippoorwill had finally presented him with a son after he had given up on his wives having anything but daughters. This was to be Jackrabbit's first major raid.

They traveled rapidly once they had put the river behind them. At one point they saw a distant campfire, and some of the young men wanted to investigate. Buffalo Caller dissuaded them. The fire might belong to a few hunters, and a hunter camp was unlikely to yield as many horses as could be expected deeper in the white men's country. Or it might belong to the Texan warrior society, in which case an attack would only stir up an unnecessary fight and gain few, if any, horses. The rangers seldom took with them more than one mount per man, and they did not easily give them up.

He knew the way well, for he had hunted buffalo all over this region south of the Clay-Colored River in the time before the white men had come to dominance. He took precautions to travel as much as possible on hard ground where tracks would not be obvious, though there was no way to avoid them altogether. When the riders came to a narrow stream that flowed in the general direction he wanted to travel, he had them put their horses into it and avoid the muddy banks, which would preserve sign of their passage. They rode until sunrise, then pulled out onto a gravel bed and took shelter in a heavy stand of scrub oak.

Buffalo Caller was well aware of the minutemen patrols that watched for raiding parties' tracks. He wished for rain that would wash away all sign, but for a long time now, the skies had yielded no moisture. The winds were dry. Given time enough, wind could destroy tracks, too. If he could not have rain, then he hoped the spirits would give him wind. It might blow dust into the eyes of the rangers so they would not see what lay at their horses' feet.

He looked critically at Broken Leg, asking how his friend was enduring the ride though he knew Broken Leg would not admit it if he were dying of pain. "Ask the young men how *they* are doing," Broken Leg replied. "I have been on many long rides before."

Too many, Buffalo Caller thought. "If you become too tired, turn back. There is no need for you to hurt yourself."

He gave men and horses a few hours to rest, then mounted and reentered the stream that would swallow their tracks. He and the others were stripped for war, traveling light so they could move swiftly when the time came. They counted on their ability to endure hunger and live off the land. They could feast when they returned home with the prizes of war.

Buffalo Caller rode far out in the lead, where he could detect any hazards before the others were exposed. He knew the risk of traveling by day, but the party could not spare the time to move only at night. They needed the visibility of a full moon for the horse-stealing phase of the trip, and it would be gone if they tarried too long on the way.

They held up once and dismounted to make themselves less conspicuous when Buffalo Caller spotted two wagons moving in a northerly direction, directly in their path. The young warriors coveted the horses that pulled the wagons, but he pointed out again that larger rewards awaited them if they would be patient and not reveal their presence too early. Once they struck, the countryside would be alerted and their only recourse would be a fast retreat with whatever booty they had managed to take.

Their third night brought them to a valley where Buffalo Caller remembered that white farmers had plowed up much of the grass to grow corn and cotton and feed for their many horses. "This is the place," he said. "We will go to the end, then come back up the valley and gather all the horses and mules we can find."

Broken Leg had lagged much of the day, catching up only at nightfall when the others slowed their pace. He slumped on his horse, plainly tired but admitting nothing. "I remember this valley. Here we killed many buffalo."

"A long time ago," Buffalo Caller said. "Now there are no buffalo, only spotted cattle." Perhaps if the white men's war continued long enough, the *teibos* would kill off one another and the buffalo would return. He had eaten flesh of cattle but found it not so strong or so rich with flavor as that of the buffalo. To his taste, even mule meat was better.

He looked up. The moon was in its brightest phase. They would need all of its light to see by as they swept the farms clean of their riding and draft stock.

Past the last farm, where the valley flattened out into a long and gentle downward slope toward a distant river, he halted and reined his pony around. "Let us gather horses." The warriors spread out in an irregular line and started back in the direction they had come. In a short time they were pushing ahead of them more horses and mules than he could count on his fingers four times over, and much of the valley still lay ahead.

This, he thought, was going to be one of the greatest raids of his life. He put aside the pain which had invaded his joints. Exhilaration overwhelmed any feeling of fatigue. He looked for his son and was pleased to see Jackrabbit riding ahead of the other young men. His gaze sought out Broken Leg, who appeared as invigorated as Buffalo Caller felt. Perhaps it was right after all that he had brought his friend.

They came to a farm where half a dozen horses and mules stood inside a closed pen. When one of the young men tried to open the gate, a rifle blasted, and for a second or two the burning of gunpowder lighted an open area between two sections of a cabin. Yelping like coyotes, two of the young men rushed the rifleman and struck him down before he had time to reload. They burst through a door. Buffalo Caller heard a woman scream in fear, then cry out again in agony. The cry was cut short.

Buffalo Caller rushed to the cabin and pushed through the door in time to see Jackrabbit dragging live coals out of a fireplace and spreading them across the rough wood floor. Buffalo Caller quickly raked the coals back onto the hearth. "White men farther up the valley might see the fire. They would know we are coming."

"I did not consider such a thing, Father," the young warrior said ruefully.

"You must learn to think, or you will not live to be an elder."

On the dog run, the other warrior was taking the fallen rifleman's scalp. He held it up for Buffalo Caller to see, along with the longer hair of the woman.

"She was with child," the warrior said. "So we have killed three."

Buffalo Caller was more interested in the fact that the echo of the rifle shot might have carried a long way up the valley. "You will have time later to show off your scalps. We are losing too much of the night."

Looking back, he almost wished he had let his son burn the cabin. He would like to burn all the cabins and leave no trace that white men had ever come. They were, to him, a curse upon a land once pure and fruitful, now despoiled by plows and cattle and hogs.

By daylight the warriors passed over a hill that marked the upper end of the valley. In front of them, strung out over a considerable distance, trotted a large band of horses and mules. Buffalo Caller tried to count them by fours but gave up after two attempts brought him two different answers. They were enough. Now the challenge would be to get them out of the country without being stopped by the white men's warriors.

He asked Broken Leg, "Are you all right?"

Broken Leg beamed with delight. "I am a young man again."

"Good, for we have two long days' ride ahead of us before we reach the river. Even the young men will be feeling old."

He was aware of pursuit, though it was tentative and did not press hard. He saw two horsemen trailing a comfortable distance behind. It would be folly for two men to attack the raiders, but they could hang back and keep the horse herd in sight, hoping for reinforcement somewhere ahead. He tried to ignore them, but after half a day they irritated him like an itch he could not scratch away.

He picked two of the young men he judged to be the most seasoned and told Broken Leg, "Keep the horses moving. We will catch up when we have swatted the gnats behind us."

He led his two warriors out into a thicket and motioned for them to dismount. They squatted on their moccasined heels to wait. Patience was drilled into potential hunters and warriors from the time they were boys. It was as much a part of their training as learning accuracy with the bow, for often they were forced to lie in wait for hours until game approached close enough to kill.

The two white riders passed the thicket. They were too intent upon the heavily marked trail to see the three men, even had the warriors not been so well hidden. One of the young men arose, and Buffalo Caller motioned for him to crouch again. "We will wait until they are well past, then we will come up behind them."

The surprise was swift and complete. The white men were unaware of danger until the three Comanches were within easy arrow range. By then it was too late even to bring a rifle into play. They fell, and the two younger men had a scalp apiece to show off when they returned in triumph to the larger group.

Buffalo Caller gave the two bodies but a quick glance, for the white men were of little interest to him once they were dead. The young warriors tied the fresh scalps to their horses' manes and took the reins of the two mounts they had just acquired. They led them into a trot, then into a lope as Buffalo Caller set the pace. They were a long while in catching up to the rest. He slipped the bridles from the horses' heads so the animals would not trip on the reins. He tied the bridles to the saddles, which he left in place. He did not like white-man saddles himself, but probably he could trade them to someone who did.

They were within half a day of the river when a group of horsemen appeared without warning over a low hill and fanned out in challenge. Buffalo Caller had begun to hope he and his party would escape unscathed, but he saw that it was not to be. He stopped and counted the horsemen, who were as yet far beyond arrow range. They might simply be aroused citizens, who sometimes fought bravely but usually not well. On the other hand they might be rangers, better organized and savage in a fight, tenacious as hungry wolves.

Several of the young warriors gathered around him, eager for combat. Buffalo Caller counted the white men a second time and knew they fell well short of the Comanches in number. He pointed to several of the warriors, including his son, and told them to put the horse herd into a run. "The rest of us will stay behind and hold back the Texans."

The young men protested. They all wanted to participate in the battle. Buffalo Caller reasoned, "We have traveled far and endured much for these horses. Do you want to lose them now?"

The young men quarreled over who should stay with the horses and who should seek the glory of killing more Texans. Buffalo Caller saw that his arguments were useless. There would always be more horses. One sought battle honors wherever the opportunity presented itself. He took a long look at the herd, which was becoming more strung out and more scattered as it pulled away from the quarreling warriors.

He could understand the young men's wish for glory. He had known it himself when he was their age. Now he had gained glory enough over the years, and he had a high appreciation for the value of horses.

Reluctantly he said, "Let us make a quick fight of it, then, so we do not lose everything we came for."

The young men yelped and shouted and charged wildly toward the Texans. Buffalo Caller thought he saw confusion in the ranks of the whites. He hoped they would scatter and run. If they did, the fight would degenerate into a race, and death would come swiftly for those whites who rode slow horses.

To his dismay, the white men stepped down from their saddles, dropped to their knees, and aimed their rifles at the warriors who bore down upon them. A quick rattle of gunfire left two horses riderless and a third horse down. Buffalo Caller saw Jackrabbit still astride and was thankful he was not one of the fallen.

He hoped the warriors could overwhelm the Texans while they paused to reload their rifles, but it quickly became evident that some had held their fire to avoid such a calamity. They spaced their shots so their line would not have all its rifles empty at one time. Buffalo Caller felt sure then that these were rangers.

The Comanche charge broke up, the warriors reeling back uncertainly. The rangers immediately remounted their horses and made a charge of their own.

A ranger spurred straight toward him, rifle in his hands. Buffalo Caller strung an arrow in his bow. The ranger's hat blew off, and Buffalo Caller was startled to see that his hair was red. Old dreams, long pushed aside but never forgotten, flashed in his mind like a flare of gunpowder. Even as he released the string and let the arrow fly he knew it would miss.

The ranger fired the rifle, but the motion of his horse spoiled his aim. Buffalo Caller heard and felt the impact of the bullet striking his pony in the chest. Before he could jump free, he was slammed against the ground. The crushing weight of the pony rolled over him, pressing him hard into the dirt. He tried to crawl free, but his leg was pinned.

He grasped desperately for the bow that had fallen in front of him. He clawed at the ground but could not quite reach the bow. He strained to pull himself forward. His heart pounded hard as he tried again to reach the bow and failed though he stretched every muscle in the effort. He felt that his medicine had soured. Helpless, he steeled himself to receive the bullet that would kill him.

The ranger's black horse was wild-eyed, nostrils flaring in excitement. In the saddle, the ranger seemed to tower above Buffalo Caller like the high walls of The People's winter encampment. Numb, suddenly cold, Buffalo Caller saw that the man was young, like the warriors in the raiding party. The black horse danced nervously, threatening to run away. The ranger drew a pistol from its holster and tried to bring the horse under control.

Buffalo Caller spoke to his spirits, asking them to be ready to receive him, for the ranger was too close. He could not miss.

He heard a shout. Broken Leg galloped up, bow in his hand, an arrow fitted against the string. The ranger whirled and hastily fired his pistol. Broken Leg's arrow drove into the young Texan's leg. With a cry of pain, the ranger dropped his rifle and bent over in the saddle, losing his hold on the reins. His horse broke into a run, away from the fight.

Instantly Broken Leg was on the ground. He tugged at the pony's rein but received no response. The horse was dead. He pushed against the body until Buffalo Caller was able to pull his leg free.

"Quickly!" Broken Leg said. "Up behind me before more Texans come."

Buffalo Caller hopped, for the leg felt numb and threatened to crumple beneath him. He retrieved his bow and shield from the ground as well as the rifle the ranger had dropped. Broken Leg jumped onto his horse's back, then leaned down, arm extended, helping Buffalo Caller up behind him. Looking back over his shoulder, Buffalo Caller could see that the rangers and the warriors had become scattered over a broad area. Firing was sporadic. The fight was winding down to a draw, neither side a clear winner.

It was just as well. The stolen horses were badly scattered too, but as the warriors regrouped they could probably recover a substantial number. The young men had had the taste of battle they had wanted, so they would be content despite losing some of their horses.

Buffalo Caller was relieved to see no sign of pursuit. Several warriors had broken away from the engagement and were coming up behind. Jackrabbit was among them. The rest would probably be on their way shortly as they extricated themselves.

He asked Broken Leg, "The ranger you wounded . . . did you see his hair?"

"For a moment. I thought I would have his scalp, but I only wounded him. It was more important that I rescue you."

"His hair was red."

"That I saw. I thought it was colored with clay."

"I have had bad dreams about a red-hair. He spoiled my medicine. He would have killed me had you not come."

"Perhaps it was your medicine that brought me."

Buffalo Caller had not considered it in that light. "Perhaps. I am glad you persuaded me to let you come, old friend. But for you, I would be with my grandfathers."

Broken Leg agreed. He would make much of it when they returned to the main camp and the boasting began. Buffalo Caller could not begrudge him the glory.

Broken Leg said, "My medicine was good today."

Buffalo Caller shuddered, the dreams heavy on his mind. "If ever I see a red-hair again, I hope you will be with me. His medicine is stronger than mine."

Rusty Shannon almost despaired of stopping the runaway horse. The heavy firing had frightened Alamo into a blind panic. Each stride brought excruciating pain, seeming to drive the arrow deeper into Rusty's leg. It had glanced off the bone. Blood flowed freely, warm and gummy to his fingers as he awkwardly holstered the pistol and grasped the shaft of the arrow. He struggled in vain, trying to pull it out.

The reins trailed on the ground, dropped along with the rifle when the arrow had struck. Reins could be a hazard. Looped, they could snag on a tree branch while a horse ran. If split, like these, a running horse could step on them, jerk his head down, and take a hard fall.

Through his pain, Rusty recognized that danger. He leaned forward, trying to grab a rein. Light-headed, he could not reach it without tumbling from the saddle. Yet he knew that at any moment Alamo could turn a somersault. Rusty stood a strong chance of being crushed beneath him.

He was aware of another horse closing from the left. He assumed the rider was a Comanche, come to finish him off. He felt helpless to defend himself, though he drew the pistol again. Blood on his hand made it feel sticky as syrup.

Tanner's shout relieved his fear. "Hold on, redhead. I'm comin'." Tanner pushed his horse up against Alamo and reached down, his bony hand grasping the reins. He dallied them around his saddle horn. "Got you." He slowly brought both horses to a stop. Alamo breathed hard, eyes rolling in the aftermath of fright. "Damn it, Rusty, you're bleedin' like a stuck shoat."

Blood had spread down Rusty's leg to the stirrup and the toe of his boot.

Tanner said, "I'll get you back to the rest of the bunch. Wouldn't want some stray Indians to catch us out here by ourselves and pick us off. Say, I'll bet that arrow hurts like hell."

Rusty's head seemed to spin. He was in some danger of falling from the saddle. He attempted three times before he managed to shove his pistol back into the holster. It tried to stick to his hand. "Damn right it hurts."

"We'll get it out soon's we can. Me and Captain Whitfield, we're pretty good at pocketknife surgery."

Pocketknife! The thought did not encourage confidence. But anything to lessen the pain.

Tanner said, "I seen you miss that Indian. You were so close, I don't understand how you kept from hittin' him."

"Alamo was faunchin' around too much." Rusty did not know how anyone could make a good shot from the back of a running horse.

"Maybe you've taken a case of buck fever. You ever shoot at anybody before?"

"Been tempted, but I ain't done it." Rusty hoped the interrogation would stop. He hurt too much to think straight.

"Captain'll want to know. Just tell him about the horse. You don't have to say nothin' about buck fever."

Rusty did not want to feel resentful of his friend, but he could not help it. "Did *you* kill any Indians?"

"Brought down a horse. Set an Indian afoot and it's almost as good as killin' him. Except he'll be back to shoot at you another day. But if it wasn't him it'd be another one. The world don't seem to run short of Indians."

It did not seem to run short of unnecessary conversation, either. Rusty tried to close his mind to Tanner's rambling. He realized Tanner was talking in an effort to bring his own excitement under control. "Yes, sir," Tanner said, "we scattered us some Comanches."

"But they're gettin' away. Looks like they've still got most of their horses." Rusty could see that much through eyes pinched with pain.

"Well, me and you can't be held responsible. We're just followin' orders. I don't hardly know who we're workin' for anyway, the state of Texas or the Confederate States of America. Ain't neither one paid us lately."

Since Texas had joined the Confederacy, its affairs had descended into confusion and controversy. State officials in Austin quarreled with national officials in Richmond over the financial responsibility for protecting the frontier. Most recently they wrangled over a new Confederate conscription law that threatened to strip the outlying settlements of the already deficient manpower needed for their defense. Texas officials resisted the law and as yet were refusing to enforce it in the western counties. Confederate authorities in Richmond saw Indians as a distant problem easily ignored while Yankee soldiers were pounding rifle butts against their doors.

Tanner led Alamo while Rusty gripped his saddle with both hands. Shock was setting in. He felt himself in danger of slipping to the ground. Tanner had to catch him and ease him back into the saddle. The ranger never stopped talking.

"Hang on, pardner. I see some of the boys gatherin' just ahead yonder. If you fall now you're apt to break that arrow off, and we won't have enough left to grab ahold of."

Rusty tried to focus on the rangers ahead, but it was like looking at them through a fog. He did not recognize the one who rode out to meet him until the man spoke and he knew the gruff voice to be Captain Whitfield's. The former sergeant had been promoted after August Burmeister's departure.

"Bring him over here under the tree, Tanner. We've got a couple others to patch up, but at least we didn't get anybody killed."

Rusty felt himself being lifted from the saddle. Though the men tried to be gentle, there was no way to move him without causing the arrow to cut deeper into the flesh. They laid him on a blanket. With the point of a knife, Whitfield ripped a long slit in the leg of Rusty's trousers. His hands carefully explored around the shaft. "It's gone most of the way through. I can feel the point stickin' out just a little on the underside. If we try to pull back on it, the head is liable to break loose and stay in there. Best thing is to shove it on through."

Tanner's voice was uncertain. "That's liable to hurt a right smart."

"But it'll be over with before he can holler. You-all hold on to him."

Rusty cried out in agony as Whitfield's strong hands pushed the shaft, and the arrow cut the rest of the way through the leg. He must have fainted for a moment, because when he became conscious again, he saw Tanner fingering the bloodied arrowhead.

Whitfield said, "Now to pull out the shaft. Hold him again."

Rusty felt a sharp pain, then the ground dropped away from under him. He was conscious of something being poured into the wound and wondering how anything wet could burn with such ferocity. Then there was a flash of fire, and consciousness left him altogether.

He had no sense of time, but he was aware that the sun was going down when he managed to open his eyes. He heard Tanner's voice. He seemed to have heard it all during the time he had been unconscious, but he supposed that was hallucination. He felt a hard throbbing in his leg and a sense of severe burning.

Tanner was saying, "About time you quit lazin' around and woke up to your responsibilities. You goin' to sleep your life away?"

Rusty looked down at his leg, wrapped with cloth. "What did you-all do, set me afire?"

"We cauterized that wound. Ain't but one way, and that's with hot steel." Tanner drew a bowie knife from a sheath on his belt, opposite the pistol he carried. "Heated this 'til it glowed red. Probably took all the temper out. It won't be much account from now on."

"I'll buy you another, if we ever get paid."

Tanner shrugged. "We're liable to be old and gray by then." He reached into his pocket. "Here's you a keepsake. You may want to use it for a watch fob." He handed Rusty an arrowhead. Rusty knew it was the one that had gone through his leg.

"I don't have a watch."

"Maybe you won't be a poor man all your life."

Captain Whitfield stood over Rusty, hands on his broad hips. "I hope you shot the Indian who put that arrow in you."

"I didn't hardly even see him. I was tryin' to shoot another one, but my horse kept dodgin'."

"I don't know that we killed any of them. We bloodied them a bit and got back a part of the horses they stole. The price was a little high, though. We've got two wounded besides you. Your leg is the worst."

The leg throbbed and burned as if a fire blazed inside it. Rusty felt as if it were about to fall off. He had a bad moment as he mulled over the thought of losing it. "How bad do you reckon it is?"

Whitfield's face creased. "Bad enough. We need to get you someplace where people can take proper care of you."

Tanner suggested, "The Monahan farm is down yonder a ways. I'll bet they'd put him up."

Rusty asked, "Monahan? Is that Lon Monahan?"

Tanner nodded. "You know him?"

"Met him on my way up to Fort Belknap, is all. Can't say I know him real well."

"They're a hotbed of unionists, him and his family, but otherwise they're good folks."

Whitfield growled. "Look around you, Tanner. This company itself is a hotbed of unionists. Most who don't favor the union have already left to join the Confederate army. You're one of the few who haven't."

Rusty knew Tanner's loyalty was to the Confederacy. He remained confused about his own. He could not in good conscience support last year's secession, yet he understood Texans' frustrations with the union. "I wouldn't want to cause the Monahan family any trouble."

Whitfield said, "You wouldn't add a speck to the trouble they've already got. You might even be a help to them."

"The shape I'm in? I don't see how."

"There's been agitation against the Monahans. Wouldn't take much to stir the hotheads into somethin' real mean. Havin' a ranger stayin' there might calm the waters."

Rusty had heard ugly stories about mob violence against unionists farther east in the state. "If it came to trouble, I don't know how much help I could be. This bad leg . . ."

"You represent the authority of the state of Texas. Most people will respect that. Those that don't . . . well, you might have to shoot one or two of them." His eyes narrowed. "Speakin' of which, are you real sure you were tryin' to kill that Indian? There's some who flinch when it comes to actually pullin' the trigger."

The thought startled Rusty. He had not considered that his own reluctance might have caused him to miss. The Indian had been pinned down, helpless, an easy target.

Too easy, perhaps. That might have been the trouble.

Whitfield said, "It's no disgrace to hate havin' to kill. I've got no use for a man who kills because he likes to do it. I'll fire him out of my company quicker than a jackrabbit can jump."

Rusty considered, then said, "It was my horse. Kept faunchin' around." But now that the question had been raised, he could no longer feel completely sure.

Whitfield started to turn away but stopped. "Maybe your life didn't depend on it just then. But you'd better be sure you can do what you have to when your life *does* depend on it. Otherwise, you're dead."

CHAPTER

ELEVEN

anner rode south to the Monahan farm. Two days later he returned to the camp at Belknap with Lon Monahan, his son Billy, and a wagon. Monahan climbed down over the right-hand front wheel and tied the lines to the brake. He walked to Rusty's tent and ducked to enter through the open flap. "Looks like you got yourself a little too close to the Indians. Didn't anybody ever tell you that they bite?"

"I guess I wasn't thinkin'."

"Soon's Tanner came and told us, we sent for Preacher Webb. He's near as good at healin' the body as at healin' the soul."

"It'll be good to see him. It's good to see *you*, Mr. Monahan."

Tanner gave Rusty a critical study. "You're lookin' mighty drawed."

Tanner had looked "mighty drawed" to Rusty ever since they had first met. He had barely enough flesh to hold his bones together. "The worst day I ever had, I looked better than you do. But you look pretty good to me right now, you and that wagon."

Monahan nodded at his son. "You hurry and spread a couple of blankets in the wagon. We'll do good to make it to the farm before dark tomorrow."

Billy complied. Rusty gritted his teeth and held his breath while Tanner and Billy lifted him. Movement set the leg to hurting badly again. Tanner threw Rusty's saddle, blanket, and few possibles into the wagon bed, then tied Alamo on behind. He said, "Before you get into another Indian fight, you'd better train this horse to mind."

"It was his first time up so close. Mine, too."

"Probably won't be the last. Now, don't you linger any longer than you have to. The state ain't payin' you to idle around."

"Or for anything else." Rusty reached over the sideboard to shake Tanner's hand. "You watch out some Comanche doesn't slip up on the blind side of you and cut your hair."

Monahan and his son climbed up onto the seat. Monahan cautioned, "It'll be rough in spots, so take a grip. The Comanches never built any roads out here, and neither has the state."

Tanner stood with narrow shoulders slumped and watched the wagon pull away. Rusty felt a tug of regret at the parting. He had been with the company more than a year now, patrolling the line, watching for Indian sign, and seldom finding any. Yesterday's engagement was the closest he had come to being in a real fight where he could see the color of the enemy's eyes. But he had enjoyed the life despite its lack of comforts, despite its sometimes monotonous routine, despite the slowness of pay scanty by any standard and irregular in arrival. He had enjoyed the bond that had grown among members of the company, riding together, camping together day after day, playing cards, occasionally racing horses.

Jim and Johnny Morris had shown him how close brothers could be, though they argued about trivial matters from time to time. Rusty had grown to regard Tanner as a substitute for the brother he never had. But Tanner had family back in the East Texas blacklands and had taken leave a couple of times to visit them. He wrote and received letters at fairly regular intervals. Rusty had received no letters except an occasional brief message from Preacher Webb, nor had he anyone else to write a letter to. When other men talked of their families, he was achingly aware that he had none.

The Monahans did not make a lot of unnecessary talk on the way south to the farm. They knew the rough ground caused Rusty considerable pain, and they did not bother him with useless conversation. The elder Monahan held the reins. He was careful to seek out the most benign terrain he could find, though much of the time he had little choice. One way was as rugged as another. Rusty managed to doze for short periods when the going smoothed out, though he remained always conscious of the throbbing in his leg.

The Monahan women met the wagon in their front yard. Geneva Monahan said nothing but pressed the palm of her hand against her mouth, her stricken eyes telling Rusty what she was thinking.

Clemmie anxiously looked over the sideboard. "My land, he looks more dead than alive. I hope you-all stopped along the way now and again to let him rest."

"Couldn't afford to," Lon replied. "If dark had caught us we'd've had to camp a second night. Wanted to get him here to your tender mercies the fastest we could."

"Let's carry him into the house. Preacher Webb ain't showed up yet. Lord knows how far Papa has to ride to find him."

By that, Rusty assumed that Clemmie's father had gone to search for Webb. He realized he had not seen Geneva's older brother or heard him mentioned. He asked, "Where's James?"

Lon and Clemmie Monahan glanced at each other before Lon answered, "We ain't sure, exactly. It's best that we don't know."

Clemmie said, "The conscript officers came lookin' for him. He had to slip away in the middle of the night. Wasn't nothin' else he could do. He didn't want to go to war against the union."

The conscript law had put many young men on the run, some who had unionist leanings and some who simply did not want to be drafted into the Confederate army. By Richmond law it had become part of the ranger mission to find and bring in conscript dodgers, though Whitfield's company had exerted itself but little in that direction. Many of the rangers might have joined the fugitives had their frontier service so far not exempted them from military service.

Rusty said, "I thought you-all made up your minds to stay here no matter what."

Lon said, "The sons of bitches was fixin' to take James away. He didn't have no choice."

Clemmie fretted, "I'm afraid Billy's next. He's sixteen. Another year or so and he'll be of age."

Rusty knew that some boys as young as fifteen and sixteen were serving, though to his knowledge it was by their own choice. He felt a surge of bitterness. "I don't know who wanted that stupid war in the first place. They sure didn't ask me what I thought."

Lon stared down at a knotty fist. "In a way, I reckon they asked all of us. Texas called a vote on secession. A majority said yes."

"But they didn't ask for war."

"I'm afraid both camps was itchin' for it. I can't fault one side more than the other, but us Monahans have always stood for the union."

"In spite of it drivin' your son away?"

"He'll be back. When this war burns itself out, people'll come to their senses, most of them. As for the rest, the hell with them."

Clemmie said, "Right now we've got a different fight on our hands. Let's quit talkin' and carry Rusty into the house. We'll take off the dirty wrappin' and see what that limb looks like."

Rusty felt a small, warm hand slip into his. Looking up, he saw Geneva's worried eyes. "Don't you fret, Rusty. We'll take care of you."

He felt better already, a little.

Removal of the binding agitated the wound. Geneva had to soak the final pair of wraps because dried blood had stuck the cloth to the skin. Rusty sucked a sharp breath beneath his teeth as the binding was pulled free.

He did not look down. He did not have to, for the grim reaction of the women told him more than he wanted to know. Clemmie demanded, "What did they burn you with, a brandin' iron?"

"A knife. Said they had to cauterize the wound."

"Roasted it, more like. But maybe they saved you from gangrene."

A dark fear had lurked in the back of Rusty's mind almost from the first. He had not permitted it to rise all the way to the surface. When no one volunteered further comment, he asked the question in a shaky voice. "You reckon I'm fixin' to lose my leg?"

Clemmie managed an answer. "Not without we give it a hard fight. I'll be glad when Preacher Webb gets here."

"I doubt he can doctor it any better than you can."

"But he's got more say with the Almighty."

They lighted a lantern and hung it on the porch in case Webb should arrive in the night. It could as easily guide marauding Indians, but nobody mentioned the risk. Rusty had just dropped off into a fitful sleep when he heard a commotion on the dog run. The door swung open, and Webb entered, removing his flop-brimmed old hat and pitching it against a wall. He did not break his stride until he reached the cot where Rusty lay in the cabin's kitchen.

Clemmie's father, Vince Purdy, followed Webb. He looked small and wizened and tired.

Clemmie explained, "We cleaned the wound the best we could and put on fresh bandagin'."

Webb placed his hand on Rusty's forehead, checking for fever. He turned back the blanket and touched the bandage but withdrew his hand without untying the knot that held it. "We'll leave well enough alone 'til mornin'. Since the Lord hasn't taken you already, maybe He's not got a place fixed for you yet."

Rusty said, "If there *is* a Lord, I was lookin' Him square in the eye. The Comanche who put the arrow in my leg was tryin' to put it in my heart."

"God has saved you for other work."

"I had my front sight leveled against another Indian. You think the Lord saved him, too?"

"The Indians are His creatures, same as we are. Maybe He has other work for that one, too."

Rusty was inclined to believe that his nervous horse was the cause for both misses, but he did not feel like arguing religion with Webb at this time of night. "It's awful good to see you, Preacher."

"And you. I'm glad you've managed to stay out of trouble, at least 'til your scrap with the Indians."

Rusty understood the reference. "I don't suppose Isaac York has drunk himself to death yet?"

"No, but he's tried." Webb frowned. "You've been away more than a year. I'd hoped you'd forgotten about Isaac."

"I can't forget him. Every time I think of Daddy Mike, I see Isaac York, too. I will until he dies, or I do."

"Leave him to heaven, Rusty."

"Or to hell."

Rusty forced himself to look at the leg when Webb unwrapped it the next morning. It was swollen, the color running from red to blue, but at least he saw nothing to indicate the onset of gangrene. Crusting had begun along the edges where Tanner's knife had seared the wound. He thought it smelled a bit too, but that could have been something Clemmie had applied to it last night.

Anxiously he asked, "What do you think, Preacher?"

"There are better things to do than burn it, but I suppose there was little choice out in the field. I'm afraid the burn will leave a bigger scar than the arrow would have."

"A scar won't bother me much if I've still got a leg."

"It'll take awhile, but I think you'll heal. The main thing to worry us now is blood poisonin'. About the only thing we can do on that is to pray."

Geneva stood beside the minister, hope in her eyes where there had been dark worry last night. "We'll all do that, Preacher."

Webb looked at her as if something about her surprised him. He turned back to Rusty. "That should help as much as any medicine we can give him. I'm not sure Rusty knows how to pray for himself."

Geneva said, "I'll teach him."

Webb smiled.

Rusty spent most of his time lying on the cot the first couple of days, for the pain from the wound reached its peak, and he was too weak to want to move much. After that he became increasingly restless, wanting to be up and doing something. The Monahan family was busy from early morning until dusk, harvesting their feed crop and picking their cotton, which would have to be hauled eastward a long way for ginning. Rusty felt guilt about requiring their attention and eating their food while performing no service in return, especially after Preacher Webb left to attend to his circuit.

Once Rusty was able to sit up for long periods, he insisted that they bring him work to do: harness he could mend, tools he could sharpen. He constructed a crude but workable crutch from a forked branch of oak that Billy brought him. He shaved off the bark and padded the top so it would not rub his arm raw. Though he moved awkwardly, the crutch enabled him to get around the house and the barn. The guilt and the feeling of uselessness left him.

One day Geneva brought him a cup of coffee at the barn, where he was grinding a new edge onto a scythe. "Maybe I can get back to the company before long," he told her.

He heard regret in her voice. "Are you in such a hurry to leave us?"

"No, but I feel like it's my duty to go soon as I'm able to ride. Every day I'm gone, others have got to make up for me. The company's short-handed."

"What if you'd been killed? They'd've had to find somebody else. Let them find somebody else now."

He said, "There's another consideration besides duty." He had not put the thought into words before, though it had come to him often enough. "Long as I stay in the frontier company, the conscript officers have to leave me alone. But if I quit it, they'll be comin' after me. Then I'll have to go fight the union or I'll have to leave the country like James did. Either way, I couldn't stay here."

"They won't take you 'til that leg heals. Maybe the war'll be over by then."

"Sounds to me like it's barely got started."

Tears welled in her eyes. "First it was James. Now we've got you and Billy to worry about. It's not fair, a bunch of old men startin' a war and makin' the young men go and fight it." She leaned against him and touched his hand. He set down the coffee cup, and she turned into his arms.

It was the first time he had held her. He felt warm and happy and greatly confused. He had never held a girl this way before.

She said, "Don't be in a big hurry about gettin' well."

His crutch slid to the barn's earthen floor. He would have to turn her loose to stoop and pick it up. He let it lie.

Another day, Rusty was leaning on his crutch, brushing Alamo's mane, when Colonel Caleb Dawkins rode up accompanied by half a dozen men. Rusty blinked in momentary disbelief, for he recognized two of them. One was Dawkins's son Pete, who had wanted to kill Rusty the day he had encountered the thieves with the Tonkawa horses. Beside Pete was the point rider who had decided against it.

Dawkins was surprised to find Rusty there. "Don't you belong in the ranger camp up by Belknap?" he demanded, as if it were his right to know and approve or disapprove.

Rusty stiffened at the challenge in the voice. "I do."

"Then why are you here?"

"Recuperatin'. Had a little run-in with some Comanches, and they came out with the best of it."

"You could have chosen a better place for healing. Don't you know this place is a nest of unionists?"

"They're friends of mine. Their politics don't matter to me."

"They should. You are sworn to uphold the laws of the state of Texas. You should be more careful about the company you keep."

Rusty found a bit of unintended humor in that comment. He studied the young horse thieves, particularly Pete. "That'd be good advice for a lot of people."

Dawkins straightened his shoulders in an attitude of authority. "We are here representing the conscription committee. As a ranger, I expect you to speak the truth."

"I always do, or pretty close to it."

"The committee has declared James Monahan a fugitive. Have you seen him?"

Rusty saw no reason to lie, though he would have had there been a reason. He owed nothing to Dawkins. "I haven't seen him since I came here."

"Do you know where he has gone?"

"Someplace else, is all I know. It's none of my business where he's at."

"As a representative of the law, every lawbreaker should be your business."

Rusty looked at the young men again. Pete appeared suddenly apprehensive. The other could not meet Rusty's eyes. The more Rusty considered it, the more he was convinced that the colonel did not know about the horse stealing.

Rusty said, "I suppose if you had a lawbreaker in your midst, you'd turn him in?"

"Unless it was a Yankee law."

"I don't suppose there's any Texas law against runnin' off Indian horses?"

The puzzlement in Dawkins's eyes indicated that he was indeed ignorant about the thieves in his midst. "Are you saying one of us steals Indian horses?"

Rusty saw nothing to be gained by telling him. "I'm just usin' that as an example. Everybody's got laws they don't like and don't pay any attention to. Even you, I suspect."

"Not I, sir. The law is the law. I abide by it, and I insist that others do the same."

Lon Monahan came in from the field, riding a bareback mule with most of the harness still on him. He rode up close enough to have reached out and punched Dawkins on the nose had he intended to. He looked as if he might be considering it. "'y God, Dawkins, I've ordered you off of this place more than once. What do you want this time?"

As before, Monahan's quick anger was in marked contrast to the cold calm in Dawkins's look and manner.

"The same as before. We're looking for your son James. He has been declared a deserter."

"How can he desert somethin' he never joined in the first place?"

"He deserted his duty."

"His duty as *you* see it. He saw it different. You're not welcome here, Dawkins, you nor any of them scalawags with you. I'm tellin' you to leave."

"When we're ready." Dawkins looked across the field, where Billy was dragging a cotton sack. "How old is that boy yonder?"

Monahan's defiance began giving way to uneasiness. "He ain't barely sixteen. Too young for you to be takin' him."

"*You* say he's sixteen. I say he looks older."

"He ain't. We've got his birth date wrote down in our Bible."

"The hand of man can make even a Bible lie." Dawkins began to rein his horse around. "Let's go take a look at him, boys. I say he looks eighteen."

Monahan stepped inside the barn and immediately came out again, carrying a rifle. He aimed it at Dawkins's broad chest. "Touch my boy and I'll kill you!"

For a fleeting moment Dawkins lost his composure. Murder flared in his eyes and made Rusty wish for his own rifle. But the moment passed and Dawkins appeared calm again, at least outwardly. It was just as well, for Lon had the upper hand.

Dawkins drew himself up into a military attitude of full attention. "We are representatives of the conscription committee, duly appointed. You are interfering with the performance of our duties."

"It ain't your duty to take an underage boy against his family's will. Now I'm givin' you a chance to git, and don't be comin' back."

Dawkins lowered his deep voice. "You'll see us again."

"If so, it'll be the same way I see you now, over the barrel of this gun." Monahan's hands were steady, but as soon as Dawkins and the men with him turned away, his hands began to tremble.

The point rider lagged, looking back as if he wanted to say something, but he thought better of it and followed Dawkins.

Rusty had forgotten his pain. It came back to him in a rush, for in his concentration on Monahan and Dawkins he had let some of his weight rest on the wounded leg. He lifted it and rubbed his hand gingerly over the bandage as if that would ease the throbbing. "I thought sure as hell you were fixin' to shoot him."

"I was. The Lord stayed my hand."

"He'll be back."

"I know. And before I'll let him have Billy, I *will* shoot him, 'y God." Monahan's face was grim. "Damn that Dawkins for a hypocrite. He's out roundin' up other men's sons for the army, but he pays the government to keep his own at home."

Rusty appreciated the irony of the situation. While Dawkins lectured gravely about law and order, his own son was stealing Indian horses without the old man knowing it.

Watching Dawkins's retreat, Rusty feared for a minute that the man was going to cut back into the field and make for Billy. Dawkins paused once, as if considering it.

Monahan raised the rifle. "He's still in range, and he knows it."

Dawkins resumed his retreat. Monahan lowered the rifle, relieved. He said, "I'm goin' out and fetch Billy."

He climbed back onto the mule and cut straight across the field, making no effort to spare the unharvested cotton from trampling. Watching, Rusty saw signs of argument between Monahan and his son, though he could not hear the voices. Presently Billy followed his father out of the field, carrying the half-filled sack on his shoulder. He resumed his argument at the barn. "But everybody around here knows I'm only sixteen."

"To Dawkins you're as old as he wants you to be. It ain't you he's really after, but he'll use you to get even with me and James. So you've got to go, son. You've got to go now, because there's no tellin' when he's apt to come back for you." Monahan turned to his father-in-law, who had come up from the house to watch in silence. He carried a shotgun, ready to support his son-in-law if the incident had built to violence. "I'd appreciate it if you'd go tell Clemmie and Geneva to fix up a big sack of grub for Billy. And roll up a couple of blankets. Soon as it's dark, he'll be ridin' out."

Billy's grandfather nodded, his thin face sad. "Just like with James. I don't know what Clemmie's goin' to say."

"Ain't much she can say. It's got to be done or we'll lose the boy sure enough." Monahan turned to Rusty. "As a ranger, maybe you ought not to see none of this. It might go hard with you if the authorities decide you could've stopped it and didn't."

Rusty shrugged. "I'm all crippled up, and my pistol is in my saddlebag where I can't get ahold of it. I couldn't stop it if I wanted to."

Monahan grunted. "You'd better tell them you wanted to, though. Tell them I held a gun on you, if it helps any." He swung the muzzle of the rifle around to point at Rusty a moment, then turned it away. "Now it won't be a lie." Monahan climbed back onto the mule. "I'll go out and see what horses I can find. Billy's got to have a good one."

"Give him Alamo if you want to. He's got a lot of endurance. He just doesn't like guns much."

"I don't think that'll be necessary. But I'll always be grateful that you offered."

The sun seemed reluctant to set, and dusk seemed hours about settling in. Rusty and Clemmie's father stood on the dog run, watching. The old man said, "I wouldn't put it past Dawkins to be hidin' out yonder, spyin' on this place. He's bound to suspect we'll be slippin' Billy away."

Rusty could hear Lon and Clemmie Monahan in the kitchen, giving Billy advice. Clemmie said, "I just wish Preacher Webb was here. He'd know just where James is at, so Billy could find him."

On leaving, James had promised to stay in touch with Webb. Webb could quietly pass James's letters on to the family, whose own mail was almost certainly being watched. The authorities would have no reason to suspect the minister.

When the sky had turned full dark, the family blew out the lamp in the kitchen, throwing the cabin into darkness. Lon Monahan led a saddled horse up from the barn. "You'd best be on your way before the moon rises. You can travel many a mile before sunup."

Billy reluctantly shook hands with Rusty, his father, and his grandfather, and hugged his mother and sisters. Lon Monahan gave him a small leather pouch. "This is good Yankee money we've kept hidden away."

The youngster accepted it tearfully. "Maybe with luck I can bring it all back."

Clemmie said, "Don't trust only to luck. Keep talkin' to the Lord. We'll be prayin' with you."

"I'll be back," Billy said, and he disappeared into the darkness. The women cried.

Lon Monahan laid his heavy hand on Rusty's shoulder. Tightly he said, "Remember, if anybody asks you, you tried to stop him."

"I'm a poor liar."

"Then don't say anything. We'll lie for you."

The women went back into the dark kitchen, shoulders heavily burdened with sadness. Lon Monahan remained outside, stuffing his pipe, puffing harder than normal. Clemmie's father leaned against the corner where the logs joined together at right angles. He kept his grief to himself, though his bony shoulders trembled.

Rusty, not wanting to intrude on their mourning, hobbled out into the packed yard, leaning heavily on the crutch. He looked toward the black horizon, where the moon was just beginning to rise. Soon it would be in full brilliance. The early stars were out. It struck him that moonlit nights were the favorite time for Comanche raids. But Indians were a minor concern at the moment. A much larger and all-consuming war had taken precedence.

He heard a faint commotion somewhere to the west, in the direction Billy had taken. It lasted but a moment, and afterward he was not certain he had heard anything. He made his way back to the dog run and found Lon Monahan with the pipe in one hand, the other hand behind his ear.

"Did you hear somethin', Rusty?"

"I thought I did, but I'm not sure." He had seen some of the Monahan horses wander down that way to graze just before sundown. A couple of them might have had a brief biting and kicking fight.

Clemmie's father said he had heard nothing. "Half the time anymore, I can't hear it thunder."

Monahan paced the dog run, debating with himself, then said, "I'm goin' to saddle up and ride down that way. Got to be sure nothin' has happened to Billy."

It was Monahan's custom to keep a night horse penned so someone could ride out each morning before breakfast and bring in the work stock. In a few minutes Rusty heard Lon ride by and saw his dark form at some distance in the moonlight. Lon soon faded from view.

Rusty said, "It probably wasn't anything. A couple of horses fightin', or maybe a cow and calf spooked by a coyote."

The old man said, "You're probably right," but his voice carried no conviction. "Can't help worryin' that the boy has run into trouble."

After a time Clemmie came out onto the dog run. "Where's Lon?"

Rusty considered lying to her, for he saw no reason to upset her needlessly. But her father did not give him a chance. "He saddled up and rode off. Thought he heard somethin' out yonder."

Clemmie caught a short breath. "Heard what?"

Rusty said, "We don't know. Probably nothin'. He'll likely come back pretty soon."

But he did not. Rusty guessed that an hour passed, and more. Clemmie came out onto the dog run several times. The last couple of times Geneva was with her. At last she said, "I've got a dreadful feelin' somethin's happened." She started walking westward. Geneva ran to catch her, clutching her arm.

"No, Mother. No! What if somethin' is out there? Indians, maybe."

"I've got to see about Lon and Billy." Clemmie pulled away from her daughter.

Rusty heard something too far out to see. "Mrs. Monahan, wait. I think I hear a horse. Lon's comin' back."

"Thank the Lord." She returned to the cabin, Geneva beside her, holding her arm again.

"See, Mother. It wasn't anything."

Rusty began to see the shape of a horse and rider. By the time they were within fifty yards of the cabin he could tell that this was not Lon Monahan, nor was it Billy.

The horseman reined up a few feet in front of the family. He seemed reluctant to dismount. Rusty hobbled up closer to see his face. He recognized the horse thief who had ridden point for the Indian remuda. The youth tried twice to speak before he managed to bring up anything intelligible. "Miz Monahan, I . . . I don't know how to tell you . . ."

Rusty moved up close enough that he could have reached out and pulled him down from the horse. "Tell them what?" When the young man seemed unable to speak, Rusty grabbed him by the knee and shook hard. "Damn it, man, tell them."

"It wasn't none of my doin'. I didn't want them to do it, but Colonel Dawkins, he . . . he said it had to be done. And he done it."

Rusty felt as if he had been showered with ice-cold water. He shouted, "Did what?"

"He hung Mr. Monahan. And the boy, too. Down yonder by the river."

Geneva screamed. Clemmie wilted. Her father caught her as she started to slump to the ground.

CHAPTER

TWELVE

Rusty could not speak. He leaned over Clemmie, who lay weeping, and Geneva, who knelt by her mother's side. The old man kept whispering, "God help them. God help them."

A little late for God to intervene now, Rusty thought. He turned to the young horse thief, who had not dismounted and showed no inclination to do so. "Wasn't there anybody who could've stopped it?"

"Nobody stops Colonel Dawkins. When he makes up his mind, there'd better not be anybody standin' in his way."

"So you didn't even try."

"Well, I told him we ought to wait, that we ought to take them to the sheriff. He cussed me for a coward and said if I didn't have the stomach for it, I ought to leave and not ever come back. So I left."

Aching inside, Rusty felt like weeping with the women, but he faced a duty that was more important. "We can't just leave them out there. Would you fetch in the mules and help me hitch them to the wagon?"

The young man bowed his head. "That's the least I can do."

Rusty had to be helped up onto the wagon seat, but once he was there, the pain subsided. He felt he was able to drive the mules. Clemmie's father sat beside him, his head down. Clemmie cried hysterically, fighting to climb up into the wagon. Her father talked her down, and Geneva held her as the wagon pulled away, leaving the women behind. Rusty rubbed a sleeve across his burning eyes.

The horse thief, who said his name was Smith, rode beside the wagon, pointing the way.

"If we run into Captain Dawkins, I'm leavin'. I'm lightin' a shuck anyway, soon as I help you bring these poor fellers in. I've got no use for a country that goes around hangin' people for not thinkin' the way they're supposed to. Like all them folks over at Gainesville."

Rusty had heard of mass hangings at Gainesville, farther east, where rumors of a unionist uprising had aroused hysteria. "Looks like the world's gone crazy."

"I'm thinkin' it was a short trip." After a long silence Smith said, "I'm beholden to you for not tellin' the captain I had a hand in runnin' off them Indian ponies. He might've hung *me*. He's hell for keepin' the law."

"The law? He just murdered a man and a boy."

"Law and order accordin' to his beliefs. He's got a fire-and-brimstone way of lookin' at things, but he's an honest man, after his own fashion."

"He's a mad dog. Does he know what his son Pete has been up to?

"God no. Fanatic as he is, he might hang Pete, too."

Twice Smith thought he had found the place, only to be mistaken. Rusty was about to despair of finding the Monahans before daylight. Then Smith said, "Light your lantern again. I think this is where they're at."

It was. Rusty had held to a faint hope that somehow Dawkins might have bungled the job, that one or both Monahans might still be alive. He raised the lantern and saw that the hope had been in vain.

The old man wheezed, "God help them."

Rusty wished Preacher Webb were here. He would be a comfort to the women, though it was too late for either him or God to help Lon and Billy Monahan. "I'm afraid God was lookin' somewhere else." He drew the wagon up under the bodies. "Grab ahold," he told Smith, "while I cut them down."

Smith was queasy about the task, taking a moment to summon the stomach for it. Leaning heavily on the crutch so it would not slip from under him, Rusty managed to slice through the ropes. Smith and Vince Purdy gently laid the pair onto the bed of the wagon. Rusty tried not to look at the dead faces, but he was compelled by a force he could not resist. Lon Monahan's eyes were half open. Clemmie's father closed them.

The old man broke down, kneeling beside his grandson, taking one still hand in both of his own. "He wasn't nothin' but a boy. How could any just man do such a thing as this?"

Smith said, "He's got a hard view of justice. It don't allow no extra room. He'd hang Jesus Christ if he thought he was in the wrong."

Rusty repeated something Lon had said once: "God save us from zealots." Caleb Dawkins was such a man, like Isaac York back home. Worse, perhaps, because York acted in the passion of the moment. Dawkins was cold and calculating.

Purdy spread a blanket over the bodies and blew out the lantern. His voice quavered. "I dread for Clemmie to see this. It'll nigh kill her."

Smith said, "I already been a witness to too much tonight. I'm fixin' to put as much ground under me as I can before the colonel changes his mind. Like as not he'll send after me."

Rusty asked, "Where'll you go?"

"West. There's a heap of rough country out yonder where no ranger or conscript officer is apt to come pokin' around. I'll find me a deep hole and wait for this god-awful war to finish."

"Watch out for Indians. They won't care whether you're from north or south, long as you're white. Especially if they catch you lookin' at their horses."

After Smith left, Purdy said, "First thing come daylight, I'll see if the neighbors can get word to Preacher Webb. At least we can see that Lon and Billy get a decent buryin'."

Rusty said, "I'll go tell the sheriff. He needs to know what's happened here."

Purdy's voice was bitter. "Ain't much the sheriff can do about it. The times favor the likes of Caleb Dawkins, not the Monahans."

Rusty traveled in the wagon, for his leg would not yet permit him to ride a horse. Halfway to town he met the sheriff and his deputy. The lawman's expression was dark and forbidding. "It's rumored this mornin' that somebody killed Lon Monahan."

Rusty's anger quickly rekindled. "Not just somebody. It was Caleb Dawkins. And not just Lon but his boy Billy, too. Taken out and hung like dogs."

The lawman grimaced. "This stupid war . . . how can you be sure it was the colonel? Did you see him?"

"No, but I talked to somebody who was with him." He repeated what Smith had said.

"Smith!" The sheriff spat the word. "The country's fillin' up with men named Smith, and most of them are lookin' back to see who's comin' behind them." Clearly, he would rather have been somewhere else. "I'll need to talk to this Smith myself. Is he still at the Monahan place?"

"No, he was afraid of what Dawkins might do if he stayed around. Said he was leavin' and not comin' back."

"I wish they'd all go, somewhere a long ways from here."

The sheriff stared at the horizon. "Ain't likely the colonel will admit anything. Not to where it would mean somethin' in court."

"But it was him. Smith told us so."

"You didn't see the hangin' yourself?"

"It was over with before me and Mr. Purdy got there. Everybody was gone except Smith."

"Unless somebody who was there is willin' to bear witness, you're huntin' bear with a switch. You've got no case."

"As a sheriff, you're supposed to do somethin'."

"I'm not a judge. All I can do is make an arrest."

"As a ranger, I could do that, too."

"But whoever you arrested, you'd have to turn him over to the local law, and that's me. Whatever happens after that is up to the court. You know what a court'll say."

Frustration burned like lye in Rusty's stomach. "So there's nothin' to be done?"

"Someday there'll be an accountin'. Caleb Dawkins will stand in judgment like all of us and answer to a higher power than any Confederate court."

"That's liable to be a long time in comin'."

"You're young, and young people are impatient. I'm old enough to know that you've got to have patience. Most things eventually come to pass if the Almighty means them to."

Rusty clenched a fist, wishing he could hit somebody. But he realized the lawman was being realistic, walking a narrow line and looking at reality rather than what should be. Another time, under other circumstances, he might act differently.

Preacher Webb arrived late in the day. Though devastated himself, he consoled the family the best he could.

Rusty grieved much as he had for Daddy Mike and Mother Dora. He told the minister, "I don't understand. There's good people on both sides in this war, and they all say God is with them."

"I'm afraid they haven't asked Him. They wouldn't like His answer."

The subject was painful to Webb, for he quickly changed it. "I see you've put the crutch aside for a cane. Your leg must be better."

"Still itches somethin' awful. Must mean it's healin'."

"Then I suppose you've thought about gettin' back to the ranger company." Webb sounded hopeful.

"Soon as I can get on a horse by myself. But I hate to leave here when the Monahans have got so much to worry about. Nice words seem empty. What's needed is a good killin'."

The minister's face revealed his misgivings. "Vengeance is mine, sayeth the Lord. You were sent away from home because you talked about killin'. If you talk enough about it, sooner or later you may actually do it."

"I believe I'd be justified."

"All the more reason to rejoin your company as soon as you can."

Rusty counted the neighbors who began showing up for the burying, a-horseback and in wagons and buggies. Aside from family, they numbered only a few more than a dozen. He understood the reasons. Many of the Monahans' friends had fallen away from them once the war began, for most favored the Confederacy. Fear was another factor. The hanging here, like the larger ones at Gainesville, had been a warning to any besides the Monahans who might have unionist leanings or even associate with people who did. Among the few who came, Rusty wondered if Dawkins might have sent a spy or two. He was a big man whose long, dark shadow reached even into the grave.

Webb was taken aback by Rusty's suggestion. He had not considered the possibility that an informer might carry word to Dawkins about those who attended the funeral. "The ones who've come are not easily intimidated. Some have family members in the Confederate service, so Dawkins can hardly charge them with disloyalty."

"Dawkins is a zealot. If he likes whiskey but you like beer, that makes you a traitor in his sight."

"Both sides have their share of blind fanatics. They're the kind who brought on this war."

Rusty said, "I've heard you pray for people to get well. Can't you pray for Dawkins to get sick? A heart seizure maybe, or at least a slobberin' fit."

"That would be a poor use of prayer, and certainly not pleasin' to the Lord."

"It'd please the hell out of me."

Those who came to the funeral avoided mentioning the way Lon and Billy had died. Any death was painful, but deaths from this brand of violence and hatred were especially hard to accept. When Preacher Webb stood over the grave and spoke of madness descending upon the land, Rusty saw several heads nod. He hoped Caleb Dawkins *had* planted a spy here. This would give him something to ponder.

The services over and the grave filled in, the visitors paid their respect to the Monahan women and children and began leaving. The sheriff and his deputy remained to the last, watching for possible trouble. There had been a worry, though slight, that Dawkins might send men to harass and throw fear into the mourners.

The lawman was looking for something else, too. He said, "I thought James Monahan might show up. I've got a warrant for his arrest."

Rusty was not surprised. "Word may not have gotten to him. There's no tellin' where he's at."

"I expect there's folks here who know exactly where he's at." The sheriff glanced toward Preacher Webb. "But I'm glad he didn't come. I'd be duty bound to take him in."

"I know how you feel."

"Do you? You're a ranger. If you see him, you have the same duty to arrest him."

Rusty had not allowed himself to think much about that. The notion was too disturbing.

Relieved that no problem had occurred, the sheriff said, "I didn't think even the colonel would be so eaten up with hate that he'd disrupt a funeral."

Rusty replied, "He hated enough to hang two men."

The younger Monahan girls had strayed off a little ways from the burial place, weeping together apart from the adults. They returned in a run, frightened. One shouted, "There's some men hidin' on the river."

The sheriff stiffened. "Where?"

The girl pointed. "Down yonder. One of them is on a big white horse."

Rusty limped out with the lawman. He could not see any men, but he saw the white horse the girl had mentioned, half hidden in underbrush. His first thought was that James had returned to watch from a safe distance as his father and brother were buried.

The sheriff thought otherwise. "Somebody's been spyin' on the funeral crowd. I see Colonel Dawkins's fine hand in this." He gave Rusty a quick look. "Where's your gun?"

"In the house."

"Good. Let it stay there. Been enough men died already." He jerked his head as a signal to his deputy.

Rusty hobbled along on the cane, trailing the two lawmen as rapidly as his sore leg would allow. Realizing they had been discovered, the men on the river emerged into the open. Rusty recognized Dawkins on the white horse, flanked by two riders he had seen before. One was his son Pete.

The sheriff said accusingly, "I thought you had more judgment than to come here, Colonel."

"I came only to observe. I did not intend to be seen."

"Then you ought to've rode a black horse. You've got no business on this place."

"I am a citizen, free to come and go as I choose."

"So were Lon Monahan and his boy."

"Lon Monahan was a traitor, and his son was fleeing conscription."

"You are not the court. You have no authority to hang anybody."

Dawkins gravely considered his answer. "Can you prove I hanged anyone?" When the sheriff did not reply, Dawkins added, "I thought not."

Rusty broke in, "One of your men told us you did it."

Dawkins eyed Rusty with contempt. "As I recall, you are supposed to be a peace officer. If you had been doing your duty, all this need not have happened."

The sheriff told Rusty, "I think you had better step back and let me attend to this."

"Attend to it, then. Arrest him for murder."

The lawman had already explained why that would do no good. He did not repeat himself.

Dawkins challenged Rusty. "You said one of my men told you. Who was he?"

"He said his name was Smith."

"Every scalawag and rascal in the country claims his name is Smith. I have no Smith in my employ."

Clemmie and Preacher Webb came down from the family burying ground, Clemmie's father and Geneva close behind. Rusty could see the two smaller girls huddled together near the new graves. Clemmie spoke in a voice trembling with anger. "Caleb Dawkins, if I'd seen it was you I'd've brought a gun, and that would've been the end of you."

Dawkins pretended he had not heard. He did not look at her.

Sternly the sheriff said, "Colonel, it'll be better for everybody if you turn around and leave here, now."

"That I intend to do. I do not wish to fight with women and children." He looked at Clemmie's father. "Or old men, so long as they sit in their rocking chairs and do not make trouble. But I suggest that it would benefit the community as well as themselves if the Monahan family would load their wagons and depart this country."

Clemmie Monahan moved forward in a cold fury. "This is our home, Caleb Dawkins. We built it from nothin', me and Lon and Papa and the kids. Before we leave it, we'll see you in hell."

Geneva stepped up beside her mother, silently adding emphasis to what Clemmie had said.

Old Vince Purdy joined her on the right. He said, "There ain't a rockin' chair on this place, Caleb, but there's guns. If you come into range after this, we'll shoot you on sight and by God leave you for the hogs."

Rusty felt the hair bristle on his neck. By the tone of the old man's voice, he meant every word.

Dawkins's face masked any feeling he might have had. "Remember what they said, Sheriff. These are dangerous people."

The sheriff said, "You'll do well to remember it yourself."

Dawkins retreated into the dusk. He did not deign to look back, but the two men with him kept turning in the saddle, afraid.

The old man eased up to the sheriff's side. He reached out stealthily, then grabbed the pistol from the lawman's holster. Before anyone could react, he pointed it at Dawkins's back.

The hammer fell on an empty chamber. The sheriff grunted as he wrested the pistol from Purdy's knotty hand. His angry voice crackled. "That was a fool thing to do."

The old man began to weep. "He killed my grandson."

Clemmie put her arms around her father. The sheriff looked at the pair, anger subsiding, sympathy taking its place. "Dawkins didn't see you do that, and I'll try to forget it myself. But don't ever pull such a stunt again. It could get you killed."

Purdy's voice was barely audible. "It'd be worth it if I could take Dawkins with me."

Clemmie Monahan said, "Thank you, Sheriff. We appreciate you standin' up for us."

"I'm just tryin' to stay in the middle ground."

Preacher Webb said, "That can be the most dangerous place of all. People shoot at you from both sides."

Clemmie had talked little all day, trying to keep her emotions under tight control. Now she turned to Rusty. "You're a ranger. Can't you do somethin'?"

Geneva protested, "Mother, Rusty's crippled up . . . can't even ride yet."

Reluctantly Rusty said, "Your mother's right. Somethin' has got to be done. Trouble is, I don't know what I can do."

In his time with the rangers he had never acted alone. He had always ridden with others and followed the orders of superiors. He wished for that guidance now. "If I arrested Dawkins, I'd have to turn him over to the local authorities. No local court'll convict him, not with times bein' like they are."

The sheriff nodded agreement. "That's the sad facts, Mrs. Monahan. The court would say that all he did was kill a unionist and a young man runnin' away from conscription. Dawkins may be called on to pay at the Pearly Gates, but not in Confederate Texas."

Rusty looked to Webb for advice. The minister had no answers. He supposed there *were* no answers.

The sheriff nodded at his deputy. "We're done here. Let's be goin'."

Webb said, "I'm glad you stood up to Dawkins, Sheriff, but you've probably made an enemy of him."

"He's not liable to forget you either. Even though you're a man of the cloth, he'll figure you've taken sides."

"My side was chosen for me when I saw Lon and Billy in their coffins."

The sheriff faced Clemmie. "After all this, are you sure you want to stay here?"

"More than ever. What's Dawkins goin' to do, hang women and children and an old man?"

"Since he's gotten away with this, I'm afraid he'll think he can get away with anything. Maybe not kill you, but he could shoot your livestock, burn you out . . ."

"He'd better not try. I'd kill him myself."

Geneva put her arm around her mother's shoulder. "This is our home. Caleb Dawkins be damned."

The sheriff regarded them glumly. "I wish I'd stayed in Harris County." He got on his horse and rode off into the dusk, his deputy spurring to catch up.

Preacher Webb did not leave immediately. Rusty assumed he wanted to help the family endure its grief and begin the healing process. Webb periodically stopped whatever he was doing and looked off into the distance as if expecting something. Rusty assumed he was watching for Caleb Dawkins to return.

"Preacher, you don't need to worry. If he comes lookin' for trouble, I'll see that he gets it."

"That's one thing I *am* worried about." Webb looked down at Rusty's leg. "You're bendin' it a lot better. I believe you'll be able to ride soon."

"You're tryin' to get me away from here and back to my company, aren't you?"

"Just as quick as I can."

"All right, we'll see. Would you please catch and saddle Alamo for me?"

The horse had not been ridden since the day of the Indian fight. He had been enjoying his freedom from work, and he made a little game of eluding Webb until the minister hemmed him in a corral corner. "Now," Webb said softly, "don't you tempt me into language I'll have to beg forgiveness for."

Once caught, Alamo was tractable enough. Rusty held the bridle reins while Webb put the blanket and saddle on. He breathed into the horse's nostrils to remind the animal who he was, in case Alamo was forgetful. He did not have an exaggerated opinion of equine intelligence. He had seen good horses lose all their training after ranging awhile with a reprobate, or even in solitude.

Handing Webb the cane, Rusty gingerly raised his left foot to the stirrup and swung the wounded leg over the saddle. A sharp stab of pain told him he was rushing things a little. He managed to put the right foot into the stirrup, but the leg hurt enough to make him wince. He removed the foot from the stirrup. That eased the pain but did not stop it. He felt cold sweat breaking out and shook his head.

"Maybe tomorrow." He dismounted carefully and rubbed the leg in an effort to stop the throbbing that had begun anew.

"I'm sorry. I didn't mean to push you."

In his concentration on trying to ride, Rusty had not noticed that

Geneva had walked down to the corral. She watched, troubled. While Webb unsaddled Alamo, Rusty made his way to the fence where she stood. He found himself leaning a bit heavier on the cane.

Anxiously Geneva asked, "You're liable to lame yourself for good, pushin' too fast. Are you so anxious to leave us?"

"No, but Preacher Webb wants me to go as soon as I'm able. He's afraid Colonel Dawkins may cause me trouble."

"Looks to me like you've hurt your leg all over again."

"Irritated it a little, is all. But I've got to keep tryin'. Can't laze around forever, bein' a burden."

"You're no burden. It's been a comfort havin' you here, especially after . . ." She looked away. "Preacher Webb is right, though. Dawkins will hate anybody who helps us. No tellin' what he might do."

"I doubt he'd take action against a ranger. He'd bring the state of Texas down on his head."

"Not if nobody could prove he'd done it, like we can't prove what he did to Pa and Billy."

The second day's effort at riding went better than the first, though it soon set the leg to throbbing again. Rusty had to dismount. He knew he could not make the long ride up to Belknap and the ranger camp on horseback, not yet. He could probably persuade someone to take him in a wagon, but he was not in a hurry about leaving. Maybe in another couple of days.

He made himself as useful as his physical limitations allowed. Preacher Webb joined the Monahan family in the field, picking cotton, cutting feed with a scythe. Rusty kept the tools sharp. Though he felt awkward and out of place, he helped around the kitchen so the women could remain longer at the outdoor chores he could not do.

Often Webb paused in his work and let his gaze search the western horizon. At first Rusty assumed he was worrying about getting back to his circuit. Then he realized the minister was watching for something. Rusty asked him once what he was looking for and received an evasive answer. He did not ask again, but he suspected he knew. Somehow the family had sent word to James.

The thought was troubling, for James's appearance would force Rusty into a painful choice.

"Preacher," he said when he had a chance to speak to Webb alone,

"I'm not askin' you to tell me anything you don't want to, but what can I do if James shows up? I'm supposed to arrest him. But the Monahan family took me in, and I don't want to be puttin' James in jail."

Webb pondered. "I didn't figure on your leg bein' so slow to heal. I hoped you'd be able to go back to Belknap sooner."

Rusty took that as affirmation. "So you do expect James to come back?"

"You would, if you were him."

"As fast as I could get here. But I'm not him, I'm me. So I'll keep Alamo in the pen tonight and start for Belknap first thing in the mornin'."

"Your leg still looks angry. Do you think you can ride that far?"

"I'll make a two-day trip of it, and rest along the way."

"I'll pray that James doesn't get here tonight."

The prayer was in vain. Rusty had not been asleep long when he awoke to the sound of voices from the cabin. After the first couple of nights on a cot in the kitchen, he had taken to sleeping in a shed to be out of the way. He laid his blankets aside and reached for his trousers.

A dark figure appeared in the doorway. "Are you awake?" The voice was Webb's. "Stay where you're at. What you don't see, you can't bear witness to."

Rusty knew. "James."

Webb's silence told him enough.

The autumn night air carried a chill. Rusty pulled the blanket around his shoulders. He had an uneasy feeling. "I ain't seen them, but I have a notion Caleb Dawkins or his bunch have been watchin' this place off and on."

"It's the dark of the moon, and James is careful."

"He'd better be gone long before daylight."

"I've already told him that."

Webb left, and Rusty drifted off into a restless half sleep. He was awakened by a quarrel in the cabin. The voices were loud in disagreement, though he could not hear the words. Later he heard a horse moving. He made it a point not to look, but he assumed the horse was James's. He felt relieved that James was leaving and Rusty could truthfully say, in the event he was asked, that he had not seen him. Soon, however, he realized the horse was traveling eastward, not to the west, where James should be going. The thought disturbed him. He threw the blankets aside and reached for his clothes.

As he pulled his boots on, an agitated Preacher Webb appeared in the doorway. "I should have known it would happen," he said.

"What's happened?"

"James has gone to get Caleb Dawkins."

"Dawkins has it comin' to him."

"Violence begets more violence, 'til there's no stoppin' place. I preached that to you when you wanted to kill Isaac York."

"Sometimes I still wish I'd done it. Where does Clemmie stand?"

"She didn't try to talk him out of it. She'd like to spit on Dawkins in his coffin."

"Can't say I'd blame her any."

"But James won't just be a fugitive from conscription. He'll be runnin' from a murder. Sooner or later somebody will kill *him*. Vince and Geneva did their best, and so did I, but James wouldn't listen to us."

Rusty felt an itching along his backside, an urge to be moving. "I should've seen James after all. Worst come to worst, I could've arrested him."

"He wouldn't have let you. You'd have had to shoot him. There wouldn't have been much point."

Rusty looked around the dark shed for his hat. "Maybe I can still find some way to stop him. Would you help me saddle my horse?"

"What'll you do?"

"Try to get to Dawkins before James does."

"But you wouldn't know where to find him."

Vince Purdy shuffled into the shed, shoulders slack, his voice grave. "I know where he'll be at. I'll show you the way."

Any doubts Rusty had about taking the old man along were quickly shunted aside by the fact that he couldn't find the Dawkins place by himself, certainly not in time to help. He picked up his cane, then pitched it atop the cot. If he could ride a horse he should not need a cane. It might just be in his way.

Though only Alamo was in the pen, several other horses stood around outside the gate, waiting for their morning feed. Purdy caught one while Rusty struggled to lift his saddle to Alamo's back. The weight bore heavily on his weak leg. Webb helped him finish saddling, then gave him a boost onto the horse's back. Rusty grunted involuntarily. The leg ached from the exertion.

"The Lord ride with you," Webb said.

"He'd do better to ride with James, and slow him down."

Geneva was there as Rusty rode Alamo out the gate. She reached up to squeeze his hand. Her voice seemed about to break. "James is not the only one at risk in this. You are, too. Be careful, Rusty."

On an impulse too strong to resist, he leaned down and put his arms around her. Urgently he kissed her on the lips, holding the kiss until he felt his lungs would burst.

"I'll be back," he said.

Striking a trot, then a lope, Purdy pointed the way across country rather than follow the winding wagon road.

Purdy worried, "If James gets there before us, I don't know what we can do."

Rusty confessed, "I don't know what we'll do if *we* get there first. But we'll do somethin' even if it's wrong."

Nothing would be without risk. If he arrested James, he would not only alienate the Monahan family but would put James in jeopardy of being dragged out of jail and lynched by the Dawkins faction. At the least, such a move would result in James's being taken by the conscription officers and forced into Confederate service. Rusty could simply warn Dawkins, but that would probably result in getting James waylaid and killed.

Mike Shannon had once told him to have confidence in himself, that he would know the right thing to do when the time came.

He wished Daddy Mike could whisper in his ear now.

The Dawkins farm was quiet. The thin moon shed but little light on it, and the eastern horizon showed no hint of sunup. He saw the dim glow of a lamp in the window of a small log structure, evidently a bunkhouse, and another in the larger house, where he assumed Dawkins lived. A milk-pen calf bawled for its mother. Rusty figured a hired hand was milking, for a lighted lantern was suspended from the rafter of a low shed nearby.

He said, "I wish we could get to Dawkins without stirrin' up everybody on the place." It had been on his mind that he might arrest the man and sneak him away before James arrived. It would be difficult to do without the colonel raising unholy hell and rousing everybody within hearing.

Purdy suggested, "We can circle around his house and slip in through the back door."

A lot of small houses in this part of the country had no back door, but Dawkins's was of a size that would surely have a second way in and out. Rusty hoped it would not be barred. Hardly anyone had locks on doors, though most had provisions for barring the way in event of an Indian raid. A normal lock would pose little difficulty for a determined Comanche.

Rusty's leg burned as if he were standing too close to a fire, but he had no choice except to bear it. He feared it might collapse when he dismounted and stood on it.

He saw a lamp burning in a back room he assumed was the kitchen.

Purdy said, "He's probably havin' his breakfast."

"Maybe I can bring him out without stirrin' up a fuss. You stay here and hold the horses."

"You're liable to need my help."

More likely, Rusty thought, he would get the old man hurt. The Monahan family had suffered enough already. "You just keep the horses ready. We'll put Dawkins up in your saddle, and you can ride behind me."

Rusty eased down from Alamo and tried his weight. The weak leg held, though it trembled a little. He drew his pistol and limped up the two steps to the back door. Just as he started to open it he heard a shout of surprise and an angry voice.

Damn it, James has gotten here ahead of us.

He pushed on the door and found himself in the kitchen. Caleb Dawkins sat at a table, a plate of eggs and ham in front of him, a half-eaten biscuit in his raised right hand. James Monahan stood facing him, holding a rifle. For a man looking death in the eyes, Dawkins seemed amazingly calm.

Not only does he have no heart, he has no fear, Rusty thought. He was at a loss to understand such a man.

He shouted, "James, don't do it!"

James involuntarily swung the rifle toward Rusty, his eyes widening in surprise. Dawkins took the momentary distraction as an opportunity to jump to his feet, knocking the chair backward to clatter against the floor. Instantly James moved the muzzle back to cover him. His eyes seemed afire.

"Don't you move, Colonel."

Rusty saw that Dawkins had no weapon, at least none within reach. He would not have expected trouble at his breakfast table.

For the first time Rusty noticed a gray-haired black woman standing in the doorway to the next room, a cloth draped over one arm, her eyes and mouth wide open. She wheeled and bolted out of sight. A door slammed, and he could hear her excited voice as she went running across the yard.

Rusty said, "Let's get out of here, James. It won't bring your daddy and brother back, killin' Isaac York."

"York?" James puzzled. Rusty realized he had spoken the wrong name. James said, "It won't bring them back, but at least I can make Dawkins pay."

Rusty heard shouting out in the yard. The slave woman had roused the farm help.

Dawkins said, "You hear that, Monahan? My boys'll be here in a minute."

"There's still time for what I came to do."

Anyone else would show mortal fear. Dawkins showed nothing. "If you shoot me, my boys won't let you get away. Pull that trigger and you're a dead man."

James said, "No. *You* are."

He squeezed the trigger, and Caleb Dawkins buckled.

CHAPTER

THIRTEEN

Dawkins fell forward across the table, tipping it, sliding to the floor, carrying the plate and cup and utensils with him. An agonized groan came from deep inside.

Rusty stiffened in shock. "James, for God's sake . . ."

The shouting from the yard grew louder. James grabbed Rusty's arm. "Come on, we'd better git!"

Rusty had no time to think. He acted by instinct, following James out the back door. His leg threatened to cave beneath him.

He heard a woman's piercing scream from inside the kitchen. He doubted that the slave woman had gotten back so quickly. The scream must have come from Dawkins's wife.

He had given little thought to the possibility that the colonel might have a wife and perhaps other family besides Pete.

Vince Purdy had brought the horses up to the steps. "What happened to the colonel?"

James declared, "He's halfway to hell. I tied my horse out yonder. We'd better ride fast." He sprinted away.

Rusty had trouble getting into the saddle. Purdy reached down and grabbed his arm, helping lift him. Angry voices arose in the kitchen. The door burst open, and someone fired a shot into the night. Rusty imagined he could hear the bullet whisper by his ear. He fired a quick shot in the direction of the house to discourage pursuit, then spurred Alamo into a hard run. Purdy was close behind him.

The woman's scream seemed to echo in Rusty's ears.

James cut in beside his grandfather. He said, "Let's ride north awhile. Lead them away from our place so they won't know it was a Monahan done it."

Rusty began to regain his composure, and with it came anger. "Don't you know you'll be the first one they think of?"

"If you've got any notion that I regret what I done, you're wrong. I've killed snakes and felt sorrier for it."

"You've left a woman a widow back there."

"My mother's a widow."

"What's more, you've outlawed yourself. You'll find every man's hand turned against you."

James's voice had a brutal edge Rusty had not heard in it before. "Anybody tries to stop me, they'll get what I gave Caleb Dawkins."

As the sun appeared, they reached a creek. Rusty looked back. He saw no pursuit, but he sensed that it was coming.

James reined up. "I'm goin' north a ways to lead them astray. You-all ride in the creek to cover your tracks 'til it's safe to go back to the farm." He frowned at Rusty. "Unless you feel like you've got to try and take me in. I'd advise against it."

Rusty swallowed. If he let James go, he would have to lie to the company captain, or at least fail to tell him the whole truth. That went against everything Daddy Mike had drilled into him about duty. "What you did was wrong. I think the world of your mother and your sister"—he glanced at Vince Purdy—"and your granddaddy. But I've got a duty. I'm arrestin' you for shootin' Caleb Dawkins."

James brought the rifle around, pointing it at Rusty.

Rusty said, "You ain't had time to reload. That rifle's empty." He drew his pistol. "But this isn't."

James stared in dismay at Rusty's weapon, then at his own. "You wouldn't kill me, Rusty."

"I wouldn't want to. I'd try to wound you instead, but my leg's hurtin' so bad I can't guarantee my aim."

Vince Purdy's jaw dropped. "Rusty, if I'd ever thought you'd do this . . ."

"I don't like it any better than you do, but I've got no choice. Hand me your pistol, Vince."

Hesitantly Purdy complied. Rusty removed the loads and handed it back to him. Purdy said, "James is a good man at heart. Had a good raisin'. He done what most anybody might do."

"I know. I came awful close to doin' the same thing myself once. But I was lucky. Somebody stopped me." Rusty pointed in the direction of the Monahan farm. "Like James said, you'd better ride in the creek for a ways. Whoever's comin', they'll follow me and James. Tell the womenfolks I'm sorry it had to be this way." He thought regretfully of Geneva. She would take this badly.

"Sooner or later your conscience'll commence to plaguin' you over this."

"It already does, but I've lived with a wounded leg. I can live with a guilty conscience. They're neither one fatal."

James argued, "If you turn me over to the sheriff, I'll be dead before dark. He can't stop Dawkins's people from draggin' me out and puttin' a rope around my neck."

"I'm not takin' you to the sheriff. I'm takin' you to the ranger camp at Belknap. I don't know what the court may do, but at least the rangers won't let a mob get you."

Purdy said, "I'm goin' along with you."

"That's not necessary. I'll see that nobody touches him."

"I'm goin' anyway, and you can't stop me."

The determined look in Purdy's eyes showed where Clemmie's stubborn nature had come from. Arguing with the old man would be like talking to a fence post.

"All right. But I have a job to do, and it's got a bad-enough taste as it is. Don't do anything to make it worse." He looked back. He still saw no sign of pursuit, but his skin prickled. "We'd better be movin'."

This was a poor way to repay the Monahan family, but duty gave him no choice.

James pointed out, "It's a right smart of a ways to Belknap."

"We'll make it."

James looked as if he had a secret he was not sharing. "Mama and Geneva told me about your leg. Reckon it'll hold up to that long a ride?"

"It's held up this far."

In the stress of the shooting and the escape, Rusty had given little thought to his healing wound. Now he became very conscious of its insistent aching. He knew putting this kind of strain on it was a risk, but he saw no option. He had to make it to Belknap. He did not point the pistol directly at James, but he motioned with it. "Let's go."

They pushed the horses as hard as Rusty dared. He could not ride fast enough to outrun the memory of the anguished scream from Dawkins's wife. The rest of her life she would carry the image of Caleb Dawkins sprawled in his own blood, just as Clemmie Monahan would have to live with the sight of her husband and her son lying lifeless in a wagon. War was hell on men, but in its way it was as bad or worse on women, he thought.

The first couple of hours went well enough, though the pain in the leg was increasing. By noon Rusty had to grit his teeth, cold sweat breaking out on his face.

James said, "I'm gettin' hungry. Ain't et nothin' since a midnight supper."

It had been longer than that since Rusty had eaten, but he doubted he could hold anything on his stomach if he had it. He was nauseous, the pain grown almost beyond endurance. "The sooner we get to camp, the sooner you can eat."

Sometime later he realized he was hunched in the saddle. He had difficulty focusing his eyes. Once he tried to throw up, but his stomach held nothing to yield. He had long since holstered the pistol for fear of dropping it.

He felt helpless when James drew up beside him and took the weapon from him. James demanded, "What makes you think you can keep somebody under arrest when you can't hardly even stay in the saddle?"

Rusty heard himself mumbling that James was still his prisoner, but he knew that was no longer true. He was James's prisoner, if James chose to take advantage of the situation.

James's voice stung. "When you needed help, my family took you in like their own. Now look how you paid them back. I ought to shoot you the way I shot Dawkins." He raised the pistol.

Purdy pushed his horse between his grandson and Rusty. He gripped the barrel of James's pistol and forced it downward. "No, James. You've caused grief enough already. Whether you can see it or not, Rusty was right in what he done."

James turned on the older man. "You didn't do me no favors either, leadin' him to Dawkins's place to stop me. My own grandpa."

"Yes, I'm your grandfather, and when you were growin' up I tried to teach you better than what I've seen from you today. I didn't teach you to kill people."

"There wasn't no war then. There is now, and it's all about killin'."

"You're not killin' Rusty."

James lowered the pistol. "No, I ain't. I ought to, but I got a feelin' from my sister that she kind of likes him. Damned if I can see why. So you can go home and tell her I let him live. He can go on to Belknap by himself."

"The shape he's in, he might not make it alone. He's liable to fall off that horse and lay there and die."

"It'd serve him right. I'm strikin' off west, across the country."

"I'll stay with him, at least 'til I can turn him over to somebody who'll see that he gets to Belknap." Purdy pulled his horse in close and embraced his grandson. "You've done wrong, but you're still family. You're still ours."

"Tell Mama . . . well, hell, you'll know what to tell her." James's voice broke. "It won't be safe to write to you, but I'll let Preacher Webb know where I'm at. He can pass the word. Maybe when this damned war is over . . ."

"I may not still be here."

"Sure you'll be here. You'll never die, you'll just turn into an old gray mule and keep on kickin'." James gripped his grandfather's thin shoulders, handed him Rusty's pistol, then turned quickly away.

The old man watched him a long time in silence. Rusty could not see his face, but he could see Purdy's body shake.

Rusty said, "There's a lot of Indians the direction he's goin'."

Purdy wiped a sleeve across his eyes and cleared his throat. "There's worse the other way." He faced around to Rusty. "I'd best be takin' you someplace."

"I'm not as helpless as I may look."

"The hell you're not. You'll never make it to the ranger camp by yourself."

Rusty lacked the strength or the will to put up more of an argument.

They rode without talking for what must have been a couple of hours before Purdy said, "I see a wagon yonder, headin' in the right direction. Hang on tight, because we're fixin' to lope and catch up."

Rusty gripped the saddle horn. He saw the wagon ahead. It appeared to be loaded with freight. Purdy shouted, and the driver sawed on the reins, halting his mules. A black man beside him reached beneath the seat and brought up a rifle, which he held defensively in front of him. Wind lifted his torn, unbuttoned jacket.

Purdy asked, "You-all goin' to Belknap?"

The driver was dressed no better than the black man beside him. He gave the horsemen a long appraisal, slowly satisfying his suspicion. "Yep. Got a load of goods to deliver."

"I've got somethin' else for you to take there. This man belongs to the ranger camp."

The driver was a middle-aged man with a sun-browned face dark as an Indian's where his salt-and-pepper beard did not cover it. He gave Rusty a second close inspection. "Looks like he's got somethin' wrong with him. Ain't no catchin' sickness, I hope."

"He took an arrow in his leg awhile back. Keeps agitatin' it to where it ain't healed good."

The freighter regarded Rusty with sympathy. "At least he's still got all his hair on. Mose, spread my blanket roll on top of the load back there so he can lay down."

Purdy supported Rusty as he dismounted, then helped the black man boost him up over the wagon wheel. Rusty settled onto the blankets that covered several wooden crates. Purdy tied Alamo behind the wagon.

The driver said, "It won't be the smoothest ride you ever had, but we'll get you there."

Rusty reached out for Purdy's hand. "I owe you, Mr. Purdy. James would've just left me out there."

"We raised him better than that, in spite of the way he talks. At least now he's goin' someplace that there won't be no conscript officers, no hangin' parties, no fanatics like Caleb Dawkins."

"Don't ever tell me where. I don't want to know."

"You may need to go there yourself someday. The way I've heard you talk, you've got union leanin's of your own."

"I don't noise them about."

Purdy handed the driver Rusty's unloaded pistol and backed his horse away from the wagon. He said, "Give this to him when you get him there. And tell them rangers to take good care of this young feller. He's a right decent sort."

The last Rusty saw of him, Purdy was headed south.

The driver held his questions as long as he could. "He says you belong at the ranger camp. I don't like mixin' into law business. You ain't an escaped prisoner, are you?"

"I'm a ranger, or what's left of one . . . if they haven't fired me for bein' gone too long."

"I'd best take you to the camp before we go into town. There's some folks in Belknap that ain't fond of the law. Feel like it messes in their business too much."

"Some business needs messin' in."

"I heard him say you've got union leanin's."

"My father fought in Mexico for the union flag."

"Well, it don't mean nothin' to me one way or the other. Washington is a long ways off from here, and Richmond ain't much closer. I make a livin'. What happens somewhere else is other folks' business."

Rusty looked at the black man. "They claim the union wants to take away everybody's slaves."

The driver shrugged. "Don't mean nothin' to me. Ol' Mose here, he's a free nigger. Saved up and bought himself, he did. They can't free him if he don't belong to nobody noway. Eh, Mose?"

"God's truth," the black man said.

The wagon hit a rut, and Rusty had to grab a sideboard to keep from being jostled off. "These crates are awful hard. What you got in them?"

The driver thought a minute. "You askin' as a ranger?"

"Not if you don't want me to."

"I oughtn't to tell you, but there's whiskey in them crates, bound for a dram house in Belknap. That's all I know and all I *want* to know. But if I was a suspicionin' man, I'd be inclined to think some of this whiskey is meant to be taken up into the territory and traded to the Indians."

"Knowin' that, you'd still deliver it?"

"If I didn't do it, somebody else would. I've got to make a livin'. Me and Mose, we've sort of got used to eatin' every day whether we need to or not."

The tent camp looked the same as the last time Rusty had seen it. The driver halted the wagon and motioned for Mose to help Rusty to the ground. "This is as far as I dast take you without gettin' me in bad with some of the boys in town."

"I'm much obliged." The leg hurt as Rusty climbed down, using the left front wheel as a ladder of sorts. It almost buckled when he reached the ground. Mose's strong hands steadied him. The black man untied Alamo from the rear of the wagon and handed the reins to Rusty. He also gave him his pistol.

The driver said, "If you see us in town, just act like we're strangers."

They just about were. Rusty never had learned the driver's name, and all he knew about Mose was his name and that he was a free black. He knew also that some of the crates contained whiskey, not illegal in Texas but a violation of union law in Indian Territory. Liquor smuggling was of interest to Texans when it encouraged Indian raids south of the river. Under present conditions of war, neither union nor Confederacy was in a position to make a strong effort against the whiskey trade.

Rusty watched the wagon pull away, then limped toward the corrals, leading Alamo. He wished he had not thrown away the cane. He would whittle a new one to use until the leg was stronger.

Tanner was at the corral, brushing a horse. Surprised at seeing Rusty, he strode out on his long, lanky legs to open the gate. "Looks to me like you rushed things a little. Leg's still botherin' you, ain't it?"

"Got tired of sittin' around doin' nothin'." Rusty unbuckled the girth and slid the saddle to the ground.

Tanner said, "You ain't missed anything here. We've rode a million miles since you been gone, and we ain't seen an Indian, hardly. Things sure been quiet."

"Been dull where I was, too." He did not feel like getting into a long discussion. He would save that for the captain.

"A few of the boys got tired of the routine and joined up with the army. Conscripters've been here, too. So far they're leavin' us alone long as we stay on guard with the company. The minute we leave, they'll be lookin' for us to go fight Old Abe."

"I've got no intention of leavin'." However, much depended upon the captain's reaction when Rusty told him about the shooting of Caleb Dawkins and James's escape from his custody. Losing a prisoner was serious business.

"Looks like the folks you stayed with fed you pretty good. Things got so bad on scout awhile back that I had to skin and eat a prairie dog."

"How was it?"

"You don't want any."

Rusty saw to it that Alamo had a little grain in a pen by himself where the other horses could not contest him for it. He squared his shoulders. "I'd better go and report in."

"We're shorthanded. The captain'll be tickled to see you."

Maybe not when I tell him everything, Rusty thought.

Captain Whitfield sat at a table, writing. He looked up as Rusty entered the tent. "Shannon. Saw you come in on a wagon. Can't you ride yet?"

"I can, some. Just can't overdo it."

"Then what're you doin' here? You could've stayed longer where you were at."

"Felt like I'd better report to you, sir." Reluctantly Rusty told him everything. He was tempted to leave out the part about taking James prisoner, then losing him, but a deliberate omission would seem the same as an outright lie.

The captain frowned. "So you had him, then lost him."

"I was hurtin' so bad I couldn't see straight. He had my pistol before I knew it."

"Do you know where he went?"

"The last I saw of him, he was headin' west. He couldn't keep up that direction too long, though. He'd be apt to run into Comanches when he got to the plains."

"Probably dropped south once he felt he was in the clear. There's a lot of conscript dodgers hidin' out on the far Colorado and the Brazos and the Conchos. Some of them've been slippin' back into the settlements and stealin' supplies, takin' horses and whatever else comes to hand. As bad as the Indians except they haven't scalped anybody we know of."

"I don't see James Monahan bein' a thief."

"Just a murderer is all?" Sarcasm coarsened the captain's voice.

"He felt like he was justified. Caleb Dawkins hung his daddy and his brother."

"The law would've taken care of Colonel Dawkins the first time it could prove somethin' on him. At least it looks like your James Monahan has saved the state of Texas the cost of that trial, but it'll still be out the cost of his own."

"It'll have to catch him first."

"It will sooner or later. Or kill him." He dismissed the subject with a wave of his hand. "It appears to me that you'd best stay around camp until that leg will let you ride the line. You can find plenty to do on foot."

Rusty was relieved that the captain was not summarily dismissing him. "Yes, sir." He felt that a salute was in order, but he had never been taught the proper way to give one. He made the effort, knowing it fell short of being soldierly.

Whitfield called to him as he was about to leave the tent. "Shannon, are you sure you didn't let your guard down on purpose, out of friendship?"

Rusty thought about it. "I don't think so." Now that the question had been posed, he could not be sure. Perhaps subconsciously he had wanted James to get away and had provided the opportunity without admitting to himself what he was doing. "I couldn't swear to it on the Bible."

"Thanks for an honest answer. Not everybody gives me one." Whitfield waved him away.

Rusty was troubled a little now that the suspicion had been aroused. After all Mike Shannon had preached to him about duty, it was possible he had compromised himself.

Tanner came up from the corrals to meet him. "You look like you're cloudin' up to rain. Catch hell from the captain?"

"No. I'm catchin' a little hell from myself."

He spent the next few days doing chores around camp, raking out the corrals, pitching hay, helping with the cooking. He even shod several horses, a job he would have expected to be particularly hard on the weakened leg. He was gratified to find that the leg was stronger day by day. It was coming back to normal, though the wound was leaving a frightful-looking mark. He had heard that Indians took pride in their scars, sometimes outlining them with paint to make them more noticeable. His was private, to remain forever concealed by the leg of his trousers.

Any damned fool could get himself wounded. The real object in a fight was to win *without* getting wounded, or worse.

Because of the frequent comings and goings of strangers, he paid little attention to a buggy pulling up to the captain's tent, accompanied by several men on horseback. He was currying a horse when an adjutant came into the corral. "Shannon, the captain wants to see you."

Rusty brushed off some of the dirt and horsehair from his clothing and followed the adjutant to the center of camp. He asked no questions. He had found that when the captain wanted the men to know something, he told them.

A broad-shouldered man sat on a chair facing the captain. His back was turned to Rusty.

Whitfield said, "This is Private Shannon."

The big man turned. Rusty's stomach seemed to sink to his feet.

Caleb Dawkins.

Dawkins was pale and seemed to have lost some weight. He pointed his heavy chin at Rusty. "That is the man, captain. Indeed it is. I saw him enter the room just before I was shot."

Rusty was speechless, his tongue stuck to the roof of his dry mouth. His hands shook a little.

The captain said, "Shannon is not the man who shot you."

"No, but he was an accomplice."

Rusty began to find his voice. "I wasn't. I went there to try and stop it."

Whitfield said, "Private Shannon told me he took the culprit prisoner but due to disability was unable to hold him."

Rusty took comfort in the tone of the captain's voice. Evidently Whitfield believed him if Dawkins did not. "I've told the truth, sir."

Dawkins said, "You ran off and left me for dead."

Whitfield said, "Private Shannon was of the opinion that you *were* dead. He left in pursuit of the man who shot you."

"That man was a Monahan, and Shannon has been thick with the Monahans all along. Are you aware, Captain, that they are union sympathizers? I suspect Private Shannon is, as well."

"We do not inquire into our men's politics. Our only interest is in their ability and willingness to face the Indians, and whatever other assignment we give them."

"You have a duty to run down fugitives from conscription."

"When we have time. The Indians are our main concern, and we are spread very thin."

"Then I shall take my case to the governor. We will see what he thinks about officers who shirk their duty and let murderers go free."

The captain's face colored. "You are free to take your case anywhere you wish, Colonel Dawkins. To hell, if that be your choice."

"I see I will get no justice here. Willingham, please help me to my feet." One of Dawkins's men lifted the big man from his chair. Dawkins trembled from the exertion. Clearly, the wound had weakened him considerably. Dawkins raised his hand to his side, his face twisting in pain. Rusty could not see why the bullet had not killed him. He guessed that James had fired in haste, without taking proper aim.

Dawkins said, "I strongly suspect, Whitfield, that your company is harboring men whose loyalties are open to question. I believe Shannon is a unionist, and it stands to reason that some of his fellows are as well. The governor will receive a full report from me, you may rest assured of that."

The captain struggled to control his anger. "Will you be equally eager to report to him that you have taken it upon yourself to hang men you believe are disloyal?"

"You should be careful in making charges you cannot prove."

"And you as well, Colonel."

Rusty stepped aside to allow Dawkins to pass, aided by the man he called Willingham. He felt conflicting emotions, on the one hand relieved that James had not become a murderer after all, and on the other a wish that he had been a better shot. It was unlikely that Dawkins would rest until either he or James was dead. Granted a wish, Dawkins would probably choose to see Rusty and James buried together.

The captain said, "Stay a minute, Shannon." He waited until the sound of horses and squeaking harness told him Dawkins was leaving. "You know, I suppose, that Caleb Dawkins has marked a target on your back. He will be pleased to put a bullet in your chest or a rope around your neck."

"He's a hopeless zealot."

"It's zealots who've brought about this war. Good men can be as dangerous as bad men when they let passion turn them into fanatics. You should be careful not to leave this camp alone. Have other rangers with you wherever you go."

"That's almost the same as runnin' away."

"There's no disgrace in runnin' when the odds are dead set against you. You live, and you fight another day."

"I guess so, but I don't like the feelin'." Another concern came to him. "Am I liable to bring trouble down on you and this company, Captain?"

"Trouble is what we're here for. We can handle it."

"In case the Monahan family doesn't already know, I'd better go warn them that Dawkins is still alive. He might take it in his head to revenge himself on them."

"You stay close. There's nothin' he'd like better than to catch you off by yourself. I'll send Tanner to warn the Monahans."

That brought some comfort, though not enough. "He knows how to find the place."

Soon Rusty was able to participate in routine patrols, short ones at first, then longer as he regained full use of his leg. Now and then the scouting trips turned up sign of Indian incursion, but it seemed more of a probing nature than any effort at full-scale invasion. A couple of times the scouts overtook the Indians and escorted them peacefully if not happily back across the river. More often, the Indians returned on their own before they were caught, usually with horses and mules and occasionally a few scalps. Once they reached the north side of the Red, they were in Union territory and out of bounds for any official Texan pursuit. Unofficial civilian pursuit was something else, more often than not bringing retribution upon innocent reservation Indians who had nothing to do with the raids.

Though he deplored the punitive expeditions, the captain understood the fear and anger that prompted them. To most white men an Indian was an Indian, just as most Indians made no distinction between whites. He said, "Whatever it costs and whoever gets hurt, we can't let up our guard. If they ever get the notion they can come across the Red and do whatever they want to without fear of punishment, they'll be here in force."

The Indians were fully aware that the white man's war had crippled the frontier defense and that settlers along the western edge were highly vulnerable. That much was gleaned from conversations with captured Indian invaders given an armed escort back to the line. It was up to the minutemen companies to block hostile incursions to whatever extent they could, lest the dam break and the frontier be inundated by a Comanche flood.

Rusty and Tanner lagged behind Captain Whitfield and two other men in a small patrol scouting far south and east of Belknap. Rusty was half listening to Tanner tell with considerable glee about finding and moving a whiskey runner's stash to see what would happen. The runner accused a rival of theft, and the two men got into a fistfight of monumental proportions in a Fort Belknap dramshop.

"You ever see them Germans make sausage down on the Guadalupe?" Tanner asked. "Them two fought one another all the way across the floor and out into the road. Time they wore theirselves out, their faces looked like a batch of that raw sausage. I laughed 'til I was rollin' on the ground."

"It don't sound like somethin' to laugh about. What if they'd killed one another, and you'd been the cause of it?"

"The world would've been shed of two whiskey runners. All they're good for is to get the Indians liquored up and rarin' for a raid. There's no tellin' how many people have died on account of them, white and Indian both."

"Still, I wouldn't have wanted them on my conscience."

"Maybe your conscience is too sensitive for your own good. You ain't never had to kill anybody, have you? Even an Indian?"

"No, I haven't."

"Time you've done it to two or three that really need it, your conscience won't weigh you down near as much."

A movement to the south caught Rusty's eye. He saw a horseman spurring a sweat-lathered horse toward the patrol. The captain and the two other rangers had already seen and had stopped to wait. The oncoming rider waved his hat. He tried to shout, but he was too hoarse for his voice to carry far.

Tanner said, "I've seen that gent before."

Rusty recognized the man called Willingham, who had been with Caleb Dawkins the day the recuperating farmer visited the camp. The man reined his horse to a rough stop and stirred a small cloud of dust. He coughed, trying to coax his voice into use. "Damn but I'm glad to see you-all. Minutemen, ain't you?"

The captain said, "We're scoutin' from Belknap. You look like you're totin' a load of trouble."

"Trouble enough." Willingham turned in the saddle and pointed in the direction from which he had come. "They raided the Dawkins farm last night. Set fire to a haystack and tried to burn the barn."

"Kill anybody?"

"Not that we know of. Wasn't because they didn't try."

"How many horses did they run off?"

"None that I know of. Ain't had time to take a count."

"Doesn't sound like the Comanches I know. Or the Kiowas either."

"Wasn't Indians atall. White men they was. Colonel says they're some of them conscript dodgers that skulk around in the timber out past the settlements. They was after the colonel personal. Searched the house lookin' for him. Scared Miz Dawkins half to death."

Rusty had a strong hunch. He pushed Alamo forward, facing Willingham. "Recognize anybody?"

"One of the boys said he thought he saw James Monahan among them. Colonel laid low and didn't see nobody, but he's dead certain it was Monahan led the raid."

Rusty had heard reports of petty thievery, blamed on men of the brush who hid out to avoid conscription officers and self-appointed hangmen like Dawkins. He had never seriously considered that James would allow himself to become a thief. But if the raid was aimed specifically at Dawkins, it took on a new and interesting complexion.

The captain told Willingham, "You lead the way. We'll borrow a fresh mount for you at the first farm we come to."

Willingham reined his horse around. "I've heard Colonel say some hard things about you rangers, but he'll be tickled to see you this time."

Rusty had noted that some people who railed at the law's interference in their own affairs were mightily pleased for it to show up when trouble arose.

The patrol spent much of the day in reaching the Dawkins farm. However strong the excitement had been the night before, the place looked calm enough now. Men were working in the fields and around the barn. Rusty saw a scorched area beside the wide barn door, and what had been a stack of hay was just windblown gray ashes.

The captain said, "I wonder how come they had to burn the haystack. Seems like a spiteful thing."

Willingham said, "They saw one of the boys run and hide himself in it. They thought he might be Colonel Dawkins, so they burned him out. Singed his whiskers but didn't hurt him."

If Caleb Dawkins was glad to see the scouts he kept his pleasure well concealed. He gave Rusty a moment's attention, then turned on the captain. "It is way past time for you-all to show up, after the trail's gone cold. You ought to've been here last night."

The captain's jaw hardened, but he remained painfully civil. "We can't be everywhere at once. There's a lot of country to cover and only a few of us to do it."

Dawkins repeated the story Willingham had told, with a few extra embellishments and a strong condemnation of James Monahan. "That boy is beating on the doors of hell, and if the law doesn't let him in, I will!"

"Willingham says they made a point of lookin' for you. How come they didn't find you?"

Dawkins glanced away, not meeting the corporal's probing gaze. "They didn't look everywhere."

Willingham had already divulged that Dawkins had taken cover beneath his porch.

The captain said, "At least nobody was killed."

"No thanks to James Monahan. You'd better bring him in. Better yet, kill him where you find him." Dawkins faced Rusty. "Lest somebody turn him loose again."

Pete Dawkins came into the house as the rangers were about to leave. "Papa, looks like we've come up short some horses after all."

Dawkins turned back to the captain. "Well, there you have it. The raid on the headquarters was meant to cover the theft of my horses."

Whitfield promised, "We'll look around and report back to you."

Rusty had no difficulty in finding the trail left by the retreating raiders. Its westward course was plain enough.

Whitfield had been circling in another direction. Finding nothing, he came to Rusty. "What did you find?"

Rusty pointed to the tracks. "No more horses than what they were ridin', the best I can see. If anybody stole the colonel's horses, it was a separate bunch and went off in another direction."

"It could have been like the colonel said. The raid on the headquarters was a diversion."

"Not to James Monahan it wasn't, if he was really here."

"These tracks lead toward the Monahan farm, don't they? I believe he was here."

Rusty could not argue the point. He believed it himself.

Whitfield sent Tanner and the Morris brothers to make a wider circle and look for tracks of stolen horses being driven away. With Rusty beside him, he delivered what information he had back to Dawkins, who waited in front of his house. He said, "We'll go talk to the Monahan family."

Dawkins grunted disapproval. "They won't tell you anything but lies. There won't be peace around here 'til that nest of unionist trash is cleaned out, from the old man down to the women and kids."

Giving in to fury, Rusty dismounted and drew back his fist. Dawkins stumbled backward, trying to avoid the blow he could see coming. The captain grabbed Rusty's arm and broke up the swing before it was completed. "Shannon, he's a wounded man."

"So am I. That makes us even."

Dawkins's cold stare said he was mentally measuring Rusty's neck for a rope.

Rusty declared, "You hurt them women and I'll kill you!"

The captain pulled Rusty away. "Let's go, Shannon. We're doin' no good here."

Rusty resisted leaving a worthy fight unfinished, but Tanner joined the captain in hustling him along to his horse. Tanner said, "Come on, redhead, before you get in trouble."

"The trouble's already here." But he reluctantly gave up the struggle and went along, looking back toward Dawkins.

Riding away, the captain said, "You have to try to put your personal feelin's aside and remember you represent the law."

"Can *you* always do that?"

"I don't go around hittin' people I don't like—unless I think it'll do them some good."

"It would've done *me* a lot of good."

"Maybe I ought to send you back to camp. If we get into a chase after James Monahan, you won't have your heart in it."

"I'll do my duty."

"I'll hold you to that."

Rusty dropped back to the rear. Tanner pulled in beside him. "Looks to me like your conscience is already weakenin' some. Would you really kill him, or are you just talkin'?"

"I hope we don't have to find out."

CHAPTER

FOURTEEN

usty was not surprised that most of the horse tracks veered well to the north of the Monahan farm. James would be too cagy to incriminate his family. But the sharp-eyed captain found a single set of tracks that led toward the Monahans'.

Rusty welcomed the patrol's brief stop for a cold supper. Though the pain in his leg had lessened to a point that he was unaware of it most of the time, fatigue brought back enough that he could not ignore it. While they ate jerked beef and hard bread, the captain asked pointed questions about James. He knew Rusty once had James in custody and lost him. Rusty suspected that most of the rangers believed he had simply let James go. Few blamed him. If Dawkins had any friends in the ranger camp, they kept it a secret.

The captain said, "By the looks of things, Monahan may have thrown in with a bunch of men from the brush."

"I feel like he was just lookin' for revenge against Dawkins."

"We can't stand back and let a bunch of men just run wild. It's our job to catch them or run them plumb out of the country."

"Run them where?"

"A lot of union sympathizers and conscript dodgers have slipped off to Mexico. Others have gone up north to Colorado or out to California. Me, I've got no wish to see James Monahan dead. I'd just like to see him gone.

I'd be inclined to look in another direction if I was satisfied he was leavin' the country."

"I'll tell his family that. They'll know a way to get word to him."

They would do it through Preacher Webb, but Rusty would not tell the captain. What he didn't know wouldn't hurt the minister.

Nearing the Monahan farm, Rusty saw Vince Purdy moving out from the house and into the dusk to meet the rangers. His stride was slow and careful. Autumn weather had summoned arthritis into his joints. Purdy's gaze settled on Rusty. "We figured on company," he said. "Didn't know you'd be amongst them."

"I go where they tell me to."

"You're lookin' a right smart better than the last time I seen you."

"I'm able to do a day's work."

"If your work includes catchin' James, he ain't here."

"Didn't figure he would be. But he's been here."

"You're the one sayin' that."

The captain spoke. "The tracks say it. He came by to let you-all know he failed again to kill Caleb Dawkins."

"Is that a fact?" Purdy had the look of an innocent child. He carefully avoided telling a lie; he simply withheld what he knew.

Clemmie Monahan emerged onto the porch. She stood with her arms folded, belligerently silent.

Geneva paused beside her mother, then came down the front steps. Clemmie called for her to come back, but Geneva walked toward Rusty. He stepped down from the saddle to meet her.

She halted a stride short and glanced back toward her mother. Her eyes misted. She reached out as if to touch him, then withdrew her hand. "James isn't here."

"I wasn't goin' to ask you." He looked regretfully at Clemmie, up on the porch. "I don't suppose she understood why I tried to take James to the ranger camp."

"She thought it was poor payment for what we did to help you."

"You feel that way, too?"

"I don't agree with you, but I can see why you felt like you did. You had your duty, and you looked at it the only way you could. Bein' family, we saw it the only way *we* could. I'm grateful you and James didn't come to shootin' one another."

"I couldn't have. I doubt he could either."

"He's still got his mind set on squarin' things with Dawkins."

"I can't blame him, but it's our job to keep him from it."

"What if it means havin' to kill him?"

"I hope it doesn't come to that."

"It might."

Clemmie called from the porch, "Geneva, you come back here." Geneva did not move.

The captain rode up almost to the steps. He took off his hat to Clemmie. "Ma'am, we're lookin' for James Monahan."

"You'll not find him here."

"I don't disbelieve you, but it is our duty to make a search."

"Then do your duty, and be damned." She turned abruptly and disappeared back into the house.

Rusty told the captain, "He'd be a fool to stay here. If we didn't come for him, Dawkins would."

"That's why we need to make a show of searchin'. It's got to look good on our report. Then Dawkins won't have any complaint comin'."

"He'll complain anyway. You heard what he said about gettin' rid of this family. He means it."

Geneva took a sharp breath. "Get rid of us? How?"

"However he has to. Whatever it takes."

She grabbed Rusty's arm. "You-all wouldn't let him do that. Would you?"

The captain said, "Not while we're here, but we're spread too thin to stay."

"We have a sheriff."

"He's got this whole county to worry about. He can't set up permanent camp here. Looks to me like you-all are in a fix." Whitfield looked regretfully at the girl. "I'm afraid with Dawkins it's gone deeper than patriotism and a difference over the war. Your brother has made a personal vendetta out of it."

Rusty protested, "It didn't start with James. It started when Dawkins hung Lon and Billy."

"It doesn't matter where it started. What matters is where it has got to now."

Rusty took Geneva's hands in his own. "I told Dawkins I'd kill him if he hurt any of you. I don't think he believed it. I'm not sure I believe it either."

The captain asked, "Is there any place you folks could go to get away from here for a while?"

"Before Pa died we promised we'd stay here no matter what."

Rusty said, "It's a promise you can't afford to keep. On account of James, you're all in danger if you stay here."

"Mother won't hear of goin'."

Vince Purdy had stood with his hands in his pockets and his head down, listening quietly. Now he interceded. "When everybody made that promise, we didn't know your daddy was fixin' to be killed. Everything is different now."

Geneva gave Rusty an anguished look. "But we've got nowhere to go. We can't live out in the brush like James. There's the young ones to think of."

Purdy took his granddaughter's arm. "We'll try talkin' to your mother. Don't know that it'll do any good." He walked with her up the steps and into the house.

Rusty faced the captain. "I'm not goin' anywhere 'til I know these folks are safe. I'll resign from the company if I have to."

Whitfield frowned. "The conscript officers'll come for you. They'll send you off to Virginia or Tennessee or someplace a long ways from here."

"They'll have to catch me first."

"You want to hide out like James Monahan?" The captain shook his head. "You don't have to resign. I'll assign you to stay and watch after these folks 'til they're out of harm's way. Our main duty is to protect the settlers."

"What if Mrs. Monahan refuses to go anywhere?"

"You'll have to persuade her. The sooner the better."

Rusty dreaded facing Clemmie. When she folded her arms and stuck out her chin, a mountain would be easier to move. He forced himself up the steps and through the door. She was in conversation with her father and Geneva, but her eyes cut him like a knife.

"You're not welcome in this house. We don't need you here."

He took off his hat. "You need me more than you know. I suppose they've told you?"

"That Caleb Dawkins thinks he's goin' to get rid of us? It'll take some doin'."

"He can do it. The war hasn't left enough law around here to stop him. Some of you are liable to get hurt, maybe killed."

"Maybe it's Dawkins who'll get killed." She threw her thin shoulders back and pointed at the door. "Git out!"

Geneva nodded almost imperceptibly, her eyes telling him this was not the time to argue with Clemmie. Rusty backed to the door, turned and went out onto the porch.

The captain asked with his eyes. Rusty said, "She ain't in a mood for talkin'. Maybe she'll see different in the mornin'."

"We'll have to leave in the mornin'. Got to see if we can overtake those other men."

The chance was slim to none, but Rusty understood. "I don't reckon you could leave Tanner here with me?"

"There aren't but five of us now. Four with you stayin' behind. Can't do it, Shannon."

They made camp on the south side of the barn, where the walls would protect them from the chilly north wind. Tanner built a small fire and warmed his hands. Whitfield had assigned him the night's first guard tour. Though their horses were penned, they were vulnerable to theft by either Indians or reckless white men.

Vince Purdy came down from the house, carrying a small cloth sack. "Thought you men might like to make a little coffee before you turn in. Brought some. Can't brag on it any. It's mostly parched grain with just enough coffee in it to give a little flavor. There's a war, you know."

"We hadn't noticed," Tanner said. He accepted the sack, opening it and smelling of the contents. "I wouldn't trade one cup of good old-time coffee for a gallon jug of whiskey. One of these days when the war is over I'm goin' to buy me a whole barrel of coffee beans and boil enough to float a boat from here to the river."

Purdy tried squatting on his heels, but his arthritic knees would not allow it. He sat flat on the ground. Rusty suspected he would need help to get up.

He asked, "You reckon Miz Clemmie will be a little more inclined to listen once she's slept on the idea?"

Purdy shook his head. "I raised me a real stubborn daughter. I'm afraid the only way to get her off of this place would be to tie her up and drag her away. But she'd turn around and come back if she had to crawl on hands and knees. Too bad James wasn't a better shot."

"We'll all have to keep talkin' to her."

"Me and Geneva been talkin', but Clemmie ain't listenin'. Looks to me like we'd best do some talkin' to the Lord."

Rusty said, "Pray for Him to drop a hailstone on Dawkins, one the size of a washtub."

Rusty stood the last watch before dawn. He observed the dimming of the stars and the first sign of light in the east, grateful that the night had passed without incident. Dawkins had probably known the rangers would be at the Monahan farm. However fanatic he might be, Dawkins would not want to risk confrontation with five armed and determined men.

Tonight, however, there would be only one. Two, including Vince Purdy. Rusty had no idea how well the old man could shoot. He knew he had been in the revolution against Mexico, but that had been nearly thirty years ago. He had scrapped with Indians in more recent times, but for all Rusty knew he might never have hit one. In all the Indian fights he had ever heard of, far more shots were fired than people wounded or killed on either side.

He watched as Whitfield and the others saddled their horses. The captain said, "I wish there was more I can do. Maybe Dawkins'll change his thinkin' when the dust has settled better."

"He's got blinders on, like a mule. He can't see but one thing at a time."

Whitfield wished Rusty luck and led out. Tanner lingered a moment. "We're never goin' to find them other fellers. Maybe I can talk the captain into comin' back here once he sees that."

"Even if he did, he couldn't afford to stay. Dawkins'd just wait him out."

Glumly Rusty watched the riders angle away to the northwest to intersect the horse tracks. He hunkered at the rebuilt fire, sipping from a cup of lukewarm liquid that had to pass for coffee in these short-ration times. He arose as he saw Geneva coming down the steps and walking toward him. He tossed out the little that remained in the cup. It had gone cold anyway.

She said, "Why don't you come to the house? I'll fix you a decent breakfast."

"Your mother wouldn't want me there."

"*I* want you there." She touched his arm. "You can't just camp out here while you wait for her to change her mind. She may never change it. Come on." She caught his hand and tugged.

He made a weak show of resistance, then gave in. "All right, but if she comes at me with a chunk of firewood . . ."

"She won't. She'll try to freeze you with her eyes, but she won't draw blood. I think deep down she knows you did what you thought was right. She just thinks you were wrong."

"So do you, don't you?"

Geneva did not reply.

Unlike the night before, Clemmie did not order him out of the house. She simply glared at him, then left the kitchen to him and Geneva and one of the younger girls slow in finishing her breakfast.

Clemmie came to the door as Rusty finished a bit of salt pork, dragging it through gravy and following it with half a biscuit. She leaned against the jamb, studying him critically. "Me and Lon and Papa and the boys built this house with our own hands. If you think I'll let Dawkins scare me into leavin' it, you're mistaken."

"He doesn't strike me as a man who makes idle talk."

"It'll be a cold day in hell."

Rusty spent the day puttering around the farm with Vince Purdy, patching a broken place in a fence, putting several fresh shingles into the shed roof to repair hail damage. Every little while Rusty would look eastward toward the Dawkins farm, wondering where Dawkins was and what type of vengeance simmered in the man's twisted mind. It seemed inconceivable that he would risk injury or death to women and children. Yet Dawkins was fanatical about the war and hated the Monahan family. Passion could easily drive such a man across the boundary between reason and madness. Daddy Mike had encountered fighters in the Mexican War and Indian campaigns who lost all sense of caution or compassion in the fury of the moment. Isaac York had been such a one.

Purdy offered, "You can sleep in the room with me tonight if you don't mind an old man's snorin'."

Rusty demurred. "Clemmie wouldn't get much rest, knowin' I was under the same roof. I'll sleep in the shed like I did before."

He did not expect to sleep much. He intended to stay awake and on guard in case Dawkins came. But weariness overcame good intentions. He dozed off slumped on the edge of his cot.

He was awakened by a shout and a flash of light, the sound of horses moving. Fighting off a lingering drowsiness, he instinctively jumped to his feet, jamming his pistol into his waistband and grabbing the rifle he had loaded and left ready. He stumbled outside, nearly falling in his haste. Flames licked at the front of the house. Horsemen fired through the windows, shattering glass. In the flickering light of the blaze he saw someone emerge from the front door with a blanket and try to beat out the flames. Whether man or woman he could not tell. Horsemen raced down upon the figure and forced a retreat back into the burning house.

Against the flames he managed to outline a rider and bring the sights of the rifle to bear. The rifle roared, and a man shouted in shock, almost falling, leaning over the saddle horn as he lost himself in the darkness.

The flames swept upward, hungrily spreading across the front of the house. Rusty tried to reload the rifle as he ran. Two horsemen bore down upon him. He dodged, swinging the rifle like a club but missing. He raised the pistol and fired once.

Vince Purdy came around from the back of the house, firing a shotgun. A horse squealed and pitched and almost lost its rider.

Someone shouted, "We've done it! Let's go!"

Sprinting toward the house, Rusty saw Clemmie burst out upon the porch, carrying a rifle. She fired into the horsemen. With a squall of pain, a rider fell to the ground. He arose, hopping. A companion reached down and pulled him up behind the saddle. They raced past Rusty, almost running over him.

Another horseman spurred to the porch steps as Clemmie tried vainly to reload the rifle. He fired at her, and she fell. Rusty shot at the rider but knew the bullet went wild.

Flames were spreading across the porch toward Clemmie. Rusty dropped his rifle and hurried up the steps, arm raised to shield his face from the intense heat. Clemmie pushed up onto her elbows, her nightgown beginning to smoke. He lifted her and carried her into the yard, away from the blaze. He felt wetness soaking through his shirt. It was Clemmie's blood.

She pointed back toward the house. "The children! Get the children out of there."

For a fleeting moment Rusty considered trying to fight the fire, but he saw that it had grown too intense. "How bad are you hit, Clemmie?"

"Leave me. Go see that the children get out."

He set her on the ground as gently as he could, then ran back to the house, again shielding his face with his arms as he hurried onto and across the porch to the front door. The thick smoke choked him. The doorknob burned his hand. Inside, the flames lighted the house brighter than daytime. He saw Geneva and one of her younger sisters, carrying all the clothing they could hold in their arms.

"Get out of this house!" he ordered.

The smallest of the girls carried the family Bible. Geneva had probably thought of that.

Flames turned them away from the back door. Rusty saw that the front door had become completely engulfed. "This way, out a side window."

He raised the window and propped it with a stick. Geneva and the girls pitched out the clothing they had retrieved, then Rusty helped them through the opening. Geneva said, "There's more clothes in that chifforobe. Hand them through to me."

"This house is fixin' to fall down around us," he said, but he opened the doors to the upright chest and grabbed everything he could reach.

The fire was roaring, engulfing the house. It was unthinkable to go back inside. Geneva asked desperately, "Where's Mother?"

"Around front. You-all come on. She'll want to know that everybody got out."

The girls cried, and Geneva's voice broke as she called for her mother. The answer came in an urgent shout from Purdy. "She's out here."

Clemmie lay where Rusty had left her, her anxious face lighted by the dancing flames. The smaller girls ran to her, sobbing. Purdy grabbed them. "Your mama's hurt. You're liable to hurt her more if you touch her."

Geneva knelt at Clemmie's side and took her hand. "How bad is it?"

Clemmie tried to answer but had difficulty in speaking. Purdy said, "Bullet hit her in the side. Might've busted a rib or two, but I don't think it got any of the vitals." He looked up as the porch collapsed in a shower of fire. "That's the wound that'll hurt her the most, I think, losin' the house."

One of the girls said eagerly, "We saved a lot of the clothes."

"And the Bible," the smallest put in.

Clemmie managed to control her voice. "Is everybody all right? Nobody hurt?"

Geneva said, "We made it out just fine. Rusty helped us."

Now that he had time to think, Rusty began to suffer from a worrisome conscience. If he hadn't fallen asleep . . .

Clemmie murmured, "Everybody is here. Thank God for that."

Out past the barn, two stacks of hay went up in flames. The raiders had taken time to touch them off before they left. Clemmie lamented, "The house is gone, and now we've got no winter feed for the stock."

If the animals had to, they could survive on grass until the spring green-up, Rusty thought. But the prospect of the family spending the winter without a roof was much more troubling. "Clemmie, we'd better see after that wound."

He started to tear the gown where the bullet had ripped through, but she shoved his hand away. "Ain't proper. Geneva can see to it."

It struck him odd that at a moment like this she should let modesty take precedence. Only the direst of emergencies had caused her even to let him see her in her nightgown.

One of the girls asked fearfully, "You think they'll come back?"

Purdy stood hunched, staring at the blazing ruin that had been their home. "Ain't much to come back for, unless they take a notion to burn the barn and shed, too."

Rusty thought they probably would have had they not encountered more resistance than they expected.

"He ought to've killed us," Clemmie said bitterly.

"He?" Rusty asked.

"Caleb Dawkins. Who else? If he wanted to be shed of us, he ought to've killed us, because we ain't givin' up. We may have to go somewhere else for a while, but we'll be back."

Geneva asked, "Where could we go?"

"I don't know, but we ain't about to roll over and die. We'll build it all back big as it ever was."

"Dawkins would just burn it down again."

"Not if he's dead. He'd be dead now if I'd just been able to get him in my sights."

Rusty looked around sharply. "Did you see him here tonight?"

"No, because if I had, I'd've shot him. He must've managed to stay back out of the light."

Thunder rumbled, and lightning streaked the northern sky. Rusty could smell moisture in the air as the wind carried the smoke away from him. He said, "Everybody better get into the shed before it starts to rain." He supported Clemmie, helping her move under the roof. Geneva and the girls brought the clothing they had managed to salvage.

A downpour began. Even under the shed, Rusty could feel the cold mist as the wind drove it inside. "Pity it couldn't have done this an hour ago. They wouldn't have been able to light the fires."

Clemmie said grittily, "*What if* is a fool's game that nobody wins. We've got to deal with things the way they are. Come daylight we'll take stock of what's left and figure out what we can do, where we can go."

Rusty knelt in front of her. "I've already thought some about that. I've got a place down on the Colorado River. It's a pretty good ways from here, far enough that Dawkins isn't apt to follow. House isn't near as big as yours was, but it'll keep you warm and dry through the winter. Ought to be grass enough for at least some of your stock, too."

Clemmie seemed not inclined to accept. "James wouldn't know where to find us."

"Preacher Webb can tell James where it's at. Could even bring him. Nobody there would know James. He wouldn't have to sneak around in the dark."

"You were all set to turn him in once. Why wouldn't you do it again?"

"If I don't see him, I won't know he's around. And I won't be there. I'll be in camp at Belknap."

Geneva pressed, "Maybe by spring the war'll be over, and we won't have to worry anymore about men like Dawkins."

Glumly Clemmie said, "Sometimes I think this war never will be over with. I can't understand the men that started it. I don't understand what they were thinkin' of."

Rusty watched the rain pounding down, drowning the fire. It had come too late. Daylight would reveal nothing of the house but blackened timbers and sodden ashes.

He said, "They sure wasn't thinkin' of the women and children, and how much it was goin' to cost them."

Clemmie held her hand against the bound-up wound. Pain put a raspiness in her voice. "If women were in charge of all the governments, there wouldn't never be no more wars."

Rusty doubted that. He had read about queens running countries in Europe, yet Europe had wars. War seemed to be part of nature, whether man, bird, or animal. He had seen stallions in vicious combat and enraged bulls trying to kill one another. Once he had happened upon two male wildcats ripping each other with fang and claw, and had watched them battle to total exhaustion. One bled to death. The other slowly limped away the winner, yet barely alive.

It seemed to him that human beings ought to be smarter than the animals, but in some ways they weren't.

The sheriff grimly surveyed the damage, a silent anger in the stern set of his jaw. "Useless. Stupid."

Rusty limped along beside him, taking stock of what had been lost and what remained. "All because of the war, I guess."

"There are some people who use war as an excuse to do what they otherwise wouldn't have the nerve for. Recognize any of them?"

Rusty shook his head. "It was dark, and things were movin' too fast."

"I know for a certainty that you didn't see Caleb Dawkins."

"No, but he must've been here. Those had to've been his men."

The sheriff grunted. "Probably were. But he wasn't with them. He was in town all night."

"How do you know?"

"Saw him myself early in the evenin'. He was playin' cards. I asked around this mornin'. They said he stayed in the game 'til way after midnight, then went home with some folks I know who wouldn't lie."

Rusty did not know what to say. He would have bet all he owned that Dawkins had been here.

The sheriff said, "He ain't normally much of a card-playin' man. Ain't got the time or the patience. He did it to make sure plenty of people saw him and could vouch for his whereabouts."

"Just the same, he arranged for the raid. You know he did."

"I'd bet my best horse on it. But unless somebody tells off on him, no court will convict him. Not now, the times and politics bein' what they are. And nobody who really knows anything is goin' to talk. Dawkins will pay them off or scare them off. He can be a scary son of a bitch."

"Scares me, sure enough. A man who'd have a house burned down around women and kids, there's no limit to what he'd do."

"And not much way to stop him, short of murder. James Monahan tried that." The lawman walked to the shed where Clemmie sat with her children. "Mrs. Monahan, I think you folks ought to get away from here for a while."

Clemmie nodded woodenly. "We've talked about it. Ain't likely we can go to any neighbors. Been a couple come to see about us, then left real quick. They're afraid of Dawkins."

Rusty said, "I've offered them the use of my farm down on the Colorado."

The sheriff stared hard at Clemmie. "You goin'?"

"Don't look like we've got much choice. The cattle can take care of themselves if we leave them here. We'd need to take the horses along because there's some people'd steal them soon as they found out we're gone."

"I know a couple of boys who'll help you make the move."

Rusty asked the sheriff, "Would you get word to the captain at Belknap that I'm takin' leave of absence while I show the Monahans to my place?"

The minutemen organization was so loose and perpetually in need of help that even a private had considerable latitude in setting his own terms.

The sheriff said, "They won't pay you for the time you're gone."

"They haven't paid me half the time as it is. I didn't join for the money."

"I figured you joined to stay out of the Confederate Army."

"Not at first. But it's a good reason to stay in."

The Monahans had two wagons, one strong and heavy, the other old and broken down so that it was used only for light work around the farm. Most of the household furnishings had been lost in the fire. The two wagons should be enough to haul whatever remained, provided the oldest did not collapse.

True to his word, the sheriff sent two schoolboys to help gather and drive the loose horses. Rusty guessed them to be fourteen or fifteen. They were too young to be conscripted into the army, though he had seen some of that age volunteer or lie about their birth dates to get in.

He felt that the boys should be warned of the possible consequences. "Caleb Dawkins may not like it, you-all helpin' the Monahan family. He might take it out on your fathers."

One boy said, "I don't see how he can. My pa is off in Tennessee someplace, fightin' the Yankees."

The other said, "My folks are dead. Worst thing he can do to them would be to knock over their tombstones. He's a little bit tetched, maybe, but not that crazy." An eagerness came into his voice. "You reckon we're liable to run into Indians? I'd sure like a chance at an Indian fight."

Bad memories stirred like a supper gone sour and rising back up. "Goin' south, it's not likely we'll see any." For the first time in a couple of days, Rusty felt a dull ache in his leg. "Fightin' Indians ain't as much fun as it sounds like."

He rode out with the two boys to round up as many of the Monahan horses as they could find. After two days of combing the country for miles around, they were still at least a dozen head short by Purdy's reckoning. "You never can be sure what-all has happened to horses," Purdy said. "Some stray, and now and then one will die on you. And then there's the wolves, them with four legs and them with two."

Rusty said, "Maybe the same wolves that got off with some of Colonel Dawkins's horses."

"Dawkins can afford the loss. We can't."

Since the war had shut off eastern markets, cattle had become dirt cheap, hardly worth a thief's efforts. Horses were far more valuable. From reports Rusty had heard, dry weather had set in down on the Colorado, so grazing was likely to be limited. His home place would probably do well just to accommodate the Monahan horses. The cattle would stay behind to shift for themselves.

"If anybody steals *them*," Purdy declared, "it'll be his own fault."

During the course of gathering the horses, Rusty was aware of riders watching from a comfortable distance. He suspected they were Dawkins's men, though they never came close enough to recognize. Dawkins would know the Monahans were leaving. Their destination would not likely be of great interest to him, so long as he knew they were on their way out. Rusty doubted he would pursue the vendetta to the Colorado River. He might if he thought James was there.

Despite the hard downpour the night of the fire, rainfall had been scarce in recent weeks, and grass showed the effects of deprivation. It would probably benefit the range to remove the horses for a while, regardless of the family's other problems.

Clemmie stood beside the wagon, her shadow stretching far across the yard in the winter morning's early sunlight. She stared at the ruins of her home. "It wasn't nothin' but a house," she said tightly. "Just a lot of wood and a little bit of glass. Wasn't no great effort to burn it down. But it won't stay down. We'll be back, and we'll build it just like it was, only bigger and better. And Caleb Dawkins can burn in hell."

Rusty supported her as she climbed up onto the seat. Geneva was already there, holding the reins. Vince Purdy sat on the older wagon, ready to leave. The youngest girl sat with him. The other was on a horse alongside the two schoolboys.

"If we're goin'," Clemmie said, "let's be gettin' at it."

Rusty sensed that she would not need much persuasion to stay here and face Dawkins down with a shotgun. But the family was without menfolk now except for Purdy. In the short run she had to do what seemed best for her young ones. There would be time enough in the future to return and make a stand, to face the challenge of the land and Caleb Dawkins.

Clemmie shouted at the team, and Geneva flipped the reins to set the mules into motion. Rusty watched the two wagons set out on the dim trail southeastward. He rode back to where the boys waited. "We'll give them time, then fall in behind. No use in them havin' to breathe the dust these horses raise."

One of the boys pointed. "We've got company yonder."

He saw a man on horseback and a man in a buggy. They made no move to approach but watched from afar. Though at the distance he could not see the faces, every instinct told Rusty the man in the buggy was Caleb Dawkins.

"Come to watch the Monahans leave," he said. "He probably feels like he drew four aces. But these folks'll be back, and we'll see who laughs loudest then."

CHAPTER

FIFTEEN

amiliar landmarks set Rusty's pulse to racing. He came to a place where he and Mike Shannon had camped once while searching for unused grazing land during a dry year much like this one. He imagined he could hear his foster father's voice telling him about the Mexican War, well-remembered old stories Rusty had heard before and wished now he could hear again.

Vince Purdy pulled his wagon up close. "Kind of early to be campin'."

"Just studyin' about better times. We'll travel a little farther before sundown."

Thoughts of Daddy Mike led him to Isaac York and the terrible day Mike was shot. Stationed far from home, away from the familiar places that triggered old memories, Rusty had managed most of the time to relegate the past to a far-back corner of his mind. Now as he returned to the land he knew so well, the memories came in a rush, resurrecting an old bitterness he had not managed to overcome.

He hoped he would not encounter Isaac York. He would stay no longer than was necessary to get the Monahan family placed. He would avoid the settlement, where he was most likely to see York. On no account would he go near the York farm for fear of arousing an impulse he might not be able to control.

His heart quickened at sight of the Shannon cabin. From afar it looked just as he had left it. Then he noticed smoke curling from the chimney. That struck him odd. He allowed himself a moment of fantasy that he would find Mother Dora there, cooking supper. He knew better, but the image brought him an inner glow before cold reality dashed it.

Preacher Webb had promised to look in on the farm once in a while to be sure the roof had not fallen. Perhaps he was there now. Rusty motioned to Geneva, who drove the lead wagon, her mother sitting beside her. "That's the place. Just pull up to the dog run so we can unload."

He rode beside the wagon until Geneva stopped the team, then dismounted and reached to help Clemmie down from the high seat. Setting her feet on the ground, she fell against him, weary and barely able to stand. Days of slow travel had put deep lines in her face and dark circles under her eyes. The trip had aggravated the wound in her side. It was good that she would finally be able to get some rest.

He watched her survey the cabin and tried to read what was in her eyes. He realized this was not an adequate substitute for the home she had lost. She said, "The place is goin' to need a right smart of cleanin' up."

Trash had accumulated and weeds had grown around the cabin, something Mother Dora would not have tolerated. The woodpile out back was too small for winter. Maybe he could talk the two schoolboys into staying an extra few days to replenish it.

He apologized. "It won't be what you've been used to, but the roof doesn't leak. At least, it didn't when I left. Come on in. Let's see who's here."

He stopped in mid-stride as a man slouched out of the kitchen and onto the dog run.

Fowler Gaskin!

Surprise left Rusty momentarily speechless. Gaskin looked as if he might have stolen his clothes from a scarecrow in a field. His dirty underwear showed through holes in the elbows of his shirt. A piece of twine served in lieu of a belt to hold his ragged trousers in place. His face had not felt a razor in ages, and his beard was stained with tobacco.

Rusty got over his surprise enough to ask, "What the hell are you doin' here?"

"I been livin' here." Fowler's questioning gaze roamed over Clemmie and Geneva and the youngsters. Rusty saw apprehension in the rheumy eyes.

"I never gave you leave . . ." Rusty broke off, for Gaskin knew very well that he was trespassing. It was useless to tell him so.

Gaskin said, "You wasn't here, and I didn't know but what you might never come back. Fightin' Indians can get a man killed."

"But you've got your own place."

"We had a storm last spring. Taken off some of my roof. I had to have a place to live."

"You could fix the roof, you and your boys."

Eph and Luke were about as shiftless as their father, but at the least they ought to be able to repair a damaged roof and keep the rain off their heads, Rusty thought.

Gaskin said, "My boys are both gone off to the army. Fightin' for Texas and the Confederacy."

That did not sound like the Gaskin boys Rusty had known, but maybe the war had given them an unexpected sense of responsibility. More likely the conscription officers had come and taken them away whether they wanted to go or not.

Gaskin added, "My old woman died, and daughter Florey run off and got herself married. I been havin' to do everything for myself. It's hard, boy, awful hard."

For someone else, Rusty would have felt compassion. But Gaskin had never done much for himself and had done nothing for anybody else, so far as Rusty knew. "You'll have to gather up your stuff and move. These folks lost their home, and I've brought them here to live 'til they can do better."

Gaskin had the cowering look of a dog just given a whipping. "I don't know where I can go. My old house ain't fit to live in."

"You can find somebody to help you fix the roof. Doesn't look like it's rained around here lately or is fixin' to any time soon."

Gaskin hunched, his voice trailing into a whine. "I'd hoped you'd turn out better, but you're just like your old daddy was. He never had no pity on the poor and helpless. I'll bet Saint Peter gave him a cussin' when he got to the gates."

Rusty had tried to summon tolerance, but it evaporated. "I said go, Fowler."

"I'll have to fetch my team. They're down by the creek."

"Then do it. I'll pile what's yours out here on the dog run."

The old man mumbled to himself as he hobbled off in the direction of the creek where two mules grazed. Rusty realized he had not seen any Shannon cattle on the way in. There should have been some. He would not be surprised to learn that Gaskin had driven them off somewhere and sold them for whatever little he could get.

Geneva helped her mother into the cabin. She turned back at the door. "We wouldn't want that old man put out in the cold on our account."

"You don't need to feel sorry for the likes of Fowler Gaskin. If he could be sold for his true worth, he wouldn't fetch six bits."

The kitchen was a mess. Rusty could well believe that Gaskin had lived here for months. It would have taken that long to accumulate so much grease and filfth. Mother Dora would be appalled if she could see what had become of her home. "I'm sorry," he said. "I had no idea the place would need so much cleanin' up."

He smelled something simmering on the stove. Squirrel stew. For a moment he felt hungry, but he quickly recovered, remembering how dirty Gaskin's hands had been. When Fowler Gaskin died, it would not be of food poisoning; he must be immune to that or he would already have gone to his reward. Rusty removed the stew from the stove and carried it out onto the dog run. "You don't want to eat that. It'd kill anybody but a Gaskin."

He crossed over the dog run and into the bedroom side. The blankets had a rank odor. Evidently they had not been washed or sunned since Gaskin had been here. Rusty rolled them and dumped them outside, along with a suit of Gaskin's clothes he found draped across a chair. Wherever they had been worn, he assumed it had not been to church.

He propped open the one window to let the chill wind draw through. He returned to the kitchen and told the women, "I'm afraid you may have to sleep outdoors another night or two. It'll take awhile to give this place a decent airin'."

He walked to the barn as Gaskin drove the mules into a pen. Gaskin brought out a set of harness. Rusty stopped him as he started to put it on the first mule. "Wait a minute. That looks like mine." He examined the harness and saw he was right. He carried it back into the barn and found an old, badly patched set he did not recognize. "That'd be yours."

Gaskin grumbled but made the change. Rusty did not want to help him harness up, but he was so tired that as he watched the old man fumble around, his patience quickly wore through. He finished the job himself and hitched the mules to Gaskin's old wagon to hasten his neighbor's departure. He watched closely to see that Gaskin did not carry off more than he had brought with him. He allowed the blankets to go, though he recognized some as having belonged to Mike and Dora. He would never want to use them. They would forever carry Gaskin's scent, in Rusty's imagination if not in reality.

Leaving, Gaskin hollered back over his shoulder. "I hope you wind up in hell someday, because that's the only place you'll find any friends."

Rusty grunted, "It'd be my luck to find him there ahead of me. Then I'd know for sure that it *was* hell."

Geneva studied him critically. "You don't seem to have much patience for a poor old man down on his luck."

"I've got all the patience in the world for folks who have a run of bad luck that isn't their fault. Like you-all. But Fowler Gaskin? He's too lazy to scratch when he itches."

After supper he started up the hill toward the oak grove that shaded the small family cemetery. Geneva stepped from the dog run. "A little late to start out huntin'."

"I'm not. I'm goin' up yonder to pay my respects to the folks."

"Mind if I walk along with you?"

Rusty was pleased at the prospect of her company. "You sure Clemmie's all right?"

"She's takin' her rest." Geneva walked out to join him, and they started up the long slope. He took her arm to give her support on the steepest part of the climb. He liked touching her.

She said, "I'm sorry I never got to meet your mother and father."

"So am I. You'd've liked them, and they'd've liked you." It was on the edge of his tongue to add, *They'd've been tickled to have you join the family*. But that would be premature. He had not seriously toyed with the idea of asking her, and he probably would not until the uncertainties of the war were behind them. There was no way to know what calamities might be thrust upon them without any doing of their own. People had little control over their own destinies in such a time.

Rusty had already told Geneva something of Mike and Dora. She watched him pull weeds from around the markers. Someone had put a carved stone over Mike's grave, fairly well matching Dora's. Preacher Webb's doing, most likely, or perhaps Tom Blessing's. He would remember to thank them.

She said, "Your father died because of his beliefs, like mine."

"A lot of people are doin' that these days. Seems like there ought to be a better way—more talkin' and less fightin'."

"That's easy to say, but would you be content just to talk to whoever killed your father?"

Old anger arose in him. "No, I guess not. I still want to kill him. I suppose that makes me a hypocrite."

"It just shows you're human. I have the same feelin's toward Caleb Dawkins, but I know I'll never kill him. Somebody else may, but I won't. And if you try hard enough, you can get past the notion of killin' the man who shot your father."

"It'll take a lot of tryin'."

He did not want to delay his return to the ranger camp longer than necessary, but he disliked leaving the Monahans such a mess to clean up for themselves. He decided a couple more days should do no harm, considering how much time he had already lost in recuperation and in the trip here. Few Indian incursions had been discovered in recent weeks. He persuaded the two boys to stay, too. They could ride back together when they had the Shannon place in better shape, the woodpile replenished, and Rusty's cattle accounted for.

It was the latter task that brought him suddenly and unexpectedly face-to-face with Isaac York. He had hoped to avoid any such meeting. But after a wide sweep failed to turn up half as many cattle as he thought should be there, he decided to ride over to Tom Blessing's place and ask if Blessing knew anything about them. He had yearned to see at least a few old friends anyway, and Blessing was at the top of his list along with Preacher Webb.

Riding up to the Blessing cabin, he saw a face he knew well, the black man Shanty. Isaac York's slave sat on a bench beside the door, soaking up the winter sunshine. Rusty reined to a stop and considered turning back. But stubbornness demanded that he not retreat. He tied his reins to a post.

Shanty stood up, his face troubled. "Mr. Rusty. You back to stay?"

"Just another day or two. Came to see Tom Blessing."

Shanty jerked his head toward the door. "He's gone someplace. Mr. Isaac's inside, waitin' for him. You ain't come for trouble with Mr. Isaac, I hope."

"Didn't know he was here 'til I saw you. I wouldn't have come if I'd known."

"I've told you before, it wasn't Mr. Isaac killed your daddy."

The old man's honest eyes told Rusty that he believed what he was saying. But Shanty was a slave, and it was unlikely York would have told him anything that might later incriminate him. "I didn't come for trouble, and there won't be any unless he starts it."

"He won't start nothin'. Mr. Isaac's a sick man. He looks different than the last time you seen him."

The door opened, and Isaac York stepped outside. "Tom," he said, then stopped, dumbfounded at the sight of Rusty. "Heard talk and thought Tom had come back." He stood awkwardly, one foot on the step, one on the ground. He made no move to extend his hand, nor did Rusty.

Rusty felt paralyzed. It had not entered his mind that he might find York here.

Though Shanty had warned him, he was surprised by York's gaunt, pallid look. The man appeared to have shrunk. His eyes seemed sunk back into his head and surrounded by darkness.

Looks like the whiskey is finally about to get him, Rusty thought. But he sensed that the problem was deeper than simply drink. *Maybe his conscience is grinding him down.*

York appeared frozen in place. "I ain't armed."

Rusty's rifle was on his saddle. "I'm not either. This is Tom Blessing's farm. I've got no wish to bloody his ground."

York eased a bit. "I never did want a fight with you. What happened to your daddy, that wasn't none of my doin'."

Rusty did not believe him, but he was determined to let the matter rest for now. Someday when the time was right he would call for an accounting, if nature did not beat him to it. York's look indicated that he might not be long for this world.

"Tell Tom I came by. He'll understand why I didn't stay."

He swung into the saddle. He felt the rifle beneath his leg. It would be easy to draw it from the scabbard and shoot Isaac York where he stood. He had to struggle to keep himself from reaching down. But York was not armed. Killing him under these circumstances would be murder, as brutal as the murder of Mike Shannon.

Another time, then. Another place. He turned Alamo around and rode away. He would not allow himself to look behind him, though his back itched with anxiety. It would be easy for York to step into the cabin and fetch out one of Tom Blessing's rifles, to shoot Rusty from behind as Daddy Mike had been shot. To turn and look would be to admit fear, and that he would not do, not for the miserable likes of Isaac York.

He felt a rising of confidence after he had ridden two hundred yards and strong faith after three. York was not going to shoot him. He wondered why.

A mile from Blessing's cabin he saw a wagon coming toward him, Tom Blessing's familiar figure perched on the seat. By this time Rusty's pulse had slowed back to normal. He raised his hand in greeting. Blessing sawed on the reins and stopped the wagon. A huge smile spread across his face.

"Rusty Shannon. Didn't know you were anywhere around."

Rusty shook with him. Blessing's big hands were strong enough to crush rock, and Rusty feared for a moment that his bones were going to break. "Just a few days. Brought some folks to stay on my place 'til the war foolishness slows down."

"You been to my house? Sorry I wasn't there. Been to the settlement to get some supplies to carry my wife 'til I get back from my trip."

"Trip? To where?"

"Up north of here, town of Jacksboro. I've been workin' for the Confederate army, buyin' horses. Supposed to meet some dealers up there the first of next week." He made a circular motion with his hand. "How about turnin' around and goin' back to the cabin with me? Wife'll fix dinner."

"I'd better not. I found Isaac York there."

Blessing's smile died a sudden death. "Rusty, I hope you didn't . . ."

"No, I didn't. Not that I didn't study on it some. Hard as it was, I left him be. For now."

"I'm glad. Lord willin', you've got a long life ahead of you. You wouldn't want to do somethin' foolish and ruin it."

"I don't see that it's foolish to want to even up the score for Daddy Mike."

"You think another killin' would make the pain go away? It'd just make you hurt different, and worse. I've killed men because I had to, and it hurts when I think about it. It'd hurt more if I knew I hadn't had to."

Rusty had talked all he wanted to about Isaac York, for even hearing or speaking the name made him sick to his stomach. He changed the subject. "I can't find near all the cattle I ought to have. You know anything about them?"

"Can't say I do, exactly, but I've got suspicions. I think Fowler Gaskin and his boys helped themselves 'til the conscript men drug the boys off to the army."

"I didn't figure they went of their own accord."

"You never heard grown men bawl and carry on like them boys did, or cuss like the old man. He kept hollerin' 'til they was plumb across the county line. Said he'd starve to death without them boys of his to take care of him."

"He wasn't goin' to starve as long as one beef critter was left on my place. Did you know he'd taken up livin' in my cabin? I had to run him off so the folks I brought would have a place to stay."

"I told him several times he had no call to be over there, but he kept tellin' me it was only temporary. I'm sorry I didn't run him off myself, but I've been away a lot, workin' for the government."

"It's done now. Come over the first chance you get and meet the Monahan family. They're good folks." Briefly he told what had happened to the Monahan men.

Blessing sympathized. "Been a many a wrong done in the name of the war. Someday folks'll have to learn to put the wrongs aside and get on with livin'."

Rusty took that as a reference to his problem with Isaac York. "It'll be hard. I don't know if I can."

"You'll have to. Either that or go to the brush with blood on your hands. I don't think you've got it in you to turn outlaw. Mike Shannon taught you better than that."

"Daddy Mike was a fighter."

"So are you. And the toughest fight you face may be against yourself."

He brooded all the way home, arriving at dusk. He turned Alamo loose and walked into the kitchen, where Geneva was almost done preparing the family's meager supper. She smiled in relief. "I was afraid you wouldn't get back in time to eat with everybody else."

"I could smell your good cookin' for the last two miles. I wasn't goin' to miss it."

He tried to smile, but he could not quite make it convincing.

She sensed his uneasiness. "What's wrong?"

"I'd figured on stayin' a few days, but I can't. First thing in the mornin' I'm startin' back."

She stared at him, holding a skillet until the handle's heat forced her to set it down quickly. "But why?"

"If I stay here I'm liable to kill a man."

"That fellow York?"

"I saw him today."

"But you didn't kill him."

"Not this time. But next time I might. It's best I don't take the chance."

She made a step toward him. "I was hopin' . . ." She broke off as her two younger sisters entered the kitchen. They left when they saw that supper was not quite ready. "What you need is time."

"I've been gone more than a year. Thought I'd put the worst of it behind me. But I saw him, and it all came back strong as ever."

"This is your home. You can't stay away forever."

"If I killed him, I'd have to. This way I'm just leavin' a few days quicker than I figured on. A few days don't make a lot of difference."

He saw a tear in her eye before she blinked it away. She said, "Everything is so uncertain in these times. A few days might be all we have."

She came into his arms. Old Vince Purdy walked in, stopped in surprise, then quietly withdrew.

Embarrassed, Geneva asked, "What do you suppose he's thinkin'?"

"The same as I am, I reckon. That it's high time I get myself back to Belknap."

He expected a stern lecture from Captain Whitfield about his having stayed away longer than planned, but the officer seemed glad to see him. He mentioned that he had lost a couple more men who decided to join the Confederate army, and only one replacement had as yet shown up.

"How we're expected to hold this line, I don't know," Whitfield said. "If the Comanches and Kiowas ever take it in their heads to come across in numbers like on the Linnville raid, there's no tellin' how far they might go. There have been rumors about Kansas Jayhawkers up in the territory, agitatin' for them to do just that."

Rusty had been hearing rumors about Jayhawkers and union activists ever since the war had started, and nothing of the kind had ever come to pass. The people who started such rumors were doing about as much to demoralize the frontier as the Comanches could.

He said, "The Indians don't need anybody from outside to agitate them. They've got reasons enough of their own." He thought especially of the Tonkawas, exiled in the midst of their enemies after long and helpful service to Texas.

Whitfield asked, "You hear any talk about horse thieves down where you went?"

"Didn't talk to many people, but Indians haven't penetrated that far in a good while."

"I'm not talkin' Indians. At least, I don't think so. Seems like there's been a mild epidemic around the settlements over east, horses turnin' up missin'. Most people blame Indians, but we haven't found that much Indian sign."

Rusty remembered that somebody had run off a number of the Monahan horses the night the Monahan house had been burned. And Caleb Dawkins had complained about missing horses after James Monahan's retaliatory raid, though Rusty was sure James had not taken them.

Whitfield said, "The army's buyin' all the horses it can get and not askin' many questions. It's not likely it's buyin' any of them from Indians. As I see it, it's white men doin' the stealin'."

"Anybody in particular?"

"There are some people around Belknap I wouldn't trust with a blind mule. Or else it's some of the renegades in the brush, waitin' out the war. They're a mix of conscript dodgers and wanted men."

Rusty wondered if he was thinking of James. "Even if they snuck into the settlements and did the stealin', those men from the brush couldn't afford to be seen. Somebody would have to help them sell the horses to the army."

"That is the way I figure."

Rusty remembered what Tom Blessing had said when Rusty met him driving his wagon. "I've got a friend back home buyin' horses for the government. He told me he's fixin' to meet some horse dealers up thisaway."

Whitfield's interest quickened. "Did he say where?"

"Town of Jacksboro." Rusty's trips along the frontier line had never taken him quite as far as Jacksboro, but he knew in a general way where it was.

Whitfield's big moustache made several contortions while he thought over the situation. "Might be interestin' if we just happened to be passin' through when those horses come in."

Defensively Rusty said, "Tom Blessing is as honest as anybody you ever met."

"Blessing? I remember that name. Seems like I even rode with him a time or two."

"He used to be a friend of old Captain Burmeister. He wouldn't be a party to horse stealin'."

"Not intentionally, but if he lives way down on the Colorado River he probably doesn't know the people at Jacksboro, or around here either. He has to take them at their word."

"For that matter, *I* don't know anybody over there."

"But I do. They've had a right smart of Indian trouble since Jacksboro got started. Nobody's apt to get suspicious if we make a *pasear* over that way lookin' for fresh Indian sign."

Whitfield took Rusty, Tanner, and the Morris brothers. They set up camp west of Jacksboro, a small farming and stock-raising town of modest log and lumber houses, hard hit in the past by Indian raids and surviving hard times on the most tenuous basis. From afar, the rangers watched Tom Blessing arrive on the second day with his wagon, a saddle horse tied behind. He raised his tent beside a set of log corrals.

Rusty said, "I'd like to go and say howdy. I've known him as far back as I can remember."

Whitfield shook his head. "I don't doubt your friend's honesty, but he might say somethin' to flush our quail. Last thing we want to do is to attract undue attention. We're out here lookin' for Indians, remember?"

The following day Rusty saw a cloud of dust. Lack of rain had left the grass short, the surface dry. Anywhere an animal walked, it left a tiny dust trail slow to settle behind it. The size of this cloud indicated many animals. He limped to the captain's tent to let Whitfield know, but the officer had already seen. He held a spyglass to his eye and focused it.

"Looks like twenty horses, give or take a few." He folded the glass, a transient smile lifting his moustache. He was not given to smiling often. "We'll wait 'til they get them penned, then mosey down for a look."

The captain seemed cool and calm. Rusty was not. Whitfield moved slowly and deliberately, as if he had all day. Rusty felt his stomach tightening with tension. Whitfield admonished him, "Never get in a hurry when you don't have to. A man in too big a hurry makes mistakes he can't afford. Let the other man be the one who makes mistakes."

The volunteers had their mounts saddled and were sitting on them, waiting, when Whitfield finally got ready. He nodded. "Leave us go and look at some horses."

Their approach went unnoticed until they had almost reached the corral. Tom Blessing had his back turned. He was examining a gray horse's teeth and asking about the animal's age. When the man beside him answered, Tom said, "His teeth tell it different. He's a sight older than that."

Tanner's horse took a notion to neigh at those in the corral. Blessing turned, eyes widening in surprise, then smiling as he recognized Rusty. "Rusty Shannon, you're about the last man I expected to see here so far from home."

The man beside him turned. Rusty recognized Pete Dawkins and somehow felt no surprise. Dawkins's face fell as his gaze swept over the rangers. Nearby, a rope in his hand, stood another man Rusty was sure had been with Pete the day they were trying to escape with the stolen Tonkawa horses.

Rusty said, "Howdy, Tom." He left it to Whitfield to advance the conversation.

Whitfield looked straight at Pete. "You are Colonel Dawkins's son, aren't you?"

Pete's only answer was an affirmative nod. He had the look of a coyote with his foot caught in a trap.

"I would assume these are some of the colonel's horses you've brought to sell?" A few bore the Dawkins brand.

Pete managed a weak "Yeah, part of them. Bought the rest from farmers around."

"I assume you have bills of sale."

Pete looked toward his horse. The man with the rope began walking toward the fence where his and Pete's mounts were tied outside. Pete said, "Got the papers in my saddlebag. I'll fetch them for you."

He climbed over the fence near his horse. Rusty heard him say something to his companion. Quickly they jerked their reins loose and swung into the saddle. They spurred the horses into a dust-raising hard run on the wagon road that ran through Jacksboro.

Tanner drew his rifle and aimed. Whitfield said, "Don't shoot. You might hit some innocent person in town."

Tanner lowered the rifle. "From what I've heard, there ain't no innocent people in this town."

"A few. Let's give them the benefit of the doubt."

"Them boys are gettin' away."

"I think we all know where they're goin'."

Tom Blessing stood gaping. "I'm just guessin', but I'd have to figure the government won't be gettin' these horses."

Whitfield said, "Not unless the government encourages horse thieves. Johnny Morris, you stay here and take charge of these animals. The rest of you, follow me."

Rusty told Blessing, "Sorry to bust up your trade."

"You-all may need a witness. I'll saddle up and go with you."

Whitfield did not have to say where they were going. Rusty knew long before he saw the big house where Colonel Dawkins lived. Several of the Dawkins farmhands stood silently watching the rangers ride into the yard.

Rusty studied one face after another, uneasy. One order from Caleb Dawkins and none of the rangers might leave here alive.

Whitfield asked an elderly black man, "Is the colonel at home?"

"Yes sir, up at his house."

Whitfield stopped and studied the house before he dismounted. "Shannon, you come with me. Tanner, Morris, Mr. Blessing, you-all stand watch out here. You may have to cover our leavin' if things don't go well."

Rusty had a pistol on his hip, but he had always trusted the rifle more. He drew it and walked to the captain's side. They ascended the few steps up to the long veranda.

A man stood just inside the doorway that led into a hall. Caleb Dawkins, who had always looked seven feet tall, seemed smaller than Rusty remembered him. His broad shoulders sagged. His face appeared the gray of riverbank mud, his eyes dull and dispirited. His voice lacked the deep resonance Rusty remembered. "Come in, Captain. The men you seek are here."

Pete Dawkins and the other man who had fled Jacksboro sat in straight chairs in the parlor. They looked as if they had been whipped. A middle-aged woman stood beside Pete and wept.

The colonel said gruffly, "Amity, you'd best leave the room."

She cried, "You can't do this to our son."

"Our son has done it to himself. You'd best go and let me talk to the captain."

The woman left the room in tears.

Pete pleaded, "Papa, please . . ."

The colonel rubbed the knuckles of his left hand as if arthritis was biting him. Gravely he said, "Pete asked me to help him get away. He told me what he'd done, he and Scully here, and some of those renegades out in the brush. They stole from others, and they stole from me." He turned on his son with a flash of anger. "For this, I've kept you out of the army." The anger left him quickly, and a deep sadness came over him again. "I have had men hung for less than what he has done. He's my son. I can't have him hung. But I can turn him over to you and let the law take its course."

Whitfield gave the two culprits a long study. "I can't say what a court might do. Stealin' horses is a penitentiary offense."

Dawkins looked at the floor. "No Dawkins has ever gone to the pen. We've always gone the last mile to uphold the law. The thought of a son of mine in that place . . ." His voice trembled.

Rusty had never thought he could feel sorry for a man like Dawkins, and he resisted it now. But a touch of sympathy came unbidden. He had a hard time putting it down.

The captain said, "I might suggest one thing. I can take him into custody and turn him over to the conscript officers. He'd do his country more good in the army than in the pen."

Dawkins walked to the window and looked out into the yard, nervously flexing his big hands behind his back. When he turned, his mind was made up. "Son, you've shamed us. You've brought dishonor on the Dawkins family name. The army might give you a chance to redeem yourself."

Pete protested, "Papa, a man can get killed in the army."

"He can get himself hung for a horse thief on the outside. So you'll go and serve your country. You too, Scully. The army'll make men of you, or it'll kill you." He walked to the door through which his wife had gone. He turned. "They're yours, Captain. Take them."

He disappeared into the hallway. Rusty heard a door slam behind him.

Captain Whitfield motioned for Pete and Scully to stand up. "You boys are under arrest. Try to run again and we'll shoot you."

Pete looked toward the door where his father had disappeared. He opened his mouth as if to shout something, then changed his mind and hung his head. "We won't run. Next time he'd hang us himself. He told us so."

Whitfield looked back toward the house as they rode across the yard. "Shannon, if you know some way to get word to James Monahan, tell him there's no use tryin' anymore to kill Caleb Dawkins. Pete has already done that."

"Colonel still looked alive the last we saw him."

"Walkin', breathin', sure. But this has hurt him worse than any bullet ever could. It'll eat on him like a cancer. It'll kill his soul."

In a peculiar way, Rusty felt that the Monahans had been avenged.

CHAPTER

SIXTEEN

HIGH PLAINS COMANCHE ENCAMPMENT, 1863

Buffalo Caller fidgeted in a vain attempt to find comfort. He had sat in the council circle so long that his arthritic joints had stiffened and were beginning to ache. A horse had stumbled and rolled over him during a buffalo hunt last fall, leaving him with chronic pains he had never felt before. If this interminable discussion ever ended, he would probably have to ask someone to help him to his feet. That was embarrassing to a man who in his prime had led ambitious raids far down into the Texas settlements and deep into Mexico. Once his war party had ridden so far that the horsemen from the open plains penetrated the edge of dark, humid forests and marveled at the excited chatter of funny-faced little people perched high up in the limbs.

Now the council was considering Buffalo Caller's proposal for an invasion on a scale not seen since the great raid that had carried him and so many others all the way to the big water, chasing terrified whites out into the surf. He was ready to do it again. It was high time that the land-hungry Texans felt once more the full fury of The People, that the blood cry of Comanche warriors rang in their ears at the moment of their deaths.

He had sensed from the first that the council did not share his enthusiasm for a massive strike. He could not understand the reluctance. He argued that the timing was perfect. Many reports from south of the Eckhoft Pahehona, the Red River, indicated that the white men had become so hopelessly embroiled in their war against one another that their defenses at home had almost fallen apart. They had sent most of their fighting men away to some distant country to kill their own kind in awesome numbers.

The white man's foolish ways would forever be a mystery. But it seemed equally foolish for The People not to take advantage of them.

Buffalo Caller voiced a strong opinion that the Texans were vulnerable enough now to be pushed back from all the lands The People claimed for their own. He was convinced that the spirits were moving to bring this about. How else could one account for the white men's destructive war against each other unless it had been willed by the spirits? How else could one explain the fact that the western line of Texan settlements was guarded only by a small and tattered group of men on horseback who had to range over long distances because they were so few and the land so large? Such a line should be easy to breach. With help of benevolent spirits, the destruction should be well under way and irreversible by the time Texan patrols discovered the signs of invasion.

Black Wing countered that several attempted penetrations of late had been discovered early and pushed back, some with painful loss of life. He felt that Buffalo Caller was much too optimistic. "You and I have both seen the Texans' settlements. Even with their war, the hair-faces have become thicker to the east of us than winter hair on the back of a horse."

Buffalo Caller argued, "There was a time we could have stopped them easily, but we waited. We thought the Mexicans would turn them back, or the land itself. But they continued to come. If we wait much longer, the white men's war will end and there will be twice as many of them. This is the time to be bold."

He used a pointed stick to draw a crude map in the sand. He indicated the course of the Colorado River, far south of the Red. "This is the Talking Water River. As a young man I hunted there. Many times since the Texans built their houses, I have gone and taken horses from them."

Black Wing knew. He had ridden along on a couple of the excursions and had acquitted himself with honor. He now owned many horses. But he cautioned, "Many more Texans live there now."

"And many more horses." Buffalo Caller hoped the appeal to greed would be persuasive if an appeal to patriotism was not. "The Texans to the south and east are not as ready as those to the north. They no longer expect us."

"But the searchers are out all the time. They will find our trail."

"Not if first we go far west, where they do not ride. Then we go far south before we turn and move into the Talking Water settlements."

"Are there not white men to the west?"

"Only a few. They are fugitives. Even if they see us, they cannot send warning. They hide from the white man's law."

Black Wing's frown told Buffalo Caller he was resistant to the whole notion. Black Wing was already rich enough in horses. And many of The People did not share Buffalo Caller's strong compulsion to drive the white man away. After all, most Comanches remained at large. Though they had lost homelands to the south, they still ranged in relative freedom across the high plains. Most had not allowed themselves to be gathered like cattle and confined to the reservation north of the Clay-Colored River, the way less resistant tribes had done, or the white men's pet dogs, the despised Tonkawas. The Comanches could still hunt buffalo unimpeded so long as they did not venture too far eastward into areas infested by the white men.

Buffalo Caller felt a sour letdown. Though the argument would go on and on, he already sensed that he would lose it. At least there was an alternative. Above all, a male Comanche was a free man, allowed to act on his own volition if the way of the others did not please him. If the council would not agree upon a huge raid, he could organize a smaller one of his own. He had always found young men ready to follow him. Seldom had they come home empty-handed. Sadly, it was true that the last time he had led warriors into the land of the Texans, he had had the misfortune of running unexpectedly into a ranging patrol. The warriors had been obliged to give up some of the horses they had taken and flee back across the river to sanctuary.

But that had not been his fault. One of the reckless young men had chased an owl from its perch and made it angry. Everyone knew that Mope the owl harbored dark spirits. The same ill luck could have happened to anyone burdened with unseasoned youngsters who did not respect the proprieties.

If he was obliged to make up his own raid, he would be careful in choosing those who went with him. He had felt compelled the last time to take some poorly seasoned men who wanted the glory without regard to the requirements.

The conversation and the wrangling went on around him, but mentally Buffalo Caller had already stood up and left. He shut out the sound of others' voices and kept counsel only with himself. Already he was visualizing the country he would cover, the circuitous western route by which he would make his way down to the Colorado River settlements with the least chance of discovery. He knew the farms where he had found horses and mules before and where he would likely find them again. But this time he would do more than simply take the white men's animals. He would make a concerted effort to take as many of their scalps as possible. Those he did not kill, he would leave frightened for their lives. The survivors would be glad to gather their families and leave the land that had been Comanchería since the time of his grandfathers' fathers.

He itched for the council to finish its deliberations, for he had preparations of his own to make. He would need, among other things, to repeat the vision quest ritual he had undertaken as a young man first seeking his guardian spirits. He would ask those spirits for a renewal of the power he had known in his youth, that he might bring down The People's full wrath upon the Texans. Granted that power, he and others would regain the land that was the Comanches' own by every right a warrior held sacred.

Unbidden, a loud war cry escaped him. He looked around quickly and saw that the rest of the council was as startled as he was. Everyone looked at him.

He was sure one of the warrior spirits had spoken through his voice. "The signs are good," he said. "Many enemies will fall."

Often in the past he had sought a vision, and usually one had come to him if he prepared himself properly to receive it. He entered the hide-covered sweat lodge naked and poured water on heated stones to force the impurities from his body, then cleansed himself in the river. His son Steals the Ponies rode beside him to the hill chosen for the vigil so he could take Buffalo Caller's horse back to the encampment.

Formerly known as Jackrabbit, his son had earned a new name after leading several young men in stealing army horses right out of the military corrals one moonlit night last fall. They had not so much as awakened a sentry. Any father would have cause for pride in such a bold stealer of the soldiers' mounts.

"Come for me in four days," Buffalo Caller said. "If the vision appears earlier, I can walk back."

He waited until his son had passed from sight, then unrolled the buffalo robe he had brought and spread it carefully on the ground. He built a small fire and lighted his pipe, blowing the smoke in each of the four principal directions, then down toward the earth and up toward the sky. He would not eat or drink until he saw a vision that would guide him. Often it came on the fourth day or night, for four was a number that held much power.

Four days was a long time, but Buffalo Caller could wait. Infinite patience was one attribute of a good warrior.

Several times recently a disturbing dream had visited him. It was an old dream, actually. He had first experienced it after the great raid on the coast, when for a short time he had held the captive boy with red hair. In the dream he had seen his old friend Antelope, warning him that the red-hair was an ill omen, that the boy should be killed before he could bring evil upon The People. But Antelope had already been dead when the dreams had begun; the Texans had regained the red-haired boy. The dreams had eventually become less frequent, though he had never quite put them out of his mind. It seemed to him, when he allowed himself to dwell on it, that the spirits were saying Antelope had been right.

It was probably true enough that red hair was a bad omen, because Antelope, a fearsome warrior, had died trying to kill the boy who possessed it. To Buffalo Caller this meant that red hair had great power. The spirits were telling him to beware of anyone whose hair was red.

Fortunately there seemed to be few red-hairs among the Texans. The rest were fair game.

Fasting was little hardship for Buffalo Caller. He had done it many times on the war trail and in quest of a vision. The discomfort was small compared to the satisfaction of a victory or being visited by a dream of good portent. The first night he slept well. His dreams were an empty succession of meaningless images. He was not disappointed. He did not expect a real vision the first night or the second. Usually they did not come to him until the body had advanced beyond the distracting sensations of hunger and thirst and the mind was open to whatever message the spirits wished to deliver.

By the close of the third day his vision was blurring because of self-imposed deprivations. He considered this good. Unimportant details faded, and he could better see the intentions of the spirits, better hear their voices above the whisper of prairie wind through the dry grass.

He was not aware of dropping off to sleep. It was as if he drifted without effort from the conscious world to one in which dreams became reality. He saw around him a great mass of warriors and more horses than there were buffalo on the plains. He saw the white man's houses and felt the ground tremble as the invaders mounted a charge upon them. He saw the warriors' mouths open wide as they raised their voices in a grand cry for victory, yet there was no sound, only silence, only feeling.

It was a wondrous thing, but puzzling.

He saw himself on the ground and saw the Texan horsemen rushing down upon him, swarming like angry bees. But most passed on, disappearing into a haze. Only one remained. Buffalo Caller realized with a start that though this was a grown man, he had the face of the boy once captured, then lost. And his hair was red like blood.

Buffalo Caller awakened to a loud shout and realized the voice was his own. He was cold, yet sweating. He looked around him but saw little in the darkness except the sparkling of the stars above and a moon round and white and bright. He gathered the robe over his shoulders to stop his trembling. He wanted to grasp the dream and hold it in his hands for study to determine what it was meant to tell him. But dreams are elusive, and the details faded before his eyes. He could hold the essence of this one: the fall, the red-haired Texan, a sense of emptiness.

He poked at the remnant of his fire, adding a few dry sticks to coax the flames, then building the blaze with larger pieces of wood. He sat hunched in the robe, staring into the flames, trying to decide what the spirits had told him. They did not always speak clearly.

He had much to ponder.

Buffalo Caller wished he had not seen the horses. The discovery threatened a premature breakup of a carefully planned expedition.

He had led his group of twenty warriors, mostly young and eager for plunder, far to the west before dropping southeastward toward the Colorado River settlements. He counted on being able to make a deep penetration, as he had done several times in the past, before his band attracted attention.

Now, from the cover of timber along the river, he peered out onto a rolling prairie where the horses were scattered, grazing. They were an inviting target. Too inviting.

Tall Eagle argued, "We have already come far. We are likely to be discovered soon, and we may be forced to turn back with hands empty. I say we should take these horses and be content."

Buffalo Caller struggled to control his temper. Only a poor leader had to shout and harangue his followers. "We agreed before we came. We would not strike a blow until we are deep in the Texan country. As we go out we will leave a trail of fire. Those who survive will run like rabbits and our land will be rid of them."

The warriors had departed the encampment days ago fired with enthusiasm, but now he was disappointed to see how easily the young men could become distracted from the larger goal by discovery of a lesser prize. He had seen wolves snarl and fight over the right to one buffalo calf when there were many more close by, easy to bring down.

"We know where these horses are," he said. "They will still be here when we return. Be patient, for there are many more horses farther on. We can have those and these as well."

He feared some of the young men would follow Tall Eagle and spoil the grander plan, for they were not bound to follow Buffalo Caller should they at any time disagree with his leadership.

Tall Eagle pointed through the trees. "There stands a white man's house. You seem more interested in blood than in horses. We can take them by surprise and kill them all, then capture the horses."

Buffalo Caller remembered this log house. He had picked up several horses and mules here once, adding them to a large band taken farther to the east. Now the chance of discovery had forced his warriors to stop riding in daylight, and they had taken cover along the edge of the river, waiting for darkness to hide them as they traveled. He had been studying the house awhile, trying to determine how many might be living there and how strong their defense might be. So far he had seen only one man, and by the way he walked he was old. He had seen two women and two or three children. He thought it probable that the young men of the family were away to the big war.

"I say we go farther, because once we strike, there will be no more surprise. Everywhere else, they will gather and wait for us. The spirits have favored us so far, but if we are foolish they will turn away."

Tall Eagle acknowledged the logic but hated to pass by an easy prize for a larger yet chancier one. "You dream. The white men will never give up our lands. There are too many, and they keep coming. We can no more kill them all than the wolves can kill all the buffalo. But we can do like the wolves and feed from them. We can take their horses. We can even take their cattle and trade them to the Mexican Comancheros."

Buffalo Caller had never understood that defeatist sentiment. He had never doubted that The People could defeat the Texans if only they would steel their hearts and minds to accept the high cost of the fight. Nothing of value was gained without work and sacrifice.

Steals the Ponies said, "My father is right. Why be content with the hooves and tail when we can have the whole animal?"

Buffalo Caller turned, pride warming him. His son was not inclined to speak often, but when he spoke he showed he had inherited his father's wisdom.

Tall Eagle gave in reluctantly. "The next time we find many horses, we will take them and turn back."

The band remained in the timber, waiting for darkness to cover their movement. Shortly before dark, another white man arrived at the cabin. Several of the people inside came out to greet him. He and the old man led the new arrival's horse to the barn and turned him loose.

The young men were pleased, because this meant one more horse for the taking. Buffalo Caller was pleased because this was one more white man to die when the time came.

CHAPTER

SEVENTEEN

usty Shannon was brushing Alamo's back when he saw a rider approaching the ranger camp in a lope, his horse lathered with sweat.

Private Tanner was leading his own horse back from the water. He jerked his thumb over his shoulder. "Feller comin' yonder must be carryin' a powerful message. He's fixin' to kill his horse."

Rusty put the brush into a wooden box and squinted. Something about the rider looked vaguely familiar. "I do believe that's James Monahan. He wouldn't come out of hidin' without there's a strong reason for it."

Tanner stopped abruptly. "Monahan? Ain't he the one who . . ."

"That's him."

Rusty tied Alamo to a tree and sprinted toward the camp headquarters. "Captain Whitfield. Somebody comin'."

Whitfield stepped out of the open-fronted tent as James slid his horse to a stop and hit the ground trying to run, stumbling in fatigue. James's anxious gaze fell immediately upon the captain. "You the man in charge?"

"I am, sir. What is your business?"

"Indians. A sizable bunch of them, a good ways west of here and on their way south."

"You saw them yourself?"

"Sure as hell did, me and a preacher. He found their trail, real fresh, and we both followed it a ways 'til we almost ran up on them from behind."

"How many?"

"Twenty or so. Enough to do a right smart of mischief."

The captain appeared convinced, yet suspicious. "You say they were a long way west of here. There's very few people to the west of this place. What were you doin' out there?"

For the first time James spotted Rusty. He made a tiny nod of acknowledgment. "Tryin' to stay out of sight."

Rusty realized that Whitfield had not seen James before and had no reason to recognize him. He wished now he had not said anything to Tanner. Though the lanky ranger was a talkative sort, he could hold his silence when necessary. Rusty intended to tell him it was necessary.

The captain said, "Why would Indians ride so far west if they are on the warpath? There are no people out there for them to raid except maybe a few camps of deserters and renegades." His narrowed eyes made the implication clear.

"Me and the preacher, we figured they were tryin' to travel without bein' seen. They'd go south, maybe down as far as the Colorado, then cut east and hit the lower settlements."

"And where is this preacher?"

"He figured to circle around and get ahead of them, then warn the folks livin' in their way. I come to fetch you and your company."

Whitfield gave the order for most of the company to be ready to ride in twenty minutes, leaving only a skeleton guard. He told James, "We'll furnish you a fresh horse. You intend to come with us, don't you?"

"Damn betcha. I got folks somewhere down yonder."

Rusty threw his saddle on Alamo. Whitfield pointed out a horse for James, and Rusty caught him. As he transferred his saddle, James said quietly, "You could've given me away. How come you didn't?"

"Looks to me like he's pretty well figured you out as it is. He's got you pegged for a fugitive from the conscript, and maybe one of them renegade horse thieves in the brush to boot. The only thing he doesn't know is that you're the man who tried to kill Caleb Dawkins."

"You goin' to tell him?"

"I'll keep my mouth shut unless he asks me. But I won't lie to him." Rusty had not forgotten that James once contemplated killing him. "You took a big chance comin' here."

"Wasn't no choice. Preacher Webb knows how to find my family and warn them. I don't know where your farm is."

Rusty jerked his head, motioning for James to follow him to his tent. "We'll pick up some grub. It'll be a long, hard ride."

James explained, "Me and Preacher Webb been keepin' pretty close touch. He was on his way out to see me when he come upon that fresh Indian trail."

Rusty put some jerky, cold bread, and coffee beans into a cloth sack. "If it hadn't been for worryin' about your family, would you have come and told us about the Indians?"

"I don't know. I'd've had to think about it awhile."

That at least was an honest answer.

Rusty counted ten rangers, including himself, plus James, mounted and ready to ride. On Whitfield's command they set out in a trot. The temptation was strong to run the horses, but the animals would tire out and break down long before they reached the Colorado. At best it would be a hard two days' ride. The captain's strategy was to travel straight south. If James's theory was correct, that the Indians would turn eastward at some point, the rangers should intersect their trail without wasting extra miles.

Rusty suggested, "Captain, I can point you to my farm down there. Not many people live to the west of it."

"Then do so, if you please."

Much later they stopped in a stream to water the horses. The captain pulled up beside James. "I don't believe I heard your name."

"I don't see where that matters."

"I've been rememberin' a description I heard. Do you know a man named Caleb Dawkins?"

James flashed Rusty a look of resignation. "I do."

"I believe you are the James Monahan who attempted to kill him. Would I be guessin' close?"

James shrugged. "Close enough."

"I can't say that I criticize your motive. I do criticize your marksmanship."

"I was a little excited. Next time I'll try to keep my head."

"It's my job to see that there is no next time. Consider yourself under arrest."

"You're not sendin' me back now, are you?"

"I can't spare the men. Do you give me your word that you'll stay with us?"

"'Til we see about my folks and them Indians. After that, I ain't promisin' you nothin'.'"

"Fair enough. But understand this: afterward, if you try to run it'll be my job to stop you. Even if it takes a bullet in the back."

"Looks to me like we understand one another." James looked at Rusty. "Is that your feelin', too?"

Rusty had let him go once, though he had little choice. "Like I told you last time, I follow orders."

They rode in silence, trotting awhile, picking up into an easy lope for short stretches, then trotting again. The pace put miles behind them quickly, but not quickly enough to ease the persistent burning sensation where Rusty's rump met the saddle. He could not put aside a fear that they might be too late.

They rode far into the night and made a dry camp, resuming the march at first light. The second night Rusty guessed that they were near the river, though he could not be certain of the distance. Whitfield ordered a halt.

Rusty argued, "If we keep goin' we ought to strike the Colorado pretty soon."

"We may do it afoot if we don't rest these horses."

James declared, "While we're restin' there's no tellin' what may be happenin' to folks downriver."

"We can't help them if we can't get there, and we'll never get there on dead horses." But Whitfield eased a bit. "We'll let them breathe an hour or so, then we'll see."

The horses may have rested, but Rusty did not, nor did James. They paced back and forth until in exasperation Tanner said, "I wisht you boys'd set yourselves down awhile. You're makin' me tired just watchin' you."

James retorted, "You ain't got folks down there to be worryin' about." He glanced at Rusty. "For that matter, neither do you."

Rusty's mind had been dwelling on Geneva since they had begun the trip. "Maybe I do. Or will have someday."

Whitfield had been lying on his spread-out blanket. He arose and rolled it, tying it behind his saddle. He was irritatingly calm. "All right, boys, time to travel."

Rusty sighed in relief. James was already in the saddle while Rusty tightened the girth he had loosened so Alamo could breathe easier. Rusty took up his position to point the way, though it was not necessary. They had been moving as nearly due south as the terrain would allow.

In about an hour he came upon a wagon road, visible in the light of the full moon. It ran generally east and west. "I know this one. It follows the river."

Shortly he was on the riverbank. "There ought to be a farm on the other side, just a little ways up."

The cabin looked black against the moonlight, and Rusty feared it had been burned. Nearing it, however, he realized he had been fooled by the deep shadow. The cabin was intact. Motioning for the others to stay a safe distance behind, he put Alamo into a walk and carefully approached the house. He listened for sounds of life, but the place was silent as a tomb.

He wished he knew how he could shout quietly. The last thing he wanted to do was make a lot of noise. "Anybody home?" he called.

No one answered. He felt a chill, fearing the worst. Perhaps the Indians had already visited. If they had been here, they almost certainly had struck other farms to the east, including his own. He moved to the door, where he found a piece of paper held down by a bent nail. He could not read it in the shadow, so he tore it off and held it up to let the moon's light fall upon it.

It said, *Indian sign. Gone to Shannon place.*

He swung back into the saddle and carried the note to Whitfield, telling him what it said so the captain would not have to waste time trying to read it in the moonlight.

Whitfield grunted. "Then let's go to the Shannon place, too."

By the stars Rusty guessed it was midnight or a little later by the time they reached there. He agonized all the way, fearing that he would find the place in charred ruins, its occupants slaughtered. Somewhat to his surprise he found himself whispering a prayer. As he rode in, James close beside him, he saw that the cabin was dark but intact. A large number of horses were held in a corral.

The Indians had not struck here. Not yet, at least.

"Thank God," Rusty said in a husky voice.

James responded, "I thank Him, too. I sure as hell do."

A shot was fired from the far side of the corral. A sentry's warning, Rusty surmised.

"Hold on," he shouted. "We're comin' in."

He recognized the distant voice as Vince Purdy's. "Who's out there?"

"It's me, Rusty Shannon. With some rangers."

"Well, come on in, and welcome. We've been expectin' company, but not you."

Several men materialized from the shadows, carrying rifles. Rusty realized that several neighbors had come together for mutual protection. Purdy pumped Rusty's hand, then hugged his grandson. "Preacher Webb told us you'd rode for help. But it's liable to cost you, son."

Rusty said, "He came here under arrest. Where's the preacher?"

"He rode on to warn others. Said he was goin' to Tom Blessing's first so Tom could help him spread the word. He ain't been back, and we been worried about him. From the sign he showed us down on the river, there was a war party came by here a couple of nights ago. They could've taken us then. We wouldn't't've known they was around 'til they was on top of us."

"They were savin' you for their return trip."

"That's the way we see it. If it hadn't been for Preacher Webb, no tellin' what might've happened."

"It still could."

"But now they won't catch us by surprise. We're fixed to give them a dandy scrap."

James asked urgently, "Is everybody all right? Mama and them?"

"Your mama's made out of rawhide. That bullet slowed her down a little, but it was a long way from killin' her."

James turned back to the captain. "I'm goin' up to the house to see my folks. Any objections?"

Rusty said, "I'll go with him." He tried to make it sound as if he were volunteering out of a sense of duty.

"Go ahead. We'll set up camp at the corrals. There won't be any horses stolen out of here tonight."

Purdy went ahead to awaken the family. Clemmie and Geneva came out onto the dog run so quickly that Rusty doubted they had ever gone to bed. With the threat of a raid hanging over them, they probably could not sleep in any case. Clemmie clasped her son in her arms and wept.

"Preacher Webb said he'd fetch you down here when he could. We didn't figure on it bein' this way." She raised her gaze to Rusty. "You got him under arrest?"

"The captain has."

She said to James, "You could take your horse and lose yourself in the timber down by the river. You could be far gone by daylight."

"I'm ridin' a ranger horse, Mama, and he's plumb give out from the trip."

"There's plenty of fresh ones in the corral."

"And bunch of men there to see that I don't take any of them. No, I'm stayin' here 'til we know the Indian trouble is over with."

Geneva took Rusty's hand and eased him off the back side of the dog run, into the shadow. She leaned to him and kissed him. "I was hopin' you'd come. I've missed you."

"It hasn't been all that terrible long since I left here."

"I was already missin' you while I watched you ride away."

Tanner came along after a while. "Captain says he'd like to see you and James Monahan down at the corral. Says you belong with the rest of the company." He gave Geneva a moment's quiet study. "Sorry to pull him away."

She said, "We can sleep now, knowin' the rangers are here."

Tanner smiled. "I expect just one of them would've done, provided it was the right one."

As he started to leave, Rusty heard a groan of complaint coming from a dark shape lying beside the cabin. A querulous voice complained, "A body can't get no sleep around here, people talkin' loud all the time."

The voice was Fowler Gaskin's.

Purdy walked with James and Rusty and Tanner. He said, "Fowler was the first one to come here after word got out about the Indians. He was scared to stay by himself down yonder in his cabin."

Rusty warned, "He won't leave 'til you run him off with a club."

"You've got to feel sorry for him. Word came a few days ago that both of his boys been killed."

"Eph and Luke? I never thought the army could get them that close to the fightin'."

Purdy looked back to be sure no one else could hear. "They told the old man the boys died in battle, but Tom Blessing whispered in my ear that it wasn't that way atall. They got in a fight over two French women in a New Orleans fancy house. That was the nearest them boys ever come to a battlefield."

Daylight brought a sense of relief, for there had been no sign of Indians. Though it was generally believed they did not like to fight at night, that was their favorite time for stealing horses, protected by darkness. Rusty saddled Alamo and made a circle around the corrals and down to the river. He saw no fresh tracks that would indicate passage by the raiding party. Unless they had decided to give the farm a wide berth, they were still somewhere downriver.

Captain Whitfield gave the men time for a quick breakfast before announcing, "I'll leave a few men here to help guard this place. The rest of us will move east and see if we can intercept the hostiles." He sought out Rusty. "I'll take you with me, Shannon. And your prisoner, too." He nodded toward James. "I want to keep him in sight."

"*My* prisoner?"

"You lost him once. He's your responsibility."

James did not change expression. He spoke softly, so that only Rusty could hear him. "You goin' to shoot me if I take and run?"

"I guess I'll have to decide about that when the time comes."

"My sister wouldn't take it kindly."

Rusty suspected James was trying to determine the depth of his feelings for Geneva. If he took a notion to run, he would have to count on their being strong. In a sense James was using his sister. That irritated Rusty. "I wouldn't take too much for granted, was I you."

James said, "If we run into Indians, I won't be much help without a gun."

The captain overheard. "If that happens, I'll give you your gun back. But not before." He looked around. "Everybody ready?" He motioned with his hand and led the way, setting his favorite dun horse into an easy trot. The rangers' mounts had received only a short rest after two hard days of travel. Whitfield was being careful not to overtax them without cause.

Rusty counted eight riders paralleling the river. That seemed the most likely route for the Indians' return.

James said, "There's twice as many Indians as there is of us."

"Daddy Mike used to tell about the big fight on Plum Creek. He said the rangers were outnumbered four or five to one, but they whipped the Comanches anyway."

"Took them by surprise, I guess."

"No, the Indians knew they were there. They just thought their numbers made them safe. They didn't expect the volunteers to hit them so fast and hard. It threw them off balance, and they never got back on their feet."

They rode by the Gaskin place. The roof had been patched, after a fashion, but it was the sort of slapdash job Rusty would have expected of Fowler. He managed to muster some sympathy for the old man in the loss of his sons despite years of grievances at Gaskin hands.

James knew little about the Gaskin family. He said, "It would be a mercy if the Indians burned that place down. Maybe the neighbors would get together and build a better one."

"They would for sure, if they could build it fifty miles away."

Farther downriver lay the Isaac York place. Rusty would rather have passed it by, for the thought of seeing York brought a bitter taste rising up from his stomach. He hoped York would not be there. Perhaps he had heeded Preacher Webb's warning and had gone to the settlement.

Captain Whitfield raised his hand in a signal for a halt. "Quiet!" he ordered. "Listen."

Rusty heard distant gunfire. The York place was under siege.

His first thought was that the Comanches would do for him what he had not been able to do for himself: administer justice to Isaac York. He took quick satisfaction in the thought, then lost it. He felt shame for letting himself harbor such an unworthy sentiment.

No comment was necessary, and Whitfield made none. He signaled for an advance and set his dun horse into a run. James spurred up beside him. "You promised me my gun, remember?"

Whitfield reached into his saddlebag and brought out the pistol he had taken when he placed James under arrest. "I'll want that back."

James made no promise.

Rusty pushed Alamo hard, trying to keep up. He suffered a confusing ebb and flow of conflicting emotions pulling him forward yet trying to hold him back. He was tempted to drop behind and leave the rescue of Isaac York to the others, but he could not bring himself to draw on the reins. Outnumbered, the rangers needed every man they had, and more. His feeling of duty to them was stronger than his hatred for York.

The cabin came into view on a slope easy water-carrying distance up from the river. The Comanches were circling it on horseback, loosing arrows at the windows and a broken door that sagged half open. A dead horse lay at the doorstep. Rusty guessed that a warrior had tried to smash the door by backing his horse into it. The rider evidently had escaped, but his mount had not.

White smoke arose from the two windows and around the door as defenders inside fired sporadically at the attackers.

The Indians spotted the incoming riders and broke their circle. They quickly formed into a group, then surged toward the rangers.

Oh, hell, Rusty thought. *They're fixing to meet us head-on.*

The sight of the oncoming Comanches, stripped down to little more than breechcloths and warpaint, shouting in defiance, set Rusty to shivering. His blood was like ice. But Whitfield did not temper his speed, nor did the other rangers. They plunged headlong toward the mass of warriors. Some of the men raised an exuberant yell to match that of the Indians.

Whitfield shouted, "Chastise them, boys! Hip and thigh!"

The Comanches split suddenly, avoiding an actual collision. They swept around the rangers, who struggled to circle about and give chase. Rusty heard the whisper of arrows and instinctively dropped down on the side of his horse. He saw a minuteman tumble from the saddle, an arrow in his shoulder. A horse fell, hit in the chest.

So far as he could see in the wild chaos of the moment, only two Comanches had rifles. One rifle fell to the ground as ranger pistols barked.

He glimpsed a large gathering of horses farther down the river, prizes of the Comanche raid.

The Indians regrouped and made a wide circle back toward the horses. They did not intend to give up their booty without a fight. The cabin door was forced open, and three men stepped out to fire at the Comanches as they passed. Rusty recognized Preacher Webb, Tom Blessing, and the slave Shanty.

He did not see York. Perhaps the Indians had done to him what Rusty had long yearned to do.

Whitfield shouted, "Keep poundin' them, boys. They can't fight us and drive their horses, too."

Rusty was uncertain for a moment which the warriors would choose. Then he knew, for they formed a long, ragged line and came forward in a run, ready for more battle. The rangers spread out to meet them. Rusty found himself at one extreme end, racing toward a Comanche who seemed to have chosen him as his specific target.

The Indian swung a war club. The stone head looked as large as both of Rusty's fists. He knew it could crush his skull. He tried to line his pistol sights on the man's broad, painted chest, but the motion of his running horse kept the barrel bobbing up and down.

The opposing riders were no more than ten feet apart when Rusty squeezed the trigger. He saw the other horse scotch at the flash, just enough to prevent the war club from striking Rusty's head as it swung in a wide arc. It hit him across the shoulder so hard that it knocked him loose from the saddle. He felt himself falling. He landed on his back, jarring most of the breath from his lungs. His hat rolled away. He looked up as the Indian wheeled his horse around and came back, swinging the club again. Instinctively Rusty brought up the pistol and squeezed the trigger, but the hammer fell on an empty chamber.

Buffalo Caller had been in high spirits over the success of the raid. Though he had been thwarted in gathering scalps—most of the farms the warriors visited were either deserted or too well defended for a frontal assault—they had done well in gathering horses. It appeared they had somehow lost the element of surprise, but most of the Texans had been more interested in saving their lives than in saving their animals. The war party had rounded up horses in more abundance than he had dared hope.

He had not been surprised when their approach to the small log cabin was greeted by gunfire. Most of the warriors had been willing to pass it by and settle for the four horses they saw in the corral, but Buffalo Caller fretted over not having taken Texan scalps. The cabin looked vulnerable, and he had led the assault.

Now they stood in danger of losing all the horses they had gathered and perhaps a few of the warriors themselves. He dreaded the blame the young men would fasten upon him. He had taken a rapid count of the horsemen approaching and had decided the whites were too outnumbered to attempt a fight. Surely they would back away. He would have to give up the attack on the cabin, but at least the raiders should be able to move on with their horses.

To his surprise, the Texans mounted a charge. There had been nothing for Buffalo Caller's warriors to do but meet it and try to break it up. He was confident the white horsemen would disperse when they saw the superior force riding down upon them. But they did not. They kept coming.

Buffalo Caller wondered what manner of madmen he was dealing with. The Texans' failure to be intimidated left him rattled, unsure what he should do.

The young warriors made the decision for him. They would try to save the horses. Surely the inferior band of Texans would realize they were too outnumbered to take the horses back. Surely they would pull aside and let the warriors pass.

But it quickly became evident that the *teibos* had no such intention. Buffalo Caller had no choice but to lead another charge. It was poorly organized and quickly began disintegrating as the opposing bodies neared one another. He looked around desperately for his son Steals the Ponies. He could not see him in the confusion of running horses and shouting men.

Buffalo Caller found himself facing a single rider. He had fired his rifle in the first charge and had not had a chance to reload. He did not trust his aim with an arrow from the back of a running horse against another moving horseman. He chose to use the war club.

He was almost blinded by the flash of the rider's pistol. The bullet missed him, but the blazing powder set his face afire. He felt his club connect with the white man's shoulder so hard that it would have been jarred from his grasp but for the leather thong that bound it to his wrist. The rider fell from his horse and landed on his back.

Buffalo Caller quickly brought his horse around for another run, determined this time to crush the *teibo*'s head. Blinking, trying to see through the lingering brightness of the flash, he raised the club, then stopped. He looked down in surprise and growing horror, for he saw what he had seen in his dream. The white man's hair was red.

Buffalo Caller burned all over. Instinct told him to smash this man quickly, for the red-hair was evil medicine. But his hand seemed paralyzed. He felt a struggle of opposing powers, his own against that of the red-haired Texan. He tried to bring down the club but could not move it.

He heard a shout and saw another white man bearing down upon him. As Buffalo Caller turned to meet the new threat, he felt a renewal of power. He swung the club back for momentum, then felt a terrible blow to his side even as he heard the shot fired. He once had been kicked by a mule, but that was nothing compared with the impact of the bullet. He almost fell from the horse. He managed to grasp a handful of mane, but he could not see to guide the animal. He could feel that it was still running, but he had no idea where it was going.

It did not seem to matter. A slow paralysis came over him. His hand loosed its grip on the mane. He knew the sensation of falling, of pain when he struck the ground. Then he was lying on his back, sunlight filtering through tree branches above and burning through the lids of his closed eyes. He felt himself drifting away as if floating in the river.

The last thing that came to him was a renewal of the vision. Once again he saw the man with the red hair. And once again the face was that of the boy he had taken for his own but had lost in the turmoil and fire of Plum Creek.

Rusty felt a terrible pain as a hand gripped the shoulder the club had struck. He cried out, and the hand jerked away. He recognized James Monahan's anxious voice before he was able to focus on the face.

"Are you shot?"

Rusty had trouble bringing out the words. "He hit me with his club. Feels like he might've busted my shoulder." He reached up to examine the source of pain. "He was fixin' to fetch me another lick when you rode up. Thanks. You saved my life."

"It ain't worth thankin' me for." James straightened up and looked around. "I'll go fetch your horse. Looks like our Indian got away, but he won't go far. I put a bullet in him."

While James rode out to catch Alamo, Tanner reined up and swung a long leg over the cantle of his saddle. He bent down to give Rusty a searching look. His anxiety faded, a smile creasing his face. "Fell off of your horse, did you?"

Rusty did not see the humor. "Got clubbed. If James Monahan hadn't come along, I'd have my brains scattered all over the grass."

"Wouldn't've been enough to make much of a mess. Come on, I'll help you up."

Rusty felt shaky on his feet, and Tanner held him until James brought the horse. Tanner boosted Rusty into the saddle. Rusty asked, "Where's everybody else? What went with the Indians?"

"Scattered to hell and gone," Tanner replied. "Looks like we busted up their party. You know how it is with Indians. They'll go off in six directions and meet up later, somewhere they don't figure we can reach them."

James observed, "They've left their horse herd behind."

Rusty was grateful for that. "But they'll be back. They'll try again. Maybe not today, but sooner or later."

Tanner said, "That means me and you can hang on to our high-payin' job." He pointed his chin toward the York cabin. "Looks like the boys are startin' to gather over there. Guess we'd best go join them."

James looked toward the river. It was only fifty yards away. "Maybe they won't notice for a while that I'm not with you."

Rusty frowned. "You leavin'?"

"I promised to stay 'til the trouble was over. It is, so I'm gittin' while the gittin's good."

Tanner said, "They'll blame Rusty for you gettin' away."

"Tell them it happened while him and that Indian was havin' their set-to. Wasn't nothin' he could do about it. Ain't much either of you can do now except shoot me in the back."

Tanner drew his pistol and studied it. "I ain't had time to reload. Don't reckon Rusty has either."

James smiled. "Then adios, Rusty. Take good care of my sister. See you when the war is over."

Rusty grimaced. "The war back east has got to end one of these days, but I'm afraid the one out here may take a lot longer. Don't let some Comanche raise your hair."

He watched James disappear into the timber, then shifted his attention to the York cabin. "Guess we'd better see what's goin' on."

Captain Whitfield stood with his hands on his hips as Rusty dismounted, his shoulder stiff. "I don't see your prisoner."

Rusty grimaced. "Neither do I, sir. Things got kind of mixed up out there for a little bit."

"Caleb Dawkins will be upset if he finds out you had him, then lost him again."

"Somehow, what Caleb Dawkins thinks doesn't mean a damn thing to me right now." Rusty rubbed his aching shoulder. He decided it was not broken, but it would probably turn black as a bucket of coal. "Anyway, he's got other troubles on his mind. And deserves them every one."

"There's no reason he has to know, unless somebody has the poor judgment to tell him. I don't know anybody in this company that short of good sense."

"Truth is, Captain, if it hadn't been for James Monahan, I'd be layin' out yonder with my head stove in. It's a lucky thing he was there."

Preacher Webb stood at the door. "Just luck, you think? Likely it was Providence that James was close by when you needed him."

Rusty shook the minister's hand. "I wouldn't be surprised."

"And it was the Lord brought you and the minutemen here in time. We were might near out of ammunition."

"I'm glad we got here, for your sake. As for Isaac York, I wouldn't care if the Indians plowed him under."

Webb stared critically at Rusty, then motioned him over to the side of the cabin away from the others. "It's time you know the truth. Tom and me, we tried for a long time to tell you we weren't sure Isaac shot your Daddy Mike. Now we know he didn't."

Rusty swallowed hard. "What do you mean, he didn't?"

"When word came about Fowler Gaskin's boys bein' killed, I went over to try and comfort the old man. He let the truth slip. Eph and Luke did it. They were afraid to sneak up close, so they mistook Mike for you. It was you they meant to kill."

"Me?"

"You'd just had a fight with them, and you whipped up on them pretty good."

Rusty leaned against the cabin wall. He felt that otherwise he might fall down. Remorse burned like a long drink of bad whiskey. "I came awful close once to killin' Isaac York."

"Hate is a heavy load to carry. Especially when it's for nothin'."

"Is Isaac inside the cabin?"

"He took an arrow. Shanty and Tom are doin' what they can for him."

Rusty dreaded going in. But it had to be done. He owed Isaac York for a wrong he was not sure he could ever set aright.

Blessing and Shanty leaned over York, stretched out on a cot, groaning. A bloody arrow lay on the dirt floor. Blessing was washing a chest wound with a whiskey-soaked cloth. Shanty was murmuring, "Don't you go and die on me, Mr. Isaac. You take a tight grip and hang on. You hear me, Mr. Isaac? I don't want to belong to somebody else." Shanty's voice broke.

Blessing said, "It's bad, but it missed the heart. He'll make it. Guess it sort of makes up for him shootin' those Indians on the reserve that time. When his time comes to die, it'll be the whiskey that kills him."

In a voice so weak as to be almost inaudible, York murmured, "Preacher, pray me through this. I swear I'll give up drinkin'."

Webb said, "The Lord expects a man to live up to his promises. Were I you, I wouldn't go makin' any I couldn't keep."

Rusty said, "Mr. York, I'm sorry."

York became aware of Rusty's presence. He struggled to find voice. "Boy, whatever troubles you've got with me, they'll have to wait."

"I've got no trouble with you. I'm sorry I ever did. I just found out what really happened to Daddy Mike."

The man's puzzled expression made Rusty realize York did not know. "I found out it was the Gaskin boys shot him."

York was slow in absorbing the information. It seemed too much to digest at one time in his weakened condition. "I had some differences with your daddy, but not nothin' I'd kill him for."

"Maybe someday I'll learn to be slow about makin' judgments. Forgive me, Mr. York?"

York began muttering incoherently as shock took hold. Shanty leaned over him again, grasping his hand. "You just take a strong grip, Mr. Isaac. I'm right here."

Webb and Tom Blessing walked out with Rusty. Blessing said, "Takes a man to admit he's wrong. Looks to me like you've grown up, Rusty."

"I reckon it was high time."

Captain Whitfield was assembling the company. Rusty shook the two men's hands.

Webb said, "You've taken a load off of Isaac York. The Lord is smilin' on you."

"He must be, because all of a sudden there's a load gone off of me, too. Come up to Belknap when you can, Preacher. There's folks up there who could sure stand some gospel-learnin'."

He mounted Alamo. Preacher Webb asked, "Anything you want me to tell the Monahans?"

Rusty shook his head. "Nope. I'll be goin' by and tellin' them myself." The rangers were riding away. Rusty spurred to catch up to them, thinking of what-all he wanted to say to Geneva and to the rest of the family.

His shoulder ached, but it was not enough to overcome the warm feeling that arose within.

He *had* a family now. He was no longer alone.

Buffalo Caller lay on damp ground. Looking up through a haze dense as smoke, he knew he was in the midst of timber along the bank of the river. He had fallen from his horse. His side burned like fire where the bullet had smashed his ribs. Carefully he pressed his hand against the wound. The blood flowed warm and much too freely. He realized his life was draining away. He did not want to die lying on his back. He wanted to push up, to meet death in a sitting position, but he lacked the strength.

He blinked, trying in vain to clear his blurred vision. He sensed that a horseman was moving toward him. One of the Texans, coming back to kill him, he thought. He felt no fear, for the *teibo* could do nothing more to him. He was dying anyway.

The voice that called softly was not that of a white man. "*Powva?* Father?"

Steals the Ponies had found him. The young warrior dropped to the ground and knelt by Buffalo Caller's side. He gave the wound a swift appraisal. "I am here to take care of you, Father."

Buffalo Caller struggled to find voice. "It is too late. Even if I could ride, my horse has run away and left me."

"We lost all the horses, Father, except the ones we rode. There will be other times and other horses."

"For you, my son. Not for me. Our grandfathers are waiting for me."

Steals the Ponies choked off a cry. It was not becoming for a grown son to weep in the presence of his father.

It was a hard thing to die, knowing his last mission had been a failure. But Buffalo Caller could feel the darkness coming over him, the long darkness from which there would be no waking. "You will keep fighting, *Ner-*

too-ahr—son. Take my bow and my shield. Every time you fight the Texans, I will be with you."

"I *will* fight them, Father. I will fight until they are gone or *I* am."

Buffalo Caller found strength to raise his hand, to touch his son's arm. "But beware the red-haired ranger. His medicine is stronger than mine. Stronger, perhaps, than yours."

He sighed then, and the long sleep closed his eyes.

Steals the Ponies remained beside him long after the breath was gone and the strong heart had ceased to beat. He did not understand what his father had said about the ranger. Perhaps Buffalo Caller would come back in a vision sometime and explain.

As darkness came, Steals the Ponies took his father into his arms and lifted him up, laying him across his pony's back. He heard a whisper of wind through the trees and thought for a moment it was the voice of Buffalo Caller, trying to reach him.

"What did you mean about the red-haired ranger?"

There was no answer. Head bowed in disappointment, Steals the Ponies realized he had heard only the wind after all.

Time had come to begin the journey. Time had come to take his father home.

BADGER Boy

FOREWORD

One of the most dreaded hazards of Texas frontier life was capture by the Indians. It happened more often than history books might indicate. Comanches in particular often took women and children captive, though they usually killed men on the spot. Women and older girls not murdered outright were almost invariably raped. Whether they continued to live or not depended upon the mood of their captors. For a majority, life proved to be terrifying, and short.

Children had a better chance for survival. For one thing, the tribe was gradually shrinking in numbers because of lives lost in battle and in the dangerous hunt for buffalo. Captives helped make up for this decrease. Boys were looked upon as potential hunters and warriors. Girls would become warriors' wives when they were old enough. In the meantime they were pressed into menial labor to help ease the work burden for Indian women.

Comanches liked to capture children old enough to endure hardship, yet young enough to be pliable, to forget their past quickly and adapt to a vastly different mode of life. Children were separated from their mothers as soon as possible to make the transition easier for their captors. Unless freed fairly soon, they usually forgot their native tongue and became, for all intents and purposes, Indian children.

In most cases families never saw or heard of captive children again. It was as if the earth had swallowed them up. On rare occasions they were ransomed by traders or rescued by the military. In one notable case a black teamster named Brit Johnson spent years doggedly searching for his kidnapped family. Finding them, he successfully bargained them free. He also freed several white captives of the Kiowa.

Children who did not soon adapt were likely to be killed. Boys in particular were often tested by severe treatment. Those not tough enough to endure it were considered expendable. However, a boy who fought his captors might be spared out of admiration for his bravery. He was seen as having the potential to become a good warrior.

One of Texas's first well-documented accounts of Indian captivity was that of Rachel Parker Plummer, taken in a raid on a civilian fort on May 19, 1836, two months after the fall of the Alamo and less than a month after the battle of San Jacinto. She was one of five whites taken that day, another being her cousin, Cynthia Ann Parker. Mrs. Plummer wrote a lengthy report on the horrors she endured. Pregnant at the time of her capture, she saw the Indians kill her baby at the age of six weeks because they considered him a hindrance to her work. She spent thirteen months as a captive. Ransomed by traders from New Mexico, she returned to her family in broken health and lived but a short time.

Much more famous is the tragic history of her younger cousin, Cynthia Ann, who spent almost twenty-five years with the Comanches, becoming the wife of warrior Peta Nocona and mother to Quanah Parker, who would be the last war chief of the Quahadi Comanches. Though offered a chance at freedom several times, she had become so thoroughly Comanche that she refused. She was forcibly "freed" in 1860 when a band of rangers under Lawrence Sullivan Ross overran her camp, killing most of its inhabitants. She was spared when it was noticed that she had blue eyes. She remembered little of English, though she recognized her name when it was spoken. Against her will she was returned to relatives. She tried to run away to rejoin the Comanches but was restrained. Brokenhearted, she never reconciled to white ways. In effect she had become a captive for the second time.

For those who returned to the white world after extended life among the Indians, the readjustment was usually difficult. Herman Lehmann was a German boy captured in the hill country when eleven years old. He became a warrior and participated in Comanche raids on the Texas settlements. He narrowly escaped death at the hands of the rangers, some of whom became his good friends in later years. Eventually returned to his people, he made a partial readjustment but maintained ties with his former captors and lived their lifestyle as much as he was able under the constraints of society.

CHAPTER
ONE

THE TEXAS FRONTIER, SPRING, 1865

Rusty Shannon saw brown smoke rising beyond the hill and knew the rangers had arrived too late. The Indians had already struck, and by now they were probably gone.

He had expected trouble, but his pulse quickened as if the smoke were a surprise. He signaled his five fellow patrol members and spurred his black horse, Alamo, into a run. He did not have to look back. The men would follow him; they always did though he had no official rank. He was a private like the rest, but they had fallen into the habit of looking to him for leadership. Nor was he noticeably older than the others. Orphaned early, he could only guess he was about twenty-five, give or take a little. A harsh outdoor life had made him look more than that. He had accepted the responsibility of leadership by default, for no one else had offered to take it.

Back East, the strong nicker of the war horse was fading to a faint and painful whinny as the tired and tattered Confederacy kept struggling to its feet for one more battle and one more loss. To Rusty's independent, red-haired manner of thinking, it was high time the Richmond government conceded defeat and let the guns fall silent. Even from his faraway vantage point at the edge of Comanche-Kiowa country he saw clearly and with pain that the war had bled both sides much too long.

The Texas frontier had a war of its own to contend with, and it was far from over.

Rusty Shannon was tall and rangy, some would say perpetually hungry-looking. Meals were a sometime thing when frontier rangers scouted for Indians. Often the men were too pressed to stop, and at other times they simply had nothing to eat.

He considered himself a soldier of sorts, though he owned no uniform. Texas had not even provided him a badge as a symbol of ranger authority. The cuffs were raveled on his grimy homespun cotton shirt, the sleeves mended and mended again. His frayed gray trousers seemed as much patch as original woolen fabric, for the long war had made new clothing scarce and money scarcer.

Red hair bristled over his ears and brushed his collar. Forced to be frugal, rangers cut each other's hair. It was often a rough job of butchery, but appearances were of little concern. Staying alive and helping others stay alive were what counted on the frontier.

Riding their assigned north-south line past the western fringe of settlement, the patrol had come upon tracks of fifteen to twenty horses at dusk yesterday. By order of Texas's Confederate government in Austin, the rangers were duty-bound to locate and take into custody any deserters or conscription dodgers who might be idling out the war in the wild country beyond the settlements.

Rusty knew the approximate whereabouts of fifty or sixty such men banded together for mutual security, but they were of little interest to him. If the Confederacy wanted them captured it should send Confederate Army troops to do the job. Five or six rangers were no match for so many brush men even if they invested a full heart in the duty, and he had no heart for that kind of business.

He had regarded secession from the Union four years ago as a grave mistake though fellow Texans had voted in its favor. He saw the war as folly on both sides, North and South. If a man did not want to take part in it, the authorities should leave him the hell alone. Officialdom did not share his view, of course. Remaining with the rangers on the frontier kept him out of the military's sight.

Freckle-faced Len Tanner had swung a long and lanky leg across the cantle, dismounting to study the tracks. "Conscript dodgers, you think?"

That was a possibility, but instinct told Rusty the trail had been made by Comanches or possibly Kiowas. Perhaps both, for they often joined forces to venture south from their prairie and mountain strongholds. The Indians were well aware that white men of the North had been at war with white men of the South for most of four years. They did not understand the reasons, or care. What mattered was that the fighting's heavy drain upon manpower left the frontier vulnerable. In places it had withdrawn eastward fifty to a hundred miles, leaving homes abandoned, strayed livestock running wild. Settlers who dared remain lived in jeopardy.

After sending one man back to company headquarters near Fort Belknap to report to Captain Oran Whitfield, Rusty had set out to follow the trail. Len Tanner rode beside him. Rusty had never decided whether Tanner's legs were too long or his horse too short, for his stirrups dangled halfway between the mount's belly and the ground. Eyes eager, Tanner said, "Tracks are freshenin'. We ought to catch up with them pretty soon."

"Catchin' them is what we're paid for."

"Who's been paid?"

The Texas state government was notorious for being perpetually broke, unable to meet obligations. Wages for its employees were near the bottom of the priority list, especially for those men in homespun cloth and buckskin who rode the frontier picket line far away from those who wrote the laws and appropriated the money.

Darkness had forced Rusty to halt the patrol and wait for daylight lest they lose the trail. He had slept little, frustrated that the raiders might be gaining time. Night had been no hindrance to the Indians if they chose to keep traveling.

Now he saw a half-burned cabin, a man and two boys carrying water in buckets from a nearby creek and throwing it on the smoking walls. He remembered the place. It belonged to a farmer named Haines. Hearing the horses, the man grabbed a rifle. He lowered it when he saw that the riders were not Indians. He focused resentful attention on Rusty.

"Minutemen, ain't you?"

Ranger was not an official term. The public often referred to the rangers as minutemen, among other things.

Looking upon two blanket-covered forms on the ground, Rusty felt a chill. The blankets were charred along the edges. "Yes sir, Mr. Haines."

"How come you always show up when it's too late?"

Rusty could have told him there were not enough rangers to be everywhere and protect everybody. The war back East had drawn away too many of the state's fighting-age men. The ranger desertion rate had risen to alarming levels, partly out of fear of being conscripted into Confederate service and partly because the state treasury was as bare as Mother Hubbard's cupboard. Even on those rare occasions when a paymaster visited the frontier companies, he never brought enough money to pay the men all that was due them.

It was futile to try to explain that to a man who had just lost so much. "We'll bury your dead," Rusty said, "then I'll send a couple of men to escort you and your boys to Fort Belknap."

The farmer set his jaw firmly. "We've got nobody at Belknap. Everybody we have is here, and here we're stayin'."

"You've got no roof over your head."

"We saved part of the cabin. We can rebuild it. You just stay on them red devils' trail."

Rusty saw only the man and the two boys. Fearing he already knew, he asked, "What about your womenfolks?"

The farmer cleared his throat, but his voice fell to little more than a whisper. "They're here." He knelt beside one of the covered forms and lifted the scorched blanket enough for Rusty to see a woman's bloodied face. The scalp had been ripped from her head. "My wife. Other one is our little girl. The Comanches butchered them like they was cattle."

"How come they didn't get the rest of you?"

The farmer looked at the two boys. They still carried water to throw on the cabin though the fire appeared to be out. "Me and my sons was workin' in the field. The heathens came upon the cabin so quick they was probably inside before Annalee even saw them. I hit one with my first shot, and they drawed away. All we could do for Annalee and the baby was to drag them outside before they burned." He looked at the ground as if ashamed he had been unable to do more.

Rusty was undecided whether settlers like Haines who remained on the exposed western frontier were brave or merely foolhardy. Either way, he would concede that they were tenacious.

Ruefully the farmer turned his attention back to his wife and daughter. "Conscript officers decided to pass me by on account of my age and my family." He cleared his throat again. "I wish they'd taken me. My family would've moved back to East Texas and been safe." He gave Rusty a close scrutiny. "You're a fit-lookin' specimen. Why ain't you in the Confederate Army?"

"I figured I was needed more in the rangin' service."

The Texas legislature had fought and won a grudging concession from the Richmond government to defer men serving in the frontier companies. But the agreement was often ignored by conscription officers who raided the outlying companies and took rangers whether or not they were willing to go. Those drafts had increased as the Confederacy's fortunes soured and its military ranks were decimated by battlefield casualties. So far Rusty had avoided the call, though he had a nagging hunch that time was closing in.

The farmer rubbed an ash-darkened sleeve across his face. His voice became contrite. "Sorry I jumped all over you. I know it's not your doin' that there ain't enough rangers. It's the Richmond government's fault, takin' off so many men to fight a stupid war a thousand miles away. And the Texas government for lettin' them get away with it. Damn them all, and double damn Jeff Davis."

There had been a time when such words could put a man in mortal danger from rope-wielding zealots determined to rid Texas of dissidents. Rusty had helped cut down the bodies of his friend Lon Monahan and Lon's son Billy from the limbs of a tree in the wake of the hangmen. Now and then in the dark of night the memory brought him awake, clammy with cold sweat and fighting his blanket. He had long harbored the same opinions as Haines but spoke them aloud only to friends he could trust. He had witnessed too much grief brought on by night-riding vigilantes like Colonel Caleb Dawkins who did not go to war themselves yet demanded that others do so or die.

The farmer cautioned, "There was sixteen, eighteen Indians. I don't see but six of you."

"We're lucky we've got six." The five who accompanied him, like Len Tanner, were men Rusty felt would stay with him if they skirted along the rim of hell. He looked again toward the bodies. He shuddered, for he had seen too many like them. "If we come across a minister, we'll send him. You'll want proper services for your folks."

"Much obliged, but I can read from the Bible same as any preacher."

The older of the two boys appeared to be around twelve, the other perhaps ten. Rusty felt sorrow for them. They would have to finish growing up without their mother. But at least they still had their father. Unlike Rusty, they had not lost all their family. Surely the war back East would sputter out before they were old enough to become soldiers.

The war here was another matter. He could see no end to it.

The farmer pointed. "I'm fearful for August Faust, my neighbor. I hope him and his family saw the smoke and forted up."

"We'll go see," Rusty promised. He signaled the patrol and set off in the southeasterly direction the Indians had taken. The tracks were plain enough to follow in a lope.

He expected more smoke ahead, but he heard sporadic firing instead. Someone was still fighting at the Faust place. When the picket cabin came into full view, Rusty rough-counted eleven Indians. Most were afoot and taking cover wherever they could. It stood to reason that a few others were behind the cabin, out of his sight. Fifty or sixty yards away, two warriors held a number of horses.

It was not normally Comanche or Kiowa custom to make a frontal assault on a well-defended position. They preferred to catch their quarry by surprise with a quick, clean strike, pulling back if resistance proved stronger than expected. Evidently that had been the case here. Almost every time an Indian raised his head, fire and smoke blossomed from the doorway or a glassless window. Someone was firing from the back as well. The raiders had the cabin surrounded, but they were a long way from taking it.

Tanner grinned. "They only got us outnumbered by three to one. We ought to crack this nut pretty easy."

The befreckled young ranger would willingly go hungry for three days to get into a good fight. He had, several times.

"Then let's be at them." Rusty drew his pistol and loaded the chamber he customarily kept empty for safety. He preferred the rifle, but it was difficult to use from a running horse.

The rangers were two hundred yards from the cabin when the Indians discovered them and ran for their mounts. In the excitement three horses jerked loose and loped away, wringing their tails. Two Indians set afoot swung up behind others. A third mounted a spare animal whose owner no longer needed him. Rusty saw an Indian lying beside a tall woodpile but did not take time to determine if he was dead.

A man with an old-fashioned long rifle stepped out of the cabin and took a parting shot. An Indian slumped forward but grabbed his horse's mane and remained astride. The man shouted, "Go get them!"

Rusty called, "Everybody all right?"

"Nobody killed." He waved the rangers on. "Get my work horses back if you can."

Horses and mules were almost as important as life, for without them a farmer had no way to plow his fields, no way to travel except to walk. The war had pulled most horses out of this region except wild bands ranging free beyond the settlements. Few farmers were equipped to catch those, much less to break and train them. And should they manage to do so, chances were that either the Indians would steal them or a government horse-buying team would come along and take them away. It would leave Confederate script or worthless promissory notes, which Rusty regarded as legalized theft.

The Indians cut immediately to the creek. Timber there was heavy enough to give them partial cover for their escape, though it would slow them as they dodged through the trees and undergrowth, the entangling briars.

Rusty said, "We'll stay out here in the open and keep up with them." Sooner or later the fugitives would have to quit the timber and ride into the clear.

Tanner turned in the saddle. "Look back, Rusty."

Two raiders had broken out behind the rangers and were racing toward the cabin. Startled, Rusty reined the black horse around. His first thought was that they intended another try at Faust or one of the other settlers who had come out of the cabin and gathered in the yard. He spurred in pursuit, intending to keep the warriors too busy.

The pair slowed their mounts and leaned down, grabbing the fallen man by the arms and lifting him up between them. Men in the yard fired a couple of futile shots.

It was a point of honor among plains warriors not to ride away from the battlefield and leave a wounded or dead comrade behind to be killed or mutilated if rescue was at all possible. By white men's standards the Comanches were savages. Though Rusty deplored their propensity for random killing, he respected their bravery. He wondered if he could muster the courage to do the same thing.

The main body of warriors crossed the creek and emerged on the other side, beyond the protective timber. They retreated northward, pursued by three rangers who were no match for them in numbers should they decide to turn and counterattack. Rusty reined up, knowing he was unlikely to catch the fugitives. He was not sure he even wanted to. They seemed to be retreating back toward the reservation, taking with them a dozen stolen horses. Even in the unlikely event that the patrol caught up and killed them all, it would make little difference in terms of the larger war between white men and red. There would still be enough to keep the fight going . . . Comanche, Kiowa, sometimes Cheyenne and others.

The black horse's hide glistened with sweat. Rusty slowed him, then brought him to a stop. The three rangers who had pursued the main group abandoned the chase and turned back. Two more Comanches left the creek and circled around them, striking out northwestward across the prairie in the wake of the others. Rusty stopped and drew his rifle but knew his shot would be wasted. A snowball in hell stood a better chance.

A single rider crossed the creek and took after the pair. Rusty recognized Tanner's lean form. He waved his hat and shouted, "Len, get the hell back here!"

He feared the Indians would lead the reckless Tanner off by himself, then turn and kill him. Fortunately the wind was in the right direction to carry his voice. The ranger drew rein and reluctantly returned.

"Damn it, Rusty, they'll keep splittin' off in little bunches, and first thing you know we'll be wonderin' where they went."

Rusty was aware of that. He had seen similar escapes in the four years he had served a frontier company. It was a familiar Comanche tactic to divide up, knowing the pursuers were seldom able to follow them all. The last small bunch, though closely trailed, would somehow manage to disappear like a puff of smoke.

Shortly he looked back over his shoulder and saw three more warriors on open ground north of the creek, racing away. They had concealed themselves in the timber until the pursuit had passed.

Tanner argued, "There ain't all that many of them. What say we show them who's the boss?"

Rusty considered his choices. "The odds are too long. We'll just keep trailin' after them so they won't turn and come back. Maybe we can crowd them into settin' the stolen horses loose."

Moving into a stiff trot, he gathered the patrol and half a dozen loose horses the Indians had taken, then abandoned under pressure. Rusty hoped these were the ones stolen from Faust and perhaps the Haines's farm.

He picked out the oldest man, whose thin shoulders were pinched, his face weary. "Mr. Pickett, if you don't mind, I wish you'd take these horses back to the Faust place. The rest of us'll pester the hostiles all the way to the river."

Oscar Pickett seemed relieved. He was too old for such rigorous duty, but he would die before he would admit it aloud. "What do you want me to do afterward?"

Even men twice Rusty's age readily took his directions. He tried to give them in a manner that sounded like friendly suggestions rather than commands. "Stay at the Haines's place awhile. Your horse needs a rest. You can come up to Belknap tomorrow." The rider appeared more tired than the horse, but Rusty wanted to spare the older man's pride.

He turned to the rest of his rangers. "What do you say we go aggravate those Comanches?"

Steals the Ponies was his name. He had stolen several this time, only to be forced to abandon some under pressure of the Texan war party that had dogged the raiders so closely. The loss nettled like prickly pear spines digging under his skin. He had contended all along that the white horsemen were too few for real warriors to run from. But Tall Eagle had assembled this raiding party, and it was for Tall Eagle to say whether they fought or retreated. The older warrior had decided at the first cabin that their medicine had gone bad because one of his followers was wounded by the opening shot. The feeling had been reinforced when they failed to take the second cabin by surprise and the *teibo* horsemen interrupted their siege.

Next time, or the time after, it would be different. The younger, more eager warriors would sooner or later pull away from Tall Eagle, for he was beginning to lose the nerve he needed for leadership. Steals the Ponies would organize his own raiding party as his father, Buffalo Caller, had frequently done before him. Then he would be the one to decide whether to attack or pull away.

His father's forays had not always been successful, but he had never turned and run like a frightened dog. Buffalo Caller had eventually died in a raid on a white settlement. His was a fitting death for a warrior.

Frustration prompted Steals the Ponies to stop for a show of defiance. Tall Eagle shouted for him to keep up, but Steals the Ponies defied him. He turned back toward the little group of white horsemen who trailed behind. They made no effort to close the distance but acted as an annoyance, like so many heelflies. They must belong to the formidable Texan warrior society known as rangers, he thought. Rangers stuck like cockleburrs.

He doubted that the white men could understand his words, but they would understand his gestures well enough. He crisscrossed his war pony back and forth in front of them, shouting insults, waving his bow over his head.

One of the white men rode a little ahead of the others. His face was dark with several days' whiskers, but he sat erect in the saddle, a young man's way. Steals the Ponies decided on a challenge. He raced toward him, waving the bow, drawing an arrow from his quiver. The other rangers quickly moved up to flank the leader. Steals the Ponies saw that the young Texan had no intention of answering the challenge.

He knew he was within range even of the rangers' pistols, but he had made a display of courage and would not compromise it by turning and running away. He was close enough to see that the rider's whiskers and shaggy hair were red.

That shook him a little. More than once, his father had told him of a troubling vision about a red-haired man. The day Buffalo Caller was killed, he had been in a close fight with a ranger whose hair was the color of rusted metal. Though someone else fired the fatal bullet, Steals the Ponies had always felt that the redhead's strong medicine was somehow responsible for his father's death.

This might not be the same man. Then again, it might. Steals the Ponies shuddered, but pride would not allow him to run. He turned slowly away from the white men, letting them know he was not afraid though they could easily kill him. For a time he held his pony to an easy pace that kept him within range if they should choose to shoot. They did not. He supposed their forbearance was a tribute of sorts to his valor. He stopped again to deliver a loud, defiant whoop, then moved on to rejoin the others.

He hoped Buffalo Caller might be watching from the spirit land to which he had gone. His father would be proud. He wished his foster brother could be here to see this, but Badger Boy was too young to ride on such an expedition. He would hear of it, though, and perhaps he would be inspired to become the greatest fighter of them all.

The warriors gave Steals the Ponies their silent approval, all except Tall Eagle. Tall Eagle rebuked him with a scowl. Steals the Ponies smiled inside, knowing the leader was jealous. The older warrior could have made the same gesture but had not chosen to do so. Perhaps he had not even thought of it. Word of Steals the Ponies' exploits would spread among The People. They would say he was a son worthy of his father and a model for his younger brother to emulate.

He had shown the *teibos* his courage. Perhaps the next white men to see him would remember and be afraid.

CHAPTER

TWO

Rusty raised his rifle to bring down the Indian who taunted him. He held the bead a moment, then lowered the weapon across the pommel of his badly worn saddle.

Len Tanner drew in closer. "You're the best shot in the outfit. You couldn't miss."

"He's got guts, paradin' himself that way."

"Ain't your fault he's got more guts than good sense. Shoot him."

"Too easy. I'd take no honor in it."

"Honor, hell! There wasn't no honor in them killin' that woman and little girl."

The warrior brought his pony a little closer. Tanner became more agitated. "Looks to me like he's askin' for you to do it."

"He's darin' me to come out and meet him in the middle ground. I'm not a schoolboy. The only dares I pay attention to are the ones I give myself." He knew if he killed the young Comanche the others would turn back and do their damndest to kill *him*. They would stand a good chance of getting it done. The price would be one ranger for one Indian. There were already so many Indians, and so pitifully few rangers.

"We bloodied them some and spoiled their party. Won't do any harm to leave them somethin' they can brag about when they get home."

Home might be the broad and mysterious high plains of Texas, the land known as Comanchería, where the wild bands still roamed free. Or it might be a reservation set aside north of the Red River shortly before the war began between the states. It was under Federal jurisdiction, which meant that any Texan who strayed upon it and managed not to be killed by hostile Indians was subject to arrest as a Confederate belligerent unless he could convince the authorities that he was trying to escape Confederate service. In that case they were likely to impress him into the Union Army. Rusty saw no net gain in that. Though he did not want to fire upon the United States flag, he would not like to fire upon fellow Texans either.

He wished the only thing he ever had to shoot at was meat for the table.

Some men with more courage than scruples periodically invaded the reservation to steal Indian horses. That fanned Indian anger at all Texans and made them more eager than ever to raid south of the Red River. Some of these horse thieves were brush men, fugitives from Confederate conscription. They used aversion to the war as an excuse, but many would have been outlaws whether there had been a war or not. It was in their nature. They seemed indifferent to the misery their forays brought upon fellow citizens.

Rusty's horse stood relaxed in the camp corral, enjoying the brushing his owner gave his black hide. Rusty stood upwind so the breeze would not carry dust and loose hair into his face. Both horse and rider had been granted a rest after days out on patrol. Rusty examined Alamo for sign of scalds or saddle sores, a hazard when a horse was used long and hard. Out here a man took care of his mount before he took care of his own needs. Everything was too far away for walking.

Len Tanner paused in brushing his own horse and gazed to the east. He pointed with the brush. "You don't reckon that'd be a paymaster comin' yonder?"

"I think they've lost the map to this place." Rusty walked to the rail fence for a better look. He wondered if the rider would make it all the way into camp before his mount collapsed of fatigue. The animal was thin. The state provided little money to pay for grain, so horses had to subsist on whatever grass they could find. Only recently had showers begun to fall after two years of drought across most of Texas.

Half of the company had deserted during the winter and early spring. Rusty could not blame the men for saddling their horses in the dark of night and stealing away. They had not been paid in months. Confederate script found little favor among the merchants of nearby Fort Belknap town anyway, even those few who still boasted about their continuing enthusiasm for the Southern cause. The last time Rusty had been sent away to buy horses for the outfit, he had felt like a thief. The rangers had authority to take the horses with or without the owners' consent, paying with promissory notes on the state government. The paper was worth more than the promise. People could save it and write letters on the back.

Tanner said, "Maybe we ought to go see what's happenin'."

"Captain Whitfield'll call if he needs us." On patrol, Rusty was nominally in charge. Anything and everything was his business. In camp, Captain Whitfield was in command, and nothing was Rusty's business unless the captain saw fit to make it so. Whitfield was a large man who carried a navy Colt on his hip, a bottle of whiskey and a Bible in his saddlebag. He was accomplished in the use of all three.

The new arrival dismounted wearily in front of the captain's tent and tied his horse to a post. He leaned against the horse, stamping his feet to improve blood circulation in tired legs. His clothes were as ragged as those of the Fort Belknap rangers. Rusty thought he recognized him as a ranger from another company.

Tanner leaned against the fence, watching. "He don't look like no paymaster. A paymaster would steal at least enough to buy him a decent suit of clothes."

Rusty went back to brushing Alamo. He could feel the ribs without pressing hard. The horse needed a month's rest on grain and green grass, but he was no more likely to get it than Rusty was to receive the pay rightfully due him.

Presently he saw Captain Whitfield walk to the mess tent and ring a bell that was normally sounded at mealtime. It was only the middle of the afternoon. Rusty jerked his head as a signal to Tanner, but Tanner had already dropped his brush in a wooden tack box and was on his way to the corral gate, burning with curiosity.

Reluctantly Rusty laid his brush aside. More Indians, he thought. He had not caught up on sleep since the last skirmish.

The company was down to a fraction of its normal strength because of desertions and a shortage of men willing and able to put up with the privations of frontier service. Of those still in the company, more than half were out on patrol.

Whitfield was middle-aged and broad of hip. He would probably run to belly if ranger rations were not perpetually meager and duty hours long. As it was he probably would not render out two pounds of fat. He tugged at a bushy, unkempt mustache while he watched seven men amble up in no particular hurry and cluster around him. Two squatted on their heels. Army officers had admonished Whitfield several times about his company's lack of military order, but he paid no more attention to them than to the buzzing of flies around the corrals. He considered it absurd to require the men to stand in a straight line or at attention. All that mattered was that they listen to him, whether he was giving orders or reading to them from the Book.

Whitfield had formerly been a sergeant and had taken over the company soon after the outbreak of war. He had inherited the captaincy when the former commanding officer, August Burmeister, had ridden north to join the Union Army. Rusty had never heard Whitfield express favor for either side in the conflict. He suspected that, like himself, Whitfield had chosen frontier service rather than take up arms against the Union. The compromise gave ease to a conscience torn between two loyalties.

Whitfield's eyes were troubled. "Boys, I've been brought some bad news."

Tanner asked, "We've lost the war?"

"Not yet, though it looks like the end is upon us, praise the Lord. Reason I've called you together is to tell you the conscription officers are on their way again."

Rusty saw nothing new in that. Conscription officers had come several times before, trying to persuade younger rangers to resign from frontier duty and join the Confederate Army. They usually left with a recruit or two.

Whitfield said, "The war has taken a bad turn, so they're grabbin' everybody they can get. Frontier service won't keep them from takin' you now if you're halfways young and not too crippled to walk or ride a horse." His gaze fastened on Rusty. "I know some of you never did have strong feelin's for the Richmond government."

Whitfield had read Rusty's mind a long time ago.

The captain said, "The position I'm in, I can't be givin' you advice. Anybody wants to leave before the conscript officers get here, I ain't stoppin' him. Just don't take any horse that don't belong to you." He stood a moment to let the message soak in, then strode back to his tent.

A tingle ran up Rusty's back. He listened to a rising buzz of conversation around him.

A young ranger said, "If they want me that bad, I reckon I'll go. War ought not to last much longer anyway."

Another responded, "They'll have to chase me plumb to Mexico."

Rusty listened to the two men argue, but they were no help to him in making up his mind. He walked to Whitfield's tent and found the captain sitting at a table, where a Bible lay open. In violation of standing orders, Whitfield was pouring whiskey from a bottle into a streaked glass. He looked up.

"Have a drink, Shannon?"

"No, thank you, Captain. I want to keep my mind clear."

"Mine is too damned clear already. I don't understand what Richmond is thinkin' of. There's women and children dyin' out here because they ain't left enough fightin' men to protect them. Now they want to take even more for a war they're fixin' to lose anyway."

"Those people back in Richmond never saw a Comanche. They don't realize the problem."

"The Book tells about times of tribulation. Lord help us, we're damned sure livin' in one." Whitfield took the contents of the glass in one swallow.

"Captain, I need to tell you . . ."

"Don't. Don't tell me a thing. What I don't know, I can't answer for. Just do whatever you feel is right and don't allow anybody else to sway your judgment."

Rusty rarely let anyone do that. "If the conscription officers find most of the company gone, they're liable to bear down hard on you."

Whitfield snorted. "What can they do? I'm too old to be sent to the army. They can't fine me because I'm as broke as the rest of you. I doubt they'd shoot me. So what's left except to send me home? I'm ready to shuck it all and go back to the farm anyhow."

"You've been a good officer. I'm proud I got to serve with you."

"Get you some grub out of the mess tent. You can't travel far hungry."

"Just a little salt, a little flour. I can probably scare up enough game to keep me in meat."

"I wish I could trade you out of that good black horse, but you'll need him worse than I do." Whitfield extended a large, rough hand.

Rusty went to the tent he shared with Tanner and several others. He rolled his bedding and his few clothes— a woolen coat, an extra shirt no less patched than the one he wore, a pair of trousers with one knee out. His small war bag held his razor and a few incidentals.

When he had first come to Belknap from the Shannon farm down on the Colorado River, he had brought considerably more with him. He had led a pack mule named Chapultepec, which his foster father, Daddy Mike Shannon, had brought home from the Mexican War. The mule was old now, but not too old to suit a deserter named Lancer, who had ridden away on him a couple of months ago.

This was one of the few times Rusty had ever seen Len Tanner looking solemn. "Where do you figure on goin', Rusty?"

"Ain't had time to figure. I just want to be gone before the conscription outfit shows up." He was reluctant to part with his longtime friend. He had few friends anymore and no family at all. "I'd be right pleased if you went with me."

Tanner considered. "I've thought about lightin' out, but like as not I'd either run into the conscript officers or the Comanches. The army might not be so bad. Maybe they'll feed better, and pay us to boot."

"I wouldn't bet a wore-out pocketknife on that."

"You can't cross the Red River onto the Indian reservation. They'd give you a Comanche haircut before your horse dried off. Some folks have run away to Mexico, but that's a far piece from here."

"I'd be a lost child in Mexico. All the Spanish I know is a few cusswords Daddy Mike brought home from the Mexican War. Reckon I'll just drift west and hope nobody is interested enough to trail me."

"You're liable to come up against some of them brush men hidin' out in the thickets. They'd as soon kill a ranger as look at him. Instead, why don't you slip down to that farm of yours on the Colorado River and marry that Monahan girl?"

Rusty warmed to the thought of Geneva Monahan. The truth was that he had already considered that possibility, but he chose not to tell Tanner. He did not want to cause his friend a conflicted conscience should the authorities press him with questions. He reached out his hand. "Be careful, Len. Don't let some Comanche lift your hair or some Yankee sharpshooter bring you down."

"Nobody's ever killed me yet."

He built a small fire in the bottom of a dry buffalo wallow, hoping it could not be seen from a distance. He did not need it for warmth but only for broiling a slice of hindquarter from an antelope his rifle had brought down. He made a poor sort of bread dough by mixing a bit of flour with water and a pinch of salt, then curling it around a stick to hold over the coals. He wished for coffee, but the war had made it scarce. Most Texans were substituting parched grain or doing without. He did not even have grain.

Before it was good and dark, when he was through, he would kill the fire. He doubted that conscription officers would be so bold as to prowl about this far from protection. There was always a risk that Comanche eyes might discover the flames, though he had seen no sign of Indians.

While he waited for his simple supper, the full weight of his situation settled upon him like a heavy shroud. He had not felt so achingly alone since he had buried Daddy Mike beside Mother Dora and turned his back on the Colorado River farm where he had spent his growing-up years. The ranger company had been a family of sorts, though its members came and went. Almost the only constants had been Len Tanner and Captain Whitfield.

His thoughts drifted to another family far away, and to the wisp of a girl named Geneva Monahan. Someday, if peace was ever allowed to settle over the land, he intended to marry her just as Tanner had suggested. Then once again he would have a family of his own. From here, and for now, that seemed a long time off.

He had ridden west from camp, intending to confuse anyone bold enough to trail after him. Tomorrow he would find a place where hard ground or thick grass should lose his tracks, then he would turn southward. To travel much farther west would take him to the escarpment marking the eastern edge of the staked plains, still the hunting grounds of free-roaming Comanche and Kiowa bands. To venture onto those broad plains alone was to flirt with death, either to wander lost and succumb to thirst or to be cut down by arrow or lance.

He was on or near what once had been Texas's Indian reserve on the Clear Fork of the Brazos River. The state and federal governments had set it up in the 1850s in hope of curbing Indian raids and encouraging the horseback tribes to become peaceable farmers and stockmen. Many of the less warlike had accepted, realizing they were about to be trampled under by an unstoppable horde of white settlers. But many Comanches and Kiowas had remained unrestrained and unreconstructed, invading and plundering the settlements at will. Rightly or not, frontier settlers blamed reservation Indians for much of the raiding. Their persistent protests eventually forced abandonment of the reserve. Its residents were given a military escort to new reservations north of the Red River shortly before war began between the states.

Rusty had been present at the removal, serving as a volunteer ranger. The haunting memory still lay heavily upon his conscience. He regretted the sad injustice of haste that did not allow the reservation Indians time to harvest their crops or even to gather their scattered livestock. They had tried the white man's road in good faith, only to be dispossessed because of acts committed by other Indians. Rusty understood why many formerly peaceable ones had later taken to raiding south of the river, or at least aiding and abetting those who did. Even so, it had been his job for most of four years to thwart them the best he could.

When he finished eating, he kicked dirt over the fire to smother it. It might have been seen despite his precautions. To sleep here was to court trouble. He rode another mile in the dusk before coming upon a narrow creek. It seemed a likely place to spread his blanket. He staked Alamo where the horse could graze within reach of the water.

He tried in vain to sleep. Heavy in spirit, feeling cut adrift from all he had known, he lay looking up at the stars and thinking of so much forever lost to him. His mind ran back over the long years to Daddy Mike and Mother Dora Shannon, the couple who had taken him in, a lost child orphaned by Indians, and had raised him as their own. He remembered a pleasant boyhood on the Colorado River farm so far from here in both time and distance. It still belonged to him by inheritance although it had been a long while since he was given leave to visit there.

He thought of Geneva Monahan, who had moved to that farm with what remained of a war-torn family, seeking refuge from the dangers of their own place nearer the frontier. It had been the better part of a year since he had last received a letter and much longer since he had seen her. He pondered his risk in traveling there to visit her and to look again at the farm the Shannons had bequeathed to him.

Finally, he thought about the years he had patroled the frontier. He thought of the comradeship, the shared perils and disappointments and occasional small victories. That it had come to an abrupt and unexpected end left in him a sense of emptiness, of work left hanging, incomplete. He had had no time to formulate plans. The most urgent consideration had been to remove himself from the conscription officers' reach. Where to go from here was the major question. He faced several alternatives, none of them to his liking.

He pulled the blanket around him, hoping morning would bring him an answer. But the question continued to nag him. He could not sleep. He got up, finally, and started toward the creek for a drink of water. Alamo snorted, acknowledging his presence.

The sight of distant firelight stopped him in mid-stride. He thought first it might be a lantern in some settler's window, but he dismissed that idea. The only cabins he had seen since leaving the ranger camp had been abandoned, their owners electing to move away from the Indian danger. No, this was a campfire. Two possibilities came to mind: brush men or Indians.

The brush men, a combination of outlaws and fugitives from military service, tended to congregate in out-of-the-way places and in numbers that kept them relatively secure against attack by either Indians or civil authorities.

Rusty stared at the distant fire and considered his options. The law be damned; he had never felt any moral obligation to pursue conscription dodgers for benefit of the Confederacy. Now that he was no longer part of the company, brush men were none of his business.

Indians were another matter. This far south of the Red, an Indian campfire almost certainly meant trouble brewing for someone. His safest course would be to saddle up now and be far away by daylight.

He told himself this was none of his business either. He no longer had any ranger obligations, no oath to live up to. If the Indians moved toward the settlements, someone else would probably find their trail. Only by purest chance had he seen this fire in the first place. Had he not been obliged to leave camp he would not have traveled this far west. If he rode away now no one would be worse off than if he had never been here.

He tried to convince himself as he saddled Alamo. He mounted and turned the horse southward. He rode a hundred yards and stopped, looking back toward the fire. He felt a compulsion to know. Were they really Indians? And what could he do about it if they were?

He followed the creek westward, holding Alamo to a walk to lessen the sound of his hooves and to avoid stumbling into deadfall timber that might make a noise. When he was as near the fire as he dared ride, he dismounted and tied the horse to a tree. He moved on afoot, stopping often to listen. He smelled the smoke and meat roasting over glowing coals. He saw figures moving about.

His skin prickled. These were Indians, right enough. He counted at least eight and reasoned that others were beyond the firelight. For a moment he entertained a wild notion of firing into their camp and giving them a scare that might make them retreat to the reservation. He abandoned that as a bad idea. In all likelihood they would swarm over him like wasps disturbed in their nest. Taking his hair might only increase the warriors' desire for more, because enemy scalps aroused a competitive spirit. Symbolizing manhood and fighting ability, they were trophies sought after and prized.

The Indians had posted no guard. This was a basic flaw in the Comanche approach to war that Rusty had never understood. He did not know if it was a sign of arrogance or simply a false sense of security. They did not normally like to fight at night, and perhaps they felt that no one else did either.

He drew away from the camp and returned to his horse. His skin still tingled with excitement. "Old feller, we wouldn't want to run into those boys in the daylight."

Prudence told him to head south, but he hesitated. The honorable thing—the responsible thing—would be to double back to the ranger camp and sound an alarm. Perhaps enough men remained there to head off this band as they had done the last raiding party, forcing them to retreat north of the Red before they could strike outlying farms or ranches. But he would be riding into the clutches of the conscription officers. It was a foregone conclusion that they would want him for the Southern army.

The image of Daddy Mike flashed into his mind—Daddy Mike and a Union flag proudly draped on the wall of the Shannon cabin. Back in the 1840s, Mike had campaigned to have Texas brought into the Union. He had fought for that flag in Mexico. He had sworn that nothing would ever cause him to fire upon it, though his passionate rhetoric had led to his being declared a traitor to the Confederacy.

Daddy Mike's fierce patriotism had been burned into Rusty from the time he was old enough to grasp the meaning of the flag. He would rather face prison, or worse, than fight against the Union to which his foster father had proudly given full allegiance.

But Rusty thought of the Haines woman and the little girl. Other settlers would likely fall victim should these raiders not be turned back. Innocent blood would stain his hands if he rode away, taking care only of himself. Even before he decided at a conscious level, he turned Alamo eastward, going back the way he had come.

Perhaps the conscription officers had not yet arrived. Perhaps he could deliver his message and steal away before anyone had a chance to stop him. Perhaps . . . But more likely they would grab him like a wolf grabs a lamb.

He gritted his teeth and put Alamo into a long trot.

CHAPTER

THREE

usty judged that it was near noon when the Fort Belknap settlement loomed up ahead. All along he had hoped he might encounter a friend and impart his information, then slip away without
actually entering camp. Unfortunately he saw no rangers or anyone
else he knew well enough to trust. Some residents of the settlement had no liking for the rangers, who interfered with their chosen work
of stealing reservation horses and running liquor to the same Indians they
stole from. He would have to take his chances.

Len Tanner's legs always looked too long for the rest of him. Ambling
out of the open corral, leading his horse, he spotted Rusty. Surprise yielded
to regret. "I thought you'd got clean away."

Rusty sensed the answer before he asked, "The conscript officers here
already?"

"Two of them, fixin' to take most of the company away. Me included."
His eyes were solemn. "What in the hell did you come back for?"

"I ran into Comanches. The captain needs to know."

"He won't have enough men left to do much about it. They're just waitin'
for the last patrol to report in so they can pick over the rest of the outfit."

Rusty flared. "Strippin' the frontier companies . . . I don't know how
they expect the settlers out here to hang on against the Indians."

"That's gov'ment for you . . . talk big about how much they care, then go off and leave you to fight the wolves by yourself." Tanner looked uneasily toward the headquarters tent. "Tell me what you want the captain to know, then fog it out of here before they see you."

Captain Whitfield stepped from his tent, a well-fed middle-aged stranger beside him. The stranger wore a Confederate uniform, nicely tailored though begrimed from travel.

Rusty caught a sharp breath and held it. "Too late. That'd be one of the conscript officers, I suppose."

Two steps behind that officer came another man wearing a badly weathered Confederate coat with sergeant's stripes. The left leg of his civilian trousers was folded and a wooden leg strapped into place at the knee.

Tanner looked as if he had contracted colic. "Head man, walkin' with the captain, calls hisself Lieutenant Billings. Acts like he owns the world. Sergeant's name is Forrest. Been to war and got his leg shot off."

Despite the wooden leg, Forrest's back was straight and unyielding as if he had been a soldier all his life. Rusty summoned up his defenses, for stern military types always made him ill at ease. Like Captain Whitfield, he had never understood or seen good reason for strict military discipline.

He feared he was going to dislike the sergeant.

Captain Whitfield's eyes revealed misgivings as he approached Rusty. "Back from patrol a little early, aren't you?"

Whitfield knew very well that Rusty had left with no intention of returning. Covering up for me, Rusty thought gratefully. "I came across a Comanche war party last night. They camped better than half a day's ride west of here."

"How many?"

"I counted eight, but it was dark. I'm guessin' twelve or fifteen."

Whitfield turned to the army officer, frowning. "This is what I've been tryin' to tell you, Lieutenant. Time you take most of my men, I won't have enough to face a small war party, much less a real invasion."

"I have my orders. The army doesn't ask for opinions. It says 'jump,' and all we can do is ask 'how high?'"

Bitterly Whitfield said, "I'd like to put that Richmond bunch out here on the picket line and let them fight off Indians for a while. They'd see for themselves that Yankees aren't the worst thing we've got to worry about."

The recruiting officer stared at Rusty, his eyes probing so hard that Rusty felt the man was reading his mind. "You said you saw the Indians more than half a day's ride from here. Isn't that a long way to be scouting by yourself?"

Stiffening, Rusty fished for a good answer. "We're short-handed." He suspected the officer sensed the truth and was trying to coax an admission of desertion. The day that happened, hell would have six inches of frost on the ground and the fires would be out.

Captain Whitfield put in, "Better one man than no men at all. And that's what it's gettin' down to."

Sergeant Forrest spoke for the first time. "How do we know these are hostile Indians?"

Whitfield replied, "Since they were removed from the Texas reservations, any Indians found inside the state's boundaries are considered hostile."

"They might just be hunting buffalo."

"This time of the year they'd go out onto the plains. They wouldn't come down this way to hunt . . . not for buffalo."

The lieutenant demanded, "When did you say that last patrol is due in?"

"They should've been here already."

"Good. We want to start back toward Austin as soon as possible."

"Can't you wait 'til we see about those Indians?"

"War does not await the convenience of anyone. We have no time for running after a bunch of bow-and-arrow savages."

Rusty felt compelled to retort, "You would if they raided *your* place and killed some of *your* family."

Billings demanded, "What's your name, ranger?"

Rusty drew himself up army-straight. "David Shannon. Folks that know me call me Rusty."

"Well, David Shannon, I don't for a minute believe you were scouting out there by yourself. I believe you were running away to avoid conscription."

Rusty did not meet the lieutenant's eyes. He had never considered himself a convincing liar, though he had known many occasions when a lie acceptably told was far preferable to the truth. "Captain Whitfield knows. He's the only man I report to."

"You'll be reporting to *me* as soon as we start back to Austin. Don't you forget that."

Rusty knew he had been trapped the minute he rode into camp. He unsaddled Alamo and began working off his frustration by vigorously brushing the sweaty black hide where the saddle had been. The lieutenant started back toward the headquarters tent, his stride victorious.

The sergeant called after him, "We're a long ways from Austin and farther yet from Richmond. A day or two oughtn't to make much difference."

Billings faced back around. "Need I remind you, Sergeant, that I am in charge here?"

"I never forget that. I was just thinkin' . . ."

"You are not here to think. You are here to obey orders."

"I don't question your authority. I just meant to remind you . . ." He stopped in the middle of the sentence.

Billings and a reluctant Captain Whitfield returned to the captain's tent. Sergeant Forrest stayed behind. He asked Rusty, "Are you sure you could take us back where you saw the Indians?"

"I could, but they wouldn't be there anymore. I figure they're headin' off yonder"—he pointed to the southeast—"where the settlements are thicker."

"If we angled across, shouldn't we run into them, or at least come upon their tracks?"

"You're forgettin' the lieutenant's orders."

"I never forget orders. But sometimes I ignore them when I see a good reason."

"You don't seem to have much fear for authority."

"It was family connections that won the lieutenant his commission. I got these stripes on the battlefield. And this wooden leg besides. After all that, there's damned little that son of a bitch can do to scare me." He walked toward the tent.

Rusty decided he was going to like the sergeant after all. As for Billings, he remembered that Daddy Mike came home from the Mexican War with a jaundiced view of lieutenants.

Rusty discovered Len Tanner silently watching him. Tanner said, "Accordin' to the sergeant, Billings has never seen war against the Yankees. Never even been out of Texas." He waited for Rusty to comment, but Rusty had nothing to say. Tanner added, "How come men that never went to war theirselves are so anxious to send other men there?"

The last patrol arrived about noon, bringing the company's strength to eleven men. Captain Whitfield walked among the new arrivals. "Get yourselves some dinner as quick as you can, then saddle fresh horses." He gave Lieutenant Billings a defiant look. "We're goin' after Indians."

Billings stepped in front of him, his right hand dropping to the butt of a pistol. "The hell you are! I am taking these men to Austin."

Whitfield spread his feet apart in a stance that said he would not be moved. Rusty had never seen him more determined. "This is my camp, Lieutenant, and you are a long way from home."

Billings whirled around, seeking the sergeant. "Forrest, put this man under arrest."

Forrest shook his head. "The captain makes good sense. I'd advise you to listen to him."

The lieutenant started to draw the pistol from its holster. Rusty took a long step forward and grabbed his hand. He twisted the pistol from Billings's grasp. The officer stared at him in fury, then turned upon the sergeant. "I'll have you court-martialed for this."

"Do it and be damned. I never intended to make a career out of the army anyway. Tell them anything you want to. Tell them I got drunk and dallied with lewd women, if that's your pleasure."

Looking around as if seeking help, Billings saw only hostile faces. He gave in grudgingly. "I won't forget this. I could have every one of you shot."

Forrest said, "You're a long way from Austin. If you want to get there, you'd better talk less and listen more." He reached for the lieutenant's pistol. Rusty gave it to him. "I know you've never had to face the Yankees. You ever been in an Indian fight?"

Billings calmed a little. "No. I have been denied both pleasures."

"I've done both, and there's damned little pleasure in either one. You can go with us or stay in camp, whichever suits you best."

"I'll go, if only to keep some Indian from killing you before I can have you properly shot."

Forrest handed the pistol back to the lieutenant, who recognized reality and holstered it.

Captain Whitfield said, "This is no time to fight amongst ourselves. If we can turn back a raid, we'll save some settler families a lot of grief. That ought to count for somethin', Lieutenant."

Billings glared at Forrest. "We'll see how it counts in a court-martial."

Whitfield delegated two rangers to remain at camp. One had reported in sick. The other was the aging Oscar Pickett, exhausted by the long patrol in which he had just participated. Rusty had to leave Alamo behind, for the horse was too tired to undertake another trip. He picked a dun confiscated from a thief caught running stolen horses down from the Indian territory. The rangers had chosen to keep most of the mounts because they lacked the manpower to go looking for their rightful owners. That had been Captain Whitfield's stated justification, at least.

The day was more than half gone. Rusty thought they would need the devil's own luck to find the Indians before dark. He did not feel that lucky. Captain Whitfield sent him out in front to scout, though any ranger could have led the way as well. Where they might connect with the Indians was anyone's guess.

Billings came forward and rode beside him awhile. Rusty suspected the lieutenant was watching him to be sure he did not seize an opportunity to slip away and avoid Confederate service. The officer seemed to have banked the coals of his anger, though he would probably fan them back to life when the mission was over.

Rusty said, "This ain't the healthiest place for you to be."

Billings growled, "As long as I am here, I want to get the first shot at the Indians."

"Like as not, *they'll* fire the first shot. And if they hit anybody, it'll be whoever is up front."

Billings contemplated that possibility and dropped back to rejoin the others. Sergeant Forrest caught up to Rusty awhile later. He rode with his peg leg secured by a leather loop tied above the stirrup. "What did you say that threw a booger into the lieutenant?"

"Just told him the man out in front is usually the first one shot."

Forrest looked back with distaste. "I wouldn't mind if he *did* get shot. Just a little bit, not enough to kill him. He would be a better educated man."

"Somebody like him has got no business carryin' authority over anybody. How come he's never gone back East to fight the Yankees, since he seems to hate them so bad?"

"The same family connections that got him his commission. He claims he's more valuable here, hunting down conscription dodgers. I'll have to admit that he's a human ferret."

"Every man to the job he's best at." Rusty stared ahead a minute, searching the horizon for any sign of movement. "Can he really get you court-martialed?"

"I've got connections of my own, and he knows it." Forrest frowned. "But *you'd* best watch him. He's got a special grudge against you. You might not make it all the way to Austin."

"Not if I get a chance to slip away."

"I'll help you if I can. But first we've got this job to see after." Billings shifted his weight. Rusty suspected that riding with the wooden leg presented some problems in balance.

Rusty had never been to Austin. He could only imagine what it was like. He asked, "What's goin' on back yonder in the settled country?"

"Did you ever see an old quilt coming to pieces at the seams, scattering threads and cotton everywhere? That's Texas. The whole Confederacy too, I would suspect. Money's not worth anything. People barter whatever they've got to get whatever they need, if they can find it at all. Local governments are falling apart. There'd be riots in the streets, only there isn't much left to riot for."

Rusty had surmised as much from rumors and from bits and pieces of news that had drifted into camp. "High time the war was over."

"Pretty soon now, I think."

Forrest watched while Rusty dismounted to study a set of tracks. Rusty soon determined that they were made by a shod horse headed west. Probably a fugitive from conscription, not the Indians they sought.

Forrest said, "You haven't spent your whole life trailing Comanches. What did you do before?"

"Seems like a long time ago, but I growed up on a farm. Farmin' is what I was best at, 'til other things got in the way."

"They've gotten in the way for all of us. We're alike in that. But we don't have the same loyalties, do we?"

Rusty knew, but he asked anyway. "What do you mean?"

"I suspect you've stayed in the frontier service to keep from going into the Army of the Confederation."

"I was just a boy, but I remember how hard Texas fought to get *into* the Union. I've never understood why it got so hell-bent to leave it."

"Slavery was part of it."

"I've got no slaves. Neighbor named Isaac York has one he calls Shanty. He's the only one I know."

"Some of the war has to do with rights that Washington tried to take away from us. Those people back East live a different life than we do out here. What gives them the right to tell us what we can and can't do?"

Rusty shrugged. "Richmond has done the same thing. I ought to have the right to stay on the farm and mind my own business, but the Confederate government won't let me. It wants me to go fight in a war that I didn't start and didn't want."

"There are times when duty overrules our individual rights."

"If we're not fightin' for our rights, then what *are* we fightin' for?"

"I can't answer that. I'm only a sergeant. What's left of one, anyway."

"You lost that leg fightin' Yankees?"

"A minié ball. Came close to dying of blood poisoning."

As Rusty had expected, darkness descended without their seeing any trace of their quarry. They made camp without fresh meat. The captain had forbidden any shooting that might alert the Indians.

In the early-morning sun soon after breaking camp, Rusty saw the Indians three hundred yards ahead, strung out in single and double file. He quickly raised his hand, signaling those behind him to halt. He did not look back, but he heard the horses as Whitfield and Forrest spurred up to join him. Lieutenant Billings seemed to have rethought his ambition to shoot the first Indian. He stayed behind.

Rusty pointed. "They've seen us. They're pullin' into a line."

Whitfield's hand jerked up and down as he counted. "Eighteen. They outnumber us damned near two to one." He looked at Forrest. "Any suggestions?"

"My old commander always said, 'When in doubt, charge.'"

Rusty could not see a good defensive position for either side. Rangers and Indians were all in the open.

Whitfield asked Forrest, "Did your commander always win?"

"He did 'til they killed him."

Whitfield considered. "Indians can count, same as we can. Looks to me like our best chance is to hand them a surprise."

Rusty said, "They've already seen us. How can we surprise them?"

"By doin' what they don't expect." Whitfield turned to Forrest. "You ready to take your old commander's advice?"

"Nothing is better than a good cavalry charge to throw a scare into your adversaries."

Whitfield turned to his rangers. "Check your cinches. You wouldn't want your saddle to turn."

The men dismounted and drew their girths up tight. Rusty glanced toward Billings. The lieutenant appeared to have taken ill.

Forrest noticed it, too. His voice dripped with sarcasm. "Pretend they're Yankees."

Billings made no reply. He wiped a sweaty hand on the gray leg of his trousers. Austin must have been looking like paradise to him.

Whitfield removed his hat and bowed his head. "Lord, we're fixin' to get ourselves into a right smart of a fight. We hope you're on our side in this, but if you can't be, please don't be helpin' them Indians. A-men."

Forming a line, the rangers and two conscription officers put their horses into a long trot. After a hundred yards they spurred into a run. The Indians shouted defiance, waving bows and the few rifles they had. Wind roared in Rusty's ears. The Comanche line began to waver as the rangers neared. Rusty sensed the Indians' confusion. Captain Whitfield had called it right; they had not expected a determined charge by an outnumbered enemy.

The rangers were fifty yards away when the Indian line split apart. A few warriors fired rifles or launched arrows wildly, then followed the others in disorganized retreat. The ranger line swept through the opening. Pistols and rifles cracked. The rangers pulled their horses around. Whitfield stood in his stirrups and shouted, "We can whip them. Give them another run, boys!"

This time there was no Indian line. Warriors were scattered, addled by the audacity of the inferior force. Three lay on the ground. A fourth was afoot, chasing his runaway horse.

Whitfield ordered, "Keep them broke up. Don't let them get back together."

The rangers themselves broke up, pursuing small groups of Indians in various directions. From the first, Rusty had concentrated on one warrior he surmised might be the party leader. He brought his horse to a quick stop, stepped to the ground, and squeezed off a shot. Through the smoke he saw the Indian jerk, then tumble from his horse.

Rusty started to reload. Billings spurred past him, shouting, "I'll finish him!"

The Indian was not ready to be finished. He rose up on shaky legs and fired a rifle. Billings's horse plunged headlong to the ground. Billings lay pinned, a leg caught beneath the struggling animal. Pressing one bloody hand against a wound in his side, the Indian limped toward him. He held a knife.

Billings cried out for help.

Rusty finished reloading, then remounted and put the dun horse into a run. The Comanche saw him coming and moved faster. Billings's voice lifted almost to a scream. "For God's sake, somebody!"

Rusty knew a running shot was chancy, but if not stopped the warrior would reach the lieutenant ahead of him. He brought the stock to his shoulder and braced the heavy rifle with his left hand. The recoil almost unseated him. The powder smoke burned in his nostrils.

The Indian fell, then started crawling. Billings struggled but still could not free himself.

Rusty slid his horse to a stop, dropped the reins, and swung the rifle with both hands. He felt the Indian's skull break under the impact of the heavy barrel. His stomach turned.

Billing's face glistened with sweat, his eyes wide. "Oh God! Are you sure he's dead?"

"Dead enough." Rusty knew the disgust was palpable in his voice, but he did not care. He dismounted, fighting an urge to club Billings as he had clubbed the Indian. "Instead of goin' after one of your own, you came runnin' to try and finish mine when he was already down. I ought to've let him gut you."

A quick look around assured him that no other danger was imminent. The war party had broken up. Warriors were fleeing in several directions, most pursued by rangers.

A single rider approached. Fearing he might be Comanche, Rusty hurried to reload his rifle. He was relieved to recognize Sergeant Forrest.

Billings's fright gave way to impatience. "You just goin' to stand there? Get this horse off of me."

Rusty glared at him. "You brought this on yourself. I wanted to keep that warrior alive."

"What for? There's still plenty of Indians. I'm ordering you, Shannon, get me out of this fix."

"Order away, damn you. I'm not in the army yet."

He tugged halfheartedly, in no real hurry. The horse's dead weight barely budged.

Billings's voice went shrill again. "Put some muscle into it. You want those savages to come back and catch me helpless?"

Rusty saw merit in that proposition. "That'd suit me, except they'd catch me, too. I turned my horse loose to save your ungrateful neck." True, he had let go of the reins, but the dun horse had stopped a hundred feet away. The excitement over, the animal was beginning to graze. Rusty saw no reason to point out that he would be easy to catch. He watched Forrest's approach.

"Maybe me and the sergeant together can get you loose."

Forrest dismounted on the right-hand side because of the wooden leg.

Billings complained, "It's about time you got here. I can't get this red-headed peckerwood to be any help."

Forrest frowned. "I saw enough to know that this red-headed peckerwood saved your life, and with some risk to his own." He leaned down to inspect the fallen animal.

Rusty said, "There's still a little life in that horse, Sergeant. You'd best watch out for his hooves if he commences to kick."

Straining together, Rusty and Forrest managed to raise the animal a little. Billings wriggled free just as the sergeant's breath gave out and forced him to turn loose.

Forrest told Billings, "Better be sure that leg's not broke." His voice sounded hopeful.

Billings rubbed the limb and found it intact though skinned and bruised. He rebuked Rusty. "You ought to've shot that Indian good and proper the first time. He wouldn't have killed my horse." Still sitting on the ground, he jerked his head quickly from one side to the other, eyes wide with concern. Looking for Indians, Rusty supposed.

"What'll I do now?" Billings demanded. "I've been set afoot."

And we ought to leave you that way, Rusty thought. It'd do you a world of good, walking back to Belknap. "There's several Indian ponies runnin' loose. I'll try to catch one for you."

"Then don't just stand there talking." Billings arose shakily and limped to where the Indian lay. He picked up a painted bull-hide shield. With the Comanche's own knife he cut a leather thong from around the warrior's neck and removed a small leather pouch. Rusty knew it would be the Indian's medicine bag, containing sanctified articles supposed to protect him from harm. They had brought him no luck today.

Billings cut two eagle feathers from the warrior's braided hair. "Too bad he wasn't wearing a headdress. That would look good hanging on my wall."

Rusty reflected that Comanches did not often encumber themselves with full headdress on a hasty raid like this one appeared to be. Billings stuck the feathers into his hatband. Rusty hoped they were infested with lice. "I'll see about catchin' you a horse."

Sergeant Forrest said, "I'll go with you."

Billings reacted with fright. "Don't go off and leave me here alone."

Rusty worked up a little saliva and spat dust from his mouth. "If any Indians show up, just lay down and play dead."

Riding away, he told the sergeant, "I almost wish I'd left him and that Comanche to sort things out for theirselves."

"Don't expect gratitude. If anything, he'll resent you more than he already does."

"After I pulled his bacon out of the coals?"

"He's a proud man, though God knows he has little to be proud about. To him you're an inferior, and you've made him beholden to you. That'll itch at him like a case of the mange."

Slowly the rangers gathered. Captain Whitfield was the only casualty. He had taken an arrow in the hip. The wound did not appear deep enough to cripple him permanently, but his ride back to Fort Belknap would be grueling punishment. Blood poisoning was always a possibility.

The captain tried to cover the pain with a forced smile. "At least we've scattered them to hell and gone."

Rusty pointed to the dead warrior. "That was the leader, I think. I was hopin' to take him alive so we could use him to make the others turn back."

Whitfield pressed a bloodied neckerchief against his hip. "We set half of them afoot. Ain't much they can do but give up the game and go back where they came from."

Typically when Comanches split they regrouped at some previously agreed-upon gathering point. Rusty could see three Indians half a mile away, moving north. Two were on horseback, a third walking.

Whitfield said, "Let's back off a ways and give some of them a chance to come get this one. Then we'll follow them so close they can't do anything except return to the river."

"We?" Rusty asked. "You'll do well just to get back to camp."

Whitfield saw the logic and nodded in reluctant agreement. "I'll take one man with me in case I fall off my horse and can't get back on by myself. I'm leavin' you in charge Rusty. You and the sergeant." He made a point of leaving the lieutenant out.

Billings was freshly mounted on a horse Rusty had caught. It was skittish, fighting its head. Rusty hoped it would keep the officer so busy staying in the saddle that he could cause no trouble. A brand on its hip indicated it had belonged to some settler before a Comanche had laid claim. Billings objected, "We've already lost a lot of time. This wasn't our responsibility in the first place, chasing somebody else's Indians."

Whitfield said, "You can go with me back to camp. The rest'll come along when they finish the job."

That suggestion was met in the same sour spirit it was given. "I intend to file a protest when we return to Austin. You people will have hell to pay."

Whitfield grimaced at the pain in his hip. "File and be damned. Take over, Rusty." He turned his horse and started away, giving no indication that he cared whether Billings came along or not.

Sergeant Forrest said, "I'll go with the rangers."

Billings accepted the decision with poor grace. "You make certain you still have all of them when you get back to Belknap."

Forrest's only answer was a grunt that could mean anything or nothing. He glanced at Rusty. "You're holdin' the cards."

Rusty nodded. "We'll do what the captain said . . . back off and give them room. If that's all right with you."

"It's all right with me if we don't see Austin before next Christmas."

They waited afoot, giving their horses a chance to rest. After a time, several warriors who had not lost their mounts returned to retrieve the man who had fallen. They lifted him and placed him belly-down on a black pony. Shortly they caught up to several who were afoot, some of them wounded. The rangers followed at a couple of hundred yards, close enough to be an irritant but not enough to present an immediate threat.

Len Tanner remarked, "To them, we must be like mosquitoes that buzz around your face but don't bite."

Rusty said, "We want them to know we could bite if they was to give us reason."

It did not appear that the Indians were going to give them reason. They trudged northward at a pace slow enough to accommodate those who had to walk.

The sergeant pulled in beside Rusty. "You were unhappy about having to kill that Indian."

"I've killed Indians when I had to. This time, I oughtn't to've had to. If we'd made him a prisoner, I figured the others would give up the raid."

"They gave it up anyway. It's my feeling that you had more reason than that."

Rusty considered before he replied. "If things had taken a different turn a long time ago, I might've been ridin' with them myself."

The sergeant's mouth dropped open. "With the Indians? But you're white."

"You've heard of the big Comanche raid on the Gulf Coast back in 1840? I was there. Just a little tyke, not much more than walkin' good. Best anybody could figure, the Indians killed my folks and carried me off. Intended to raise me for a warrior, I guess. Later on, when volunteers hit the Indians at Plum Creek, Mike Shannon and a preacher named Webb found me on the battleground. Mike and Dora Shannon gave me a home."

"Do you remember anything about your real folks?"

"Just a foggy picture, is all. Never could even remember their names. And nobody ever found out who they were."

"Tough, being left an orphan at that age."

"The worst of it is not knowin' who I am. By raisin', I'm a Shannon. By blood, I have no idea. I see strangers and wonder if they might be kin. I might have kinfolks livin' right down the road from me and I wouldn't know it. Sometimes I wonder if I'm kin to *anybody*. It's like there's a piece of me missin', and I'll never find it."

"Everybody needs family. Without family, a man is like a leaf loose on the wind."

"My real folks couldn't have done better by me than the Shannons did. They treated me like I was their own. But if it hadn't been for the fight at Plum Creek, chances are I'd've been raised Comanche. Or I'd be dead."

"So you feel a kinship to the Indians."

"Don't know as I'd call it kinship, exactly. After all, they must've killed my real folks, and they've killed lots of other good people. But I could've become a Comanche myself if it hadn't been for luck."

"Maybe it wasn't luck. Maybe the Almighty had other plans for you."

"I don't think He planned for me to go back East and shoot at Union soldiers."

"I've suspected all along that you're not much in sympathy with the Confederacy."

"When Daddy Mike came home from the Mexican War, he hung an American flag on the wall where we'd look at it every day. He never wanted to forget what him and others like him went through to get Texas into the Union. Even after Texas seceded, he never backed away from that."

"So now the Shannons are gone and you've got nobody."

"There's a young woman down on the Colorado River. If this war ever gets over with . . ."

"Good for you. When a man spends his life alone it seems like he shrivels up inside. We all need somebody."

Rusty grimaced. "Nobody knows that better than me."

At last the visible remnants of the Comanche raiding party reached the Red River. Rusty was reasonably sure the rest would come along soon, or perhaps had already crossed at some other point. Once the Indians reached the far side, the rangers rode up to the river to water their horses. Rusty was careful where he let his mount step. The Red was notorious for quicksand. The riverbed was wide, but the river itself looked deceptively narrow. Much of the water seeped along just beneath the wet sands, out of sight.

The sergeant eased up beside him. "You know, don't you, that the other side is Union territory?"

"It's also Indian territory."

"But the Indians we trailed have gone on. If someone from this party were to cross, there's nothing I could legally do to make him come back."

Rusty grasped what the sergeant was trying indirectly to say. His skin began to itch. "I've got no business on the other side. No Texan has."

His mind ran back to the sorrowful time when he had been among a party of volunteer rangers escorting friendly Indians across the Red River against their will, throwing them off a Texas reservation they had been promised would be theirs forever. He had felt ashamed, though he understood the settler anxiety that had led to Indian removal. The intervening years had not lessened his feeling of guilt. To go across the river now would reopen old internal wounds, even if the Indians did not inflict new external ones upon him.

The sergeant said, "If we happened to look the other way, you could slip free and go wherever you want to."

"Where I'd most like to go would be my farm down on the Colorado River."

"Other conscription officers might find you."

"There's a lot of timber down there. I'd make them hunt awful hard."

"Then I'd suggest you hang back when we start east. I'll make it a point not to be watching you."

"You'll be in trouble with Lieutenant Billings."

"A mite more won't make any difference. The day the war is over I'll be leaving the army anyway. It doesn't have much place for a one-legged soldier."

Rusty reached for the sergeant's hand. "Maybe in better times we'll see one another again."

"That'd pleasure me." The sergeant turned to address the other rangers. "Anybody share Shannon's leanings?"

Len Tanner said, "If you can stand my company, I'll string along with you, Rusty."

"Thought you'd decided to go to the army."

"I'm afraid I'd have to kill that Billings before we ever got to Austin. At least notch his ears and teach him the ranger code of conduct. I expect there's some silly law against that."

"I'd be tickled to have you."

No one else offered to stay behind. With luck, Rusty thought, the war might be over before any of these men reached the battlefields back East.

Aside from his farm, far away, almost every possession he had was on his back or tied to his saddle. But he had been obliged to leave his black horse behind. To try to retrieve Alamo now was too risky. Returning to camp a second time would ask more from good luck than one man was entitled to.

To the sergeant he said, "Please ask Captain Whitfield to watch out for my horse. If the outfit breaks up he can take Alamo home with him. I'll find him when this foolishness is over with."

"I'll tell him."

The sergeant motioned for the men to move out.

Tanner said, "I'm only sorry that we'll miss seein' the big explosion."

"What explosion?"

"The lieutenant when he finds that we slipped out of his hands. He's liable to swell up like a toad and bust wide open."

Rusty watched the departing riders, then cast a glance back over his shoulder toward the river. He felt uncomfortably exposed out here in the open. A prickly feeling ran along his spine.

"I've got a notion somebody's watchin' us. We'd best be travelin', too."

"You lead, and I'll foller."

CHAPTER

FOUR

en Tanner was unusually quiet. Most of the time the lanky ranger had much more to say than Rusty thought necessary. He would ramble aimlessly, sometimes stopping in the middle of a sentence and jumping to a totally unrelated subject. That he was quiet now indicated he felt as conflicted as Rusty about their sudden leave-taking.

After one of the long silences Rusty asked, "Wonderin' if you did the right thing, comin' with me?"

"I'm *always* wonderin' if I've done the right thing. I've been known once or twice to make a mistake."

"I can't imagine when that was."

"What'll we do when we get to that farm of yours?"

"We'll plow and plant, and keep our eyes peeled for conscript officers."

"You still got the Monahan family livin' on your place?"

"Been a long time since I heard from them, but they're still there as far as I know . . . Mother Clemmie and Geneva, and the two younger girls. And Clemmie's old daddy, Vince Purdy."

"It's a damned shame what Caleb Dawkins done to Lon Monahan and his boy Billy . . . takin' them out and hangin' them like horse thieves, and for no reason except they didn't want Texas to leave the Union. There was lots of people agreed with them."

"And some of them died for it."

The memory was still bitter as quinine. Rusty tried to keep it pushed back into the darkest corner of his mind, but sometimes it intruded, ugly and mean. Farmer Lon Monahan had been too vocal for his own good, persisting in voicing unpopular political opinions at a time when Confederate zealots like Colonel Caleb Dawkins made such expressions potentially lethal. Rusty had helped cut the bodies of Lon and his son Billy from the tree where they had been lynched. An older Monahan son, James, had fled to the West, beyond reach of Dawkins and his night-riding patriots.

Too late to save the Monahans, the extreme fanaticism had diminished as the war's casualty lists had grown and its hardships had spread disillusionment to the outermost reaches of the Confederacy.

Tanner smiled. "That Geneva's a pretty little slip of a girl. If you hadn't already put a claim on her, I'd do it myself. How long since you heard from her?"

"Got a letter a year or so ago. There was probably more that never reached me. No tellin' what went with our mail."

"At least you'll be seein' her pretty soon."

"If she's still on the farm where I left her and her folks." Because he had not heard from her in so long, he could imagine all manner of misfortunes that might have befallen the surviving Monahans.

Tanner said, "Wish I had a girl waitin' for *me*. I never knew how to act around women, or what to say."

"It's hard to picture you not havin' somethin' to say."

"Always seemed like when I opened my mouth the wrong words came out. By the time I knew what I ought to've said, the girl would be gone."

"I was awkward around Geneva 'til we got used to one another. After that, things just seemed to come natural."

Tanner considered awhile, then asked, "Did you and her ever . . ." He left the question unfinished.

Rusty's face warmed. "She ain't that kind."

Tanner looked sheepish. "I was only wonderin' if you ever talked about marryin'."

"Oh. Well, it was understood, sort of. I never felt like I ought to ask her as long as the war was on."

"Maybe you should've. Things can change when you're gone for a long time."

Rusty fell silent, trying not to think about the violent deaths of Lon and Billy. He preferred to recall Geneva, to bring her image alive in his mind. He tried to hear the music of her voice and see her as he had first seen her long ago.

Tanner's edgy tone shook him back to sober reality. "I thought we was all by ourselves."

Rusty jerked to attention. His skin prickled as five horsemen pushed out of a thicket. One cradled a rifle across his left arm.

Tanner pulled on the reins. "At least they ain't Comanches."

"Just the same, they don't look like they've come to bid us welcome." Dismounting, Rusty slipped his rifle from its scabbard. He stood behind his horse to shield himself. Holding the weapon ready across his saddle, he watched the oncoming riders.

Tanner followed his example, eyes tense but not afraid. Tanner was seldom afraid of anything he could see. "Brush men?"

"I don't know who else would be so far out this way." Rusty did not like the riders' somber expressions. The black-bearded man carrying the rifle pushed a little past the others. He gave first Tanner and then Rusty a hasty appraisal that brought no friendliness into his sharp black eyes. He leaned forward, focusing a fierce suspicion on Rusty.

"Who are you men, and what's your business?"

If these had been Comanches, Rusty would have no doubt about their intentions. The fight would already be under way instead of hanging in the air like electricity before a storm.

"Name's Shannon . . . Rusty Shannon. This here's Len Tanner. We're headed for my farm."

"Ain't no farms out this way."

"Mine is down on the Colorado River."

"You're a long ways from home. How come you so far west?"

The other riders were unshaven, which added to their formidable appearance. None had a beard as black as the leader's, however. Rusty sized them up as probable army deserters, conscription dodgers, or simply fugitives from the law for various and sundry crimes. "We didn't come to cause trouble. We had no idea there was anybody around."

One man spoke hopefully, "They got honest faces, Oldham. They don't look like conscript officers."

"Now, Barlow, you know you can't tell what a conscript officer looks like. They don't wear a uniform, most of them." Oldham cut his sharp gaze back to Rusty. "Maybe you're rangers."

Another rider pulled a paint horse up beside the leader and gave Rusty and Tanner an accusing study. His eyes reminded Rusty of a wolf's. He was a youth of eighteen or nineteen, his uneven whiskers patchy, soft, and light in color. "They *are* rangers, big brother. I seen both of them over at Fort Belknap."

The paint had gotch ears, a sign it had probably belonged to Comanches at one time. Rusty could only guess how this youngster came by it.

Tanner admitted, "We *was* rangers. They was fixin' to drag us into the army, so we taken French leave. Like most of you, I'd judge."

"That don't hold no water with me, Clyde," the youth said to Oldham.

"Me neither, little brother."

The one called Barlow said, "It could be the truth. Lately the army's been grabbin' everybody that ain't missin' an arm or a leg, right down to boys and old men."

Clyde Oldham objected, "Then again, these could be spies, sent to find us and bring the army."

The youngster declared, "Only safe thing is to shoot them." He seemed eager to start.

Barlow pressed, "What if they ain't spies?"

Oldham scowled. "Then we've made a mistake. Too bad, but I never heard nobody claim that war is fair. Half the time it's the wrong people that get killed."

Rusty saw agreement in the other men's faces, all but Barlow's. He leaned his rifle across the saddle and drew a bead on Oldham's broad chest. He tried to keep his voice calm. "We're liable to take more killin' than you'll want to do."

Barlow raised a hand, his palm out. "Let's don't nobody do nothin' hasty. If you say you ain't rangers anymore, I say we ought to take your word . . . for now. How about you two comin' along with us?"

"We've got plans of our own."

The Oldhams and two others cautiously moved up a little, trying to form a semicircle that would prevent escape. Rusty pivoted the rifle barrel from Clyde Oldham to his younger brother. "You-all stop where you're at."

Tanner whispered, "There ain't but five, two for me and two for you. We can share the other one."

Rusty thought it would be a poor consolation to die knowing they had won the fight. "We don't want to kill anybody."

Barlow said, "We don't either." He seemed to be speaking to his friends more than to Rusty and Tanner. "We came here to stay out of the war. Ain't no point in startin' one of our own."

The younger Oldham looked to the men on either side of him. He echoed Tanner. "Ain't but two of them. You-all afraid?"

Clyde Oldham cautioned, "*You'd* better be, little brother. You've got a rifle aimed right at your belly."

"Well, I ain't afraid." The youth's eyes gave away his intention just before he brought up a pistol and pointed it toward Rusty.

Rusty muttered, "Oh hell!" and triggered the rifle. Through the smoke he saw young Oldham jerk back as if kicked by a mule. In reflex the youth fired his pistol. The paint staggered and fell, dumping Oldham on the ground. He had shot his own horse.

Tanner shouted, "Don't anybody make a bad move. I still got a load in this gun."

Clyde Oldham left the saddle quickly and knelt over his younger brother. "Buddy!" he cried. The dying horse was kicking. Oldham dragged the youth away from the flailing hooves.

The other three men stared as if they could not believe what they saw. Tanner said, "You-all throw them guns to one side before you get off of your horses." They complied.

Rusty was momentarily in shock. He had acted by instinct. He had not had time even to take good aim. Now he saw the blood and knew it was of his own doing. He felt sick.

Tanner calmly told him, "We're still deep in the woods. You better reload that rifle or draw your pistol."

"I hope I didn't kill that kid."

"If you didn't, you taught him a hell of a lesson." Tanner moved slowly from behind his horse, keeping his rifle trained in the direction of the brush men. Clyde Oldham had laid his rifle on the ground. Tanner tossed it away and did the same with the pistol the younger Oldham had dropped. He leaned over the fallen youth, then looked up at Rusty.

"You hit him in the arm. It's a hell of a mess."

Rusty gathered his wits and reloaded his rifle. Oldham had ripped his brother's sleeve to expose the wound. The arm was shattered. The youth groaned, his face draining white in shock.

Oldham cried, "He'll bleed to death."

Rusty handed his rifle to Tanner. "Not if I can help it." He wrapped his neckerchief above the wound as a tourniquet. He twisted it tightly until the blood slowed. Anger began to rise. "Damn it to hell, I didn't want this. But he was fixin' to shoot me."

Oldham showed no sign that he had heard, or if he heard, that it made any difference. "Little brother, don't you go and die on me. Don't do it, I say."

The only answer was a deep groan.

Rusty managed to choke the blood flow down to a trickle. "I don't suppose anybody in your camp claims to be a doctor?"

Barlow said, "There's a preacher comes to see us now and again, but he ain't there right now."

"A preacher?" Rusty felt a sudden hope. "Would his name be Webb?"

"That's him. You know him?"

"From as far back as I can remember."

The more he looked at young Oldham's smashed arm, the more he despaired of saving it. At this point he would not wager two bits that the youth would even survive. "Ain't much more we can do for him out here. You-all better get him back to your camp."

Clyde Oldham looked up, hatred in his eyes. "You think we'll just let the two of you ride away?"

"That's all we wanted in the first place. The rest of this was your own doin'."

Tanner stepped between the men and the weapons they had tossed away. "You can come back later to fetch these."

Rusty heard horses and looked up. Six or eight riders came loping out of the thicket toward them. His heart sagged, and for a moment he felt defeated. Then he recognized the man riding in the lead. Hope began a tentative revival.

Tanner raised his rifle. Rusty motioned for him to lower it. "James Monahan is with them."

Tanner hesitated. "Last time you and him met, you didn't part real friendly."

"He's the best hope we've got. We can't fight our way past all that bunch."

James brought his mount to a rough stop, raising a small cloud of dust. "We heard shootin'. What the hell happened here?"

Barlow jerked his head toward Rusty. "It was Buddy Oldham's fault. He tried to shoot this ranger."

James recognized Rusty. His reaction was less than cordial. "Damn it,

Rusty Shannon, can't you go anywhere without takin' trouble with you?" James examined the wounded arm and looked up at Rusty, his eyes critical. "If you had to shoot him, couldn't you just crease him a little?"

Rusty knew it would be poor politics to say he had aimed at the heart. "I didn't want to shoot him at all. He gave me no choice."

James turned on Clyde Oldham, his voice severe. "You're his big brother. Looks like you could've kept him jugged and stoppered."

"He's always had a mind of his own."

"Damned pity he never used it much." James looked up at the men who had ridden with him. "Let's get him to camp and see what more we can do. Mack, we'll put him on your horse. You can ride behind the saddle and hold him on." He faced Rusty again. "Did you have to shoot Buddy's horse, too?"

"He did it himself."

James nodded. "That don't come as any big surprise." He helped Clyde Oldham and Barlow lift the half-conscious boy into the saddle. The man named Mack sat behind the cantle, one arm holding Buddy in place. James jerked his head at Rusty and Tanner. "You-all come and go with us."

Rusty saw no choice. "We're keepin' our guns."

"Be careful whichaway you point them."

Riding, Rusty studied Geneva's brother. James had been forced to leave home early in the war and live by his wits in a wild area where the only people he encountered were Indians and fugitives like himself. The strain had put a haunted, desperate look in his eyes. Rusty knew him to be near his own age, mid- to late twenties, but James had the appearance of a man closer to his forties.

Rusty wanted to ask him a dozen questions, most having to do with Geneva, but this did not seem the time.

James broke the silence. "You still a ranger?"

"Not since yesterday." He explained the circumstances under which he and Tanner had left the company.

James said, "You took a long time about doin' the smart thing."

"It wasn't smart. We just didn't see where we had any choice. We were tryin' to explain that when Buddy-Boy decided to commence firin'."

Clyde Oldham said bitterly, "He couldn't have hit you. He never could shoot worth a damn."

"I wish I'd known that."

Oldham seemed to be making an effort not to cry. "I brought him out here to protect him, to keep the war from takin' him. And now this . . ."

Rusty had no answers left. A thousand of them would not change what had happened. He asked James, "Are you the chief of this camp?"

"This camp ain't got no chief. Every man is free to come and go, to do what suits him as long as he don't hurt somebody else. We stay together for mutual protection against the Indians, the army, and the rangers." His eyes narrowed. "Especially the rangers."

"You don't need to be concerned about the rangers anymore. There's not enough left to guard a jailhouse, much less to raid a brush camp. I'd worry a lot more about the Indians."

"Worst they've ever done is make a try for our horses. Raidin' parties ride a long way around a camp as big as ours."

Rusty had heard talk about a large gathering of brush men far west of Fort Belknap, near the ragged breaks that marked the eastern edge of the staked plains. He supposed the fugitives moved camp from time to time for security.

Tanner muttered, "We've got ourselves into a dandy fix. We ought to've fought when we had the chance."

Rusty said, "I'd've ridden fifty miles extra to stay out of their way. All we can do now is keep our eyes open."

The brush men rode ahead but watched lest Rusty and Tanner turn and run. The situation reminded Rusty of two fighting bobcats locked in a sharp-clawed embrace from which neither dared try to break away.

Tanner asked, "What'll we do when we get to wherever we're goin'?"

"We'll dance to whatever tune the fiddler plays."

Rusty smelled wood smoke before he saw the camp. A number of horses grazed on a rolling stretch of open prairie, accompanied by a slack-shouldered boy who appeared to be asleep in the saddle. Rusty's attention went to a long-legged mule. Recognition brought a surge of pleasure that for a moment shoved aside his concern over their trouble. "Yonder's old Chapultepec."

Tanner said, "Looks like him, all right."

The mule looked up as the horsemen rode past, but he went back to grazing.

Tanner shrugged. "Didn't recognize you. I suppose old mules are forgetful, like old people."

"He'd've noticed if I'd been ridin' Alamo. They always got along good together." Rusty thought about the deserter who had stolen the animal from the ranger camp. "Lancer must be here, too. I owe him a busted jaw for stealin' Daddy Mike's mule."

James Monahan stopped and waited for Rusty to come up even with him. "You know that mule?"

"My old daddy brought him home from the Mexican War. A deserter named Lancer stole him awhile back. Me and him are fixin' to talk about that."

James frowned. "It won't be much of a conversation. Lancer is buried where we had our last camp." He pointed northwestward. "He was a hard man to get along with. Every time somethin' didn't suit him, he threatened to go fetch the rangers. One of the boys got a bellyful of it."

Rusty said, "I'm goin' to want my mule."

James did not reply. Rusty took that as a sign James was not sure he and Tanner would ever leave this place.

He had seen ranger camps and army camps. This looked like neither. It was a haphazard scattering of canvas tents and rude brush shelters strung along the banks of a creek. Half a dozen campfires sent up their smoke, and the smell of roasting meat made him aware that he was hungry.

Hell of a thing, Rusty thought, thinking about my stomach when I ought to be thinking about my hide.

Tanner remarked to James, "It don't look like you-all's cup has run over with prosperity."

"At least we ain't takin' orders from Richmond, or Austin either. We're still free men."

Free seemed a questionable description. The brush men were free in the sense that they were neither in the army nor in jail. But their situation hardly met Rusty's definition of freedom. Hostile Indians roamed to the north and west. To the east, the Confederate government considered them traitors. The only relatively open course was to the south, toward a distant foreign border. Those willing to flee to Mexico had done so much earlier in the war. In a sense, those who remained here were confined to a huge prison without walls. They were refugees, hiding, moving periodically lest they be discovered and overrun.

Almost immediately Rusty and Tanner were surrounded by more than a dozen men. He knew his rifle would be useless. At best he might shoot one man before the rest swarmed over him. Tanner's expression said he was still willing to fight if Rusty gave him the sign. Rusty shook his head.

Somebody demanded, "James, where'd you find these rangers?"

Rusty did not know the speaker's name, but he remembered the face from among the men who used to loaf around the dramshops at the Fort

Belknap settlement. He looked about, hoping to see other familiar faces. Surely some of the men he remembered deserting from the rangers would be among this group.

Clyde Oldham pointed to his brother and said Rusty had shot him . . . shot him down in cold blood. Someone grabbed Rusty's rifle, jerking it from his hand before he could react. Tanner tried to hang on to his, but two men dragged him from his saddle, landing on top of him as he hit the ground. They took his rifle and his pistol.

Rusty felt hostility radiating from the men who surrounded him. He was reminded of the hatred Caleb Dawkins and other Confederate zealots had shown toward the Monahan family, hatred that had culminated in two hangings. His pistol was still in its holster on his hip, but if he tried to draw it he would not live to pull the trigger.

It would be useless to argue that the army had become too small and too weak to indulge its time searching the wide West Texas wilderness for a poverty camp like this. It was likely that most of these men had hidden out through a major part of the war. Many had probably suffered during the early period when fanaticism had inflicted injustice upon those whose loyalties were suspect. They would not easily believe that the long war had sapped the energy and resolve of even the most extreme, like the hangman Caleb Dawkins. Most Texans now simply wanted to put the conflict behind them and rebuild what they could from the wreckage of war.

James stood in front of Rusty's horse. "You'd just as well get down. I'll see that nobody does anything to you."

Though hostility was strong in the faces Rusty saw uplifted toward him, the men seemed willing to accept James's leadership. James extended his hand. "Just for safety, maybe you'd better give me your pistol."

Rusty grasped it stubbornly. "I believe I'll keep it."

He expected an argument, but James made what in other circumstances might be regarded as a faint smile. To the men around him he said, "Leave him hold on to it. He knows better than to try and do anything." To Rusty he added, "I'll give you ranger boys credit for guts, even if not good sense."

Rusty was surprised to see a couple of women and half a dozen children in the camp, families uprooted by the war.

James said, "First thing, we'd better see what we can do about Buddy."

Young Oldham was carried into a tent and laid down on some blankets. James went to his knees beside him and gave the wound a closer examination. He loosened the tourniquet to let the blood flow. It had slowed considerably from before. His face was grave as he looked up at Clyde Oldham. "Ain't nothin' holdin' that arm together but a little skin. The bone is busted into a dozen pieces. It needs to come off."

Oldham's voice went shrill. "Amputate? But what can he ever do with just one arm?"

"Live, maybe. Otherwise, he ain't got a jackrabbit's chance. If I was you, Clyde, I'd go out yonder and find somethin' to drink. You don't want to watch this."

Oldham's stricken gaze fastened on Rusty for a moment before he walked away from the tent. A friend put an arm around his shoulder and said, "Come on, Clyde. You need a shot of whiskey."

James beckoned to Rusty. "You did the shootin'. It's your place to do the cuttin'."

Rusty had treated bullet and arrow wounds, but he had never cut off an arm or leg. James held the blade of a skinning knife over a campfire, then handed it to him. Sweat trickling down his face and burning his eyes, Rusty severed what remained of the arm.

Young Oldham screamed. His brother turned to come back, but his friend held him. "We both need a drink, Clyde."

Rusty felt sick at his stomach. He fought to keep everything in it from coming up.

James said, "You'll need to tie off those veins."

"I'd better let you do it." Rusty walked out of the tent and leaned against a tree while his stomach emptied itself. Barlow joined him, kicking dirt over the vomit. "There's a spring down yonder. You can wash the blood off. Then I know where there's a jug. It ain't good whiskey, but there ain't no good stuff to be had."

Rusty doubted he could keep the whiskey down.

Barlow said, "The kid ought to live, if shock don't kill him, or blood poisonin'. Or he don't bite himself like a rattlesnake."

Kneeling by the spring, actually just a slow seep in the bank of the nondescript creek, Rusty dipped his hands into the cold water. The blood would wash away, but not the memory. "Why did that button have to play the fool?" he demanded. "This damned war . . ."

"Some people are bound to be fools, war or no war. Buddy-Boy never did have brains enough to pour water out of a bucket. You said somethin' about headin' for your farm."

"We were, 'til we ran into this outfit." Rusty looked to the west, where the sun was rapidly sinking toward the horizon. "Are we prisoners?"

"Depends on how you look at it. Some of the boys probably wouldn't want to see you leave just yet."

"Clyde Oldham might decide in the middle of the night to shove a knife between my ribs. Especially if his brother takes a turn for the worse."

"I'll keep an eye on Clyde. Anyway, if he wanted you that bad, he could follow and kill you the first time you stopped."

Rusty clenched a fist. "He could've sat on that little brother of his if he'd tried to."

"It's like I said about fools. Those two tried to kill an army recruiter. That's when they skedaddled to the brush."

James came out of the tent, his hands bloody. Rusty started to approach him, but an angry look in James's face turned him back.

Damn it all, Rusty thought, I didn't ask for this.

He wanted to ask James about Geneva and the rest of the family, but he decided it would be prudent to wait.

Somebody shouted, "Yonder comes Old Man Timpson."

Rusty squinted. He made out the figure of a rider leading two pack horses a quarter mile from camp.

Barlow took joy in the sight. "The old man brings us supplies. People here have got folks back in the settlements. They send what they can . . . flour and salt, powder and lead. And news . . . the old man is our main way of keepin' up with what's goin' on back yonder. Him, and now and again Preacher Webb."

"This is a long way for Preacher Webb to travel."

"He answers his callin'. There's some people here who need a strong dose of preachin' any time they can get it."

Rusty agreed. "There's been a right smart of raidin' and horse stealin' laid at these men's door."

"There's a few sour apples like them Oldham brothers, but you can't blame everybody. Most of these are decent people. The war put them in a bad situation, that's all. When it's over they'll go back to where they came from and tend to their own business."

"*Most.* But what about those who use the war as an excuse, the ones who would've been renegades even without it?"

"Time'll weed them out. They'll rob the wrong citizen or steal the wrong horse."

"You could've weeded them out yourselves."

"We need them. When the war is over we won't need them anymore."

Men of the camp surged forward as Old Man Timpson rode in. He flipped the pack horses' lead rein to one of them.

Somebody shouted, "I hope you brung us some coffee."

The old man's voice was hoarse. He was weary from a long ride. "Sure enough, along with flour and salt and such." He coughed, trying to clear his throat of dust. "But I brought somethin' a lot better than any of that."

Barlow spoke up, "I don't know nothin' better than coffee."

"I brought news." The old man took off his hat and bowed his head. "Praise God . . ." He paused, taking a deep breath. "The war is over."

Shouts erupted among the men, moving through the camp like a whirlwind as the message was relayed from one to another. Timpson dismounted slowly and carefully, then clung wearily to the saddle, his aging legs stiff. He explained that General Robert E. Lee had surrendered and the Confederacy was no more.

Rusty had sized up Barlow as a farmer, for he had the strong, broad shoulders of one used to hard and heavy work, his large hands probably accustomed to gripping the handles of a plow. Yet this big man stood without shame and let tears roll down his whiskery cheeks in front of everybody. He murmured, "I had begun to think we never would live to see this day."

He turned toward the crowd. "Friends, looks to me like we ought to join together and give thanks . . . thanks to Him who has delivered us from this terrible ordeal."

He stood with hat in hand, waiting for the remainder of the crowd to gather. The two women clutched their husbands' arms and wept. Many men knelt while Barlow said his prayer. His voice gained strength as he spoke.

"Lord, Thou hast watched over us and brought us through four long years of misery. Now we bow to offer our gratitude. Thou hast brought us deliverance from the evil that has rent families asunder and torn our country apart. We ask Thee now to give us errant children guidance as we undertake to bind up the wounds. We beseech Thy blessings upon the widow, the orphan, the soldier crippled. Bring us together and make us whole again, we ask in the name of Him who died for our sins, Amen."

Rusty shivered as he pondered the significance of the old man's news. He had sensed the end coming, yet it seemed unreal that the years of agony had come to an end.

Barlow asked Timpson, "Does this mean we can go home?"

"It means there's no Confederate government to say you can't."

Tanner gripped Rusty's shoulder, jubilation in his eyes. "That high-and-mighty Lieutenant Billings can't have got halfway to Austin yet. Wouldn't you love to see his face when he finds out?"

Rusty felt more awed than jubilant. "This means we didn't really have to quit the ranger company."

Clearly, that idea had not occurred to Tanner, but it did not give him pause. "There may not be a company left anyhow. If there's no more Confederacy, there's no more government."

"If there's no government, there's no law." The thought brought a chill to Rusty. He could visualize criminals banding together, ranging over the country with impunity, taking what they wanted, smashing anyone daring enough to stand in their way. "There's *got* to be law."

"It's just so much paper if there ain't nobody to carry it out."

Rusty wished they had not quit the rangers. "Len, we've got to go back."

"Where?"

"To the camp at Fort Belknap. Captain Whitfield may need us now more than ever."

Tanner's face fell. "I was countin' pretty strong on goin' home and seein' my folks."

"Duty, Len. I don't see we've got a choice if we ever want to hold our heads up again."

"I never saw anybody so hell-bent on duty."

"Then go on south without me. I know what I've got to do."

"I've already had to save your life once or twice. You'll probably get yourself killed if I'm not around, so I'll go with you. But damn it, Rusty, that sense of duty will be the death of you someday, I swear it will."

Rusty felt a strong hand grip his arm. He turned to a grim-faced James Monahan.

James said quietly, "Now's your chance to get out of camp while everybody's mind is on somethin' else."

A quick glance showed Rusty that nobody seemed to be paying any attention to him and Tanner.

"We'll catch our horses and go. But first I want to ask you . . ."

Impatiently James declared, "You ain't got time to ask questions, and I ain't got time to answer any. Git while the gittin's good."

Reluctantly Rusty had to acknowledge the wisdom in James's advice. He was bursting with questions about Geneva, but they would have to wait.

"All right, let's go, Len. But I'm takin' Daddy Mike's old mule."

James jerked his head toward the place where the two rangers' horses were tied. "Take him and be damned. But whatever you do, do it quick."

CHAPTER
FIVE

A t first the ranger camp appeared deserted. Captain Whitfield's tent was still standing. The others had been struck, the canvas folded and stacked on the ground. Wooden stakes lay in a pile.

Riding in, Rusty saw only a few ranger horses grazing free. He gave a quick, happy shout as he recognized Alamo among them. The horse nickered at Chapultepec. Rusty slipped the loop of a rawhide reata around Alamo's neck and petted the black horse before leading him into camp with the mule. "Old friend, I was afraid somebody with light fingers might've taken a fancy to you." To Rusty, a thief was a thief, whether he decorated his head with a hat or a feather.

Tanner grunted. "Place looks like everybody died."

"Bound to be somebody around."

"We might've come for nothin'. But at least you got your horse back."

That in itself was justification enough for returning, Rusty thought. "Maybe the captain's still here."

He found Whitfield taking his rest on a cot inside the stained old canvas tent. It struck Rusty that he had never seen the captain idle in the daytime. But he had never seen Whitfield take an arrow in the hip before, either.

Whitfield arose slowly, wincing in pain from the wound. He seemed drawn, his eyes dull as he shook Rusty's hand, then Tanner's. "I thought you boys took off for the tall timber."

Rusty said, "We heard about the surrender. What's happened to the company?"

Whitfield made a sweeping motion with his hand. "You can see about all that's left. Billings and the sergeant took most of them away before word came about the war. The others didn't see much point in stayin' around after we got the news. If you-all came back with any hope of gettin' paid, forget it. Even if they gave it to you, a barrelful of Confederate money wouldn't buy you a plug of tobacco."

Rusty said, "We gave up on pay a long time ago. We just thought you might need us."

"If somebody was to commit cold-blooded murder on the street in Fort Belknap, we couldn't do anything about it. We've got no authority."

"We could still turn back Indians if any tried a raid. We wouldn't need anybody's authority for that."

"We'd need more manpower. It's all finished, boys. If you've got a home to go to, you'd just as well head thataway. I'm goin' myself, soon as Oscar Pickett fetches a wagon so I can load up the state's property and keep these rascals around here from stealin' it."

The prospects were troubling. Rusty said, "I don't see how a country can get along without law."

"Texas was part of the Confederacy. That's gone. It'll take the Federals awhile to set up their own government. 'Til then, except for maybe a little local law, everything is left hangin' between the devil and the deep blue sea."

Rusty felt cold. "So it's every man for himself."

"If I was a robber or a horse thief, I'd be pickin' in tall cotton right now."

Rusty told the captain about the brush camp, now in the process of breaking up.

Tanner said, "There's men in that bunch would skin their grandmothers for six bits a hide."

"Not much we can do about them now."

Tanner pointed his chin at Rusty. "He done somethin'. Shot one of them, he did."

"By accident?"

Rusty shook his head. "I did it on purpose. Had to. But I'm hopin' he lives."

Tanner said, "You better hope he don't. He may come after you some-day. Even with one arm, he could still blow a hole through you."

Whitfield frowned. "There was a time we might've broken up a camp like that, but I didn't want to. Most of them were just tryin' to stay out of the army. Now they're not my problem anymore. As long as they don't bother me or mine, I won't bother them."

Rusty asked Whitfield, "Do you think you can travel with that wounded hip, even in a wagon?"

"As long as it's in the direction of home, I can grit my teeth and keep goin'."

Home. The word held the warmth of spring sunshine.

"It'll be safer, travelin' in a bunch. Me and Tanner will wait here with you 'til Oscar Pickett gets back. Then we'll ride along with you as far as we can."

Rusty could see in Whitfield's eyes that the wagon's jolting hurt him, but the captain voiced no complaint. Rusty had once suffered through the ordeal of a long ride after a Comanche arrow had driven deeply into his leg. Tanner had cauterized the wound with a red-hot blade. It still pained him to remember, though the searing probably saved his leg. Healed now, the scar was still large and ugly, and it sometimes itched enough to drive him to distraction. He could imagine what the captain was going through.

Oscar Pickett hunched beside Whitfield, his age-spotted, arthritis-knotted hands gripping the reins. Two of Whitfield's horses and the mule Chapultepec trotted behind, tied to the wagon by long reins. In the wagon bed were folded tents, what few supplies had remained in camp, and Whit-field's and Pickett's personal possessions. These were too meager to strain the capacity of the canvas war bags in which they were stowed.

Rusty and Tanner rode beside the wagon, Rusty leading the unclaimed dun horse he had used before recovering Alamo. They came to a burned-out cabin, its blackened ruins slumped in a heap near a seeping spring.

"Good place to water and rest the horses," Rusty observed. He was more concerned with giving the captain a rest, but he knew better than to say so. Whitfield's pride would make him insist on traveling farther.

The captain offered no complaint. He said, "I remember the folks who lived here. Jackson was their name. Indians kept wartin' them 'til they decided to go back to East Texas. Then the Comanches came and burned the cabin. Figured that would keep the family from ever comin' back."

Rusty figured the Indian victory would be short-lived.

"If the Jacksons don't," he said, "somebody else'll claim this land. Once the soldiers start comin' home, this country will settle up again, heavier than it was before."

Whitfield made no comment.

Rusty said, "They'll need law to protect them."

Whitfield shook his head. "I've been the law long enough. I just want to go back to whatever's left of my own place and enjoy some quiet for a while."

Tanner put in, "Them's my sentiments, too. We ought to think of our own selves for a change. All the work we done, all the ridin' we put in, and what's it got for us?" He held up his left arm. His bony elbow poked out through a long tear in the ragged sleeve. "Ain't even got a decent shirt."

So far as Rusty knew, Oscar Pickett had no home to go back to. At his age, his prospects appeared limited. Rusty took it for granted that the captain would see to the old ranger's welfare, giving him a place to stay in return for whatever work Pickett was able to do. Otherwise Pickett was likely to end up in some demeaning job like swamping out a dramshop just to feed himself and have a roof of something more substantial than leaky canvas to turn aside the rain.

Rusty felt a hollowness inside as he contemplated his own future. He had the farm. He could pick up a handful of its rich soil and know it was something substantial, something that was his. And he was confident that Geneva would stand by his side. But everything else was an unanswered question. Texas, along with the rest of the Confederacy, had lost the war. It was only a matter of time until the Federals moved in troops to take over whatever remained of a government. Where would the defeated Confederates fit in, or would they fit in at all? What punishments might they suffer at the hands of the victors?

Rusty had never taken up arms against the Union, yet in his won way as a ranger for the state of Texas he had been an agent of the Confederacy. Would he be subject to punishment? If so, what would the punishment be? These nagging questions ran through his mind, seeking answers but only stirring up more questions.

He voiced some of his concerns to Whitfield, who lay in the shade of a tree beside the slow-yielding spring. The captain said, "They can't line us all up and shoot us; there's way too many. Ain't enough jails between here and Cape Cod to put us all behind bars. We'll make do somehow as long as we're livin' and breathin'. Even if they burned us out like Sherman did in Georgia, there's always the land. They can't burn that up."

They had unhitched the wagon team and led them to the water. Rusty took them back for a second chance to drink after their rest, then hitched them to the wagon again. "We'd best be gettin' on. It's a long ways to the Colorado River."

He began seeing familiar landmarks he associated with the Monahan farm. They brought memories rushing back. He tried to concentrate on Geneva, but thoughts of her led to the chill of remembered violence. He relived the brutal lynching of Lon and Billy Monahan and a frightening nighttime raid that had culminated in the Monahan house going up in flames.

Tanner said, "I'll bet you're thinkin' about that Geneva girl."

Rusty had been struggling with bitter memories of Colonel Caleb Dawkins and his son Pete, but he did not feel like arguing with Tanner over technicalities. "Didn't know it showed."

Len suggested, "We could swing by the old Monahan farm, maybe spend the night there."

Rusty dreaded the feelings such a visit would inevitably stir up. "It'd add some miles, maybe cost us an extra day. Wouldn't likely be much left there anyway. Dawkins and his bunch left a lot of it in ashes."

"Been a right long while since we heard anything about Caleb Dawkins." Tanner smiled hopefully. "You don't reckon somethin' awful might've happened to him?"

"I doubt it. But he may not be gettin' much sleep."

"On account of the Federals comin' in?"

"On account of James Monahan. Now that the war is over he's free to come and go wherever he wants to. If it was me that hanged his daddy and brother, I'd have a crick in my neck from watchin' over my shoulder."

"The captain said there won't be much law for a while. James could dice old Dawkins up into little bitty chunks, and nobody could do a damned thing to him."

"There's always his son Pete and the rest of the Dawkins people. Once a thing like that gets started, it's hard to stop 'til everybody's sick of it . . . or everybody's dead."

Tanner pondered that proposition in unaccustomed silence awhile. "If I was you, the first thing I'd do when we get to your farm would be to unsaddle my horse. The second thing would be to ask that girl to marry me. Come to think of it, I might leave the horse saddled."

"It's been more than a year since I saw her. Me and her have got a lot to talk about first."

"You've got the rest of your lives to talk."

"A thing like marryin', you've got to work up to it. You don't just ride in after a year and say, 'Howdy, girl, let's go find Preacher Webb.'"

"If it was me, I would. I'd carry her off someplace where nobody could find us, and I wouldn't turn her a-loose 'til we both had to come up for air. I don't know as I'd even wait for the preacher."

"A man would if he had any respect for the girl. Or for himself." Rusty would not admit to anyone that at times he entertained such fantasies about Geneva, with or without marriage. Usually he tried halfheartedly to suppress the images, then gave up the attempt and took pleasure in letting them run free. It was guilty pleasure, but pleasure just the same.

No, he would wait for Preacher Webb. But the preacher had better not be long in coming.

Rusty and Len Tanner rode a little ahead of the wagon that carried Captain Whitfield and Oscar Pickett. The captain hunkered down on the wagon seat, enduring his pain without complaint though it showed in his pinched face, his half-closed eyes. Rusty called back to him, "Hang on, Captain. We don't have far to go."

"I'm fine," Whitfield lied. "Just fine."

Ahead lay the timber that fringed the Colorado River. A dim twin-rutted trail led toward the nearest crossing that a wagon could ford without danger of floating downstream. Rusty had ridden there many times, usually with Daddy Mike, occasionally with Preacher Webb, accompanying the minister on his circuit. It was pleasant to remember when he could keep from dwelling on the sad truth that those times were over and would never come again. Mike Shannon was gone, and age would be overtaking Preacher Webb. Rusty doubted that the minister could hold up to the rigorous pace he had set for himself in earlier times, carrying the gospel to the forks of the creek and beyond. Traveling that once had been a joy for him must now have become an ordeal. Yet Rusty knew Webb persisted, traveling more slowly and paying a price in weariness for every mile.

Rusty began to see mares and colts bearing the Monahan brand. The family had brought their horses down from the old place to Rusty's because of the certainty that they would quickly be stolen if left behind. No one had an incentive to steal cattle except an occasional one to butcher for beef. War had made horses scarce and valuable even as it resulted in an over-abundance of unclaimed cattle.

He noticed several cows with calves bearing his brand. He had not been here to burn it on them, so he credited the Monahans. They had been looking after his interests as well as their own. It was a pity the cattle had no monetary value.

Sight of the fields helped lift his melancholy. They were green with growing corn, with forage for the stock. The Shannons' old double log cabin came into view. It was easy, seeing the place, to fantasize that Daddy Mike and Mother Dora would be waiting there for him as they had done so long. Rusty was tempted to put Alamo into a lope, but reality intruded. The pleasant dream was quickly gone. Familiar landmarks aroused old memories, one on top of another.

Rusty crossed a creek where he and Daddy Mike once had ridden with a band of local farmers trailing a Comanche raiding party. They had not managed to overtake the Indians; they rarely did. Farther along, Rusty had helped bury a murdered woman. The Comanches had taken the woman's small son, but no one had ever found a trace of him. He had disappeared like the Indians themselves onto the open plains of Comanchería.

Daddy Mike . . . sometimes it was hard to realize that four years had passed since he died, yet at other times, remembering the uncounted miles Rusty had traveled since, the many rivers he had crossed, it seemed an eternity. The deaths of Daddy Mike and Mother Dora had left him with an acute sense of abandonment, of being alone in the world. That feeling of isolation had brought him to bond with the Monahans. They were not truly his kin, but they and Preacher Webb were the nearest to it that he knew. When he married Geneva he would become a part of their family. He needed that sense of belonging.

At the farthest end of the field, a man followed a mule and a moldboard plow. The distance was too great for recognition, but Rusty assumed this would be Geneva's grandfather, old Vince Purdy.

A girl was hoeing in the garden. For a fleeting few moments Rusty thought she was Geneva. He spurred ahead, then drew Alamo to a stop as he realized this was one of Geneva's sisters. The two younger girls had grown up during the war years. He had hardly known them the last time he had been here.

The girl saw the horsemen and the wagon. She dropped the hoe and climbed over the log fence that enclosed the garden. Lithe as a young deer, she raced barefoot to the cabin. She was shouting, though Rusty was too far away to make out the words.

By the time he and Tanner reached the cabin, Clemmie Monahan stood on the dog run. She was a small, thin woman of perhaps ninety pounds, so slight that she looked as if a high wind could sweep her away. Rusty knew from experience that her appearance was deceiving. She had a will of pure steel and a backbone to match it. Her two younger daughters stood on either side, beaming with delight. Rusty struggled with his memory a moment before he recalled that the older of the two was Josie. The younger was named Alice.

Clemmie had taken it badly when Rusty had arrested her son James long ago for an attempt on Caleb Dawkins's life in revenge for Lon and Billy. She had mellowed in the years since, and he hoped she had put the incident behind her. That she greeted him with a thin smile gave him hope.

"You-all get down and come in," she shouted.

Rusty dismounted and removed his hat. "Clemmie," he said by way of greeting.

"Rusty," she answered. Neither seemed to know much more to say at first. While he tried to decide how to continue the conversation, he stared at the two girls, hardly believing the change. Josie looked a great deal like her grown sister and appeared to be about as old as Geneva had been when Rusty had first met her. Alice was a pretty girl of fourteen or fifteen.

Josie declared, "I told them it was you, Rusty. I recognized you from as far as I could see you."

He was glad she could not read his mind and know that he had had trouble remembering her name.

He said, "I expect you-all have heard that the war is over."

"We heard," Clemmie responded. "Now maybe the menfolks will be comin' home . . . them that survived." She coughed away a catch in her throat. "I'm right glad to see that you're one of them, Rusty."

Tanner was on the ground, stretching his long legs. Pickett had brought the wagon up near the cabin's dog run. He and Tanner helped the captain to the ground.

Rusty looked past Clemmie, hoping to see Geneva somewhere. "You remember Captain Whitfield, don't you? And Len Tanner? This other feller is Oscar Pickett."

"I remember them all. Welcome, gentlemen, to our house." She glanced back quickly at Rusty. "I should've said, 'To Rusty's house.' It's his, not ours."

"It's yours as long as you want it," Rusty said. He gave the girls a second looking over. "My, but you two have changed a lot in a year."

Josie smiled, looking even more like Geneva. "It's been longer than a year." She studied him up and down. "You're thin. Haven't you been eatin'?"

"When I could. Been times I couldn't."

Clemmie made a sweeping motion with her hand. "Then we'd better get busy and fix you-all a good dinner. Come on in."

Captain Whitfield limped, each step bringing pain. Clemmie frowned. "What's happened to you, Captain?"

"A Comanche had nothin' better to do than to put an arrow in my hip, is all. It's healin', thank you."

"It'll heal quicker once we put some food into you."

Rusty watched her stir up a blaze in the fireplace. He could not hold the question any longer. "Where's Geneva?"

Clemmie looked up in surprise, her expression slowly turning to one of regret. "I guess you never heard."

A cold knot suddenly built in Rusty's stomach. "Heard what?"

"She's up yonder at our old place. Her and her husband."

Rusty caught hold of a chair. "Husband?"

"She's married. Been married since winter."

Pete Dawkins poked at the campfire with a dry stick, his backside prickling with impatience. Somewhere in the distance he heard a bugle, but he gave it no attention. He had heard far too many bugles since he and his friend Scully had been hustled unceremoniously into the Confederate Army. There had been no bands to play stirring martial music, no pretty women waving at the departing soldiers. They had been marched out of Austin in the middle of a driving rain without fuss and feathers and with damned little if any showing of respect. It was almost as if they were prisoners, not soldiers.

The truth was that he and Scully would have been prisoners had they not become soldiers. Pete's hardheaded old daddy had been responsible for that. All on account of a few horses. Hell, the old man had lost more to colic than Pete and Scully had taken. He would probably have considered them stolen by the Indians and have forgotten them had it not been for the nosy damned rangers and that army horse buyer in cahoots with them. What was his name? Blessing, that was it. Tom Blessing. And the rangers. One of them he had encountered before and had gotten to know better than he wanted to. Rusty, they called him. Shannon, that was the last name. Rusty Shannon. He did not know the ranger captain's name, but he would remember that face and that bushy mustache if he lived to be a hundred.

If it hadn't been for them he wouldn't be here. He would still be in Texas, raiding the reservation north of the Red River for Indian horses and making himself wealthy enough that someday he could snap his fingers in Old Colonel's face and tell him where he could go.

And what in the hell was he still doing here anyway? Word had come days ago that the war was over. What was the use in having an army if there was no longer any war to fight? But the officers were waiting for specific orders from higher authorities. They had not allowed any soldiers to leave.

Scully stared at him from the other side of the small fire. "You tryin' to poke them coals to death? You look like you're fixin' to cloud up and rain pure vinegar."

"Just thinkin'."

"They can court-martial a soldier for thinkin'. You're supposed to leave the thinkin' to them and do what they tell you to."

"Right now they're thinkin' I'm goin' to stay here and act like a good soldier, but they're mistaken. I'm fixin' to up and leave this outfit. I'm goin' back to Texas."

"They shoot deserters."

"That was when there was still fightin' goin' on. They got no reason to keep me now, and no reason to hunt for me if I'm not here when they call the roll in the mornin'."

Scully looked around furtively to be sure no one was listening. "Would you take me with you?"

Pete hesitated in answering. He felt he could make better time alone, looking out for no one except himself. On the other hand, Scully had always been useful so long as he had Pete around to do most of the thinking for him. If anything, he was a better hand than Pete when it came to handling horses. It was as if his mind were on about the same plane of intelligence as theirs.

"I guess you can go provided you keep up. I ain't waitin' for you if you fall behind or get yourself into any trouble."

Scully's reply was curt. "The only trouble I ever got into was by followin' you."

True, they had a good thing going back home when they were gathering Indian horses from the reservation and selling them in the Texas settlements to farmers or to the Confederate Army. But they had come up short after one trip up north of the river, and Pete had seen no harm in adding a few of the old man's horses to the mix. Caleb Dawkins was already richer than one man had a right to be.

Pete knew Old Colonel's temper, for he had felt the lash of it many times, growing up. But he never gave a moment's thought to the possibility of getting caught, or of Caleb Dawkins giving him and Scully a choice between the army and the state penitentiary.

Choice hell! About like choosing between getting shot and getting hanged.

If it had been anyone except Dawkins's own son, the outcome might very well have been the rope. Old Colonel was hell on hanging people. Like them Union-loving Monahans.

Scully asked, "If we left right now, how far you reckon we could travel before daylight?"

"Eight or ten miles if we hustle. A right smart farther if we was a-horseback."

Two horses were tethered on the picket line, out beyond the light of the company's several small campfires. They belonged to the captain and the lieutenant, the only men in the company allowed to ride.

Scully said, "Are you thinkin' the same thing I am?"

Pete nodded. "The officers have ridden far enough. We ain't been paid, and we ain't goin' to *be* paid. The least the army owes us is a horse apiece."

He and Scully gathered up what few belongings they had, including their rifles. Pete led the way to the picket line. He drew a bowie knife from his belt, ready to cut the rope.

His blood went cold at the sound of a gun hammer being cocked. A voice demanded, "Who goes there?"

He saw the dark shape of a guard just in front of him, too near to miss if he fired a shot. Pete shivered.

"Who are you?" the guard demanded again. Pete recognized the gruff voice of a company sergeant.

"Just me," Pete said weakly. "I was lookin' for the latrine. Guess I got turned around in the dark."

"Well, you just turn around again. Already been two men tried tonight to take the officers' horses. The next one I'll personally shoot, and I'll bury him in the ditch we dug for the latrine."

Pete backed off, bumping into Scully. His fear gave way to frustration as he retreated. It had not occurred to him that other men in the camp were considering desertion, just as he was, and that they had caused a stiffening of the guard detail.

Scully whispered, "What'll we do now?"

"We'll walk. Sooner or later we'll find somebody careless with his horses."

He found the road that led west. Anger made his stride long and purposeful. His mind went back to the black day that the rangers had caught him and Scully with stolen horses. He wished he had Rusty Shannon here right now. He would gladly beat him within an inch of his life, then shoot him in the belly. Maybe someday.

CHAPTER

SIX

Rusty felt as if a mule had kicked him in the belly. He sank into the nearest chair. "Geneva's married?"

Clemmie sensed the depth of Rusty's shock. Her voice was sympathetic. "A man named Evan Gifford. She said she wrote and told you."

"I never got the letter."

She pulled a chair up nearby and faced him, taking one of his hands. "I wish I'd known. I'd've found an easier way to tell you."

"There isn't any easy way." He could not meet her gaze. He looked down at the rough floor. He lost his voice for a minute. He swallowed hard to get it back. "I hope he's a good man."

"You can take comfort in that. He is."

Both girls spoke at the same time. "He sure is," they agreed. Rusty got the impression that either would have been happy to have married him.

Too bad one of them hadn't.

Clemmie said, "Evan took a Union bullet in his chest. They sent him home to die, only when he got there he found he didn't have a home anymore. He showed up here with one foot in the grave. We cared for him the best we knew how."

"Sounds like you done right good." For the moment, he wished they had not.

"When he was able, he commenced helpin' around the place. That corn and that feed you see growin' out yonder, he done a big part of the plantin', along with Daddy Vince. Branded your calves for you, too."

Rusty turned so they could not see the anguish in his face. His long-nourished dreams were slipping away from him. He was powerless to grab them and bring them back. He looked through the open door. "I see Vince out yonder, ridin' a mule in from the field."

"It's early for him to be quittin'. Probably saw you-all and thought he'd better come to the house. Visitors mean trouble, oftener than not."

One in particular, he thought, by the name of Evan Gifford. "You-all've had trouble?"

"No Indians lately, but there's been horse thieves. There's them that represent the army and give you worthless paper for them. Then there's them that don't bother with paper, they just run off whatever they can find."

"At least the army shouldn't bother you anymore. I imagine it's breakin' up fast."

"There's enough of them others, though. And there's already been soldiers cut loose afoot and hungry, tryin' to scavenge a livin' wherever they can. You can't expect them to stay hungry without puttin' up a struggle. The law is apt to be scarce, so everybody'll pretty much have to take care of theirselves."

"Who *is* the law around here these days?"

"The regular sheriff went off to the army, so folks elected a man by the name of Tom Blessing. Know him?"

"Tom Blessing." The name brought memories that would have been pleasant were he not still in shock over Geneva. "He was a friend of Daddy Mike's. And he was the man who first put me into the rangers."

Clemmie's eyebrows went up. "You're grateful to him for that?"

"It was the best thing that ever happened to me." He saw Vince Purdy nearing the barn. That gave him an excuse to get out of the cabin. Perhaps in the open air he could clear his head and get a grip on his feelings. "I'll go meet Vince and set his mind at ease."

Purdy rode the plow mule, carrying the long reins coiled in one hand. He was taller than his daughter Clemmie but built along the same spare lines. His work-toughened hands seemed too large for the rest of him. Every year of his long life was etched deeply in lines that spider-webbed his thin, weathered face.

He grasped Rusty's hand with bone-crunching strength that belied his age. "You home for good?"

"For better or for worse." Rusty figured he had already heard the worst. He motioned toward the field. "The crops look good."

"Rains've been fair enough, and we've watered them with a goodly amount of sweat. You ought to have a good harvest."

"Not me. You. You-all planted and worked the fields. Whatever comes off of them rightly belongs to you."

"With the war ended, I figured we'd soon be goin' back up to our own place."

"I don't see any need to hurry. At least you'd ought to stay here 'til the fields are cut."

"We've got fields up yonder, too. Evan and Geneva can't handle all that work by theirselves."

Evan and Geneva. Hearing the names spoken together jolted Rusty anew. "Maybe James will be able to help them, now that he's free to travel."

Purdy's eyes brightened. "You've seen him?"

Rusty told him of their brief encounter in the brush men's camp. "I expect that camp broke up fast."

Some of Purdy's years seemed to have lifted from his thin shoulders. Humming, he began removing the mule's harness. "James comin' home . . . Everything's fixin' to be fine from now on out."

Rusty leaned against a fence and turned away with his eyes closed. They burned as if he had rubbed pepper into them. "Yeah, fine from now on."

Rusty talked Captain Whitfield into staying a few days and resting before he finished his trip. His hip gave him pain enough that he was amenable to the idea. Clemmie and the girls seemed to enjoy waiting on him. Rusty rode with Tanner around the farm, searching beyond his own boundaries for cattle bearing his brand. He rough-counted about fifty head, double what Daddy Mike had owned and what had been here when Rusty rode off to join the rangers.

Tanner said, "Looks like the folks taken good care of things for you."

"I never had a moment's hesitation. I knew what they'd done with their own."

"I'm sorry that girl let you down."

Rusty was immediately defensive on Geneva's behalf. "She didn't let me down. She hadn't made me any promise and didn't owe me nothin'. From what Clemmie says, she didn't even know if I was still alive. None of my letters ever got here."

He brought up the subject of the calves at the supper table, thanking Vince Purdy for branding them.

Purdy said, "Couldn't've done it by myself. Evan helped me, and Preacher Webb pitched in every time he came by." He glanced up at Clemmie. "Which has been right often."

Clemmie suppressed a smile.

Purdy said, "The girls helped a right smart, too. They're both good hands whether it's with a cow or a plow."

Rusty thanked them. Josie said, "It's the least we could do. You gave us a place to go, away from Caleb Dawkins and his men."

Clemmie said sharply, "We've agreed never to mention that man's name in this house. What a scorchin' he's got comin' when the devil gets his turn."

Purdy said, "It ain't no big thing, holdin' on to cattle. Nobody wants them much anyway. Not unless it's a milk cow. Our old Spot's been missin' for over a month. Somebody's probably milkin' her right now, and I'll bet it ain't no Comanche Indian."

Rusty said, "I think I remember her. Mostly white with brown spots, and a stub horn on the left . . . no, the right side?"

"That's her. I've hunted high and low. It's like she fell in a big hole and covered herself up."

"You talked to all the folks around us?"

"Nobody's seen her."

Rusty had a suspicion, but he would not voice it, not yet. "I've been neglectful," he said. "I ain't made a circle yet to visit my neighbors. I don't even know if they're all still around."

Clemmie's face wrinkled. "There's one that's been around a lot more than I would've liked."

Rusty thought he knew. "Sounds like Fowler Gaskin."

Gaskin had lived just a few miles from the Shannons for years, to their continual misfortune.

Clemmie said, "That old sneak has got it in his mind that I ought to be in the market for a new husband. If there wasn't but one man left alive on the face of God's earth and it was him, I wouldn't let him within smellin' distance of me. And I can smell him a long way."

Gaskin had been a thorn in Daddy Mike's side, always borrowing without asking, never bringing anything back, always looking to ride instead of walk if he could manage it at someone else's expense. Clemmie said, "You ever see a pig that would wiggle in with other litters and steal milk from every sow in the pen? That's Fowler Gaskin."

Vince Purdy scowled at mention of the name. "I've had to threaten to wallop him with a singletree to make him leave Clemmie alone."

Clemmie might be well into middle age, but to her father she was still a young girl who needed protection. Though she might not weigh enough to sink in deep water, Rusty suspected she could swing a mean singletree herself if the need arose.

Rusty said, "I'll go talk to Fowler. Me and Tanner."

The last time he had seen the Gaskin cabin, part of it had been damaged by a windstorm. Repairs had been done in a makeshift manner, but now the whole cabin leaned to the south and seemed in danger of collapse.

Tanner observed, "He's propped a log against the eaves. That's the only thing holdin' it up. That and the south wind."

"He'd rather bleed than sweat. Never do for himself what he can wheedle someone else into doin' for him. Never buy anything if he can borrow it. And never remember to take back anything he borrows."

"You mean like a milk cow?"

"I'd not be surprised."

Gaskin's droop-tailed hound announced the horsemen. Gaskin stepped out through the cabin's sagging door and stood slouched in front, a long rifle in his hand. Rusty wondered idly who he had "borrowed" it from. Gaskin reminded Rusty of a scarecrow, gaunt, bent-shouldered, his tangled beard a mixture of black and gray, streaked with tobacco juice that had dribbled down his chin. His red-rimmed eyes were far from friendly.

"Rusty Shannon. Back, are you?"

It was not much to say after such a long time, but in Gaskin's case Rusty was not interested in extended conversation. "Back. I see you're still here."

It would have been too much to ask of good fortune to find that Gaskin had left the country. "I think you met Len Tanner a time or two."

Gaskin hardly looked away from Rusty. "You a ranger now, or a soldier?"

"Neither one. Our company disbanded."

"Just as well. I never seen the rangers stop an Indian raid yet, not 'til after the damage was done."

Rusty felt the burning of resentment. The rangers had turned back a number of attempted raids before they were able to materialize. Nobody other than the rangers themselves knew it had happened. "You still livin' here by yourself?"

Gaskin's voice broke into a whine. "You know I am. Them two good boys of mine gave up their lives fightin' for the Confederacy."

Rusty knew better. The Gaskin boys had been absent without leave and were killed in a New Orleans bawdy house fight. He was not sure Fowler Gaskin was aware of that. If he truly believed his sons had died on the battlefield, it was just as well to leave him that illusion. If he was lying to save humiliation, Rusty saw no point in picking the scab from an old sore.

"I don't suppose you've seen anything of a milk cow that belongs to the Monahan family?"

"They done asked me about that cow. I'll tell you the same as I told them. If I ever see the old hussy, I'll give her a whack on the rump and send her home."

Rusty heard a sound he had not encountered in a long time, the bleating of lambs. "You got sheep?"

"Ain't nothin' wrong with sheep," Gaskin said defensively. "Confederate money ain't worth nothin', but you can always swap wool for somethin' you need. Them's dogie lambs in that pen. Lost their mamas."

Rusty's faint suspicions began to take on larger dimensions. "What you feedin' them?"

"Whatever I've got. Lambs ain't choosy."

Rusty and Tanner rode down to the pen, Gaskin following suspiciously. Rusty saw half a dozen lambs. He asked Tanner, "You know anything about sheep?"

"Not much. Just that they don't smell good, is all."

Rusty would guess these lambs were two or three months old, all in excellent flesh. Whatever they had been fed, they were thriving. Over in the corner of the pen was a stanchion large enough for a cow.

Sheep manure came in small pellets. Scattered around the pen were large patties, some of them fresh.

Rusty said to Gaskin, "You must have some awful big sheep."

Gaskin looked nervous. "They're big enough."

The cabin was within easy water-carrying distance of the river, which was fringed with heavy timber and thick underbrush. Rusty saw cow tracks leading off in that direction. He saw boot tracks as well.

He told Gaskin, "Since you don't know anything about that cow, we'll be movin' along."

"You-all come back sometime." The tone of Gaskin's voice said that he hoped they never would.

Rusty and Tanner circled around and came into the timber downriver, where Gaskin was unlikely to see them. They rode along the edge of the water, back in the direction of the cabin. If they found what Rusty expected, it would not be far from the pens. Fowler Gaskin was not likely to walk any farther than necessary.

He found the spotted cow staked on a long rope that allowed her room to graze and to reach the water. She gave the horsemen a docile bovine stare as Rusty dismounted and looked her over. Examining her udder, he noted that the teats showed small tooth marks.

"Just about lamb size," he muttered. He assumed that Gaskin had been staking the cow out of sight and leading her up to the pen for the dogie lambs to suckle.

Tanner said, "I'll bet that old heifer put up a fight the first time or two he put them lambs on her."

"Probably thought they were the funniest-lookin' calves she ever saw. That's what the stanchion was for, so he could tie her up good and tight 'til she got used to the lambs."

The rope was attached to a strong sapling. Rusty untied it, coiled it, and got back on the horse. The cow followed him as he put Alamo up the riverbank and across a narrow strip of pasture.

At the front of the cabin he hollered for Gaskin. The old man came out, his jaw slack with disappointment as he saw the cow.

Tanner shouted, "Look what we found down yonder. She somehow got a rope around her neck and tied it to a tree."

Whatever Gaskin was trying to say, it caught in his throat.

Rusty said, "It's about time them lambs were weaned onto grass, don't you think?"

Gaskin found voice, and it was shrill. "I'll have the sheriff on you, takin' a man's cow."

"I'll go tell him myself and save you the trip."

Gaskin turned and reached back through the cabin door and brought out the long rifle.

Len asked, "You don't reckon that old man's crazy enough to fire that thing at us, do you?"

Rusty had not considered that Gaskin might actually be crazy. The notion was not far-fetched. "I sure wouldn't stop and ask him." He spurred Alamo and forced horse and cow into a long trot.

Clemmie beamed as Rusty led the cow into the yard. She walked around the animal, petting her, rubbing a hand along the smooth hide. "I'm sure glad to see you back, old girl."

Rusty explained the circumstances. She said, "Daddy was over at the Gaskin place a couple of times, thinkin' she might've strayed in that direction."

"She strayed all right, with a little help."

"How come you figured it out so easy?"

"With Fowler Gaskin for a neighbor, nothin' is safe unless it's nailed down tight or too heavy to carry."

He did not worry about Fowler Gaskin carrying his complaint to the sheriff. Tom Blessing knew the old reprobate as well as Rusty did. But mention of Blessing set Rusty to thinking he should ride over and visit Daddy Mike's old friend. He intended to take Len Tanner along, but Len seemed to be enjoying himself hoeing the garden with the two girls.

He told Rusty, "These Monahan sisters are different. Somehow I can talk to them without my tongue tyin' itself up in a bow knot."

"They're still just kids."

"Kids? Maybe you've been hurtin' so bad over Geneva that you ain't taken a close look, especially at Josie. Country girls turn into women fast. Ain't no make-believe like with them town girls, no flirty put-on."

Rusty did not need Tanner to remind him of Geneva. She was never far from his thoughts.

"Well, you keep choppin' those weeds and don't get too close to the girls. You wouldn't want their mother comin' after *you* with a singletree."

Tom Blessing was a large man whose natural leadership drew others to follow him no matter how long or difficult the trail. He had led local volunteer minutemen companies in pursuit of raiding Indians and by example had been a strong moral force in the community. Daddy Mike had always looked up to him, and Mike Shannon had not been one to give honor where honor was not due. He had always said Tom Blessing's word was like gospel. Blessing had been present when Mike and Preacher Webb had found a frightened little red-haired boy on the battleground at Plum Creek back in 1840. Later it seemed he was never far away when the Shannons needed help.

As a boy, Rusty had looked upon Tom Blessing with an awe that had never entirely left him though now he stood as tall as Blessing and could look him squarely in the eyes.

Blessing had added a wing onto his cabin since Rusty had last been there. It was typical of him that he never let "well enough" alone. He was not content with existing conditions if he could see a way to improve them.

Rusty saw him saddling a horse in a log pen beside the barn and reined Alamo over that way. Blessing reacted with surprise upon recognition but methodically finished buckling the girth before he stepped around from behind the gray horse and waved a huge hand. "Thought the Indians might've got you, or you'd plumb left the country."

Rusty dismounted and accepted Blessing's bruising handshake. "Never saw a place I liked better than here." He studied the gray horse. It took a big one to carry a man like Blessing. "Looks like I caught you fixin' to go someplace. I wouldn't want to hold you up."

Blessing frowned, considering before he spoke. "I got a message from Isaac York. Asked me to come over to his place as quick as I could. I'd invite you to go with me, but I remember that you held a heavy grudge against him."

"That was a long time ago. When I found out I was mistaken, I told him I was sorry." Rusty had long believed York had fired the shot that killed Mike Shannon. He had been almost to the point of shooting the man before he discovered that the blame lay elsewhere.

"Then you're welcome to come if you're of a mind to."

Rusty was a little surprised that York was still alive. York had fought a long and hopeless battle with whiskey. Neighbors had placed bets on when he would lose the inevitable fight with the final bottle.

"Still drinkin' as hard as he used to?"

"I'm afraid so. Last time I saw him, I doubted he'd make it home. If it hadn't been for Shanty, he probably wouldn't have."

Shanty was York's slave. More than that, he was York's friend, almost the only one the man still had after years of alienating his neighbors.

Rusty said, "I still owe Isaac for all the bad things I said about him. I'll go with you."

Blessing nodded his approval. "You show your good Shannon raisin'.

Takes a strong man to admit he's been wrong." He mounted the gray horse and started off, Rusty pulling in beside him. They talked of old times, shared experiences on the trail when Blessing had headed up the local volunteer minutemen and Rusty had gone along as a green youngster eager for his first real fight. He had never been that eager again, not after seeing blood.

Blessing had helped Rusty and Captain Whitfield break up a horse-stealing ring. He had been buying remounts as a civilian representative of the Confederate Army when Caleb Dawkins's son Pete had driven a sizeable bunch into Jacksboro to sell. They proved to have been stolen, some from Caleb Dawkins's own remuda. Facing his prideful father's wrath, and a choice of prison or military service, Pete had reluctantly enlisted in the Southern Army.

Rusty said, "I hear you're the sheriff now. I don't see you wearin' a badge."

"The last sheriff lost it someplace. Anyway, everybody around here knows who I am."

"What if you run into outlaws and they don't know you?"

"They'll get acquainted with me quick enough."

York's cabin was plain, without even such embellishments as a small porch or a yard fence. York had no family beyond the slave Shanty. His wife and daughters had been killed by Comanches years ago. He had tried to drown his bitterness in whiskey ever since. He seethed with hatred for Indians, no matter their intentions, no matter their tribe, and embraced any opportunity to kill them.

A dog's barking brought a slight figure to the cabin door. Rusty recognized the aging slave. The talk was that his mother had belonged to Isaac York's father, and he and Isaac had grown up together. Some people whispered that the two might be half-brothers. Technically Shanty was York's property, but in practice he was more a caretaker and protector. Had it not been for Shanty constantly watching over him, dragging his contentious master out of a fight before it went too far, sobering him up before it was too late, Isaac probably would have gone to his grave years ago.

Shanty bowed in the deferential manner drilled into him from the time he had learned to walk. His lean body was bent under the weight of hard times. His big-knuckled hands were disproportionately large, bespeaking a lifetime of manual labor. "Mr. Blessing, it's a mercy you've come. Mr. Isaac's mighty low." The voice was soft and seemed near breaking. Shanty looked at Rusty a moment before coming to recognition. "Why, you're that Shannon boy. Been a long time. Only you don't look like a boy no more."

"Nobody stays young long in this part of the country. Sorry about Isaac."

"I'm afraid the Lord's fixin' to call him to Heaven."

Rusty was not sure Heaven was Isaac's true destination. He was about to ask if a doctor had seen Isaac, then remembered that the nearest thing to a doctor anywhere around was Preacher Webb. Primarily interested in ministering to souls, Webb had a considerable practical knowledge about healing bodies as well.

Shanty said, "Last we seen of Preacher Webb, he was headin' west. Said he had a flock out yonder in need of a shepherd."

That might have been a reference to the brush men, Rusty thought. One had mentioned occasional visits by Preacher Webb.

Shanty's eyes reflected a deep sadness. "There's lost sheep in need of him right here. I hope he comes in time."

A weak voice called from inside the cabin. Shanty motioned toward the door. "He's been frettin', Mr. Blessing, wonderin' when you'd come."

Rusty followed Blessing into the cabin. Shanty came behind him. Rusty's eyes adjusted slowly to the gloom indoors. Isaac York lay on a cot, his face drawn, his eyes hollow and showing but little life. He extended a trembling hand to the sheriff. "Tom. I was afraid you wouldn't get here in time."

"I'm here now, Isaac. What can I do for you?"

York's gaze lighted on Rusty. He was momentarily surprised. "Shannon? Rusty Shannon?"

"It's me, Isaac."

York's voice was hoarse. "I never killed your daddy. Me and Mike didn't get along, but it wasn't me that killed him."

"I know that. I'm sorry I ever thought otherwise. I wish I could take back every bad word I ever spoke about you."

"I'm glad you come. You can be a second witness."

Blessing asked, "Witness to what?"

"I want you to write me a will. I'd do it myself, only my hands shake too much. There's some paper over on that table, and a pencil."

Blessing found a sheet of paper and used the bottom of a tin plate to give it a firm backing. "What do you want me to write?"

York looked toward Shanty, who leaned his bent frame against the log wall. "I want you to say that I am of sound mind and body. Well, maybe the body ain't sound, but my mind is clear. I want you to write down that I am givin' Shanty his freedom. No *ifs*, no maybes. I want it known that he don't belong to me or to nobody else."

Rusty saw that gesture as unnecessary. Abraham Lincoln had declared the slaves free, and if they weren't already they would be when the first Yankee soldiers showed up.

"Another thing," York said, "everything I own, this farm, this cabin, the little bit of money I've got . . . it all goes to Shanty."

Blessing's eyebrows raised a little. "There's liable to be talk."

"In my shape, what do I care about talk? Shanty ain't a slave, not anymore. He's worked hard on this land. By all rights, it's his."

"You mentioned money."

"There's a can with Yankee silver in it. A little over a hundred dollars, buried out by the corner post of my cow pen."

"You don't have any blood kin that you'd want to leave somethin' to?"

"Used to have a brother over the Sabine in Louisiana. We ain't seen one another in years. He never even answered my letter when I buried my family. So to hell with him."

Blessing wrote slowly and laboriously, then handed the paper over to Rusty. "That look to you like what he said?"

Rusty glanced quickly over the scribbling. "You got it just fine."

York reached for the paper, pencil, and plate. With shaking hand he signed it. "You-all witness it. Make it to where no lawyer can mess with it."

Blessing signed beneath York's name and passed the paper to Rusty. "You've done good by Shanty. I'm proud to've known you, Isaac."

"I ought to've given him his freedom years ago."

Shanty's voice quavered. "I thank you, Mr. Isaac."

Isaac relaxed, seeming to sink deeper into the bed. "Some people ain't blessed with any real honest-to-God friends in a lifetime. I've had one, at least."

Outside, Blessing turned sharp eyes on Rusty. "You got any idea where Preacher Webb might be found?"

"Ain't seen him, but they tell me he comes by my place to visit the Monahan family pretty often."

"If he shows up, I wish you'd tell him to get over here as quick as he can. I doubt he can do much about Isaac's sickness, but maybe he can help the poor feller die with his soul at ease."

"I'll watch for him."

Blessing looked worried. "I'm afraid Isaac ain't thought all this through."

"He's leavin' Shanty a good farm."

"May be leavin' him trouble, too. There's some folks won't take it kindly."

"It's Isaac's farm to do with as he pleases."

"He won't be here to take the punishment, but Shanty will."

"You're the sheriff. You can help him."

Blessing's eyes narrowed. "Maybe, maybe not. Looks to me like the state government is comin' unraveled. Maybe we can hold the county together. I'll keep tryin' to do my job 'til the Federals come and tell me I'm not sheriff anymore."

Blessing's comment was like an echo of the concerns Rusty had heard from Captain Whitfield. "Do you really think they'll do that?"

"I don't know. I've never been on the losin' side of a war before. We weren't exactly gentle with Mexico. Maybe the Yankees won't treat us kindly either."

"Captain Whitfield says they can't hang us all, and they don't have prisons enough to pen us all up."

"But they can make life pretty miserable. Best thing for a while is stay close to home and tend to business like I always did. Keep the peace the best I can 'til they tell me otherwise."

"You won't have any rangers to back you up."

"I don't even have a deputy. He went off to the war, and the county hasn't hired anybody to take his place."

Rusty considered awhile. "If you need help, let me know. I'll come runnin'."

"Thanks, but the county's got no money to pay you."

"I didn't get paid for most of my ranger service either. They sent us a little flour and salt and sometimes coffee. They allowed us a place to roll out our beddin'. That was about all."

"I hope you're not sorry I got you into it in the first place."

"No. If I'd stayed here I'd have most likely shot Isaac York, thinkin' he killed Daddy Mike. I always felt like I was doin' somethin' useful, bein' a ranger. I'll miss it."

Blessing turned wistful. "Once the Federals have been here long enough to see how bad we need the rangers, maybe they'll organize them again."

"If they do, I'll be ready."

"You've barely got home and you're already talkin' about leavin' again. Rangerin' can be a hard life, even harder than farmin'."

"How long can a man stare at a mule's hind end before he starts gettin' a little crazy?"

CHAPTER

SEVEN

pproaching home, Rusty saw Vince Purdy and Oscar Pickett with a mule in the cornfield. Tanner and the two Monahan girls were hoeing weeds at opposite ends of the garden. Tanner turned away, but not before Rusty saw a bruise on his cheek and a darkening around one eye. He asked Josie, "What happened to Len?"

She and her younger sister exchanged quick looks. "He stumbled and hit himself in the face with the hoe handle."

The younger girl giggled.

Rusty thought two and two stopped short of being four. He led Alamo to where Tanner worked. He waited for Tanner to volunteer an explanation, but none came. Rusty had to ask him.

Tanner reluctantly admitted, "I tried to kiss that Josie. You know she's got a fist like a mule's left hind foot?"

Rusty could imagine Clemmie chasing Fowler Gaskin, swinging a singletree at his head. "She's her mother's daughter."

"All that time in the rangers, I thought we were protectin' helpless womenfolks. I pity the poor Indian that runs afoul of the Monahan girls."

Rusty returned to where the two girls stood watching. "Len tells me it wasn't a hoe handle that bruised his face."

Josie blushed. "He kissed me without even askin'."

Rusty smiled at her embarrassment. "I'll remember that if I ever feel like kissin' you."

Her eyes sparkled. "The difference is, *you* won't need to ask me."

Rusty rode Alamo to the barn. He noticed a strange horse in the pen. He tied his own horse to the fence and walked toward the cabin. Clemmie was sharing a bench with a man on the open dog run. Recognition brought Rusty a surge of joy.

"Preacher Webb!" He rushed to offer his hand. Webb had been like a foster father to him, second after Daddy Mike.

Webb stood up, carefully stretching his back as if it ached. That would not be surprising, considering the long miles he rode to carry the gospel's light to every dark corner he could reach. Rusty gripped the minister's hand so tightly that Webb winced.

"Careful, Rusty. These old bones are turnin' brittle." The knuckles were swollen with arthritis.

Rusty was taken aback to see that wrinkles had bitten deeply into the minister's face. The war had aged everyone more than its four years should justify. "Looks to me like you're still tryin' to carry the weight of the world."

"The Word is never too heavy for these arms to bear, even if one of them *is* crippled."

Webb's left arm had been broken in an Indian fight long ago. It had given him trouble ever since. He was thinner than when Rusty had seen him last. His hair seemed grayer and his eyes careworn in spite of what he said about the joy of carrying the Word.

Rusty sobered. "I just came from Isaac York's. You're needed real bad over there."

Webb's smile died. "For doctorin', or to preach a funeral?"

"I'm afraid that depends on how long it takes you. When I left, it didn't look like Isaac had much time left."

"I've expected this, sort of." Webb turned. "Clemmie, I'd meant to stay longer."

Clemmie clutched his arm. Regret colored her voice. "Next time."

He patted her hand, then set off toward the barn. Rusty had to lengthen his stride to keep up.

Webb said, "I took a look at Captain Whitfield's wound. It seems to be healin' right well. He's anxious to go on home."

Rusty had been with Whitfield so long that seeing him leave would almost be like watching a good friend die. Distances being what they were and the farm likely to tie him down, he might not see the captain again for a long time, if ever.

Len Tanner would probably go when Whitfield and Pickett did. Rusty dreaded parting with him, for they had ridden together a long time. However, given Tanner's little run-in with Josie, it might be just as well. Staying here, being constantly reminded of his humiliation, would be for Tanner like an itch he could not scratch.

Saddling his horse, Webb asked, "How did you know about Isaac?"

"I went with Tom Blessing to witness Isaac's will."

"He's never talked to me about havin' any kin."

"He's leavin' everything to Shanty."

Webb reacted much as Tom Blessing had. He seemed troubled. "Isaac may have burdened Shanty with a load of grief too heavy for his old shoulders."

"I don't know who would bother him. These are God-fearin' people around here . . . or used to be."

"Some who call themselves God's children have notions they didn't learn in church."

"They won't hurt Shanty. There's a bunch of us will see to that."

"I'm afraid Isaac didn't realize the trouble he might be stirrin' up."

Or maybe he did, Rusty thought. York was a bitter man who had little liking for his neighbors.

Webb started to mount his horse but paused. "Clemmie says you didn't know about Geneva bein' married."

Rusty looked away. "No, I didn't."

"I wrote you. I guess you never got the letter."

"We seldom got much mail."

"Are you goin' to be all right with it?"

"I *have* to be, don't I?"

"You're still young, and there's lots of nice young women out there. You'll find one."

"I don't know that I'll be lookin'."

"Then maybe she'll find *you*."

Clemmie was still standing on the dog run when Rusty returned to the cabin. Her worried eyes were fixed on Webb, riding away toward the east. She said, "He looks awful tired. He should think of himself for a change."

"I don't believe he knows how."

"He ought to quit travelin' so much. He needs somebody to take care of him."

Like you, for instance? Rusty resisted speaking the thought aloud.

She said, "I'm afraid he'll die all alone out on some trail with nothin' but his horse and his Bible."

"He's a man of the cloth. He'd consider it a fittin' way to go."

Her mouth tight, Clemmie retreated into the kitchen. Rusty considered following after her but could not think of anything helpful he might say.

Vince Purdy and Oscar Pickett came in from the field, Vince riding the plow mule, Pickett carrying a hoe over his thin shoulder. Rusty walked out to meet them. He unsaddled his own horse, then helped remove the harness from the mule. Purdy said, "Preacher left here in a hurry, seems like."

Rusty explained. Purdy looked with concern toward the cabin. "Clemmie figured on him stayin' a day or two."

"He'll be back."

"But then he'll be gone again. She sets a lot of store by him."

"It appears that way to me."

"It ain't like she's forgot about Lon and Billy. She never will. But there comes a time when folks have got to pick up and move on, live for the livin' and not for them that's gone. What is it the Bible says? Don't look for me in the graveyard because I've gone on to a better place?"

"Somethin' like that." Rusty had never done much reading in the Book, though Mother Dora had read a lot to him when he was small. There had been times when things he saw happen around him made him wonder if the Word applied to Texas. He had seen too many good people die, like Daddy Mike and Mother Dora, Lon and Billy, while others like Caleb Dawkins and Fowler Gaskin lived on. That seemed a contradiction of the Scriptures.

Reconciling to the loss of his foster parents had taken him a long time. Even yet, something heard or seen or felt would bring them suddenly to mind. Remnants of old grief would sweep over him, reviving a painful sense of aloneness. That feeling had been renewed and intensified by his loss of Geneva. "It's easy to say we ought to put such things behind us. I wish doin' it was as easy as talkin' about it."

Captain Whitfield came onto the dog run as the men approached the cabin. He had left his cane inside. "Oscar, would you be ready to leave here in the mornin'?"

Pickett seemed pleased. He had evidently expected this. "Ready any time you are, Captain."

"We've abused these good folks' hospitality too long."

Rusty assured him, "You could stay here all summer and not wear out your welcome."

"I'm rarin' to go and make sure nobody has carried off my farm."

It did not take long for the three men to load their belongings after an early-morning breakfast. They had little to take with them. Whitfield tugged at his big mustache, eager to go, yet reluctant to say good-bye. He took a hard grip on Rusty's hand.

Rusty said, "Sir, it's been a pleasure and a privilege to serve under you."

Whitfield blinked a couple of times. "Looks to me like the state government has fallen to pieces. I don't know when it may ever decide that Texas needs to reorganize the ranger force. But if anybody asks me, I'll tell them you'd make a good officer."

Whitfield gave Rusty's hand another shake, then turned quickly and climbed up into the wagon. Oscar Pickett said, "I better git too, before he runs off and leaves me."

"You take good care of him." Rusty figured the two old rangers would take care of each other.

Len Tanner hung back after Pickett set the wagon in motion. He twisted the reins in his hand and stared at the ground. "Damn it, Rusty, this is hard."

"I know. I feel the same way."

"I'm anxious to go see how Mama and Daddy are gettin' along. But don't you be surprised if I show up around here again one of these days."

"I'll be lookin' for you."

Tanner glanced toward the sisters on the dog run. "You watch out for them girls. They could hurt a man."

He gripped Rusty's hand, then mounted and spurred off after the wagon. He looked back once. Rusty could not tell whether Tanner was looking at him or at the girls.

When Rusty looked at them, he saw Geneva.

He attended Isaac York's funeral more out of guilt than out of liking for the man—that and respect for the aging Shanty. It weighed on his conscience that he had so long blamed the innocent York for Daddy Mike's death. But York had been easy to dislike for his disagreeable manner, his violent temper.

Fewer than two dozen neighbors and people from the settlement came to see York laid to rest. To find good words to say about the deceased, Preacher Webb skirted gingerly along the boundary between fact and fiction. Funerals were one place where a minister had license to stretch the truth a little.

Ropes lowered the plain wooden coffin into the grave. Rusty gazed at Shanty's solemn face and considered the infinite patience the black man must have had to live with and serve someone who had so many negative traits. Of course, as a slave Shanty had had no real choice. But even a slave's tolerance must have its limits. Now he was legally free. But Rusty wondered if at heart he could ever be free from slavery's legacy of dependence and self-doubt.

No one claiming to be a relative showed up for the service. That was to be expected, for York had never said much about his kin. He had mentioned a brother in Louisiana, but no one around the settlement knew just where the brother lived, if indeed he was still alive. The only known survivor, then, was Shanty. Only a few people filed by after the service and extended their sympathies to him. As a former slave, his feelings were not widely regarded as being of much importance.

Tom Blessing was among the exceptions. He said, "Shanty, you'll need to come to the courthouse the first chance you get. There'll be some papers need signin' before this land can be deeded over to you. Since Isaac made me executor of his will, I'll see that they're ready and waitin' for you."

"I'm obliged, Mr. Blessing."

"I'll need your last name. I don't believe I ever heard it."

"I don't recollect as I ever had one. They just called me Shanty. That was all."

"You can take Isaac's name then. I'll make out the papers in the name of Shanty York."

"Shanty York suits me fine, sir."

Fowler Gaskin pushed forward, scowling. "You'd give a nigger a white man's name?"

Blessing was taken aback. "It's an old custom for slaves to take the name of their masters."

"Not where I come from it ain't."

Rusty wondered why Gaskin had come to the funeral unless he hoped to pick up something useful when nobody was looking. Gaskin had disliked Isaac York, and York never had a good word for him. That was one point on which York and Rusty had long been in full agreement. Rusty said, "Maybe you ought to go back where you came from, Fowler."

Gaskin turned on Rusty. "You'd like that, wouldn't you? Well, I'm stayin' where I'm at. But it don't set right with me, knowin' I got a nigger for a neighbor."

"You always did. He's been there longer than you have."

"But he never owned the land. He was just what the Lord intended for a nigger to be. A white man's property."

Gaskin gave Shanty a contemptuous look and stalked away toward a lank mule he had tied nearby.

Rusty moved to Tom Blessing's side. "What Fowler Gaskin thinks don't amount to a damn."

"But look around you. Even some people who don't like him agree with him on this."

"They'll get used to it. With the war over, there's a new day comin'."

Blessing's mouth drooped at the corners. "The war is over, but I'm afraid the fightin's not."

Steals the Ponies was troubled. Two Comanche warriors returning from a clandestine visit to relatives on the reservation had brought interesting news that raised many questions but offered few answers.

He interrogated them at length, distrusting their report. Much of the word that circulated among people on the reservation proved after a time to be false. The whites were worse tricksters than the coyote.

"How do you know the white men's war is finished? Who told you?"

"My cousin," said Wolf Eyes. "He heard it from a shaman."

"Shamans are always seeing things that are not there. It is what they do."

"But this one went to the long-knife post at Fort Sill. He was told by those who heard it from the soldiers. The *teibos* of the North defeated those of the South."

Despite his distrust of whites, Steals the Ponies found the report plausible. But even if true, its meaning was uncertain and therefore troubling.

Wolf Eyes said the war's end had aroused consternation among the many peoples who lived on the reservation and in the territory beyond. Some, like those near-whites known as Cherokees, had been divided in their loyalties, many fighting alongside men of the north, others allying with the South. What the Cherokees did was always a source of puzzlement to Steals the Ponies. They walked along the white man's road in the way they lived and thought. He did not consider them to be of the same race as the Comanche.

He had been told that the whites saw all red men as being of one people, though reason proved that it was not true. Comanches had little in common with the Cherokees or the others who had migrated from some distant eastern land and tried to make themselves white. To suggest that Comanches had anything in common with the accursed Apaches was an insult. To Steals the Ponies, each tribal group was a race apart. The Comanches were *The* People, the chosen ones, a superior race. All others were allowed to live or willed to die at the discretion of the True Human Beings.

Steals the Ponies had heard old men say the world was large, that it would take many seasons to ride all the way across it on even the fastest horse. His father had told him of visiting a great water, so wide he could not see the far side. The elders said there were many more races of men than he had ever heard about, and each race had its own manner of speaking. One would reason that they must have a common sign language like the plains people so they could make themselves understood to strangers. He had noted, however, that most white men did not seem to have the same signals as The People. They moved their hands a lot as they talked, but the meanings were lost to him.

Nor could he distinguish much difference between white men, though the elders claimed they were of many races. They all looked more or less alike except that some were hairier than others. Their talk was gibberish, as empty as the chatter of the gray cranes that wintered around the many playa lakes shimmering on the plains after a season of rain. How they understood one another was beyond his imagining. It stood to reason that one had to be born white to talk that way, and one had to be born Comanche to know The People's language.

Yet, Steals the Ponies had a foster brother who was white. His father had captured him on a raid and brought him home as a small boy. At first Badger Boy had babbled in the white man's undecipherable tongue. Now nine or ten summers old, he spoke Comanche almost as if he had been born to it.

Steals the Ponies wondered if he would ever understand life's puzzling contradictions.

After lengthy consideration, he told Wolf Eyes, "The white men have fought each other a long time. It is not reasonable that they would stop now while so many on both sides still live. We shall go and see for ourselves."

Wolf Eyes was more than willing, for the ranger warrior society had thwarted the last two raids in which he had participated. "How many of us will go? Do you think we will bring back many horses?"

"There will be only the two of us. We go to look, not to fight."

Wolf Eyes became dubious. "What is the use in just looking?"

"So we will know for certain."

"And once we know, what then? Is it good for us, or is it bad, that the white men no longer fight each other?"

Steals the Ponies considered. "I fear it will not be good. If the Texans no longer war against the men of the North, they may make more war against The People. If the ranger society and the long knives make peace with each other, they may join together to fight us."

Wolf Eyes remained disappointed that a pony raid was not to be part of the expedition. "Perhaps if some *teibos* should attack us and we kill them, we may take their horses."

"It is my intention that we see but are not seen. We leave tomorrow, before the sun."

He traveled light on such trips, not wanting to encumber his horse with excess weight. He packed dried meat strips and pemmican in a leather pouch and tested his bowstring to be certain it would not break should the unforeseen force him to use it.

A boy moved up beside him in the firelight. "You are going somewhere, big brother?"

"Not far, Badger Boy. I will not be gone for long."

"Would you take me with you?" Badger Boy was always begging to go somewhere, but he was still too young for any mission that involved danger. He had earned his name by fighting to a standstill all the other boys who tried to pick on him. Steals the Ponies considered Badger Boy an appropriate name because the lad had that animal's unyielding temperament when provoked. He fought with a badger's tenacity.

"Not this time. You must grow some more." Steals the Ponies placed the flat of his hand against the top of the boy's head, then raised it. "When you are this high, then you can go."

The fire blazed up unexpectedly, and Steals the Ponies was reminded that the boy's eyes were much lighter in color than his own. In daylight they were blue. Steals the Ponies had long ago become accustomed to that fact, yet now and again it struck him as if for the first time, reminding him that he and the boy were not of the same blood.

"This is your new brother," Buffalo Caller had said when he brought the young captive home. "Teach him so he will forget the white man's ways."

At the time the boy had been four or perhaps five summers old. Steals the Ponies had resented him. He had beaten him when Buffalo Caller was not there to see. But the boy had fought back with the ferocity of a cornered bear cub, gradually gaining his adoptive brother's respect and eventually his love. Steals the Ponies had become his protector against those who would antagonize him. Badger Boy had grown strong for his age, able to exact a painful price from anyone tempted to taunt him because of his light-colored skin and blue eyes. Seldom anymore did anyone try.

So far as Steals the Ponies could determine, the lad had forgotten his white past, his blood parents, even the white man's language. He was as Comanche-born.

Steals the Ponies said, "I promise that when you are ready I will take you on a raid deep into the white men's country and you will have many horses."

"I am ready now."

Warily eyeing the horizon for a sign of anyone on horseback, Steals the Ponies rode across what had been the ranger warrior society's camp. The corrals remained as he remembered. He had stolen horses out of them more than once. Now they were empty, the gates sagging open. Where the ranger tepees had stood, he found only square areas of hard-packed earth.

Wolf Eyes suggested, "Perhaps you are mistaken. This may not be the place."

"It is the place. I have taken ponies from this corral while the rangers slept."

The two warriors had made their way here by the light of the moon, skirting the nearby settlement. He had no wish to stir up the white men and set them into pursuit. This was only a mission of discovery. Clearly, the rangers had evacuated the camp. But where had they gone? Surely they had not been killed off, for word would have spread like wildfire sweeping the prairies under a dry west wind. He suspected their removal had something to do with the end of the white men's war, but it was unlikely the rangers had abandoned their war against The People.

The last attempted raid had shamed him in the eyes of the camp. Though outnumbered, rangers had caught the warriors by surprise and routed them ingloriously. He and his followers had been forced back across the river empty-handed, with fewer horses than when they had started. The failure still rankled. Like Wolf Eyes, he itched for redemption. But unlike his companion, he could be patient when patience was called for.

Wolf Eyes suggested, "If the rangers are gone, it will be easier for us. There will be no one to keep us from going among the settlements and taking the farmers' horses."

Steals the Ponies was not so confident. Perhaps the rangers had relocated to a larger camp. If the white men were no longer fighting among themselves, more might choose to join the struggle to drive The People onto the reservation. It appeared obvious that they intended to take over all the old hunting grounds and either violate the earth with their steel-pointed plows or chase off the buffalo and substitute their spotted cattle. Such a thing was a blasphemy too profane to be tolerated.

Wolf Eyes asked, "What do you want to do?"

"We shall find if the rangers have truly left or if they are still somewhere around. You have been telling me you want to take horses. You saw those that graze near the white men's houses?" He pointed in the direction of the settlement that was Fort Belknap.

"There did not seem to be even a guard."

"We shall rest in the timber until night. Then we shall take the horses and see if the rangers come after us. If they do not, we will know they are no longer anywhere near."

"And if they are not?"

"Then when the grass is cured and the moon is full, we shall come back. We shall take all the horses we want and show the hair-faced *teibos* that this land belongs to The People."

CHAPTER
EIGHT

I t had been a long, wearisome walk for Pete Dawkins and his friend Scully. They had quietly taken leave of their company in the middle of the night without bothering to notify the officer in charge. Pete had seen no reason to disturb the captain's sleep. Everybody had been mourning the loss of the war, declaring the Confederacy crushed, complaining that no one was going to be paid what was due him. Pete saw no reason to stay around for formalities or to surrender to some damned Yankee outfit. For all he knew, the defeated Confederate soldiers might be herded into a prison camp. If he had been willing to go to prison he would not have joined the army in the first place.

He and Scully had made a futile effort to liberate two horses from the officers' picket line but had found them too well guarded. He doubted that anyone would be shot for deserting a collapsing army, but they might be shot for trying to get away with someone else's horses. The two had made their getaway afoot, hoping for better luck somewhere along the road. Pete had always felt that luck was not a matter of waiting for something good to happen on its own. A man made his own luck, grabbing whatever came to hand.

"Scully," he said, "do you remember that good little blaze-faced sorrel I had, the one we found just wanderin' around loose on the Tonkawa reservation?"

"I remember it like to've got us scalped."

"I sure wish I had that little horse now." Pete sat down at the side of the dusty wagon road, checking the soles of his shoes. "Got a hole wore almost through. I'd be about as well off barefooted." He removed the offending shoe and rubbed his foot. Its bottom was tender where the leather had worn thinnest.

Bad as they were, the shoes were no worse than the rest of his clothing. What once had been a gray uniform was now only a couple more rips away from being rags, stained, crusted with dried sweat and dirt. The knees were out of his loose-hanging trousers. Missed meals and loss of weight had caused him to punch a new hole in his belt so he could draw it tighter. The cuffs of his tattered shirt flopped open, the buttons gone.

He said, "You'd think somewhere we ought to be able to borry a couple of horses."

"Like we borrowed from the Tonkawas?"

A buyer had come along with genuine Yankee money in his pocket, and Pete had sold the horse. In his estimation it was too good an animal for a blanket Indian anyway. It had also been too good for the buyer, but Pete had been unable to track him and steal the sorrel back, though he tried.

Scully grunted. "Horses seem awful scarce around here. Reckon the war took up all anybody could spare."

"I'd settle for a hog-backed mule if I could get off of my feet for a while."

Pete had worried little about pursuit, even before they crossed out of Louisiana into Texas two days ago. He had seen many Confederate soldiers straggling along the roads, trying to make their way home. Nobody seemed to question whether or not they had deserted their companies. An army had to be fed, and the Confederacy seemed unable to continue doing that. Better that the men scatter and try to take care of themselves. That was Pete's opinion anyway, and lots of Texans seemed to share it. Opinion was about all most of them had left to share.

Pete and Scully had been able to shoot enough game for at least a bare subsistence. True, it was hard to fill up on squirrel, and it became tiresome day after day, but it was better than starving. Yesterday afternoon they had managed to catch a farmer's fat shoat without attracting attention. They had feasted last night on roast pork several miles beyond the farm where the shoat had come from. The meat was gone now, and Pete was hungry again.

"You'd think somebody would take pity on a couple of soldiers who went and done the fightin' for them," he complained. "Ain't nobody offered us nothin'."

"Don't look to me like anybody's got much *to* offer us. This whole country's poor as a whippoorwill."

"Their own damned fault for startin' the war." Pete had no high-flown notions about the glory of the Confederacy. He and Scully had not joined the fight out of loyalty and patriotism. Pete's father, Old Colonel Caleb Dawkins, had given them no real choice after they were caught with stolen horses, some of them his own.

The memory still rankled Pete, still roused him to occasional fits of anger when he let himself dwell upon the old man's grim ultimatum. As an alternative to prison, Caleb Dawkins had sent Pete and Scully to become targets for Yankee guns.

"Redeem yourselves," he had declared. "Expiate your guilt by serving your country."

Pete had developed an elemental survival strategy. Any time the guns sounded, he fell into a ditch or crawled up against protective trees or a stone wall. He would remain there, his head down, until the firing stopped. Be damned if he intended to die for someone else's grand cause. His only loyalty, his only obligation, was to Pete Dawkins.

After resting awhile, the two men resumed their weary westward march. Pete was not sure just where they were, but the wagon road showed every sign of being well used. Surely it must lead to someplace where opportunity awaited a man keen enough to recognize it.

Scully wiped sweat from his face onto his tattered sleeve. "Reckon we'll live to reach your daddy's farm?"

"We'll get there."

"If he's still down on us like the last time we seen him, we may wish we'd gone someplace else."

"I worked like a nigger on that farm when I was a boy. The old man owes me for that. And he owes us both for packin' us off to the army over nothin' more than a few broomtails we borried from him. I figure to collect, then move on west."

"Collect what? If he's like everybody else we've seen, he's got the seat hangin' out of his britches. Probably couldn't buy us a pint of whiskey if it was ten cents a gallon."

"I know better. Bad as he hated the Union, I know he buried a bucket of Yankee gold and silver under the woodpile back of the house. Seen him myself when he didn't think anybody was lookin'. That'll spend right handy when me and you get to California."

"You think he'll just stand there and let you take it? He's got the tem-

per of a sore-footed badger. We was with him when he hanged them Monahans, remember? A meaner-eyed son of a bitch I never seen, even if he is
your daddy. I think he might be just a little bit crazy."

Sometimes Pete wondered why he put up with Scully. His partner was
always asking questions, always expressing doubts even when everything
appeared clear as crystal. Someday, when he didn't need him anymore, Pete
would ride away and leave him afoot to manage on his lonesome. Like as
not, Scully would wind up in jail before the chickens went to roost.

Just at dusk they trudged into the edge of a small farming town. Pete
saw no sign bearing its name, but the name did not matter. A town was a
town. He observed a tired-looking woman bent over a washboard and tub.
Behind her, wet clothes hung on a line, flapping in the evening breeze. He
guessed she was a professional washerwoman. A regular housewife should
have finished her family wash earlier in the day unless she had a terribly
large family.

Pete said, "Late as it is, them clothes won't be dry enough to take in
the house before dark. Ought to be somethin' there that'll fit us."

"They don't look like much."

"They're better than what we've got on. We'll circle back this way after
a while."

"How far do you think we'd get, afoot like we are?"

"Maybe when we leave here we won't be afoot."

"Takin' other people's horses is what got us into the army in the first
place."

"And it'll get us away from here. Stay close to me and maybe you'll
learn somethin'."

"I learned a lot the last time."

From up the street Pete heard singing. He thought at first it might be
from a saloon, and the thought made him thirsty. But he soon realized the
music was not the kind that went with whiskey. Lamplight spilled from the
open windows of a frame church. Several horses were tied on the street outside, along with a few buggies and wagons.

Scully quickly surmised what was going through Pete's mind. "Stealin'
horses is bad enough, but from a church?"

Pete smiled. "Now, where would you find more cheerful givers than in
a church house?"

Scully followed, as he always did. Pete made a hasty choice for himself
and pointed to another for Scully. "That saddle may be big for you, but
you'll grow into it when we start eatin' regular again." He tightened the

cinch, for the owner had loosened it to let the horse breathe more easily during the services. He mounted and jerked his head. "Come on, we don't want to be hangin' around here when the sermon is over."

"*Hangin'*? That's apt to be the outcome if they catch us."

"Ain't nobody goin' to. Dark as it is, they won't have any idea which-away we went. Let's go back and get us them clothes."

Pete was glad to find that the woman had gone into the house. Even with the help of distant lamplight, it was difficult to see the clothes and judge their size. To improve the odds, Pete picked a couple of shirts and two pairs of trousers. They were still damp. He laid them across the pommel in front of him. "Hurry up. Don't be so damned picky."

There would be time to change clothes when they were well away from town. "Let's be movin'," he said, "and put this town behind us before they take up collection down at the church house."

The Dawkins farm lay just ahead. Much as he might deny it, Pete had begun looking forward to seeing it again. He had been in his early teens when Old Colonel had built the big house. It was often an unhappy place, but home nevertheless. His father sometimes treated him as if he were a black slave in the fields. His protective mother, on the other hand, had tried to shelter him and ease his wounded pride when she thought the colonel had been too harsh. He learned early how to manipulate her. He was never able to manipulate his father.

Caleb Dawkins had been brought up to believe in supplementing the sermon with the lash. He bore scars from his own boyhood and visited their like upon his son. He believed in bending the twig in the direction he wanted the tree to grow. But Pete had thwarted him. He grew in his own direction.

The nearer they came to the house, the more nervous Scully became. Some of that nervousness was contagious, but Pete would not acknowledge it for a hundred dollars in Yankee silver.

Pete tried to ease Scully's fears. "Who knows? He may even kill the fatted calf."

"More likely he'll meet us with a shotgun. It near tore the heart out of him to admit what you done."

"What *we* done. You was mixed up in it as deep as I was."

"But it was your idea."

"We're stayin' just long enough to get us a fresh outfit and maybe some better horses. And to dig up that can of gold and silver from under the woodpile."

"He may have dug it up already."

"He's too tight. He'd let it lay there and rust before he'd spend it. I'm takin' it for all the work I done on this place and never got paid for."

"What if he puts up a fight?"

"He's an old man, and I'm tougher than when I went into the army. I can whip him."

"You didn't talk this brave the last time."

Pete gave Scully an angry look. Scully was getting too free with his mouth. One of these days he was liable to earn himself a good stomping. That would teach him to stay in his proper place. "I'll handle the old man, don't you worry yourself about that."

In truth, Pete had no idea what the reception would be or how he would react to it. He thought he would try being politely formal. That would please his mother and make her easy to handle. It might be unexpected enough to keep the old man off balance as well. If it did not work, military service had taught Pete a few things, like standing up for his rights so long as that stand did not put his life in jeopardy. He knew there was a time to be bold and a time to back away. He could always try boldness if being polite did not disarm Old Colonel.

One of the slaves came out from the barn and stared in surprise. "Marse Pete? Can that be you?"

"Sure as hell is, Jethro." Pete dismounted and held out the reins for the servant to take. It occurred to him that by order of the Union government Jethro was no longer a slave. It was possible no one had told him, certainly not the colonel. Pete could not imagine Jethro or any other slaves staying around here under the Dawkins thumb if they had an alternative. "Is the colonel up at the house?"

Jethro nodded solemnly. "He stays up there a right smart anymore, since old missus died."

The news struck Pete hard. The words came painfully and sounded like the croaking of a frog. "Mama's gone?"

"Taken to her bed last winter and never got up again."

Scully said, "Damn, Pete, but that's tough."

Pete turned and leaned against his horse, trying to get his emotions under control. Maybe the colonel had written him a letter but he had never received it. Or, just as likely, the stubborn old bastard hadn't even tried.

The first rush of grief passed, and anger took its place. Pete clenched his fist. If his suspicion was correct, he had found one more reason to hate his father.

He turned back to Jethro. "Ain't nothin' wrong with the colonel, I suppose?" He hoped there was.

"He's down in his mind, what with old missus dyin' and the war bein' lost. But he's a strong man. He'll do a lot better, seein' as you've come home."

Don't bet on it, Pete thought. More than likely he'll throw a conniption fit.

"Put our horses up for us, Jethro. We're goin' to the house." He walked away without looking back, knowing the servant would obey and Scully would follow. He held his gaze on the open front door, wondering if the colonel had seen him and would come to meet him. He halfway hoped for a cordial reception, though he knew it was unlikely.

He was right. He stepped through the door and stopped a moment, letting his eyes adjust to the near-dark interior. The drapes were drawn, but he could see the colonel seated in the parlor, his huge bearlike body completely filling his favorite chair. Holding a glass of whiskey, the colonel stared at him with eagle eyes that offered no sign of welcome. As always, his was a formidable presence. Pete had seen strong men shake when the colonel confronted them.

Despite his intention of taking a strong initiative, Pete felt his face warming, his heartbeat quickening.

Damn it to hell, he was still a little afraid of the old man. He hoped the colonel could not see it.

Pete walked up almost within touching distance, trying to muster voice to speak. Caleb Dawkins spoke first, in a tone like a pronouncement of doom. "You back legally, or did you just run away?" Dawkins's scowl matched his voice.

"The Confederacy is breakin' up. Wasn't no use stayin' around for the funeral."

"I'm surprised you didn't try to run away sooner and get yourself shot for desertion."

Pete had a sinking feeling. He had hoped his father might have softened a bit. Clearly, he was still the same bull-headed son of a bitch he had always been. "I didn't know about Mama. You ought to've written to me. I'd have come."

"If you hadn't been a horse thief, you'd have been here to start with."

The colonel's gaze went to Scully for only a second, then back to Pete. "I see you're still runnin' with the same trash as before."

Scully took a step backward, toward the door. Pete summoned enough nerve to command, "Stand firm, Scully. We've got a right to be here." He surprised himself a little. Emboldened, he stepped to the small table beside the colonel's chair and picked up the bottle of whiskey from which Dawkins had filled his glass. Pete tipped it and took a long swallow. "You used to buy a better brand of bourbon."

Dawkins said, "How would you know? I never gave you any."

"I took it when you wasn't lookin'."

"Like you took my horses." Dawkins finished what was in his glass and set it down. "Where do you plan to go from here?" The implication was plain enough: He did not intend for Pete to remain.

That stiffened Pete's stubborn streak. "What makes you think I figure on goin' anywhere?"

"I don't intend to let you stay here."

"I'll stay if I decide I want to. Me and Scully both."

"I'll have the law on you."

Pete thought he sensed a weakness in the colonel's voice. It was time to play his trump card. "It's pretty soon goin' to be Yankee law, and I don't think you'll want it pokin' into what happened over at the Monahan farm. Me and Scully was there, remember?"

Colonel Dawkins tried to stare Pete down, but he was the first to pull his gaze away. He went to the whiskey bottle and refilled his glass. He drank most of it in one huge swallow. "We did the patriotic thing. Those Monahans were traitors."

"Not the way the Yankee law will see it. You sure won't want to stand in front of a Yankee judge and jury while me and Scully tell what happened."

"You can't testify against me without implicating yourselves."

"They got a word for it. *Coercion*, I think it is."

For the first time Pete could remember, he had his father pinned against the wall. He could see conflicting emotions in the old man's eyes: resentment, defiance, fear.

He declared, "Like I said, we're stayin' if we want to. The way I figure it, this farm is part mine. When you're gone, it'll all be mine."

Defiance won out, but not by a wide margin. The colonel's eyes crackled with anger. "Stay and be damned. But keep out of my sight."

"This farm ain't *that* big. You'll be seein' a lot of me. And every time you see me, remember the way you treated me when I was a boy and couldn't defend myself. I ain't a boy no more."

Dawkins met Pete's gaze, and this time he held it. "If I didn't know how good a woman your mother was, I'd wonder if you were truly my son."

"Take a hard look, because your face is a lot the same as mine. I'm yours, and I've decided I can be just as stubborn mean as you are. I worked and sweated like a field hand to make you wealthy, and now I'm claimin' my share." Pete jerked his head at Scully. "Come on. I'm takin' my old room back."

Later he had Jethro muster three of the hands and led them to the woodpile behind the big house. "You-all throw all that wood over here," he said, pointing to an open piece of ground. When the wood had been moved, he dug the toe of his shoe into the soft earth. "Grab your shovels and start diggin'."

Scully stood by with hands on his hips. "You sure you remember just where the colonel buried that bucket of money?"

"I'll remember it to my dyin' day."

Scully motioned toward the back porch. Colonel Dawkins stood there, staring. "This could *be* your dyin' day. I do believe that old man'd shoot you, son or not."

"There was a time he would've, but somethin's been took out of him. Maybe it's losin' the war, or maybe it's losin' Mama, I don't know. He acts as mean as ever, but look in his eyes and you'll see he ain't the man he was."

"I looked in his eyes, and they still scared me."

The hole was four feet deep when a field hand's shovel struck a rock. He raised up, sweat rolling down his face. "Ain't nothin' more down here."

Pete's confidence began to waver. Scully said, "Maybe your memory ain't as good as you thought it was."

Pete reluctantly admitted, "Maybe I missed it by a foot or two. Dig the hole out wider, thisaway."

At last Colonel Dawkins stepped down from the small back porch and strode out to where the woodpile had been. He challenged Pete, "You think you're mighty smart, but you're making a fool of yourself."

"The hell I am. I saw you myself, buryin' a whole bucketful of Yankee money. I figure by rights it's mine because of all the work I done around here for nothin'."

"You're several months too late. I already dug it up."

Pete felt as if an ax handle had struck him across the stomach. "What did you do with it?"

"I gave it to the cause. The Confederacy needed it to buy guns in Mexico."

Pete wanted to believe his father was lying, but he knew instinctively that he was not. Though the old man would not have spent that money on himself or any of his family, he would squander it on a lost cause. "You fool! You damned old fool!"

Triumph glowed in Caleb Dawkins's eyes. "When I saw the men start digging, I knew why you wanted to stay. You weren't content just to steal horses from me. You were going to steal my money, too. Well, now there's nothing here for you except a lot of hard work. So, when are you leaving?"

Pete gritted his teeth. "That'd tickle you plumb to death, wouldn't it? But this country owes me, and one way or another I'm goin' to collect. If not from you, then from anywhere and anybody I can." He turned angrily on Jethro. "Fill that hole up before somebody falls in it."

Scully said, "It looks like a grave to me."

The colonel walked back into the house. Pete kicked a clod of dirt and broke it into a dozen pieces.

Scully said, "Seems like there ain't much use in us stayin' around here."

"At least we got a roof and beds and somethin' to eat. And I've found out the old dog barks loud but ain't got any teeth left. So we'll stay. Even a blind hog finds him an acorn now and then."

"We ain't blind hogs."

"So there's no tellin' what acorns we may find."

CHAPTER

NINE

Every day or two, tired and hungry ex-soldiers stopped by Rusty's farm. Most had not been released officially. They had simply declared themselves finished with war and had struck out on their own without a by-your-leave. They were ragged, hungry, and afoot, too proud to ask outright for a meal but grateful for anything offered. Some were making their way to homes farther along. Some had found that they no longer had a home and were looking for a place where they might start afresh. Open country to the west offered land almost free for the taking if a man were willing to accept the challenge of low rainfall, few neighbors, and the risk of Indian raids.

No matter where they came from, the refugees carried essentially the same reports. Hard times had fallen upon Texas with a vengeance. Confederate money would buy nothing, and Yankee money had long ago been spent. Commerce, what little there was, had to be conducted on a barter basis. Local governments were for the most part in a state of collapse.

Rusty gave what he could to the transients, grateful not to be among them. The cabin was reserved for Clemmie Monahan and her two younger daughters. Rusty and Grandpa Vince Purdy slept beneath a shed out beside the barn. Soldiers were welcome to spend the night beneath that roof. If they were too tired to go on, they were given welcome to stay and rest.

At least there was food. The spring-planted garden was yielding vegetables. Beef was plentiful and without monetary value because cattle had
run free and mostly unclaimed during the war, multiplying without limits
beyond those imposed by drought and the available grazing.

Rusty listened with interest to the soldiers' stories. They reminded
him of tales Daddy Mike Shannon had brought home from the fighting in
Mexico. Names and faces were different, but the recent war seemed much
the same as the one before, bloody, frightening, and often maddeningly
futile.

"Seemed sometimes like the generals was just playin' a game, and they
used us soldier boys like checker pieces," said one veteran, his face scarred
by an exploding shell. Using a broken-off stick, he drew a circle in the dirt
at his feet and punched a hole in the center. "This here'd be a gun
emplacement. We'd run the Yankees off from it, then they'd build up a little stronger and chase us back. We'd drive them away again, like a bunch of
schoolboys playin' tag. Then the officers would decide we didn't need the
position anyway, and they'd move us someplace else. Long as we cost the
Yankees more than they cost us, the generals seemed satisfied. I never seen
many of *them* bleed."

"Hell of a way to run a war," Rusty sympathized. "It was a lot that way
with us rangers and the Indians. We'd cut them off and chase them back
across the Red River. Then they'd get together and come again when they
were ready. Nothin' ever got settled for good. Still hasn't."

The soldier's eyes seemed haunted, his hair and beard grayer than his
years would justify. Rusty blamed the war for that.

Clouds had built, black and threatening. Lightning streaked. A loud
clap of thunder startled the soldier so that he ducked and whirled around.
Sheepishly he apologized. "I didn't go to act like an old woman. I still see
Yankees under every bush."

"They haven't found us out here yet." But they would, Rusty knew. It
was only a matter of time before the Federal government would send soldiers and civilian regulators past the forks of every creek, to the end of the
last wagon track.

The soldier worried, "When they do, they ain't apt to look kindly on us
old rebel boys. Especially after what happened to Lincoln."

It was said that Lincoln had been urging leniency toward the beaten
Confederates. Now, in the bitter aftermath of his assassination, it was
widely speculated that the proponents of vengeance would take over, that
the Southern states were in for harsh retribution.

Rusty said, "Nothin' much we can do except wait and see. I just hope the war doesn't start all over again."

"I ain't waitin' to see. I'm travelin' west 'til I can soak my sore and achin' feet in the Pacific Ocean. And if I can catch me a boat, I may go all the way to China. Everything around here has been stood on its head. You know you got a neighbor that was a slave? Face blacker than the ace of spades, and now he owns a farm."

"That'd be Shanty. Sure, I know."

"I spent last night at his place. Treated me kind, he did. Even said 'sir.' But I was glad to get away from there without any trouble. I know some hard-headed old boys back home who wouldn't hold still for such as that. I wouldn't want to be there when they come callin'."

"Everybody around here has known Shanty for years. They won't bother him."

"Maybe you don't know everybody around here as well as you think. I ran into an old man on the road, name of Gaskin. When I told him where I'd spent the night, he fell into a cussin' fit."

"Fowler Gaskin is all wind. Nobody listens to him."

"Well, you know your neighbors. I don't. If I was that Shanty, though, I'd sleep with one eye open."

Rusty remembered Tom Blessing's misgivings when Isaac York had dictated his will.

Maybe I'd best go talk to Tom the first chance I get, and make sure there's nothing going on that I haven't heard about, he thought.

He had known the Monahan family would not remain indefinitely. They had come seeking refuge from Caleb Dawkins's violent fanaticism. That danger had ended with the war. For a while Clemmie had been saying they should soon return to their own farm to piece together whatever remnants they could find of their past lives. Each time Rusty saw her step out onto the dog run and look hopefully to the northwest, he knew she was looking for her son James.

It was raining the night he came. Rusty had been watching the darkening clouds during the afternoon, fearing they might pass over without shedding a drop, or at least more than a light shower. But weather was unpredictable. Drought or flood, anything was possible. The farmer's life was always subject to the vagaries of wind, rain, and sunshine.

Coming in from the field, he saw the two girls harvesting vegetables in the garden, holding them in their aprons, carrying them to baskets set at the end of the rows. Sometimes their sudden appearance caught him off guard and gave him a start, making him think of Geneva. Especially Josie, who looked the most like her older sister. Josie came to meet him at the garden gate, her long hair blown by the wind.

She said, "Looks like we're fixin' to get a frog-stranglin' rain. We thought we'd better gather what we could."

"I'll pitch in and help you."

Josie smiled. "We'd like that."

An hour or so later they were seated at the supper table. The cabin door had been closed against the damp wind that came with the rain. It was suddenly flung open, and James Monahan stood there, his clothes dripping water. Lightning flashed in the sky behind him, making him look like some malevolent apparition.

Clemmie jumped up so quickly she overturned her chair. She kicked it aside in her eagerness to reach her son. Shouting with joy, she threw her arms around him, oblivious to the fact that his clothing was soaked. The girls hugged him when their mother stepped back. Old Vince Purdy grabbed James's hand and pumped it vigorously.

Clemmie said, "We been prayin' for this day."

James said, "I wish you'd prayed for dry weather. My wagon like to've bogged down, and I'm wet to the hide." His gaze drifted to Rusty. A little of his old reserve remained, but he shook Rusty's hand. "I do appreciate you givin' the folks a place to live for so long."

Rusty shrugged. "The whole outfit might've dried up and blowed away if they hadn't been here. They took good care of things while I was away."

"I'm glad you got past the brush men all right. Some of them turned kind of peevish when they found out you'd slipped away."

"How was that Oldham boy when you left camp?"

"Alive but not kickin' much. His brother wanted me to tell him where you live. I told him I thought it was somewhere over on the Trinity River." That would be a long way from the Colorado.

"Thanks. I don't want any more trouble with them. I wasn't lookin' for the trouble I already had."

Clemmie did not know what they were talking about, or care. She demanded of her son, "The war's been over for a right smart while. Where've you been all this time?"

"Up at our old place, helpin' Geneva and Evan build you a new house. It's finished, Mama, and waitin' for you." He looked at his sisters and grandfather. "For all of you, any time you're ready to go."

Clemmie clasped his hands. "We've been ready for the longest time." She looked apologetically at Rusty. "This place has been good to us, and Rusty's been more than generous. But it ain't the same as home."

"The new house ain't as fine as the one Caleb Dawkins burned down, but it'll keep the rain off of your head."

She asked, "Is the old cabin still standin', or did Caleb Dawkins go back and burn it?"

"It's still there, such as it is. Geneva and Evan been livin' in it." James peeled off a wet jacket and hung it on a peg. "Have you heard from Geneva lately?"

Clemmie shook her head. "Ain't been any mail since I don't know when."

"She's in a family way. Goin' to make a grandmother of you before the snow flies."

Rusty swallowed hard, then walked out onto the dog run, watching rain pound the hard-packed ground and run-off water move in small brown rivulets down toward the swelling creek. He stopped beneath the edge of the roof and felt the wind-blown spray wetting his face. He shook, suddenly cold, and wished the rain could wash away the grief that came with the slow dying of old dreams.

He was still on the dog run, sitting on a bench, when James finished his supper and came out to join him. James stood beside him, looking out into the rain.

Rusty said, "Back there in that brush camp you could've told me Geneva was married."

"I never got around to it. We had other things pressin' on us, remember? And pretty soon you were gone."

"I never thought but that she'd wait for me."

"She hadn't heard from you in a long time. For all she knew, you were dead."

"I wrote to her. The letters never got through."

"You ought to've found a way to come and see her, even if you had to desert the rangers. But you didn't, and Evan came along, lookin' like he was fixin' to die. Geneva cared for him like a nurse. You know how it is, a man and a woman together so much. You weren't here, and he was. Nature just took its course."

Rusty doubled a fist. The war, the damned war. It had cost everybody far too much.

James argued, "Evan works hard, he loves her, and he makes her smile. For a long time she didn't have much to smile about."

"The war was hell on everybody, even those who never went to it. Sooner or later, it came to *them*."

An old bitterness pinched James's eyes. "The Monahans sure suffered their share."

"It may be hard on Clemmie, goin' back where so many sorrowful things happened."

"It'll pass. She's got a will like an iron hammer." James started toward the kitchen door but stopped. "Your feelin's for Geneva will pass too, if you'll let them."

Rusty felt a deep ache. "I'd figured on askin' her to marry me."

"When a man really wants to do somethin', he'd ought to go ahead and do it. Time has a way of takin' things away from you if you wait too long."

"So I've found out."

"I used to lay awake nights, thinkin' about killin' Caleb Dawkins. But I decided that was too quick and easy for what he done, so I'm lettin' him wait and sweat over what I'm goin' to do and when I'm goin' to do it."

"What *are* you goin' to do?"

"Nothin', just let him worry himself to death. That way the revenge will last longer."

James went back into the kitchen side of the cabin. In a little while Josie came out. Her shoulders were slumped, her eyes downcast.

Rusty said, "I thought you'd be happier, seein' your brother."

"He's come to take us home."

"That's what you've been waitin' for, isn't it?"

"It's what Mama's been wantin', and Alice and Grandpa. But I like it here."

"Nothin' is as good as home."

"Too much happened there, too many bad things. Everything here has been good, 'til now." She turned toward him, her eyes sad. At this moment she looked more than ever like Geneva. "You don't want us to leave, do you, Rusty?"

"I've got used to havin' you-all on the place. It'll be lonesome when everybody is gone. But I guess it had to happen sometime."

"I'd rather stay here. You'll need somebody to cook for you and sew and keep the garden."

Rusty smiled indulgently. "I'm afraid Clemmie would never stand still for such as that. You a young woman, me a man . . . it'd give folks an awful lot to gossip about."

"It wouldn't be anybody's business."

"That's when people *really* talk, when it's none of their business."

Presently James and his grandfather returned to the dog run. The rain seemed to be slacking off. That suited Rusty. He had rather not have so much that it drowned out part of the field.

James said, "First thing come mornin', me and Grandpa will start gatherin' up our horses."

When the Monahan women and Vince Purdy had moved to Rusty's place to wait out the war, they had brought their band of mares with them. Unattended at the deserted Monahan home place, the whole bunch would have disappeared in short order. As it was, their numbers had increased.

Purdy said, "Young'un, you got no idee how much trouble we had holdin' on to them. Army horse buyers kept sniffin' around, worse than the Indians. They'd offer Confederate scrip that everybody knowed wasn't worth a bucket of cold spit. At least the Comanches never bothered tryin' to lie to us. They just taken what they could find and went on their way."

Purdy tamped tobacco into his pipe. "Me and Clemmie let the buyers take a few snides now and again, but we managed to keep the best of the bunch hid out to the west of here. We'd go to talkin' about Indians, and no government people ever got the nerve to venture that far."

Rusty said, "I've seen where most of the mares are runnin'. I'll help you round them up."

James nodded. "You've got work of your own to do. But we'd be obliged."

Rusty said, "And I'll help you move your folks back home. I'll go along with you."

"We couldn't impose on you that far."

Rusty said, "I'm thinkin' of the risk. Don't you think it was kind of dangerous, you comin' down here all by yourself?"

"Durin' the war I traveled by myself a-plenty of times to visit the folks, and I had conscript officers and sheriffs lookin' to catch me. Now I don't have to fret about them no more."

"There's always a chance of runnin' into Indians."

"Done that, too. I always had a faster horse than they did."

"This time you came in a wagon. What if you-all ran across Indians on your way home? You couldn't outrun them. How long would you last in a fight, just two men and three women?"

"Long enough to do them some damage." But Rusty could tell by James's expression that he was struggling with new doubts.

James said, "One more man *would* help the odds. If you think this farm can get along without you, we'd be tickled to have you come with us."

"The fields are goin' to be too wet to work anyway."

The younger of the girls rode with her mother on the wagon James had brought. Josie rode on horseback alongside Rusty and her brother James, driving the mares, colts, and a bay stallion. Vince Purdy drove a second wagon piled high with family belongings. It was one the Monahans had brought with them when they fled Caleb Dawkins.

Rusty had not heard of any Indian incursions in a while, but the possibility could never be dismissed. Another potential problem was the defeated ex-soldiers straggling across the country. Most were harmless, but some were hungry, frustrated, and desperate enough to do almost anything. Tom Blessing had told Rusty about a couple of murders supposedly committed in the course of robbery.

He would deny it even to himself, but one reason he had volunteered to join the Monahans on this trip was that he burned to see Geneva. He realized that seeing her might hurt worse than *not* seeing her. Still, the compulsion was too strong to put down. He could rationalize that the family needed the extra protection his presence would afford, but in some secret corner of his mind he knew that was not his primary reason for going.

He caught James studying him critically, and he suspected Geneva's brother saw into that secret corner.

The first day passed without incident. The mares and colts had to be held back, limited by the lumbering pace of the wagons. They would move well ahead, then the riders would stop and loose-herd them to graze until the wagons caught up.

Josie rode a sidesaddle belonging to her mother. Rusty told her, "You sit real good on that thing."

"I rode with Grandpa Vince a lot, lookin' after the mares. 'Til Evan came, I was Grandpa's main outside help except when Preacher Webb stopped by, or James slipped past the law to spend a day or two with us."

Her face was deeply tanned, for she had spent a lot of time in the sun and wind. Rusty had seen her ride horseback and maneuver a plow, though he had noted that she knew her way around the kitchen, too. A Texas farm woman—or girl—was expected to be able to work like a man without forgetting she wasn't one.

He said, "Looks to me like you can do whatever you set your mind to."

She grinned. "I was hopin' you'd see that."

Rusty saw cattle bearing the Monahan brand. He told James, "If cattle were worth cash money, you'd be in good shape."

James nodded. "I managed to slip back here now and again when nobody was lookin'. Gave me a chance to see after the cattle my family had to leave behind when they refugeed down to your farm."

"Looks like they increased."

"Cows didn't know there was a war on. Kept havin' calves every year. There's cattle runnin' wild over this country, no brands or earmarks, just waitin' for somebody to put a claim on them."

"They're not worth runnin' after."

"But one day they *will* be worth somethin'. I'm figurin' to burn a brand on as many as I can catch."

The procession was nearing the Monahan home place when Rusty saw two horsemen a few hundred yards ahead. The pair quickly moved into the cover of nearby brush.

Rusty turned. "James . . ."

"I saw them." Frowning, James rode quickly to his sister. "Josie, you get back with the wagons. Tell Mama and Grandpa to keep their eyes open. Be ready to run for that ravine yonder."

She nodded soberly. "Indians, you reckon?"

"We'll find out pretty soon. We'll hold the mares here 'til the wagons catch up."

Rusty and James brought the mares and colts to a stop but did not let them spread out to graze. Rusty drew his rifle from its scabbard and placed it in front of him. He watched the brush for movement.

It came, finally. As the wagons drew up even with the herded mares, the two riders emerged into the open. James squinted. "At least it ain't Indians."

Watching the horsemen's approach, Rusty relaxed his tight hold on the rifle. He did not place the weapon back into the scabbard.

Clemmie and Vince Purdy asked no questions, but Purdy had brought a rifle up from beneath his wagon seat. Clemmie held a big Colt Dragoon in her lap. It looked as if it might weigh a quarter as much as she did. She said, "Probably just a couple of soldiers lookin' for a meal. That's all right, as long as they ain't after anything else." She jerked her head toward Josie. "You stay close by me and your sister."

James had ridden out a little ways to intercept the two riders before they reached the wagons. Rusty eased forward to join him.

James muttered a low oath. "Damn! Do you see who's comin' yonder?"

Rusty was unable to recognize either rider at the distance. James growled, "It's Caleb Dawkins's son."

"Pete? Last I knew of him, the old man sent him off to the army."

"Too bad some Yankee didn't get a clean shot at him."

"I expect Pete was careful not to offer them much of a target."

Pete Dawkins reined up short, giving Rusty and James a disapproving scrutiny before he spoke. "Thought at first you-all might be Indians with stolen horses, wantin' to add ours to the bunch. Then we saw the wagons and knowed different. Now that I see who you are, I almost wish you *had* been Indians."

Rusty waited for James to speak, but James held silent, his eyes smoldering with an old hatred. Rusty said grittily, "We're glad to see you, too."

Rusty recognized the second rider as Scully, who had been with Pete when the rangers caught them stealing horses. Pete hungrily studied the Monahan mares. The thought behind his eyes was easy to read.

He said, "People been tellin' me the country is near stripped of horses. That's a likely lookin' bunch of mares and colts you got."

James declared, "We've got them, and we're keepin' them."

"Ain't you afraid some slick-fingered Comanches might run off with them?"

Rusty said, "All the slick fingers don't belong to Comanches. I remember the day we caught you two with some horses you forgot to pay for."

Pete's eyes flashed resentment while his mouth curved into a forced smile. "An honest mistake. We misread the brands."

James said, "These all carry the Monahan brand, big enough for a blind man to see."

Scully had not spoken. He seemed content to let Pete do the talking. Rusty judged him to be a follower. He would follow Pete all the way to hell if that was the direction Pete chose to go. It probably would be, sooner or later.

Pete turned his attention to Rusty. "You still a ranger?"

"There are no rangers, as far as I know. The outfit broke up."

"Ain't that a shame!" Pete's smile turned genuine. "Won't be no laws around to beat up on us hardworkin' farmboys."

James patted the palm of his hand against the rifle across his lap. Malice was in his voice. "There's still guns, and there's still rope. You remember about rope, don't you, Pete?"

Pete's smile died as quickly as it had come.

James added, "Since we won't have any regular law, it'll be up to all of us to administer justice accordin' to our own lights. I remember the way the Dawkinses did it."

"You threatenin' me, Monahan?"

"Just lettin' you know I've got a long memory. Now, if you're through visitin', we've still got a ways to go."

Pete pulled aside, and Scully trailed after him like a pup. Rusty and James set the mares to moving. Rusty turned in the saddle, making certain Pete and Scully did not follow. "I didn't like the way Pete was lookin' at your horses."

"I liked it. First time he makes a try for them, he's liable to disappear off the face of the earth, and everybody'll wonder what went with him."

"Everybody but you?"

"Everybody but me."

"Maybe it's just as well I'm not a ranger anymore. I'd hate to be the one sent to take you in."

"I'd hate it, too. I wouldn't like havin' you on my conscience."

CHAPTER

TEN

The Monahans' new house was simple, constructed of logs and built in the traditional double-cabin fashion with an open dog run between the sections, much like Rusty's own. Clemmie's reaction could not have been more enthusiastic if it had been the governor's mansion. She leaned forward on the wagon seat, straining to see better.

"We're home, children," she exclaimed to her daughters.

Josie sat on her horse beside Rusty's Alamo. She had contrived to ride near him most of the trip. She said, "We're not children. At least I'm not."

She was not, though Rusty thought she would probably always seem that way to her mother. She was blossoming into a handsome young woman.

Some of the older mares had seemed to perk up during the last miles of the trip. They held their heads higher and quickened the pace.

James said, "They remember. They're glad to get back."

Vince Purdy had told Rusty a few mares had caused problems in the first weeks after the original move down to Rusty's farm. They kept trying to return north to what had been their home. They became accustomed to their new range after a time but evidently never forgot where they came from. One problem now, for a time at least, would be to keep younger mares from trying to return south to the Colorado River. Horses had been known to travel hundreds of miles, following their instincts to go back where they came from. Occasionally a horse stolen by Indians would escape and turn up at the home corral weeks or even months later.

Rusty looked hopefully toward the open dog run, thinking Geneva might walk out to greet her mother and sisters. He burned to see her. But the only person he saw was a man he realized must be her husband. Evan Gifford opened a corral gate to receive the mares, then strode toward the wagons with a hand raised in welcome.

Josie said, "You'll like Evan."

Rusty doubted it.

"You-all light and hitch," Gifford shouted. He raised his arms to help his mother-in-law, and then Alice, down from the wagon. Rusty studied him, hoping to find something to dislike but seeing nothing beyond the fact that he had won Geneva while Rusty was busy elsewhere. Gifford appeared to be about Rusty's own age. The effects of war showed in his face, in the seriousness of his eyes. A narrow scar across his right cheekbone could have resulted from a saber slash or a bullet.

If a bullet, Rusty thought, why could it not have been an inch farther in? He immediately felt guilty. Such a thought was unworthy of him. He wished no one dead, least of all a soldier who fought for his country.

Clemmie looked around worriedly. "Where's Geneva? There's nothin' wrong with her, is there?"

Gifford tried to reassure her, shaking his head. "She's in the cabin, takin' her rest. Been havin' some low days. Preacher Webb says it's normal, what with her condition."

Clemmie brightened. "Preacher's here?"

"In yonder with Geneva."

Clemmie turned toward the older structure in which Geneva and her husband had made their home. It had been the Monahan family's first dwelling years ago, replaced eventually by a larger house.

Gifford asked, "Don't you want to look at your new home first?"

"It'll still be there when I'm ready. I need to see after my daughter." Clemmie hurried through the door, calling, "Geneva, we're here." Alice trailed close behind.

Rusty helped Josie dismount from her sidesaddle. Smiling her appreciation, she clung to Rusty's arm longer than necessary, then followed her mother and sister.

Still on horseback, James followed the mares into the corral. Rusty waited a moment for the dust to settle, then closed the gate behind them. He heard Vince Purdy ask Gifford, "You sure Geneva's all right?"

"Preacher don't seem worried. A neighbor lady's been comin' over regular. Geneva'll do better now that she's got her family around her. She's missed them."

"And we've missed her," Purdy said. He went into the cabin.

Rusty offered a handshake. "I'm Rusty Shannon."

Gifford accepted the gesture without hesitation. "Pleased to meet you. Geneva and her folks have spoken of you. I already know a lot about you."

"I never knew about *you* 'til just a little while back."

Rusty hoped his voice betrayed no resentment. His feelings were badly confused. He told Gifford, "Ever since I got home, Clemmie's been itchin' to get back here and pick up where she left off."

"Nothin' will ever be the same as it was, but she'll bow her neck and make the best of what there is. These Monahans are a strong-minded bunch."

"I know for certain that James is." Rusty looked toward Geneva's brother, still in the corral busily inspecting the mares. "We came across Pete Dawkins. He been by here, him or his daddy?"

"No, they've taken a wide round dance of this place. James let it be known that he wasn't lookin' for trouble, but if any came at him he'd go meet it halfway. Everybody knew he was talkin' about the Dawkinses. I imagine the word got to them."

"Pete gave the mares a long and hungry look."

Gifford's eyes hardened. "If any turn up missin', me and James will know where to look first. And we'd better not find them there."

Rusty sensed that there was no false bravado in Gifford. He meant what he said. That was a strong point in his favor.

The hardness left Gifford's eyes. "I owe the Monahans a lot. You have any idea what it means not to have anybody, no family . . . nobody?"

Rusty felt a flicker of an old sadness. "I do. I've been there myself." Still am, he thought.

"The army sent me home, so shot up they thought I'd die. But I found I didn't have a home to go back to. Ma and Pa had both passed away. My only sister had sold the place. Then she took down with the fever, and she was gone, too. I was like a lost child 'til the Monahans took me in. Nursed me like I was their own. Got me back on my feet."

"Old Colonel Dawkins had killed Lon and Billy. Like as not you filled an empty space for the family."

"They sure filled an empty space for *me*." Gifford looked away, trying to find the right words. "I have a notion you and Geneva were sort of close. Close enough for marryin'?"

"We never talked about that. Anyway, it was a long time ago, before you came. That's over and forgotten about." The lie almost choked him.

"I'd like to have you for a friend, Rusty, but I'd need to know I've got no reason to worry."

"You don't." Though his heart was not in it, Rusty extended his hand again. Gifford took it, then beckoned with his head. "Come on, let's go in. Geneva's had time to say howdy to her folks by now."

The bedroom half of the cabin was separated from the kitchen side by an opening over which a common roof extended. Rusty followed Gifford through the narrow door. He steeled himself, not sure what his feelings would be when he saw Geneva.

She sat on the edge of a bed, tinier than he had remembered, though her stomach was visibly extended. Alice was brushing out Geneva's long hair. Clemmie and Purdy had pulled wooden chairs up close. Geneva's features were as fine as he remembered. He thought her face looked pale, but it was hard to be sure because the room was semidark. Rusty felt warmth rise in his face, and for a moment he wished he had not come.

She smiled at him. "Welcome back, Rusty." She extended her small hand. Hesitant to take it, he held it gently as if it were an eggshell. She seemed frail.

"You look mighty good," he said. He felt anew the aching sense of loss. It used to be easy to talk with her. Now he felt awkward, especially with her husband standing beside her. He saw a look of affection pass between the two and wished for some excuse to leave this crowded room. The air seemed close and hard to breathe.

She said, "Rusty, when I didn't hear from you for so long, I thought you were probably dead. We heard about some awful Indian fights."

"There were some rangers killed, but none of them were me." He realized too late how unnecessary that sounded.

For the first time he noticed Preacher Webb standing back in a corner. Rusty suspected Webb was aware of his discomfort, for after a minute the minister placed a hand on Rusty's shoulder. "It's been awhile since I ministered to my flock down your way. I hope sin has not broken loose amongst the lambs."

"Not so much that a sermon or two wouldn't fix it."

"It's time I went back down there. I may ride with you when you're ready to go."

"It'd pleasure me to have your company."

Rusty turned back to Geneva. "I know you've got a lot of family visitin' to do. I'd best go see after my horse."

Geneva took his hand again. "Don't be in a hurry to leave."

He saw nothing to stay for. He had come mostly because of a compulsion to see her again. Now he had seen her, and it still hurt as badly as *not* seeing her.

The minister followed him out onto the dog run. He looked back to see if anyone might hear. "Maybe you oughtn't to've come. It's like pickin' at an old sore after it's healed over. Or *has* it healed?"

"One reason I came was to find out. And I guess it hasn't."

"There's times a man has got to turn loose of what's past, no matter how bad it hurts."

"I know. I'm leavin' here come daylight tomorrow mornin'."

"I'll ride with you, Rusty. It'll be like old times."

Nothing would ever again be like old times, but Rusty was grateful for whatever part of them he could salvage. He thought of the occasions in his youth when he had ridden with Warren Webb on the minister's preaching circuit. "I'd be tickled to have your company."

"I'd need to stop and deliver a couple of sermons along the way."

"A sermon or two might do me a world of good."

At breakfast, Clemmie expressed sorrow about their leaving. Rusty suspected her distress was over Webb's departure more than his own. She said, "I do wish you-all wouldn't hurry away. We just barely got here."

Webb said, "Rusty's got work to do at home, and I've got sheep wanderin' around lookin' for their shepherd."

Clemmie took the minister's hand. "You've got a flock here that loves to see you come and hates to see you go." Almost as an afterthought she added, "You'll always be welcome too, Rusty. You made your home ours for a long time. Now our home is yours."

"I'm obliged." Rusty thought he would probably wait awhile. Maybe someday he could look at Geneva without aching inside.

He was tightening the cinch on his saddle when Evan Gifford came around from behind Alamo, looking for a chance to speak without anyone else hearing. "I know you're concerned about Geneva. So am I. But Preacher says he thinks she'll be all right. Says it's pretty much normal, bein' her first baby."

"Preacher's a good doctor."

Again, Gifford seemed to fish around for the words. "I can tell by the way you looked at her, there was a lot of deep feelin's. I want you to know that I love her . . . that I'll never hurt her . . . that she'll never have reason to shed a tear over anything I do."

Rusty swallowed hard. "Nobody could ask for more than that. I hope you both live for a hundred years, and every year is better than the one before it." He put out his hand and forced a weak smile. "She made a good choice."

Gifford walked away. Preacher Webb had come up in time to hear. He gave Rusty an approving nod. "I know it hurt to say that. It takes a strong man, sometimes, to recognize the truth and to speak it."

"Then let's be gettin' started while I'm still feelin' strong." Rusty put his foot in the stirrup and swung up onto Alamo's back.

Josie stood in the open gate. Rusty saw tears in her eyes. She said, "I wish you'd stay, but I know why you can't." She glanced back toward Geneva, who stood in the dog run of the older cabin.

He said, "I'll be back one of these days."

"I know you will, because one of these days I'm goin' to marry you, Rusty Shannon." She turned and hurried toward the new house.

Preacher Webb gave Rusty a quizzical look. Embarrassed, Rusty said, "She's too young to know her own mind."

Webb smiled. "She's a Monahan. Monahans are *born* knowin' their minds."

James and Vince had turned the mares out of the corral at daybreak. Rusty and Webb rode through them as they scattered, the older mares seeking out remembered favored grazing places, the younger ones exploring their new range.

Rusty caught sight of two horsemen a quarter mile away. The pair were still.

Webb saw them, too. He squinted hard. "Maybe they're soldiers workin' their way home."

Rusty could not see the men clearly enough to recognize them, but he noted that the horses were the same colors as those Pete and Scully had been riding. "That'd be Pete Dawkins and his runnin' mate. Probably hatchin' a scheme to make a run at the Monahan mares some dark night."

"Maybe we should go back and tell James."

"James already knows. We ran into Pete on our way up here."

"The Monahans have already suffered too much at the hands of the Dawkins family."

"I have a notion it's the Dawkinses' turn to suffer at the hands of James Monahan."

The people of the band knew him as Badger Boy because he had a badger's belligerent response when other boys picked on him. And pick on him they had, in the beginning, for he seemed a misfit among those near his own age. His eyes were blue where theirs were brown or black, his skin lighter than theirs. He had found that the best way to stop others from bedeviling him was to hit back stronger than he was struck, resorting to a preemptive strike from time to time to keep his tormentors off balance.

Gradually they had learned to show him respect, though it was obvious that he had not been born of The People.

He had only hazy recollections of a time when he was not living among the Comanches. He was dimly aware, more from stories heard than from things remembered, that he had been taken in a raid on a *teibo* settlement when he was no more than four or five summers old. He remembered his Comanche father, known as Buffalo Caller. No one spoke that name anymore because it was the way of The People not to voice the names of the dead lest their spirits be disturbed.

He vaguely remembered a Texan father and mother. The years had all but erased any memory of what they looked like or anything they had said. Yet, buried somewhere deep in his consciousness was a faint memory of raw terror that came to him now and again as in a dream. He knew within reason that his white parents had been killed, for they would not otherwise have yielded him up. None of The People had ever told him anything of his origins. He sometimes wished he could recall more. That remembered fear rose up as a barrier, blocking him from probing deeper into the dark shadows of his past.

Buffalo Caller had taken him as a son but all too soon had died a warrior's death at the hands of the rangers. Steals the Ponies had shouldered the responsibility of becoming both brother and father to the boy. He had taught Badger Boy how to make a boy-size bow and the arrows that went with it, how to ride, how to hunt. He had refined the youngster's fighting skills, though most had come instinctively as a defense against other boys tempted to taunt an outsider.

Now they stepped aside rather than face his fists, or sometimes a leather quirt or heavy stick, whatever he could lay his hands on. Older people often said within his hearing that he might well become the fiercest warrior of them all. But they added that he had to wait, to bide his time and get his full growth.

He thought he had waited long enough. He had listened to his brother and other young warriors make plans for a raid on the Texan settlements, and he wanted to go.

The thought seemed only to amuse Steals the Ponies. Condescendingly he pulled one of the boy's long braids. "Your legs are still too short. You could not keep up."

"But you will be riding, not walking. My legs are long enough for riding a war pony."

"A short-legged pony perhaps."

Badger Boy felt anger rising hot in his face. Steals the Ponies took the idea as a joke, but Badger Boy was in earnest. "I would not fall behind. If I do, you can leave me. I can find the way by myself."

"The Texans would laugh at us. They would say The People must have no warriors left if they bring a boy on a mission of war."

"I hear that Mexican Talker is going. He is not but this much taller than me." Badger Boy made a gesture with both hands to illustrate the small difference. Mexican Talker, like himself, had been brought into the band as a captive, taken as a boy in a raid on a Mexican village. He was dark-skinned and black-eyed, so that strangers looking upon him could easily assume he was Comanche by blood. Only when he spoke would they know otherwise, because he still had the accent of one who had learned another language first. Badger Boy had a bit of the same problem. A few words never came out quite the way he intended. People said it was because of his Texan birth.

"Mexican Talker is older than you. He has made his quest and found his medicine. No, Badger Boy, you must wait awhile longer."

Badger Boy reluctantly conceded to himself that his brother would not allow him to ride out with the others when they invaded the white men's settlements. So Badger Boy began planning how he would slip out of the encampment and go anyway.

CHAPTER
ELEVEN

t took Rusty somewhat longer to get home than he expected because Preacher Webb was much in demand along the way. Isolated settlers rarely had a chance to hear the gospel unless they read it themselves.

Clemmie Monahan had once said, "Others may know the words, but Preacher Webb knows the Master."

The two stopped for the night at the house of a farmer Rusty had met and Webb knew well. The farmer seemed overjoyed.

"Preacher, I been beggin' the Lord to send you, and damned if He didn't do it. I was afraid there wasn't a chance in hell . . ."

Webb's warm smile turned to a concerned frown. "Somebody sick?"

"No, nothin' like that. My daughter needs marryin'. Her young man come home from the army about a month ago. Now, she's a good girl, and all that. Me and her mama brought her up accordin' to Scripture. But her and her feller hadn't seen one another in three years, and . . . well, I'm afraid they've done planted a crop, if you understand my meanin'. It'd be a shame for it to sprout before the bonds are tied right and proper."

Rusty saw that Webb was trying to suppress a smile. He could not control his own. He turned to brush Alamo's sweaty hide.

Webb said, "Don't think bad of them, Hank. Sometimes our human nature outwrestles our convictions. Back when preachers were a lot scarcer,

I can remember performin' a marriage and then baptizin' the infant, both in one ceremony."

"It's only been a month, so it ain't gone too far. But I think the Lord would be a damned sight better pleased if you was to do it up accordin' to the Book."

"Would tonight be soon enough?"

"They'd sleep with an easier conscience. Me and Mama would sleep better, sure enough."

The farmer's wife lamented that her eldest daughter should be married in a church, with nice decorations and organ music, or at least a piano. The farmer declared, "Ain't no need for a lot of folderol when the horse has already got out of the stable."

That brought a sharp retort and an unspoken promise of retribution from the wife, but the farmer seemed unfazed. He sent the younger sons and daughters out to pick wildflowers. That, he said, was decoration enough. The ceremony, short and simple, was performed in the open dog run of the family cabin. Two of the bride's sisters sang a hymn, not well but with conviction.

Webb reached that part of the service in which he said, "If any man knows a reason why this couple should not be joined in holy matrimony, let him speak now or forever hold his peace."

The farmer looked around fiercely as if expecting someone to voice an objection. The only people present besides family were Webb and Rusty. Webb pronounced the couple man and wife.

The farmer grinned, finally. "Preacher, I hope you drawed that knot good and tight."

Webb watched the couple kiss. "When I marry them, the knot always holds."

Rusty had been impatient at first, wanting to leave, but now he relaxed and enjoyed the easygoing family atmosphere. It was evident that the new son-in-law was accepted into the circle, and that he felt secure in it. Rusty envied him. These people were not the Monahan family, yet they had much in common as frontier folk facing up to whatever hardships their isolated life imposed upon them and grateful for whatever small pleasures they managed to wring from it. If they had concerns about Indians, or about whatever changes might be imposed upon them as the Federals took over in Texas, they seemed able to put them aside and enjoy the amenities of the moment.

As he and Webb retired to their blankets beneath the wagon shed,

Rusty said, "They seem like contented folks. I'd hate to see anything bust up what they've got here."

"People like these won't stay busted. Their ancestors fought their way across the Alleghenies and down through the old Southern states. This generation has made it all the way out to the far edge of Texas. They've been beaten down and some of them killed, but those that survived always got back on their feet. Time and again, they've stood shoulder to shoulder with the Lord and fought the devil to a standstill."

"I guess the key to it is family."

"And you're thinkin' you don't belong to one."

"All the family I ever had is gone."

"If you're just lookin' at blood, I don't have a family either. But all the people I minister to, all the friends I've made along my circuit, even the strangers I come across . . . they're my family. They're kin because we've walked the same ground. We've shared the same experiences. Look at it that way, Rusty, and you'll see that you've got family, too. A mighty big family."

"I wouldn't count Fowler Gaskin. Or the Dawkinses."

"Fowler's like the uncle nobody wants to claim, the one they forget to invite to family gatherin's. Caleb Dawkins thinks he hears the voice of God, but he's just talkin' to himself. Still, saint or sinner, they're all our brothers in the sight of the Lord."

The first thing Rusty noticed was that the weeds had gotten somewhat ahead of him. The second was that the mule Chapultepec did not come to the barn at the usual time.

"I guess he got used to me bein' gone," he told Webb. But morning came without the mule showing up. Rusty saddled Alamo and rode a wide circle without finding sign of the lost animal.

Webb said, "Maybe he's just strayed a little farther than usual. Mules have a way of knowin' what you want them to do, and they do the opposite."

Rusty remembered the Monahan milk cow. "Any time somethin' comes up missin' around here, I see the fine hand of Fowler Gaskin. He probably got wind that I was gone. You've got to nail everything down tight to keep him from walkin' off with it."

Webb said, "I'll ride over there with you. The mood you're in, you may say or do somethin' you'll be sorry for afterwards."

"I've never spoken a cross word to Fowler that wasn't justified. But you're welcome."

They rode in silence, for they had exhausted just about all subjects for conversation on the long and often interrupted trip back from the Monahan farm. Passing Gaskin's field, Rusty saw that weeds threatened to choke the crops.

"If Fowler took my mule, he didn't use him to plow out his corn," he said. "Probably rode him to town to get whiskey."

"Don't condemn a man 'til you know he's guilty. Be tolerant."

"When it comes to rascals and thieves, I don't see where tolerance has got much place."

Rusty's first impression was that the old cabin leaned a little farther than the last time he had seen it, but he decided that was his imagination. Were it not for a couple of logs leaned up at an angle to brace one wall, it probably would have collapsed by now. Fowler Gaskin sat in a wooden chair beside the front door, a jug at his feet.

He started to arise, then sat down heavily as if his legs would not support him. He blinked, trying to clear his eyes. "You come makin' trouble again, Rusty Shannon? And who's that you got with you?" He blinked some more. "Oh, howdy, Preacher. Didn't know you right off. Sun got in my eyes."

Rusty did not waste time. "I come lookin' for my mule. You got him?"

Rusty's sharp tone brought an equally sharp reply. "You see him anywhere around here? I already got one old wore-out mule. What would I want with another?"

Webb spoke softly. "Rusty doesn't mean to accuse you, Fowler. He's just worried about Chapultepec. I don't suppose you've seen him wanderin' around?"

"Ain't seen him and ain't lookin' for him."

Gaskin's voice was relatively calm. Rusty thought the old man might be telling the truth, for once. Usually the guiltier he was, the more loudly he protested his innocence.

Gaskin reached down for the jug. He let the stopper fall from his hand but made no move to retrieve it from the ground. "You been over to the York place and asked that nigger Shanty?"

Rusty said, "No, you were the first one that came to mind."

"You're like your old daddy . . . always quick to accuse a man." Fowler scowled. "I been tellin' everybody: There ain't nothin' safe around here as long as that Shanty stays amongst us."

"Shanty's never hurt anybody."

"No? Them niggers are always sneakin' around, stealin' whatever they can find. I'd bet a gallon of good whiskey that you'll find your mule over at his place."

"I don't believe Shanty would steal from me."

Gaskin dragged his sleeve across his mouth. "He may not be around here much longer to steal from *anybody*. I heard that some fellers rode over there last night to tell him he'd be a sight healthier somewheres else. It ain't fittin', a nigger ownin' a farm same as a white man."

Webb showed a sudden concern. "What fellers?"

"I ain't sayin'."

Rusty demanded, "Where were *you* last night?"

"You ain't a ranger no more. I don't have to tell you nothin'."

Rusty was instantly convinced that Gaskin had been with whomever had visited Shanty's place. "If you did that old man any harm . . ."

"You're accusin' me again. Go over there, why don't you? Like as not that's where you'll find your mule."

If I do, Rusty thought, it'll be because you put him there. He said, "Let's go, Preacher." He reined Alamo around without waiting.

The minister had to push to catch up with him. "I can read your mind. You're thinkin' Fowler might've taken the mule over there to make Shanty look like a thief."

"I didn't know it showed so plain."

"I doubt Fowler has that much imagination."

"Maybe I *am* blamin' him too quick, but I don't put anything past that old reprobate."

He felt a special responsibility to the former slave, partly, at least, because he had wrongly accused Shanty's former owner, Isaac York, for so long. Crossing the land that had been York's and now belonged to Shanty, Rusty saw no sign of his mule. He had hoped he would not. That would have provided ammunition to those who agitated against Shanty's presence, even though Rusty would not have believed the passive-natured old man to be a thief.

He saw Shanty in his field, plowing with a mule much younger than Chapultepec. The corn stood tall, and the cotton looked green and promising. The farm was in sharp contrast to what Rusty and Webb had seen at Gaskin's.

Webb said, "This shows what a man can do when he's on the good side of the Lord."

"Shows what he can do if he's willin' to work." Rusty reined Alamo toward the field.

Seeing them, Shanty appeared apprehensive. He reined the plow mule to a stop and took off his hat, lifting and holding it to shade his face and block out the sun's glare. He looked ready to turn and run. Recognizing the visitors, he resumed plowing to the end of the row, then halted the mule and stepped to the rail fence to greet them.

He took off his hat again and bowed in the deferential manner he had learned in boyhood. "Good afternoon, Mr. Preacher, Mr. Rusty."

Rusty saw an ugly welt across Shanty's dark face. It appeared to have been left by a quirt or a whip. Anger seized him.

"Who did that to you?"

Shanty blinked as fear came into his dark eyes. "I'm all right. Ain't nothin' been done that won't heal."

Webb dismounted. With thumb and forefinger on Shanty's chin, he turned the black man's head one way, then the other, examining the mark closely. "That cut deep enough to bring blood. Have you put anything on it?"

"Some bacon grease with a touch of salt in it. That's all I had."

Anger made Rusty tremble. "Anybody who'd do a thing like that . . ."

Shanty shrugged with the resignation to which he had been conditioned all his life. "They just figured to scare me some, is all. And I reckon they done that."

"Warned you to get off of this place?"

"That seemed to be the main thing on their mind. Said I don't belong here, and if I don't want somethin' worse than that whip I'd better leave. But I got nowhere to go."

"This place belongs to you fair and square. They've got no right to run you off."

Soberly Webb said, "Rights don't matter when the devil's at work. Don't forget what happened to Lon and Billy Monahan."

"Tom Blessing's the law. I'll go talk to him. No tellin' what they might do the next time."

Webb said, "It wouldn't be a bad idea if you took Shanty home with you where you can watch out for him. I'll go see Tom."

Shanty demurred, gently but firmly. "I thank you gentlemen, I surely do. But I got crops here and a few critters to see after. I can't just be goin' off and leavin' them."

Rusty said, "It's dangerous for you here 'til we get this thing squashed."

Shanty shook his head. "Ain't nothin' happens without the Lord's will. I'll talk to Him about it."

Rusty considered a moment. "You're dealin' with people who don't spend much time listenin' to the Lord. But they'll listen to me or pay the price. Who were they, Shanty?"

Shanty looked down, avoiding Rusty's eyes. "They come at night. Had their faces covered."

"I'll bet Fowler Gaskin was amongst them."

"Like I said, I didn't see no faces. I wouldn't want to bear false witness against nobody. The Commandments is plain on that."

"Damned cowards, whippin' an old man that can't afford to defend himself. Let's see them try and whip *me*."

Webb warned, "Better get ahold of yourself. The mood you're in, you might shoot somebody."

Shanty pleaded, "I wouldn't want nobody killed on my account. This little old place ain't worth that."

Rusty realized Webb was right; in his present state he just *might* shoot somebody. He had come frighteningly close once with Isaac York, and he would have done it the night the Monahans were lynched if he could have reached Caleb Dawkins. On both occasions he had felt chilled afterward, realizing how near he had come to doing murder.

Webb said, "You talk to Tom Blessing. I'll stay with Shanty. I don't think anybody would molest him with me as a witness."

Rusty felt more like staying, but he recognized Webb's wisdom. "I'll go see Tom."

He wondered how much legal authority the sheriff had since the breakup of the Confederacy. But Tom Blessing's challenging presence bespoke authority whether backed by law or not. He had only to walk into a crowd to draw its full attention.

Rusty had not visited the settlement since his return home. Physically it had not changed much. It was a farming community with a plain two-story stone courthouse, a cotton gin, a general store, and three dramshops. The dirt streets were quiet, though he noticed an unusual number of men loafing in front of the store, the saloons, and a blacksmith shop. Some wore remnants of Confederate uniforms. Most had a hungry look, for they had come back from the war to find employment scarce and money scarcer. A couple of strangers gave him a hostile stare for no good reason he could think of except perhaps that he seemed to carry purpose, and they had none. To a barefoot man, the owner of an old pair of boots appears rich.

He had ridden first by the Blessing farm, where Mrs. Blessing had told him her husband was in town. Rusty entered the sheriff's office. The high windows were open, but the breeze outside was not strong enough to carry through the room. The place was oppressively warm.

Tom Blessing worked at a stack of papers, his face beaded with sweat. He laid them aside and stood up, shoving out his big, rough hand. "I hope you brought a few dollars to town, Rusty. This place ain't been blessed with fresh money in six months."

"I haven't got ten cents."

"If somebody was to spend a hundred dollars in Yankee silver it'd circulate from one hand to another and wipe out most of the town's debts before dark."

Rusty did not feel like making small talk. "There's been trouble out at the York place."

"Shanty?"

Rusty told what he and Webb had found. "They're liable to kill him next time, or try to. But that farm belongs to him. They've got no call to run him off of it."

Blessing listened, his blue eyes troubled. "Ever since Isaac left him that place, I've been afraid of somethin' like this."

"What're you goin' to do about it?"

Blessing turned up his work-roughened hands. "I could camp out at Shanty's shack and hold off trouble for a while, but I couldn't stay forever. There's just one of me. They'd wait me out and hit him after I left."

"What's the use in havin' law if it can't be enforced?"

"I'm not sure how much law there is. Governor Murrah has gone south to Mexico and taken a bunch of state officials with him. He figured when the Yankee troops move in they'd put him in irons. Like as not, they would. For all I know, they may come and put *me* in irons."

" 'Til they do, you're still sheriff."

"Even if I throw somebody in jail I couldn't take a case to trial. I don't think the Federals recognize any Texas courts right now."

"Kind of like havin' an empty gun and no shells."

"It's quiet here compared to some places. There's been riots in Austin and San Antonio, places like that. A lot of soldiers came home with empty pockets and feel they've got a right to whatever they feel like takin'. Been folks killed fightin' over property that don't amount to a damn."

"The Confederate government never paid much attention to us out here except for the conscript officers. Maybe the Yankees won't either."

"We won't know where we stand 'til they move in and take over."

"We may not like it."

"It's what we get for losin' the war."

It never was my war in the first place, Rusty thought. He knew Blessing had felt allegiance to the Confederacy, so he did not give voice to what was in his mind. "This still doesn't answer what we're goin' to do about Shanty."

Blessing studied him intently. "You were a ranger, Rusty. A good one, from everything I saw and what I've heard. How would you feel about bein' a deputy sheriff?"

"You just said you don't have much authority left. A deputy would have even less."

Blessing walked to a wooden rack attached to the wall. He selected a rifle and lifted it out. "Even if the government goes all to pieces—and it might—there's still authority in this."

Rusty was hesitant. "I don't know . . ."

"The rifle is yours if you want it. I doubt you'll ever get any cash wages."

"When I was a ranger I got paid mighty seldom and mighty little. But why would I want to be a deputy sheriff?"

"For one thing, there's Shanty. In case of trouble, the backin' of my office might keep you out of jail."

Rusty saw some points in favor of the proposition. "I wouldn't want to be away from my farm too much."

"I'm at mine most of the time."

Rusty feared if he gave himself a chance to consider he might decide against it. "I'll do it."

"Good." Blessing fished in a desk drawer and brought out a badge. "This came from a county over in Arkansas, but if anybody gives you trouble you'd best hit him before he has time to read it anyway. Raise your right hand."

Blessing administered a short oath of his own making, then shook Rusty's hand. "Anything you feel like you need to do, tell them I told you to." He smiled in satisfaction. "Once the word gets around that you're a deputy, maybe nobody'll have the nerve to steal your old mule again."

Rusty was surprised. "What about my old mule?"

"You've missed him, ain't you?"

"Yep. I figure Fowler Gaskin's got him hid out."

"Fowler's guilty of enough stuff to earn him his own hot corner in hell, but not this time. A stranger came ridin' in the other day on Chapultepec and tried to swap him. Everybody in town knows that mule. Been plannin' to take him out to you but haven't had time to do it."

"Where's the thief now?"

"In jail. Thought I'd give him a few more days to repent, then turn him loose. There's not likely to be a session of court 'til the Yankees come."

Rusty warmed with remorse. "I'd've taken a paralyzed oath that Fowler Gaskin done it."

"You can bet he's done worse things we don't even know about. Someday when he's called to Judgment he'll have more use for a fire bucket than for angel wings."

Leading Chapultepec, Rusty arrived at Shanty's cabin a little before dark. Preacher Webb sat on a bench in front, watching. Rusty saw no sign of trouble, but he asked, "Anything happen?"

Webb stared at the badge on Rusty's shirt but made no comment about it. "Nobody's goin' to do anything in the daylight. Two men came within a couple of hundred yards and stopped to look. Then they rode on."

"Recognize them?"

"My eyes aren't what they used to be. If they ever were." Webb shifted his attention to Chapultepec. "Where'd you find your mule?"

Rusty told him. Webb nodded in satisfaction. "I don't think either man I saw was Fowler Gaskin."

Rusty realized Webb was indirectly preaching him a little sermon about rising too quickly to judge.

Shanty was in the cabin, starting to fix a small supper. He was quick to see the badge. "You the sheriff now? What happened to Mr. Tom?"

"He's still the sheriff, at least 'til the Yankees come. He made me a deputy. Said that'd give me a stronger hand in case of trouble."

"I don't see why anybody'd trouble theirselves over this little old place. It barely growed enough to make a livin' for me and Mr. Isaac."

Rusty saw no tactful way to explain that the land itself was not the issue, but rather the fact that it was owned by a black, a former slave. He suspected Shanty knew the real reason he was being harassed but was trying to deny it to himself. "These are mean times. There's people who would kill a man for a pair of shoes, much less a farm."

It went against Shanty's kindly nature to think the worst about anyone. He was probably trying to delude himself as well about the danger he faced. "I'll be all right. Ain't no need of you-all puttin' yourselves out on my account."

Rusty brushed the comment aside. "Me and Preacher will sleep in the shed. It's too late to go back to my place tonight."

Shanty made no further argument. "We'll be havin' somethin' to eat directly."

After supper Shanty took down an old banjo from the wall and played a couple of pieces. As the room darkened he lighted a candle and asked Webb to read to him from the Scripture. Webb held the Bible open, but Rusty sensed that he was reciting from memory. He knew the text so well that the Book was more for display than for reference. Shanty listened, nodding in silent agreement.

Shanty said, "If I wasn't so old I'd learn myself to read. It'd be a comfort, knowin' I could go to the Good Book any time I wanted to."

Webb said, "You can talk directly to the Lord any time you want to. He's always listenin'."

Rusty stood up, turning his right ear toward the open door. "I hope He's listenin' right now, because I hear horses."

Webb blew out the candle. "I suppose it means trouble."

Rusty said, "I don't remember the last time anybody brought me good news at this hour of the night." He picked up the rifle Tom Blessing had given him. "Shanty, if there's any shootin', lay flat on the floor. Whatever you do, don't come outdoors." He turned to Webb. "You got a gun?"

"I prefer to use the Word."

"If these are the same old boys that whipped Shanty before, they ain't likely to listen to no sermons. But they'll pay attention to this rifle."

For a minute or so Rusty did not hear the horses moving. He wondered if he might have been wrong, that the riders might simply have been travelers passing by. Then he saw several small points of fire bobbing about.

"What in the world?"

Webb said, "They've lighted torches. They intend to burn this cabin."

Rusty counted six horsemen and a man on a mule. He thought on Len Tanner, who would have liked these odds. He wished he had the fight-loving Tanner at his side instead of the peaceable Preacher Webb.

He heard a hammer cock and looked back in surprise at a pistol in the minister's hand. "Thought you didn't have a gun."

"I said I *prefer* to use the Word. But sometimes you have to get their attention before they'll listen."

Rusty heard a shout, and the horses moved into a run. The men screeched and yelled as they came on, the torches weaving and dancing. A man in front fired a pistol toward the cabin. Their aim was to terrify Shanty into submission.

Rusty wondered that he felt no fear. Instead his earlier anger returned, rising like a brush fire. He lifted the rifle to his shoulder. When the leading horse was fifty feet away, he squeezed the trigger. Propelled forward by momentum, the stricken animal tumbled. He spilled the rider onto the ground almost directly in front of Rusty. Rusty dropped his rifle and jerked a pistol from its holster. He grabbed the hooded man by the collar and jammed the muzzle against his head, hard enough to break skin.

He shouted, "The rest of you stop where you're at or I'll splatter his brains all over you. If he's got any."

The other riders reined up. One cried out angrily, "Who the hell are you?"

"I'm a deputy sheriff, and I'm placin' all of you under arrest." It was a bluff. If they decided to ride him down they could do it in an instant. But about one thing he was not bluffing. He hoped they believed he would blow the lead rider's brains out, because he meant it.

The downed horse kicked a few times. By the flickering light of the torches Rusty saw a whip tied to the saddle. He knew it was intended for Shanty.

He had no time for regret over killing the horse. He had shot Indian mounts to set their riders afoot. A horse was a surer target than the man on its back. Remorse could trouble him later when he had leisure to indulge in it.

The men still in the saddle hesitated, uncertain. All wore sacks over their heads with holes punched to see through. A familiar voice growled, "You think you can stop us all by yourself?"

Preacher Webb moved into the torchlight, holding the pistol up where they could see it. "He's not by himself."

"Preacher? Who the hell told you to butt in? This ain't Sunday meetin'."

"I declared war on Satan a long time ago, and it's his work you're about tonight."

Another horseman glanced at his fellows, still uncertain. "We didn't come here to do battle with a preacher, or even a deputy sheriff. It's got nothin' to do with you. We come to put a nigger in his place."

"We're all children of God, Shanty no less than the rest of us. A hand raised against him is a hand raised against a child of God."

The man on the mule said, "We didn't come here to listen to no preachin'. We come to do a job." He pushed forward.

Rusty jabbed the pistol against the leader's head hard enough that the man shouted in pain. "Boys, back off. He'll kill me sure."

Grittily Rusty said, "As sure as hell." He raised the muzzle toward the horsemen. "Whatever guns you've got, drop them on the ground."

The men looked at one another, each waiting for someone else to start. One said, "Don't you let your finger twitch on that trigger, deputy. That's my cousin you got there." He dropped his weapon, and the others followed suit, all but the mule's rider.

Rusty jerked the sack from the head of the man he had been holding. He recognized the face, though the name would not come to him. He said, "The rest of you, take off those hoods. I want to look at you."

He had to put the pistol back against the leader's head before the others complied. The man on the mule wheeled about and beat a hasty retreat. The animal's tail switched furiously as the rider quirted him.

Rusty knew the mule. He had seen Fowler Gaskin riding it lately. It was like Gaskin to start a fight, then step back and let others take the consequences.

Most of the men who remained were strangers to Rusty. "Do you know them, Preacher?"

"Most of them." Webb looked regretfully at the leader, who still had the muzzle of Rusty's pistol near his ear. "I'm sorry to see you here, Jedediah Hoskins. As many times as we've prayed together, I thought better of you."

Rusty could not have called Hoskins by name on a hundred-dollar bet, but that was natural, considering how long he had been absent in the ranger service. He said, "I didn't know most of you before, but I'll know all of you the next time."

He stepped back from Hoskins, who turned on him angrily. "Since when did the law go to sidin' with niggers?"

"Black or white, right is right and wrong is wrong. It doesn't make any difference."

"Makes a difference to us. You can't be here all the time, deputy. We'll be comin' back."

"If you do, I'll know who to go lookin' for."

"What about our guns?"

"I'll sack them up and take them to Tom Blessing. When you work up the nerve, you can get them from him." Along with a sermon stiffer than Preacher Webb ever gave, he thought.

Hoskins frowned over his dead mount. "That was a good horse. It'll be hard to find another."

Rusty said, "It was either him or you. I figured you'd rather it was him."

Hoskins and his cousin struggled to retrieve the saddle, having to lift the animal's dead weight. Hoskins handed the saddle up to another rider and mounted behind his cousin. He looked back angrily as they rode away.

Preacher Webb moved over beside Rusty. "We didn't make any friends here tonight."

"I don't need friends like them anyway." Rusty turned toward the cabin. "Who was the feller I had ahold of?"

"Jed Hoskins. He and his cousin Mordecai took up farms to the south yonder a ways. It was after you went up to Fort Belknap."

"I want to remember them two."

Shanty had ventured outside. He gave the dead horse a moment's sad scrutiny. "Pity for an innocent animal to die like that."

"Might've been better to've shot the man who was on him," Rusty said, "but there would've been all kinds of trouble."

Webb said, "There's trouble anyway. You can see now that you're not safe here, Shanty. They'll keep comin' at you 'til you leave . . . or 'til somebody's dead, most likely you."

Shanty seemed finally to accept the minister's judgment. "Best that I be goin'. But this is home. Won't no other place ever be the same."

Rusty said, "I told you before, you can stay with me. It's not far. We can ride over here and work your farm together. I'll help you with your fields, and you can help me with mine."

"That'd be a kindness, but you don't owe me nothin'."

"I owe Isaac. Since you're his only heir, I owe you."

Preacher Webb nodded approval. Shanty said, "I'll tote my share of the load, and that's gospel."

His thin shoulders did not appear capable of carrying a heavy load, but Rusty knew better. He had seen him work. "You'll do fine, just fine."

Shanty went into the cabin and began to throw a few things together. "Be all right if I fetch my old banjo along? I'll try not to be no bother with it."

"Bring it. That cabin could stand to hear some music."

CHAPTER
TWELVE

adger Boy sat with the children at some distance from the fire. He listened to the drum and watched the dancing by his elder brother and fifteen warriors who had volunteered to accompany him on his raid. Resentment gnawed at him like hunger in an empty belly. Steals the Ponies had belittled his pleading that he be allowed to go along. His shadow was not yet long enough, his brother had said. That in itself was humiliating, but the fact that Steals the Ponies said it with a laugh only compounded the wrong.

No one could say with certainty how many summers Badger Boy had lived, but the best guess was nine or ten. The top of his head came to his brother's shoulder, and Steals the Ponies was relatively tall by the standards of The People. Badger Boy had seen warriors smaller in stature ride out to strike the Texan settlements or to invade the scattered ranches and tiny pueblos of northern Mexico. Perhaps they *had* been a little older, but that did not mean they were better riders, better fighters.

Badger Boy could not help wondering if his brother's reluctance had to do with the fact that the boy was Texan by blood, not Comanche. But he felt Comanche. All he knew was Comanche ways. Whatever he might once have known about the white man's world had been forgotten or at least pushed back into some deep corner of his memory where he could not reach it.

The dance was meant to strengthen the warriors' *puha*, the mystical power that would improve their chances of success. It was also intended to bolster their resolve and confidence. They did not lack for exuberance. They sang and shouted as they danced to the strong beat of the drum. Consternation and terror would tear like wildfire through the lodges of the Texans before these men returned to the encampment.

Badger Boy had heard pessimistic old men lament the passing of the good times. They were saying, though others strongly disagreed, that the white men were coming in ever-increasing numbers and that the days of The People as free-roaming hunters and raiders would soon be over. Wolf That Limps, highly honored for past brave deeds but too arthritic to ride far anymore, had told of a vision in which he saw the buffalo only as scattered bones. White men's spotted cattle grazed the buffalo range, thick as fleas on a camp dog. He saw no Comanches anywhere, just white men with their plows and cows.

"I do not know what we have done to offend them," Wolf had said, "but the spirits have turned against us."

Steals the Ponies contended that Wolf was an old man whose stomach had soured, that he had eaten spoiled meat and his vision had been nothing but a bad dream. Badger Boy wanted to believe that, but the dark predictions filled him with foreboding nevertheless. If he waited until he was as tall as his brother, it might be too late. There might be no more raids. He wanted to go now.

Wolf had not said where The People had gone in his vision, simply that they were no longer here. Perhaps they had returned to the place from which tradition said they had come, a hole deep in the earth. If that were so, the spirits might never call for them to emerge again, and Badger Boy's chance at being a warrior would be gone forever.

He wanted to go now, and go he would.

Later he lay awake, listening to his brother snoring nearby. He did not understand how Steals the Ponies could sleep so soundly, knowing that sunrise would find him on his way to the settlements. He supposed his brother had already ridden the war trail enough times that it no longer stirred the high excitement it once did.

Badger Boy wanted to sleep but could not. He squeezed his eyes shut, trying to force sleep, but soon he found himself staring up at the stars through the smoke hole in the tepee's top. His skin prickled with eagerness to be on his feet and moving.

Steals the Ponies and his companions made plenty of noise about their predawn leaving. They had no qualms about awakening the entire camp. On the contrary, they wanted everyone to know. A major benefit of being a warrior was the acclaim one received. Reticence was not a virtue among fighting men.

Badger Boy watched his brother and the others mount their war horses in the pale light that preceded sunrise. Steals the Ponies rode over to him and leaned down for a final few words.

"Do not grieve. You will be going with us sooner than you think."

"Sooner than *you* think," Badger Boy said, too softly for his brother to hear.

He watched the men walk their horses through the center of camp, receiving the cheers and plaudits of those who could not go. They led a few extra horses to be used as remounts in the event any of those they rode were worn out, crippled, or killed.

While most of the crowd was watching the spectacle and vicariously riding with the warriors, Badger Boy entered the tepee and picked up the items he had laid out: his bow, his quiver and arrows, a leather lariat, and a supply of dried meat sufficient to last him many days provided he did not eat much. He slipped out the back side, where the bottom of the buffalo hide covering had been rolled up to allow circulation of air at ground level. He glanced around quickly to be sure no one had seen him, then trotted toward the horse herd.

He stopped twice, turning to look back, making sure he was not followed by anyone who might try to stop him. He could still see the tepee he shared with his brother. He feared he might not share it much longer, for Steals the Ponies had taken a strong fancy to a young woman of the village. He was talking about marrying her when he returned from the raid, for he was confident he would bring back many horses. Her father would be pleased to accept a new son-in-law who brought him many horses.

Badger Boy did not see why a man needed a wife. From observation he was aware that a man had physical need for a woman, but he knew a woman's favors were not difficult to obtain for one honored as a warrior. He had awakened many times deep in the night to find that a young woman had voluntarily entered the tepee and joined his brother upon his blankets. A man did not *have* to marry. He did not have to put his brother out of the tepee just so he could bring in a woman to stay.

However, since that appeared to be the probable outcome and Badger Boy would soon be living alone or perhaps sharing with other youths too young to ponder marriage, it seemed all the more appropriate that he be allowed to participate in the raid. And if he could not have his brother's approval, he would go without it.

He had planned this for some time. For several days he had slipped out before full daylight and studied the horse herd. He had found that most horses formed habits of behavior. At night, each had its own place to sleep within the group. Though the herd was moved frequently from one area to another for fresh grass, daylight would find each animal in more or less the same location relative to the others.

Steals the Ponies had taken his best war horse with him. But Badger Boy had long thought his brother might be overlooking the merits of a particular roan he had brought back from an earlier foray. This roan could usually be found near the perimeter of the herd each morning, on the north side near two other geldings with which it had formed a bond.

Stealthily, like the wolf, Badger Boy had practiced slipping among the horses and catching the roan without stirring up the rest of the herd or the two sleepy-eyed boys who stood night watch. So far he had not been caught. He did not plan to be caught today.

The roan had become accustomed to Badger Boy's morning routine. It pointed its ears toward him as he approached but showed no sign of concern. Badger Boy quickly had one arm around the horse's neck and fitted a rawhide bridle over its head. Though surprised, the roan did not resist or try to turn away.

Badger Boy held still a minute, making sure where the two night guards were. He located both on the far side, paying no attention that he could see. He felt sure one was asleep, and the other was not far from it. He led the roan to the edge of the herd in a slow walk. The roan's two friends followed. He stopped and raised his hand quickly. The pair halted, their ears following him as he continued leading the roan away.

He kept looking back over his shoulder, trying to keep the roan between him and the two guards so they would not easily spot him if they should happen to look in his direction. Only when he had reached a stand of small timber did he begin to breathe easily. Only then could he feel confident that he was getting away with his plan.

He had reconciled himself to the certainty that Steals the Ponies would be unhappy with him. He knew he was probably in for verbal and perhaps even physical abuse at his brother's hands and from his brother's companions. But by the time they saw him and knew what he had done, it would be too late to send him back. He planned to follow unseen until they were in the settlements. From that point, Steals the Ponies would see that it was safer for him to remain with the warriors than to try to find his way back alone through the white man's country.

He mounted bareback, his bow and quiver and the lariat slung over his shoulder. He wore no decoration, no feather in his hair, for he had not yet earned the right. He had not yet been on the customary vision quest during which a young man waited for a guardian spirit to visit him, to endow him with the medicine that would guide him on his life's journey. He had asked the shaman to advise him, but the shaman had said he did not yet have enough years to seek power.

Badger Boy had a feeling the shaman had never liked him, probably because of his lighter skin, which he considered a mark of impurity. The shaman was given to strong counsel against bringing outsiders into the tribe, diluting the blood that made the Comanches *The* People, superior to all other races, white or red. If it were in the shaman's power he would see that Badger Boy never received a vision, never received the intercession of a guardian spirit. He might even try to saddle the lad with a dark spirit that would work against him.

Badger Boy felt that he could do well enough for himself without the aid of that evil-eyed old man, his potions and talismans and witchery. He had seen the shaman perform his rituals over the sick. Sometimes they recovered and sometimes they did not. In a few cases he suspected the old man had willed them dead, and they had died. There was a question in Badger Boy's mind whether the shaman had allied himself with benevolent spirits or with those of the darkness.

Unfortunately the shaman's negative views were shared by some others influential in the band, like the warrior Tonkawa Killer. Badger Boy hoped his participation in this raid would demonstrate that his white skin was not a liability.

His first impulse was to ride hard and get himself some distance away from the village in case someone should miss him and come to fetch him back. But who was likely to miss him? If he rode too fast he might overtake his brother and the war party prematurely. He would almost surely suffer punishment for his transgression, then be sent back, shamed.

Steals the Ponies had always counseled him that patience was essential, that haste too often led a warrior to a downfall. Though Badger Boy itched to move with more speed, he slowed his pace once he felt he was well clear of the village and any strong likelihood that someone would come after him. He knew Steals the Ponies and the others would not push their horses hard and risk wearing them down. The time to push would be on the return, when there was likely to be pursuit.

In the beginning the trail was easy to follow. The riders made no effort to conceal it, for here in the heart of Comanchería there was no enemy to elude. He knew that as they moved closer to the settlements the tracks would challenge him. Fortunately his brother had taught him much about trailing, whether it be for game or for enemies.

Badger Boy sometimes boasted that Steals the Ponies could trace the shadow of a hawk across bare rock.

For three days the trail led southward. Badger Boy began to wonder if his brother might have changed his mind about the Texan settlements and be heading for Mexico instead. He was disappointed, for he had much more curiosity about the Texans than about Mexico. However, the fourth day the trail abruptly shifted eastward. His brother's strategy became clear. He had remained well west of the settlements until he had led his fighters as far south as they needed to go. Now they were riding directly toward the Texans' farms. Badger Boy found anticipation exhilarating.

He was also feeling hunger. He began to understand what he had been told about the rigors of the war trail. He had eaten too deeply into his short supply of dried meat the first days. Now he had but little left. He summoned a strong will against a temptation to eat it all, to quell at least for a while the pangs that seemed to tie his belly into a knot. He realized he must not succumb to a desire for momentary relief at the expense of the larger goal.

He managed to put an arrow through a rabbit, which he roasted for a while over a tiny fire, then eagerly consumed half raw.

The first log cabin stopped him cold. He tied the roan on the far side of a small hill, out of sight, then lay on his belly in grass atop the hill. He studied the farm with an insistent curiosity. The sight prompted fleeting memories, so quickly come and gone that he could not quite grasp them and hold them for inspection. He vaguely remembered that he had lived in such a cabin once, not much different from the one he observed now. He remembered playing in the yard, riding a long stick and pretending it was a horse.

He could almost see a man and a woman in his mind's eye, but they were as elusive as the other memories. Hard as he tried, he could not bring them into focus.

Perhaps it was just as well. That was another life, gone forever. He had attuned himself to a different life among The People. Those others, whoever they might have been, were strangers to him. The spirits probably preferred that they remain so.

He saw a wagon standing empty beside a shed. He remembered riding in one long ago. It had to have been before his time with the Comanches, for he had never seen a wagon since Buffalo Caller had taken him. He had seen no Texans either, except a couple of captives. One had been a boy younger than himself, kept to raise by another band. The other had been a woman. The last he had seen of her, some warriors were dragging her away. He could only imagine what had become of her. He remembered being strangely affected by her screams as if he had heard them before. A wizened old grandmother had warned him not to show concern, for unwarranted sympathy might mark him unfit to be trained as a fighting man. Nothing that happened to a Texan woman could ever be punishment enough for injuries the Texans had done to The People, she said.

He studied the wagon a long time, wishing he might ride in it. Then perhaps he could summon a clearer memory of the last time. He noted that the wagon had four wheels. He had seen ox-drawn carts with two big wheels, brought out onto the plains by Mexican *Comanchero* traders from somewhere west. In them they brought all manner of fascinating trade goods. Later they would return to wherever they came from, the trade goods exchanged for cattle, horses, and especially mules the warriors had taken from the Texan settlements. Comanches had little use for mules, considering them much inferior to the horse, but they had found them valuable for trading.

He understood that the Mexicans did not like the Texans. Steals the Ponies said they had warred and the Texans had won. He wished he could have seen the fight. It was claimed that they had great guns many times larger than the rifle for which Steals the Ponies had once traded a horse and three mules to the *Comancheros*. It was said these guns made a noise louder than thunder. That was hard for Badger Boy to imagine.

He saw a woman come out into an open passageway between the two sides of the cabin, her long hair flowing in the wind. At the distance he had no idea if she were young or old, but something about her gave him pause, stirred unexpected feelings he could not understand. Curiosity would have carried him closer for a better look, but caution won out. In a field some distance beyond the cabin he could see a farmer at work. It was likely he had a rifle that could wound or kill at a much greater distance than Badger Boy's bow and arrows.

The raiders had made their trail much more difficult to follow once they reached the edge of the settled country, but Badger Boy knew they had passed this way. More than likely his brother had marked this place to be struck on the return journey. Then perhaps Badger Boy would get a closer look. He eased down the far side of the hill and remounted the roan. He set him into a gentle trot.

His mind turned back to the cabin and the people who lived there. He tried to reconcile them with fleeting wisps of memory that had long haunted him, tiny fragments of a past life.

An uneasy feeling came upon him. He had long recognized that he had strong instincts, premonitions about things not yet seen. Even forewarned, he almost rode upon a man and a boy in a wagon. Badger Boy saw them at about the same time they discovered him. His heart leaped. He could never explain to Steals the Ponies how he had been so careless. The man reached quickly behind the seat and brought up a firearm. The sound of the blast indicated it was a shotgun. Dust kicked up where the shot fell short. Fortunately Badger Boy was out of range. He hoped the man did not also have a rifle, for it could carry death much farther.

Badger Boy jerked the roan horse around and kicked him into a hard run, trying to get into the cover of a wooded draw before the *teibo* could fire again. As he reached the thick brush, he heard another shot. It was no more effective than the first, but the sound made his heart pound hard. Never before had anyone attempted to kill him. He found himself sweating, his mouth dry.

Warriors were not supposed to know fear, but Badger Boy was afraid. He looked back, thinking the man might come after him. He realized the wagon made pursuit difficult, for the roan could travel where wheels could not. He began to get a grip on his nerves, though he still felt as if his thumping heart had risen high in his chest, almost in his throat.

Steals the Ponies would be ashamed of him. He was ashamed of himself.

Later, when he had time to gather his wits, he realized he had made a mistake that could endanger the raiders. By allowing himself to be seen he might have started an alarm that would move more quickly than the warriors. The Texans might be ready and waiting.

He was so weighted down with anxiety and remorse that he allowed himself to become careless again. Riding through an oak thicket, he sensed movement on both sides, a rush of hooves. Horses charged at him, and he heard a battle cry. A warrior raised a club over his head. He checked himself, but not in time to prevent his horse from colliding with Badger Boy's. The roan staggered. Badger Boy grasped desperately at the mane to keep from being knocked off the horse's back.

An angry voice lashed him like a whip. "Badger Boy! Why are you here?"

He looked into the furious eyes of Steals the Ponies. He could not find voice to speak. His brother repeated the demand.

Struggling for breath, Badger Boy managed, "I wanted to ride with you."

"I told you many times, you cannot."

Tonkawa Killer pushed up close, a quirt in his hand, fury in his face. "Do you not know that you have endangered us all? What if you had been seen?"

Badger Boy swallowed. He had rather take a beating than admit what he had done, but to hold his silence would be the same as lying. "I was. A man shot at me."

The fear that had plagued him was confirmed in the accusing faces of the warriors who surrounded him.

Tonkawa Killer shouted, "You are a fool!," and swung at him with the quirt. Though the quiver of arrows absorbed some of the force, the lash bit deeply into his flesh. He cried out in pain before he could catch himself. A warrior was supposed to bear punishment without complaint. He bit his tongue as the quirt burned him a second time.

Steals the Ponies pushed between him and Tonkawa Killer. "That is enough. We cannot undo what has been done."

Tonkawa Killer said, "He is not one of us. He has the pale skin of a Texan, and he always will."

Badger Boy fought against a rising of tears. He looked into his brother's eyes, searching for a sign of forgiveness but finding none.

"Some of us may be killed because of your recklessness. Now we have to decide whether to go ahead or turn back."

Tonkawa Killer scowled. "Go back without horses? The village would laugh at us."

Steals the Ponies shook his head. "That is better than hearing the women cry because some of us do not come back at all."

Tonkawa Killer made a quick search of the warriors' faces. "Perhaps you should take your Texan baby back to the village. I will lead however many want to continue the raid."

Steals the Ponies had to concede the obvious, that most were not ready to give up what they had begun. They had invested too many days and nights already. "Either we all go back or we all go ahead. I can see that most of you want to go ahead, so that is what we will do."

Tonkawa Killer demanded, "What about that boy? He may already have spoiled our medicine. We cannot take him."

"We have no choice. We are too far into the Texan country to send him back alone."

Badger Boy began feeling better. This was what he had counted on all along, that they would have to let him remain with them. "Give me a chance to fight. I will do whatever you say."

Steals the Ponies glared at him. "Yes, you will, or I will let Tonkawa Killer wear out his quirt on your back."

His back already burned severely. Though he could not see it, Badger Boy sensed that the quirt had cut deeply enough to bring blood. He had been willing to shed blood on this raid, but he would have expected it to result from battle, not from punishment. Shame made him realize how small he really was, how badly out of place here among men who had proven their maturity and earned the right to go against the Texans.

Steals the Ponies frowned at him, then looked at the roan. "You are disobedient and you are foolish. But at least you have good judgment about horses."

That was small comfort, but even a grudging compliment was welcome in the face of so much blame. Badger Boy made it a point to ride close to his brother and as far as possible from Tonkawa Killer.

Steals the Ponies sent out "wolves" to scout the white men's farms for horses as they rode eastward. On their return they would pick up as many as they could gather without undue risk. The scouts brought back reports that they were not finding many horses. They brought back other reports that visibly disturbed the raid leader. The Texans were gathering what horses they had and holding them in corrals or herding them under guard. Moreover, the settlers seemed to be banding in numbers at certain points as if for defense.

Steals the Ponies called the men together in council under a bright, full moon. "The Texans act as if they know we have come among them. I do not know how they learned this"—he glanced at Badger Boy—"but our risk is greater now."

Tonkawa Killer did not mince words. "It is because of that child." He pointed at Badger Boy. "He allowed himself to be seen. We had as well have an owl in camp."

The owl was considered a malevolent spirit, a harbinger of misfortune, even death.

Steals the Ponies argued, "It could be that some sharp-eyed Texan noted our tracks. It is impossible to cover the trail of so many, however we may try."

Tonkawa Killer was not placated. "Our medicine has gone bad. Kill the boy and perhaps it will be good again."

Steals the Ponies was shocked. "Kill one of our own?"

"He is not one of us. He is a Texan. You cannot turn a mule into a horse."

Badger Boy drew close to his brother. He searched the faces of the warriors, wondering if any seriously considered what Tonkawa Killer said. He was unable to read their expressions in the moonlight. Steals the Ponies pushed himself protectively in front of Badger Boy. "This boy is Comanche now. If there is to be killing, let it be of the *real* white men, not my younger brother." He put extra emphasis on the word *brother*.

Killing of Comanche by Comanche was almost unheard of. But if it did occur, it would call for vengeance by the victim's kin. Steals the Ponies made it clear he considered Badger Boy to be of his blood.

Tonkawa Killer made a placating motion with his hands. "I will not hurt him. But if the spirits move against him, I will not interfere."

Steals the Ponies looked up at the full moon. "The light is good. Let us see how many horses we can gather."

CHAPTER
THIRTEEN

he exhilaration of the raid overrode Badger Boy's shame. Though Steals the Ponies ordered him to remain a safe distance behind, he was able to hear the commotion. Scouts had found horses corraled in a log pen. It appeared that several farm families had gathered for mutual protection. The first inclination had been to pass the place by because of the difficulty of getting at the guarded animals, but the challenge was too strong for proud men to ignore.

Steals the Ponies and two others crept to the corral and cut the rope that bound the gate. They had pushed most of the horses through the opening before one of the Texans woke up to what was happening and fired a futile shot. Steals the Ponies leaped upon one of the stolen horses bareback and pushed the others into a run. The rest of the raiders fell in behind, whooping, shouting to bring the horses to a full gallop. Badger Boy was among them, yelling as loudly as any.

Several warriors dropped back to intercept any Texans foolish enough to pursue. Badger Boy would have joined them had they not included Tonkawa Killer. Instead he remained with the main body, driving westward. The bright moon yielded light enough for them to see where they were going.

From far behind, Badger Boy heard a few shots, followed by silence.

Steals the Ponies ordered the horses slowed so they would not exhaust themselves and be unable to make the long trip to Comanchería. After a time the rear guard caught up.

Tonkawa Killer was disappointed. "They turned back when they saw us. They never gave us a chance to kill them."

Steals the Ponies replied, "There will be others. They are like flies on the buffalo."

The night yielded a dozen more horses from a field. Two men on horse-back stood guard, but they fled toward a cabin when the Comanches charged at them. Tonkawa Killer and two of his friends managed to over-take one and knock him from his horse. Once he was on the ground, the struggle lasted but a moment. The man's scalp and his horse were taken as prizes.

In the false dawn that preceded sunrise, the raiders came upon another cabin. There appeared to be only two horses both in a corral. Steals the Ponies ordered Badger Boy to remain with the main group and help hold the horses already taken. Badger Boy itched to follow his brother, but he had disobeyed once. He would not do so again.

Tonkawa Killer and two friends crept to the cabin. Light showed from inside. Badger Boy heard a desperate shout then a woman's scream. It began in fright and escalated into agony.

He felt cold inside. As had happened the time he heard a captive woman's cry, he trembled for a reason he could not quite fathom. The scream aroused a memory, a clutch of long-subdued fear. He had heard such a scream before but did not know when or where. He remembered a feeling of panic, and some of that gripped him now. It was like trying to recall a dream after morning's sunlight has driven it deeply into the shad-ows. He found his hands shaking and puzzled over the source of his fear. It was not for himself, and it was not for the white woman dying in that cabin. But he could not remember who it *was* for.

He must not let anyone know. He must conquer this weakness lest it diminish him in the eyes of the others.

Steals the Ponies brought the two horses to add to those already taken. Tonkawa Killer caught up shortly, showing off two fresh scalps. One had hair long as his arm.

Steals the Ponies asked, "Do you feel better now?"

Tonkawa Killer grunted. "She was young. I wanted to bring her with me, but she got a rifle. I had to kill her." He held the weapon in front of him. "The rifle will be of more use."

Surprise was the Comanche's favorite tactic of war. But now and then the white man applied it against the Comanche with equal success. Badger Boy had heard old men tell of a great raid that took a huge war party all the way to the big water and left a coastal town in flames, yet was smashed by a smaller Texan force that caught the retreating column by surprise.

He was unprepared for the sudden *teibo* attack upon the stolen horse herd. Steals the Ponies had taken most of the raiding party to sweep a couple of farms a little ways off the line of march. He had left Badger Boy and half a dozen warriors to continue driving the horses so no time would be lost. It was obvious that the countryside had been aroused, for some farms had been found suddenly deserted and others too heavily defended to risk frontal attack.

Tonkawa Killer was in charge of the horse guard. Badger Boy wished it had been somebody else—anybody else—for he was convinced that Tonkawa Killer meant him harm.

The horses moved along in a steady trot, and all seemed to be well with the world. Even so, Badger Boy was vaguely uneasy. His instincts were trying to tell him something, but he could not analyze what it was. He tried to put his fears behind him by imagining how it would be when they reached the encampment. Though he was yet a boy and had joined the raid against orders, surely he would be allowed to share in whatever honors the village might bestow upon the party. He had proven himself worthy to ride with men.

In a heartbeat the world turned upside down. He did not see where the Texans came from. Suddenly they were there, shouting, shooting, racing at him. The loose horses panicked and turned back, breaking into a hard run. Instead of being behind them, gently pushing, he was in front of their wild stampede, in some danger of being knocked down and trampled. He waved his arms and shouted, trying desperately to turn them, but he made no more impression than did the quail which flushed from tall grass before the pounding hooves.

He gave way to panic, as on the day the white man fired at him from the wagon. This time there were many white men, more than he had time to count, and it seemed they were all firing at him.

The roan horse did not wait for Badger Boy to decide what to do. It turned and broke into a hard run away from the shooting, away from the stampede. Badger Boy pressed hard with his knees and clung to the mane to keep from falling off. He knew he should stand his ground and fight. That was what Steals the Ponies would do. But he had no control over the horse. He freed his grip on the mane and brought his bow down from his shoulder, drawing an arrow from the quiver and fitting it to the string. He found a white-man target coming up swiftly beside him. The roan jumped a small bush just as the arrow flew. Badger Boy knew he had missed.

He saw a flash from the white man's pistol and braced himself for a bullet that did not come. The Texan missed, too. While Badger Boy struggled to fit another arrow, Tonkawa Killer raced alongside the Texan and dealt him a strong blow with his war club. The Texan fell and rolled. Looking back, Badger Boy saw him jump to his feet and begin dodging the oncoming horses. Then he was lost in the dust.

Because he was watching behind him, Badger Boy did not see the fallen tree ahead. The roan horse attempted to leap over it but struck a hind foot on the dead trunk. He went down headfirst and rolled over. Badger Boy cried out involuntarily as the horse's weight slammed upon his leg. He heard the bone snap and felt a stab of pain more terrible than anything he had ever known. The roan stepped on Badger Boy's stomach as it staggered to its feet. The air went out of his lungs. He gasped for breath.

For a moment, through the dust, he saw a dark figure looming over him and thought it must be a Texan come to finish him. He was too numb for fear.

The face was Tonkawa Killer's, and it was malevolent. "You have spoiled our medicine, white boy. Now die!" Tonkawa Killer swung his club. Badger Boy turned quickly aside so that the blow missed his head but struck his shoulder. Then Tonkawa Killer was gone.

Badger Boy heard the horses race by on either side of him, going around the downed tree that had caused the roan to fall. Hooves kicked dirt in his face and barely missed him. He tried to crawl farther under the tree but could not move. He felt paralyzed, his lungs burning in a desperate search for air, his broken leg ablaze with pain.

Then he saw another horseman, this time not a Comanche. He looked up at the Texan, at the rifle in the man's hand, and he closed his eyes, waiting to die.

———

Rusty Shannon had hoped he had seen the last of Comanche raids. Tom Blessing said it had been more than a year since hostiles had penetrated this far down the Colorado River. Now that the war was over and new settlers were occupying regions farther west, it seemed that this area should be well buffered. Yet Tom Blessing had come to him on a sweat-lathered mount and shouted, "Grab your rifle and saddle your horse. There's Indians about."

Preacher Webb was among a dozen men who rode with Blessing. He looked tired and old.

The black man Shanty had been staying at Rusty's, sleeping on the open dog run so long as the weather was favorable, working his own farm only when Rusty could be with him. He said, "I'll fetch our horses, Mr. Rusty." He turned toward the corral.

Blessing raised a hand to stop him. "Catch your horse, Shanty, but you won't be goin' with us. The women and children are gatherin' at my place. They'll need every man we can spare to protect them."

Shanty was too old and stove up to be out chasing Indians on horseback, though he could fire a rifle and take up a defensive position as well as anyone. "Yes sir, Mr. Tom, if that's what you'd rather I do."

"I'd be much obliged."

Rusty appreciated that Blessing was protecting Shanty's feelings, first by telling him he was needed and second by not making a point of the old fellow's age and limitations. Blessing's large frame and commanding presence masked a benevolent spirit.

Jed Hoskins rode with the group. Rusty remembered him from the aborted raid on Shanty's place. Hoskins grumbled, "Damned darkey won't be any help. They could scalp every last woman and child before he'd come out from under the bed."

Shanty gave no sign that he had heard, though Rusty knew he must have. A life in slavery had taught him to endure indignity without protest lest indignity turn to physical violence.

Rusty knew nothing he might say would alter Hoskins's opinion. He asked simply, "Your ear still sore?" That was a reference to his having jabbed the muzzle of his pistol against Hoskins's ear at Shanty's place.

Hoskins did not answer.

Rusty wished Preacher Webb would stay with the women and children too, for he was looking none too strong. But Webb's medical experience would be needed if anyone was wounded on this mission.

A milk-pen calf was kept confined so its mother would come to the barn twice a day to be milked and to let the calf suck. Rusty turned the calf out to find her so it would not starve in case he was gone for several days. It stared in bovine confusion at the unaccustomed freedom and nosed at the closed gate, trying to get back in.

Shanty observed, "Freedom can be a hard thing to get used to. But it's harder yet to give up, once you've had it."

As he rode, Blessing explained that a farmer farther west had come upon an Indian and fired at him with a shotgun. He was too excited to aim straight.

Rusty asked, "Was he sure it was an Indian?"

"Said he wasn't wearin' much but breechcloth and moccasins, and he had a bow slung across his shoulder. Afterward some of the neighbors went scoutin' and found tracks. Looked like there might've been twenty or thirty passed by, goin' east."

"Goin' for where they expect to find the most horses," Rusty guessed. The invaders might be disappointed, for the war had taken away large numbers. Years would pass before they could be bred back up to earlier levels. "Any notion where the Indians have got to?"

"Somewhere east. We'll keep ridin' 'til we run into them."

That happened sooner than Rusty expected. A farmer came toward them, vigorously kicking a saddle mule's ribs, pushing for all the speed the animal could muster. The man waved his hat and shouted. Foam formed around the bridle bits, and the brown hide glistened with sweat.

"Comanches! Must be a hundred of them!" The farmer's eyes seemed to bulge. He turned halfway around in the saddle, pointing behind him. "Drivin' a bunch of horses. Must be a hundred of those, too."

From past experience Rusty suspected that the man's excitement caused gross exaggeration in the numbers, both of Indians and of horses. The earlier report had indicated there might be twenty or thirty Indians.

Blessing wasted no time on foolish questions. "How far?"

"Two, maybe three miles behind me. They been killin' folks right and left. Must've killed a hundred by now."

Blessing's expression indicated that he too, suspected the account was exaggerated. "We'll see if we can head them off. You want to go with us?"

The farmer looked over the group. Blessing had picked up several men, bringing the number to eighteen. "There ain't near enough of you. There's a hundred of them, maybe two hundred."

Blessing nodded as if he believed. "Tell you what do: you keep ridin', spread the word so nobody gets caught unawares."

The farmer needed no further encouragement to set the mule into a run again. He was quickly gone, dust rising behind him. Blessing turned to the men. "You heard what he said. I don't think there's near as many Indians as he claimed, but anybody who wants to turn back is free to do it."

Rusty looked at Preacher Webb, hoping he might, for the minister was obviously weary. But neither Webb nor anyone else showed an inclination to leave.

Blessing was pleased. "Then let's go find us some Comanches."

They were easily found. Rusty saw the horse herd first. A rough count showed him about twenty head, a fraction of the farmer's wild estimate. For the Comanches, this raid had been slim pickings. Moreover, only half a dozen Indians rode with the horses. Rusty suspected the raiding party consisted of considerably more, but the others were probably away looking for additional horses.

Blessing said, "I don't believe they've seen us yet. Let's don't give them time to think about it." With a wave of his hand, he led the charge.

Rusty took a quick look around to locate Preacher Webb. He wanted to keep the minister in sight, lest he get off to himself and end up in trouble.

The Indian horse guards were taken by surprise. They tried to come together, but the Texans were among them too quickly. To one side a small rider on a roan horse tried to join his companions. He was cut off by Jed Hoskins, who gave chase. The rider loosed an arrow at Hoskins but missed. Hoskins in turn fired his rifle but without effect. A second Indian cut in from behind, swinging a war club. Rusty gave chase, hoping to ward off the warrior, but he was too late. The club struck the farmer and knocked him off his horse. The Indian whirled about to finish the job but saw Rusty coming and changed his course.

The fallen Hoskins pushed shakily to his feet.

Rusty shouted, "You all right?"

Hoskins waved Rusty on. "Go get them!"

The farmer might have lacked tolerance, but he had nerve. Rusty continued the pursuit. The smaller Indian, out in front, turned to loose another arrow. His horse tried to jump a fallen tree but did not quite clear it. The roan went down, tumbling over its rider. It got up, shook itself and ran on, limping a little.

The second Indian paused a moment, leaning toward the one who had fallen. Rusty thought for a moment that he tried to strike the one who had fallen, but that made no sense. The warrior rode away, abandoning his companion.

Hell of a friend, Rusty thought. Usually Comanches did everything they could to rescue their own.

The downed Indian tried to crawl away, dragging a broken leg. A quiver had spilled most of its arrows in the fall, but the Indian grabbed at one, then felt around desperately for his bow. Not finding it, he flopped over on his back, grasping a knife in one hand and an arrow in the other. He jabbed them threateningly at Rusty.

"Figure on goin' out fightin', do you?" Rusty said, knowing it was unlikely the warrior understood him. Then, in surprise, "You're nothin' but a shirttail kid."

The Comanches trained them early, but this one appeared too young to be out on a raid. The boy's skin was lighter in color than most Comanches. Wide blue eyes tried to show defiance but betrayed mortal fear.

Rusty's spine tingled. "You're a white boy!"

He stepped down from Alamo. Again the boy jabbed at him with the knife, but Rusty remained out of reach. He waited until the arm was extended full length, then grabbed the wrist. Twisting hard, he took the knife from the lad's hand and broke off the arrow.

"Boy, who are you? And how come you ridin' with Comanches?"

The youngster shouted harshly, the words alien to Rusty.

Hoskins trudged through the dry grass, his legs moving heavily. Sweat rolled down his face. "You got you one, Shannon. How come you ain't killed him yet?"

"Look at him. He's no Comanche."

Hoskins leaned over for a close look. The boy struck at him with his fist. The farmer stepped back. "He's got a white skin sure enough, but underneath it he's pure Comanche."

Rusty tried again. "You got a name, boy?"

The lad made no sign that he understood.

A wisp of faint memory touched Rusty like the brush of a transient breeze. "Comanches stole me from my real folks a long time ago. Like as not, that's what happened to him."

"Maybe so, but raise a dog pup with wolves and you can never get the wolf out of him. Better if he was to die right now."

"But he won't, not unless a broken leg can kill him."

"They've turned him into a savage."

Sympathy welled up in Rusty, deep enough that pain came with it. "I could've been where he is if Mike Shannon and the preacher hadn't grabbed me."

"The way I heard it, the Comanches didn't keep you long enough to hurt you much. Looks like they had this young'un long enough to ruin him for life."

Rusty heard horses and looked up, hand tightening on his rifle until he recognized Preacher Webb and Tom Blessing. Blessing leaned partway out of the saddle for a better view of the boy. "Looks like you've caught yourself a bear cub."

"Take a close look at him. He's white."

Preacher Webb dismounted heavily, fatigue pressing down on his thin shoulders. The boy stared up at him with frightened eyes that no longer tried to show fight. Plainly, he expected to be killed.

Rusty asked, "Remind you of anything?"

"Reminds me of you, a long time ago back at Plum Creek. But you were a lot younger than this." Webb knelt over the youngster. "Do you speak English, son?"

The boy did not reply.

Webb tried again. "Do you have a name? Do you remember your mother and father?"

The blue eyes flickered. Rusty thought the words might have registered, at least a little.

Webb pressed, "Your mother? Do you remember your mother?"

The boy's lips tried to form the word, though no sound came.

Webb looked up. "I believe he understands the word *mother*. Maybe he can remember more if we keep at it."

Tom Blessing dismounted, excitement rising in his face. "I think maybe I know who he is. Remember the time, Preacher—you were there too, Rusty— when we trailed after Comanches who had taken a woman and a boy? That was before the war started. We found the woman dead, but we never did find the boy."

It had been the first time Rusty had seen the results of murder. He remembered the shock, the stomach-turning sight of a woman butchered, her scalp taken.

Webb said, "I'd ministered to the family, even baptized their baby boy. Their name was Pickard. I even remember the name they gave their boy. Andrew. They called him Andy. Andy Pickard."

The boy's eyes widened at the name. His lips moved as he tried to form a word. He made a couple of efforts, then managed, "Andy. Andy." He drummed fingers against his chest. "Andy."

A chill ran all the way down to Rusty's boots. "Then he's the one we hunted for but never found."

Blessing said, "Looks like it. You were lucky we found *you* so quick. He wasn't as lucky."

"Maybe his luck is fixin' to change. Preacher, what can we do about that broken leg?"

"Set the bone if we can, and tie a splint on his leg so it stays set. It'll hurt him real bad for a minute."

Rusty nodded at Hoskins. "Me and you will hold him while Preacher sets that leg."

Hoskins was dubious. "He's liable to bite. A man could get hydrophoby."

Blessing said, "I'll hold him, me and Rusty. You see if you can find a broken tree limb that'll do for a temporary splint."

The boy cried out and struggled as if he thought they meant to kill him. Rusty and Blessing held him tightly.

Webb said, "Now." He jerked the leg. The boy convulsed, then went limp. "Fainted dead away. It's just as well. He won't be fightin' me while I brace up his leg."

The farmer found nothing suitable. Webb placed Rusty's rifle flat against the leg and bound it with strips of cotton cloth torn from a jacket he had carried behind the cantle of his saddle.

Blessing asked, "What'll we do with him?"

Rusty said, "If somebody'll go fetch a wagon, we'll take him to my place. Me and Shanty'll look after him."

Hoskins warned, "Like as not you'll wake up dead some mornin' with a knife between your ribs."

Rusty said, "I don't see how I can do anything else." He turned to the minister. "I've been where this boy is. I look at him, and I see me layin' here in his place. Do you understand, Preacher?"

"I do. But this boy is not you. He's been raised to fight. Like as not he's been raised to hate you and me and everybody white. He may never get past that."

"You're a preacher. No matter how bad a sinner may be, you give him a chance, don't you?"

"That's part of the callin'."

"I'm a long ways from bein' a preacher, but I've learned a lot from followin' you around. I've got to give him his chance, like the Shannons gave me."

Distant shots told Steals the Ponies that the horse guard had come under attack. To their disappointment, he and the warriors he had taken with him had managed to find only six more horses. The Texans seemed not to have many, and most of those were too well protected to take without higher cost than the raiders were willing to pay. He had begun to worry about the reception they would receive when they returned to the encampment with less booty than expected.

Now a darker worry burdened him. He had left his brother where he had thought he would be safest. It appeared his judgment had been terribly wrong. He felt a fear for Badger Boy that he had never felt for himself.

"Leave the horses," he shouted, and turned in the direction from which he had heard the shouts. Most of the other warriors objected. It seemed cowardly to abandon the few they had obtained. "Had you rather lose them all?" he responded with anger.

Several men stubbornly held to the stolen horses. Steals the Ponies led the rest toward the sound of the shots. He had left Badger Boy in the care of Tonkawa Killer, as fierce a fighter as he knew. Tonkawa Killer hated the boy, but surely he would live up to the responsibility Steals the Ponies had placed upon him.

Driving the horses, the warriors stayed in or near timber as much as they could. Steals the Ponies could only guess how much opposition the Texans had mounted against them. From the cover of trees he watched a considerable number of Texans moving westward, driving a dozen horses before them. That represented about half the ones the raiding party had left under guard. He assumed that Tonkawa Killer, Badger Boy, and the rest had gotten away with the others. He felt a little better, though much anxiety lingered.

A wagon appeared to carry someone covered by a blanket. A Texan, he thought, perhaps wounded or, more to be preferred, dead, as all Texans should be.

He reasoned that the horse guard must be somewhere to the north, more or less where he had left them. When the Texans had passed out of sight he signaled the men behind him to move on. He pushed his horse into an easy lope, well out in front of the others.

He hoped to find that Badger Boy had not only survived unscathed but had acquitted himself in a manner befitting a warrior. If so, the other men should no longer chastise him for his disobedience.

He neared a tree-lined creek. A horseman rode out from the timber at some distance upstream and signaled. Much as Steals the Ponies looked forward to seeing that his brother was all right, he dreaded facing up to the fact that they had only six horses to show for their foray, plus whatever number the guard had managed to keep. This would reflect badly on his leadership and perhaps make it more difficult for him to recruit warriors for future raids.

Riding down to where the horse guard waited in the bed of the creek, he knew by their hang-dog look that they were ashamed for having failed him. But he felt that he had failed himself. To redeem his standing he would have to do something spectacular the next time.

He did not see Badger Boy. His throat tightened.

"Where is my brother?"

Nobody answered. The men who had stood guard on the horses looked away from him, most staring at the ground.

"Tonkawa Killer! Where is my brother?"

Tonkawa Killer sat up straight and defiant on his horse. "The last time I saw him, he was running away."

Angrily Steals the Ponies pushed his mount against Tonkawa Killer's, forcing the warrior to back away. "You lie! He would not run."

"I told you many times, he was never one of us. He is a Texan. Perhaps he ran to the Texans."

"He would not do that. Never would he do that." Steals the Ponies swept the other horse guards with eyes fierce as an eagle's. "Did anyone else see him? Did anyone see him run away?"

No one answered. Most looked off as if he were lashing them with a whip. He felt fire in his face. He *would* lash them if he had something more formidable than a quirt.

"Perhaps you let the Texans kill him, and you did nothing to help."

Tonkawa Killer remained defiant. "Go look for yourself if you do not believe us."

The rest of the warriors arrived with their six horses. Steals the Ponies chewed on his anger a minute. "Go on, the rest of you. See if you can keep these horses, at least. I am going to look for my brother."

Tonkawa Killer said, "Look for him in a Texan lodge, among his *true* brothers." His tone was charged with contempt.

Heart heavy, Steals the Ponies began backtracking the horse guard's line of retreat. He was aware of the danger that he might suddenly confront Texans doing the same thing in a reverse direction, but he had no choice. He must take that risk.

After a while he saw a horse grazing alone. Holding his breath until his lungs burned, he closed the distance quickly. He recognized the roan Badger Boy had been riding. The horse looked up, alert ears pointed forward.

Steals the Ponies grabbed the trailing rein, then circled the roan, looking for dried blood that might indicate his brother had been shot. He saw none. That raised his hopes a little. His anxious gaze scanned the countryside, searching for Badger Boy.

Shamans sometimes claimed they had heard animals talk, but Steals the Ponies never had. He wished the roan could talk to him now.

"Where is he? Where did you leave him?"

The roan tried to lower its head to graze again, but Steals the Ponies held the rein too closely. "You will lead me back to where you lost him."

He tried to pick up the roan's trail, but it was lost amid the tracks of so many others. He reasoned that all had come more or less the same way, so he followed the broader trail. He checked every brush motte, thinking a wounded Badger Boy might have dragged himself to the shade. He found nothing.

He came finally to a set of wagon tracks. Boot marks and crushed grass indicated that several men had moved around afoot. The wagon had circled and retreated in the same general direction by which it had come. He thought it probably was the one he had seen earlier, carrying some wounded Texan.

He had no interest in wounded Texans. The more of them, the better. Dead ones would please him most of all.

For a fleeting moment he considered the possibility that the Texans had found Badger Boy and carried him away. He dismissed the notion immediately. It was the way of the Texans to kill any Comanche where they found him and leave him lying where he fell, meat for the scavengers.

The sun touched fire to thin clouds stretched along the western horizon. Steals the Ponies realized darkness would be upon him soon. He urged his horse into a faster trot, tugging sternly at the rein by which he led the roan. Somewhere his brother lay injured, perhaps even dead. Steals the Ponies had to find him.

But he did not. He spent a sleepless night beside a small seep and at first light was up again, searching in ever-widening circles. For two full days he rode back and forth, looking for tracks, watching for Texans.

Not until late evening of the third day did he yield to the inevitable. Badger Boy was almost certainly dead. Otherwise Steals the Ponies would have found him by now.

It was painful to think of his brother's body being set upon by wolves or by the buzzards that seemed to await patiently the death of every living thing. But he did not know what more he could do. He felt he had searched every piece of ground where the warriors and the Texans had ridden.

Shoulders hunched, his head low, he turned northward. It was a long way to the Red River, and beyond it to where the encampment lay. He would think of Badger Boy every step of the way.

It was good that his father Buffalo Caller was not here to witness his failure. He would be ashamed, as Steals the Ponies was ashamed. Stronger even than the shame was grief for a brother lost.

CHAPTER

FOURTEEN

Rusty knew the jolting of the wagon must cause the boy intense pain, and he imagined he could feel it himself. He turned in the seat. "Grit your teeth, Andy Pickard. We'll be home after a while."

Jaw clenched, the boy stared up at the sky and made not a whimper. The Comanches had taught him stoicism. Rusty wondered what else they had taught him.

Because so many men had sent their families to Tom Blessing's place for mutual defense, it was agreed that the procession would go there first. The Texans drove before them those stolen horses they had managed to recover. The ones lost would have to be regarded as a tax of sorts, payment for living where Indian raids had to be accepted as a cost of business.

From a distance Rusty could see no one at Blessing's. Then, as the inhabitants recognized that the oncoming horsemen were not Indians, they began emerging into the open. Several riders spurred ahead, anxious to see about the women and children they had sent or left there for safety.

Among them was Jed Hoskins. Whatever his shortcomings, Rusty decided, he was devoted to his family. Relieved men embraced wives and children. Rusty had no one there except Shanty. The old man limped out to meet him.

"Who's that you got in the wagon, Mr. Rusty?"

"A boy by the name of Andy Pickard."

Shanty's eyebrows lifted in surprise. "How come he's dressed up like an Indian?"

Rusty explained. "We're takin' him home with us 'til his leg mends, and 'til we can get word to his kinfolks to come and fetch him."

Tom Blessing had said he was fairly sure the boy's father had relatives down on the lower Brazos River, somewhere around old San Felipe.

Shanty leaned over the wagon and reached in as if to test the binding that held Rusty's rifle in place as a splint against the broken leg. The boy struck at him and shouted defensively. Shanty drew back. "He snaps like a young pup that's been beat on."

Rusty heard a familiar voice call his name. "Rusty Shannon! Damned if your hair ain't got redder than it already was."

Rusty knew the speaker before he turned and saw him. "Len Tanner, I thought you'd gone back home for good."

The lanky former ranger grabbed Rusty's hand so hard he made the knuckles hurt. "The trouble with home is that after you've been gone too long it ain't home anymore."

"How come you here at Tom Blessing's?"

"Joined in with some fellers trackin' Indians. This is where we ended up." He peered into the wagon bed. "Just heard about your Indian boy. He don't look so fierce."

"Don't lean in too close. He's liable to take a chunk out of you."

"How you goin' to talk to him? You don't speak Comanche."

"He seems to recognize some words. I figure the language will gradually come back if we talk to him a lot."

Tanner said, "I'm better at talkin' than you are."

Rusty could not argue with that. "Then come home with us, why don't you?"

"Us?"

"Me and Shanty." He pointed toward the black man. "He's been stayin' at my place."

Tanner hesitated, then extended his hand. It was not common for white to shake hands with black. Old ways faded slowly.

Jed Hoskins walked up, his face solemn. "Shanty, I want to talk to you."

Rusty stiffened, expecting trouble. He thought of his rifle, still tied to the boy's broken leg. But he had his pistol on his hip.

Hoskins said to Shanty, "My wife told me what you done."

Rusty prepared himself to step protectively in front of Shanty.

Shanty said, "I didn't do nothin' much."

"Saved my young'uns. I'd call that a right much."

Rusty stared in disbelief as Hoskins stuck out his hand toward the black man. Hoskins had a shamed look. "I've said some mean hard things agin you. I take back every one of them."

Surprised, a little flustered, Shanty accepted the handshake.

Hoskins turned to Rusty. "Wife says my young'uns and some others got restless bein' cooped up like chickens. They went outside to play and strayed off too far. All of a sudden a bunch of Comanches showed up. Of course they was mainly lookin' for horses, but they'd take a scalp from a kid if they couldn't get one from a grown man.

"Shanty was out there keepin' an eye on the children. He put himself and his rifle between the Indians and the young'uns 'til they got back in the cabin. Like as not he kept some of them from bein' killed or carried off."

Rusty did not know what to say. Shanty seemed struck dumb, too. He made a slight grin and shrugged his shoulders.

Fowler Gaskin had waited out the Indian danger with the women and children. He listened in angry disbelief. "What he done wasn't so much. I'd've done the same thing."

Hoskins turned on him. "You was here. Why didn't you?"

Gaskin stammered. "I . . . I didn't have no rifle."

"There was rifles around. You could've got you one. But they say you hunkered down in a corner and covered your head." Hoskins turned to the larger group of men. "I want everybody to understand: from now on, any-body who bothers this boy"—he pointed at Shanty—"has got me to whip." He turned a fierce face toward Fowler Gaskin.

Rusty thought it ironic that old Shanty was being called *boy*. But it was the way of the times. He voiced agreement with Hoskins. "What he said goes for me, too."

Shanty seemed embarrassed by the attention. He looked at the ground.

Rusty told him, "That means you can go home if you want to, but you're welcome to keep stayin' at my place. Me and you have worked right good together."

Shanty welcomed the offer. "I reckon I'll stay at least 'til we get the crops in. Looks to me like you'll need help takin' care of that Indian boy." He pointed his chin toward the wagon.

"He's not Indian."

"But he thinks he is."

"He's liable to be a handful, sure enough."

Shanty held up both palms. "I've got two hands, both of them strong."

Preacher Webb said, "I'd better stay with you too, at least a couple of days. Got to watch that youngster's broken leg."

It was in Rusty's mind that the Comanches might set enough store in the boy to come looking for him. "The more of us the better." Himself, Shanty, Webb, and Tanner . . . they could make a good showing should it come to that.

Crowd opinion was that the Indians were unlikely to return, but it seemed the better part of valor to be prepared. Trying to outguess Comanche tactics was risky. Most agreed it was wise to remain at the Blessing farm overnight and not begin scattering until morning. No one wanted darkness to catch him halfway home.

That gave Webb plenty of time to remove the makeshift splint. He returned the rifle to Rusty, replacing it with two thin strips of pine. The Pickard boy bore the treatment in sullen silence.

Webb said, "The leg's swollen and hot. Goin' to be right painful for a while. Got a black bruise on one shoulder, too. Probably from the fall."

Everyone, particularly the children, showed a strong curiosity about the boy. They clustered around, studying him, commenting at length. The youngster tried to show them a fierce face, but his eyes betrayed fear and pain.

Webb said, "I think he's still got it in his head that we may kill him." He addressed the boy directly. "Nobody's out to hurt you, lad. We mean you well."

Tanner remarked, "You could put him in a circus and advertise him as the wild boy. He'd draw a crowd."

Rusty felt compassion. "All this attention is keepin' him agitated. We need to get him away from the crowd. Then maybe he'll settle down."

The next morning, still using the borrowed wagon, they set out for Rusty's farm. The women had made a sympathetic fuss over the Pickard boy, which seemed to distress him. The children were mainly inquisitive, some trying to talk to him, others simply chattering about him. All seemed only to add to his confusion. The boy appeared relieved to be getting away from so many strange people.

Rusty drove the wagon. Len Tanner rode close beside him on a bay horse. It was a long-legged animal, befitting its rider. Rusty said, "I didn't expect to see you back, especially so soon."

Tanner shook his head. "It don't take long to catch up on kinfolks. After about a week everybody seemed to be sayin' the same things over and over again. Even Mama and Papa. I'd figured I could help them through their old age, but they got too much family helpin' them as it is. And then there's them Yankee occupation soldiers. They got this far up the river yet?"

"Ain't seen them. I guess they've gone to the more settled places first." Rusty had heard that Union troops were scattering across the state, imposing Federal authority through martial law.

Tanner spat. "They'll get here soon enough, then you'll wish they'd never left Ohio or Massachusetts or whatever foreign country they come from. Insolent, overbearin' . . . you'd think they never won a war before."

"I notice that bay horse you're ridin' has got a U.S. brand on him. Bought him from the government, did you?"

"Not exactly. Borried him, you might say. I needed to leave in a considerable hurry, and I seen him tied to a hitchin' post. Saddled and all, like he had Len Tanner's name on him."

Rusty put mock accusation into his voice. "Stealin' horses. And you used to be a ranger."

"I don't lay any claim to him. If the government wants him it's welcome to come and get him. I won't give them any trouble."

"Sounds like you're already *in* trouble."

"Just a little difference of opinion with a Yankee sergeant, is all. I was sittin' in the grocery quiet and peaceful when he come in and wanted to see my parole pass. I told him I didn't have one because I never had been a Confederate soldier. Told him I'd been a ranger. He couldn't see no difference. Said if I couldn't show him a pass he was fixin' to drag me off to the Yankee compound.

"Well, after a polite discussion he ended up on his back, all covered in flour. Barrel got turned over durin' the commotion. He said he'd see to it that I saw the front end of a firin' squad. Acted plumb serious about it. This horse looked faster than the plug I'd been ridin', so I taken the borry of it. Thought it was a good time to go visit some of my old friends."

"You're welcome to stay here as long as you want to."

"'Til the first Yankee soldiers show up. I've seen enough of them to last me awhile."

Badger Boy felt strange lying in a bed that stood on legs. He stared up at a ceiling of wood instead of buffalo hide. It did not even have a smoke hole in the center like the tepees to which he was accustomed. He vaguely remembered having lived in a cabin much like this one. He conjured up a hazy image of hard-packed dirt floors, of climbing a stairway into a loft above an open dog run. And there had been people. He wished he could remember them better, but when he reached for them they faded like dust carried away on the wind.

He wanted to get up and move around, but his leg was immobilized by the splints the Texan shaman had tied against it to hold the broken bone together.

He knew the man must be some sort of shaman. A number of people had stood with him, heads bowed, speaking to whatever guardian spirits watched over the Texans. Badger Boy reasoned that theirs must be different from those of the Comanches. How could the same spirits serve both The People and their enemies?

He longed to escape this trap that had snared him, but his leg was tightly bound and so painful he could not move. He realized that if he untied the splints the leg would collapse under his weight. They had taken away his breechcloth and moccasins and had given him a long cotton shirt much too large. To him it resembled a woman's dress, no fit garment for a fighting man.

His early fears had subsided, but he remained distrustful. Despite these Texans' display of concern, it was possible they were holding him prisoner until they were ready to torture him to death, as he had seen Comanches ceremonially torture captives, especially Apaches. If this came to pass he was resolved not to cry out or let them see fear. He could be at least as brave as any Apache. He was determined to die with the dignity worthy of a warrior. Somehow, he felt that Steals the Ponies would know. Perhaps his adoptive father, Buffalo Caller, would look down from the spirit world and know, too.

The red-haired man who had captured him walked into the small room. Badger Boy had heard others call him Rusty. He had no idea what the name meant. He sought but did not find any sign of hostility in the man's countenance. On the contrary, the Texan seemed worried about him. This was difficult to understand in an enemy.

Rusty said, "We'll have dinner directly. You hungry?"

Badger Boy recognized some words here and there. He knew *dinner* meant food. He understood *hungry*. He reasoned that he had known the Texan language before he became a Comanche. Bits and pieces came back to him as he listened to the men talk. When no one was in the room he tried to speak the words to himself. Some came easily. Others twisted his tongue.

It did not really matter whether he remembered the Texan language or not. If they did not kill him, he intended to escape. When his leg mended enough that he could walk without the splints, he would steal away and return to his true people. At times he entertained a fancy that Steals the Ponies would find him and take him away, though this hope did not stand up well when he thought soberly on it. It was probable that his brother had given him up for dead. His only hope for freedom lay in his own efforts. Time, then. He had been taught patience, necessary to a hunter and a warrior. He would bide his time and wait for strength.

Meanwhile he observed the four men who held him captive, trying to figure out who and what they were. The old one they called Preacher was, of course, some manner of shaman, for he spoke often to his gods. The tall, skinny one they called Tanner talked a lot, though Badger Boy had difficulty understanding enough words to find meaning in the one-sided conversation. The old man with the black face and hands puzzled him considerably. He could not remember ever seeing a skin so dark, not even among the Mexicans who sometimes came from the far west to trade among The People. The black man played for him on an instrument he called a banjo. The music was strange, yet he remembered hearing its like before.

Most worrisome of all was the one called Rusty. His red hair troubled Badger Boy. Steals the Ponies had told him about a warning from Buffalo Caller not long before his father's death. The old warrior had told of a Texan with red hair, carrying medicine stronger than his own. Years earlier, Buffalo Caller had captured a small Texan boy who had hair the color of rusted iron. Some days afterward, disaster had fallen upon Buffalo Caller and all The People with him. Texans had recovered the boy. From then on, Buffalo Caller had regarded red hair as a dark omen, a hostile power to be avoided. Steals the Ponies had seen a red-haired Texan in the fight that gave Buffalo Caller his fatal wound.

Badger Boy wondered if this might be the same man. Of the Texans he had observed since his capture, this was the only one who fit the description.

Often when one or more of the Texans came to look at him, he feigned sleep. Not when they brought him food, however. Once the pain diminished, his appetite returned with a vengeance. He did not recognize much of what they brought him to eat, but he found it mostly flavorful.

When Tanner told him, "You're startin' to fatten up, boy," Badger Boy understood. He was beginning to understand more words every day. He reasoned that they had been buried somewhere in his memory. Hearing them now was bringing them back into his consciousness. He began speaking some of the words, like *dinner, supper, water, meat.* After a few efforts he was able to say them easily.

One day Rusty, Tanner, and the black man Shanty brought him a pair of long sticks carved from limbs of an oak tree. Each had cloth wrapped as padding around a fork at its tops. Rusty placed the sticks beneath his own arms, demonstrating their use. He said, "These are crutches, so you can start gettin' around a little."

Badger Boy did not know the word *crutch*, but he realized the purpose of the sticks.

Len Tanner declared, "It ain't good to lay on your back too long. You'll petrify."

The old black man carefully lifted Badger Boy to a sitting position. Rusty and Tanner then positioned themselves on either side of him and brought him to his feet. Badger Boy felt weak, the room swaying around him, his leg hurting. But the two men's strength gave him confidence to remain on his feet and place the crutches beneath his armpits.

Rusty said, "Now take ahold," showing him how to grip the handles firmly attached by rawhide at arm's length. "All right, now, walk. We'll hold on to you. We won't let you fall."

Badger Boy understood the meaning and most of the words. "I walk," he said. He took a step and would have fallen had the two men not had a firm grip.

Rusty said, "Try again. You'll get the hang of it."

This time Badger Boy took a step without feeling that he was about to fall. Gaining confidence, he took another and another. The two men relaxed their holds, though they did not relinquish them altogether.

Shanty declared enthusiastically, "You're doin' fine, boy. The Lord is lookin' down and smilin' on you."

Badger Boy reasoned that the Lord must be one of the Texans' gods. He had heard Preacher Webb talking to Him from time to time, though he had never heard a reply. The Comanches' spirits often spoke to them in the voices of birds and animals. He reasoned that the Texans' gods must dwell farther away, though if that were the case he did not understand how they could hear Webb speak.

They were a strange lot, these Texans.

After a few steps the men released their hold entirely, though Rusty remained near enough to catch him if he fell. Badger Boy ventured out onto the dog run and felt the coolness of the breeze. The bright sun made his eyes pinch at first, though he found the light pleasant once they had accommodated to it. He had spent too many days in the room's close confinement.

Tanner said, "Beats hell out of stayin' indoors, don't it?"

Not sure of the proper reply, Badger Boy said, "Beats hell."

Rusty grinned at Tanner. "Good thing Preacher Webb has gone away to sermonize. He'd scorch you good for corruptin' an innocent boy."

Tanner said, "First things I ever learned as a young'un was the cusswords. A few *damns* here and there don't hurt anything. Sometimes they're like a tonic."

Badger Boy understood only the general meaning of what they were saying, but he sensed that it was in good humor. He allowed himself a faint smile. It had been awhile since he had felt like smiling about anything.

Tanner noticed. "He's tryin' to grin. Some people don't think Indians have got any humor at all."

Rusty said, "They just don't know."

"The trouble is, what an Indian is most apt to grin about don't bode no good for a white man."

Shanty was not smiling. "Preacher Webb wouldn't like to come back and hear this boy usin' mean language. We need to teach him proper so he'll find favor in the eyes of the Lord."

There was the Lord again, Badger Boy thought. If these Texans put so much store in Him, perhaps he should learn a little about Him, too. He needed all the gods and beneficent spirits he could summon, for he would require help to get away from here and return north where he belonged.

In time he more or less had the run of the place, within the limits imposed by his broken leg. He was able to get out of bed by himself, tuck the crutches beneath his arms, and go as far as the barn and livestock pens. He stayed away from the hog pen, for the mud-loving hogs had a smell like something four days dead. He saw that Rusty owned cattle, but those did not interest him. They were smaller and appeared more vulnerable than the buffalo. He found their meat less flavorful. Perhaps worst of all, they seemed dependent upon the Texans' care. Buffalo did not depend upon anybody. They ranged proud and free. They were brother to The People, like the wolves and the other wild animals of the plains.

The horses interested him a great deal more, partly because he loved horses in general, but more importantly because they were his hope of getting away from here as soon as he healed enough to ride. He noted that Rusty's favorite was a large black horse he called Alamo. He was not young, but he appeared sound, and strong enough to carry a rider all the way to Comanchería without stopping often for rest. Then there was the long-legged bay of Tanner's. From conversation he had been able to understand, he gathered that Tanner had stolen it somehow from the blue-coated soldiers. That elevated Tanner's standing in his eyes. A good horse thief was to be admired.

It pleased him to think how proud Steals the Ponies would be if Badger Boy came riding into camp on a fine Texan horse after having escaped from captivity. His brother might even stop calling him Badger Boy and give him a name befitting a man.

He leaned against the fence, staring northwestward, trying to visualize the way he and the other warriors had come. He had noted landmarks along the way, though a lot of the country had a monotonous sameness that led to confusion. He wondered if he could find his way home without getting lost.

A big worry would be the possibility of recapture, or even of being killed by the first whites who saw him. He had heard reports among The People that the white men had ended their long war against one another. He had understood enough talk by Rusty and the others to know it was true. He gathered that the warrior society known as rangers had been disbanded, which he considered especially fortunate. The People had always respected them more than the soldiers because when they engaged in a battle they clung like wildcats, with tooth and claw. The tall man Tanner talked about damnyankee soldiers, expected to arrive at any time. Badger Boy understood the word *soldiers*, but he was unsure about *damnyankee*. Tanner used the word as if it were an obscenity.

One afternoon while Badger Boy sunned himself in front of the cabin, Preacher Webb rode in. He had been absent for several days. He tied his horse and walked directly to Badger Boy, smiling. "Sunshine is the Lord's great healer, son. You're lookin' better every day." He leaned over close, reaching out as if to touch Badger Boy's long braids. He had tried more than once to persuade the lad to cut his hair white-man style. Badger Boy had resisted firmly each time, fighting off the scissors. The Texans had taken everything else that marked him as Comanche. He did not intend to let them cut his hair.

Webb said, "You need a good washin'. You've got company comin' tomorrow."

Washing, Badger Boy understood. *Company*, he did not.

"Somebody comes?"

"Kin of yours. I located your uncle down by San Felipe."

"Uncle?" Badger Boy did not understand.

"Your father's brother. His name is Pickard, like yours. Jim Pickard."

Badger Boy spoke the name. He had easily become used to being called Andy, for he dimly remembered having been called that before. He was less sure about the name Pickard. "Jim Pickard," he said, trying to find something familiar in it.

"Maybe you called him Uncle Jim."

"Uncle Jim. Uncle Jim." Nothing aroused any memories.

"Maybe when you see him. He's your family."

"Not my family. My family Comanche!"

"Well, we'll get you cleaned up in the mornin'. We don't want him to see you lookin' like a wild . . ."

Webb broke off, and Badger Boy had no idea what he had been about to say.

"Where this San Felipe?"

Webb pointed to the east. "Yonderway."

"Far?"

"Pretty far. Took me most of two days to get back."

"My uncle, he takes me?"

"I expect he will. We all figure the best place for you is with your own kin."

Rusty came in from the field. Badger Boy heard Webb tell him, "The boy's uncle stopped off at Tom Blessing's to rest his team tonight. I thought I'd better come ahead and let you know he's on his way."

Rusty stared at Badger Boy, his thoughts unreadable.

Webb went on, "Tom's not the sheriff anymore. The Federals turned him out. Appointed one of their own."

"Then they're takin' over lock, stock, and barrel."

"There are soldiers everywhere east of here, settin' up provisional local governments. They've appointed their own man governor in Austin."

"If Tom's not the sheriff anymore, then I reckon I'm not a deputy. Never saw a dime anyway, so it's no big loss." He turned back to Badger Boy. "First thing in the mornin' we'll get you shined up for your uncle."

Badger Boy bordered on panic but tried to keep from showing it. He was already a long way from The People. A trip to this place San Felipe would take him even farther and vastly increase the odds against his reaching home without being caught.

He had not intended to make the break quite this soon. His bad leg needed more healing time. But a change in circumstances was forcing his hand.

"Tomorrow. Tomorrow I get clean."

He lied. By tomorrow he intended to be a long way from here.

CHAPTER

FIFTEEN

adger Boy ate hardly any supper. His stomach was in a turmoil. He watched the evening shadows lengthen and wished darkness would hurry.

Tanner noticed, for he could put away a prodigious amount of food himself. "You ain't eatin', boy. Sick?"

Preacher Webb said, "Probably excited. He seemed awful surprised when I told him about his uncle."

Rusty had said little. Mostly he had stared at his plate, picking at his food. "I know it's the right thing, sendin' him back amongst his own. But I'd like to know they'll take good care of him. What did you think of his uncle, Preacher?"

"It's hard to tell about a man the first time you see him. I noticed a family Bible on the table, and it was not dusty. That speaks well for him, I think."

Tanner declared, "I've seen some Bible thumpers you couldn't turn your back on. Present company not included, Preacher."

Rusty said, "I've gotten used to havin' Andy here. Place'll seem different when he leaves."

Badger Boy wished they would quit talking and go to bed.

They did, eventually. Badger Boy made all the motions of bedding down, but when the room was dark he sat on the edge of the bunk, staring into darkness. He listened for snoring. It seemed forever in coming. When it came he recognized it as Tanner's.

He knew he should wait a little longer, to be safe, but anxiety gnawed at him like a wolf gnawing a bone. Before dark he tried to find his breech-cloth and moccasins without arousing suspicion, but Rusty had put them away too well, or perhaps had even destroyed them. He had to content himself with wearing the long shirt. He was used to riding almost naked anyway. The question was whether he could ride, or even mount, with the splints on his leg. He knew he must try.

He moved slowly lest the crutches make a noise and awaken someone. He moved out of the room and onto the dog run, stopping often to listen. He could still hear Tanner's snoring. Shanty had been sleeping in the dog run, and Badger Boy circled around him carefully. He reached the barn, wondering which horse had been kept penned for the night. It was Rusty's habit to keep one up so he would not be afoot the first thing in the morning. Badger Boy hoped it would be Alamo.

He was disappointed. He found Tanner's long-legged bay instead. Well, the bay would have to do. At least those legs ought to carry him a good distance in a hurry. The main problem would be getting on him, for his back was a long way from the ground.

Badger Boy did not bother with a saddle. He was used to riding bareback, tucking his knees under a rope tied loosely around the horse's chest. He had a little trouble with the bridle, for he was not accustomed to dealing with the steel bits. Their sound, grating against the horse's teeth, was disconcerting.

Ordinarily he would grab a handful of mane and spring up onto the back, but the splints kept one leg immobilized. He tried a couple of times but could not achieve enough height. He led the horse close to the fence and attempted to climb far enough up the rails that he could slide over onto the back. That too, proved futile.

He saw but one alternative, and it was risky. He had to remove the splints. He hoped the bone had knitted enough to handle the strain. Leaning against the fence, he untied the wrapping Webb had put around his leg. The pine slats fell to the ground.

Gingerly he tested his weight. The leg felt as if someone had driven a spear though the bone. Cold sweat broke out on his face, and he found his palms were wet as well. He dried them on the long shirt and pulled the horse up close to him. Taking a deep breath, then gritting his teeth, he tried to spring up onto the bay's back.

He did not make it. He felt himself sliding down but was unable to stop. He intended to let the good leg take the impact as he struck the ground, but the broken leg caught much of it. It collapsed, and he fell on his stomach. The sudden movement spooked the horse. It jerked away from him and ran halfway across the pen before stopping to look back, snorting in its excitement.

Badger Boy did not know if he had rebroken the bone. The pain was excruciating. He lay helpless, unable to push up from the ground far enough to gather his legs under him. He wanted to cry out in agony but would not allow himself the weakness.

A shadow fell across the moonlit pen. Looking up, he saw the outline of a man with a rifle or shotgun.

"No shoot! No shoot!" he called.

The voice was Shanty's. "Andy, is that you layin' there? What in the Lord's good name you tryin' to do?"

Shanty knelt at Badger Boy's side. "You done taken all the wrappin' off. Wouldn't surprise me none if that leg is busted plumb in two again."

That was Badger Boy's fear, too.

Shanty stood up and cupped his hands around his mouth. "Mr. Rusty! Preacher! You-all needed out here by the barn."

He started to help Badger Boy to his feet but thought better of it. "We better leave everything like it is 'til the preacher man looks at you." He shook his head, showing disapproval. "Tryin' to skedaddle, wasn't you? I figured some Indian was tryin' to take Mr. Tanner's horse. Guess I wasn't all that far wrong."

Badger Boy hurt too badly to try to decipher all Shanty said. He knew the gist of it.

Rusty, Webb, and Tanner all arrived at the same time. Webb picked up the fallen splints and leaned them against the fence, then carefully ran his hand up and down Badger Boy's leg. Badger Boy winced. He tried not to make a sound, but an involuntary groan escaped him.

Webb said, "Maybe the bone held together. It's God's mercy if it did. Let's carry him back up to the cabin. Real careful now. That bone's as flimsy as an eggshell."

Rusty demanded, "What did you do it for?"

Badger Boy ground his teeth together in an effort to fight down the pain. "No want to go with uncle. Want to go home."

Tanner tried to make light of it. "Don't you know they hang horse thieves?" Badger Boy had surmised that Tanner stole the bay from the bluecoats, but he hurt too much to appreciate the ironic humor.

Badger Boy lay awake most of the night, the leg throbbing, allowing him no mercy. Webb had wrapped the splints around it again after satisfying himself that the bone had not broken anew. He had said, "The Comanches raise their boys to be tough. Anybody else, that leg would be in two pieces."

Badger Boy was unable to hold breakfast in his stomach. After a couple of tentative bites, he quit.

Webb said, "We'd best be about gettin' you cleaned up."

Badger Boy would much prefer to bathe in the creek, but the splints and his injured leg precluded that. He took his bath out of a tin pan, slower and less satisfying. Done, he put on a clean shirt that Rusty brought him. It was much too large. The sleeves were considerably longer than his arms, so he had to roll them up. The tail of the shirt reached past his knees. He had seen boys at Blessing's cabin wearing long shirts and nothing else, no trousers, not even a breechcloth. To him it still looked like something for a woman, not a man.

"Why uncle come?" he asked. "I no know him, he no know me."

"You're blood kin," Shanty said. "Everybody ought to be with their blood kin."

Badger Boy had seen no one else whose face was black like Shanty's. "You got blood kin?"

Shanty seemed taken aback. "Someplace, I expect. I was sold away when I was just a young'un. But you got a chance to be with your own folks now. You'd ought to be happy."

Badger Boy would be happy only when he got back with The People. Since last night's failure, he knew it would be somewhat longer than he had expected. Now that he had grudgingly accepted his situation, he began to feel some curiosity about the man who was his Texan father's brother. Brothers often looked much alike. He wondered if seeing his uncle would help him remember his Texan father's face.

"When uncle come?"

Rusty stood on the dog run, shading his eyes. "I see Tom Blessing on horseback, and somebody in a wagon. Let's get Andy out here in the daylight." They moved him to a chair on the dog run, the splinted leg extended straight out. Rusty gave Badger Boy a quick inspection. "Now, you be on your best behavior, and smile."

Badger Boy could not smile on command. He had to feel like it, and he did not feel like it. Anxiety put his stomach in turmoil. His uncle was coming to take him away, farther than ever from the Comanche stronghold. Hampered by his leg, Badger Boy would not be able to put up much resistance. His hands shook. He tried to hide his nervousness by folding them together.

Tom Blessing trotted ahead. The other man hauled up on the lines and stopped a team of mules that pulled his wagon. Blessing dismounted to greet his longtime friends first, then turned to Badger Boy. "Got somebody who's traveled a long ways to see you. Andy Pickard, this here is your Uncle Jim, come to fetch you home."

It was the white man's way to shake hands, but Badger Boy did not want to. He did not want anyone to see how his hands were shaking. He managed a noncommittal nod to the man who climbed down from the wagon and approached him.

Uncle Jim stopped a bit short to give Badger Boy a critical study. He did not speak directly to his nephew. "Can't say I see much of my brother in him. Maybe a little around the eyes. I'm afraid he's taken after his mother a right smart more."

Preacher Webb offered, "I remember his mother. She was a handsome woman." Most women looked handsome to old bachelor Webb.

"If you like them skinny. I always liked to see a good stout corn-fed woman myself. They can usually outwork a skinny woman two to one."

Webb seemed a little put off. "If a workhorse is all you're lookin' for."

"Just bein' practical, Preacher. Life is hard in this country, and a weak woman can't tote her share of the load. Good looks wear off pretty soon. Strong hands and a strong back, that's what a Texas woman needs."

Badger Boy listened intently, trying to understand. He stared at Pickard's face, hoping to see something that would bring back a memory of his father. The voice had a faintly familiar quality, but he saw nothing in the face to bring patchy old images back into focus. He gathered that his uncle was saying something unfavorable about his mother. Though he barely remembered her, he felt a rise of indignation.

No Comanche would insult his own mother or allow anyone else to do so. His face warming, Badger Boy tried to think of the Texan words to express his disapproval. All that came to him was Comanche, and he used that in an angry voice.

Pickard narrowed his eyes in disapproval. "He's speakin' Comanche. How come you-all ain't taught him to talk civilized?"

Rusty's voice was sharp. "It's comin' back to him a little at a time. He can talk some when he wants to."

"And how come he's still got those Indian braids in his hair? I'd cut them off first thing. He may still *be* a heathen, but he don't have to look like one."

Webb said, "We've tried to cut his hair. He won't let us."

"Since when do you let young'uns set the rules? If he gave me any sass I'd quirt the heathen out of him. And I'd start with that hair." He stepped closer to Badger Boy and pulled a skinning knife from a scabbard on his belt.

Badger Boy feared his uncle meant to stab him. He recoiled, wishing for a weapon. Pickard caught one of the braids. Badger Boy realized he meant to cut it off. He jerked free, then lunged at Pickard's throat. He knocked Pickard's hat off before the splinted leg betrayed him. He fell forward, his hands striking the ground first, his chin following an instant later. He was stunned.

He heard Rusty's angry voice. "Back off, Pickard. Leave the boy alone."

"You saw how he came at me. Damned savage, that's what he is."

Webb lifted Badger Boy to his feet and helped him fit the crutches beneath his arm. "The boy's still confused. The Indians have had him since he was little."

Pickard's face was flushed with rage. "There was murder in his eyes. He's past all salvation. Keep him around white folks and he's apt to kill somebody."

Rusty said, "You've got to give him time."

Pickard picked up his hat and dusted it against his leg. "Time for what, to do murder? He'll never change. Maybe we'd all be better off if you'd shot him in the first place and put him out of his misery."

Tom Blessing seemed to swell up even larger than his natural large size. "We'll have no talk about killin'. And this boy is your own kin!"

Pickard pointed. "Look at him. He ain't white anymore, he's got the killin' heart of a Comanche. If he ever was any kin of mine, he ain't no more."

Anger flared in Rusty's eyes. "I've changed my mind. I'm not lettin' you take him with you."

"I don't *want* to take him with me. Think I'd let him slit the throats of all my family? Or maybe ravage my daughters? And even if he didn't, what would my neighbors think, me keepin' a wild savage and callin' him kin? I'd probably have to chain him up like a dog."

Fists clenched, Rusty moved close enough to breathe in Pickard's face. "Then maybe you'd better get in your wagon and go back where you came from."

"I'll do more than that. I'll tell the bluecoat army about him. I'll tell them to come get him and put him on the reservation where he belongs. He'll never be nothin' but a wild Indian."

Webb and Tanner and Blessing all moved toward Pickard. He backed off, his hands raised defensively. His eyes cut from one man to another. "Four against one ain't a fair deal."

Rusty growled, "The others are stayin' out of it. It's just me and you, if you want it that way. The boy's no animal to be put in a cage."

"That's just what he is, an animal."

Badger Boy was amazed that the two men would threaten a fight over him. He had not understood all that was said, but he knew his uncle meant him no good and Rusty had come to his defense. That did not seem logical inasmuch as his uncle had a blood tie to him. This reinforced his long-held acceptance that Texans were a strange lot. Trying to make sense of them could give a man a headache.

Tom Blessing pushed between Rusty and Pickard. His was a formidable presence when he was aroused. "Now, men, you're liable to do somethin' you'll both hurt for tomorrow." He took a viselike grip on Pickard's shoulder. "Mr. Pickard, I think you'd best get in your wagon and start home. It's a long ways to San Felipe."

Pickard stomped toward the wagon and climbed up onto the seat. "That boy's a menace. My advice is that you send him back to them wild Indians where he belongs. Or give him to the Yankee army. They've probably got a place for the likes of him." He whipped the mules into a trot.

Tanner gave Badger Boy a look of pity. "Might be better he *was* back with the Comanches."

Rusty shook his head. "Don't say such a thing where he can hear it. You'll give him more notions like he had last night."

"He's still got them. It don't take a smart man to know what he's thinkin' when he stares off to the north and shuts you out like you wasn't there."

Rusty turned to Tom Blessing. "You don't really think the Yankees would take him away and force him to the reservation, and him white?"

"There's no tellin'. They might. Or they might try to turn him into a bluecoat Indian scout."

"He's just a young'un yet."

"There was many a young'un killed in the war. In any case they won't bother askin' me or you what we think. They didn't ask me my feelin's when they took my sheriff's job away; they just slammed the door. We're a defeated enemy."

Rusty fixed a worried stare on Badger Boy. "Andy Pickard, I don't know what we're goin' to do with you."

Badger Boy wondered, too.

Preacher Webb walked up beside Rusty. "That boy doesn't seem half as disturbed over this as you are."

"He's too young yet to know how it can hurt, not havin' any kin in the world. But I know."

Rusty walked halfway out to the shed and stood awhile, staring at nothing in particular. When he came back, he appeared to have come to a difficult decision. "Tanner's right. You'd be better off runnin' free with your Comanches than penned up with strangers on a reservation. Soon as you're fit to travel, I'll take you."

Webb said, "He won't be able to ride for a while yet."

"We'll wait 'til he can."

"You can't take him all the way back to the Comanches. They'd almost surely kill you."

"How else can I get him there?"

"You can take him as far as the Monahan farm, and maybe as far as the Red River. He can make the last part of the trip by himself."

Rusty frowned, studying the proposition. "In the long run this may be the wrong thing to do, but in the short run I can't see any other way. Bein' a captive on the reservation would be like dyin' an inch at a time."

"Sometimes you have to get through today the best you can and trust tomorrow to the Lord."

Rusty looked toward his field. The crops were almost all in. "Won't be much for somebody else to take care of if I'm gone for a while. Len, you've got nowhere to go. Wouldn't you like to winter here?"

Tanner shrugged. "It's better than campin' in some brushy draw when the northers come down. But hadn't you rather I'd come with you?"

"I'd rather you were here, watchin' over the farm."

Shanty said, "I ain't in no hurry about movin' back home. I can stay here with Mr. Tanner and look after my own place just the way I been doin'."

Rusty nodded his gratitude. "I don't know how long I may be gone."

Tanner said, "It won't matter. This place'll be waitin' for you when you get back. Me and Shanty won't let old Fowler Gaskin tote it away."

In another week Webb removed the splints. "Test your weight real careful and trust in the crutches."

Badger Boy was delighted. He found that he could move the knee a little. Though it caused pain, it was a welcome pain. He had feared that the leg might remain stiff forever. "Pretty soon no more crutches."

"Don't get in too big a hurry. Rome was not built in a day."

Badger Boy wondered who Rome was.

Shanty and Tanner both grinned to see Badger Boy without the splints. Rusty was not smiling. If anything, he appeared regretful. "Why you not glad for me?" Badger Boy asked.

"I am, in a way. But I'm not anxious to see you leave us. I was hopin' maybe you'd change your mind if you stayed here long enough."

"My mind not change."

Getting rid of the splints meant a change of clothes. Webb said, "He can wear somethin' decent now instead of that long shirt."

Badger Boy was ill at ease in the white-man shirt and trousers Rusty gave him. A floppy old hat dropped down to his ears and had to be stuffed out with strips of newspaper to fit comfortably on his head. He kept his moccasins because they fit his feet better than anything the men could offer.

Webb observed him with reserved satisfaction. "Except for the braids, he looks like a farmboy from anyplace. Nobody'd take him for a Comanche."

"I *am* Comanche," Badger Boy declared. "Clothes no change." He turned to Rusty. "When we go?"

"Another week. Maybe two. We've got to know you can stand a long ride."

Badger Boy sensed that Rusty continued to hope he would change his mind and stay. But when the north wind blew at night he imagined he could hear the voices of his People, calling. Nothing was going to change his mind.

Three saddled horses and a pack mule stood waiting. Rusty shook hands with Shanty, then Tanner. "In case somethin' drastic comes up, Len, you know where I'll be."

Tanner smiled. "Tell them Monahan girls Len Tanner said howdy. And kiss them for me, if you've got the nerve."

The Monahan girls. Mention of them brought the image of Geneva, and the pain that went with it. "Kissin' the girls is more in your department."

Shanty was somber. "Be watchful, Andy, and take care of yourself."

Tanner gripped the boy's hand. "You ever get tired of that Indian life, come see me. There's lots more things I can teach you."

"Damn betcha."

Webb said dryly, "I think you may have taught him too much already."

Rusty was able to follow a well-defined wagon trail for better than half the day, but then he had to turn off of it when it shifted due westward. He angled across country, toward the northwest.

Webb rode alongside him, Andy trailing a little ways behind, Indian style. Webb said, "Years ago, the first time you ever rode with the volunteers, we followed Indian raiders along this same route."

Rusty nodded solemnly. "That's right. We camped for the night yonder where the trail crosses the creek. But we're not stoppin' there this time. I've got another place in mind for tonight's camp."

Webb's voice became anxious. "You sure you know what you're doin'?"

"I'm takin' a chance. He's been havin' trouble rememberin'. This may jog his memory."

"Some memories are best left buried."

"Not when you need them to tell you who you are."

Webb shook his head in doubt.

For a time Rusty feared darkness might catch them before they reached the place he was aiming for, but then he saw the line of small trees and knew he had reached the creek crossing he remembered with such terrible vividness.

Andy had sat slumped in the saddle, looking as if he might even be dozing. Now he sat up straight, looking around with serious interest. "This place. I think I been here."

He pointed to a tree that apparently had been bent out of shape as a sapling and had grown crookedly into something like a question mark. "That tree. I remember."

"One tree looks about like another."

"Not that one." Badger Boy's face became increasingly grave. "Bad place."

"Bad? How so?"

"I don't know. Feel bad spirits here. Damn bad."

Preacher Webb frowned. Tanner's teachings had left an indelible mark on the boy's speech.

Rusty said, "We'll camp here for the night."

The lad's eyes looked fearful. "Something happen here. Something bad."

"Do you remember it?"

Andy shook his head but kept looking around anxiously as if he saw or felt something the men could not.

Webb suggested, "Maybe we ought to move on a little farther."

Rusty said, "There's wood here, and water. Been others camped here before." He helped Andy down from the saddle and handed him a long stick whittled into a rude cane to aid him in walking now that he had left the crutches behind. The boy seemed reluctant to venture out.

He leaned on the cane and kept watching as if he expected something awesome to rush at him out of the trees.

Rusty and Webb took what they needed from the mule's pack. Webb built a small fire while Rusty led Badger Boy to a small pile of rocks beneath a tree. Rusty's skin went cold as he remembered. "I came this way once with Preacher and Tom Blessing and a bunch of others, trailin' a Comanche war party. They had taken a lot of horses. But worse than that, they had stolen a woman and a small boy."

He waited, watching for a reaction. He was not sure he saw one. He said, "They killed the woman here. This is where we found her, and where we buried her. We never found any sign of the boy."

Andy remained silent. Rusty was not sure he understood until the youngster asked, "That boy . . . him me?"

"Yes."

"How come I no remember?"

"You were young. And maybe you tried hard *not* to remember."

Andy seated himself on the ground, favoring the weak leg. He sat staring at the unmarked grave. He said nothing. Rusty waited for him to react, to speak, but no words came.

Eventually Webb called, "Coffee's ready if you are."

Looking back over his shoulder, Rusty walked to the fire and poured coffee from a blackened can into a tin cup.

Webb asked, "He remember anything?"

"Can't tell. It's like he's in a trance or somethin'. Indians have got a way of sensin' things they can't see. He may have gotten that from them."

Rusty's cup was half empty when he heard something, a sort of low whine, then a wail. He turned quickly to see the boy bent over, face in his arms, his body trembling. Rusty dropped the cup and hurried to him.

Andy cried out in anguish. "Mama! Mama!" He wept bitterly.

Rusty knelt and put an arm around him. "It's all right, Andy. It was a long time ago."

Preacher Webb tried to squat down on the boy's other side, but his knees were too stiff. He remained standing.

Rusty said, "Seems like he finally remembered."

"A boy so young couldn't stand lookin' into hell. He put up a high wall to shut it out. Now you've made him see over that wall."

Later, Andy stared into the small blaze of the campfire. Rusty and Webb had finally prevailed on him to eat a small supper. "This place . . . they stop here with us. They eat a horse. Then they take Mama . . ." He squeezed his eyes shut. "Many times she screams. I try to go to her, but they whip me. Long time . . . no more screams. I cry, they whip me. I make myself not cry. They don't whip me no more."

Rusty said, "At least now you remember who you are."

"I am Andy Pickard. All the same I am Badger Boy. How can I be two people?"

Rusty had no answer.

Webb said, "I knew your mother, Andy. She was a good woman. Your daddy was a good man, too."

"Not same as uncle?"

"Not the same as your uncle."

"Good. Damn uncle. No like."

Before they left camp the next morning they stood beside the grave. Rains had caused some of the rocks to roll away, and Rusty had replaced them neatly.

Badger Boy was solemn. "My mother . . . why my people do this to her? Why they kill her but keep me?"

Rusty shook his head. "They're different from us. There's a lot us white people will never understand."

"I am white, but I am Comanche also. Why I not understand?"

CHAPTER

SIXTEEN

They were a couple of hours short of the Monahan farm when Andy said, "Something moves, there." He pointed to the west.

Rusty could not see anything. "Where?"

Andy pointed again. "Somewhere there. I feel it."

"Feel it? You sure it's not your imagination?"

Then Rusty saw horsemen straggle from a ragged row of trees a few hundred yards away. He reined up. "He's right, Preacher. See them?"

Webb had his own reins drawn tight. "Not until just now." He glanced at Andy with wonder. "Son, you've sure got sharp eyes."

"Not see." He touched his hand to his chest. "Feel it here."

Rusty asked, "Indians?"

Webb frowned. "Can't be sure at the distance."

Andy said, "Not Indians. White."

"If it's holdup artists, we haven't got much worth stealin'."

Webb said, "We have three horses and a mule. For some, that would be enough."

Rusty studied the terrain. It was open in all directions out to the trees. "If they come at us, this is a good place as any to stand them off." He dismounted. "Come on, Andy, I'll help you down."

The boy seemed unperturbed. "We fight?"

"Not unless they bring a fight to us." Rusty checked his rifle. Webb stood behind his horse, resting his own rifle across the saddle.

The horsemen hesitated briefly, perhaps discussing the situation, then moved cautiously across the open prairie. Rusty counted five. As they closed the distance he could see three blue uniforms. He lowered his rifle. "Soldiers. One's hunched over like he's hurt."

Webb said, "Andy, you might ought to stick those braids under your hat. We didn't bring you this far to have the army take you away from us."

Two riders were in civilian clothes. They sat awkwardly, hands tied to their saddles. Two soldiers held rifles ready for action. The third straightened up with some difficulty. Rusty recognized the uniform of a lieutenant. He lowered his rifle and stepped forward.

"You-all come on in. We're peaceful."

The two enlisted men were black. One wore sergeant's stripes. The officer's dusty coat showed a dark bloodstain on the shoulder. A bulge indicated a heavy bandage beneath it. The lieutenant's face was drained to a pale clay color.

Both prisoners were heavily bearded. Rusty looked a second time before he recognized them. "Pete Dawkins!" The other man was Dawkins's running mate Scully.

The lieutenant glanced apprehensively toward the two enlisted men. He seemed reassured to see they had not relaxed their stance with the rifles. He asked Rusty, "You know these prisoners?" His cautious manner told Rusty it would be better to deny any acquaintance.

"I wish I could say I don't. It's been my bad luck to know them for several years."

The officer eased a bit, though the two troopers remained stiffened for a possible fight.

Rusty asked, "What've they been up to this time?"

Cagily the officer said, "I hope you have no interest in setting them free. My men would drop you in a moment."

"No need to worry about us. I arrested Pete myself once, when I was with the rangers. He was stealin' horses."

"Then he's still at the same trade. He's just not very good at it."

"Who'd he hit this time?"

"A good Union family just north of here. Horse people."

"By the name of Monahan?"

"That's right. The Monahan men fought them off, but this Dawkins wounded one."

"Which one? Do you know the name?"

"Evan Gifford. Are you acquainted with him?"

Rusty grimaced. "I know his wife. Good woman. They're good people, all of them. How bad was he hurt?"

"They said he was wounded worse in the war and got over that. He will recover from this."

Rusty knew his compassion should be for Evan Gifford, but most of it was for Geneva. He imagined how it must have shaken her to see her husband brought in shot, again. "Damn you, Pete, haven't you Dawkinses caused the Monahans grief enough?"

Sullen, Pete Dawkins looked past Rusty as if he could not see him. Scully's head was down, his shoulders pinched in an attitude of despair.

The lieutenant said, "We had some trouble capturing these two. They killed one of my troopers and put a bullet through my shoulder."

Rusty said, "You look like you could use some help. We'd be glad to be of service to you."

The officer's eyes were hopeful. "You say you're a ranger?"

"Used to be. They cut us loose when the war ended. I'm Rusty Shannon. This here's Preacher Webb. The boy's Andy Pickard."

"My father knew the rangers in the Mexican War. He said they would charge hell with half a bucket of water."

"They did, several times. Where are you headed with these two?"

"Back to the Monahan farm to get positive identification."

"The Monahans'd gladly hang Pete for you . . . by his toes, by his neck, any old way you want it done. And I'd be glad to help them."

"Any hanging will be up to a court."

The lieutenant seemed about to slip out of his saddle. He grabbed his horse's mane to steady himself.

Rusty stepped forward to catch him in case he fell. The two black soldiers instantly aimed their rifles at him. The sergeant warned, "Don't you touch Lieutenant Ames."

The lieutenant coughed. "It's all right, Bailey. He's trying to help."

"Yes sir," the sergeant said, but he did not shift the rifle's muzzle away from Rusty.

Rusty knew it would be wise not to make any more quick moves. "Lieutenant, you'd better get off of that horse and rest awhile. When you're up to it, we'll escort you to the Monahans'."

"I've come this far. I can go the rest of the way. We ask for no favors."

"We were headed there ourselves. You favor *us* by takin' Pete Dawkins away." He explained how Colonel Caleb Dawkins, Pete, and some hired help had lynched Lon and Billy Monahan early in the war for the family's pro-Union sentiments.

Ames glared at Pete. "A rebel hangman. He has that much more to answer for."

"You sure you're strong enough to keep ridin'?"

"I'm strong enough. Two Johnny Reb bullets didn't kill me at Chicamauga. I'll survive one from a bushwhacking horse thief."

The lieutenant pulled in beside Andy as Rusty climbed back onto Alamo. "I've forgotten what he said your name is, young fellow."

The youngster gave Rusty a querulous look. "Andy."

Rusty feared Andy's halting use of the language would give him away, but the boy said nothing more.

The sergeant poked his rifle in Pete's direction. "Move out, you backshooter."

Pete growled, "I don't take bossin' from no nigger."

The lieutenant snapped, "Then you'll take it from me. Move out, like he says, or I'll shoot you myself."

Scully was usually a follower, but he started first.

Pete said defiantly, "You ain't hanged me yet. My old daddy's got influence. Ain't no jury around here will ever convict me for killin' a nigger."

The lieutenant said, "It won't be a local jury. You killed a soldier, so you will be tried by a military court."

Clearly, Pete had not considered that possibility. He looked as if the officer had struck him with a club. Scully slumped lower in his saddle.

Rusty felt a glow of satisfaction. "Pete's not worth the price of the rope that hangs him. But I'd be glad to make the investment."

"The government will provide the rope."

"I haven't seen many soldiers yet, but they tell me you-all are spreadin' out across the state."

"As rapidly as we can. It's our job to begin the Reconstruction of this country and to keep the peace no matter how many we have to shoot."

Rusty nodded in the direction of the sergeant. "Are all your soldiers black?"

"A lot of them."

"Then peace may not be easily kept. Black soldiers will be like a red flag to some folks."

"I'm afraid that's the idea, though I am not proud of it. The powers that

be are determined to humiliate the defeated rebels. One way is to place former slaves in a position of authority over them."

"They'll get a bunch of soldiers killed."

"The shameful part is that the officials don't care. No price is too high,
so long as someone else has to pay it."

"You know who'll pay the most. The blacks."

"Yes, just as they carried the burden of slavery."

The Monahan farm broke into view. Pete Dawkins became agitated.
"You ain't goin' to let them Monahans at me, are you? They're crazy . . .
James and that hateful old woman. They'd kill me and not bat an eyelash."

Preacher Webb's face reddened. "You'll not speak ill of Clemmie Monahan in my presence."

"Put a curse on me, why don't you?"

"I am a minister. I do not practice witchcraft. Any curse that's on you,
you've put it there yourself."

With a lifetime of help from Colonel Caleb Dawkins, Rusty thought.

The lieutenant said, "No one is going to kill you, Dawkins, not until
the duly appointed time. Then it will be the army's responsibility."

Andy waited until the lieutenant and the two troopers were out of hearing. He whispered, "Those soldiers, they Shanty kin?"

Rusty realized the boy had seen few if any blacks. "I'd hardly think so."

"Same tribe, look like."

All the way up from Rusty's farm, Geneva had weighed heavily upon his
mind. She had carried him to the extremes of high anticipation, then of
dread. Hearing about her husband's injury had only complicated his feelings. He wondered how well she was coping with what must seem an over-
abundance of bad luck.

He hoped his own hurt had healed enough that he could look at her
without falling apart inside.

Andy was being stoic, but Rusty could see in his weary eyes that his leg
pained him, that only willpower kept him in the saddle.

The lieutenant said, "I've been trying to draw your boy into conversation. He doesn't talk much, does he?"

"The trip's worn him out. He needs a few days of rest before he goes on."

"Goes on to where?"

"Back to his folks." Rusty hoped Ames would be satisfied enough to stop asking questions. He seemed to be, for he fell quiet. He looked even wearier than Andy. The wound in his shoulder was wearing him down.

Vince Purdy, the grandfather, was the first person Rusty saw. Working in the garden, he paused and leaned on his hoe, staring at the incoming riders. Rusty's attention went to Josie Monahan, picking tomatoes and holding them in her apron. She hurried to the new log house.

"Mama! We got company comin'!" She emptied the tomatoes into a basket on the dog run, then turned to watch the visitors' approach. "I see Preacher Webb. And Rusty Shannon. Looks like soldiers with them."

Clemmie Monahan stepped out past the dog run, shading her eyes with one hand. She beamed at sight of the minister and gave Rusty a tentative nod. The smile died as she recognized the two prisoners. Reining Alamo to a stop, Rusty heard her declare, "They'll not bring Pete Dawkins into this house!"

Webb dismounted and embraced her. "Pete's a prisoner. He can't hurt anybody."

"But I may hurt *him*. Put him in the barn out yonder, or the shed. Even the root cellar. But not in this house where I've got to look at him."

The lieutenant gave her a weak salute. "We'll not trouble you with him more than we have to, ma'am. We'll keep him out of your sight."

Clemmie stepped into the yard. Her agitation over Pete turned to solicitude for Ames. "You're hurt. Come on into the house and we'll see what we can do for you."

"I'm obliged, ma'am, but first I have to see to my men, and to my prisoners."

Rusty climbed down. "I'll help your troopers, Lieutenant. You go with Clemmie . . . Miz Monahan."

Clemmie put her arms around Webb again. "It's good to see you, Warren. Come on in. Josie, go unsaddle Warren's horse for him."

Josie's eyes shone as she stared at Rusty. The glow was infectious. The resemblance to her older sister grew stronger each time he saw her.

Clemmie noticed Andy still sitting on his horse. "Get down, boy, and come in." She asked Webb, "Who is he?"

"His name's Andy Pickard. I'll explain about him later."

Clemmie called again, "Come on down, Andy."

Andy seemed shy. "Rusty, I stay with you."

Rusty saw that the attention made the boy nervous. "You can help me unpack the mule, but be careful about that leg." He helped Andy to the ground. He shouted to Clemmie, "We'll be comin' along directly."

As he turned, he found Josie standing in front of him, blocking his way. She asked eagerly, "You stayin' awhile?"

"It all depends."

"You can stay for a hundred years as far as I'm concerned. I was afraid you'd forget about us."

"You know I could never forget the Monahans."

"Does that include me?"

"You're a Monahan."

"But I'm *Josie* Monahan. I'm not Geneva."

He thought he knew where the conversation was going, and he tried to head it off. "I hear Geneva's husband got in the way of a bullet again."

"He's laid up over in the old house."

"How bad is he hurt?"

"He's in considerable pain, but he'll heal."

"And Geneva?"

"She's in pain too, for him."

"A bad piece of luck for both of them."

"But they've got the baby. That makes up for a lot. Geneva had a boy, you know."

"Nobody told me."

Rusty was not sure what he ought to feel. Geneva was a mother now. That put her even further beyond his reach. He had known of her pregnancy since last spring, yet he had never accommodated to the hurt, the feeling of loss. He had tried to put it aside and not deal with it. Now, one way or another, he *had* to deal with it.

Josie said, "You'll want to see the baby. It's beautiful."

"That's no big surprise. It has a beautiful mother."

"And a good-lookin' daddy. It takes two, you know."

"They get along well together, Geneva and Evan?"

"He worships the ground she walks on. And he should. After all, she's my sister. I'll want my husband to worship the ground *I* walk on, someday."

Unexpectedly he felt like smiling. "Then you'd better be careful where you step. There's been horses by here."

Sergeant Bailey asked Rusty, "You know a safe place where we can hold these prisoners for the night? I expect the lieutenant will want to travel on come mornin'."

Rusty pointed toward a shed. "Ought to be a couple of good stout posts you can tie them to. It may not be comfortable."

"They ain't got no comfort comin' to them." Bailey prodded Pete with the rifle.

Pete complained, "You wouldn't tie me to a post, would you? I wouldn't be able to sleep at-all."

Bailey was not impressed. "You'll soon be gettin' all the sleep you ever need. Come on, Private Cotter. I'll let you do the tyin'."

Josie said Evan and her brother James had come across Pete and Scully driving off some of their horses. In the gunfight that followed, Evan had taken a bullet in his arm. Another bullet had creased James's leg. "Didn't hurt him much. It was just enough to make him good and mad. He'd have followed Pete and Scully all the way to hell if he hadn't had to take care of Evan. Lieutenant Ames came along with his patrol and took over the chase."

"Knowin' James, I expect he's still mad."

"Mad enough that we'd better keep him away from Pete Dawkins."

"Pete has spilled it for good now, killin' a soldier. Old Colonel Dawkins is liable to take this mighty hard."

Bitterness crept into Josie's voice. "He's got it comin' to him for the grief he's caused this family. But the word is that he disowned Pete. Drove him off of the place with a black-snake whip."

"You've got to feel a little sorry for the colonel, all by himself now on that big farm."

"The word we're hearin' is that it won't be his much longer. The Federals are layin' taxes on him that he can't pay. They've got it in for him because he preached so strong for the Confederacy and rode roughshod over everybody who didn't agree with him."

"Sounds like some people are still fightin' the war."

"In some ways, I'm afraid the war's barely started. Texas is in for a lot of grief."

Andy's limp was so severe that Rusty told him to sit down. The boy slumped on a wagon tongue, his eyes dull and weary.

We ought to've waited another week before we started, Rusty thought.

He turned the horses loose and fed them. Beneath the shed he found Pete and Scully sitting on the bare ground, their arms behind their backs and tied to two sturdy-looking posts.

Pete complained, "This ain't no way to treat a white man."

Rusty grunted. "It's no way to treat any man. But then, you're not much of one."

Sergeant Bailey's eyes crackled with hatred. "Pity his mama didn't take him out the day he was born and drown him like a sack of kittens. Private Wilkes was a good soldier. Didn't deserve to get shot in the back. Lieutenant didn't deserve a hole in his shoulder, neither. And all for a no-account like this."

It struck Rusty that Pete had better keep still, or he might be in more danger from Sergeant Bailey than from any of the Monahans.

James Monahan strode into the shed, his face clouded for a storm as he sought out Pete Dawkins. He towered over the bound prisoner. "Pete, I ought to cut your throat right where you're sittin'."

Pete's eyes went wide in fear.

Sergeant Bailey said sternly, "He's the army's business now. You dassn't touch him."

James fumed. "I know, and I won't. But I'd like to." He stuck his finger in Pete's face. "I hope they send out invitations to your hangin'. I'd ride five hundred miles bareback to watch it." He strode angrily back toward the house.

Rusty said, "Andy, we'd just as well go, too."

The boy pushed himself up from his place on the wagon tongue. Rusty was disturbed to notice that the braids had slipped from beneath Andy's hat and lay on his shoulders.

Bailey noticed, too. "I've seen some light-skinned Indians. Is this boy half Choctaw or somethin'?"

Andy took offense. He thrust out his chest. "Not Choctaw, Comanche."

The sergeant's suspicions rushed to the surface. "You ain't fixin' to sell him or make a servant out of him, or somethin' like that, I hope. Lieutenant Ames, he wouldn't stand still for nothin' of that kind."

Rusty saw it was too late to put the cork back in the bottle. "Andy's white, but the Comanches raised him. He wants to go back to them. I'm helpin' him get there."

Andy nodded, silently vouching for Rusty. The sergeant still seemed to have reservations.

Rusty said, "I'd sooner you didn't say anything to the lieutenant."

"There ain't nothin' slow about Lieutenant Ames. He sees things for hisself."

"We've been afraid the army might try to take Andy and send him to a reservation, or maybe an orphanage . . . somethin' like that."

Bailey looked intently at the boy. "Long as this is what he really wants . . ."

Andy nodded. "I want to go home."

"Then I don't see where the army's got any business messin' around with him. And I don't think Lieutenant Ames would either."

The other soldier listened but never spoke. Rusty judged that he had come out of slavery, where no one had asked his opinion or even considered that he might have one. Whatever suited Sergeant Bailey would suit him, too.

Pete Dawkins was not so compliant. "Damn anybody who'd send a white boy back to the Indians. Ain't you got no pride in you, Shannon?"

"You're a horse thief and a hangman. I don't see where you've got any call to talk to me about pride. Even your old daddy's ashamed of you."

"My old daddy might be wrong about a lot of things, but he was right about the Confederacy. Now we got Yankee soldiers overrunnin' the country, makin' white folks take orders from niggers. It's a hell of a world the Monahans and all you Union-lovin' scalawags have took us into."

Bailey knelt beside Pete, malice in his eyes. "I wonder, did Cotter get them ropes tight enough? I think I'll take another hitch on them."

Pete cursed. "You damned black crow, you're cuttin' off my blood."

"Be glad I ain't cuttin' off nothin' else. I am sore tempted."

Rusty had to walk by the old log house to get to the newer one where most of the family lived. Andy limped along beside him. Geneva stood in the open dog run. Rusty stopped in mid-stride, looking at her. All the old pain returned for a moment, all the burning inside. He touched his fingers to the brim of his hat. "Howdy, Geneva. You're lookin' real fine."

She really did, he thought. He was not just paying an empty compliment.

She said, "You brought in Pete Dawkins."

"The soldiers brought him in. Preacher and Andy and me, we just came with the soldiers."

"I hope they had to shoot him a little, the way he shot Evan."

"I'm afraid they didn't, but the army'll give him what he's got comin'."

"Rusty, I'd like you to see my baby."

"I was on my way up to the house." He did not really want to see the baby right now. It would remind him too much of old plans and dreams gone irretrievably astray. But he could not refuse her. "Just for a minute." He nodded for Andy to follow him.

Evan Gifford lay on a bed, his legs covered by a blanket. His arm was heavily bandaged. Geneva said, "Look who just came, Evan."

Gifford extended his good hand. "I heard you brought in Pete Dawkins."

Rusty accepted the handshake. "The soldiers did. I had nothin' to do with catchin' him."

"I was lookin' him square in the eye when he did this to me." Gifford lifted the wounded arm an inch. "Another second and I'd've shot him instead of him shootin' me. But at least we gave him a good scrap, and we didn't let him get our horses."

Rusty remembered his earlier favorable judgment of Evan Gifford. Geneva had married a fighter.

Damn it, he thought, why can't I find something to hate about him?

Gifford asked, "Seen our baby yet?"

"Geneva was fixin' to show me."

The baby lay in a small handmade wooden crib. Geneva beamed as she lifted a corner of a blanket to reveal the tiny reddish face. "Ever see a prettier one in your life?"

"I can't say as I've seen that many."

Andy said nothing but observed the baby with curiosity.

Geneva said, "I think he's got Evan's face. Some of the family say he has my eyes. What do you think?"

"I'd have to study him awhile."

The baby's blue eyes were open but did not seem to be focused on anything in particular. Geneva kissed its tiny forehead. "It's about time for feedin'. I'd invite you to stay, Rusty, but it's not exactly a public event."

Rusty's face warmed. "No, I'd expect not." He tried not to allow himself the mental picture, but it came nevertheless.

"Me and Andy will be goin' on."

He paused at the door for one more look at Geneva. She began unbuttoning her dress from the top. He turned quickly away.

Andy said, "Baby has red face. Like Comanche baby."

"I think that's the way they all look at first."

"Pretty woman. Why you don't have a woman?"

Josie stood in front of the new house, waiting. "You saw Geneva and the baby. I can tell by the look on your face."

She did not have to say what she was thinking; he could read it in her eyes. He said, "I never had any claim on her. She's married now, and to a good man. I'm happy about that."

He was not, and he knew Josie knew it.

She said, "You just haven't made up your mind to turn a-loose yet. But you will. And when you do, I'll be here."

"You deserve better than to be a substitute for somebody else."

"I'd settle for that, at first. But I think I could make a man forget he had ever wanted anybody besides me."

"I doubt I'd be that man."

"We'll just have to wait and see, won't we?"

Andy looked from one to the other. It was obvious he had no idea what they were talking about.

The boy was the object of quiet curiosity at the family supper table. It would have been impolite to wear his hat in the house, so the long Comanche-style braids were in plain view. Rusty was not concerned about the Monahans' acceptance, but he was a little worried about Lieutenant Ames. He was haunted by what Jim Pickard had said about the army perhaps forcing the boy to a reservation or into an institution.

Ames put his fears to rest. "I have seen other white children taken from Indian captivity. He is hardly the first. I assume he is some kin of yours, Shannon?"

"By experience, not by blood. The Comanches took me when I was too little to remember much, but I was freed after a few days. Andy spent better than four years amongst them."

"So now you are trying to fit him back into white society."

"No sir. I'm takin' him back to rejoin the Comanches." He watched for what he thought was the inevitable adverse reaction. But Ames pondered in silence, his face devoid of expression that might indicate what was in his mind.

Rusty added, "His blood kin rejected him. The Comanches are all the family he's got. I wish he'd stay with us, but if it can't be of his own accord maybe he'll be better off back where he came from."

"For now, perhaps. But what of the future? The sun is going down on the Indians' free times. They're being crowded off of their hunting grounds. They'll soon be so decimated by war and hunger that they can no longer remain independent. Assuming he is not killed in battle before then, what will become of him?"

"I've laid awake at night worryin' about that."

"But you are still taking him back?"

"I can't chain him up. If I don't take him he'll run away. If he's goin' anyhow, it's best I travel along and be sure he makes it."

"You may not get back. What assurance have you that the Indians will not kill you?"

Rusty glanced at the minister. "Preacher Webb has friends in high places."

"He's riding with you?"

"No. This is as far as he goes."

Webb said, "But my prayers will go with him."

James Monahan had held quiet through the meal, listening, hiding his thoughts behind half-closed eyes. "Prayers are all right, but sometimes an extra gun carries more weight. I'll go with you if you like, Rusty."

"If it comes to usin' guns, a dozen of us wouldn't be enough. No, it's best it be just me and Andy. When I've taken him far enough that I'm sure he can finish the trip alone, I'll turn back."

Josie raised a hand to her mouth. "But you'll be all alone out in Indian country."

"When I was a ranger I spent a lot of time in Indian country."

"At least you had a badge then."

"I never did. There weren't enough to go around. The best I ever had was a piece of paper. Badge or paper, neither one meant a thing to the Comanches. It still wouldn't."

Josie arose and quickly left the room, holding a handkerchief to her eyes as she stepped out onto the dog run. Clemmie pushed away from the table, intending to follow. Preacher Webb touched her hand, stopping her. "Clemmie, I think someone else should go and talk to her." He looked at Rusty.

Rusty remained seated for a moment, trying to decide what he could say. He still did not know as he walked out where she stood. "Josie . . ."

She looked away from him. "I didn't go to act like a baby. It usually takes a lot to make me cry."

"I know, but you're borrowin' trouble that may not ever happen. Chances are I'll never see an Indian. I'll take Andy across the river. From there he ought to have no trouble finishin' the trip alone. I should be back in three or four days."

"When do you plan to leave?"

"Andy's worn out. That leg is troublin' him. He needs a few days' rest before we start."

"A few days." She squeezed the handkerchief. "That's better than no days at-all."

"Josie, I don't want you takin' too much for granted. I like you, but anything past that . . ."

"Past that . . . who knows? After all, we do have a few days."

Clemmie and Preacher Webb walked out. Clemmie raised a lighted lantern to give her daughter a moment's anxious study. "Is everything all right out here?"

"It's all right, Mama. I didn't mean to break up everybody's supper."

"Most people eat more than is good for them anyway." Clemmie swung the lantern. "Come on, Warren, I want you to take a look at that new colt."

Rusty and Josie watched them walk past the shed and out to the barn. The lantern light disappeared.

Josie asked, "When a preacher gets married, can he just do the marryin' himself, or has he got to find him another preacher?"

"I don't know. Guess I never thought about it."

"Been a Methodist minister by here a couple of times lately. I have a feelin' Mama and Preacher Webb will be needin' him. I reckon a sprinklin' preacher can tie the knot as tight as a deep-water preacher, don't you?"

"I suppose it's mainly up to the couple how strong the knot is."

"When I get married, that knot'll be so strong that wild horses couldn't pull it apart."

Rusty bedded down in the barn, along with Andy, Preacher Webb, and Lieutenant Ames. He was awakened in the night by Andy shaking his shoulder. Andy whispered, "Something wrong."

Rusty pushed up onto his elbow, peering into the darkness and seeing nothing. "What?"

"Don't know. Spirits, maybe."

"Spirits! More likely you heard an owl hoot."

He had noticed that owls made Andy nervous. Comanches were wary of them.

He heard horses running. The sound came from beyond the corrals. He flung his blanket aside and pushed to his feet. His first thought was an Indian raid.

Ames awakened. "What's the matter?"

Rusty hurried to the barn door to look outside. He saw nothing amiss, but he was fully alarmed.

He saw a dark figure lurch from the shed and fall to his knees, moaning. Rusty ran to him. Sergeant Bailey rasped, "Tell Lieutenant Ames. Them prisoners have got away!"

CHAPTER
SEVENTEEN

xploring with his fingers, Rusty found the point of a nail protruding through the post to which Pete Dawkins had been tied. Webb's lighted lantern revealed frayed fragments of rope indicating that Pete had rubbed his bonds against the nail until he had worried his way through them and freed his hands.

Sergeant Bailey's head was bloody. He told the lieutenant, "Private Cotter was on guard. Must be he went to sleep, or maybe Dawkins was just too sneaky for him. Busted him over the head with that shovel yonder. Then he busted me before I could get my rifle."

Ames gave vent to strong Yankee profanity. "I ought to've stood guard on them myself. Damned little sleep this shoulder has let me get anyway."

Bailey lamented, "Him and his partner, they got off with our guns."

Private Cotter would never stand court-martial for losing his prisoners. He was dead.

"Probably never knew what hit him," Rusty said.

Bailey rubbed his forehead and looked at the blood on his hand. "Thought he'd killed me too, like as not. He didn't know how hard my head is."

The lieutenant clenched a fist. "That's two of my soldiers he owes the army for."

The commotion had aroused James Monahan. He had hurried down from the new house, buttoning his britches. He found that the fugitives had run the extra horses out of the corral, but the animals had gone only a few yards and stopped. James easily drove them back into the pen.

He declared, "Pete owes this family too, more than he could pay in a hundred years. I'll get him, Lieutenant." He looked at Rusty. "You goin' with me or not?"

"I'll be ready in two minutes."

"It'll take me five. Preacher, how about you saddlin' my dun horse for me while I run back to the house and get my gun?"

The lieutenant protested, "It's a long time until daylight. You can't see the tracks."

"I know the first place he'll head for. If me and Rusty don't find him there, at least we'll have that much advantage when the sun comes up."

The lieutenant argued, "He's the army's prisoner. It's my place to recapture him."

Rusty said, "With all due respect, you're not strong enough to travel ten miles. We'll bring him back for you, either in the saddle or across it."

"I can't give you any legal authority . . ."

Rusty said, "I never officially got mustered out of the rangers. I've got papers that say I am one whether there's still a ranger force or not."

"You'd be laughed out of a civilian court, but a military court might accept it if I testify that I approved." He glanced at James. "How about you? Any history with the rangers?"

"No, I was hidin' from them most of the time."

While Rusty caught Alamo, Webb saddled James's horse. Sergeant Bailey saddled and mounted his own leggy black.

Rusty told him, "Pete fetched you a bad lick with that shovel. You've got no business ridin'."

"I don't ride on my head. You say you know where he's goin'. Let's be gettin' started."

Andy stood watching. "I go, too?"

Rusty wondered about the instinct that had awakened the boy. Perhaps he had heard something but did not realize it. Or perhaps his time with the Comanches *had* given him some sort of sixth sense. "No, you stay here. Keep off of that leg as much as you can, and don't go anyplace 'til I come back."

Rusty and James did not have to compare notes. Both guessed Pete's first destination would be his father's farm. Even granted that the old man had disowned him and thrown him off the place, Pete would probably go there for fresh horses and, likely as not, to take any money his father might have. In times of trouble he had always run to Colonel Dawkins.

They put their horses into an easy lope for a while, then slowed to a trot. Sergeant Bailey was impatient to keep up the faster pace. "I ain't so bad hurt."

Rusty said, "We've got to think about the horses. We're liable to have to chase Pete a lot farther than his daddy's place."

James added, "He's bound to figure somebody is grabbin' at his shirt-tails. He'll be makin' all the tracks he can."

As they rode, James asked Rusty how things were at his farm down on the Colorado. Rusty told him they had managed a good harvest, but what they produced would be mainly for their own consumption. Barter trade was limited. There was no cash market at all.

James said, "Me and Evan spent a lot of the summer catchin' and brandin' wild cattle. Nobody paid much attention to them through the war, so they've multiplied. They're there for the takin'."

Rusty replied, "But they're not worth a continental. About all you can sell is hide and tallow. Even to do that, you have to be on the coast where the boats can load it up."

"That's now. By next year it'll be different. There's a cash market for cattle in Missouri, live and on the hoof. They'll pay in Yankee silver. Soon as the grass rises in the spring, I'll gather everything I can rustle up and drive them to Missouri."

"All that way afoot?"

James nodded. "Before the war lots of cattle were driven to Missouri and Illinois and down to New Orleans. I heard of a bunch that was walked all the way to New York City."

"That'd take time."

"Time we've got a-plenty of. Money we don't. You can't do much farmin' in the winter. You could be out puttin' your brand on unclaimed cattle same as me and Evan."

Rusty found the proposition interesting to contemplate. "It'd be somethin' to do."

James said, "In fact, I don't see no reason we couldn't throw our gathers into one good-sized bunch. By summer we'd be back from Missouri with our pockets jinglin' and the goose hangin' high. Who knows? I might even buy the Dawkins farm off of them Yankee tax collectors."

Rusty found himself warming to the idea, though he knew it was a long shot. "It's a far piece to Missouri. We'd better not be spendin' it 'til we get it in our pockets."

James grinned. "Half the fun is in thinkin' about what you're goin' to do with it. You can spend it a thousand times before you get it. When you have it, you can't spend it but once."

Scully kept looking over his shoulder into the darkness. "I tell you, I been hearin' somethin'."

"You hear your own cowardly heart beatin'," Pete declared. "Ain't nothin' behind us but a whippoorwill and an owl or two. We killed both of them nigger guards. Ain't nobody goin' to miss us 'til daylight."

"Then what are we pushin' these horses so hard for? I can feel mine givin' out under me already."

Pete said, "We'll get fresh ones from the old man. Then we'll head north up into the Nations. Won't nobody find us."

"There's lots of Indians up there. Some of them are apt to remember when we borrowed horses from them."

"Them Indians don't know one white man from another. We could tell them we're Ulysses S. Grant and Robert E. Lee. They wouldn't know the difference."

Scully argued, "As many times as we've run from Indians, I ain't none too keen about goin' up there amongst them."

"We'll stay where the peaceful ones are, the Cherokees and the Choctaws and such. We won't have no truck with the Comanches." Pete brightened as a new idea struck him. "Who knows? We might even set ourselves up as horse traders. Instead of borrowin' Indian horses out of the Nations and sellin' them in Texas, we could take Texas horses up into the Nations."

"Evenin' up the score?"

"Sure. We'd be the Indians' friends. And in return, they'd protect us if anybody came snoopin' around."

Scully was unconvinced. "Sounds good, but there's still many a mile between us and the Nations. How do you know your old man will give us anything? Last time, he was fixin' to shoot us both. If we'd stayed five more minutes, he would've."

"He's about done. You notice how he's shrunk up lately? Losin' Mama, losin' the war, has took the guts out of him. We won't *ask* for nothin'. We'll just take what we want. He can't do nothin' about it, the shape he's in."

"He ain't too weak to pull a trigger."

Pete shrugged. "But the will to do it ain't in him anymore."

Dawn was only a pink streak across the eastern sky when they rode into the Dawkins corrals. Pete's heart jumped as he heard a wooden gate strike against a post, and he brought up the army rifle he had taken from the black sergeant. He saw lantern light at the cow shed and realized one of the house servants was already doing the morning milking.

Pete's pulse slowed. "It's only old Jethro. Ought to be a couple of night horses in the pen yonder. Let's go get them."

Scully had spooked even worse than Pete. "You don't reckon he'd have a gun, do you?"

"Jethro wouldn't know which end the shot comes out of. Get ahold of yourself."

"I guess I'm nervous bein' this close to your old man. I can't help but remember how he was when we hanged them two Monahans. I never saw a man so cold and hard. He scared the hell out of me."

"Used to scare me too, but no more. Ain't nothin' left of him but a hollow husk. A good strong wind would blow him plumb away."

Two horses had stood in the corral overnight. The morning had become just light enough that Pete could see to rope them out, the smaller of the two for Scully, the strongest for himself.

Scully complained, "This one don't look like he'd go all the way to the Nations. Lucky if he gets across the county line."

"Stop belly-achin' and throw your saddle on him. If we come across a better one somewhere, we'll make a swap."

The lantern came bobbing along, its faint light dancing off the corral fence. A dark figure climbed up onto the second rail and held the lantern at arm's length.

"Who you-all? What you doin' there?"

"It's just me and Scully. We're tradin' horses."

"Marse Pete? Old Colonel ain't goin' to be pleased. You remember what he told you, that he'd shoot you if you was to ever come back."

"Well, I'm back just the same. You go on up to the house and roust him out. Tell him I want all the vittles me and Scully can pack behind our saddles. And any cash money he's got in the house. We'll be there soon as we finish saddlin' up."

Jethro climbed down, muttering. "Old Colonel, he sure ain't goin' to be pleased." He went trotting off toward the big house, splashing milk from his bucket.

Pete snickered. "Right there is proof enough that the Yankees are crazy. Settin' the slaves free! Jethro would starve to death like an old pet dog if he didn't have somebody to feed him and tell him what to do. When Papa dies, or when he loses this place, what's goin' to become of people like Jethro?"

"I'm more worried about what's goin' to become of me and you. The army's got a long memory."

"For them nigger soldiers? I'll bet none of them could even sign their name to the company roster. They'll be forgotten about before we get to the Nations."

Scully's nervousness had been getting under Pete's skin. Even after Pete had freed himself from his bonds and had broken the first guard's head with a shovel, Scully had been whimpering that they would never get away, that they were sure to be hanged for what he had done.

"We were goin' to hang anyway," Pete had argued. "They can't do it to us but once."

The second soldier had come awake just in time for Pete to give him the same treatment. Pete then had cut Scully loose, gathered the soldiers' rifles, and saddled the first two horses he could catch. Daylight had shown both to bear the U.S. brand.

"Now we *are* in trouble," Scully had complained. "We've stolen army horses."

"The worst they can do is use a heavier rope."

Pete did not walk when he could ride. Though it was a short distance from the corrals to the big house, he mounted the fresh horse he had just taken. Scully followed along, leading his.

Caleb Dawkins met them at the door, standing in it to block their entry. He seemed smaller now than Pete had remembered him. He had lost weight, his clothes were hanging loose. His shoulders had a tired slump as if he carried a heavy yoke. "I told you the last time, Pete, you are no longer welcome in this house."

"Jethro tell you what I want?"

"He told me. I have nothing here for you. Go, before I summon all the hands and have you forcibly thrown off of this place."

"You'd better not summon anybody you wouldn't want to see dead." Pete flourished the army rifle. "You're standin' in my way, old man. I'm comin' in."

He gave his father a push. The colonel stepped back, almost losing his balance. Pete felt exhilarated at his sense of new power. For most of his life, his father had only to give him a fierce look and Pete would shrink away. Colonel did not even have to say anything.

The old man's already dead and doesn't know it, he thought.

"I told Jethro to sack us up some grub. Where's it at?"

"I told him to forget it. If you came empty-handed, you'll leave the same way."

Frustration boiled into anger. "Damn you, old man, you owe me somethin'. I'm your son."

"A fact that a heavy heart has brought me to regret."

Pete jerked a thumb toward the kitchen door. "Scully, go in yonder and see what you can find. Hurry up." He turned back to his father. "You keep tellin' me how poor you are, but I believe you've still got money stashed away. I want it."

"All the money I had went to the cause. You know that."

"I just know you *told* me that, but I think you lied. Now, where've you got it?"

"It's a sorry state you've come to, Pete, that you'd rob your own father. I'm only glad your mother isn't here to see how low you've let yourself sink. You're on the run again, aren't you?"

"It's none of your concern if I am. You've already disowned me, so what difference does it make?"

"What did you do, steal some more horses?"

"Killed some nigger soldiers, is all."

"So now you've moved up to higher crimes. You've added murder to the list."

"It ain't murder, killin' a nigger. The country's overrun with them as it is."

"But if they were soldiers the Federals won't rest 'til they have a noose around your neck."

"There was thousands of soldiers killed in the war. What's three more, especially with them bein' black?" Pete took a threatening stance. "Now, where's that money at?"

Tears glistened in the colonel's dull eyes. "You'll find a metal box in the bottom of my desk yonder."

Pete took three quick strides and flung open the double doors in the lower part of the rolltop desk. He grabbed the box so eagerly that it slipped from his grasp and fell heavily to the floor. He lifted it to the desktop and nervously fumbled with the latch. He flipped the box open and plunged his hands into stacks of neatly banded currency. He yelled exuberantly. Then the yell broke off. His face fell.

"Confederate money!" He ripped the bands off several bundles before he turned in disbelief. "Confederate, every damned bit of it. But where's the real money?"

"That's it. That's all there is."

Pete let a handful of currency float to the floor. "You fool! You damned old fool! You were richer than Croesus, and you let it go to hell for a crazy notion."

"Not crazy. You wouldn't call it crazy if we had won."

Pete could not contain his rage. He drove his fist into his father's square chin. Colonel Dawkins staggered back, grasping at a chair. He missed it and fell heavily to the floor.

He made no effort to get up. He lay there, rubbing his hand across his bleeding mouth, then looking at it. In a voice so weak Pete barely heard it, he said, "I remember when you were eight, and you took diphtheria. You would have died, but your mother and I would not allow it." Bitterly he shook his head. "Better you had died an innocent boy than to become what you are."

Pete shouted, "Hurry up, Scully. We got to be movin'."

Scully came out of the kitchen with a cloth sack. "Didn't find much. Some bacon, some cold bread. Not even any coffee."

"It'll do. Let's go."

His father still lay on the floor, gasping as if he could not catch breath enough to fill his lungs. Pete barely yielded him a glance as he rushed out the door. He ran toward his tied horse, which took fright and pulled back hard against the reins. Pete had difficulty mounting him. Once in the saddle, he slapped the horse across the shoulders with the long reins. "Settle down, damn you!" For a moment it looked as if the animal would pitch.

"You want to run, you jughead?" Pete turned northward and drummed his heels against the horse's ribs. He had no spurs. "Then damn you, run!" He lashed the animal's shoulders again.

Scully had trouble keeping up. He struggled to tie the sack of food with his saddle strings while his own mount jumped a ditch and galloped after Pete's. "For God's sake, Pete . . ."

Pete let his horse run a mile or so before he slowed to an easier lope, then a long trot. Scully caught up, complaining as usual. "You're goin' to kill these horses."

"Never let a horse think he's boss or he'll take advantage of you every time."

"How far back do you reckon the army is?"

"Wasn't nobody left but that lieutenant, and he took my bullet in his shoulder."

"But there's them Monahans, especially that James. And Rusty Shannon. They'd kill us on sight, give them half a chance."

Pete growled, "I wish you'd shut up. You tryin' to turn me into a coward, too?" Scully's fears were beginning to get to him, though he hoped it did not show. Scully would probably go limp as a rag doll if he saw that Pete was weakening. What little strength the man had left, he was borrowing from Pete.

Pete kicked his horse back into a lope. "Since you're so damned scared, we'll pick up the pace."

After a time he began to sense his horse's stride becoming more labored. He knew he should slow down, but Scully's fear was infectious.

That next hill yonder, he thought. We'll stop and look back when we get to the top of it. If we don't see anybody, we'll rest the horses.

His horse never made it to the hill. He stepped in a badger hole and went down, slamming Pete to the ground. Pete arose on hands and knees, struggling for breath, coughing at the dust in his throat.

Scully was frightened. "You hurt, Pete?"

"I'm all right. Catch my horse. Don't let him get away."

"He ain't goin' noplace. He's crippled."

The animal limped heavily, favoring its right forefoot. Pete was dismayed. "Damned stupid horse!" He was angry enough to shoot the animal, but his rifle lay on the ground where the fall had spilled it. Legs wobbly, Pete walked over and picked up the weapon. He saw that the barrel was clogged with dirt. Firing it would be dangerous. It might explode in his hands.

Scully was long-faced. "What we goin' to do now? Your horse ain't fit to go on. If we try to ride this one double we'll break it down before we get to the river."

Pete quickly made up his mind. "We won't ride it double. Get down, Scully."

"Get down? What for?"

"Because I said so." He swung the rifle's muzzle toward his partner. "Get down."

Scully reluctantly complied. "What're you fixin' to do?"

Pete took the reins from Scully's hand and swung into the saddle. "I'm takin' your horse."

"But what about me?"

"What *about* you? I'm sick of your bitchin' and complainin'. I ought to've left you behind a long time ago."

Scully's voice was near the breaking point. "What'll I do?"

"You'll walk like hell if you know what's good for you. Run, if you can. Or find you a hole somewhere and pull it in after you." He reined Scully's horse around and started north.

For a while he could hear Scully's voice, pleading, as Scully tried to run after him. He put the horse into a lope and soon outdistanced his partner. When he finally looked back he saw Scully sitting on the ground, a picture of despair.

Rusty did not know what to expect as he rode in to the Dawkins place. Several of the colonel's field hands were gathered in front of the big house. They seemed heavily burdened. Rusty nodded at James and the sergeant and rode up to the group. He expected hostility but saw no evidence of it. The men appeared saddened.

He said, "We're lookin' for Pete Dawkins. You-all seen him pass this way?"

One man took a step forward. Rusty had encountered him before, though he could not remember his name. The black man said, "He done come and gone. Him and that Scully. Caught fresh horses and left yonderway." He indicated to the north.

"How long ago?"

The man looked at his companions and shrugged. "A right smart of a while. Ain't got no watch."

"Didn't say where he was headed?"

"Didn't say nothin' much to any of us. Might've said somethin' to the colonel. I wouldn't know."

"Maybe we'd better go talk to the colonel."

"I'm afraid you're too late. Ain't nobody goin' to talk to the colonel, not ever again. He's dead."

A cold chill ran through Rusty. "Pete killed him?" He found that hard to believe, even for Pete.

"No sir. But Pete knocked him down. Colonel never got up. Had him a heart seizure after Pete left. Wasn't nothin' I could do for him. He was gone before I could even finish sayin' the Lord's Prayer."

Rusty looked at James. In view of the long enmity, and the fact that Dawkins had hanged his father and brother, Rusty expected James to be glad. Instead, he seemed regretful.

James said, "I've thought of a hundred ways for the old devil to die and wished for every one of them. But this way never crossed my mind."

Sergeant Bailey had not spoken. Beyond the little conversation he might have overheard, he knew nothing about the violent history between the Dawkins family and the Monahans. He said, "We're settin' here. He's travelin'."

James's voice was bitter. "He'd *better* travel. Just one good shot at him, that's all I ask for. Just one good shot."

Rusty said, "We need to bring him in alive."

"We didn't promise that. You told the lieutenant we'd bring him back either in the saddle or tied across it. If I can get just one good shot, he'll be across it."

Rusty realized James had no intention of bringing Pete back alive. He looked for Bailey's reaction.

The sergeant said, "He's goin' to die anyway. Why not save the army some money?"

Rusty led the way out. The tracks were easy to follow, for Pete had made no apparent effort to hide them. They indicated that his and Scully's horses had run hard for the first mile or so, then slowed. The course was due north.

"Headin' for the Red River the quickest way they can," Rusty speculated.

James nodded. "Probably think they'll be safe when they get to the Nations. But they've stolen a way too many Indian horses. If any of them so-called friendlies recognize them, their lives won't be worth a Confederate dollar."

They came at length upon a crippled horse, standing with its head down. It turned away, trying to move on three legs.

Grimly James said, "Pete and Scully must be ridin' double. They're as good as dead now." He rode over for a closer look at the lame horse. He drew his pistol to shoot it but changed his mind. "I don't think its leg is broke. Just taken a bad sprain."

Rusty removed the saddle and bridle, dropping them to the ground so the horse could move unencumbered.

A little farther on, a man afoot spotted them about the same time they saw him. He began to run, stumbling, falling, getting up, and running again. James spurred ahead of Rusty and Bailey, his pistol in his hand.

"If that's Pete . . ."

Rusty soon saw that the fugitive was Scully.

James shouted, "Stop, Scully."

Scully darted to the left. James fired at the ground just past him. Scully darted back to the right. James fired again, the bullet kicking up dirt at Scully's feet. Scully dropped to his knees and began to cry.

"Don't shoot me! I never killed nobody!"

Rusty thrust the pistol into Scully's face. "Where's Pete?"

Scully had trouble controlling his voice. "He crippled his horse. He took mine and went on. Bound for the Nations."

James glanced at Rusty. "Just like we figured."

Rusty asked, "How far ahead is he?"

"I don't know. An hour. Maybe two."

"By the tracks, he's been pushin' hard."

"He don't care if he kills a horse. He just cares about gettin' away."

Rusty beckoned James and Bailey to one side. "What'll we do about Scully? Anybody want to stay and watch him?"

James said, "I vote we shoot him right here."

Bailey said, "The lieutenant would be right put out about that. Anyway, it's the other one we want the most."

Rusty turned to Scully. "We're goin' on after Pete. You start walkin' back to the Dawkins place. We'll pick you up there."

James protested, "How do we know he won't keep walkin'?"

"Because he knows the army'll hunt him down and hang him like a sheep-killin' dog."

Scully cried, "I never killed nobody. The army's got no call to hang me."

"Then you wait for us at Dawkins's. Maybe Sergeant Bailey will testify for you."

Scully looked at Bailey and trembled. "You'll tell them it was Pete done it all? You'll tell them I didn't do nothin' to get hanged for?"

"I'll tell them what I know. I can't do no better than that."

Following Pete's trail was not a heavy challenge. Even the few times Rusty temporarily lost it, James or Sergeant Bailey quickly picked it up again. There was no mistaking Pete's intention. He was headed for the Red River as directly as the terrain would allow him to travel.

And there was no mistaking James's intention. He meant to kill Pete on sight. The fierce look in his eyes made a chill run down Rusty's back.

Rusty said, "There's no tellin' what we may run into if we have to follow him over to the other side." He had become acutely aware that they had left in too much of a hurry to be concerned about supplies. Hunger was beginning to gnaw at him. He suspected Bailey was running a fever, though the sergeant had not complained. But James had a determined look that said he would follow Pete across hell and out the far side if he had to.

Coming upon a freighter camp, they stopped only long enough to wolf down some cold bread and red beans and sample some weak coffee extended with parched grain. The boss freighter wore what was left of a Confederate uniform. He glared at the sergeant, but James's manner was grim enough to make him swallow whatever negative feelings he might have about black soldiers. His only comment was, "There's some places you won't want to go as long as he's with you."

James said, "To catch the man we're after, we'll go wherever we have to."

"If you catch him, I hope you ain't goin' to let that darky take him in. It's a damned poor white man who'd do that."

James's eyes narrowed dangerously. "When we catch him, he'll be *beggin'* us to let that darky take him in."

As they left the freighter camp, picking up the trail again, Rusty reminded James, "We promised the lieutenant we'd bring him in."

"*You* promised him. I didn't. If we bring him back alive there's too many ways he can cheat the hangman. Bring him in dead and there won't be no appeal, no bond, no parole."

"Even Pete Dawkins deserves his chance in court."

"You still talk like a ranger. There ain't no rangers anymore. You're just another civilian, same as me."

Rusty thought back on his former ranger commanders. August Burmeister and later Captain Whitfield. Badly as they might have hated a man like Pete Dawkins, they would have made every reasonable effort to bring him in for a jury's judgment rather than impose judgment of their own. "I guess I'm still a ranger at heart. If they're ever reorganized, I'll be the first in line to join up."

"Fine, but I'm not burdened with all that righteousness. If I get Pete in my sights, I'll kill him."

Rusty looked to Bailey for his opinion. Bailey said, "All I promised was that we'd bring him back. I didn't say what shape he'd be in."

They came at last to the river. The sign indicated that they were not far behind Pete. Horse droppings were still fresh. The rust-colored river was at low ebb, much of its water running unseen beneath the red sands. Only one narrow channel toward the center of the broad riverbed showed a current. The tracks were deep and bold.

Rusty took a deep breath, fighting back dread. He had crossed this river more than once, farther west. His experiences on the other side had invariably been unpleasant. This time, he felt, would be no different. "All right, let's be after him."

The horses' feet sank deeply into the wet sand and made a sucking sound as they lifted for each next step. The tracks almost instantly filled with water behind them. The three men had crossed only a quarter of the wide riverbed when James stopped.

"Somebody's comin' yonder."

On the north side of the river a rider came pushing his horse for all the speed he could summon. A dozen horsemen were in close pursuit. All seemed to be yelling.

James declared, "That's Pete, by God." He raised his rifle.

Bailey mused, "Looks like he's roused up half the Nations."

Pete plunged his horse into the shallow water. He hammered his boots against the animal's ribs and looked back over his shoulder. Rusty knew he had taken a rifle from Bailey, but he evidently no longer had it. He must have dropped it in his panicked flight.

From across the width of the river Pete's urgent voice rose almost into a scream. "Help me! For God's sake, help me!"

James muttered, "I'll help you. I'll shoot you right where you're at." He brought the rifle to his shoulder.

Rusty grabbed James's arm. "No. The Indians will think you're shootin' at them. There's way too many for us to tackle."

The Indians rode into the river after Pete, rapidly gaining on him. Pete's pleas made Rusty's skin go cold.

Midway across, the Indians overtook Pete and circled around him. Rusty heard one more high-pitched scream. Pete's horse broke free and splashed toward the three men on the south edge of the river. Pete was not on him.

James said, "They're liable to come for us next." He raised his rifle again but did not point it.

Three men might cut down some of the Indians but could not get them all. Rusty shivered, and not from cold.

The Indians turned back toward the north bank, still yelling in triumph. Behind them, half buried in the wet sand, lay a lifeless lump. The river ran redder as it moved around and past Pete Dawkins.

The three watched in silence as the Indians moved northward. Finally Bailey said, "We promised the lieutenant we'd bring him back."

James said, "I'm afraid there ain't enough left of him to *take* back."

Rusty rode out to intercept Pete's horse and lead it to the south bank. It belonged to the army. "We'll need it for Scully." He did not look again at whatever remained of Pete Dawkins.

CHAPTER
EIGHTEEN

Lieutenant Ames walked fifty yards out to meet them as they rode up to the Monahan farm. He gave Scully only a quick glance. "I don't see Dawkins. Did he get away?"

Rusty said, "No, he didn't get away."

"You killed him, then?"

"*We* didn't. He ran into some old Indian acquaintances. They saved the army some time and money." He glanced toward James. "May have kept some other folks out of trouble, too."

Ames gave Scully a second look. "At least you brought back this one."

"We'll want to talk to you about him, but we can do that later." Rusty looked beyond the officer, toward the two houses. "Everything been all right here while we were gone?"

"Fine. Your Comanche boy is a lot stronger. Evan Gifford was out of bed this morning, walking around. And it appears there is to be a wedding in the family."

Rusty blinked. "A weddin'?" Alice was too young. And Josie? Surely not Josie.

"Clemmie and your minister Webb have decided to throw in their lot together."

Rusty smiled. "Been awhile comin'."

James said, "Everybody's known it for a long time, everybody but *them*."

They unsaddled the horses and walked to the house. Andy stood just past the dog run, Josie a step behind him. Andy came down to meet Rusty halfway across the yard. He barely showed a limp.

"I am strong now, Rusty. I am ready to go."

Rusty wished he could think of a new argument against it, but they had already talked the subject to death without any weakening that he could see on Andy's part. Regretfully he said, "All right. Tomorrow, then."

Josie caught Rusty's hands. "Tomorrow?"

"I've argued myself hoarse, but a promise is a promise."

"I thought you were goin' to stay a few days."

"Pete Dawkins spoiled that. Maybe when I come back."

"*If* you come back."

"I will, I promise. I wouldn't want to miss seein' Preacher and Clemmie get married."

"Maybe that'll give you some notions of your own."

It was time to change the subject. "I'm dry to my toes. Reckon there's some coffee in the kitchen?"

"If there isn't, I'll make some. Come on in the house."

Directly across the Red River lay the Indian reservations, but Rusty knew Andy's band was unlikely to be there, submitting themselves to military supervision and agency regulations. They would range free farther west on the Texas plains, wherever the buffalo grazed. Time had come for the autumn hunt to lay in meat for the long winter ahead.

Rusty and Andy were three days out from the Monahan farm. Andy had left his white-man clothing behind. He was back in his Comanche breech-cloth as he had been when Rusty first saw him, bow and quiver slung over his shoulder. The two had taken their time, sparing the horses and watching for sign of hunting activity. They had begun encountering buffalo in scattered herds, but they saw no indications of slaughter. Though Indians typically utilized virtually all of a carcass, they left enough remnants on the killing and skinning ground to show they had been there.

Rusty said, "There ain't really that many Comanches when you spread them around over a country as big as this. And landmarks . . . ain't many of them either. Are you sure you can really find your people?"

"They have many camping grounds. I know them all. You bet I find them."

Andy's use of the language had improved in the days he had spent with the Monahans. Rusty attributed that to coaching by Josie and Alice, but Andy said old Vince Purdy had shown a strong interest in him, too. He had taken the boy hunting and fishing and taught him a little about managing the garden.

"Good people," Rusty told him. "You'd find there's lots of fine folks like the Monahans if you'd give us a chance to show you."

He knew he had little chance of changing the boy's mind, but he had not given up trying. He would not give up until Andy rode off and left him. Rusty had already ridden farther than he had intended, hoping for something that might turn Andy around.

"You enjoyed yourself at the Monahans', didn't you?"

"Much. They make me remember more. I remember better now my mama, my daddy. The Monahans much the same my mama and daddy."

"If your real folks could talk to you now, they'd say you belong with your own kind. They'd tell you to stay with us."

"They come to me in a dream, but they do not talk. My brother come in same dream and say I come back to Comanches. I hear my brother."

Andy pointed to buzzards circling far to the west. This was almost the time of year when they would begin drifting southward, but no chilly northers had prodded them yet with the first hint of winter. The buzzards were at such a distance that Rusty had not noticed them. Andy had a keener eye, or perhaps a more highly developed sensitivity to the subtle messages of nature.

"How'd you know they were there?" Rusty demanded. "I can barely see them even after you pointed them out to me."

"The spirits, I guess. Somehow I know."

"The spirits tellin' you anything else?"

"They say my people somewhere over there. They kill buffalo. They say it is time you turn back, or maybe my people kill *you*."

Rusty's backside tingled. Several times Andy had demonstrated that he possessed instincts beyond Rusty's understanding, an ability to sense presences he could not see.

"I can't just ride off and leave you by yourself."

"But it is what you said. We talked much about it."

"Talkin' about it ahead of time is one thing. But it's different when you get there and face havin' to do it. I'll always feel like I abandoned you."

"Abandoned?" Andy puzzled over the meaning of the word. "You keep promise, is all."

"Damned poor promise, the more I think about it." Rusty looked again toward the buzzards. "Maybe we ought to ride over there and have a look. It may not be a buffalo kill after all."

"I wish you turn back now."

"Just a little farther, Andy."

It was fully a mile to where the buzzards floated about. Two dark gray wolves skulked away as the horsemen approached. The wind carried an unmistakable smell of rotting flesh.

Scattered over a couple of hundred yards of ground were the leavings of a buffalo kill, heads, horns, intestines strung out by scavengers. Straight lines marked where travois had been used to haul the meat and hides. Rusty slapped at flies that buzzed around his face. "Let's get away from here."

They circled around upwind, away from the flies and the stench. "Looks like we've found your people. Or at least where they've been."

"I find them easy now. Better you go."

Rusty felt a catch in his throat as he faced Andy. "This is a lot harder than I figured." He offered his hand. "If you ever decide you want to change, you know where I live."

Andy accepted his hand, then pointed southeastward where scrub timber lined a small creek. "You go to trees, hide 'til dark."

Rusty's eyes burned as he turned away and touched spurs gently to Alamo's hide. When he had first found Andy, he had no thought that he would ever become so attached to the boy. He had assumed that relatives would soon come and fetch Andy away, and that would be the end of it. Rusty was, after all, a bachelor lacking in experience helpful in raising a youngster beyond what he could remember of his own raising by Daddy Mike and Mother Dora. He tried not to look back, but he could not help it.

What he saw made his heart leap. Andy was racing toward him. Behind Andy, Comanche warriors were running their horses hard.

Andy was shouting at him, but the wind tore the words away. The message was plain enough: run for the timber. Rusty put Alamo into a lope as Andy drew abreast of him. He said, "Didn't your spirits tell you about them?"

"Don't talk. Run."

"But they're your people. What're *you* runnin' for?"

"For you. We get to trees, I turn back and talk to them. Out here, they kill you first, then they talk."

The timber was thin, for the creek was narrow and barely running. Rusty slid Alamo to a halt, jumped to the ground, and grabbed his rifle.

Andy looked with disfavor at the weapon. "You don't shoot. They kill you sure."

Rusty knew it would be futile to fight. He might knock down two or three, but they would have him in a minute. Still, he wanted them to know he could. He wanted each warrior to contemplate the possibility that he might be one of the unlucky two or three.

The Indians stopped short of the timber and spread out in a ragged line. Andy said again, "You don't shoot. I go talk."

"You better talk real good."

Rusty could feel the pulse pounding in his neck. Dust choked him. He had to struggle for breath as he watched Andy ride out toward the Indians, one hand held high. The line contracted as the warriors drew back together to receive him. It soon became obvious that most recognized him. They greeted him as one lost and returned from the dead.

Rusty began to breathe easier. But it was one thing for them to accept Andy. He was a blood brother. Rusty was a blood enemy.

The conference continued awhile, then Andy turned and rode back toward Rusty. His face was grim. Rusty's hopes sagged.

Andy regarded him a moment before he spoke. "I tell them what you do for me. They say they don't kill you yet. They want council first."

"What would you give for my chances?"

"Tonkawa Killer is very bad man. He wants to kill you now. Others say wait, talk to my brother. My brother will help."

"I take it your brother's not here, but Tonkawa Killer is."

"My brother hunts. Will be in camp tonight."

Rusty weighed his options and found them dismal. If he broke and ran he would be lucky to get two hundred yards. To fire into that bunch would amount to the same quick suicide.

"I'll go along, I guess."

"Give me rifle so they know you don't fight."

"The minute I turn loose of this rifle, I'm helpless."

"You helpless now." Andy reached out. Grudgingly Rusty handed him the weapon.

"You were right, Andy. I ought to've turned back yesterday. But I just couldn't."

"Not be scared. My brother fix."

Don't be scared. Easy to say for somebody who had never had to ride into a bunch of Comanche warriors with *kill* in their eyes. Rusty's skin crawled as if worms burrowed under it. The warriors quickly closed around him. He picked out one who appeared the most hostile and looked directly into his black and glittering eyes, trying to stare him down. It did not work.

Andy said, "That one is called Tonkawa Killer. Always he hates me. Calls me Texan boy. Wants me dead."

"Damned sure wants *me* dead. Look at him."

"When I break my leg, Tonkawa Killer there. Says it is good I die. Hit me with war club."

"He don't look happy to see you back."

"Afraid of my brother. He thinks I tell."

"You're goin' to, aren't you?"

"First I hear him talk. Then maybe I tell."

The Comanches conferred among themselves. Andy listened without comment. When the conference broke up, four of the warriors left the others and came to Rusty. They pointed northward and motioned for him to get on his horse.

Andy said, "The others go hunt some more. These take us to camp. Wait for my brother."

Rusty noted darkly that Tonkawa Killer was one of the four. "He looks like he might change his mind and kill both of us."

"Too afraid of my brother."

"Your brother must be a curly wolf."

Andy did not know the term. "No, his name means Steals the Ponies."

The warriors did not tie Rusty's hands. In their place, he thought, he might have done so. On the other hand, there would be no point in his trying to run. Where could he go? They would kill him in a minute.

He had been in enough Indian fights that the thought of another held no terrors, but never had he found himself trapped and helpless like this.

Only a damn fool . . . , he thought. Yet he knew he would take the same risk again if he felt it necessary for Andy.

The Indian camp was bustling with activity. Dogs barked at the incoming riders. Women were cutting buffalo meat into strips to be dried on racks hastily constructed of limbs and branches from trees along a nearby stream. Others cleaned the flesh from buffalo hides to be turned into robes and clothing and tepee coverings. The work stopped temporarily as women and children came to stare at the new arrivals. Tonkawa Killer shouted a few angry words. The crowd backed away but did not completely disperse.

Several women came and made a fuss over Andy. Everyone in camp seemed to know him. From their reactions, Rusty knew they had considered him forever lost. Only Tonkawa Killer appeared displeased at the boy's apparent resurrection from among his forefathers. If hate-filled looks could kill, Andy would have died a hundred times.

The women brought freshly cooked meat. Andy accepted it with pleasure. He motioned for Rusty to join him. The meat was not thoroughly cooked, but Rusty was too hungry to be choosy.

The first hunting party arrived awhile before sundown. Andy listened to the conversation, then told Rusty they had located another herd of buffalo, but it was too late in the day to begin a fresh kill. They would return in the morning for the slaughter.

"My brother is with others. He comes soon." Andy had a nervous eagerness about him. He walked to the edge of camp and stared off to the west. Rusty started to follow him but stopped when one of the warriors made a menacing gesture that told him to sit down. He sat.

There was no mistaking the arrival of Steals the Ponies. Apparently he had been told of Andy's return, for he raced ahead of the other hunters and galloped into camp without regard for the dust he raised or the roasting meat that it settled upon. He leaped to the ground. Andy ran to him, showing but little of his limp. They threw their arms around each other.

Rusty had long been told that Indian men were too stoic to cry. He saw that he had been misinformed. Steals the Ponies pushed Andy out to arm's length, tears in his eyes, and looked him over from head to foot as if he could not believe what he saw. Andy was telling him something in a language Rusty could not understand. He pointed to his leg, showing where it had been broken.

Tonkawa Killer broke into the joyous reunion. He pointed his finger at Andy, his voice loud and accusative. Whatever he said, it aroused anger and denial from Andy and a heated argument from Steals the Ponies. Watching, Rusty thought the quarreling men were about to come to blows. Steals the Ponies pushed himself in front of Andy and took a protective stance.

Tonkawa Killer pointed again, said a few words more, then turned on his heel and stalked away. Steals the Ponies shouted something after him, but Tonkawa Killer made a show of ignoring it. Several warriors followed him, evidently taking his side in the argument.

Cold dread settled in the pit of Rusty's stomach.

Andy led his brother to where Rusty sat. Rusty stood up, trying to look as if he had no concern. Steals the Ponies stepped close and lifted Rusty's hat from his head. His eyes widened.

Rusty asked, "What's he lookin' at?"

"Your hair. It is red. My brother say red hair big medicine."

"Is that good or bad?"

"Good for me. You save me. Maybe not good for my brother."

"Tell him I don't mean him any harm. Tell him I want to be his friend." Rusty dropped his voice. "Tell him I want to get the hell away from here." He did not like the look of the conference Tonkawa Killer was having with his adherents.

Steals the Ponies and Andy went into another conversation while Rusty watched their faces and tried to decide whether it meant good news or not.

Andy turned. "My brother and me take you out of camp. We ride with you 'til you are safe from Tonkawa Killer."

"Tell your brother I am much obliged. I'm ready to start any time he is." Right now would not be too soon.

Steals the Ponies said something to one of the hunters. They brought up Rusty's and Andy's horses. Steals the Ponies made a motion for Rusty to mount. He did, quickly.

"Better get me my rifle, Andy."

Andy fetched it but handed it to Steals the Ponies. "Better my brother hold it. Give back when all is good."

Rusty felt naked and vulnerable without the rifle, but this was no time to bog down in details. "Sun'll be gone pretty soon. I want to put a lot of miles behind me while it's dark."

As they started to leave camp, Steals the Ponies turned to shout something at Tonkawa Killer. Whatever he said, it drew a response of raw malice.

Rusty said, "Looks to me like those two are ready to kill one another."

"Comanche never kill another Comanche."

"Never?"

"Never. But Tonkawa Killer says I lie, cause him big shame. Says I am not Comanche. He glad to kill me. Glad to kill you, too. Only scared of my brother."

"Tell your brother I hope he has a long and happy life."

Rusty was relieved when he put the sight and smoky smell of the Indian camp behind him. He kept looking back, half expecting Tonkawa Killer to build his nerve and come in pursuit. He suspected Steals the Ponies had the same suspicion, for the Indian also kept watching their back trail.

They had ridden perhaps three miles, and the sun was at the horizon line, the shadows long and dark across the open buffalo prairie. Ahead lay the same narrow creek in which Rusty and Andy had taken refuge from the first set of hunters. The line of small timber looked black against the sun-gilded grass. Somehow Rusty felt that the creek was far enough from camp to be a safe haven. Beyond it, he should be all right.

Steals the Ponies reined up and spoke sharply to Andy. He handed Rusty's rifle to the boy, who passed it on to Rusty. Rusty saw alarm in Andy's eyes, though so far he had seen no reason for it.

Four Comanches rode up out of the creek bottom and stopped in a line. At one end, Tonkawa Killer brandished a lance.

Evidently they had circled around without allowing themselves to be seen. Rusty shivered. "Looks like he's not as afraid of your brother as you thought he was."

Steals the Ponies said something. Tensely, Andy translated. "My brother cannot shoot Tonkawa Killer. You can."

"There's three more besides him."

"They not fight. Come only to see."

Rusty threw the breech open. He felt a jolt as he saw that the chamber was empty. One of the Comanches had removed the cartridge. He fumbled in his pocket for another.

Tonkawa Killer made a loud shout and came charging. Rusty had trouble fishing out a cartridge while trying to watch the Comanche rushing at him. He saw the lance point bobbing, a dark scalp hanging from the shaft. He knew he was too slow.

He was aware of a swift movement beside him. Andy's bowstring sang as an arrow flew. It made a dull thump driving into Tonkawa Killer's chest.

The lance point dropped, digging into the ground. Tonkawa Killer was jerked half around, then toppled from his horse. The animal brushed by Rusty and ran on.

It happened so quickly that Rusty had time only to draw one sharp breath, then it was over. Tonkawa Killer lay threshing on the ground, fighting against death but rapidly losing. He shuddered and went still.

"My God, Andy."

The three Comanches at the creek seemed ready to charge, but Steals the Ponies rode forward and spoke sharply. The argument was over almost before it began. Two of the Indians dismounted and picked up the body while the third caught and returned Tonkawa Killer's horse. Casting hating glances at Andy and Rusty, they laid the lifeless warrior across the animal's back and led him toward camp.

Steals the Ponies watched them closely, his eyes grave. Andy's hands shook uncontrollably. He could not take his eyes from the small pool of blood where the downed warrior had lain. He had never killed a man. That he had done it now, and that the man he killed was Comanche, filled him with horror.

Steals the Ponies placed his hands on Andy's shoulders. "It is an awful thing you have done, little brother."

Andy wept. "He was about to kill Rusty."

"Now his brothers must try to kill you. You chose a Texan over your own. From now on, you will be an outcast."

"He took care of me. I could not let him die."

"It is easy to watch an enemy die. It takes a brave man to stand aside and allow it to happen to a friend. But sometimes it must be done."

"Rusty risked his life to bring me home."

"This is no longer your home. It never can be again."

"What can I do?"

"You were born white. We made you Comanche. Now you must be white again. By what name does your red-haired friend call you?"

"Andy. The name my mother and father gave me."

"You are Badger Boy no more. You must be Andy now, and for however long you may live."

Andy placed a hand against his heart. "I will always be Badger Boy. I will always be Comanche."

Steals the Ponies embraced him. "To me you will always be Badger Boy. But to the others . . . it will be as if you never lived. You must never return here."

Tears rolled down Andy's cheeks as he clung to his Comanche brother.

Steals the Ponies said, "Go now, you and the red-hair. Go far while the night can hide you." He tore free of Andy. "Go. Forget."

"I will not forget."

"Then remember what is good in Comanche ways, but find your place in the white man's world." Steals the Ponies remounted his horse and rode off into the dusk. Shoulders sagging, Andy watched him until he disappeared.

Rusty's heartbeat gradually slowed to near normal. His mouth was dry as powder. He rode down to the creek and dismounted. He knelt and cupped his hands, sipping from them as the cold water trickled between his fingers.

Andy came down to join him, his face mirroring his anguish. "My brother says I must go with you now." His voice broke. "I go with you, or I die."

Rusty knew it was his fault. Reluctant to cut the tie with Andy, he had ridden too far into a hostile land. "I'm sorry."

Andy rubbed an arm across his eyes. It came away wet. "Too big to cry."

"Sometimes it's the best thing you can do." Rusty hugged the boy and let him cry himself out.

"My brother says I must be white now." Again Andy placed his hand against his heart. "But here, always, part of me will be Comanche."

And you'll never be sure just who you really are, Rusty thought darkly. He knew, for he had been there.

The boy pulled up onto his horse and reined it into the creek. "Soon be dark. We go long way in dark."

Rusty's throat was tight as he moved to catch up. More to himself than to Andy, he said, "A long way. But you have the longest road to travel."

THE

WAY
of the Coyote

FOREWORD

The end of the Civil War did not end the problems on the Texas frontier. In some ways it intensified them. The ranger force had more or
less disintegrated with the slow demise of the secession government. Like the rest of the old Confederacy, Texas was virtually
broke and could not consistently pay its employees, much less meet
all its other obligations. Indian problems remained as troublesome as ever.
During the war, when so many young men went away to the army, many
never to return, the Indians had taken advantage of weakened defenses and
in some areas drove the line of settlement back fifty to seventy-five miles.

Many men, some loyal to the Union and some simply unwilling to
serve in the military, hid out on the fringes of settlements, "in the brush,"
so to speak. A percentage of these brush men turned to outlawry, preying
on weakened communities and outlying farms and ranches with near
impunity because law enforcement had broken down. Whereas rangers
before the war had concentrated principally upon Indians, by the time the
war was over they were spending more and more of their energy and meager resources dealing with outlawry.

Under the reconstruction government imposed on Texas, the rangers
went into limbo for almost ten years. They were replaced after a fashion by
a force known as the state police, formed under the loose supervision of a
federally approved governor. Many of these were honorable men, doing

their best under trying circumstances. However, a minority were corrupt and oppressive, subverting the law to their own profit and purposes, abusing citizens without cause. They gave the state police a sour reputation and made Texans yearn for the return of the rangers under a more benevolent government.

The excesses of reconstruction embittered many basically honest men and prompted small individual rebellions in various parts of the state. The temper of the times made citizens resentful of the federal army, especially black soldiers sent with the express purpose of humiliating the defeated Confederates. Newly arrived opportunists took over local governments and cheated citizens out of their property through fraud and confiscatory taxation.

During this postwar period a new brand of banditry arose led by such notorious figures as Bill Longley and John Wesley Hardin. Many of these men were psychopathic and might have been outlaws even if there had been no war, no reconstruction. Others started out to avenge wrongs real or imagined and became hopelessly entangled in a life of violence. An embittered citizenry often looked upon these men as heroes, rebels still fighting a war long since lost.

The Texas government reorganized at the end of reconstruction. In 1874 it created two battalions of Texas Rangers, giving them at last an official name and their now-famous star-in-a-circle badge. They were better led and more efficient than before. By this time the Indian raids were almost over, and the rangers were able to concentrate on combatting outlawry. They had plenty of it to contend with, for Texas during reconstruction had become a haven for fugitives from all over. Unlike local lawmen, the Rangers were not constrained by county lines and concerns about jurisdiction. Telegraph lines and expanding railroad services gave them better communications and more mobility.

This was the beginning of the glory years, when these hard-riding horsemen and their admirers spawned the larger-than-life legends of the Texas Rangers. As the state's great folklorist J. Frank Dobie said, if some of these stories were not true, they *should* have been.

CHAPTER
ONE

An old arrow wound in Rusty Shannon's leg had been aching all day, but the sudden appearance of Indians made the pain fall away.

"Them damned Comanches," he declared to the boy. "They don't ever give up."

Sitting on his black horse, Alamo, he squinted anxiously over the edge of a dry ravine toward half a dozen horsemen three hundred yards away. They milled about, studying the tracks marking the way Rusty and young Andy Pickard had come.

An afternoon sun glared upon the summer-curing grass. Open prairie stretched to the uneven horizon like a wind-rippled sea. To run would be futile, for both horses had come a long way and were as tired as their riders. This ravine was the only place to hide, though it seemed more likely to be a trap than a refuge.

"They're comin' on," he said. He drew the rifle from its scabbard beneath his leg.

Dread was in the boy's eyes. "It is for me they come, not you. I go to them."

"Hell no! I didn't bring you this far . . ."

He did not finish, for the boy drummed moccasined heels against his horse's ribs and put it up out of the ravine before Rusty could move to stop him. Andy could easily be taken for an Indian. His hair was braided. He wore a breechcloth and carried a boy-sized bow. A quiver of arrows lay across his back, a rawhide strap holding it against his shoulder. He made no move to bring the bow into use.

He stopped his pony and looked over his shoulder as Rusty spurred to catch up. The boy said, "You stay back. They are friends of the one I shot. They want me."

Andy avoided speaking the name of Tonkawa Killer. To do so might anger the dead man's dark spirit and spur it to mischief against the living.

Rusty checked the cartridge in the chamber. "Maybe this rifle can convince them they don't want you all that bad." He stepped down, putting the horse between him and the oncoming Indians. He steadied the barrel across the saddle.

The boy's eyes widened. "Don't shoot. They are my people."

"Not if they're out to kill you. They're not your people, and they sure ain't mine."

Andy Pickard had been taken from a Texas settler family as a small boy and raised Comanche. Rusty guessed him to be around ten, too young to carry such a heavy burden on thin shoulders. His sun-browned skin gave him an Indian appearance, but in close quarters his blue eyes would give him away. They were deeply troubled as he watched the warriors move toward him and Rusty.

"They come because I did a bad thing," Andy said.

He had violated a basic tribal taboo; he had killed a Comanche warrior. Now he was subject to retribution in kind by the dead man's friends and family.

Rusty said, "You had to do it. That evil-eyed Comanche was set on killin' the both of us." His hand sweated against the stock of the rifle. Andy might foolishly consent to yield himself up, but Rusty had no intention of letting him. "Soon's they come in range, I'll knock down a horse. Show them we mean business and maybe they'll turn back."

"They not turn back."

As the Indians came close enough, Rusty thumbed the hammer. The click seemed almost as loud as a shot.

Andy said, "Wait. They are not Comanche."

Rusty's lungs burned from holding his breath. He gasped for air. "Are you sure?"

"They are Kiowa."

Rusty wiped a sweaty hand against his trouser leg. "I don't see where that's any improvement." Kiowas shared the Comanches' implacable hostility toward Texans. Rusty had seen people killed by Kiowas. They were no less dead than those who fell to Comanches.

The boy said, "Kiowas no look for me. I go talk."

He did not ask for Rusty's approval. He raised one hand and rode forward. Surprised, the Kiowas paused for council. Rusty quickly remounted and caught up to Andy.

"Damn it, young'un, you're askin' to be killed."

The boy did not respond. Instead, he began moving his hands, talking in sign language. The motions took Rusty by surprise, but they amazed the Indians more . . . a white boy communicating in the silent language common to the plains tribes. Rusty kept a strong but nervous grip on the rifle, careful not to point it directly at the Indians. He was keenly aware that several stared at him with hating eyes that bespoke murder. It would not take much to provoke the thought into the deed.

One Kiowa responded with hand signals. A single thick braid hung down over a shoulder, past his waist, the hair augmented by horsehair and fur. The other side was cut short to show off ear pendants of bear claws and a shining silver coin. Rusty sensed a gradual easing of the Indians' attitude. He saw grudging acceptance, though he perceived that some warriors remained in favor of hanging his scalp from a lodge pole. Red hair was a novelty to them.

He said, "They must think it's strange to see a white Comanche boy."

"There are others. Not just me."

Like Andy, numbers of Texan and Mexican children had been taken captive and raised Comanche. Such forced adoption was one way the tribe offset losses caused by war and accidents of the hunt.

Andy said in a low voice, "I tell them you are my white brother. We been to trade with the Comanche."

"Let's bid them good-bye before their thinkin' changes."

The boy resumed the sign talk. The only part Rusty understood was when he pointed southeastward and indicated that to be their chosen direction. The Kiowas quarreled among themselves. Rusty could tell that a couple of the youngest favored freeing the boy but killing his white brother. Fortunately the older warriors prevailed.

Andy said, "No look back." He set his pony to moving in a walk to demonstrate that he had no fear.

Rusty forced himself to stare ahead and not turn in the saddle. He wished he could be certain the two hotheads were not following. After a couple of hundred yards Andy let his pony move into an easy trot. Rusty sneaked a quick glance. He was relieved to see that the Kiowas were riding westward, all of them.

He wiped his sleeve across his face to take up the cold sweat that stung his eyes. "You sure pulled our bacon out of the fire that time."

"Bacon? We got no bacon." Andy's puzzled look showed that he did not understand. Many expressions went over his head. He had only lately begun hearing the English language again after years of exposure only to Comanche.

Rusty said, "We've still got a ways to go before we can take an easy breath. We'd better ride into the night as far as these horses can travel."

Andy looked back over his shoulder toward the broad prairie and everything he was leaving behind. He appeared about to weep.

Gently Rusty said, "I know it's hard. Go ahead and cry. Ain't nobody around to hear you but me."

Andy squared his shoulders. "I would hear."

The Red River was behind them, but caution prevailed upon Rusty to stop occasionally and survey their back trail. The boy asked, "You think they follow so far?"

Rusty saw no sign of pursuit, yet experience had taught him not to place too much trust in appearances.

"Depends on how bad they want you."

Another long look to the north showed him nothing to arouse anxiety, at least no more than he had carried in the pit of his stomach during the days since he and Andy had hurriedly left the Comanche encampment. They had been two solitary figures on the open plains. The Llano Estacado was a haven to the horseback tribes but remained a forbidding mystery to white Americans, a blank space on their maps. It was a vast country of few landmarks and few tracks. It could swallow up a stranger, lose him in its immensity, and doom him to slow starvation. But for several years it had been the only home Andy Pickard could remember. He kept looking behind him.

"Back there . . . I belong."

Rusty understood the boy's painful dilemma. "Them Comanches would kill you in a minute."

The thin voice quavered. "Most are friends."

"It don't take but one enemy to kill you." Rusty had been through this argument several times during their flight. He knew the boy remained strongly tempted to turn about and take his chances. Perhaps at his age he did not fully comprehend the finality of death.

Rusty had seen much of death in his thirty-something years on the Texas frontier. Comanches had killed his own parents and had taken him when he was but three or four years old. From that point his experience had diverged from Andy's, however. Texan fighters had recovered Rusty a few days after his capture. He had been raised by a childless pioneer couple and given their name, Shannon, because he knew no name of his own.

Years later he had followed his foster father's example and attached himself to a frontier company of rangers patrolling the outer line of settlements, guarding against Comanche and Kiowa incursion. He had remained a ranger volunteer during the four years of civil war. That service had exempted him from joining the Confederate Army and fighting against the United States flag old Daddy Mike Shannon had defended with his blood in conflict against Mexico.

Hardship had robbed Rusty of his youth, giving him the look and bearing of a man ten years older. His hair was the color of rusted metal, untrimmed in weeks and brushing uncombed against a frayed collar. A heavy growth of red-tinged whiskers hid most of his face, causing a deceptively fierce look belied by the gentleness in his voice. "It's tough to turn your back on everything you've known, but you're white. You belong amongst your own kind."

Andy placed his hand against his heart. "Here, inside, I am Comanche."

Another boy might cry, but Andy's Indian-instilled pride would not allow him to give way to that much emotion, not outwardly. Inwardly he could be dying and not show it. Even when Rusty had first found him lying flat on the ground with his leg broken and given up for dead, Andy had not cried.

Rusty said, "You'll feel better when we get to some friendly faces."

Andy clenched his teeth and looked away.

Dusk revealed a campfire several hundred yards ahead. Rusty's first instinct was to circle widely around it, but he reasoned that Indians were unlikely to build so visible a fire this near to settlements.

Andy asked, "The Monahan farm?" That had been Rusty's first announced goal.

"We're not far enough south yet."

If it were still wartime Rusty would suspect that the camp belonged to deserters from the Confederate Army or men trying to escape conscription officers. But most of the hideout brush men had dispersed peacefully when war's end removed any reason for isolating themselves.

He said, "I'd pass them by, but we ain't eaten a fit meal in days. Maybe they even got coffee."

He recognized a chance that these might be outlaws. Defeat of the Confederacy had left legal authority badly diminished at state and local levels. The wartime brush men had grown accustomed to living like coyotes, constantly on the dodge from Confederate authorities. Now a minority had turned to raiding isolated farms and villages, stealing horses and whatever else came easily to hand. The risk of punishment was slight where law enforcement was scattered thin and rendered toothless by lack of funds. The Federal occupation forces appeared more interested in punishing former Confederates than in suppressing the lawless or pursuing hostile Indians.

Rusty made out the shapes of two wagons. These gave him reassurance, for outlaws were not likely to encumber themselves with anything that moved so slowly. He reined up fifty yards short of the fire to shout, "Hello the camp."

Several men cautiously edged away from the firelight. An answer came. "Come on in."

Rusty sensed that several guns were aimed at him. He kept his hands at chest level, away from the pistol at his hip and the rifle in its scabbard. "We're peaceable."

"So are we." The reply came from someone who moved back into the flickering glow of the fire, holding a rifle at arm's length. Once Rusty could see the lanky, hunched-over form and the long unkempt beard, he was reasonably sure he had encountered the man before.

He asked, "Don't I know you from around Fort Belknap?"

The man peered closely at Rusty. "I've freighted goods over that way."

"I was in the ranger company. Served under Captain Whitfield. And before him, Captain Burmeister."

"I remember Whitfield. A good and honest man. But there ain't no rangers since the war ended. What you doin' way off out here in the edge of Indian country?"

"Dodgin' Indians."

"Us, too. We're huntin' buffalo. Saltin' humps and tongues to barter back in the settlements." Barter was almost the only method of exchange in Texas since war's end. Spendable money was as scarce as snow in August. The man turned his attention to Andy, his eyes narrowing in suspicion. "What you doin' with that Indian kid?"

"He's not an Indian. They stole him when he was little. Tried makin' him into a Comanche."

"He's got the look of one. I don't know as I'd want to run into him in the dark."

"He's a good kid. Just not quite sure yet who or what he is."

"I'd put some white-boy clothes on him as quick as I could. Else somebody might shoot him for an Indian. Rescued him from the Comanches, did you?"

"It's more like he rescued me. You-all got any coffee? I'd lease my soul to the devil for some fixin's like we had before the war."

"We've got a little coffee cut with parched grain. Best we can do. Mix it with whiskey and it ain't too awful. Got some beans and buffalo hump, too. You look kind of slab-sided."

"Much obliged. We're as hollow as a gourd."

Andy had not spoken. He dug into his supper like a starved wolf.

The hunter watched him with interest. "The boy's got the manners of a wild Indian, all right." The comment was matter-of-fact, not judgmental. "You've got a lot to unlearn him before you can make him white again. He some kin to you?"

"No, the only kin we've found is an uncle. He looked Andy over and turned his back on him."

"Probably figured he was too far gone to civilize. You figurin' to finish raisin' him?"

"Somebody's got to."

"I wouldn't want the responsibility. How did he fall into your lap?"

"He came down into the settlements on a horse-stealin' raid."

"That young'un ain't old enough."

"He sneaked off and followed the raidin' party. Didn't let them see him 'til it was too late to send him back. Horse fell on him and broke his leg. That's the way I found him."

"He looks all healed up now."

"We kept him 'til he was, me and some friends of mine. But he was homesick for the Comanches. If I didn't take him back he was fixin' to slip off and go anyway. So, bad as I hated to, I took him."

"What's he doin' here now?"

"A few of the tribe weren't happy to see him back. He had to kill one so we could get away."

The hunter frowned darkly. "Awful young to have blood on his hands. It's hard to wash off."

"Wasn't none of his choosin'."

"If I was you, I'd turn him over to the Yankee army. I've heard they've got schools for Indian boys back East someplace."

"But he's white. Reckon I'll keep him and do the best I can."

"I'm glad it's you and not me."

Rusty explained, "When I look at him I see what I could've been. The Comanches stole me once, just like him. If the Lord hadn't been lookin' my way, I'd be Comanche now myself. Or dead."

Rusty sipped with pleasure the mixture of bad coffee and bad whiskey. "Andy's got a long, twisty road ahead of him. But I want to give him the same chance I had."

The hunter said, "I ain't heard him speak. Has he forgot how to talk English?"

"It's comin' back to him. He just needs time."

"I've known a couple of boys the Indians taken and kept for years. Never could purge all the coyote out of them. They was like a broke horse that has to pitch once in a while no matter how long he's been rode."

"Nothin' comes easy if it's worth anything."

"Just so you don't expect too much. You're dealin' with damaged goods." The hunter started to tip the whiskey jug, then remembered his manners and offered it to Rusty. "You'll probably need a lot of this before you get that boy raised. You got a woman?"

"I'm not married."

"Too bad. Sometimes a woman's influence can help in tamin' a wild one. Got any prospects?"

"The one I wanted married somebody else."

When Rusty and Andy had finished supper, the hunter said, "You-all are welcome to spend the night. Just one thing . . . are them Comanches huntin' for this boy?"

"There's a chance a few still are." Rusty sensed what was on the man's mind. Andy's being here might put the camp in jeopardy. "Maybe it's best we move on a little farther."

"No, you-all stay. We'll double up the guard. If there's any Indians prowlin' about they're apt to give us a try whether the boy is here or not. We won't let him fall back into their hands."

Rusty warmed with gratitude. These men were strangers, yet they were offering an orphan boy their protection. "I'm much obliged."

The hunter shrugged. "We've got the Federals comin' at us from one side and Indians from another. And scallywags that dodged the fightin', pushin' and shovin' now to get onto the Union tit. Us old Texas rebels have got to stick together."

Rusty had never considered himself a rebel. On the contrary, he had harbored a quiet loyalty to the Union all through the war, though it would have been dangerous to make an open display of that loyalty. Hundreds who did so had died at the hands of Confederate zealots. He saw no point in mentioning this now that the war was over. They were all considered Americans again, though many had lost their basic legal rights of citizenship, including the vote.

He said, "I'll stand my share of the guard."

"Figured that. I wouldn't expect no less out of a ranger." The hunter grunted. "You reckon we'll ever get the rangers back again?"

"Not anytime soon. The Federals have a hard opinion of anything they think smells Confederate. They bristle up at the thought of Texans ridin' in bunches and packin' firearms."

The night passed without incident. Rusty and Andy ate breakfast with the hunters. As Rusty saddled his horse, the leader jerked his head, summoning him to one side.

"You remember me tellin' you about them two boys that came home after years amongst the Indians? One of them eventually went to the bad. Killed a man and tried to run off back to the Comanches. There wasn't no civilizin' him. Posse had to shoot him like a hydrophoby dog."

"It won't be like that with Andy."

"Don't take him for granted. Watch him, or one mornin' you might wake up with your throat cut."

The hunters spared Rusty enough meat and salt to last until he and Andy reached the Monahan family's farm. He intended that to be the first stop on the long trip back to his own place down on the Colorado River. Andy seemed increasingly concerned after they resumed their journey.

"The man say maybe somebody shoot me for Indian."

"Nobody's fixin' to shoot you. Just the same, I'll be glad when we get you into different clothes. And we need to cut that hair."

Andy touched one of the long braids that hung down his shoulders. "Cut? What for?"

"They draw attention. Lots of folks don't trust anybody that looks different." The hunter's warning weighed heavily on Rusty's mind.

"I *am* different. I am not ashamed."

"I'm not sayin' you should be. Ain't your fault the Comanches stole you."

"It was a good life."

"But not the life you were born to. Me and Daddy Mike and the preacher trailed after the war party that stole you, us and a bunch of volunteers. We never could catch them. It was like the wind picked them up and carried them away. I don't suppose you recollect much about that."

"A little only."

It was well that the boy did not remember much. Rusty remembered more than he wanted about the long pursuit, the shock of first blood when they came upon Andy's kidnapped mother cruelly butchered on the trail. Before that, he had never seen a person dead at Indian hands. In the years since, he had seen many. Back East there had been but one war, between Confederates and the Union. Here on the Texas frontier there had been another, against Comanche and Kiowa. He was grateful the Eastern war was over. He could see no end to the one closer at hand.

Through no fault of his own Andy was caught in the middle, whipped about like a leaf in a whirlwind. Rusty had experienced a similar inner conflict, a similar confusion of loyalties during the war between the states.

He said, "It's not like you've got any druthers. At least you know what your real name is. I had to borrow mine."

Andy fingered the braid again. Sternly he said, "I will wear white-man clothes. I will talk white man's talk. But I do not cut my hair."

CHAPTER

TWO

usty heard cattle bawling. The sound told him they were being gathered or driven in a place where he would not expect that to happen. Landmarks indicated he was yet north of the Monahan farm. This was still buffalo range on those occasions when migration drifted the grunting herds across it. They grazed the grass short, their sharp cloven hooves crushing its remnants into the ground, to be revived when the rains came again. It was home to deer in the brushy draws and antelope on the open prairie. Now and then a band of wild horses passed through, led by a blood-bay stallion, ranging free. It also provided forage for scatterings of cattle lost or abandoned during the war years, the offspring unbranded and subject to claim by anyone willing to gather them.

Up to now, few settlers had risked their lives by staking claims this far beyond white neighbors. That would invite a visit by war-painted horsemen from the plains. But more people would be coming soon, Rusty thought. Thousands uprooted by war were seeking new homes and a new beginning. After four years of agonizing conflict between North and South, the frontier would seem a lesser hazard.

Dust swirled over three riders pushing sixty or seventy cattle toward a line of brush that marked the course of a sometime creek. Rusty first thought the men might be cattle thieves, but reflection dispelled that notion. Cattle were not worth stealing these days. They had multiplied to a point of becoming more nuisance than asset, difficult to sell because few people had money to pay even if they wanted them. They were plentiful enough that anyone needing beef and willing to risk exposure to occasional Indian raiding parties could venture out and get it at no cost beyond the effort expended in the chase.

At sight of Rusty and the boy the riders quickly pulled together in a defensive stance. They eased as the two approaching horsemen drew near enough for recognition. James Monahan rode forward while the other two held the herd together. He was of about Rusty's age, a little to one side or the other of thirty. Like Rusty he could have been taken for forty. The harshness and toil of frontier farm life, compounded by war, had left his face deeply lined, his eyes haunted. He sat soldier-straight in the saddle, however, in an attitude that could be taken for either pride or defiance. Knowing James, Rusty considered it an even mixture.

Rusty was not disappointed by James's noncommittal nod. Their relationship at times had been strained by differing attitudes toward the law. James said, "About decided the Comanches had put you under." His gaze shifted to the boy. "Thought you was takin' Andy back to his Indians."

Rusty rubbed his beard. It had begun to itch. He needed a bath and a shave. "Things came unraveled. Looked for a while like neither one of us was goin' to make it out."

James stared at the boy and grunted. "It was a mistake takin' him back in the first place. He never belonged with the Comanches."

"It was what he wanted."

"A boy his age don't know what's best for him. That's the reason there's mamas and daddies."

"Andy tried to fit into white-man ways, but he'd been with the Indians too long."

"Think it'll be any easier for him now?"

"Maybe not, but the bridges are burned down behind him."

James turned to the sad-faced boy, and sympathy edged into his eyes. "Sorry things didn't work out, Andy. You're welcome to stay with us Monahans as long as you want to. My sisters were considerable taken with you. So was my mother."

Rusty said, "We'll stay a few days to rest our horses, then we'll go on down to my place. The farther I get him away from the Comanches, the better."

"You think they'd come for him?"

"Several of them were itchin' to cut his throat. We had to leave there in a hurry."

"What could a kid like him do to make them that mad? It's not like he would've killed anybody."

"That's the whole trouble. He did."

James blinked, staring hard at the boy.

Rusty said, "He did it to stop one of them from killin' me."

James's expression turned to approval, something Rusty had found that he did not give lightly. "Then I reckon he'll do to keep." He surprised Andy by gripping his hand. "You're not the first who's had to come runnin' to help Rusty Shannon out of a tight spot. He's got a knack for fallin' into holes he can't climb out of by himself."

Rusty said, "I've pulled *you* out of one or two." He nodded in the direction of the herd. "What're you doin' with those cattle? You couldn't swap the whole bunch for a sack of tomcats."

"Not here, but we're figurin' to take them where they *are* worth somethin'. We're gatherin' as many as we can, me and Granddad and Evan Gifford. Come spring I'll get some help and drive them to Missouri. They ought to fetch a bucketful of Yankee silver."

Rusty admired the spirit. Some people were content to sit around and bemoan what the war had cost them. James Monahan was not. Even if the plan did not work out as hoped, it was better to be busy doing something constructive than to idle away the coming winter indulging in self-pity and recriminations.

James said, "The boy's goin' to need a lot of learnin'."

"I'll school him the best I can."

"Teach him all you know. That oughtn't to take long."

"Mainly what I know is rangerin', and I'm a fair hand with a plow. I'll teach him what Daddy Mike taught me."

"You think you can turn an Indian boy into a farmer? I can't see you bein' content to stay on a farm yourself, not for the rest of your life. You've spent too much time on horseback."

"There's no call these days for rangers, so I'll be a farmer."

"The day the call ever comes, you'll drop that plow like it was on fire."

Rusty did not argue the point, but he could not foresee that call coming anytime soon. To the authorities his ranger service branded him a Confederate, though a strong reason for his being in that service had been his loyalty to the Union. To have declared that loyalty at the time could have caused him to be lynched, as James Monahan's Unionist father and brother had been lynched early in the war.

James said, "If you're not in a hurry, you're welcome to ride along with us to the farm. These cattle move slow, so we'll be out another night."

Rusty looked back. He saw no one. "It'll do our horses good to slow down."

"Won't hurt you none either. You look like a hundred miles of washed-out trail." James turned toward the cattle. Rusty and Andy followed.

They came first to Vince Purdy, James's grandfather, a Texan carved out of the old rock of revolution and the Mexican War, bent now from years of labor and hardship but stubbornly refusing to let anything break him. His knotty old hand still took a steely grip that threatened to crack Rusty's knuckles. "I'd given up on you," he said. "Figured the next time I seen you we'd both be playin' a harp."

"I can't even play a fiddle."

Purdy's pale eyes fastened on Andy. "Couldn't you find his people?"

"We found them, but we couldn't stay. It's a long story."

The old man looked southward. "We'll have plenty of time to hear it before we get these cattle home." Several had their forelegs hobbled with rawhide strips so they could not run. "They're wild. They want to turn and go back to where we brought them from."

Like Andy, Rusty thought. "It's a wild country."

"It won't always be. I'd give a lot to be a young man again . . ." Purdy stared off toward the horizon, his aging eyes reflecting youthful dreams still alive and stirring.

The other man was Evan Gifford, married to James's sister Geneva. Rusty had wanted to marry Geneva himself but had waited too long to ask her. Seeing Gifford always stirred up an aching sense of loss. Still, he would reluctantly admit that her choice had been a good one. Gifford, badly wounded in Confederate service and sent home to Texas to die, had fought his way back to his feet. The Monahan family had come to regard him as one of their own. Like them, he accepted hard work and frontier hazards as challenges to be met head-on. Rusty could understand how Geneva had become attracted to him. In his defiant outlook and unflinching convictions, he reminded Rusty of Geneva's murdered father. James and Evan Gifford could have been brothers instead of brothers-in-law.

Rusty forced the regrets aside and shook hands. "How's the baby, Evan?"

"Stout. You can hear him holler for half a mile." He glanced at Andy, but unlike James and Purdy, he asked no questions. He accepted what his eyes told him. "Geneva was uneasy about you . . . we both were. Preacher Webb and us, we prayed for you and the boy."

Rusty feared Evan could read in his eyes what was in his mind. "I didn't ask James about the rest of the family." It was an oblique way of asking about Geneva without directly mentioning her. Evan had never shown signs of jealousy, and Rusty did not want to stir up any.

"They're fine. We're about finished gatherin' the crops. Gettin' fixed for the winter."

"So now you're puttin' the Monahan brand on these cattle."

"It's better than sittin' around worryin' about the Yankee occupation."

"Maybe you're so far out on the edge that the Yankees won't bother you much." Rusty doubted they would trouble the Monahans anyway. Their loyalty to the Union had been well known during the war. Too well known, for it had killed the father and one son and had driven James into exile west of the settlements. Evan was potentially vulnerable, however, because he had served in the Confederate Army.

A horseman alone could travel forty or fifty miles in a day, depending upon how hard he wanted to push and how much he was willing to punish his horse. A herd of cattle did well, however, to move ten or twelve. The day was well along when Rusty and Andy joined the drive, but James pushed a few more miles before he called a halt.

"If we get them wore-out enough, maybe they won't feel like runnin' tonight," he said. "By tomorrow night we'll have them at home."

Rusty asked, "Once you get them there, what's to keep them from driftin' right back where you found them?"

"Hired a couple of ex-soldiers to see that they don't go far."

"How can you afford to pay anybody?"

"Can't. Times are so hard that some people are glad to work for three meals and a dry place to roll out their blankets. I promised them a share of whatever we get for the cattle next year."

"And if you get nothin'?"

"They won't be any worse off than we are."

James's shirt was a case in point. It had been mended so many times that it was hard to discern which parts were original material and which were patches. "Stupid damned war," James said. "All them fiery speeches, all them bands a-playin'. Look what it brought us to."

Rusty countered, "I was no more in favor of it than you were. I thought Texas already had war enough."

James cast a glance toward Andy, riding beside Vince Purdy on the other side of the herd. The boy and the old man had struck up a friendship during Andy's brief stay at the Monahan farm before going north to seek his adopted people. "How likely are those Comanches to come huntin' for Andy?"

"I think we threw them off of the trail. They'll have no idea where to look."

"You said he killed somebody."

Rusty shifted in the saddle, resting one hip while he placed extra weight on the other. The old arrow wound in his leg often pained him when he became tired. "You remember me tellin' you about the raid he went on with his Indian brother and some others down to the Colorado River country? There was a warrior by the name of Tonkawa Killer. He hated Andy for bein' white. When Andy's horse fell on him and broke his leg, Tonkawa Killer tried to finish him. Thought he had done it.

"In the scatteration after the raid, they couldn't find Andy. Tonkawa Killer told them he had seen the kid turn coward and run away. When Andy showed up with me at the Comanche camp he made Tonkawa Killer out a liar. You never saw a madder Indian. Andy had no choice but to put an arrow in him. Now he's got Comanche blood on his hands. It's like he's been orphaned a second time."

James listened soberly. "He'll feel better after Mother Clemmie fills him up with hot vittles and fresh milk."

"It'll take more than good cookin'. What he really needs is family."

"You can play big brother to him."

"I'll try, but I'm not sure how. I never had a brother before."

James said, "I did." Bitterness pinched his eyes. "The rebels took him away from me."

"Those that did it are gone now."

"Into the hottest fires of hell I hope. I'd be willin' to go there myself if I could get at them again. I'd keep pokin' them with the devil's pitchfork 'til I knew they were well done."

"Don't rush it any. We'll all get there soon enough. I want to stay around awhile and see what happens to Texas."

One of James's younger sisters opened the corral gates, then moved back toward the main log house to avoid spooking the cattle with her long skirt that flared in the wind. They balked anyway, suspicious of the opening. A brown dog came running through the corral, barking, and almost spilled them all. James shouted at him to go back, and the dog retreated. A young heifer saw him as a wolf and instinctively chased him. The rest of the cattle followed her into the corral. Evan Gifford closed the gate before they realized they were trapped. They milled around the fence, stirring dust, slamming against the logs and looking in vain for a way out. From a safe vantage point, the dog kept barking. The heifer hooked at the fence, trying to reach him.

James growled, "I've got half a mind to kill me a dog. He ain't worth two bits Confederate."

Vince Purdy warned, "If you hurt that dog, Clemmie and the girls will burn the beans for a month."

Rusty's gaze followed Evan Gifford as Evan tied his horse and strode toward an older, smaller log cabin where Geneva waited in the roofed-over dog run between the structure's two sections, holding a baby in her arms. Envy touched him as the couple embraced. The emotion was futile, but he could not help it.

She ought to've been mine, he thought darkly. That baby ought to've been mine.

It would be easy to resent Evan, but he could blame no one. Duty had called upon him to neglect Geneva in favor of his ranger service. Duty had called upon her to tend a badly wounded soldier. Nature had ordained the result.

The girl who had opened the gate started back now that it was closed. She walked at first, then picked up her stride. She called, "Rusty? Is that really you?"

He felt buoyed by the sight of her. Her smile was like sunshine breaking through a cloud. "It's me, Josie."

She seemed unsure whether to laugh or cry. "I couldn't tell for certain, all those whiskers." A tear rolled down a smooth cheek spotted with tiny freckles. She reached up and gripped his left hand in both of her own. "We'd begun worryin' you wasn't comin' back."

"For a time, it looked that way to me, too." He found himself compelled to stare at her. Josie was looking more and more like her older sister Geneva, the same bright eyes, the same tilt of her chin.

She glanced toward Andy, riding beside her grandfather. "You brought him back." It was less a statement than a veiled question.

"Things didn't work out for him."

"I'm sorry, and then again I'm not. He's probably better off."

"It's hard to convince him of that."

She asked hopefully. "You stayin' with us awhile?"

"Long enough to rest the horses." He rubbed his face. "And to shave my whiskers. I feel like a bear fresh out of its winter cave."

"You look fine to me. You always look fine to me."

Rusty's face warmed. Josie had a forward manner that disturbed him even as he admitted to himself that he liked it. He said, "These cattle are raisin' a lot of dust. Oughtn't you go back to the house?"

"A little dust won't hurt me. I'm not so fragile. Someday, when we're married, you'll see that."

Rusty's face warmed more. She meant it. He felt a little guilty, wondering if the interest she aroused in him came only because she reminded him of someone else.

A tall man with slightly bent shoulders moved out from the main house, limping a little as if each stride hurt. He stopped beside Josie and extended a wrinkled hand to Rusty.

Rusty said, "Howdy, Preacher. Didn't know if you'd still be here." For all the years Rusty had known him, bachelor Warren Webb had ridden a long and punishing circuit, testifying to his faith and carrying messages of hope wherever scattered settlers had no regular church. He never had accumulated much for himself. He was always giving it away to someone needier. During the war he had remained impartial, serving staunch Confederates and Unionist brush men alike. He had retained the respect of them all, assuring them that heaven still existed despite the hell they found on earth.

The minister smiled. "I live here now. It may surprise you to know that I've married Clemmie Monahan."

Rusty grinned. "Everybody knew it was comin', everybody but you and Clemmie." He grasped the minister's hand again, firmer this time.

Preacher Webb and Daddy Mike Shannon had found Rusty on the Plum Creek battlefield in 1840 after volunteer rangers and militia challenged a huge Comanche raiding party. Rusty had been but a toddler, frightened and confused by the gunfire, the chaos that thundered around him. Over the years he had considered Webb the best friend he had, after Mike and Mother Dora. "I'm pleased for you, Preacher, you and Clemmie both."

Clemmie was the mother of James and Geneva and of the younger sisters Josie and Alice. Rusty could see her standing ramrod-straight in the open dog run between the two main sections of the larger house. She was a small woman tough as rawhide. Though the war's hatreds had cost her a husband and son, she remained unbroken, fiercely defensive of the family that remained to her. Rusty thought it good that she and the minister had married. They were strong-willed people, and together their individual strengths were doubled.

Webb turned his attention toward Andy. "You couldn't find his people?"

"We found them."

Webb's eyes indicated that he guessed much of the story. "At least the boy's among friends here."

"He's feelin' kind of low. He needs you to talk to him the way you talked to me that time at Plum Creek."

"You were younger and easier to comfort. He's been in purgatory longer than you were."

"He never looked at it as purgatory. Livin' the Indian way came natural because he couldn't remember much else. Now he's lost that. He's got no solid ground to plant his feet on."

"You'll be takin' him south with you, I suppose."

"In a few days. He's got kind of used to things down there, and the people. I hope you haven't given his clothes to somebody." Andy had shed his white-boy clothing for breechcloth and moccasins when he had left here to go back to Comanchería.

"They're still here, just like he left them." Webb suggested, "If you'd leave him here the girls would treat him like a younger brother. They'd enjoy teachin' him to read and write. And Clemmie needs somebody like him to help make up for losin' Billy and Lon."

"She's got *you* now. And she's still got one son."

"James is a grown man. He travels his own road. She needs a boy who'll need *her.*"

Rusty did not ponder long. "This is too close to Comanche country. It'd be easy for him to take a notion to go back and test his luck. They'd likely kill him."

Webb frowned. "I guess you feel a special kinship to him, seein' what you both have gone through."

"We have a lot in common, and I've got no blood kin anywhere that I know of."

"Maybe it's no accident that he fell to you. The Lord knew you'd understand Andy in ways nobody else would."

"I hope gettin' into regular clothes will help him make the change. But he says he's not cuttin' his hair."

Webb shrugged. "Leave him somethin'. He can't change everything overnight."

Rusty thought back on the buffalo hunter's dark admonitions. "Do you think he can *ever* change it all?"

CHAPTER
THREE

Among the Comanches, Andy Pickard had earned the name Badger Boy because he had that small animal's fiercely defensive attitude when threatened or abused. He had made it a point to strike back for every blow struck against him. When circumstances did not allow him to do it immediately, he would await his chance to administer punishment. No insult was forgotten or allowed to go unanswered indefinitely. After a time the abuse stopped. Those who would maltreat him learned that retribution was certain, even if occasionally postponed.

He faintly remembered that he had been called Andy long ago, but hearing that name still caught him off guard at times. He had an uneasy feeling of not knowing for certain who he was. His life before capture by the Comanches seemed distant and unreal, like a dream dimly remembered. He could grasp only fragments, while most of it drifted out of his reach.

He was ill at ease among most of these white people who wanted to be his friends. When Rusty was reluctantly taking him north to rejoin The People, they had stopped to rest awhile at the Monahan farm. Andy had perceived a special bond between Rusty and this family, a bond that had to do with the white men's war and the misfortunes it had brought upon them all. In vague ways these people conjured up hazy memories of a white mother and father whose faces Andy could no longer bring into focus but whose voices echoed faintly in his mind.

He could not discern what was memory and what was illusion. The Comanches placed heavy importance upon dreams. Perhaps what he thought he remembered of his Texan family was no more than that, a persistent dream that haunted him like a mischievous spirit. It seemed to offer secrets but dangled them just beyond his grasp.

Memory or dream, it kept coming back while he was with the Monahan family. And sometimes in the middle of the night he woke up in a cold sweat, remembering his Texan mother's screams as she died.

Comanches had killed her. That he knew, yet he held no malice against them. After all, they had taken him in. Buffalo Caller had claimed him as a son, and Steals the Ponies, after resenting him for a time, had accepted him as a brother. The People had become *his* people.

After awakening from a nightmare he would lie with open eyes, mourning over having left them, wondering if somehow he might yet find a way to rejoin them without jeopardizing his life. No way presented itself, but he clutched at the hope.

Andy stayed close to Rusty as much as he could. When Rusty was not available, he turned to Vince Purdy. The Comanches had taught him respect for elders, and Purdy had a gentle nature as well as a wise countenance. Andy felt comfortable in the old man's presence. He wanted to feel the same way about Preacher Webb, for the minister seemed tolerant and understanding. However, when he spoke about religion he left Andy confused. Webb's teachings seemed different in many ways from those of the Comanches. So far as Andy had been able to determine, the two religions had little in common except belief in a central great spirit who oversaw the world.

Clemmie Monahan reminded him in some particulars of his adoptive mother, Sparrow, widow of Buffalo Caller. She had always been busy, flitting from one task to another like a hummingbird, never settling for long. Clemmie's many attentions to him were well meant but smothering. She treated him like a child, and he did not consider himself a child. He had ridden with older warriors on a raid, though without permission. That should qualify him as grown, or nearly so. Clemmie's daughters were much the same, especially the youngest, the one called Alice. The oldest daughter, Geneva, was kind but did not overwhelm him. She had a husband and a baby who commanded most of her time.

Rusty had spoken little about Geneva, but Andy perceived that there once had been a strong attachment between the two. He saw it in the way Rusty watched her when she was not looking and quickly cut his gaze away if she glanced in his direction.

In this respect he found little difference between white man and Comanche. He had observed Steals the Ponies's disappointment when a young woman he favored had chosen someone else. He saw the same futile longing in Rusty's eyes. Unlike Rusty, Steals the Ponies had put his disappointment aside and sought the favor of another.

As much as possible Andy tried to remain outdoors, away from the attention of the womenfolk. He enjoyed watching the men brand the cattle they had gathered and brought to the farm. A man named Macy, a former soldier for the South, was accomplished with the reata, a long rawhide rope. From horseback he would cast a loop around an animal's hind feet and drag it to a fire. While a couple of men held the struggling creature down, James Monahan would pull a long iron bar from the blazing wood and draw his brand on the bawling animal's side. Rusty said it was the letter *M*. He promised that once Andy learned all his letters, he would be on his way to reading and understanding the talking leaves of books and newspapers.

Andy understood that when enough cattle had been gathered, James intended to drive them to a faraway place called Missouri and exchange them for money. He could not fathom white men's obsession with money. It was worthless in itself. It could not be eaten. Silver coins could be used as shiny ornaments on necklaces and bracelets and such, but they had no other practical purpose that he could see.

Still, he was told that they could be traded for food, for horses, even for land. It seemed a poor exchange. But white people had strange ways.

He heard James tell Rusty, "You can't do much farmin' from now 'til spring. You and Andy could cow-hunt down yonder this winter like we're doin' here. Come spring, throw your gather in with ours and I'll take them north. The bigger the bunch, the more buyers they ought to draw."

Rusty acknowledged, "I've been thinkin' about it."

That pleased Andy. He had pictured himself wasting the winter days sitting in Rusty's cabin, studying books, learning to read and do ciphers. He would much rather be on horseback chasing wild cattle. Living among The People, he had been considered too young to go on a tribal buffalo hunt. Only grown men were privileged to participate in the excitement. Andy had been compelled to remain with the women and children, watching the action from afar, then moving in to the killing ground for the unpleasant skinning and cutting of meat. Though cattle seemed a less dangerous challenge than buffalo, at least he could share in the pursuit.

Talk in the evenings often turned to politics, which did not hold Andy's attention long. He understood little of it. He could tell that it meant a great deal to Rusty and the Monahans, however.

James said, "I'm hearin' that the military has set up a provisional government for Texas. General Reynolds has appointed his own people to office 'til the state can hold an election."

Evan Gifford said, "But I hear they may not let us old Confederate soldiers vote—me and Macy and Lucas here." He pointed to the men who worked for the Monahans. Lucas bore a jagged battle scar across his arm. Working, Lucas might roll up the other sleeve, but never the one that covered the mark. Andy thought that strange. Such a scar would be regarded as a symbol of honor among Comanche warriors. The more scars, the higher the honor.

James said, "They've been thrashin' the vote question around. One time I hear that everybody can vote if they'll take an oath of allegiance. Next time I hear that soldiers of the Confederacy are disqualified. Just goes to show why there ought to be a law against war. Maybe even a law against laws."

That too gave Andy pause. Among the Comanches, war was highly regarded. Only battle and the hunt gave a young man the chance to gain honor and respect. He had heard older men discuss what a calamity it would be if they killed all their enemies and had no one left to fight.

James declared, "Local sheriffs and judges do the best they can, but nobody knows how much authority they've got under the occupation. Thieves and outlaws run free and nobody does much to stop them."

Rusty nodded. "They need to organize the rangers again."

James said, "No chance. Last thing the Federals want is to give guns and authority to old Confederates."

Andy had heard much talk and wonderment among The People about the war between white men of the North and South. They had taken advantage of the increased opportunity for raiding into the settlements because so many young white men had been drawn away to the distant fighting, weakening the Texan defense.

He had seen a few Yankee soldiers. They looked no different from Texans except for the blue uniforms and that some had black skins. He knew only one black man, a former slave named Shanty who lived near Rusty's farm. He had found that Shanty's color did not rub off like paint, as he had thought it might.

Andy did not understand why Yankees and Texans would fight one another. It was not as if they were different in the way Comanches and Apaches were different. War between those tribes seemed natural because they had so little in common and all wanted to hunt on the same land. So far as he could determine, white men of the North had little interest in coming this far to hunt.

Josie Monahan was trying to teach Andy his letters and to print his name. During his earlier visit she had coached him on the use of English, helping him remember bits of the Texans' language. He still felt awkward, often struggling for a word that seemed determined to hide from him in a far corner of his mind.

She said, "If you'd talk Rusty into stayin' longer, I'd have time to teach you out of the first reader."

He guessed that the first reader must be a book. He wished he could learn to read without having to study so much. Studying made his head hurt.

He suspected that Josie was less interested in teaching him than in keeping Rusty around as long as she could. It was plain that she had strong feelings for him. He was not sure to what extent Rusty shared those feelings, though in his view if Rusty could not have one sister he should be contented with another. They looked much alike, and the younger one was not encumbered with a husband and baby.

He had seen more than one Comanche warrior who was disappointed in his first love but had taken the next youngest sister and found her more than satisfactory.

Josie had taught Andy to recite the alphabet from *A* to *Z*. Now she began trying to teach him the look and sound of each letter. She drew one on a slate.

"That's an *H*," she said. "It makes a 'huh' sound."

It was like no word Andy knew in either English or the Comanche tongue, but he repeated after her to keep her from becoming impatient. "What's it for?" he asked.

"Lots of words start with *H*, like *harness* and *house* and *horse*. If you use enough imagination you can almost see a horse in that letter. See his body and his legs?"

"His head, his tail, they stand straight up."

"I said you have to use a lot of imagination." She wiped the slate and made a single vertical mark. "That's the next letter, *I*."

"Don't look like nothin'."

"*I* means me, myself. If you use your imagination, you can see your own picture in that letter."

Andy shook his head. "Where my arms and legs?"

She said, "In the picture, you're standin' sideways."

Andy heard Rusty chuckle. Preacher Webb was wrapping a clean cloth around a rope burn on Rusty's right hand after having applied hog grease. Macy had been trying to teach Rusty how to use the reata in catching cattle. Rusty had thrown a loop around a young bull's horns but had made the mistake of letting the rawhide rope play out through his hand.

Andy had learned that Preacher Webb was a medicine man of sorts, though he had none of the feathers and rattles and powders that tribal shamans used. He spoke no incantations beyond a simple "Lord willin', that'll get better. But your hand won't fit a plow handle very good for a while."

"Won't be much plowin' to do anyway with winter comin' on. I expect I'll spend most of my time gatherin' unclaimed cattle like James has been doin'."

Webb glanced toward Andy. "I hope you'll spend some time teachin' Andy to read and write. Josie has made a start."

"I'll do the best I can. When it comes to books, I'm only middlin' myself."

Webb said, "Teach him out of the Bible. That way he'll learn two lessons at one time. I doubt he's studied much religion where he's been."

Rusty replied, "The Comanches have religion. Not the same as you teach, but I guess it fits them all right."

Webb's wrinkles deepened. "Teach him anyhow. When he's old enough, the Lord'll show him what's right."

Andy wondered if that meant going on a vision quest. Among the Comanches, when a boy came of age he went out alone to seek guidance from guardian spirits, usually in a vision. Only when he had experienced such a vision could he be considered truly a man.

James Monahan burst through the front door, his face dark with trouble. "Rusty, we're fixin' to have company. Where's your gun?"

Rusty looked quickly at Andy, then stepped toward his rifle leaning in a corner. "Comanches?"

Andy swallowed. They've come for me, he thought. He could imagine them cutting his throat for what he had done to Tonkawa Killer.

James said, "No, it ain't Comanches. It's the Oldham brothers."

Rusty's worried look told Andy that the name Oldham had a dark connotation. Rusty picked up the rifle, flinching at the pain in his burned hand. He seemed to debate with himself about whether to stand the weapon back in the corner. He said, "Maybe they've come to realize that I was forced into what I did. Maybe if I don't have a gun in my hand this time, I won't need one."

James warned darkly, "I doubt they've realized a damned thing. They're bullheaded, ignorant, and mean as snakes." He lifted his own rifle from its pegs atop the fireplace. "At least step back into the bedroom out of sight 'til I take the measure of their temper." He did not have to check his rifle. He kept it loaded all the time.

Andy could not remember hearing anyone mention the name Oldham before. He looked at Josie, hoping she might explain, but she only stared in silence at the front door, fear in her eyes.

"Who the Oldhams?" he asked.

She shook her head, bidding him to silence. He turned to watch the door. Boots struck heavily on the porch, and a large man entered the room. He had a rough face that reminded Andy of a defiant Apache captive he had seen once. A smaller man followed. He had but one arm, his right sleeve pinned below the shoulder.

The two men stopped. The larger one looked in surprise at James's rifle. "What's the matter, Monahan? A man'd think we're horse thieves or somethin'."

He carried a pistol in a leather holster high on his right hip. The smaller man wore one on the left side.

James considered before he answered, "I knew who you were when I saw you ride in, Clyde. What I don't know is why you're here."

"Just passin' through the country. Thought we'd sleep in your barn or under your shed tonight. Looks like it figures on rainin'."

James thought again. "Ordinarily we wouldn't turn anybody out to sleep in the rain, but this ain't an ordinary situation. I want you-all to take off them pistols and hand them to my granddaddy."

Clyde Oldham blinked in astonishment, resisting a moment, then giving in. "Never heard of such a thing." He unbuckled his belt and handed the weapon to Vince Purdy. The one-armed man held out until Purdy extended his hand.

Clyde complained, "We've visited better houses than this, and nobody ever told us to hand over our guns."

James said, "We want to head off trouble before it can start. You-all ain't the only guests we've got. Come on out, Rusty."

Rusty stepped from the bedroom. Andy watched the Oldham brothers' faces change, eyes widening in surprise, then narrowing. Clyde exclaimed,

"Ranger Shannon!" He stared in disbelief. "I hoped somebody had killed you long before now."

"Been some wanted to. Your brother Buddy-Boy tried as hard as anybody."

Clyde's voice was gritty. "And look what you done to him. He's only got one arm."

"What else could I do? He was fixin' to kill me."

The younger brother's face filled with hatred. "Looks like I'll still have to." He extended his hand toward Purdy. "Give me back my gun, old man."

Purdy stepped away, maintaining a tight grip on the pistol. "I reckon not."

Clemmie Monahan quickly sized up the situation. She said firmly, "There'll be no sheddin' of blood in this house. The war is over."

Andy looked from one face to another in confusion. The tension was tight as a bowstring. He could only guess at the root of it.

James stared fiercely at Clyde Oldham. "I was there at the brush camp when it happened, remember? Your mutton-headed brother took it on himself to declare Rusty a Confederate Army spy and try to shoot him. Damned lucky Buddy-Boy didn't lose more than an arm."

Rusty said, "I don't want any trouble here on my account. It's better if me and Andy go."

Josie protested, "Go? But why? A couple more weeks and I'll have Andy talkin' and readin' pretty good."

Rusty said, "It can't be helped."

Josie argued, "It was wartime when all that happened. We're at peace now."

Rusty said, "Not everybody." He looked at Clemmie. "The war brought too much grief to this place. I don't want to be the cause of any more. We'll leave soon as we can throw our stuff together."

Josie said, "You're not the one in the wrong here. Let *them* leave."

Rusty shook his head. "If they go first, they'll just stop out yonder and lay in wait for us."

Buddy-Boy's eyes reminded Andy of a wolf closing in on a crippled buffalo. "We just might, for a fact."

Rusty shrugged. "You see how it is. So me and Andy will leave. I don't think the Oldhams are Indian enough to trail us."

James said, "We'll take them cow-huntin' with us tomorrow. They can work for their keep."

Clyde protested, "We ain't your slaves."

James lifted the muzzle of the rifle a couple of inches, just enough to get the Oldhams' attention. "You're our guests. We wouldn't think of you-all leavin' before you've wore out your welcome."

Tears glistened in Josie's eyes. "Don't go, Rusty. Please."

Rusty started to reach out to her, then dropped his hands. "We'd figured to leave in a day or two anyhow. This is just a little quicker than we thought."

Clemmie said, "Come into the kitchen, Josie. We'll fix up some vittles for them to take along."

Reluctantly Josie turned away, pausing in the door for a look back.

James said, "You-all can leave at first light."

Rusty shook his head. "No, we'll leave now. No use takin' a chance on somethin' goin' wrong."

Buddy-Boy gave Rusty a look that could wound if not kill. "A rabbit can run far and fast, but a patient wolf always gets him sooner or later."

Rusty's eyes were sad. "It was you and your brother that brought on the trouble. I didn't want any of it. But if you ever bring any more trouble to me, I won't stand still and be a target." He jerked his head. "Come on, Andy."

As he walked out the door Andy heard James say, "Clyde, you and Buddy-Boy set yourselves down. My sisters'll fix you some supper."

Clyde sat in sullen silence. Buddy-Boy said something in an angry voice; Andy could not make out the words. But James's reply was clear. "I'm a damned sight better shot than Rusty is."

Vince Purdy and Preacher Webb came out to the barn to watch Rusty and Andy saddle up. Vince nodded toward lightning flashes in the east. "I'm afraid you're fixin' to get wet."

Rusty said, "That's all right. The country needs rain to make winter grass. Might make our tracks hard to find, too."

Webb said, "Normally I hate to speak ill of anybody, but there's not much good to be said about those Oldhams."

Vince was in a mood for a fight. "You sure you don't want to stay and have it out with them? Leavin' only puts things off to another day."

Webb said gravely, "Killin' is a mean thing in the sight of the Lord, but I believe there's times He knows it needs to be done. God forgive me for sayin' this, Rusty, but it would've been better if you'd killed the both of them that day. You may still have to do it."

"Not if they don't find out where I live."

"Nobody here will tell them anything."

Evan Gifford and Geneva heard the commotion and came out of their cabin. They waited as Rusty and Andy led their horses back toward the main house. Geneva said regretfully, "You're leavin' early."

Rusty could not look at her without a feeling of loss. "Somethin' came up."

Evan said, "The Oldham brothers. I was with James when they rode in. If there's anything I can do—"

"Much obliged. You can help James see that they stay here awhile."

Andy noted that Rusty gave Geneva a long look before he pulled away and moved on toward the main house. Clemmie and the girls came out from the dog run. Josie said, "We've put somethin' together for you and Andy to eat on the way." She handed Rusty a canvas sack and managed to hold on to his hand. He did not immediately pull it away.

Rusty said, "I'm obliged to everybody. I'm sorry we brought trouble to your door."

Clemmie said, "Trouble is no stranger here. You've helped us through the worst there ever was. We'd do anything we can for you."

"You wouldn't do murder. That's what it might take to settle with the Oldhams."

Rusty shook hands with the men, except for James, who remained in the house to watch the brothers. Clemmie and both girls hugged Andy. It made him uncomfortable.

Josie said, "Mind now, Andy, you keep studyin'."

He promised her he would, though he had reservations.

Riding away, Andy turned to look back at the lantern light in the windows. He said, "That Josie, she likes you. Likes you pretty good."

Rusty did not answer.

Andy said, "Those Oldhams don't. You think they like to hide and kill you?"

"I'd bet my horse and saddle on it."

"Why we don't hide and wait for *them*? Kill them easy."

Rusty gave Andy a look of disbelief. "That's not the way honest men do things."

"It is Comanche way. Kill them, you fix everything."

Rusty grunted. "I've got a lot more to teach you than just how to read."

CHAPTER
FOUR

COLORADO RIVER, TEXAS, 1871

Six years had passed without war, but they had not brought peace. They had brought a reconstruction government but not reconstruction.

The blacksmith rolled the wagon wheel out for Rusty to see. He leaned it against his broad hip and said, "There she is, a few spokes, a new rim, and she's as good as when that wagon first came out of the shop that made it."

The original wheel had buckled when Andy brought the team a little too fast down a rough hillside. He had a youth's weakness for speed. "It'll do fine," Rusty said. He dug into his pocket, wishing he did not have to spend any of the dollars he had received for cattle he sent up the trail with James Monahan. It seemed there were never enough dollars to cover his needs and still pay the heavy taxes imposed by the occupation government.

The blacksmith remarked, "You've taught that Andy boy readin' and writin', but you ain't taught him much about caution. He's whipped most of the young fellers his size around here and some a right smart bigger. Still got a lot of Indian in him."

"Lord knows I've tried. He's got no notion about consequences. Do it now and think about it later, that's his style."

More than once since he had been living with Rusty Andy had taken a horse, a blanket, and very little else and disappeared without offering any explanation. After several weeks he would return thinner, browner, and silent about where he had been. Threats of punishment had no effect.

The responsibility weighed heavily on Rusty's shoulders like a hundred-pound sack of feed. Sometimes he wondered if he had assumed a load he was not equipped to carry. He observed, "At least Andy makes friends of most of the boys after he's whipped them."

"I've been afraid he'd get hisself killed before you could finish raisin' him. He'd be sixteen, maybe seventeen now wouldn't he?"

"The best we can guess."

"Ever talk about goin' back to the Comanches?"

"Not anymore, but now and then he gets moody. He stares off to the north, and I can guess what's in his mind." At times Andy would be sitting in a room with Rusty or riding alongside him on horseback but seem to be miles and years away.

The blacksmith said, "He sure needs a woman's influence. You got any prospects?"

Rusty sidestepped the question. "Do you hear somethin'?"

Shouts arose from down toward the mercantile store.

The blacksmith turned his right ear in that direction. "Sounds like a fight. I'd bet you a dollar that Indian of yours is in the middle of it."

Rusty said, "I've got no extra dollar to throw away." He set out down the dirt street in a brisk trot, ignoring pain from the old arrow wound in his leg. He muttered, "Damn it, I can't turn my back for five minutes . . ."

There was hardly a young man living in or around the settlement who had not made his peace with Andy, often after a stern comparison of knuckles. But now and then a new one turned up.

The first face he saw was that of Fowler Gaskin, longtime neighbor, perpetual thorn in the side of Daddy Mike and now of Rusty. Old Fowler called himself a farmer, though he farmed just enough to stave off starvation. Rail-thin and sallow-faced, he was perpetually hungry-looking. For miles around, neighbors dreaded his visits because he seldom left without taking something with him whether it was offered or not. Nothing he borrowed ever seemed to find its way home unless the owner went and fetched it. Half the time it was not to be found, even then. Gaskin would have broken it, sold it, or traded it for something else.

Gaskin was shouting, "Git him, Euclid! Git up and show him. We don't let no damned halfway Indian come to town and act like he's as good as a white man." Tobacco juice streamed from Fowler's lips and glistened in his gray-speckled beard.

Though Euclid Summerville was several years older than Andy and forty pounds heavier, he lay pinned on his back. Andy sat astraddle and pounded on him while Summerville waved his hands futilely, trying to ward off the blows.

He was Gaskin's nephew. Rusty used to believe that Texas could never produce specimens of humanity as worthless as Gaskin's late sons, but Summerville had proven him wrong. He was as lazy as his uncle, sharing the old man's bad habits and contributing a few of his own. Rusty had heard speculation that he had been more than friendly with Gaskin's homely daughter. If that was so, he hated to think what manner of offspring the inbreeding might produce.

"How I wear my hair is my business," Andy declared. "Now say you like it just the way it is."

Summerville choked as he tried to answer. "Damn Indian son of a bitch!" He face was red enough to suggest he was about to go into some kind of slobbering fit.

Andy gave Summerville's arm a strong twist. "Say it."

"All right, all right. I'm sayin' it."

Gaskin stepped in closer to protest. "Git up from there and whup him, Euclid. You can do it."

Obviously Summerville could not. His dusty face, already pudgy, was beginning to swell from the punishment. Blood trickled from the corner of his mouth. Andy pushed to his feet and stepped back. Stooping to pick up a pocketknife, he started to close the blade, then reconsidered and broke it off against a hitching post. He pitched the ruined knife to Summerville.

"Next time you try to cut off my hair, I'm liable to cut off somethin' of yours."

Gaskin shouted, "Where's the law when you need it? This damned Comanche needs to be throwed in jail."

A bystander said, "Euclid started it. You'd better tell him to pick on people his own size from now on. The smaller ones can beat the whey out of him." Several onlookers laughed.

For the first time, Gaskin took notice of Rusty. "You Shannons! Damned Unionists and Indian lovers, the lot of you."

Rusty managed to contain his rising temper. "You'd better go home, Fowler, and take Euclid with you. He's liable to pick a fight with some schoolgirl and get beat up again."

Gaskin could see that none of the crowd showed sympathy for his nephew. He muttered to himself and jerked Summerville's arm. Near exhaustion, Summerville almost fell. "Come on," Gaskin said. "We got better things to do than furnish entertainment for the town loafers."

Summerville mumbled some halfhearted excuse, but it was not intelligible. The community did not have a high regard for his mental abilities.

Watching them leave, Andy dusted himself off, then sucked at a bleeding knuckle.

Rusty said crisply, "Haven't you ever seen a fight you could back away from? You're lucky Euclid didn't stick that blade between your ribs."

"He tried to cut off my braids."

"You'd save a lot of trouble if you'd cut them off yourself."

"I've told you before, I won't do that."

Rusty had not pressed that argument much. For most of six years Andy had been resolute against giving up this remaining symbol of his life among the Indians. He wore the same plain clothes as most other farmboys, but the braids and moccasins remained, marking him as someone different.

Turning to leave, Rusty saw a man striding in his direction, his expression stern. The badge on his shirt marked him as a member of the recently organized state police force.

"You two!" the lawman said curtly. "You ain't goin' nowhere 'til I've talked to you."

Rusty bristled but tried not to show it. "Talk. We're listenin'." He regarded the man as having been misled into an exaggerated view of his own importance.

"I heard there was a fight in the street just now." The policeman glared at Andy. "By the looks of you, you was in the middle of it."

Andy held stubbornly silent. Rusty said, "There wasn't much to it, just a little difference of opinion. No blood spilled, hardly."

"It's my job to keep the peace. Looks to me like the war ought to've given you rebels enough fightin' to last you for twenty years."

By that, Rusty guessed the man had not fought for the Confederacy. He had probably either dodged conscription or had gone east and served with the Union, which in the eyes of most old Texans branded him as a scalawag. Since the reconstruction government had organized its own police force it had tried to obtain officers free of Confederate connections. Some were well-meaning and honest citizens. Some were not worth the gunpowder and wadding it would take to send them to Kingdom Come.

Rusty had a gut opinion about this one. He said, "You know how it is when you throw a couple of bull yearlin's together. They've got to see who's the toughest. Wasn't no harm done."

The officer demanded, "Who else was involved?"

"I believe he's already left town. Anyway, he learned his lesson. I doubt he'll pick on Andy Pickard anymore."

The officer scowled at Andy. "Boy, you look old enough to get acquainted with the inside of the jailhouse. Remember that the next time you come to town." He walked away.

Relieved to see him go, Rusty warned, "Next time it's liable to be a troop of soldiers instead of one state policeman. We'd best be gettin' home. I'm lookin' for Len Tanner to come back most any day now."

Rusty and Tanner had ridden together as rangers before and during the war years. They knew enough about one another to earn each a medal or to put them both in jail.

The lanky, freckle-faced Tanner bit the end from a ragged, home-rolled cigar and lifted a tallow candle from the table to light it. His gaze followed Andy Pickard, walking out onto the dog run of Rusty Shannon's log cabin. He said, "I'd swear that boy's grown a foot since last I seen him. Next time I look, he'll be a man."

Rusty argued, "Look again. He just about is. Anyway, you've only been gone a couple of months."

Tanner had ridden to East Texas to visit his kinfolks, which he regarded as duty more than pleasure. "What you feedin' him?"

"Same as what I eat, and I ain't growed a bit. Just get a little older every day."

"How old is Andy now?"

"Old enough to beat the stuffin' out of Euclid Summerville, and him a grown man."

"Grown, maybe, but not much of a man."

Tanner stretched his long legs out in front of him and leaned back in his wooden chair, which squeaked under the strain. Rusty had braced it with rawhide strips because dryness had loosened its joints. "First time you brought Andy here I didn't think you could ever make a white boy out of him. But damned if he don't talk pert near as good as me and you."

"He reads faster than I do, and writes better, too."

"That ain't sayin' no hell of a lot." Tanner grinned, enjoying his little joke. Rusty saw no reason to spoil his fun. He knew Tanner did not mean it maliciously.

Having no home of his own and no evident ambition toward acquiring one, Tanner spent much of his time with Rusty and Andy. He came and went as the whim struck him. He helped with the farm and the cattle enough to earn his keep. He was a good hand when he wanted to be, but he never put his heart into work with plow and cow as he had done while serving as a ranger.

Tanner said, "Wish I'd seen the fight. Looks like there'll always be some Comanche in him."

"I'd like to have a Yankee dollar for every scrap those braids have got him into. Reminds me some of Daddy Mike. He was bad about fightin', too."

"Mike finally got killed."

Rusty sobered. "Yes, he did."

He contemplated that possibility for Andy but rejected the notion. He could not allow such a thing to happen, not so long as he had breath in his body.

Andy came back into the room, visibly disturbed. "Rusty, come look. Somethin's happened to the moon."

"How could anything happen to the moon?"

Andy's voice quavered. "Looks like it's burnin' up. Come see."

Rusty and Tanner exchanged dubious glances, but both arose from their chairs and followed Andy outside. Andy pointed upward. His voice was shaky. "There. See?"

The moon had dulled and turned the color of red clay, all except for a silver rind on one edge.

Andy shivered. "Maybe it's an omen. Another war, or somethin'."

Rusty laid a comforting hand on the youngster's shoulder. "It's just an eclipse."

"What's an eclipse?"

"They say it happens when the earth throws its shadow across the moon. And once in a while the moon passes in front of the sun. I've seen chickens go to roost in the middle of the afternoon. It don't mean anything."

"The medicine men would say—"

"Medicine men see omens in just about anything that's out of the ordinary."

Tanner stared at the moon. He had let his cigar go out. "Looks kind of spooky to me, too."

Half the time Rusty could not tell whether Tanner was joking or not. He glared at his friend, wishing he wouldn't reinforce Andy's misgivings. "Maybe the schoolhouse has got a book that tells about things such as that."

Andy argued, "Books can't tell you everything. I remember one night an owl lit on top of Raven Wing's tepee. The medicine man wanted to do a ceremony and take the curse off of him. Raven Wing said he'd have to wait because he needed to go and find a lost horse. Turned out an Apache had it, and he killed Raven Wing. Books don't tell you that about owls." Andy looked at the moon again. "If it burns up, the nights'll be awful dark."

Rusty perceived that the silver edge was growing larger. The shadow was slowly passing from the moon. "Look. It's comin' back."

Tanner said, "You're right. Appears the fire is goin' out."

Rusty started to argue. "There never was any fire. It was just . . ." He realized Tanner was pulling his leg. The skinny former ranger enjoyed a practical joke almost as much as he enjoyed a good meal or a lively fight.

"Someday, Len, the Lord is goin' to smite you hip and thigh."

"The yeller-leg Yankee government has done smote me. Made me pay a tax on my horse and even charged me two dollars just for bein' alive. Poll tax, they called it, and I ain't got to vote even once."

"Two dollars must've come hard for you."

"Too hard. I didn't have it to give them, so they made me work on the road for two days. I thought they made slavery illegal."

"Not when it's for taxes."

The Federals had imposed their own handpicked government on the state. They had agreed to let most Texas men vote provided they take an oath of allegiance to the Union. But when the election did not go the way they wanted they nullified the results. Now the graft-ridden state government was spending three times more than its predecessor and had raised taxes to an alarming degree.

Texas had three political parties. The Democrats were mostly former Confederates, many still disenfranchised. A group of Union loyalists called themselves Moderate Republicans. They tried to live up to the name through reconciliation with former enemies. However, a larger group known as Radicals dominated state politics, holding the governor's mansion and a majority of the legislature. They were more intent on punishing Confederates than on rebuilding the war-weakened economy. Governor Edmund J. Davis had legal power verging on dictatorship.

Rusty said, "There's too many people on both sides who won't admit the war is over. They've never given up fightin' it."

Tanner agreed. "Neither side trusts me and you very much. One bunch is down on us because we didn't go into the Confederate Army. The other thinks bein' rangers was the same as bein' Confederate soldiers."

"I just try to mind my own business and not mix into quarrels that don't concern me. The mess will straighten itself out sooner or later."

Tanner argued, "How do you mind your own business when people keep tryin' to draw you into a fight? I ran into a bunch of old rebels the other night. They accused me of bein' a Unionist because I didn't go into the army. I had to talk fast to keep them from takin' a whip to me."

"I know. Some Union men stopped here last week. Said they were lookin' for Ku Klux. More than likely they'll come again."

Tanner shook his head. "In some ways it was better when there was an honest-to-God war. At least you had a pretty good idee where people stood. You wasn't bein' whipsawed by politicians and wonderin' when somebody was fixin' to shoot you in the back."

Andy put in, "It's like that with the Comanches. About the only friends we've got are the Kiowas, and we're not always sure about them. Old men say even the Kiowas used to be our enemies."

Rusty caught the *we* and *our.* Andy often let things like that slip without realizing it. "When're you goin' to decide that you're not a Comanche? You never were."

He tried to guess what Andy was thinking. The boy's face was often a mask, revealing little in his eyes or his expression. It worried Rusty that much of the time he had no clue to what was going through Andy's mind.

He had just as well *be* an Indian when it comes to hiding his feelings, Rusty thought.

Andy returned to the dog run to look again at the moon.

Tanner asked, "You ever get to feelin' maybe you done the wrong thing, that you ought to've left him to be a Comanche? Now he's betwixt and between, not quite one and not quite the other. Like me and you."

Rusty could not argue. "Hell of a shape for anybody to be in."

"Hell of a shape for *Texas* to be in."

Rusty reined his mule to a stop and turned loose of the plow, raising a hand to the brim of his hat to help shade his eyes. He was not surprised to see a dozen men riding in from the direction of the settlement. It was safer these days to travel with company. Groups of riders had become commonplace, some on legitimate business, some up to no good. He could tell from a distance that these were white, not Indian. "Stay there," he told the mule, though he knew it would not move a foot without being compelled to.

He walked to a rifle leaning against the rail fence that protected his cornfield from cattle. He cradled it across his left arm, trying not to appear threatening but letting them know he was of a mind to defend himself.

He recognized one of the riders and growled under his breath. Fowler Gaskin, and behind him his nephew, Euclid Summerville.

Some of the others were known to Rusty, but some were not. They were grim-faced as they rode up to the rails and stopped. Gaskin stared at Rusty with all the malice he could muster. He had hated Daddy Mike, and after Mike's death he had transferred that hatred to Rusty. The old man could not be happy without hating somebody.

Summerville demonstrated less hostility. It took energy to hate properly, and he was not one to put out that much effort without a pressing need.

Gaskin demanded, "Where's that Indian kid that likes to beat up on people?"

Rusty had sent Andy out with Tanner to look for two strayed mares. "You know he's not an Indian, so why don't you stop callin' him one? Anyway, he's not here."

"Damned good thing. He always makes me feel like he's fixin' to put an arrow in my gut."

Rusty said nothing that would dispel the old man's misgivings. Because of Andy, Gaskin seldom came around anymore. Rusty wanted to keep it that way.

A broad-shouldered man edged his horse forward. He was some twenty-five years older than Rusty and looked every day of it. Rusty had encountered Jeremiah Brackett many times in town, though he had never had occasion to visit the man's farm. "Shannon, we heard you had some Unionist visitors the other day. I'd like to know what they wanted and what you told them."

Brackett had been an officer in the Confederate Army and wounded more than once. Not all of his wounds had been physical. It was said around the settlement that no one had seen him laugh since the war.

Rusty said, "They wanted to know if I'm a member of the Ku Klux. I told them I'm not and don't know who is. They argued amongst theirselves about whether to thank me or shoot me. Then they went on their way."

A couple of the Unionists had not believed him and had advocated burning down his cabin as an object lesson, but the more levelheaded restrained them. Rusty chose not to mention that. It might give some of these yahoos the same notion. Both sides occasionally burned the homes of those with whom they disagreed. It had become an almost-accepted method of expressing political opinion.

A younger man beside Brackett demanded, "Are you sure you didn't tell them anything?" A long scar on one side of his face marked him as Brackett's only surviving son, Farley. It was said he had taken a deep saber cut while riding with Hood's brigade. Like his father, he was reputed to be carrying internal scars as well.

Rusty said, "I didn't know anything to tell. I'm just tryin' to be a farmer and mind my own business."

Fowler Gaskin accused, "Everybody knows you kept a Union flag in your cabin through the war. That's how come you stayed in the rangers, so you wouldn't have to go off and fight like them two poor boys of mine."

Rusty declared, "Daddy Mike brought that flag home from the Mexican War. It had bullet holes in it, and some of them bullets were shot at him."

As for Gaskin's "poor boys," they had been killed in a New Orleans whorehouse fight. Rusty never had decided whether the old man knew the truth and was covering it up or if he actually believed his sons had died on a battlefield. The facts were well known in the community, but perhaps no one had ever felt mean enough to disabuse Gaskin of his illusions.

The elder Brackett said, "A man can't sit on the fence all his life. Sooner or later he has to come down on one side or the other."

Rusty shook his head. "The war's been over for six years. Ought not to be but one side anymore. We're all Americans."

"I have not accepted their damned Yankee oath, and I do not intend to. The war is not over, it's simply taking a rest. When the South rises again there will be no fence for you to sit on." Brackett started to turn his horse away but paused for a last admonition. "I suggest from now on you be very circumspect in your associations."

Summerville appeared disappointed. He waved a rawhide quirt. "I thought we was goin' to whup up on him a little. And that Indian kid, too."

Brackett gave Summerville a look of disgust and turned away. His son and the others followed him, all but Summerville and Gaskin. Rusty had a feeling they had not been invited to join the party; they were not the type Jeremiah Brackett would normally associate with. They had simply tagged along, hoping to participate with the others in what they dared not try alone.

Summerville lamented, "We come a long ways not to do nothin'."

Gaskin spat a stream of tobacco. Much of it fell back into his gray-and-black whiskers and glistened in the sun. "There'll come a better time."

Rusty had been a little apprehensive when the whole bunch sat there facing him. The apprehension was gone now. Neither Gaskin nor Summerville had the nerve to make a move against him without a lot of backing.

Summerville said, "Uncle Fowler, I thought they was goin' over yonder and talk to that nigger Shanty next. They ain't headed that way."

He pointed in the direction of a small farm that a former slave had inherited from his longtime owner. Shanty was well along in years but still managed to put in a good day's work. Quiet and inoffensive, he had tried to avoid trouble from those who objected to seeing a black man own a farm, even a small one like his. To people who had that attitude, a black was fit only to labor for someone white.

Rusty warned, "You leave Shanty alone. If you do anything to hurt him, you'll see more of me than you ever wanted to."

Gaskin said, "The nigger'll keep for another day." His voice dropped ominously. "Or some dark night."

Rusty raised the rifle a little. "You heard what I said."

"I heard. But I don't put much store in any white man who'll speak up for a darkey. Especially a white man who wouldn't go fight like my boys done."

More than once Rusty had felt a strong temptation to throw the truth in Gaskin's face, and that wish came to him now. But he held his tongue. He said, "You'd better whip up to a lope if you're goin' to catch your friends. You've wore out your welcome here."

Andy and Tanner rode in shortly before sundown, penning the two strayed mares they had gone out to find. Rusty looked the animals over, then bridled one of them.

Tanner said, "It's late to be goin' somewhere. Night's comin' on."

Rusty saddled the mare while he told about the visitors. "Fowler Gaskin let it slip that they're thinkin' of callin' on Shanty. I'll see if he'd like to come over here and stay with us for a spell."

It would not be the first time Shanty had stayed at Rusty's farm. Night riders had threatened him before.

Andy had developed a strong bond with the former slave. He had never understood how anybody could be hostile toward someone who kept to himself and caused no trouble. He asked, "What they got against Shanty? He never hurt anybody."

Rusty tried to explain. "He's not white. There's people who don't think anybody but a white man ought to own property. It makes them nervous to see somebody like Shanty able to do for himself."

"That don't make any sense."

"You're right, but there's no talkin' to folks who feel that way."

"The Comanches been makin' it on their own since the first grandfathers came up out of the earth. And some of the dumbest people I ever saw are white."

Rusty shrugged. "Bein' wrong doesn't keep them from bein' dangerous. Especially to somebody like Shanty, an old man livin' by himself. All his life he's been taught to hunker down like a rabbit and not fight back."

Shanty had been at Rusty's place when Rusty first brought Andy home with a broken leg. His was one of the first friendly faces the confused and frightened boy had seen since being left behind by a Comanche war party. Shanty had remained close while Andy's leg slowly healed. Though unable to read, Shanty had patiently coached Andy in the use of the language, reviving early childhood memories buried during his years with the Indians.

Andy's face twisted. "They'd better not do anything to Shanty. I'll kill them."

Rusty frowned. "You shouldn't talk so free about killin'. Some people might think you mean it."

"I do mean it."

The look in Andy's eyes disturbed Rusty. He *did* mean it.

Len's right, Rusty thought. There's still a streak of Comanche in him. He may never lose it.

Andy said, "I'll go with you."

"No, you stay here. Chances are there won't be any trouble. And if there *is* any, I don't want you in harm's way. Len, you keep him here."

CHAPTER

FIVE

Approaching Shanty's log cabin, Rusty wondered how anyone could begrudge the old fellow this humble home, this modest parcel of farming land. As the only slave of a hard-drinking Indian fighter named Isaac York, he had lived here longer than most people around him. No one had objected to his presence so long as he belonged to a white man. It was only after his dying owner had willed him this little place that objections had arisen. In recent times, as many whites lost their own land to punitive reconstruction measures, those objections had intensified. A widespread feeling had developed that the government favored former slaves, taxing them lightly if at all, while it tried to crush former rebels under the weight of confiscatory levies.

Though darkness approached, Rusty saw the old man still working in his small rail-fenced garden. Shanty grew almost everything he needed for subsistence, even a small plot of scraggly tobacco. He was not often indoors during the daytime except to eat or to get out of the rain. Age had slowed him so that it took longer to finish the work necessary even for a small place like his.

During the time he had spent at Rusty's, he and Rusty had swapped labor, alternating between the two farms. The main concern had been that someone always be nearby, that Shanty not be left to face potentially hostile visitors alone. For a time, that danger had seemed to pass. Now, like smoldering coals fanned by a rising wind, old animosities had flared anew. Rusty felt that it had less to do with Shanty as an individual than with general unrest stirred up by the seemingly endless Federal occupation that continued years after the cannons had fallen silent. Men feeling oppressed sought to vent their frustrations. Freed slaves became an easy target for their anger.

A brown dog of amalgamated ancestry wriggled through the rail fence and trotted out, barking either a welcome or a warning. Rusty was not certain which until the animal wagged its tail so vigorously that its whole body shook.

Shanty ambled to the gate rather than risk fragile limbs by climbing over the fence. "Hush up, dog. Mr. Rusty," he said by way of greeting, "you're travelin' late." His smile showed a wide row of perfectly white teeth. So far as Rusty could see, he had never lost one.

"Somethin' came up. You been havin' any company?"

"Company? This place ain't on the road to nowheres in particular. Nobody much ever comes by."

"The ones I've got in mind wouldn't come friendly. They travel in packs, like wolves."

"Oh, *them*. I don't count them as company. There was five or six by here a couple nights ago. Mostly wanted to know if I belong to the Freedmen's Bureau. I told them I don't belong to nothin'. I don't hardly ever leave this place."

The Freedmen's Bureau had been organized ostensibly to benefit former slaves. In Rusty's view it had been subverted to the ambitions of white opportunists exploiting the people they claimed to aid.

He pressed, "They didn't hurt you none, or threaten to?"

"A couple of them talked about burnin' down my cabin. The others said wait and see if I was goin' to be a good nigger or not. One of them offered me a hundred dollars in Yankee silver to sell him this farm."

"What did you tell him?"

"I told him I didn't have no other place to go. How much is a hundred dollars, Mr. Rusty?"

"Not near enough. Not even in Yankee silver."

"That's what I figured. I'd probably use it up in a year or so, and then where'd I be?"

"Just another poor soul trampin' around the country. Isaac York didn't mean that to happen, and neither do I. You'd best stay at my place 'til this all blows over."

"But I got my field and my garden—"

"We can come over here every few days and take care of things like we did that other time."

Shanty shook his head. "I don't want to be a burden. I've tried not to be a bother to anybody. Most folks around here seem friendly enough to me."

"You'd be no burden, you'd be a help. Seems like there's always plenty to do."

Shanty patted the dog. "Ol' Rough here, he's used to this farm. I'm afraid if I taken him someplace else he'd up and run off."

"Keep him tied for a couple of days. He'll adjust to the change."

"I'll do some thinkin' on it." Shanty looked westward, where a red sunset was rapidly fading. "Gettin' on toward dark. Late for travelin'. You'd just as well stay all night."

Rusty considered. Given time, perhaps he could convince Shanty that he needed to get away from here. "I'm much obliged."

"Then I'll be fixin' us a little supper. You mind corn bread and sowbelly?"

"Long as somebody else is fixin' it, anything sounds good to me."

For years, Shanty had slept in a shed while his owner slept in the cabin. Now that he owned the farm, Shanty slept indoors. He offered to share the cabin with Rusty, but it was small. They would have to move the table and chairs out into the yard to make room for spreading his blankets on the floor.

Rusty said, "I'll sleep outside. I can hear better if somebody is comin'."

"Whatever suits you is plumb fine with me."

Rusty stayed up until late, sitting on a bench just outside the door, watching, listening.

Shanty came out with an old banjo and played a couple of tunes. Then he lapsed into silence, helping Rusty listen. "Ain't nobody comin'. Don't you reckon you'd ought to be gettin' some sleep?"

"I'm rememberin' another time I stayed here, and night riders came with a notion of runnin' you off."

"You ran *them* off, you and the sheriff."

"But this is a different bunch, and Tom Blessing ain't the sheriff anymore."

"The Lord has always watched over me. He'll keep on watchin'."

"I've seen bad things happen to people who didn't watch out for themselves because they thought the Lord was doin' it for them."

"Well, when the time comes that He wants to call me home, I'm willin' to go. I leave things to Him and don't let worry mess with my sleep."

Rusty found himself smiling. "If Preacher Webb was to ever give up the ministry, you could take up where he left off."

"I can't read the Book."

"You don't have to. You know it by heart."

Rusty lay on the shed's dirt floor. The dog came up and licked his hand. Rusty said, "Go lay down."

The dog circled a couple of times, finding a spot that suited him, then settled with his head on the edge of Rusty's blanket. Rusty doubted that he was of any practical use, like a horse or a mule or a milk cow would be, but he provided company for Shanty. For an old man living alone, that was probably a considerable comfort.

The dog's barking awakened Rusty. For a moment, while he blinked the sleep from his eyes, he thought the dog had probably rousted a varmint come to raid Shanty's chickens. Then he heard hoofbeats. He had slept in his clothes, except for his boots. Hastily he pulled them on and got to his feet, rifle in his hand. He did not know how long he had been asleep, but he doubted that anyone traveling at this time of night was burdened with honorable intentions. He walked out to where the dog had taken a stand.

"Easy, boy." The dog kept barking.

The moon's pale light showed him several riders. He could not be sure, but there were at least six or seven. He brought the rifle up and cocked the hammer. The horsemen abruptly reined up. All had their faces covered.

Rusty challenged them. "You-all are way off of the main road."

Someone exclaimed, "Who the hell—"

Someone else said, "It's Shannon. What business do you have here, Shannon?" The voice was filtered through a cloth sack covering the speaker's head.

"I'm visitin'. What about you-all?"

"We've come visitin', too. Where's that nigger?"

"I sent him away for safety." Rusty found it easy to lie in a worthy cause. "Looks like you've missed him."

"We'll see for ourselves."

Rusty raised the rifle to his shoulder.

The rider said, "You wouldn't shoot a white man."

"Maybe, and maybe not. But if you move any closer, you'll be sittin' on a dead horse."

A raspy voice spoke from behind the leader. "Rusty Shannon, you're a damned nigger-lovin' scallywag."

He would recognize Fowler Gaskin's voice if it spoke from the bottom of a well. Rusty said, "If you know me that well, Fowler, you know I'll do what I say I will. If you-all came here for mischief, you'd best turn around and go back. If you were just ridin' past, then you'd best circle around and give this place a wide round dance."

Gaskin argued, "He's by hisself. He can't get us all."

Rusty said, "No, but I could get one or two. Why don't you come up front, Fowler, where I can see you better?"

Gaskin did not budge from his position in the rear.

The leader said, "I still don't believe you'd shoot a white man."

From out in the moonlight Rusty saw two dark shapes rise up as if from the ground. He turned quickly, thinking someone had circled around him.

He heard the click of a hammer. A shotgun blasted, loud as a cannon in the night. The leader's horse jerked back and twisted around, tumbling its rider. The sack came off of the man's head. Rusty recognized the younger Brackett scrambling to get to his feet.

Gaskin shouted, "It's that crazy Indian kid. Look out, he'll kill somebody!"

Rusty realized that Andy had followed him but had remained hidden. The other figure had to be Len Tanner.

Tanner shouted, "I got me a rifle here, too."

Farley Brackett turned angrily toward the men behind him. "Gaskin, this ain't like you said. Wasn't supposed to be nobody here but that nigger."

Gaskin argued, "How'd I know Shannon'd show up, him and them others? I ain't responsible for that."

Brackett said, "No use cryin' after the milk's been spilt. This'll keep for another day . . . or another night."

After one lie, the next came even easier for Rusty. "I know who most of you are. Anything happens here, I'll know where to go lookin'."

Brackett reined his horse around. "So will we, Shannon. If them Yankee soldiers hear about this, we'll know who to blame."

Rusty had no intention of getting mixed up with Yankee soldiers, but he chose not to say so. Let these yahoos worry about it, he thought.

The riders retreated, the sound of hoofbeats diminishing as they disappeared into darkness. The dog trailed after them, barking them on their way, as self-important as if he had routed them single-handedly.

Rusty turned as Andy walked up to him. His voice was sharp. "Boy, you could've got yourself killed."

"Not by them. They're cowards."

"That's the most dangerous kind there is. Cowards take every advantage they can. What possessed you to trail after me?"

"You acted like you were afraid for Shanty. I figured I could help."

Rusty glared at Tanner. "Thought I told you to keep him at home."

"Andy's got too much Indian in him. When he makes up his mind to do somethin', all hell can't prize him loose. Wasn't nothin' I could do but come along and try to keep him from gettin' hurt."

Shanty came walking up. He had put on trousers, but he was barefoot. He held a shotgun.

Surprised, Rusty asked, "What were you goin' to do with that thing?" He had never seen or heard of Shanty picking up a firearm except to kill something for the cooking pot.

"I was afraid they might hurt you, Mr. Rusty."

"Thanks," Rusty replied, "but the only thing hurt was some feelin's. You know they had a notion to give you a whippin'. They'll do it yet if you stay here."

Shanty stared off in the direction the visitors had taken. Rusty sensed that he was assessing the danger not only to himself but to his friends. Shanty said, "Even if I was to go with you, they'd still know where I was at."

"But you won't be by yourself."

Reluctantly Shanty accepted the inevitable. "I'll gather up my needfuls first thing in the mornin'." He looked toward the dog, which had returned from seeing the riders off. "I don't know how Ol' Rough will take to movin'."

"Ol' Rough doesn't have the Ku Klux on his tail."

Riding toward Tom Blessing's cabin, Rusty heard hammering and reined Alamo toward a shed that served as a blacksmith shop, among other functions. Blessing stood before a glowing forge, beating a heated horseshoe against an anvil. He had removed his shirt. His long underwear was streaked with sweat and dirt. As Rusty dismounted, Blessing lifted the horseshoe with tongs and dipped it into a wooden tub half full of water. It sizzled. Blessing raised a big hand to shield his face from the steam.

He was a large man in advanced middle age, a contemporary of Daddy Mike and Preacher Webb. Tall, broad-shouldered and all muscle, he looked at home beside a blacksmith's forge. He said, "Git down, Rusty. You come to get ol' Alamo shod? The coals are hot."

Blessing grasped Rusty's hand. He had a crushing grip that made Rusty's bones ache. "Me and Len Tanner took care of that already."

Blessing seated himself on a bench in the shade and rubbed an underwear sleeve across his grimy face. He said, "I heard a little rumor over in town."

"What kind of yarn are they tellin'?"

"I didn't get this from anybody who was there. At least they didn't own up to it. But the story was that your boy Andy threatened some citizens and fired off a shotgun."

"Not *at* anybody. He fired it into the air to get their attention."

"He got it, all right. Nobody's admitted to bein' there. I don't imagine they want to explain what they were doin' at the time." He frowned. "What *were* they doin'?"

"A bunch of them figured on whippin' Shanty, or maybe worse." He explained his own role in the incident, then Andy's and Tanner's. "The boy puts a lot of store in him."

"Most folks around here respect Shanty, but there's always a few . . . You know who they were?"

"I told them I recognized them, but I didn't. Nobody except Fowler Gaskin and his nephew." He purposely neglected to mention Farley Brackett, for the man's father had a generally favorable reputation around the community even if he was extreme in his feelings toward the Union.

Blessing considered. "I'm not the sheriff anymore, not since the carpetbaggers took over. There's not much I can do. Not officially, anyway."

The Unionist state government had fired Blessing and appointed a new sheriff from among its own ranks. That gentleman had disappointed his sponsors by leaving between two days, taking with him several thousand dollars in Federal specie. They had appointed another who did not steal but seldom ventured beyond the town limits for fear of tangling with someone who did not appreciate the majesty of the law. To talk to him about Shanty's situation would be a waste of time.

Blessing said, "Let's mosey up to the house. My wife's gone to see some of the grandkids, but me and you ought to be able to brew us a pot of coffee."

Blessing's cabin was of a standard double type. An open dog run separated the two main sections, a common roof tying them together. A loft above the dog run had been sleeping quarters for the Blessing boys until they came of age. They had to remain hunkered down to keep from bumping their heads against the low ceiling. As they grew up to their father's height, that became a considerable problem. One by one, they had left home.

A longtime neighbor to the Shannons, Blessing had been with Daddy Mike and Preacher Webb as part of the Texan force that struck a huge Comanche raiding party at Plum Creek in 1840. They found there a small white boy, barely old enough to talk and unable to tell them anything more than that his name was Davy. His red hair had soon earned him the nickname Rusty. As far back as he could remember, Blessing had been an important part of his life.

Blessing said, "After I heard the rumor, I rode by Shanty's cabin to make sure he's all right. Didn't see hide nor hair of him."

"He's over at my place. I thought it was best if he stayed with us 'til this foolishness is done with."

Blessing's wrinkles deepened. "That could be a long time. The way things are goin', with the Unionists and the Freedmen's Bureau on one side and a lot of hardheaded rebels on the other, I wouldn't be surprised none if the war busted out again."

"Sure makes me wish we had the rangers back."

Blessing said, "That's one reason Austin set up the new state police force. They're supposed to take the rangers' place, only with a different name and with Union people headin' them up."

"Most Texans ain't takin' kindly to a Unionist police force."

"At least the state police don't wear them damned blue uniforms of the Yankee army." Blessing's sympathies still lay with the rebels, though he seldom expressed them beyond his circle of closest friends.

Rusty said, "The question is whether the police will enforce the law or just keep chastisin' folks for the war."

"If they could get the right kind of men . . ." Blessing studied Rusty intently. "People like you, for instance. You spent a long time with the rangers. You could help put the state police on the gospel path."

"I doubt it. Lately both sides have come around to take my measure. Neither one seems to like me."

"There's some good men in the state police. They're not all bad."

"It wouldn't be the same as the rangers. The Unionists lean too far in one direction. As for the other side . . . some of them want to run Shanty off of his land. You know he won't fight back. He doesn't want to cause trouble."

"He causes trouble just by bein' there. He can't wash his skin white."

Rusty said, "He's a harmless old man. All he wants is to be left alone."

"It's liable to take some funerals before that can happen. But I've still got a little influence. I'll ride around and offer a few folks a Preacher Webb sermon . . . with a little smell of hellfire and brimstone."

"You'd best watch your back, Tom. There's some folks that might not dare to face you, but they'd be willin' to shoot you when you're not lookin'."

"It's been tried. Hasn't worked yet."

Rusty finished his coffee and shook hands, then started for the door. Blessing said, "Wait." The look of regret in his eyes told Rusty that he was about to say something he disliked.

"Rusty, that Indian boy of yours—"

"Why does everybody keep callin' him an Indian?"

"He acts like one in so many ways, like the scraps he keeps gettin' into."

"He hasn't had many fights lately."

"That's because he's already whipped just about everybody who might challenge him. People are talkin' about him, Rusty. They wish you'd send him away."

"What if Daddy Mike and Mother Dora had sent *me* away?"

"With you it was different. You hadn't been with the Indians long enough to pick up their ways. That Andy, though . . . folks are wonderin' when he's goin' to pull out a scalpin' knife and start takin' hair."

"I'll talk to him."

"I wish you would. There's a few people who might take it in their heads to do somethin' regrettable. I'd hate to see him put in the ground."

CHAPTER
SIX

Len Tanner stepped out of the lamp-lighted cabin and spread his blanket in the dog run. Straightening up, he shouted, "Rusty, you better come look."

Excitement in Tanner's voice brought Rusty to his feet and out into the open space between the two sections of his cabin. Against the night sky, just at the horizon line, he saw a red glow.

Tanner said, "I don't think *that* is any eclipse."

Rusty muttered an oath. "It's the right direction to be Shanty's place." He slammed the flat of his hand against the log wall. "They're burnin' him out."

"Good thing we brought him home with us."

Shanty heard the voices and ventured from his sleeping place in the shed. Andy had taken to sleeping there, too. Shanty looked at the glow, then hurried barefoot to Rusty's side. "Lordy, Mr. Rusty, they're burnin' down my place."

"I'm afraid that's what it looks like."

Andy came up, shoving his shirttail into his trousers. He wore buckskin moccasins. "If we hurry, maybe we can put the fire out."

Rusty shook his head. "By the time we got there, the cabin'd be burned to the ground. And whoever's done it, they might be waitin' to ambush Shanty or anybody else who rides in there."

Andy argued, "We can't just stand here and do nothin'."

Rusty stared at the glow, deploring his helplessness. "Best we wait 'til daylight so we can see what we're gettin' into."

Andy seemed more agitated even than Shanty. "One thing we *can* do. The people that done this, they've got houses, too."

Rusty knew what Andy was driving at. "A house for a house?"

"Seems fair to me."

"The law doesn't work that way."

"Don't look to me like the law works at all."

Shanty's shoulders slumped. Always thin and spare, he seemed to shrink even smaller. "I ain't never done nothin' against nobody."

Rusty said, "You're a free man. Nobody owns you, and some folks can't accept that."

"I ain't free if people won't let me alone. I wish Mr. Isaac was still livin'. They wouldn't burn the place if it was still Mr. Isaac's."

Rusty started to say Isaac York was white. But he knew Shanty was well aware of the reason for the hostility.

Shanty said, "They wouldn't do nothin' like this if you was to say *you* own me."

"The war settled that question. Nobody owns anybody anymore. That's the law."

"I wisht there hadn't been no war. I wisht things could go back to what they used to be. Them wasn't really bad times."

"You didn't have freedom then."

"Don't seem like I got much freedom now."

Rusty bade Andy and Shanty to stay back while he and Tanner circled around the blackened ruins of the cabin and made certain no one had set up an ambush. Tanner said, "Looks safe to me. They done their dirty work, then cleared out."

The chimney stood like a tall tombstone above the charred remnants. By contrast, the shed was only moderately damaged. Though it had been set afire, the flames had flickered out. Chickens pecked in the dirt, oblivious of the carnage about them. The shed had been their roosting place.

Len pointed. "Yonder lays Shanty's plow mule."

He gave vent to his anger as he rode up to the dead animal. It had been shot and left to die slowly, for the ground was torn up where it had lain and kicked in agony while its blood drained away. "Any man who would do this ought to be gut shot and left to fight off the buzzards."

Rusty nodded solemnly. "They didn't find Shanty. They had to take it out on somethin'."

He shivered, picturing Shanty lying here instead of the mule. On reflection, he figured they would more likely have shot Shanty at the cabin and burned him with it.

He signaled for Shanty and Andy to come in. Shanty stopped to study the cabin ruins, then came out and looked down at the dead mule. "Poor ol' Solomon. *He* wasn't black like me, he was brown."

Rusty said, "But he belonged to you."

"I ought to've been here. They wouldn't have done this to him."

"They'd have done it to *you*."

Andy clenched his fists, his face reddened. "Ought to be somethin' we can do about this."

Shanty said, "The Lord keeps a tally. Come Judgment Day, He'll call on transgressors to settle their due."

Tanner added, "He'll send them to hell."

Andy demanded, "Why wait on the Lord? Why don't we give Him some help and do it ourselves?"

Despite lectures on the subject from Preacher Webb, Andy had never quite grasped the white man's concept of a fiery hell. The vision of eternal damnation was not part of Comanche tradition. The Comanche preferred immediate punishment, duly witnessed. He said, "I've heard of the Kiowas tyin' a man to a wagon wheel and burnin' him alive. I can believe in that kind of hell."

Shanty dismounted and stood in anguish where the cabin door had been. "Me and Mr. Isaac, we built this with our own two hands." He raised his palms and looked at them. "Wasn't nobody else, just us. He'd be mighty grieved to see this."

Rusty thought Shanty was too old to be raising a cabin anymore, at least by himself. "We'll help you build it back, but we'd best wait awhile. They'd just burn it again."

Tanner said, "What this country needs is for Preacher Webb to do the honors at a few good funerals."

Rusty demurred. "There's been too many funerals already. The wrong folks got buried." He rode out to the dead mule and drew the loop of a rawhide reata tight around the animal's hind feet. He dragged the mule off a couple of hundred yards, out of sight from the burned cabin. There he found Shanty's milk cow, killed as the mule had been.

Shanty's dog Rough would probably have been shot too, had Shanty not tied him to a post at Rusty's place. The dog had kept trying to run off back to the home it knew.

The raiders had flung a few torches over into Shanty's garden, but the plants had been too green to burn.

Rusty rode back to where the others waited. He said, "You-all go on home. I've got to make a visit."

Tanner said, "You fixin' to call on Fowler Gaskin? This has got his earmarks all over it."

"Fowler can wait. There's somebody else who might listen to reason. I'll give him a try."

Like most farms in the Colorado River country, Jeremiah Brackett's had suffered hard times. Some of the old rail fencing that enclosed his main field had been replaced, but long stretches threatened to collapse, supported by temporary bracing that was makeshift at best. Recovery from the war had been slow and painful and was far from complete.

Rusty's acquaintanceship with the man was limited. Brackett apparently had brought some money with him when he settled on this land several years before the war. He had built a home larger than most in the area and had plowed a lot of grassland into fields. Fortune's warm smile had turned cold during the war, however. Becoming an officer himself, he had urged his sons to join the Confederate service. His wife had bitterly blamed him after two of them died in battle. The third son, Farley, had been so badly warped by the war that he rebelled against all authority. Toward the end he had deserted the army and taken up with fugitive brush men hiding beyond the western settlements. Now he rode precariously along the hazy-edged line that divided law and outlaw.

Brackett had paid heavily for his allegiance to the Confederacy. Rusty could respect that; the same had happened to many of his friends. But some, like the Monahans, had paid an even heavier price for their opposition.

Passing a field, he noticed a young black man guiding a moldboard plow drawn by a pair of mules. Rusty lifted one hand in a modest show of friendliness, receiving a nod and a white-toothed smile in return.

Evidently Brackett did not hate all blacks. Or, if he did, his hatred did not prevent his using them.

The house, of rough-hewn lumber, had gone for years without fresh paint. Remnants of white still clung, emphasizing patterns of grain in the exposed and darkened wood. Like much else he saw, it bespoke a long, slow fall from prosperity.

In front of the house stood a wooden carving of a boy in a jockey's uniform, holding a brass ring for tying a horse. Like the house, the carving had lost most of its original paint. Rusty dismounted and tied Alamo's reins to the ring after first checking to be sure the hitching post had not rotted off at ground level. One of the plank steps yielded under his weight. It was cracked and needed replacement.

Beyond the front door a woman stood in semidarkness just inside a hallway. He tipped his hat. "Miz Brackett?"

The woman moved closer, into brighter light. "I am *Miss* Brackett. Is there something we can do for you?"

"I'm lookin' for Jeremiah Brackett."

He could see now that the woman was actually a girl of perhaps fifteen or sixteen years, too young to be Brackett's wife.

She said, "My father is somewhere out in the fields. He'll be home directly for dinner. You'd be welcome to stay and eat with us."

Rusty was hungry, but he felt his mission was too awkward for him to break bread with these people. "I'm much obliged for the hospitality, ma'am. I'm afraid I can't stay."

She said, "You'd be Mr. Shannon, wouldn't you? I've seen you over in town."

Rusty could not remember that he had ever seen the girl before, though he probably had. She was in that period of rapid change that comes just before womanhood. He found her face pleasant, her faint smile reinforced by friendly brown eyes.

He said, "I don't recollect hearin' that Mr. Brackett had a daughter." Unmarried ladies were scarce, even ones this young. They were outnumbered by unattached bachelors persistently striving to alter their marital status. Unless a woman was homely enough to frighten hogs and had a disposition to match, she stood scant risk of becoming a spinster.

"My name is Bethel," she said. "It comes from the Bible."

"Mine is Rusty. I don't expect you'll find it in the Book." He turned to look toward the fields. "I'll go hunt for your father."

She raised her arm to point, and he noticed that her sleeve had been mended, its cuffs fraying, the fabric faded. She said, "I think you'll find him over yonderway, in that field past the oak trees."

Turning away, he thought there ought to be at least enough money to buy that girl a decent dress. But he knew the reality was otherwise. Six years after the war, much of rural Texas was still flat on its back. Or, at best, up on one elbow.

He had made a modest amount of money gathering unclaimed cattle and throwing them into herds that James Monahan trekked north to the railroad, but it had been extremely difficult to hold on to much of it. He bought little, but what he did buy was high in price. Taxes had risen to near impossible levels. He was convinced that reconstruction officials were deliberately taxing old settlers off their land so they or their friends could have it. The stronger the tie to the Confederacy had been, the higher the taxes were set.

Jeremiah Brackett stood in the edge of the field, watching a black man follow a plow and team of mules. He became aware of Rusty's approach. For a moment his gaze went to a rifle leaning against the rail fence, but it was some distance away. He gave Rusty a second look and evidently saw no imminent threat. He picked his way through rows of corn, careful not to crush any growing plants.

"Howdy, Shannon. You've come to see me?"

That seemed obvious to Rusty, but he guessed it was a strained way of being polite. He dismounted. "I have. Wanted to ask you where you went last night."

The question seemed to surprise Brackett. "Nowhere. I was at home. I am at home just about every night. Where would you have me be?"

"Thought you might've gone over to pay Shanty another visit."

"I rarely visit my white neighbors, much less one of so dark a hue." Brackett peered intently as if trying to read what was back of Rusty's eyes. "I suspect you are about to tell me that something has happened."

"Somebody burned down his cabin."

Brackett blinked as if the news was unexpected. "Was he in it?"

"No, I'd taken him home with me. But I figured you knew that."

"I had no reason to know."

"Figured your son Farley would've told you."

"Farley hasn't been there since the night your Indian boy fired a shotgun and got him thrown from his horse."

"Andy didn't shoot *at* him. He just wanted to be sure he had everybody's attention."

"He had it, and that is a fact. The boy is a menace."

"Some folks must figure Shanty to be some kind of a menace too, the way they keep tryin' to run him off."

"We don't need his kind in this country."

Rusty nodded toward the black man with the plow. "I've seen three of them in your fields."

"That's different. They're working for me. They have no claim on any of the land."

"Where do they live?"

"In a cabin out by my barn."

"Then they're livin' a whole lot closer to you than Shanty is. How come he puts such a burr under your blanket?"

Brackett's face twisted. "If you were any kind of a white man you wouldn't have to ask. Working for somebody is one thing. For a darkey to own land is something else. It is like saying he is equal to the rest of us. That, I cannot accept. Those people were brought here to serve. Let one become too independent and the others start thinking they should be, too. Worst thing Lincoln ever did was to free those people. Everybody was a lot happier before that."

"Except maybe the slaves."

"They had plenty to eat and a place to sleep, probably far better than in Africa. Now there are hundreds of them adrift without work, without a place to sleep or anything to eat unless they steal it. Do you think freedom has made *them* better off?" Brackett waved a hand toward the man with the plow. "Do you know why I'm out here watching him? Because if I don't, he'll stop at the end of the row and lie down in the shade. Left on their own, they'd not work enough for their own subsistence."

"Shanty has done all right on his own."

"But it was given to him."

"Whatever that little place amounts to, Shanty made it so with his own muscle and sweat. His master was drunk more than he was sober."

Brackett shrugged away further argument. "I see I am not going to sway your opinion, and certainly you are not going to sway mine. I know nothing about the burning of that darkey's cabin. You'll have to take my word on that."

Rusty did not want to believe him, but something in Brackett's eyes told him he spoke the truth. He asked, "What about your son Farley?"

"I regret to say that Farley was in jail last night. Some altercation with a state policeman."

"You wouldn't have any idea who did burn Shanty out?"

"Ideas do not stand up in court. You have to show proof."

"Not always, not in a Yankee court." Rusty decided upon a flanking approach. "It has the look of somethin' Fowler Gaskin might do, him and his dim-witted nephew." He watched in vain for anything in Brackett's expression that might reinforce his suspicion. He decided the farmer must be a good poker player.

Brackett said, "Fowler Gaskin is a lazy, ignorant lout, and no confidant of mine."

Rusty nodded. "At least there's *somethin'* we can agree on. It's a mystery to me why good men die young while reprobates like Fowler Gaskin live on and on."

"Perhaps it is because the Lord wants no part of him, and hell is already filled up with Unionists."

Rusty said, "Those who fought for the Union side were honest in their opinions."

"They were wrong. And if you sympathized with them—which seems to be the case—then you were wrong."

"Looks like we've about used up our conversation." Rusty put his foot into the stirrup.

"Wait a minute." Brackett raised a hand. "It's about dinnertime, and you're miles from home. You're welcome to stay and eat with us."

That caught Rusty by surprise. "You're invitin' *me?*"

"I have never turned a hungry man away from my door, be he white, black, or somewhere between."

"I'd figured myself lucky if I got away from here without bein' shot at."

"I even fed the tax collector, though he made me sell off more than half of my farm so I could keep the rest."

"That's a second thing we can agree on. I don't like the governor's tax men either."

A bell clanged at the house. Rusty saw the black man stop the mules in the middle of a row and begin to unhitch them. Brackett said, "That's Bethel, letting us know that dinner is about ready."

Brackett had evidently walked to the field. Rusty saw no horse for him to ride. The plowman rode one of the mules and led the other, but Brackett made no move toward the second mule. Either he did not like to ride mules or he would rather walk than ride beside the black.

To keep from outdoing the host, Rusty also walked, leading Alamo. Brackett showed an interest in the animal.

Rusty admitted, "He's gettin' up in years, and I wouldn't take him out anymore if I was called on to chase Indians. But he's still the best horse I ever had just for ridin' the country and workin' stock."

Brackett gave Alamo a look of approval. "You can tell a lot about a man by the horse he rides."

Rusty, by the same token, had always been able to overlook at least some faults in a man who took good care of his horses.

Brackett's daughter stood on the porch, one hand shading her eyes as she watched for her father's coming. Brackett stamped his boots against the bottom step, dislodging a little field dirt. He said, "I brought company for dinner."

"I figured you would. I set an extra plate." She motioned toward the open door. "You-all go on ahead. There's a fresh bucket of water and some soap on the back porch."

Brackett led the way. Rusty saw a black woman and a white one in the kitchen. He surmised the white woman was Mrs. Brackett, but she did not turn to greet him. He heard Bethel say, "They're here, Mama." He heard no acknowledgment. Perhaps Mrs. Brackett did not care for company. Or, from what he had heard, she no longer cared for Mr. Brackett.

Bethel was pleasant through the meal, passing food around the table, asking Rusty if he needed anything else. Mrs. Brackett took her place at one end, but Rusty soon realized she had not once looked toward her husband. She had probably been a handsome woman in a younger, happier time, but her face had frozen into a bitter, pinched expression. She kept her attention focused on her plate and the food immediately in front of her.

He caught Brackett glancing at his wife, pain in his eyes.

Bethel made polite small talk, seemingly oblivious of the wall of silence that stood between her parents. But the forced quality in her voice told Rusty she was achingly aware of it.

The war had cost this family dearly, but it had cost others just as much. He pondered the wide contrast—and the parallels—between the Bracketts and the Monahans.

Mrs. Brackett arose from the table before the others had finished. She picked up her plate and utensils and disappeared into the kitchen. Brackett stared after her, saying nothing.

Uncomfortable, Rusty pushed back his chair. "I'm much obliged for the good dinner, but I'd best be headed home." He started to pick up his plate, but Bethel signaled him to leave it.

She said, "I'll take care of it, Mr. Shannon. You needn't bother."

He sensed that she was sparing him another meeting with her mother. Or perhaps it was her mother she was sparing.

Brackett said, "Come back any time, Shannon. You're welcome here so long as you don't bring up politics."

Bethel followed Rusty out onto the porch. In a quiet voice she said, "I hope you'll pardon my mother's behavior. She hasn't been the same since my brothers died. She blames Papa for that." She looked intently into his face.

"It's odd, but you look a little like them, especially John, the oldest. I think my mother saw that."

He twisted his hat in his hands. "I'm sorry about your brothers."

"We still have Farley." She looked away as if mention of the name brought sorrow. "He follows after calls that the rest of us can't hear."

Riding away, he felt sympathy for the Brackett family . . . Mrs. Brackett, driven inward, still unable to reconcile herself to the loss of two sons. Bethel, trying to bring even false cheer into a house that had no cheer at all. And Jeremiah Brackett . . . Rusty felt that he could bring himself to like the man, even granted that he had some unreasoning attitudes.

His thoughts turned to Bethel's comment about her brothers, and the fact that Rusty resembled them a little. Could it be . . . no, surely not. No one had ever been able to determine who Rusty's real parents had been. It was taken for granted that they had fallen victim to the great Comanche raid. It was probable he had blood kin somewhere, kin who did not know he existed.

But the Bracketts? No, the chance was too slender to contemplate. He probably resembled a lot of people. For most of thirty years he had lived without knowing who he was. He thought it unlikely that he would ever know.

He wished he could. Occasionally he awoke from a dream in which he could almost see the faces of his real mother and father, could faintly hear his mother's voice singing to him. At such a time he felt adrift, alone in a world of strangers.

CHAPTER
SEVEN

ndy Pickard sat on his moccasined heels in the shadow of his horse, his attention focused on an open spot where the grass was thin and short. Chopping weeds in the garden, Shanty had eyed him awhile. Finally, laying down his hoe, he moved through the open gate and walked out to join Andy.

He asked, "Where'd you leave Mr. Len?"

"Me and him found that lost milk cow of Tom Blessing's. She'd had a new calf. Len took her home. I don't expect he'll come back tonight."

"And Mr. Rusty?"

"Out lookin' for a couple of strayed horses."

Shanty bent to see what was holding Andy's attention. "What you studyin' so hard, boy?"

"Ants."

Puzzled, Shanty asked, "What's to look at with an ant? One looks the same as another. I don't pay them no mind long as they ain't crawlin' up my britches leg."

"These are fightin' a hell of a war."

Shanty frowned at the word *hell*, but Andy had taken to using it so casually that there seemed little chance of breaking the habit.

"It's passin' strange," Shanty said, "how easy it is for a young feller to learn words he ain't supposed to say, and how hard for him to learn the gospel."

Andy pointed. "They're killin' one another by the hundreds."

Shanty's interest quickened as he braced his hands against his thin knees and leaned down. "I see what you been lookin' at. Dead ants layin' all over. They're just like people. This whole country to share, and they fight over one little bitty piece of ground."

"I remember a medicine man tellin' about watchin' a big ant war one time. Said it went on from daylight 'til the sun went down. Said he saw more dead ants than there was stars in the sky."

"That's a lot of ants."

"He said it was a sign from the spirits. The winnin' ants was Comanche, he said. The losin' ants was the Texans. Said pretty soon the Comanche nation was goin' to rise up and take back everything the white men stole, clear to the edge of the big water. Then everything would be like it was in the old days when the Comanches drove the Apaches out."

"I don't reckon he said when that was goin' to happen, seein' as it ain't yet?"

Andy sensed that Shanty was not taking the prediction seriously. "It's bad luck to make fun of a medicine man. They say some can turn a man into a crow or a bullfrog, even a snake."

"You ever seen it done?"

"No, but I've heard tell."

"I don't reckon you know a medicine man who can turn a black skin white? If I was white, maybe I could live over at my own place and not have to burden nobody."

Andy brushed away two ants that started to crawl up on his moccasins. "No tellin'. Medicine men have a lot of power. They know how to reach spirits nobody else can talk to."

Shanty frowned. "Listen at you, talkin' about spirits and such. Preacher Webb'd be mighty disappointed. He's taught you all about the Good Book and tried to help you put away them heathen notions."

"Who's to say they're all wrong? I expect Preacher Webb is closer to the Lord than anybody I know, but when I was with The People I saw things he nor no other white man could explain. Not everybody talks to the Lord the same way. I'll bet before your folks was brought to this country they talked to Him different than what you do."

Shanty mused. "When I was a shirttail young'un, before I was sold off,

I remember my granddaddy tellin' about a far-off place way across the water. Said *his* daddy was a king before the slave catchers come. Said he fought the chains and took many a bad whippin', but he never did give up the notion of bein' a king. Died claimin' he still was."

"Then by blood rights you'd ought to be a king yourself."

"King of what? A little old dirt farm that I dassn't even go to unless I got somebody with me?" Shanty pointed to the ground. "If I was an ant—if my people was ants—they'd be the ones gettin' whipped yonder, the ones with their heads bit off. And I'm afraid your medicine man was wrong about which ones was Comanche and which was white. It's the Comanches that's losin'. Or fixin' to."

Andy noticed his horse beginning to paw the ground and realized ants were climbing up its legs. He brushed them off and led the horse out of harm's way. "We ought to be smarter than ants. Looks like we could figure out some way to divvy up the land and not fight over it."

"That's been tried. Never did seem to work. There's too much difference in the way white folks and Indians look at things. I remember once the government started a reservation up on the Brazos River. Folks blamed a lot of the Indian raids on tribes from there. Maybe they was right and maybe not, but it didn't make no difference. The Indians was forced off of the reserve and pushed up north of the Red River. Even the peaceable ones."

Andy said with a touch of pride, "The Comanches I was with never let the white men put them on a reservation in the first place. They still run free."

Shanty's brow furrowed. "I hope you ain't thinkin' you'd like to go back and run with them."

"The notion strikes me sometimes. I've got no kin here that wants me. I ain't forgot the time my uncle came and looked me over. Said even though I was a Pickard, like him, I was too savage to live with his family. He went off and left me."

"Folks here have treated you good . . . Mr. Rusty and Mr. Len, Tom Blessing, and them."

"That makes it hard, in a way. Every time I take a notion I'd rather be Comanche, Rusty or somebody does me some special kindness. Then I don't know whichaway to turn."

"Don't forget that it was Indians who killed your real mama and daddy."

"I was too little to remember much about that. Mostly I just remember that the Comanches gave me a good life." He grimaced. "I guess it's easier bein' an ant. They always know which tribe they belong to."

Shanty straightened his back and groaned at the pain the move brought him. "Everybody wants to live to get old, but it sure don't come cheap." He turned his head and stared off down the wagon road. "We got company comin'. He's runnin' like he had Indians chasin' him."

Andy did not recognize the rider at first. "Looks like he's pushed his horse about as far as it can go."

Shanty nodded. "A man don't abuse an animal that way without he's got reason."

The bay labored for breath, sweat lathering its hide. Andy thought the horse might go to its knees when its rider brought it to a stop. The man slipped from the saddle and almost went down from fatigue. Andy judged him to be about Rusty's age, though his eyes were hard in a way that Rusty's never were. A scar cut through the whiskers on one side of his face, all the way up to the corner of an eye. Andy guessed he had probably earned it in a fight. It was a scar a Comanche warrior would envy.

The visitor paid no attention to Shanty. He acted as if the black man were invisible. Laboring for breath, he said, "This is Shannon's place, ain't it?"

Andy said, "Yep, but he ain't here."

Looking closer, he realized he had seen this man the night the riders had come to challenge Shanty. He remembered the scar. Rusty had said his name was Farley Brackett. Andy immediately felt a rising antagonism.

Brackett said, "I don't need Shannon noway. I just need one of his horses." He looked at Andy's. "That one will do."

Andy took a tight grip on the reins. "Not this one. I can see how you've treated yours."

"Couldn't help it. I've got Federal soldiers comin' behind me. And the state police."

"Anyway, I been ridin' mine, and he's tired. He wouldn't carry you far."

Shanty lifted his hat to arm's length, shading his eyes. "I don't see nobody back there."

The fugitive seemed irritated that Shanty made so bold as to speak to him. "They're comin', and they're hell-bent to stretch my neck."

Though Andy had seen little of the state police, they had been the topic of much conversation. Most people seemed to regard them more as an oppressive arm of the Federal military than as an independent law-enforcement body like the old-time rangers had been.

Shanty said, "Even if you was to have a fresh horse, you look mighty tuckered yourself. Best you lay low and let them go on by."

The man acted as if he had not heard. He was probably not used to listening to black people's opinions. Andy didn't like the man, but he figured anyone who had aroused the state police and the Federal troops must have redeeming qualities.

He pondered the advisability of the question, then asked, "You kill somebody?"

"Best you-all don't know what I done. Just give me a fresh horse."

Shanty said, "I seen a blue roan down on the river awhile ago. Ought to be easy caught."

Brackett looked to Andy for confirmation, not trusting Shanty. Andy said, "I don't know what Rusty would say."

Brackett declared, "It don't matter what he says. I need me a horse." He looked back for evidence of pursuit. "Them Yankees will ask if you've seen me."

Andy said, "If we don't watch you leave, we can't tell them whichaway you went."

The man looked suspiciously at Shanty. "You won't let this nigger tell them?"

"Shanty and me'll both be too busy to see where you go."

Brackett remounted and soon disappeared amid the trees and low brush that screened the river from view.

Andy said, "Maybe you shouldn't have mentioned that roan. Looks to me like Rusty's lost a horse."

Shanty smiled wickedly. "You know that roan ain't much account. He may not even outrun them Yankees. Mr. Rusty's been talkin' about swappin' him off."

Andy shaded his eyes. "I see the soldiers now, just like he said. I don't know if I can lie to them." Beyond a little creative boasting of their exploits in battle, Comanches had taken pride in veracity.

"Ain't hard to tell a lie if you set your mind to it. From the time I was a young'un I learned how to bow my head and make a big grin and tell folks what they wanted to hear. Had to, else somebody was apt to take a quirt to me."

Andy saw a fleeting resentment in Shanty's eyes, reflecting a lifetime of suppressed reaction to neglect and mistreatment. It troubled him to realize that despite his concern for the Comanche viewpoint he had never fully considered Shanty's.

Shanty said, "If you don't want to lie, ain't no reason you have to for Farley Brackett. Whatever trouble he's in, he got in it by hisself. You don't owe him nothin'."

Andy wrestled with his conscience. "I don't owe the soldiers nothin' either."

It occurred to him that if he and Shanty remained where they were some sharp-eyed trooper might notice the fugitive's tracks leading toward the river. He said, "Let's walk over to the corral and wait."

As he expected, the soldiers veered toward the corral, missing the garden and whatever trail the scar-faced Brackett might have left.

Blue-coated troopers had always made Andy uneasy. He remembered warrior accounts of fights with them before the conflict between North and South. Since returning to Texas after the war the soldiers seemed not to bother much about Indians, even when the Indians came raiding. They appeared more interested in complicating life for those Texans who had supported the South.

Though Rusty had never borne arms against the Union, the soldiers and Federal officials treated him as if he had. That added to Andy's mistrust.

Shanty spoke softly and with confidence. "Stand easy. They ain't apt to do nothin' to a boy of your age, nor to a gentleman of color."

"I ain't afraid of them. Me and half a dozen Comanche warriors could whip the whole damned bunch."

"The rebs thought thataway, too."

The troopers were black, their officer white. Andy recognized from his insignia that he was a lieutenant. Two other white men were in civilian clothes. Andy assumed they were state policemen. He was almost certain he had seen them somewhere. One had a pinned-up sleeve.

The officer raised his hand, signaling the soldiers to stop. He gave Shanty a quick, dismissive glance, shifting his attention to Andy. He demanded, "Whose farm is this?"

The superior attitude tempted Andy to tell the officer to go to hell. He deferred to better judgment. "It belongs to Rusty Shannon."

The civilians showed surprise at the name. One leaned forward in the saddle. "Shannon, you say? Him that used to be a ranger?"

"He was. But not anymore."

The man smiled. "Well, I'll be damned. I had no idee what part of the country he was in." The smile was cold.

Andy suddenly remembered when he and Rusty had made a fast

departure from the Monahan farm to avoid a potentially violent showdown with two men named Oldham. This was Clyde Oldham. The man with one arm was the brother everybody called Buddy-Boy. Andy's skin prickled.

The lieutenant stared hard at Andy, first at his braided hair, then his moccasins. "What kind of a Hottentot do you call yourself?"

"My name's Andy Pickard. I ain't no Hottentot, whatever that is."

"One might think at first glance that you had escaped from the reservation."

A black sergeant pushed forward. "I've heard talk in town, sir. This young man was raised by the Comanches."

The officer sniffed. "He does not appear to have left them far behind. Where is this Rusty Shannon?"

Andy's face warmed. He felt no inclination to answer.

Shanty broke the silence. "He's out huntin' for horses, sir. I expect he'll be comin' along directly."

The lieutenant gave Shanty a closer study than before. "I take it that you work here, boy."

"Can't get a lot of work out of an old man like me, but I live here."

"Does Shannon pay you?"

"Well, no sir, but you see—"

"Boy, don't you know slavery is forbidden anymore? You need not work for anyone unless you are paid for it."

Andy could not hold his anger. "Night riders burned Shanty out of his own place, and there wasn't none of you yellow-legs anywhere in sight."

"Young man, you are addressing an officer of the United States Army."

Shanty whispered, "Careful. Soldiers been known to carry people away, and some never was heard from again."

"I ain't afraid of no soldiers." He dismissed any thought of telling the truth about Farley Brackett.

The officer frowned darkly. "I can see that you are too young to have served in the rebel army, but that kind of attitude got your elders into a war they could only lose."

Andy clenched his fists. "Not my *Comanche* elders. They whipped you bluecoats every time they met you."

The officer turned to the sergeant. "You say you've heard about this lad. I take it Shannon is not his father."

"Way I heard it, the boy's folks got killed by Indians. I don't 'spect him and Shannon is blood kin."

The lieutenant nodded as he looked back at Andy. "So Shannon uses you for free labor, just like this poor darkey. We'll look into that. But right now we have more pressing business. We are on the trail of a fugitive. If you'd seen him, I don't suppose you'd tell us?"

Angry, Andy wanted to say he had not, but the reply seemed to swell in his throat. It would not come out.

Shanty feigned innocence. "What sort of a man you talkin' about?"

The civilian spoke up. "His name is Farley Brackett. He shot a state policeman."

Because the fugitive was a son of Jeremiah Brackett and had once tried to do Shanty harm, Shanty had no real cause to lie for him. But he said, "A feller come by awhile ago, ridin' like there was Indians after him."

"Heading west?"

Shanty hesitated. Andy quickly said, "He was when we seen him." That was a half truth. Brackett had been traveling west when he first appeared.

The officer accepted the statement. "Then we'll be on our way. Don't forget to tell Shannon we'll be back to have some words with him."

Clyde Oldham leaned forward in the saddle. "Tell Shannon that the Oldham brothers have got some words for him, too. He'll remember us."

The lieutenant said, "Shannon can wait. Right now we have to try to catch Brackett."

Oldham turned in the saddle as the others started away. "Me and Buddy'll be back. That is a promise."

Andy watched the soldiers and the Oldhams move off.

Trouble in his eyes, Shanty asked, "Who are these Oldhams? What they got to do with Mr. Rusty?"

"Seems like they had bad trouble a long time ago. Now they know where Rusty lives."

Shanty worried, "Maybe we made the trouble worse, lettin' them soldiers go in the wrong direction."

"Maybe so. I've got no reason to like Farley Brackett, and you have every right to hate his guts."

"Hate just burns a hole in your belly. Like that Farley. Folks say the war turned him ornerier than a badger in a trap. He was probably cocked and primed to shoot that state policeman."

"I kind of wish now I'd told the soldiers the truth. Lyin' don't set well on my stomach."

"You didn't lie, exactly. You just didn't tell them all of it. Other people's quarrels are best left alone. Most of us got troubles enough of our own."

Once the soldiers were well gone, Brackett emerged from the timber by the river. He was riding the blue roan. As before, he spoke to Andy and paid no attention to Shanty. "I'm obliged to you for sendin' the soldiers on their way. And I'm obliged for the horse trade." The scar-edged eye twitched.

Andy said, "Don't thank us 'til you've rode that roan awhile." He frowned. "Just curiosity, but how come you to shoot a state policeman?"

"It needed doin', and I didn't see nobody else fixin' to."

"You'd best not tarry long. The soldiers'll figure out pretty soon that they're draggin' an empty sack."

Brackett said, "If you happen to see my old daddy, tell him that snotty policeman ain't goin' to be messin' with him no more."

The soldiers and the Oldhams had ridden westward. Brackett rode southward, quickly disappearing. That puzzled Andy a little. "I figured he'd go north. There wouldn't be as many people up that way to tell the soldiers where he went."

Shanty said, "Don't matter. People south of here ain't tellin' the soldiers nothin' neither. Especially since it was a state policeman he shot. Them old rebels lost the war, but they didn't lose none of their will."

CHAPTER
EIGHT

Andy had just finished milking when Rusty came in about sundown, leading a bay horse on a rawhide rope. It was the horse Farley Brackett had been riding. Andy and Shanty met him at the corral.

Rusty seemed puzzled. "Found him down by the river. You-all know anything about him?"

Andy saw that Shanty was waiting for him to give the answer. He said, "Farley Brackett came by awhile ago in a hurry to make a swap. He took that blue roan. Looks to me like you got the best end of the trade."

"Not hardly." Rusty turned the horse around. "Look at the brand on his hip."

It was a US. Andy slumped. "Army horse. I didn't notice that." He glanced at Shanty, who shook his head. Shanty could not read, so the brand might have meant nothing to him even if he had seen it.

Rusty asked, "What was Farley doin' with an army horse?"

Reluctantly Andy explained about the shooting of a state policeman.

Rusty said, "And you lied to the soldiers?"

"Not exactly. Just sort of."

Shanty offered, "I'll lead that horse back down to the river and hide him to where them soldiers won't see him."

Rusty looked westward. "Good idea, but it's too late. They're already comin'."

Andy could see the horsemen approaching. He said, "One more thing you better know before they get here. The Oldham brothers are with them."

Rusty's face fell. He said something under his breath, then, "Bad luck. I was hopin' they'd never find out where I live."

"What's more, they're state policemen."

Rusty expelled a long, painful breath. "That gives them authority to do just about anything they want to."

Horses and men looked whipped down and subdued. Questions were unnecessary. Andy wondered how far west they had ridden before they accepted the fact that Brackett had given them the slip. He understood why Federal soldiers had managed so little success in trailing Indians. Anyone with watchful eyes could have seen the fugitive's tracks leading down toward the river, then turning about and heading south.

The army sometimes employed friendly Indians such as the Tonkawas to do its trailing, but there had been no Indian with the lieutenant's detail.

Rusty raised one hand in a civil but less than enthusiastic greeting. The lieutenant's gaze fastened immediately upon the bay horse.

Rusty said, "I found him down on the river. Looks like the man you were after left him and took one of mine."

The lieutenant cast a suspicious eye in Andy's direction. "How could he do that without somebody seeing him?"

Rusty said, "By swappin' in the timber, out of sight from up here."

The lieutenant was suspicious to the point of belligerency. He pointed a finger at Andy. "You and that darkey claimed the fugitive rode by here and went west."

Andy fumbled for words. "That ain't exactly what we said. He was ridin' west when we first seen him. We didn't say whichaway he went after that."

"We didn't find any tracks to the west."

Rusty said, "Like as not your man doubled back. Even a coyote is smart enough to do that."

Clyde Oldham fixed a hard gaze on Rusty. His brother beside him, he pushed up abreast of the officer. "Sounds thin to me, Lieutenant. Remember, Shannon was a ranger under the rebels. I'm bettin' he helped Brackett get away and put that boy and that nigger up to lyin' for him."

Shanty declared, "Mr. Rusty didn't do no such thing. He wasn't even here."

The lieutenant showed no inclination toward believing. He jerked his head at the black sergeant. "Ride down toward the river and see if you find any tracks."

Andy watched nervously as the soldier walked his horse along, looking at the ground. If the sergeant had good eyes, Andy thought, he was likely to pick up Brackett's trail. Surely enough, the trooper paused a minute, riding back and forth, then proceeded to the river. In a little while he returned and saluted the lieutenant. "Tracks are clear as day, sir. They go from here straight down to the river. By the looks of it, he changed horses and rode back up this way. Never went west at all."

Clyde Oldham declared, "This is the horse that Brackett stole off of the street after he shot the policeman." He turned a wicked gaze on Rusty. "What do you say now, Shannon?"

"Looks like I've lost a horse."

The younger Oldham had a malevolent grin. "You're fixin' to lose a lot more than a damned horse."

Clyde Oldham's eyes were cold as he looked at the lieutenant. "We've found Shannon in possession of a stolen horse, an army horse at that. Looks clear to me that he aided and abetted an escapin' criminal."

The lieutenant addressed Rusty. "I had intended to come back and talk to you about other matters, such as not paying that darkey for his labor, or this young man either. But now we have a more serious violation to consider." He glanced at Oldham. "Inasmuch as this affair began with the shooting of one of your fellow policemen, the army defers to the state. You may make the arrest."

Clyde's eyes seemed even colder. He drew a pistol and pointed it in Rusty's face. "Much obliged. Rusty Shannon, I arrest you as an accessory after the fact."

Rusty argued, "Lieutenant, this man and his brother have an old grudge against me."

Clyde said, "Damned right we do. He's the Confederate ranger that crippled Buddy." He waved the pistol. "Get your hands up, Shannon."

Rusty said, "I don't have a gun on me."

"Just the same, raise them hands. High."

Andy felt the blood rise in his face. He tried again to intercede. "Rusty wasn't even here when that feller came by."

The lieutenant pushed his horse in front of Andy. "Young man, if you interfere any further your youth will not be taken into account. I can have you sent away to a correctional institution where they will work the wild Indian out of you . . . or beat it out."

Shanty said, "The boy's right. Wasn't none of Mr. Rusty's doin'."

The black sergeant was the only one who even looked at Shanty. The white men did not acknowledge his presence. Shanty protested directly to the sergeant, who studiously looked away, his jaw firmly set, and pretended not to hear.

The lieutenant finally acknowledged Shanty by giving him an order. "Boy, put Shannon's saddle on that bay horse. Mr. Oldham and his brother will take him to town while the rest of us pursue our fugitive."

Shanty gave Rusty a plaintive look. Rusty nodded for him to do as the officer ordered. Shanty soon brought the bay horse. Clyde motioned with the pistol's barrel. "Mount up, Shannon. We got a ways to ride."

Rusty shrugged in futility and swung into the saddle. "Andy, you and Shanty take care of things while I'm gone."

Buddy Oldham motioned for Rusty to start moving. "You're liable to be gone a long time. You may *never* come back."

The tone of his voice sent a chill down Andy's spine.

The lieutenant led his soldiers out toward the place where the sergeant had found the tracks leading southward. It would soon be dark, so they would not be able to follow the trail long.

Shanty worried, "Ain't nothin' to keep them Oldhams from shootin' Mr. Rusty in the back. They can claim he tried to get away in the dark."

Andy's belly went tight. He felt that it would be his fault if something happened to Rusty. "Let's catch up and go along. Maybe they won't do him no harm if we're there to witness."

Darkness fell by the time they saddled their horses and started. They set off in the direction the Oldhams had taken. They had not gone far before two pistol shots echoed through the trees.

Andy swallowed hard. "They've already done it." He put the animal into a hard run. He could hear Shanty behind him, trying futilely to catch up.

He heard Clyde Oldham's voice somewhere ahead. "Shannon! Where the hell did you go?"

Buddy Oldham called, "Shannon! Goddamn you!"

The two turned at the sound of Andy's and Shanty's horses. Clyde declared, "We had to do it, Lieutenant. Shannon was fixin' to get away." His voice changed abruptly as he realized these were not the soldiers. He aimed his pistol at them. "You stop where you're at or I'll shoot you both."

Andy drew rein. His voice almost broke from rage. "What did you do to Rusty?"

Clyde regained his composure. "I don't have to explain nothin' to a mouthy kid nor a nigger." He lowered the pistol when he saw that Andy and Shanty were not armed.

Buddy said excitedly, "He ran off, but I know I hit him. Like as not he's layin' dead out yonder somewhere."

Andy seethed. "If he is, you'll have a lot to answer for."

"I got a duty to shoot an escapin' prisoner. Anyhow, he shot me one time."

Andy said, "Folks around here think a lot of Rusty Shannon. If you've killed him they'll hunt you down like a sheep-killin' cur."

"I got the law on my side."

"Carpetbag law."

"Law just the same."

Clyde Oldham holstered his pistol. "You don't need to explain nothin' to the likes of them. We'll go and fetch help. Come mornin' we'll find Rusty Shannon no matter where he's at." He pointed a finger at Andy and Shanty. "You two better go home and stay there if you know what's good for you."

The brothers rode off into darkness. Shanty said, "Them Oldhams ain't goin' to let him live. We got to find him first."

The moon had not yet risen. Andy could barely see past Shanty. Anxiety made him shake. "He may be wounded and down."

They rode in a walk, calling Rusty's name. Andy worried, "We could go right past him and not know it."

"We can't wait for the moon to rise. He could bleed to death by then."

Andy felt cold all the way to his boots. "If he dies I swear I'll nail the Oldhams' scalps to the courthouse door."

"This ain't no time to be talkin' like a Comanche. Better you talk a little to the Lord."

A horse nickered. Andy turned toward the sound. "Rusty! Rusty, can you hear me?"

He came upon the horse. In the darkness he could not see the color, but he knew he had found the government bay.

Shanty pointed. "There, Andy."

Andy saw a dark shape on the ground. He dismounted quickly, but Shanty reached Rusty first. "Still breathin'," he said. "Mr. Rusty, it's me and Andy."

Rusty was on his stomach. He groaned. Andy dropped to his knees and reached to touch him. He drew his hand away, sticky with warm blood. "Took a bullet in his shoulder. From the back, I'd guess."

He jerked his neckerchief loose and pressed it against the seeping wound.

Shanty said, "Let's turn him over real easy. See if the bullet came out the front."

It had. At least the slug was not lodged in Rusty's body.

Andy felt like crying but managed to choke it off. He forced the words. "Rusty, we have to move you away from here. Think you can ride?"

The only answer was a groan.

Shanty said, "We got to get him to the house."

"They'll look there in the mornin'."

"Where else can we go?"

Andy thought a minute. "Tom Blessing's. He'll know what to do." Andy touched Rusty's arm. "Rusty, can you hear me?"

The voice was weak. "I hear."

"We'll take you home and get the wagon. Then we'll haul you to Tom Blessing's. Think you can ride if we hold on to you?"

Rusty murmured, "Try."

Shanty brought the bay horse and helped Andy lift Rusty to his feet. Andy had to place Rusty's foot in the stirrup. The two managed to boost him into the saddle. Shanty held him in place while Andy mounted his own horse, then Andy took over.

Andy said, "Grit your teeth, Rusty. It won't be long."

Rusty drifted in and out of consciousness. Andy held on to him but came near losing him once. "Grab on, Shanty. He's about to fall."

The cabin was a welcome sight as the moon emerged. They eased Rusty down and carried him inside. Andy worked to stop the bleeding and bind the wounds while Shanty went out to fetch the wagon and team.

Andy felt compelled to keep talking whether Rusty heard him or not. Otherwise he would break down and cry. "Damn it all, Rusty, it's my fault. I ought to've let them have Farley Brackett. Better him than you."

Rusty made a small cough. Throat aching, Andy said, "Hang on. Hang on tight. Don't you be goin' off and leavin' with me owin' you so much." He rubbed a sleeve across his eyes.

Rusty did not respond. Andy decided it was better that he remain unconscious. Perhaps the trip would not hurt him so badly.

Andy and Shanty carried Rusty outside and placed him on blankets spread in the bed of the wagon.

Shanty fretted, "A wagon won't be no trouble for the Oldhams to follow."

"We'll use the town road as far as we can. I doubt they can tell one wagon track from another."

Tying two horses on behind, they started toward the road that led to the settlement.

Rusty lay quiet and still, reacting only when the wagon hit a bump that jarred him. Andy remained on the road awhile, then turned onto a lesser-used trail that led to Tom Blessing's place. He stopped for a minute and made an effort to brush out the tracks.

Past midnight, he saw the cabin ahead.

He said, "We're there, Rusty. We've made it." He did not know if Rusty heard him.

A dog barked. A man emerged from beneath a shed. Andy recognized the lanky form of Len Tanner. "Len," he shouted, "come a-runnin'."

Barefoot and in his long underwear, Tanner came in a trot. "What's the trouble?"

"Rusty's been shot. Go rouse Tom Blessing, would you?"

Tanner demanded, "Who done this to him?"

"Clyde and Buddy Oldham. Go, would you?"

"Oldham?" Tanner spat the name. He hurried away, cursing the Oldhams, all their antecedents and any progeny they might ever have.

Rusty regained consciousness enough to ask where they were. Blessing came out of the bedroom side of the double cabin, buttoning his britches, bringing his suspenders up over his shoulders. He was barefoot and without a shirt. Tanner trotted alongside him, looking thin enough for a strong wind to blow him away.

Blessing peered into the bed of the wagon. "How bad is it?"

Rusty had become completely aware. He managed a raspy answer. "I ain't dead yet."

Blessing slid strong arms beneath him. He shouted at his wife to bring a light to the door, then set some water on to boil in the fireplace. He carried Rusty inside the bedroom. To Andy, Blessing seemed an old man, yet he had the strength of a bull. Mrs. Blessing held a lantern, setting it down on a table as her husband gently placed Rusty on the warm bed the couple had just vacated. She hurried to the cabin's other side to stir the coals in the fireplace and set a kettle of water on.

Blessing cautiously unwrapped the binding and examined the wounds.

Andy told him, "The bullet went plumb through. He lost a right smart of blood before we could stop it."

Shanty said, "It was God's mercy that he didn't bleed to death."

Andy explained about the fugitive Brackett, about the soldiers and the Oldhams.

Tanner swore. "Me and Rusty ought to've shot them damned Oldhams years ago when we had the chance."

Blessing grunted. "Now they're state policemen. They can get away with just about anything."

Andy said, "You've been the sheriff. You know the law. What can we do?"

"Not much. The state police and the military just barely tolerate us old rebels."

"But Rusty never was a rebel, and he had no part in Brackett gettin' away. I don't see how they'd have a case against him."

"The law is whatever the carpetbag courts say it is. As long as men of the Oldhams' caliber wear a badge, Rusty has a sword hangin' over his head."

Andy clenched a fist. "I wish I could bring the Comanches down here."

Blessing pointed out, "They'd hit a lot of the rest of us, too. No, we've got trouble enough as it is."

Mrs. Blessing washed the wounds with water as hot as her hands could stand it. Her husband poured whiskey into the bullet hole, front and rear. Rusty arched his back and sucked air between his teeth.

Blessing said, "I wish Preacher Webb was here. He can heal the body as well as the soul."

Mrs. Blessing replied, "If he *was* here, he'd wonder how come we keep whiskey in the house."

Shanty had watched gravely but said little. "I doubt the Lord minds folks takin' a little nip, long as it's in a healin' way."

The rough handling had brought Rusty to full consciousness. Blessing asked him, "How'd this happen?"

Rusty struggled with his answer. "I had a notion what they were goin' to do. When I heard the hammer click I set the horse to runnin'. I reckon the first flash blinded them. They couldn't see where I went."

Andy worried, "When they can't find you, they'll start figurin' all the places we might've took you. How long before they come here?"

Blessing finished wrapping the wounds with clean cloth. "Not long.

Some damned fool is bound to tell them me and Rusty have been friends since the battle of Plum Creek."

"Where can we take him?"

Rusty said, "The Monahan place."

Tanner nodded vigorously. "Back when we was rangers, Rusty caught a Comanche arrow in his leg. The Monahans took care of him 'til he was on his feet. They'd do it again."

Blessing cautioned, "The Oldhams might guess where he went."

Tanner's face twisted ominously. "It'd be their own fault if they did. Was Clyde and Buddy-Boy to go up there, they might not come back. Them Monahans get real serious when they're provoked."

Blessing said, "Rusty would have the benefit of Preacher Webb's doctorin'."

Andy remembered, "It's a long ways. It'll take several days in a wagon."

Rusty said in a weak voice, "I can make it."

Tanner declared, "Sure you can. Damned if we'll let the likes of Clyde and Buddy-Boy do you in."

Rusty reached up to touch Andy's arm. "Len knows the way. He can take me. I wish you and Shanty would stay and watch out for the place."

Andy felt a rush of disappointment at not going. "Whatever you want."

"Fowler Gaskin will carry off everything but the dirt if somebody's not there."

Andy's disappointment was quickly overcome by the realization that he was being trusted with heavy responsibility. "We'll take care of things, me and Shanty." He looked to Shanty for support.

Tanner asked, "You sure Andy's man enough?"

Rusty grunted. "He's almost grown."

Andy thought if he were still with the Comanches he would be taking scalps by now. He would start with the Oldhams'. He decided not to say so because it might be taken for immature blustering.

Mrs. Blessing said, "I'll be fixin' us some breakfast. Andy, there's ham in the smokehouse. Fetch a shoulder in here for Rusty and Len, would you? I'll put some salt and flour and coffee together."

Like most settlers along the river, Tom Blessing let hogs range free. Butchering was done on cold winter days and the meat slow-smoked in a small log structure behind the cabin. It took a minute for Andy's eyes to adjust to the darkness. He found the mixed smells of pork and charred wood pungent but not unpleasant. He chose a cloth-wrapped shoulder and lifted it from its hook.

Returning to the cabin, he found Rusty on his feet but supported by both Tanner and Blessing. Rusty said, "I believe I can sit up if you'll put me on the wagon seat."

Tanner said, "And go to bleedin' again? You'll lay down on them blankets and not give us no argument. I don't aim to dig a grave for you all by myself."

After a hasty breakfast the two men got Rusty safely situated in the wagon bed. Rusty looked with concern at Andy and Shanty. "The Oldhams may talk pretty rough. Shanty, you'll see that Andy keeps a cork on his temper, won't you?"

Shanty said, "We'll do just fine, Mr. Rusty. Don't you worry yourself about us."

Andy said, "I'm sorry, Rusty. I'd give anything not to've brought this trouble on you."

"Don't you be feelin' guilty. With the Oldhams, if it hadn't been this it would've been somethin' else. You just step careful and don't fall into any trouble."

Andy watched the wagon move away in the first pale light of morning, Len's horse tied on behind. He did not want anybody to see him choke up, so he took a broom from the dog run and began to brush out the tracks.

Blessing watched him quizzically. "You aim to sweep all the way to the Monahans'?"

Andy recognized the futility of what he was doing. "I can brush out the trail for a little ways, at least. I don't want anything to be easy for the Oldhams."

Blessing pointed to clouds building in the east. They would hide the sunrise. Andy saw a few faint flashes of lightning, so far away that he did not hear the thunder. Blessing said, "Looks like we may get some rain after a while. If we do, it should take care of the tracks. You-all like a little more coffee before you start home?"

Shanty shook his head. "We need to hurry and get there before the Oldhams do. Me and Andy got to figure out a lie to tell them."

Andy said ruefully, "It was a lie that started all this."

They had not been home long before Clyde and Buddy Oldham appeared with several men on horseback. Andy recognized none of them except Fowler Gaskin and his nephew, Euclid Summerville. Fowler had long and loudly proclaimed his allegiance to the Confederacy, though he had been quick to take the oath of loyalty to the Union once it was clear the rebel cause was lost and there might be advantages to reconciliation. Now he rode beside the state police, symbol of the occupation. It stood to reason that he would join the search for Rusty, given the long enmity between them.

Only the Oldhams wore badges, but the others all bore a gravely officious look that told Andy they had a high regard for their authority.

Clyde leaned forward in the saddle, his face as stormy as the clouds that rose behind him. "All right, where's he at?"

Andy and Shanty glanced at one another. "Who?"

"You know damned well who I mean. Rusty Shannon."

Andy said, "Couldn't you find him with all this bunch to help you?"

"Buddy hit him last night. He couldn't have got far without help."

"We ain't seen him." Andy found that the lie spilled out easily. In the Comanche culture the coyote was regarded as a trickster, always trying to lead humans astray. The People looked upon it with a mixture of dismay and admiration. Playing the role of the coyote gave Andy a wicked satisfaction.

Clyde said, "I figure you're hidin' him. We're goin' to look around."

Andy shifted his gaze to Gaskin. "Just don't carry away anything that don't belong to you."

Clyde gestured. "Search the place, men. Don't overlook nothin'."

Some went into the cabin. Andy was glad he had thought to burn the bloody pieces of cloth that would have been a giveaway. Others went to the barn and shed. Gaskin and Summerville headed straight to the smokehouse. Gaskin came out carrying a ham.

Andy said, "Just because you're runnin' with the scalawag state police don't mean you got a right to steal."

Buddy Oldham said, "Keep it, Gaskin. When we get through with Shannon, he ain't goin' to care about one little old ham. He ain't goin' to care about *nothin'*."

Emboldened, Summerville went into the smokehouse and fetched another.

Shortly the men gathered in front of the cabin, empty-handed except for Gaskin's hams. Clyde's temper had not cooled. "Seems to me like I saw a wagon under that shed yesterday. I don't see it there now."

"You don't?" Trying to appear innocent, Andy looked again at Fowler Gaskin. "There's thieves everywhere."

One of the riders pointed out, "I see fresh wagon tracks leadin' off yonderway."

Buddy's voice crackled. "I wounded him. He couldn't have rode far on his horse. One of you—maybe both of you—hauled him someplace. Tell us where you took him."

Neither Andy nor Shanty spoke. Buddy lifted a quirt from his saddle-horn. He rode forward, lashing Shanty first. Andy saw the next strike was coming at him and tried to shield his face. The quirt stung like fire across his cheek and down his shoulder. He looked up, burning with anger but determined to take the next strike like a warrior, without flinching.

Summerfield shouted, "Hit him again. And that nigger, too."

One of the policemen rebuked Buddy. "Headquarters ain't goin' to take it kindly, you quirtin' a darkey. You'll have the Freedmen's Bureau down on us."

"Mind your own business. I'm tryin' to make them talk."

"They ain't goin' to. Look at the fire in that kid's eyes. Right now he's pure-dee Comanche. He'd cut your gizzard out and feed it to you."

Clyde Oldham said reluctantly, "Back off, Buddy."

The policeman said, "Oldham, looks to me like we ought to be huntin' Farley Brackett instead of wastin' so much time on Shannon. The worst he did was let Brackett have a horse to get away on."

Andy declared, "He didn't even do that, and Oldham knows it. He's tryin' to get even for somethin' that happened back in the war."

Buddy raised the quirt as if to strike Andy again.

The policeman caught Buddy's arm. "Been enough whippin' done. We're fixin' to get caught in a frog-stranglin' rain. I'm for goin' back to town."

The others seemed to agree. Clyde trembled with rage. "You-all quit-tin' on us? Then me and Buddy'll keep lookin' by ourselves."

"If you keep on lookin', it'll *be* by yourselves."

Clyde cursed them to no avail. All turned and started riding away except Fowler Gaskin and his nephew. Gaskin advised Clyde, "Between Rusty Shannon and the Comanches, they've plumb ruined that boy. You ought to take that quirt and make a Christian out of him."

Andy said sarcastically, "You're a great one for usin' a whip on people. And burnin' cabins, too."

Gaskin said, "We ought to burn this one. Teach them all a lesson."

Summerfield offered, "I'll do it, Uncle Fowler."

Clyde said, "Forget it. I got plans for this place. I'll need that house."

The four were so intent on Andy that they did not notice Shanty ease into the cabin. He came out with a rifle and a look of determination. "You-all are about done here, ain't you?"

Gaskin's voice went shrill. "Aim that thing somewheres else. Damned fool nigger, you're liable to touch it off and kill somebody."

Shanty agreed. "Sure might."

Gaskin began backing his horse away. Shanty swung the muzzle toward Clyde and Buddy.

Fear leaped into Clyde's eyes before he could check it. He said, "We ain't goin' to get nothin' out of these two. Let's see if we can follow them wagon tracks."

Shortly after they turned away, the rain began. It started with large drops, widely scattered, then became a drenching downpour. Andy and Shanty stood in the dog run, beneath the roof. Wind carried a cool spray into their faces. It eased the burning where Buddy's quirt had stung Andy's cheek.

Shanty looked closely at Andy's face. "That quirt marked you pretty good."

"It'll pass."

Shanty said, "With this rain, they ain't goin' to follow no tracks for long."

"Maybe they'll all drown."

Rusty and Tanner were probably caught in the same heavy rain, Andy thought. At least they had slickers and a tarp. The Oldhams, Gaskin, and Summerville didn't. Maybe they *would* drown.

He grinned. His cheek no longer burned so badly.

But Shanty spoiled his good feeling. He said, "It ain't done yet. Looks like them Oldhams ain't goin' to rest 'til they ruin Mr. Rusty, or kill him."

CHAPTER
NINE

Andy was chopping a seasoned live-oak limb for firewood while Shanty took the shade on the dog run after a day's work in the field. Andy said, "That feller hidin' down by the river is gettin' careless. I've seen him twice."

Someone had been camped in the timber for the last three days, watching the cabin. Andy knew it was probably an Oldham or some other state policeman assigned to the duty. He said, "Maybe I ought to go and invite him up for supper."

Shanty smiled but dismissed the idea. "That'd just make the Oldhams madder than they already are. They don't think we know anybody's down there."

"They're liable to take root and grow if they're waitin' for Rusty to show up."

Andy returned to his wood cutting. It struck him that in a Comanche camp, gathering wood was woman's work. But there was no woman here, and he had seen little sign that Rusty was looking for one. He remembered that the Monahan daughter named Josie had taken a shine to him. Maybe she would have time and opportunity to work on him now while he was hurt and helpless.

He had not gotten a good look at Jeremiah Brackett the night a group of riders visited Shanty's place, so he did not recognize him when the man came riding up on a long-legged sorrel horse. A wagon followed. Andy was intrigued to see that a girl was driving it.

At least they were not state police. He walked out to meet them, the dog Rough trotting ahead of him, barking. Shanty remained beneath the dog run, mending harness.

"Howdy," Andy said to the rider. "Light and hitch." It was a greeting he had often heard Rusty address to visitors.

He judged the horseman to be well into his late fifties, maybe even his sixties, roughly the same as Tom Blessing. Except for a stiff military bearing he had the look of a hardworking farmer, not a man from town.

The visitor said, "I'm Jeremiah Brackett." He gave Andy's braids a moment's quiet attention. "You'd be the young man my son told me about."

"Andy Pickard. I suppose your son is Farley Brackett."

"He is. It seems the Brackett family owes you-all a horse. We always pay our debts. I brought this one in exchange for the one Farley took from you."

Andy walked around the sorrel, giving it a close inspection. "He's a sight better-lookin' than the roan your son took. You're gettin' the short end of the trade."

"Farley said that horse almost got him caught by the state police. He would have shot him, but that would have left him afoot."

The wagon stopped. Brackett unsaddled the sorrel and threw his saddle behind the seat. He said, "This young lady is my daughter Bethel."

Andy stared at the girl, trying to remember the rules of behavior Rusty and Shanty had lectured him about. He removed his hat. He struggled for the proper words. "Damned pleased to meet you, ma'am." His face warmed. He knew he had made a mess of it.

He had not seen a lot of girls to compare her by. He thought she might be the prettiest he had ever looked upon, though his notion of what constituted *pretty* tended to change with each new one he saw. He tried to remember if he might have encountered her in town. It seemed to him that if he had, he wouldn't have forgotten.

She said, "Your name would be Andy, I suppose. I've heard about you."

He wondered what she had heard. Probably not good if she had heard it in town. He said, "Don't believe them. There's an awful lot of liars in this country."

"It wasn't *all* bad. We appreciate what you did for my brother."

Shanty came out from the dog run. Andy nodded in his direction. "It was Shanty's doin' as much as mine."

Brackett grunted. "I'll pay him for it. I don't want to stay beholden to a darkey." He reached in his pocket and withdrew a silver coin. He handed it to Shanty. "Here. This is yours."

Bethel gave her father a quick look of disapproval, then turned away.

Shanty fingered the coin, his eyes confused. "What's this for?"

"For your part in helping my son escape. It should buy you a pint of whiskey."

"I ain't a whiskey drinker, sir."

"Well then, some tobacco or whatever you like. It's Yankee. Anybody in town will accept it."

Shanty tried to give back the coin, but Brackett waved him away. "Keep it. We're even now."

Andy felt he should extend the hospitality of the house, such as it was. "We've got some coffee inside. Or some fresh buttermilk I just churned last night."

He immediately wished he had not admitted that. Churning was something else that would have been woman's work in a Comanche camp except that the Comanches did not have milk and butter.

Brackett climbed into the wagon. His daughter moved over on the seat and handed him the reins. He said, "Thank you, but we should be getting back. There is always more work to do than time to do it."

The girl gave Andy a thin smile as her father turned the team around. "Come and see us."

"I'd like to." Watching them leave, he thought, First time there's a reason. Maybe if he studied on it he could *find* a reason.

Shanty was still rubbing the coin between his thumb and forefinger. "I didn't see him give *you* nothin'."

Andy shook his head. "He didn't."

"Then how come him to pay *me?*"

Andy knew. Brackett would feel compromised if he owed a debt to a black man. Unable to think of any painless way to explain it, Andy decided to let Shanty figure it out for himself.

He did, and quickly. Shanty drew back and sailed the coin as far as he could throw it.

The Oldhams' state police gave up any pretense of secrecy in their watching post by the river, but they did not give up the stakeout. By the time Brackett and his daughter pulled away from the cabin, a rider was already trotting his horse up to overtake them. He circled the cabin and stopped the pair. After questioning them a few minutes he let them proceed and came back to where Andy and Shanty stood watching.

This was a deputy, not an Oldham. He looked disappointed. "Thought that might be Shannon."

Andy said, "You'll have to get up mighty early in the mornin' to catch Rusty. But keep on tryin'." He had wanted to needle the deputies and, if possible, the Oldhams, but Shanty had advised against it.

The deputy said, "Just followin' orders. Clyde says do it, and we do it. Tell you the truth, I'm gettin' almighty tired of campin' down there by the river."

"Come on up here, why don't you, where you can watch us a lot closer? Spread your blankets in the dog run. Even eat with us if you'll bring the grub."

"Clyde and Buddy would raise hell. Can't get friendly with the enemy, they'd say."

Andy said, "Don't it hurt your conscience, workin' for the state police, takin' orders from people like the Oldhams?"

"It's a livin'. All our officers ain't like them. Most of them are honest men just tryin' to do a dirty job the cleanest way they can."

"Like houndin' Rusty when you know he didn't do anything wrong?"

"That's Clyde's doin'. He's got the authority, and he's friends with a judge who goes along with whatever he wants to do. They've squeezed the old rebels around here for all they could get out of them. Stole some farms and stuck most of the money in their pockets, except for what they sent to Austin to keep the higher authorities happy."

"You could quit."

"I've got a family to feed. I grit my teeth and look the other way."

"This reconstruction government won't last forever. What'll you do when it's gone?"

"Been thinkin' about California. Maybe there's still some gold left out there. Ain't none in Texas. But 'til I can save enough to make the trip, I'll bide my time, do what Clyde tells me and hope I don't have to help him starve any widders and orphans."

He started to ride away but stopped and turned back. He seemed to have a hard time getting the words out. "I oughtn't to be tellin' you-all this, but I think you deserve to know. Clyde's fixin' to steal this place from Shannon the same way he's stole them others."

The statement hit Andy in the stomach. "How could he do that?"

"Rig the tax books, say that Shannon ain't paid all his assessments. It's worked for him before, him and his judge. You-all had just as well pack up whatever you'll want to take with you. There ain't no stoppin' him."

In a moment of anger Andy thought there was one way. He considered whether he should shoot Oldham in the head, in the chest, or in the belly. Any of the three would do the job. But he knew it was a futile notion.

Preacher Webb had often spoken about the wages of sin. Watching the deputy ride back toward the river, Andy said, "Yonder goes a man who hates the sin, but he's willin' enough to take its wages."

Shanty replied, "I'm glad I won't be wearin' his shoes when he walks up to the Golden Gates."

"He's wearin' better shoes than me and you."

"I'd rather be barefooted."

Andy was almost finished with his chores when he recognized the blue roan horse approaching from the direction of the Brackett farm. It was too far to identify the rider. "Company comin'," he called. His first thought was that the elder Brackett was bringing back the roan.

"Damn! I'll bet he wants to take Long Red." That was the name Andy and Shanty had given to the sorrel.

Shanty arose from his wooden chair and entered the kitchen. He was back in a moment with the rifle. "Hope it ain't Clyde Oldham, comin' around to hound us again."

"He wouldn't be ridin' that roan. Anyway, I saw him down on the river awhile ago, watchin' this place." He squinted. "That's not Old Man Brackett after all. It's his son Farley. They look a right smart alike."

"Him that caused us all this trouble?" Shanty made no secret of his disliking for the man. He handed Andy the rifle. "Mighty reckless, showin' hisself when the police are huntin' all over for him."

"Maybe he's come to thank us for that roan horse."

"He never looked like a man spillin' over with thankfulness."

Brackett reined up a little short of the cabin and studied the rifle with misgivings. The eye at the upper end of his facial scar was squinted almost shut. "Ain't no need for that."

Andy said, "I hope not, but I'd use it if you was to give me cause."

Brackett raised a hand, signaling peaceful intentions. "You and that nigger played a mean trick on me, puttin' me onto this roan. He ain't worth six bits in Yankee silver."

Andy shook his head. "You didn't do us no favor either, leavin' us with a horse that had a US brand on it. That's caused us no end of hell."

"So I've heard. I'm sorry for what happened to Shannon."

"Bein' sorry don't take Clyde Oldham off of his back, or ours."

"Ain't nothin' I can do about it."

"You could surrender to the state police. You could tell them how it really was. Then Rusty could come home."

"I'd just as well put a gun in my ear and pull the trigger as to give myself up to that bunch."

"Then what did you come here for?"

"Just wanted to say I appreciate you puttin' the soldiers off of my trail."

Andy said, "I'm wishin' now we hadn't done it."

Brackett leaned down to look closer at Andy. "That's quite a mark on your face."

"Quirt. Buddy Oldham did it."

"I'd like to take a bullwhip and write my name across his back with it. Him and all the others."

Andy said, "You've got trouble enough, shootin' a state policeman."

"He lived. Guess I'll have to try again."

Andy felt relieved. At least Rusty could not be charged as an accessory to murder. "After you do, run some other direction, would you? Don't come by here."

A smile flickered and was quickly gone. "If there's anything you need, go talk to my old daddy. If he's got it, you can have it."

Andy said, "He brought us a horse. We don't need nothin' else from him. But you might need a little advice from *us*."

"What's that?"

"Don't go down by the river. Clyde Oldham and one of his deputies are there watchin' to see if Rusty comes back."

"The hell you say!" Brackett looked toward the river. "I don't see anybody."

"We're not supposed to either, but they get careless now and again."

"You want me to go down there and shoot them?"

"Looks like you'd get tired of shootin' policemen."

"I ain't yet, but I guess this time I'll be movin' on." Brackett set the roan into a trot and disappeared around the cabin.

Relieved at his departure, Andy drew a deep breath. Shanty wiped a sleeve across his face.

Andy's relief quickly faded as he saw Clyde Oldham and a deputy riding up from the river. He growled, "Preacher Webb says trouble likes to travel in pairs." He cradled the rifle in his arms.

Oldham spat a stream of tobacco juice and gave Andy a fierce scowl as he approached. "That wasn't Rusty Shannon, was it?"

Andy said, "The shape you left Rusty in, he couldn't ride like that."

"Then who was it?"

"He didn't mention his name."

Oldham clenched a fist. "If it's somebody carryin' messages to Shannon . . ."

Andy tried not to betray his surprise as he saw Farley Brackett ride out from behind the cabin and move up behind Oldham. Oldham heard and turned quickly, then froze, gaze fixed on a pistol in Brackett's hand.

Brackett said, "No, I ain't Shannon."

Andy swallowed hard.

Oldham stammered, fear rising in his eyes. He raised his hands. "Brackett. Where? . . . How? . . ." His voice choked off.

Brackett reached forward and took Oldham's pistol from its holster, then the deputy's. "Don't worry, I ain't made plans to kill anybody today unless I'm provoked. For what it's worth, the time I stopped by this place and took a fresh horse, Shannon wasn't even here. Besides, what I did wasn't much."

"You shot a state policeman."

"He oughtn't to've messed with me and my folks. But I didn't kill him."

"You tried."

"Yes, I did. Some days I can't shoot worth a damn. Anyway, you've got nothin' to blame Shannon for. I stole his horse, same as I'm fixin' to steal yours." He nodded at the deputy. "You heard what I just said? You can bear witness to it."

The deputy looked uneasily at Oldham. "I heard."

"Don't forget it, or I'm liable to come lookin' for *you* on one of the days when my shootin' eye is sharp." He nodded toward the roan. "Now, Deputy, I wish you'd take the saddle off of this horse and put it on Oldham's."

Oldham sputtered. "You'd leave me afoot?"

"You'll have the roan. I warn you, though, he ain't much of a horse."

The deputy switched saddles. Brackett looked Oldham's brown horse over and nodded approval. "Too good for a state policeman. The roan is more your caliber."

Oldham fumed. "I'll get you someday."

"Be damned careful that I don't get *you*." Brackett mounted and rode away in a stiff trot.

Left without a weapon, Oldham could only stare, his eyes smoldering.

With a touch of malice, Andy said, "You want to stay for supper? We'll be servin' crow."

Shanty frowned at him.

Oldham said, "It don't make any difference what Farley Brackett says, I'm still goin' to get Shannon."

Andy protested, "But you heard him say Rusty wasn't here to give him that roan horse. He just took it."

Oldham acted as if he did not hear.

Four weeks had passed without word from or about Rusty. Andy was uneasy, but he knew it would not do for Rusty or the Monahans to write a letter. Any mail would almost certainly be opened and read by the Oldhams or the Federally appointed postmaster.

He found that in a perverse way he enjoyed the present situation except for being concerned about Rusty's condition and a continuing guilty feeling that he was responsible for it. He felt a sense of being on his own and given a high level of responsibility. With the Comanches the equivalent would be if he were allowed to participate in running of the buffalo or raiding into Texas settlements and Mexico. The Comanches did not count birthdays quite as white men did. A boy became a man when he proved he could carry his weight. For some, that could be as little as fifteen or sixteen summers. For others, it took longer.

Shanty came into the cabin's kitchen, carrying a slab of bacon from the smokehouse. His eyes were troubled. "Andy, did you hear my dog barkin' last night?"

"No. At least, he didn't wake me up."

"Me neither. I slept real good. But there's some hog meat missin' from the smokehouse."

Andy's first thought was that whoever stood guard at the river might have run out of meat and decided to replenish his supply. That idea gave way to a more likely answer. "Fowler Gaskin or his nephew Euclid. Clyde let them take those hams from us the day they came lookin' for Rusty. They probably figure they've got the law's blessin' to do it again."

Shanty said, "Can't always trust that fool dog to raise a ruckus. Maybe I better take to sleepin' out by the smokehouse."

A delicious thought came to Andy. "I wonder if anybody's got a wolf trap we could borrow."

"There's some over at my place, in the old shed. Me and Mr. Isaac used to do a bit of winter trappin'. Mostly for coons and ringtails and such, but now and then we caught us a wolf."

"I'm thinkin' more about catchin' us a hog. Your field probably needs weedin' again. We'll go over there tomorrow."

They had been working at Shanty's farm every few days, taking care of the field and garden. Because the cabin had been burned, they had been going early in the morning, then returning to Rusty's place late in the day to do the chores, fix supper, and sleep. Before they started home Andy sorted through several steel traps hanging in Shanty's shed, picking two of the largest. He set one of them, then tripped it. The jaws snapped hard enough to break a dry stick he used to trigger the mechanism.

"Not strong enough to bust an ankle," he judged, "but he's liable to hop around on one foot for a few days."

"Kind of mean, don't you think?" Shanty tried to sound dubious, but Andy could see mischief in his eyes.

"Not half mean enough for the likes of Gaskin."

Though he doubted that Fowler or Summerville would show up so soon, he set a trap that evening just inside the smokehouse door. Entering in darkness, the thief was not likely to see it until he put his foot in it.

Andy checked on the trap the next morning. It was just as he had left it. For safety he tripped it. He set it again the second night, and again no one came.

The third night Andy awakened to a loud cry of surprise and pain. He stepped out onto the dog run in time to see a spider-legged figure dancing furiously in the dim light of the moon, a chain clanking as it dragged behind him.

The voice was Fowler Gaskin's. A second voice quavered. "What's the matter, Uncle Fowler?"

Gaskin launched a formidable string of profanity. "Fetch my horse, you damned idiot!" Howling, he dropped to the ground and labored to free his foot. He cast the trap as far as he could throw it and limped to the horse Summerville led up.

"You sons of bitches!" he shouted toward the cabin. His voice was shrill. "You dirty sons of bitches!" He fired a parting shot toward the cabin. Andy heard the slug smack into a log.

He grinned. "Fowler Gaskin, that'll teach you to stop suckin' eggs."

He had not seen Rusty's black horse Alamo in a couple of days and set out after breakfast to search for it. Toward noon he found it with a couple of the neighbors' plow horses grazing in a draw, tributary to the river. "Come on, boy," he said, dropping a rawhide loop over Alamo's neck, "you better stay closer to home or somebody like Fowler Gaskin is liable to hook you to a plow."

He expected to see Shanty working in the field or the garden, but instead he was at the cabin, loading something into one of two wagons that stood nearby. Two men were leading harnessed teams up from the river, where they had evidently been taken to drink.

One of the men was tall Tom Blessing. The other, who looked much like him but was younger, Andy recognized as a son. Blessing saw Andy coming but continued leading his team to the front wagon.

Andy dismounted and extended his hand. "Howdy, Tom." He nodded at the younger Blessing. "What brings you-all over here?"

Tom Blessing's face was grim. "Bad news. Clyde and Buddy Oldham are fixin' to take over this farm and everything on it."

Andy felt as if his stomach were turning over. He remembered what the deputy had told him. He had not really believed it could happen. "How can they do that?"

"I heard about it in town. Clyde claims the records show that Rusty is way behind on his taxes."

"Rusty's paid all the taxes they asked for. It took just about everything he got for sendin' cattle north."

"Tax records are easy to alter if you've got the keys to the courthouse. My son and I hoped we'd beat the Oldhams out here and haul off everything Rusty might want to keep."

Shanty came out with an armful of blankets. Blessing's son had Rusty's plow in his wagon, along with all the harness and tools from the shed.

Tom Blessing said, "Pity we can't take cabin and all."

Blood hot in his face, Andy demanded, "What about the field? The crops are half grown already."

Blessing replied, "Pity, but I reckon the Oldhams'll get the benefit of all that. You want to help me empty the smokehouse? No need in leavin' the meat to them."

Andy trembled with outrage. "And I thought Fowler Gaskin was a thief. Ain't there somethin' we can do?"

"I don't know what. Clyde has got the scalawag government on his side."

"We could shoot him," Andy said.

Shanty shook his gray head sadly. "That's the Comanche in you talkin'. Killin' ain't the way the Lord meant for folks to doctor what ails them."

"Once it's done, it's damned sure permanent."

"So is a hangin' rope, and that's what you'd get. Them Oldham brothers are like a pair of hungry wolves."

"No, they're just coyotes."

"Anyway, it ain't for me and you to decide. Best let Mr. Rusty know what's happened and see what he wants."

They soon had the two wagons loaded with about everything not too heavy to lift or too bulky to carry. Andy said, "It's up to me to go tell Rusty about this. He ain't goin' to take it kindly."

Blessing nodded. "Kindly or not, he'll have to take it for now. Maybe someday when things change he'll find a way to get the farm back. At least there's this much the Oldhams won't get."

Andy gazed in the direction of the plot where Rusty's Daddy Mike and Mother Dora lay. "He won't even own the ground where his folks are buried."

Blessing's expression was grave. "I can imagine what old Mike would say. He was a fire-eater, that one. But it finally got him killed." He climbed onto the wagon.

Shanty asked, "What about me? Where will I go?"

Blessing replied, "With me, Shanty. You can stay at my place 'til things straighten out."

Shanty hesitated. "Andy, you goin' to go tell Mr. Rusty?"

"He's got to know."

"Like as not them Oldhams'll figure on that. They'll follow you. They won't be satisfied 'til they've killed him dead."

"I'll wait 'til night, and I'll ride in the edge of the river a ways so they'll have hell findin' my tracks." He reached up to shake Shanty's hand, then Blessing's. "I don't know when I'll be comin' back. A lot'll depend on what Rusty wants to do."

Blessing said, "Tell him we'll be back and gather up all of his livestock that we can find. We'll drift them west to some empty country I know of. I doubt the Oldhams will find them any time soon."

Andy stood hunched in sadness, watching the wagons roll away. For six years this place had been home to him, at least the only home he had. He felt the same emptiness as when he had turned his back on Comanchería. There were times when he wondered if dark spirits dogged his steps and did not mean for him to have a home.

The cabin appeared almost empty, bereft of most of its handmade furniture except for the beds, too cumbersome for the wagons. The cooking ware, the cups and plates, were gone. The smokehouse was empty except for a large slab of bacon Andy had saved for his trip north. He had kept back salt, coffee, and a small sack of flour so he could make bread on the trail. These he carried out to the corral and placed in a wooden trough near his saddle. He planned to ride the Brackett sorrel, Long Red, and use Alamo as a packhorse. For no amount of money would he leave Rusty's favorite mount to be taken by the Oldhams or perhaps Fowler Gaskin, whichever showed up first.

Clyde and Buddy Oldham arrived awhile before sundown, accompanied by a sour-faced deputy. Clyde dismounted and waved some folded papers in Andy's face. "I got eviction papers for Rusty Shannon. Since I know he ain't here, I'm servin' them on you. These papers tell you to vacate."

Andy feigned ignorance. "What do you mean, vacate?"

Buddy spoke up sharply. "He means get the hell off, and the quicker the better." Buddy lifted the quirt from the horn of his saddle and raised it.

Clyde blocked the blow with his arm. "He's still got a mark from when you done that before, and it didn't do no good. He may be half Indian, but I expect he understands English when it's spoke good and plain. Put your stuff together, boy. You're leavin' here."

"Where do you expect me to go?"

"Back to the Comanches, for all we care. That's probably where you belong."

Andy knew argument was futile, but he did not want to give in to them without raising a little dust first. "You've got no right to this place. It's Rusty's, and it belonged to his folks before that. What if I don't want to leave?"

"Then I'll turn Buddy loose with that quirt. He's only got one arm, but you know it's a strong one."

While the deputy waited with Andy, Clyde and his brother walked up to the cabin. They paused a moment at the dog run to look at the empty iron hooks on which fresh meat often hung, wrapped in canvas. They then went into the kitchen. Clyde was out again in a moment, crossing quickly over to the bedroom side. He stayed there but little longer before striding down from the dog run and marching angrily toward Andy.

"What the hell has happened here? Where's everything gone?"

Andy continued to feign ignorance. "I been away most of the day. Maybe Fowler Gaskin paid us a visit. He never leaves without takin' somethin'."

"Gaskin hell! Everything on this place belongs to me. These papers say so."

"You just now served them. 'Til you did that, I reckon everything still belonged to Rusty." Andy knew little about legalities, but that seemed logical enough.

The deputy put in, "I told you I seen a couple of wagons earlier in the day. They left here loaded."

Buddy declared, "Somebody tipped this Indian off. Whoever it was needs a good stompin'."

Clyde said, "We'll save the stompin' for Rusty Shannon, when we find him."

Buddy said eagerly, "Stomp on him awhile, then shoot him."

Clyde looked toward the field. "What was in the house wasn't worth much anyhow. They couldn't carry off that plowed ground out yonder. It's ours."

He turned again to Andy. "We'll be back first thing in the mornin'. You better not be here. Come on, Buddy, we're headed to town."

Andy watched them so long as they were in sight. Though they left by the town road, he had a strong hunch they would circle back and keep a lookout on him. Clyde was surely shrewd enough to guess that Andy would go immediately to notify Rusty what had happened. All he and his brother had to do was follow.

He raked banked coals in the fireplace and coaxed the flames with dry shavings, then built up a blaze with larger pieces of wood. He broiled bacon on a stick and waited for night.

In the dark of the moon he packed blankets and food on Alamo and saddled Long Red. He had built up a big fire, hoping the watchers would think he was still in the cabin. For a while he had entertained the notion of burning the cabin so the Oldhams could not have it. He gave that up as a bad idea. The cabin was Rusty's main tie to the memory of Mike and Dora

Shannon. He would not want it destroyed, even to keep it from the hands of his enemies.

Besides, Andy held out hope that Rusty would eventually find a way to get the farm back. He would appreciate having the cabin remain intact.

He swung into the saddle and tugged on the lead rope. "Come on, Red, Alamo. We're goin' north."

CHAPTER

TEN

There was no clearly marked trail at first, but Andy did not need one. He had confidence in his sense of direction and his memory for landmarks. As he had told Shanty, he rode a couple of miles in the edge of the river, then found a gravelly bank on which he could quit the water without leaving obvious tracks. He traveled until he figured it was past midnight, then halted for a dry camp. He had eaten his supper in the cabin.

He hoped the Oldhams had not noted his departure. Even if they guessed his direction and started at daylight, he should be several hours ahead of them.

Awakening at daybreak, he glanced around to be certain where he was. He had a good memory for places. More than once during the years he had lived with Rusty, he had become helplessly homesick for the plains and had slipped away alone, returning to Comanche land. There he had lived off the land and watched The People's camps from afar, wishing but not daring to enter. He had been like an estranged family member who still felt the kinship but knew the path to reconciliation was too treacherous to try.

He prepared a hasty breakfast of bacon and bread wrapped around a stick and broiled over a low flame. The bread tasted flat, so he salted it a little and made it more palatable. Shanty had taught him how to bake corn dodgers on the flat side of a hoe, but here he had neither hoe nor cornmeal. Looking behind him he saw no sign of pursuit, but he was uneasy. He felt instinctively that the Oldhams were back there somewhere. They might be greedy, they might be vicious, but they were not altogether stupid. Sooner or later they were bound to cut his trail.

Andy followed a route he had ridden with Rusty. He remembered he had also ridden this way, though southbound, following his Comanche brother Steals the Ponies and several other young warriors intent upon a horse-stealing raid. Because they considered him too young they had not let him ride with them, but he had followed at a distance. He had not allowed himself to be discovered until they were too deep in the Texan country to send him back. Misfortune had dogged him, however. In a running fight his horse fell on him, breaking his leg. That was when Rusty Shannon found him and carried him home.

Andy had relived that event a thousand times in his mind. He toyed with the fantasy that it had never happened, that he had never reentered the white man's world and traveled the white man's road. He often wondered where he would be now and what he would be doing. By this time he fancied that The People would have accepted him as a warrior and a skilled hunter of buffalo. He would ride with pride through camp after each exploit, knowing The People were watching him and telling stories of his deeds.

He had been called Badger Boy, but surely by now he would have earned a nobler name reflecting his status as a man. He would not be just that Indian-looking young'un, Andy Pickard, getting into fights at the settlement, a kid whose blood kin had rejected him and who lived as a ward of Rusty Shannon. Among the Comanches, he would be a man worth noticing.

At least now he was on a mission worthy of him, to warn Rusty of danger and perhaps to help protect him from his enemies. The responsibility was heavy, a little daunting, yet exhilarating.

Late on the first full day of travel he came upon a creek. He had known it would be there, yet he had not allowed himself to give it much thought beforehand. Now, suddenly, the sight of it took him back six years. He remembered what Rusty had shown him then, and he shuddered. This was a bad place.

His instincts pressed him to cross the creek hurriedly and ride on, but something within would not allow him that avoidance. It was as if other hands took hold of the reins and guided the sorrel horse against his will.

He watched for a landmark tree. He almost rode past, for it had fallen since his last visit. It lay dry and broken on the ground. A scattering of chips indicated that travelers had chopped up much of it for campfire wood. He rode a small circle and found the mound of stones just as he remembered them.

Stomach cold, Andy made himself dismount and tie Alamo's lead rope to the horn of his saddle. He hitched Long Red to a sapling at the top of the creek bank. He stood at the grave, skin prickling, his throat swelling to a rush of confused feelings.

This was where his white mother had died.

Rusty had told him how he and Daddy Mike and others had ridden this way, following the trail of a war party. The Comanches had taken many horses and carried with them two prisoners, a small boy and his mother. Here the pursuing Texans had found the woman cruelly butchered. Lacking digging tools, Rusty and Preacher Webb had covered her with stones the best they could.

They had not overtaken the warriors, and they had given the captive boy up for dead.

That boy had been Andy.

Rusty had shown him the place, hoping it would revive memories of his life before the Indians had taken him. Here Andy had imagined he felt the spirit of his mother, and images suppressed during his years with the Comanches had come rushing, overwhelming him. He had relived the horror of her death. He had tried ever since to rebury that memory, but the specter rose up now and then in the dark of night, chilling him, destroying any chance of rest.

Logic told him he should hate the Comanches for what they had done, but he could not. They had killed his original family—his mother and father—then in compensation had given him a new family, making him one of their own.

As he looked down at the grave now, a grief long denied came welling up. He tried to remember his mother as she was before her capture and not as she had been in the last terrifying moments of life. He could not quite see her face, but in his mind he could hear her voice. He remembered that she used to sing a lot. He tried to remember the songs. It was like trying to grasp a fluttering butterfly that remained teasingly out of his reach. As with the details of her face, the old melodies eluded him.

He said, "Mother." The word seemed strange on his tongue. He said it again, knowing he must have spoken it to her often when he was small. He had had an Indian mother too, but he had addressed her as *Nerbeahr*, in the Comanche tongue.

"Mother," he said, feeling choked, "I wish I could remember more. It's just not there. I wish . . ." But there was nothing more to say.

A faint smell of smoke drew him back to the reality of the present. For a panicked moment he wondered if the Oldhams had outthought him, if they had already been here. Perhaps Clyde had guessed where Andy was headed and had cut around him. He found a disturbed spot on the ground beneath the creek bank, near the edge of the water. Campfire coals still smoldered beneath a cover of sand, which appeared to have been kicked over it to snuff it out.

The sorrel horse nickered, its alert ears pointed forward. Taking a quick breath, Andy saw a dozen riders spill over the top of the bank where it made a bend fifty yards away.

One glance told him they were Comanche. It was not Clyde and Buddy Oldham who had camped here.

Heart pounding, he ran for the horses, jerked the reins loose and swung into the saddle. He had to tug on the lead rope to get Alamo moving. The warriors shouted eagerly, yelping like coyotes. Andy set the sorrel into a run but quickly realized he had no chance. Though he turned Alamo loose, he saw that the Indians would overtake him in a minute.

Mouth dry, blood racing, he turned to face the threat. Trying to remember one of Preacher Webb's prayers, he made a show of dropping his rifle. He raised his hand as a sign of peace, or at least of resignation.

In the Comanche tongue he shouted, "Brothers. I am Comanche. I do not fight you."

They quickly circled around him. Several held bows with arrows fitted and ready to fly, but they hesitated.

One ventured nearer than the others, eyes narrowed with suspicion. "You are white. How is it you call us brothers? How is it you know our words?"

Andy swallowed hard. They could drive a dozen arrows into him before his heart could beat twice. He hoped they would give him time to speak. He hoped also he could remember the words, for he had not used them in a long time. He said, "I was raised to be Comanche." For emphasis he took off his hat and lifted one of his braids. "My heart is still Comanche."

The one he assumed to be the leader said, "We do not know you."

"I do not know you either." Andy struggled with the language. "But it may be that you know my brother. He is called Steals the Ponies."

Someone spoke from the edge of the circle. "I know such a man. Was not his father known for finding buffalo when others could not?"

"That is right." Steals the Ponies's father had been known as Buffalo Caller, but one avoided speaking the name of the dead lest it disturb the sleeping spirit. Andy said, "The one who was his father was a great hunter. So is Steals the Ponies a great hunter, and a brave warrior."

The leader was not quite satisfied. "How is it that you are white and you wear the clothes of a white man if you were raised Comanche?"

Andy's heartbeat began to ease. That they even listened to him was a favorable omen. He drew a deep breath and explained briefly the circumstances of his capture as a small boy. "It was here at this place," he said, "that those who took us killed my white mother. Then the one who was Steals the Ponies's father carried me away. I became Comanche." He told how years later he had foolishly followed his brother's raiding party, had broken his leg and had been found by friendly Texans.

He said, "They have tried to make me white again." He touched his hand to his heart. "But I do not forget that I am also Comanche."

The leader's face twisted as he pondered such an unfamiliar concept. "I do not understand how two men can live in one body. What medicine makes this possible?"

"It is not easy," Andy admitted. "For a long time I have had to follow the white man's road. But I still know the Comanche ways."

"Why have you not left the Texans and come back to The People?"

Andy was slow to reply, unsure how his answer might be received. He said only, "There was trouble. I cannot return." He did not want to tell it all, that he could not return because he had killed a fellow Comanche.

The leader speculated, "You were too young to have stolen another man's wife. Perhaps the trouble was over horses."

Andy sensed that this would be accepted. Technically he did not confirm that horses had been the cause, but he did not challenge the suggestion. He made a grunt which could be taken in any way the warriors chose.

The leader laughed. "At least it was over something of importance. A good horse is worth fighting for." The laugh faded. "Why are you here? Where do you go?"

Andy knew he could not explain the complex political struggle between the reconstruction government and the former rebels, for he did not fully understand it himself. He simply related that he was on his way to warn a friend and benefactor that men of bad spirit were after him.

The leader asked, "Can your friend not fight for himself?"

"He has been wounded. He will need help."

"Perhaps *we* can stop these bad spirits. We have taken horses on this trip, but we have not yet taken scalps."

Andy felt a surge of enthusiasm. The Indian side of him thought how perfect it would be if the Oldhams were brought down by Comanches. No one could blame Rusty or Andy for that. But a white man's doubts intruded. Not even Clyde and Buddy deserved to die the kind of death the Comanches could administer when their blood was up. "They may not come this way."

"But they might. We had started to make camp. You will stay with us. We want you to tell us how it is to live in the white man's country."

Andy felt trapped. He had no assurance that the Oldhams were trying to follow him. Though there had been enough travel along this way to beat out a faint wagon trail, they might not be using it. They might have realized where he was going. If so, they could miss this place by miles, circling and hurrying on ahead of him. But he could see that the Comanches had no intention of letting him proceed. Not yet. Perhaps when they were all asleep he could steal away in the dark. He would have to control his impatience, difficult as that might be.

The Indians stirred the fire they had hastily smothered and kindled the coals back into life. They took Andy's slab of bacon, though if divided equally it would not be large enough to provide much for each man. Most yielded their shares to the leader and a couple of the men who seemed closest to him. The rest ate typical Comanche traveling rations, dried meat pounded almost to a powder and combined with fat, berries, and nuts, whatever had been available at the time it was prepared. They shared this with Andy.

It reminded him of earlier times, and for a change it was pleasant. But it was not nearly so tasteful as what Shanty cooked up back home, or even Rusty.

Len Tanner, by contrast, could not boil water without giving it a scorched flavor.

Andy tried to feel at ease, but it was difficult so long as one warrior kept glaring at him and sharpening his knife.

He learned that the leader was known as Horse Runner, a name probably earned either snaring wild horses or stealing tame ones. Horse Runner and several others pressed him with questions. They exhibited much curiosity about the white man's world and the puzzling things they had seen on their forays through the settlements. Why did the white man tolerate the weak taste of his beef cattle when buffalo meat was available, so much stronger and more flavorful? How could he not be sickened by the stench of his pigs? How could the white man bear to live in a wooden tepee that could not be moved when the campsite became fouled with waste and when his horses had eaten off all the grass?

Most of all, why did each white man lay personal claim to one piece of land when the Great Spirit had provided so much to roam over and to share?

Andy felt that each question was a personal challenge, that he was called upon to defend the white man's ways. That meant these raiders did not entirely accept him as Comanche, just as many people around the settlements did not fully accept him as white.

He explained, "In the white man's eyes, to own land is a thing of honor. It means he is free and does not have to do as another bids him."

"But *we* are free," Horse Runner argued. "We do not have to do as any man tells us unless it is our wish. Yet we do not each claim one piece of land." He made a long sweep with his hand. "Together, we own it all."

You own it until the white man decides to take it, and he will, Andy thought. "All people do not have the same ways," he said.

Horse Runner grunted. "The whites are not true human beings. I do not understand how you can live among them."

"There are some bad ones," Andy conceded. "But there are many more who have good hearts."

"If their hearts are good, why do they take away what is ours? We won this land. Our grandfathers fought many battles to take it from the Apaches. The white man has no right."

Andy could see the inconsistency in Horse Runner's viewpoint. Rusty would say the Comanche had won the land by conquest from weaker people and now was losing it the same way to a stronger people. But nevertheless Andy's sympathy lay heavily with the Comanche.

He was relieved of the necessity for further argument when a young warrior hurried down the creek bank, motioning excitedly. "Three horsemen come. They are *teibo*."

White men. Andy moved up the bank far enough to see over the edge. The riders were three hundred yards away. They could not see the danger that awaited them, for the warriors had camped beneath the creek bank, out of sight. He wondered that they did not detect the smell of wood smoke, for the breeze was moving in their direction. They were blissfully complacent. Carelessness was a white-man trait that had brought many to a sudden death.

The warriors quickly caught and mounted their horses. Andy sensed the electricity of their excitement, though they remained quiet so they would not alarm their quarry too soon.

Horse Runner said, "Get on your horse and ride with us. Three good scalps are there for the taking."

"They may not be the right ones."

"It does not matter. They are Texans."

Andy wished he could be somewhere else, anywhere else. He had killed once and regretted it ever since. Though he occasionally made bold talk, he had no real wish to bloody his hands again, especially on strangers who had done him no wrong.

He squinted, trying to see more clearly. His breath stopped for a moment. One of the horsemen was Clyde Oldham. Andy had learned to identify him at almost any distance by the way he sat a little off-center in the saddle, comfortable for him perhaps but tiring to his mount. Another rider had but one arm. This must be Buddy Oldham. The third was probably the deputy who had been with them before.

Horse Runner grabbed the back of Andy's shirt and almost lifted him onto the sorrel horse. "Come on," he shouted. "You may take one of the scalps." Given no choice, Andy mounted as Horse Runner and the other warriors scrambled up the creek bank.

Around him, the men began whooping and yelping, eager for the kill.

The three riders instantly saw their peril and jerked their mounts around, whipping them furiously. Hooves pounded the earth and sent clods of dirt flying behind them.

Andy soon realized that the race was uneven. The Oldhams and the deputy rode grain-fed horses, whereas the warriors' mounts subsisted on grass. Andy found himself ahead of the Comanches, for the sorrel was stronger than their horses. But his incentive for catching the Oldhams was less compelling than the Oldhams' for getting away.

The chase stretched for more than a mile before it became obvious that the white men would escape. Andy began drawing on the reins. Most of the Indians pulled up on either side of him. A few were still determined to continue the contest though it was clearly lost.

Horse Runner eased to a stop, patting his mount on the neck in recognition of a good though unsuccessful run. He said, "At least we gave them a scare. They will tell their grandchildren about it."

Except they will probably claim to have killed half the Indians, Andy thought. "They will keep running until dark."

"Were they the bad spirits you spoke of?"

"They were."

"It is unfortunate we did not catch them."

"It is," Andy said, though he felt more relieved than disappointed. He would have had no stomach for watching the warriors murder the Oldhams and the deputy. That would rekindle old and bitter memories of the brutal way his mother had been butchered near here.

He could not be sure Clyde and Buddy would give up and go home. Once they recovered from the scare they might well continue their quest for Rusty, though they would probably circle far around this place.

At least this incident had given Andy time.

The Indians straggled back toward the creek. The last holdouts gave up the chase and trailed behind. Horse Runner said, "Would you like to go with us?"

"To the reservation?"

Horse Runner snorted. "The reservation? We still live free, as our fathers lived free." He motioned toward the north. These warriors came from the open plains where few whites so far had penetrated much beyond the outer fringes. To Texans it was still an unknown land. The only outsiders who entered with little trepidation were Mexicans from mountains and valleys to the west. They came in great groaning two-wheel carts, carrying trade goods to exchange for buffalo hides and dried meat, as well as horses and mules and cattle taken from the Texans' settlements.

Occasionally these *Comancheros* had ransomed white captives. Andy remembered a time when one had tried to bargain for him, but Steals the Ponies had refused even to consider giving him up.

He said, "I cannot go with you. I still must go to my friend. Those who hunt for him will probably keep trying to do him harm."

"Look for us if you ever want to return to The People. You will be welcome, Badger Boy."

He waited until the Comanches had gone to sleep. It was a weakness of theirs as warriors that they often did not bother to post a guard at night. Andy managed to get his horses and slip away. He did not stop to rest until he had put many miles between him and the Indians.

He decided not to mention this encounter. Even Rusty might not understand how Andy could join hostile Comanches in pursuit of white men. Too, if he reported this horse-stealing party, Texans were almost certain to organize a pursuit. He might be responsible for casualties on both sides.

No, he would keep his mouth shut.

CHAPTER

ELEVEN

Rusty kept rubbing his shoulder, trying to convince himself it had healed, but the wound was still inflamed around the edges and sore to the touch. He remembered it had taken a long time for his leg to recover from his arrow wound years ago. Even when the pain was gone, the shoulder would not soon regain full strength.

Damned poor farmer I am going to be, he thought.

He had been concerned about the farm, about how Andy and Shanty were getting along down there by themselves. He had wanted to send Len Tanner back to see about them, but Tanner had thrown himself into the routine here on the Monahan place and seemed in no hurry to go south again. Besides, he had taken down with a bad case of infatuation for the youngest Monahan daughter, Alice. She had blossomed into a pretty young lady with sparkling eyes and a laugh like music.

Tanner had expressed concern about several young men of the area who went out of their way to visit the Monahan farm more often than any legitimate business would seem to call for. "Somebody's got to keep an eye on Alice," he told Rusty. "She's too innocent to know what them young heathens have got on their minds."

"And you figure you're the one to keep her innocent?"

"Somebody has got to."

Maybe he *was* the one, Rusty thought. In some ways Tanner was about as innocent as any grown man he had ever known. As loyal a friend as anyone could hope for, Tanner had pulled Rusty out of tight spots more than once. But he was inclined to talk more than he listened and to jump into deep water before he considered whether or not he could swim. That had made him a good ranger when there was a necessity for fighting, but it also got him into some fights that need not have happened.

James Monahan had returned after being gone a couple of weeks, searching for cattle he might buy and put on the trail to Kansas. In the first years after the war he had been able to gather unclaimed cattle that had run wild, unattended during the conflict, but those had become scarce. Other men had observed James's success in converting them into cash and had followed his example. Now it was rare that an animal as much as a year old turned up without someone's brand already burned on its hide. James and brother-in-law Evan Gifford had turned more of their time and attention to breaking out additional land, expanding the farm's cultivated acreage.

The family's costly pro-Union stance during the war had finally turned to their benefit. The reconstruction government, often punitive in its relations with former rebels, treated the Monahans with respect in view of the heavy price they had paid for loyalty. It did not burden them with the high property appraisals and ruinous taxes often levied against others.

Rusty fretted over not being able to help with the physical labor. He spent his days finding small tasks he *could* manage such as mending harness and sharpening tools. He could not swing an ax, but he could fetch light armloads of firewood into the house after someone else cut it, usually despite protests from Josie Monahan. Clemmie Monahan's second daughter had appointed herself his nurse, his overseer, his guardian.

Josie took half the wood from his arms to lighten the load before he could dump it into a woodbox beside the cast-iron stove. She scolded, "Rusty Shannon, you'll never get well if you don't give yourself time."

"I don't like idlin' around. I want to earn my way."

"You earned your way with this family a long time ago. Now you go sit down in yonder and get some rest."

Rusty seated himself in a rocker in the front room. He could hear Clemmie in the kitchen, telling her daughter, "You treat him like you were already married. There'll be time enough to give him orders after you've stood together in front of Preacher Webb."

"I don't remember Papa ever takin' orders from you. For that matter, I don't see Preacher Webb doin' it, either."

"Your father did, and so does Warren Webb. I've just tried to give my orders in a way to where they think it was their own idea."

Rusty smiled. He was aware that Josie had set her cap for him years earlier, even when he was involved with her older sister Geneva, now Evan Gifford's wife. From things said and not said, Rusty knew several young men had tried to court Josie, but she had offered them no encouragement. At least a couple of these had transferred their attentions to the youngest sister, causing Len Tanner considerable loss of sleep.

Rusty would admit to himself, but to no one else, that he enjoyed Josie's attentions. Perhaps it would be easier if she did not remind him so much of Geneva, for he would know his feelings were for Josie herself. Yet, if she did not, he might have no such feelings. It was hard to be sure of his own mind.

Tiring of the rocker, he walked out onto the dog run. The log house was still relatively new, built after the war to replace an older one burned one night by Confederate zealots in a show of spite against the Monahans. A porch had recently been added to extend the dog run's shade.

A boy of six rode a pony into the yard. He swung a rawhide rope over his head and cast it at one of Clemmie's hens, missing by a foot but setting the hen into a squawking fit. This was Geneva and Evan's son Billy, named after the Monahan son killed years ago with his father for the family's Union leanings. The Giffords had a second child, a girl about two years old. Rusty suspected Billy had been sent outside to play so he would not awaken his sister.

The boy had been riding horseback as long as he had been walking. He was most often somewhere close to his great-grandfather, Vince Purdy, riding with him or walking alongside him when the old man worked in the field. The patient Purdy walked slowly to let the boy keep up with him, though Billy's short legs forced him to take a lot more steps. Sometimes Purdy pulled out a pocket watch James had brought him from a cattle trip to Kansas. He held it to the boy's ear and let Billy grin over a little tune it played.

Watching them together reinforced Rusty's acute sense of the value of family, and his own lack of one.

Vince is going to make a cowboy out of that kid, he thought. It was by no means the worst thing that could happen to him. Right now Texas was pulling itself up by its bootstraps from war's economic depression. It was doing so mainly with cattle and cotton. This was a little far west for cotton because of the cost of transporting it by wagon to distant railroads. If rails were one day laid across this part of the country, the arable lands would turn white with ripe bolls, he thought.

He watched Billy make a run at a cat. The loop went around it, but the cat was gone before the boy could jerk the slack.

Purdy walked up and patted his great-grandson on the leg. "You're doin' fine, Billy. Only what were you goin' to do with that cat when you caught him? He would've clawed you somethin' fierce. Come, let's see if you can rope the goat."

"If I do, will you let me hear the watch?"

"Sure. We'll find out if it plays Dixie." It wouldn't, of course. James had bought it in Kansas for his grandfather. That was Yankee country.

Billy laughed and rode off after Purdy, hunting for another target. The boy's got no fear, Rusty thought. The Monahan blood ran strong in him. He could imagine the pride crusty Lon Monahan would have felt in his grandson had he lived to know him.

A troubling thought came unbidden. Billy could have been his own. Rusty would have married Geneva Monahan had frontier duty not called him away too soon and kept him too long.

From almost as far back as he could remember, he had been acutely conscious of having no real identity. No one had ever been able to discover who his parents had been or if he had other kin. Mike and Dora Shannon had been like family, but theirs was not a blood tie. He had felt a strong attachment to the Monahans, yet they were not of his own blood either.

Andy Pickard was an orphan too, but at least he knew who he was. He had blood kin. In spite of the fact that they had rejected him, it must be a comfort of sorts to know they existed. Rusty would always have to wonder about his own.

Preacher Webb came in from the field, shirt darkened with sweat. He stopped at the cistern and drew up a bucket of water. After drinking liberally from a dipper, he joined Rusty on the porch and said, "The Lord has sent us another beautiful day."

Rusty agreed. "But sometimes I think he sends us too many. We could stand a little more rain."

"This has always been a one-more-rain country. It always will be. But most of the time He provides just enough. How's your shoulder?"

"Better every day. I feel like I'll be able to start back home most any time now."

"Are you sure you should? The trouble you got away from will still be there waitin'."

"I've been afraid it would come up here lookin' for me. I don't want it to spill over and hurt the Monahan family."

"You've helped them through their troubles in the past. They'd help you through yours now."

"It's better if they don't have to. After so much grief, the sun is finally shinin' on them. I'd hate to see them run afoul of the state police on my account."

Josie stepped out onto the porch for a quick look at Rusty. "Good. You're sittin' down. I was afraid you might've found yourself another job to do."

Webb smiled. "I'll keep an eye on him."

Webb watched her as she went back into the house. "I wonder if you know how much she thinks of you, Rusty."

"I think so. I just don't know what to do about it."

"She'd marry you in a minute if you asked her."

"What if somebody else was still on my mind? That wouldn't be fair to her, would it?"

He did not feel he had to be more specific. He was sure Webb understood the feelings he had long carried for Josie's older sister.

The minister said, "That's a question you might need to do some prayin' over."

"I've tried, but I've never heard the Lord say anything back."

"He speaks not to the ears but to the spirit. You'll hear Him when you're ready." Webb stood up. "I'd best return to the field. That plow won't move by itself."

"I wish I could do it for you. I feel like a broken wheel on a wagon."

"We all have an appointed place in the Lord's plan. It isn't always given to us to know just what it is. Yours will be revealed to you when it needs to be."

Concern about the Oldham brothers had everybody on the place watchful. Vince Purdy limped into the front room where Rusty was seated in the rocker, trying to read a romance novel Josie had handed him but making little headway. He did not relate to the genteel ballroom adventures of English society.

"Rusty, somebody's comin'. One man, leadin' a horse."

"Just one man? I doubt it's an Oldham. They generally ride together." Travelers had passed by the Monahan farm almost every day he had been here. Nevertheless he rose, trying to ignore the pain in his shoulder. He reached for his pistol, hanging in its holster from a wooden peg.

He found Len Tanner standing protectively at the edge of the porch, rifle in his hand.

Rusty said, "I doubt you'll need that."

"Rather have it and not need it than need it and not have it. You never know when you'll see a son of a bitch that needs shootin'."

Preacher Webb approached from the direction of the field. "You won't neither of you need a gun. That's Andy Pickard comin' yonder."

"Andy?" Rusty squinted, trying to see better. It seemed to him that his vision was not completely recovered from several days' fever caused by the wound. "What do you suppose—"

Tanner said, "It won't be good news. Nobody travels this far to tell you somethin' you want to hear."

Rusty walked out to meet Andy as he neared the barn. Webb, Purdy, and Tanner followed him. Andy was riding an unfamiliar sorrel and leading Alamo. The black horse had never been used as a pack animal before. It was probably a wound to his pride, Rusty thought.

Andy drew rein but seemed reluctant to dismount. His dark expression indicated that Tanner had been right. Rusty asked, "What's wrong back home? Somebody killed?"

Andy said, "Not yet, but somebody ought to be." He swung a moccasined foot over the sorrel's back and dropped to the ground. He licked dry lips and looked toward the cistern at a corner of the house. "I sure need a drink of water. Used up my canteen a good ways back."

He drank two dippersful, then poured a third over his head. "Rusty, they've taken your farm away from you."

Rusty's first reaction was disbelief. "They can't do that." But doubt set in. He felt as if Andy had struck him with the butt of a rifle. "How could they?"

"The Oldhams came out with some papers that said they could. Told me if I didn't want a good quirtin' I'd better hit the trail in a trot. So I trotted." He rubbed a hand across his face. "I already had a taste of Buddy's quirt."

"What became of Shanty?"

"He went with Tom Blessing. We cleaned out the cabin, and Tom hauled off everything that wasn't nailed down tight. Said him and his boys would gather all your stock they could find and try to get them out of the Oldhams' reach."

"Good old Tom. I never had a better friend." Rusty glanced at Webb and Tanner. "Except you-all."

Andy said, "Wasn't nothin' we could do about the land, though. We couldn't move that."

Rusty felt a weight growing heavy and cold in his stomach. He told Andy, "You did what you could. That's all anybody could ask. Maybe there's somethin' we can still do about the land." At the moment he had no idea what that might be.

Andy said, "I asked Tom. He didn't know of anything. The law goes along with whatever the Oldhams want to do."

Tanner declared, "There's one thing we *can* do. We can shoot us a couple of Oldhams and tell the law they bit one another like rattlesnakes."

Preacher Webb watched with misgivings, probably wondering if Rusty took Tanner seriously. Rusty said, "Don't worry, Preacher. I found out a long time ago that a shootin' doesn't settle anything. It just muddies up the water."

Andy grimaced. "One more thing I hate to tell you. The Oldhams were followin' me, at least at the beginnin'."

"You reckon they still are?"

"I saw them turn back, but they might not have stayed turned back. They wanted you awful bad."

Tanner said, "If they're still comin', we ought to go and meet them. Nobody would ever have to know what went with them. Not many would even ask."

Webb pointed out, "That would not get Rusty's farm back. If the Oldhams disappeared it would revert to the government."

Tanner complained, "Every time I come up with a good idea, somebody shoots a hole in it."

Webb said, "You'd best go to the house, Andy. I expect you're hungry. We'll take care of your horses."

Rusty looked at the sorrel. It was unfamiliar to him. "Where'd you get him?"

Andy said, "Jeremiah Brackett brought him to pay for the roan his son took. He's a heap sight better horse than that roan was. You can be proud of him."

Rusty shook his head. "No, *you* be proud of him. He's yours."

Andy grinned, but the grin did not last long. "We'd better keep watchin' for them Oldhams."

Len Tanner came the next morning to warn of approaching strangers. Standing on the porch, eyes pinched, Rusty counted seven horsemen. "You don't reckon the Oldhams have fetched along a posse?"

Tanner grunted. "Might figure that's the only way they can drag you away from this place."

When the riders were close enough, Rusty determined that the Oldhams were not among them. A gray-bearded man of military bearing rode slightly ahead of the others. Something about him struck Rusty as familiar.

"Captain Burmeister!" he yelled.

The leader gave Rusty a moment's close scrutiny. "Private Shannon?" He shifted his gaze. "And Private Tanner, if my memory correct is."

There was no mistaking the voice and the accent, or the gray mustache turned up on the ends in the Prussian military style. Rusty and Tanner had served in a ranger company headed by Captain August Burmeister before the war began. After long service to Texas, Burmeister remained loyal to the Union and vocally opposed secession. He resigned at the outbreak of the conflict and rode north in hopes he could join a Federal army unit.

The old captain dismounted painfully, his legs stiff. He extended a gnarled hand, knuckles swollen with arthritis. "The time has been long, but no handsomer you are, either of you."

Rusty quickly surveyed the other six men. They had the grim and determined look he associated with those who enforced law. "Are you a state policeman now?" he asked.

Burmeister shook his head. "I am of a special ranging company set up by Governor Davis. Not rangers of the old kind, exactly, but also not state police. We are sent to the frontier to do what we can about the Indians."

James Monahan and Evan Gifford had walked out from the corral. Rusty introduced them to the captain, who remembered James from before. James said, "We hear about Indian trouble in other places, but there ain't been any around here lately."

Burmeister said, "Settlers have reported a raiding party not far from here. Comanches, they think. They have with them some stolen horses."

James pressed, "How close to here?"

"Reports say not far. A little south."

Andy had come out to listen. Rusty noticed that he seemed ill at ease. "Blood brothers of yours, Andy?"

With reluctance Andy said, "They could be. I ran across some Comanches on my way up here. They were the reason the Oldhams turned back."

Burmeister demanded, "You saw that? When, and how far from here?"

"Three days ago, two days' ride."

Rusty asked, "Why didn't you say anything?"

"I figured they were on their way out of the country anyhow."

James declared, "They could be anyplace. And if you saw one bunch, there could be others."

Evan looked around quickly. "The pony's gone. Where's Billy?"

Tanner said, "The wagon team didn't come for feed last night. Vince said him and Billy was goin' out to find them and bring them in."

James's eyes narrowed with concern. "We'd better go fetch them back. If there's Comanches prowlin' about, we don't want to have anybody out there."

Evan did not wait. He ran to the corral to throw his saddle on a horse. Rusty started to follow, but James stopped him. "You're not in shape to ride. You and Preacher stay and look out for the womenfolks."

Rusty knew James was right. He did not argue.

Andy said firmly, "I'm goin'."

Rusty watched as Andy saddled the sorrel horse. "I wish you'd told us about the Indians," he said.

"They treated me good. I was afraid if folks went chasin' after them somebody was apt to get killed, white and Comanche both."

"I still wish you'd told us."

"This colonel, is he a good man to follow?"

"As good as ever won a commission."

James finished saddling. He told Rusty, "With any luck we'll be back in a little while. No use sayin' anything to Mama and them. It'd just get them all roused up. We can tell them about it when we've got Billy and Granddad back home."

Rusty watched them ride out . . . James, Evan, Andy, Tanner, and the cowboy named Macy, who had made himself a home here since soon after the end of the war.

Turning, he saw that Preacher Webb had his head down, whispering a prayer.

CHAPTER
TWELVE

ndy hung back a little, stricken with remorse. Hindsight told him he should have mentioned running into the Comanche party, but at the time it had seemed prudent not to do so. Horse Runner and the others had said they were on their way home. Whatever damage they had caused was over and done with. It could not be undone. Andy had seen nothing to be gained by setting off a pursuit that might result in casualties for both sides.

One of Burmeister's men quickly picked up the trail left by Purdy and Billy. Burmeister told James, "When we see that your people are safe, we will go on and try the Indians to find."

James said, "That wagon team has always been inclined to stray off, but they don't generally go far."

Because Tanner had put in lengthy service with Burmeister before the war, he took advantage of the opportunity to renew an old acquaintanceship. Riding beside the captain, he talked of his experiences and Rusty's in the intervening years. Tanner's natural tendency was to go into considerable detail, repeating some parts for emphasis and adding modest embellishments from time to time in the interests of a better story.

Burmeister told Tanner that after leaving the ranger post near Fort Belknap he had ridden up into Kansas and offered his services to the Union

Army. His long years as a ranger had given him solid experience in campaigning. He had put this to use in training troops.

Tanner said, "I hope you wasn't with none of them Yankee outfits that kept tryin' to invade Texas." A few had succeeded, mainly along the lower Rio Grande, but others had been beaten back after paying a heavy price for their effort.

"*Nein.* Texas was too long my home. I asked not to raise arms against it."

"How come now you're servin' Governor Davis's carpetbag government?"

"The word *carpetbag* I do not like. An outsider I am not. The word *reconstruction* is better. It means to build back, to fix what is broken."

"Some are breakin' more than they fix." Tanner told what he knew about the confiscation of Rusty's farm.

Burmeister listened with interest. He said, "Too often those who stand first at the trough are those who did not the work or the fighting."

The tracker, forty yards out in front, raised his hand as a signal for a halt. He turned back, his expression grave. "Captain, you better come."

Andy did not like the look in the tracker's face. Neither did James and Evan, for they spurred out ahead of Burmeister. Andy trailed with the rest of Burmeister's men. He heard James shout in dismay and jump to the ground, then kneel beside a body.

Evan cried out in anguish, "Where's Billy? For God's sake, somebody find Billy."

Andy knew whose body it would be, though James and Evan and Tanner blocked it from his view.

Burmeister raised a hand. "Everybody else stay back. We must study the tracks."

Evan called out, "Billy! Billy, where are you?"

James covered Vince Purdy's bloodied face with his neckerchief, but not before Andy saw that the scalp had been taken. He felt stunned. His throat was blocked so that he could barely breathe. Misery settled over him like a suffocating blanket.

If only I had said something, he thought.

He had brought the Oldham trouble upon Rusty by something he had done. He had brought this trouble to the Monahans by something he had *not* done.

The tracker and Burmeister moved ahead of the others, searching the ground for a sign. Tanner joined them, for he had shown himself to be better than average at reading tracks. They conferred among themselves, then rode back to where James and Evan knelt beside Purdy's lifeless body.

Burmeister said, "I fear the boy is taken."

Tanner said, "There's his bootprints where he jumped down to see about Vince. And here you can see where they drug him a little ways. Then the prints stop. They must've put him back on his pony." Tanner looked at Andy. "They've taken him the same way they took you once, and like they took Rusty a long time ago."

Andy's eyes burned. For a while he wished he had let Tonkawa Killer finish him years ago.

Evan jumped to his feet, trembling. "We've got to catch them. We've got to get him back." He rubbed a hand across his eyes. "My God, how can I tell Geneva?"

James folded his grandfather's arms across the thin chest. "There ain't no easy way, but you've got it to do. Take Granddad home and tell her." He checked Purdy's pockets. "They even took his watch."

Evan said, "I can't go home now. I've got to find my boy."

James accepted his brother-in-law's decision. "All right, I'll go and help you." He turned to the cowboy Macy. "You take Granddad home. It'll be up to you to break the news to Mama and them. Andy, why don't you go with him?"

Andy had already made up his mind. He felt a heavy weight of guilt for what had happened. "You'll need me if there's parleyin' to be done. I can talk to them."

"I wish you'd parleyed with us about the Indians you saw."

Andy saw blame in James's eyes, or thought he did. He could understand that. James could not blame him half so much as he blamed himself.

Burmeister detailed one of his special rangers to go with Macy. "When you are done at the Monahans', you will go to the neighbors. Warn them. Tell them Indians prowl about."

The ranger made a poor excuse of a salute. "Yes sir, better to do it a little late than not do it at all." He looked straight at Andy. Andy looked at the ground.

Burmeister pointed his finger at the tracker, a gesture so small that Andy almost missed it. The tracker made a nod equally small and turned to pick up the tracks. Burmeister said, "Private Tanner, it comes back to me that you were better than fair at trailing."

"Yes sir, I was middlin' good."

"Then go forward and help Smith." He nodded toward the tracker. "Do not however get in his way. You are good, but he is better."

Tanner accepted this with an ironic smile, taking no offense.

Burmeister waited until Smith and Tanner were fifty yards ahead, then put his horse into an easy trot. The rest followed his example without his having to give an order. Burmeister beckoned Andy with a quick jerk of his head. "Ride beside me. We will talk."

Andy complied, though he could not imagine that he and this old German frontiersman had much to talk about.

Burmeister asked, "Know you much of history?"

This seemed no time to talk of history, but Andy said, "I read about the American revolution in a book. All those people are dead now."

"The people are dead, but history is alive. What happened before will happen again. If we know what people have done before, we know what they may do again."

"You mean we'll have another revolution?"

"I was thinking of a time . . . it is now thirty years past . . . when a big battle we fought with the Comanches. We found at Plum Creek a small boy with red hair, Stolen, you see, by the Indians. Then many years after, when that boy was a man, he found another boy who had been taken by the Comanches. That was you. Now the Indians have a third boy. Perhaps you can help find him as Private Shannon found you and as the rangers found *him*."

"You're sayin' Rusty paid his debt, and now it's time for me to pay mine?"

"We all have debts to people of the past. We cannot go back to those people, so our debts we pay to people who live now. Somewhere . . ." he pointed skyward, ". . . there is a bookkeeper."

Andy felt crushed by the heavy weight of his new debt. "I don't know how I can ever pay enough. Vince Purdy was killed and Billy stolen because I didn't tell anybody I had seen Indians. But if I had told, and a bunch had rode out to chase them, there might've been even more people killed. I wouldn't have wanted to be the cause of that either." He lowered his chin in frustration. "I wish somebody would tell me what I ought to've done."

"Always do what you think is right. Most times it will be so. The other times we leave to God."

"You sound like Preacher Webb," Andy said. He intended it as a compliment.

Though tracks indicated that the Comanches were driving as many as a dozen stolen horses in addition to the ones they rode, they had ways of making those tracks suddenly disappear. It would seem as if horses and men had simply evaporated. At such points much time would be lost while the two trackers circled farther and farther outward until they picked up sign again.

Evan seemed about to come apart. James remained close, trying to reassure him that they would find his son. To Andy they seemed more like blood brothers than brothers-in-law. Andy remembered what Rusty had told him about Evan's fighting for the Confederacy and almost dying of the wound that sent him home from battle. Yet this was almost certainly the most important fight of his life. Andy wanted to go to him and tell him how sorry he felt about Billy, but he could not bring himself to do it. Words were not enough.

By nightfall it was obvious that the pursuit would be difficult to sustain. Only the rangers had provisions. The others had ridden out from Monahan headquarters in hopes they would quickly find Purdy and Billy. They had not taken time to pick up food, canteens, or blankets. Though the rangers would share the food they carried, it was clear that all would soon depend upon what they could obtain from the land itself.

Most maps were sketchy about details of the country beyond the settlements and military posts. Some had large areas virtually blank except for the word *Comanche*.

James hunched over a small campfire built in a shallow hole so the flames might not be seen from afar. He said, "We're comin' into country I don't know. Never came this far huntin' wild cattle. Len, did you ride over it in your ranger days?"

Tanner nodded. "That's too long ago. Hard to remember landmarks. And we was too busy trailin' Indians to stop and draw maps."

Both men turned toward Andy. Tanner said, "Maybe you know it from when you rode with the Comanches."

Andy was heartened by their acknowledgment that he might have some value on this quest. He would not have been surprised had they ordered him away. "Parts of it. We moved here and yonder, followin' the water and the buffalo."

Burmeister joined the conversation. "Most important is the water. They must have water for their horses. We must have water for *our* horses."

Their general direction was northwestward. The farther they traveled, the more critical water sources would be. A spring rich in flow on one trip might be reduced to a bare seep or even dried and caked mud on another. Creeks that ran bank-full after a good rain often went dry within a matter of weeks, or even days. One reason Texans had made slow headway in penetrating the plains homeland of the Comanches was that the Indians always knew where the water was. Texans rarely did.

By noon of the second day the horses were suffering. Andy remembered a spring where The People had camped a couple of times. But he did not know how to make the dried-up spring produce water.

"Rum luck," James complained, punching at the dry mud with the pointed end of a broken willow branch. All he raised was dust.

One of the rangers told Burmeister, "These horses are stretchin' their limit. We'll be walkin' home if we try to push them any further."

Evan protested, "We can't just give up. For all we know, Billy might not be more than a mile or two ahead of us."

Burmeister said, "He might not be ahead of us at all. You know the Indians have split. We do not follow as many today as yesterday. Those we follow now perhaps do not even have your boy."

Evan turned away from the others, fixing his eyes on the northwest. He trembled in silence. James placed a comforting hand on Evan's shoulder. "They're right. Besides, Billy ain't their boy. But he's *our* boy. Me and you will keep up the hunt."

Andy said, "And me."

Tanner said, "I'll stay with you."

Evan did not reply except with his eyes.

Burmeister was sympathetic, but he was a realist. "Think, gentlemen. How many times have Indians brought captives this far, and how many times has anyone been able a rescue to make?"

James argued, "But he's our own. We can't just back off and leave him in their hands."

"It will take much patience, but always there is a chance. We will alert all Indian agents to watch and listen. Sometimes they ransom captives if they can find them. And there are traders from New Mexico who go among the Indians. They are at heart decent people, most of them. We will find a way to let them know. It is not unknown that they buy captives and send them home."

Evan said bitterly, "That means you're givin' up."

"Not giving up. We go back to make a fresh start."

James said, "Time you show up here again they could carry that boy halfway to Canada."

"But they do not go to Canada. They will stay on the plains. And as long as they are on the plains there is a chance we find him. Have faith."

Four people glumly watched Burmeister turn back. The rangers left what provisions they had not already consumed as well as most of their ammunition.

Tanner said, "Don't get the notion old Captain is afraid. He ain't, and never was."

Evan retorted, "But he's left us."

"He gave you his reasons. Don't sell him short. One day when you think the world has slid within two feet of hell's rim, he'll come ridin' up with guns in both hands."

James turned to Andy. "You knew where this water hole was. There wasn't no way you could know it didn't have no water in it. Do you remember where the next one is at?"

Andy wished he could be more sure. "I think so."

"Point us the way."

He went by instinct as much as by memory, fearing all the way that they would find the place dry. These little pop-up seeps and springs depended heavily upon recent rainfall, and that could vary widely. He had seen rains cut a new gully in one place while dust continued to blow on the other side of the hill. That brought up one of the points that made it difficult for the Comanche side of him to understand the white man. The horseback Indians were always mobile. They could pack up and follow the rains. The white man tied himself to a specific piece of ground whether rain fell there or not.

No one had said anything in a while. Andy supposed the others were as dry-mouthed as he was, and as weary. His lips felt brittle and about to crack open. He could feel fatigue in the sorrel horse beneath him.

He felt a jolt of relief as he saw the tops of a few willows at some distance ahead. He had guided them right. At least the hole was there. There might or might not be water in it.

James seemed inclined to rush ahead and find out. Tanner quietly restrained him. "Might be some of Andy's cousins up there. They may be his kin, but not ours."

Evan said, "Billy could be there."

Tanner nodded. "There, or a hundred miles from there."

Andy said, "You-all wait. I will go." He peeled off his shirt, handing it and his hat to Tanner. "I won't look so much like a white man." He set Long Red into an easy walk. The horse had perked up. He probably sensed that water waited.

He caught the smell of wood smoke before he saw the camp. He slipped to the ground and tied his reins to a tall weed that would not hold the horse for even a moment if it should decide to travel. He saw nothing that would hold better.

Carefully he walked in the direction of the willows. He dropped to his belly and crawled to the top of each rise as he came to it, lifting his head slowly, surveying the ground ahead. Finally the water hole and the camp were in full view. There were no tepees. This was a temporary transit camp for whoever was down there. He counted two horses grazing among the willow trees. Beyond them several oxen had their heads down in the green grass. Two Mexican carts stood near the water. They appeared to be piled high with goods, though the cargo was covered with canvas.

Comancheros, Andy realized. These were the people who came out of villages in eastern New Mexico to trade among the Comanches, the Kiowas, and whatever other tribes they might come across.

Andy retreated carefully to his horse, then returned to where the others waited. "There are people at the spring. Mexican traders. I don't know if you want to go among them."

Evan spoke quickly. "The captain said *Comancheros* might be able to buy Billy back."

James said, "What would we pay them with? I didn't bring any money. Even if I had, it wouldn't be near enough."

"We can promise to pay them when they deliver Billy to us at the farm."

"More likely they'll deliver *us* to the Comanches. You've been around them, Andy. What do you think?"

Andy wished he had an easy answer. "It's a risk. The People have traded with them a long time. I don't know that they've ever completely trusted them. But the Mexicans don't completely trust The People, either. You never catch one far from his guns."

Tanner said, "We can parley with them, at least. If we don't like their looks, I reckon we can shoot them."

James gave Tanner a quizzical look. "You talk a lot about shootin' people, but how many have you ever really shot?"

"I don't keep count on such as that. Maybe a hundred, a little over or a little under."

A practical question came to Andy. "Any of you talk Mexican?"

Tanner claimed he did, but Andy knew his knowledge was limited to a scattering of individual words, most of them profane. Evan said, "My daddy fought in the Mexican War. He was always against any of us learnin' their language."

Andy pointed out, "These yonder may not talk English."

James said, "If they're tradin' with the Indians, at least one of them ought to talk a little Comanche. You can auger with him, Andy."

Andy felt uplifted by the responsibility. "I'd better go first. They'll likely take me for an Indian long enough for me to talk my way in. I'll signal you-all when it's time to follow."

Evan said anxiously, "Ask them if they've seen Billy."

Andy rode boldly into the camp, holding one hand high and shouting a Comanche greeting. Four Mexican men quickly materialized, all armed. They had evidently been napping on blankets in the shade of the willows.

One stepped a little ahead of the others, raising his hand in guarded response to the greeting. Peering from beneath the sagging brim of a frayed sombrero were suspicious eyes so dark as to be almost black. He did not appear to be an old man, though heavy black whiskers and a thick mustache covered most of his features. His clothing had been patched and patched again and matched the color of the earth. "*Quién es?*" he demanded.

Andy answered him in Comanche. "I am known among The People as Badger Boy. Who are you?"

The dark eyes blinked as the man weighed the likelihood of a gringo boy speaking Comanche. "I am Pablo Martínez. Your talk is Indian, but your eyes are blue."

"I was stolen and raised among the Comanches."

The Mexican appeared to weigh the account carefully before conditionally accepting it. "It is not uncommon. I have seen it."

Andy said, "Three friends of mine wait to come in. Would you share the water?"

"God has provided it for all."

Andy turned and signaled. He watched anxiously for the reaction when the Mexicans realized these were not Comanches.

"*Tejanos,*" Martínez exclaimed. He raised his rifle but stopped short of the shoulder.

Andy said, "They mean you no ill. They come to harm no one. They search for a missing boy."

"There is none in this camp."

"But perhaps you have seen him?"

"One sees many children in an Indian camp."

The other three Mexicans gathered beside Martínez, ready either to shake hands or to start shooting, whatever he decided upon. Andy was aware that the people of eastern New Mexico had no love for Texans in general. A Texas Confederate army had invaded them early in the Civil War and, though soon defeated, left bitterness in its wake.

Like Martínez, these three appeared to have been lifelong strangers to prosperity.

A few moments of awkward silence passed; then Andy introduced James, Evan, and Tanner.

Martínez switched languages. "I speak some the English. Better than I speak Comanche. What is this about a boy?"

Evan eagerly told him about his son. "If you've been tradin' in Comanche camps you might've seen him."

"One sees many captives, some Mexican, some gringo. Not all want to go home."

Andy understood that from his own experience, but it would be different with Billy. "This one would want very much to go home."

James told Martínez, "If you're in good with the Indians, we'd like you to take us to them and ask about the boy."

"*Señor*, it would be most dangerous."

"We'd pay you if you'd find him for us."

"Pay?" Martínez's mood escalated from indifference to interest. "How much? You have it now?"

James ran his hands into his pockets. "We brought no money with us. But we would pay you when we get home with Billy."

Martínez seemed to be giving the matter deep consideration. "Water your horses, and yourselves. Then we eat together. You like buffalo?"

Andy did, though he had tasted little in his years apart from the Indians. Tanner said, "Ate a many a pound of it ridin' with the rangers. Ain't but few things tastier when you been livin' on water and air." Any kind of food sounded good to Tanner.

Evan had a more urgent priority. "Then we will talk?"

Martínez nodded. "Then we talk."

The Texans had used up the few provisions Burmeister had given them, so all they had eaten since yesterday was one prairie chicken divided between them. They wolfed down the roasted buffalo. For drink the Mexicans offered strong coffee, boiled with sugar.

Andy remembered being present when his band had traded with such people at the foot of a great escarpment, its dark rock walls steep and forbidding. The stream that meandered past was known as the River of Tongues because many languages were spoken there by the various tribes that gathered to barter. An informal truce kept old enemies from battling.

They might try to kill one another on the way there or the way back, but it was bad manners to attack even a lowly Apache while commerce was under way. Plains Indians were dedicated traders, and unnecessary violence got in the way of business.

A similar honor system protected the Mexican traders at the site, though it was hardly unknown for warriors to trail after them and rob them on their way home. With luck, goods taken from one set of *Comancheros* might be foisted upon a second set unaware of the robbery. Such doings were generally frowned upon, however, not so much on moral grounds as on the practical consideration that traders might be discouraged from coming again. One should gather the prairie hen's eggs without killing the hen.

Evan was the first to finish eating. He trembled in eagerness to talk about recovering his son. Martínez pointed out the many difficulties involved, not the least of which was finding the boy in the first place. The Comanches tended to scatter across the plains in many small bands. They had their pick of dozens of campsites, most known only to themselves.

Martínez said, "Then, if he is found, he may not be for sale. For money the Comanche has no use. He cannot eat it. He cannot go to town like you and I and spend it. You must offer him something he will want more than the boy. Usually that is horses. A Comanche can never get enough horses."

James said, "Then horses is what we'll give him. How many you reckon it'd take?"

Martínez shrugged. "Who can say? If he is a young warrior and has not many horses, he will be happy with a few more. If he is old and has many horses, a few will not interest him. He will require many more."

Andy could see obstacles no one else had brought up. For one, how would the horses be delivered? It was unlikely the Comanches would ride openly down to the Monahan place to receive them, risking not only treachery by the Monahans but attack by other whites who would know nothing of the trade and would simply consider them invaders. For the Monahans to attempt to drive the horses up into Comanche country for delivery would involve the same general risk.

As he saw it, both sides would have to trust the *Comancheros* to make the delivery. He wondered if either would have so much faith. But when Martínez suggested that path of action, James and Evan agreed without squandering much time on consideration. Tanner remained out of the conversation because he had lost no boy and had no horses to offer.

To Andy the best answer seemed simple: find him, steal him, and get the hell away from there.

Martínez said, "We will travel among the bands, my friends and I. We ask questions—carefully. If we find him, we bargain. If a trade is made, I will come for the horses. Without doubt the Indians will want to see horses before they let the boy go. When I get the boy, I take him home to you."

Evan insisted, "Couldn't you bring him when you come for the horses? Tell the Indians we won't cheat them. Tell them we're honest people."

"How can I tell them when I do not myself know you until today? No, they will believe when they see horses, and then only."

Evan spoke to James. "We'll need first of all to know that Billy is all right. When we see that he is, you'll go home and bring the horses. I'll stay with the Indians so they'll know we don't mean to pull any tricks."

It would take only one disgruntled warrior to put a knife or an arrow into Evan. Andy was impressed with his willingness to accept so much danger. He wondered if his own white father would have done as much. He wanted to believe he would, had similar circumstances arisen. In all probability he had had no chance.

Martínez raised both hands. "Wait, gentlemen. You talk as if you would go with me. That you will not. You will go home and wait."

James demanded, "Why can't we go with you?"

"Think. Many a warrior would rather have three *Tejano* scalps than a few horses. The first Comanches we find would surely kill you. They might kill me also for letting you ride with me."

Andy said, "He's right. It's better the Indians never see you. But it's different with me. I'm the one who ought to go with him."

James argued, "You're a Texan, too."

"But The People will accept me as Comanche. Whoever has Billy, I can talk to them. I can make sure he's all right. And I think I can make them believe me when I promise they'll get their horses."

Evan said, "That's too much to ask of you." Though he protested with his words, Andy could see in his eyes that he was desperate for Andy to go.

Andy said, "I owe you. Billy wouldn't be where he is . . . none of us would be where we are . . . if I'd told about runnin' into that raidin' party."

Martínez looked from one to another, trying to understand. He had no reason to know how much Andy blamed himself, or why.

Tanner studied Andy with strong misgivings. "Rusty told me to look after you. How am I goin' to do that if you ride off and leave me behind?"

Andy tried to smile, but it did not work. "All this time I thought I was lookin' out for *you*."

CHAPTER

THIRTEEN

The horses were hungry as well as tired. All afternoon they hardly raised their heads from the grass upon which they were staked. Andy took a careful look at Long Red, examining his legs, his hooves.

"No tellin' how far we'll have to travel," he told the horse. "I don't want you goin' lame on me." He rubbed a hand over the animal's back in search of possible saddle sores.

Tanner complained, "I've half a mind to stay with you. Rusty'll raise hell with me for lettin' a boy go on a man's job."

"I'm not a boy anymore, and you know why you can't go. You'd get yourself killed. Maybe the rest of us too. Tell Rusty the only way you could've stopped me was to shoot me."

"You don't hardly even know Billy."

"I know his folks. I know he belongs with them, and he'd be with them now if it wasn't for me. And I can remember enough to know what he's goin' through. They'll be whippin' on him to see if he shows fight."

"If he doesn't?"

"They may decide they can never make him into a warrior. Like as not they'll kill him."

"That might've already happened. What we've done, and what you're fixin' to do, could go for nothin'."

"I'm bettin' on him showin' enough fight that they'll want to keep him." Andy had seen the boy's pony take him under some low-lying limbs and knock him out of the saddle. Billy had immediately gotten up, used some language his mother would not have wanted to hear and gotten right back on. He had used his quirt a little heavier than necessary.

Tanner said, "If they decide he'll do to keep, they may want more horses than the Monahans can gather. It might take the whole Yankee army to pry him loose."

"We don't want soldiers gettin' into this. Billy would be the first person killed."

Tanner gave up with great reluctance. "Then I reckon it's up to you and that Martínez. Keep a sharp eye on him. I ain't trusted Mexicans since the fall of the Alamo."

"You wasn't even born then."

"I started distrustin' them *before* I was born."

Andy was not sure what James and Evan had promised Martinez as a reward for his part in finding and recovering Billy. Money, probably, or part of the horses. It didn't matter. In the dark of the night, wrapped in a thin blanket he had brought tied behind his saddle, he had time to think, to consider the probabilities. The more he examined them, the more problems he saw.

The odds were heavily against finding the boy in the first place, though Andy intended to press the hunt however far it led him. He stood a worrisome chance of falling among some of Tonkawa Killer's vengeful friends before he found Billy. They would probably murder him, leaving Rusty and the Monahans to forever ponder two mysteries: whatever became of Billy, and what happened to Andy Pickard?

He ate but little breakfast. The coffee seemed sour on a stomach already in turmoil from worry and lack of sleep.

Against their will, Tanner, James, and Evan saddled their horses and prepared to ride south. Evan squeezed Andy's hand so hard the bones felt as if they would break. Tears welled in Evan's eyes. His lips were pressed shut. He could not speak.

Andy's throat tightened. "If there's any way—"

James said, "We don't want you dyin' for a lost cause. Been too many people done that already."

Tanner almost crunched Andy's shoulder with a grip stronger than the former ranger probably realized. "You've been a damned good boy, Andy. Don't you do nothin' foolish and get yourself killed before you have a chance to become a damned good man. If things get too hot, peel off and run like hell. Won't nobody blame you."

Andy knew he would blame himself. "Tell Rusty . . ." What he really wanted to say would not come. Instead he said, "Tell him that when we get Billy back, we'll go home together and shoot Clyde Oldham."

"A deal." Tanner forced a smile. "And I'll shoot Buddy-Boy."

Watching the three ride away, Andy felt desperately alone despite the presence of the four Mexicans.

Pablo Martínez busied himself breaking camp and gave Andy time to recover from the stress of parting. Finally he said, "No Indians come here today. We must go to the Indians."

The cart men had the ox teams hitched. Andy said, "I'm ready." He led Alamo to the spring to let him drink. Martínez was not certain they would reach another watering place before night. They might be forced to a dry camp. Each cart carried a wooden barrel freshly filled so the animals would not suffer.

Andy had seen only a little of what was in the carts, but he assumed it would be the usual trading goods that Indians had come to regard as necessities: blankets, cooking utensils, knives, and such. It would include luxuries to which Indians had become somewhat addicted: sugar, coffee, tobacco. Very possibly it might include rifles and ammunition.

He hoped it would not include whiskey, but he had to accept that possibility. When whiskey entered the picture, the unwritten rules against violence at the trading place had been known to go up in smoke.

Andy had never considered how much slower an ox team traveled than did horses or mules. They plodded along, straining in their heavy wooden yokes. He wondered if anything could excite them. A horse or mule team would occasionally take fright and bolt from something as innocent as a rabbit suddenly jumping up in front of them. The oxen looked half asleep.

For the likes of these, the white man would trade the buffalo. Andy grimaced at the thought.

He remembered that when he lived with the Indians on the plains, the wind rarely died down completely. It blew now out of the west, warm and dry. It was not unpleasant. The movement of air kept the sun from feeling quite so hot as it otherwise would.

He had time now, as he had last night, to assess the hazards and consider his possible moves. He saw little point in devising detailed plans. He could make only the wildest guess about the situation that might confront him when and if he and the Mexicans found Billy. In the beginning, at least, he would have to let Martínez take the lead. Andy saw few options for himself unless for some reason the whole business fell apart. Then he would play whatever hand luck presented to him.

Martínez gestured for Andy to ride beside him. Martínez was mounted on a long-legged fine-boned brown horse that Andy took to be a Thoroughbred. Martínez seemed proud of him, for he put on a show of turning the animal one direction and then another with almost no pressure on the reins. "I won him in a race at Taos," he said. "He is of the *sangre puro*, the pure blood. Where did you get that sorrel?"

"Got him in a trade. Don't have no idea about his blood. I expect it's red, same as any other horse."

"You ever been to New Mexico?"

The Comanches had traveled over wide areas, but they had little knowledge of or interest in boundary lines. "I suppose so. I don't know where it starts."

"We come from a place called Anton Chico. A valley between the mountains. We farm, we raise sheep, we trade. A very long time my people have lived in that valley. Maybe longer than the Comanche has been in this country, who can say?"

Andy had once assumed that the Comanches had been in Texas since the mountains were built and the rivers set to running, but Preacher Webb had told him it was not true. They had migrated south from somewhere far up in the big shining mountains in the very early 1700s. Somewhere, probably by stealing from the Spaniards, they had acquired the horse and soon were able to roam wherever and however far they wanted to go. They had become the most fearsome warriors on the plains.

Martínez said, "First we were Spanish. Then there was war between Mexico and Spain, and they told us we were Mexicans. Then there was war between Mexico and the *Estados Unidos*, and they told us we were Americans. Always, people from outside come and try to tell us who we are. We *know* who we are.

"Do you wonder that we do not trust people from the outside? They never come with good news. Always they come to take something, like the *Americanos* and the Texans."

"The Comanches do the same thing, don't they?"

"In the past. But the way to make an enemy not be your enemy is to trade with him. Get him things he cannot get from somebody else. Then your enemy is his enemy. Long time ago we had much trouble with the Apaches. Not much anymore. They are afraid the Comanches will come and help us."

"But you trade with the Apaches too, don't you?"

"Better to trade than to fight. The Indian thinks he is different, but he is like all other men. Get him to want things. Get him enough of these things to keep him wanting more and he will do as you bid him. You think these oxen want to stand and wait for the yoke each morning? They do it because they know they will be fed. Feed them and they will serve you. Stop feeding them, and soon they are gone."

"You ever quit bringin' goods to the Indians, they're apt to come after you with a scalpin' knife."

"A little danger is to life as salt is to the meat."

Andy could see a serious flaw in Martínez's reasoning. "When you trade with the Comanches and Kiowas for whatever they steal out of Texas, don't you know that makes them raid and steal even more?"

"It is for the Texans to take care of themselves. When they came into our valley in the last war they fancied themselves better than anyone else. *Damned greasers*, they called us. Took what they wanted, did as they pleased. What is it to us if the Indians make them fight a little?"

"My friends are Texans. How is it you agreed to try to rescue the boy for them?"

"I am a merchant. I sell what others want to buy. The boy is trade goods, like coffee and sugar."

Andy frowned. The *Comanchero* was being bluntly honest. Martínez had never met Billy. The boy meant nothing to him except in terms of market value. At least Andy knew where the man stood. In event of crisis he was not likely to stand hitched.

Martínez kept a close watch on the horizon as if he expected Indians to appear at any time. None did. Before night he approached what Andy remembered had been a weak seep in the side of a usually dry creek bed. Martínez rode ahead to look it over. He returned, the slump of his shoulders telling the story before he came close enough to speak. "No water. Too long no rain."

The water barrels would have to suffice.

Andy asked, "No Indians either?"

"No Indians."

Andy put down disappointment. Reality told him he should not expect to overtake Billy's captors so soon, but one could always hope for a stroke of good fortune.

After a meager supper of tortillas, beans, and a bit of buffalo meat, he told Martínez, "I'm goin' off out yonder by myself awhile. Got to think."

Martínez made a faint smile. "You expect some Indian spirit to whisper in your ear?"

"Maybe. It don't hurt to be listenin'."

"I will tell my priest about you. He will pray for your heathen soul."

Preacher Webb probably would not approve either. Andy was not sure what he believed and what he didn't. He had heard so many conflicting opinions about gods and spirits, those of the white man as well as of the Indians, that he was hopelessly confused. He knew only that he had observed the wise men of the tribe wandering off to meditate and seek truth wherever they could find it. Sometimes they claimed it had found them.

He did not have time for a proper vision quest. He was old enough. If he were still with The People he would probably have undergone one or more such searches by now. The proper way would be with the aid of a dependable shaman, who would purify him and give him instructions. Then, in some isolated place where he would not be distracted by small things, he would fast and pray and go through the specified procedures for as long as four days and nights. If he were fortunate, at some point a benevolent spirit would visit, counseling him, perhaps revealing his future. Such an experience was regarded as a rite of passage to manhood.

He could not expect all this in a single night, but he could lose nothing by laying himself open to whatever spirits might be roaming about in the darkness. He could only hope they would be of a kindly nature and not malevolent. It was well known that malevolent spirits were always on watch for the unwary. Even Preacher Webb recognized their evil presence and preached for vigilance against their snares.

He had no tobacco, so he could not perform the smoke ritual except with a small campfire. He tried to blow and push the smoke in each of the four cardinal directions, then down to the earth and up to the stars. He sat back and waited.

He was still waiting at daybreak. He awoke with a start, aware that the eastern sky was turning pink. No voice had spoken to him, no vision had appeared. He tried to remember if he had dreamed. Sometimes visions were elusive and came disguised as dreams. He remembered only loose and random fragments, none that made any sense.

He trudged back to camp, where the smell of coffee told him the Mexicans were making breakfast. Martínez gave him a questioning glance. "Any message from the Comanche spirits?"

Andy did not want to talk about it.

Martínez said, "You are probably too much white. It is better you look for your white-man spirits in church."

"I've tried. Maybe they don't like the Comanche in me any more than the Comanche spirits like me bein' white."

Martínez lifted a crucifix from beneath his shirt and fingered it. "No people of your own and no God. You wander like a soul lost in darkness. You are to be pitied, Badger Boy."

The use of his Comanche name, though in English translation, startled him a little. For a long time he had heard no name except Andy other than in his brief meeting with Horse Runner's party on his way to the Monahans'.

The oxen complained but stepped into their proper places as Martínez cracked his whip. They slung their heads in brief protest, then submitted to the yoke. Andy wondered if their necks might be perpetually sore from the burden. They had long since developed heavy muscles and a thick hide to compensate. The wooden cart wheels groaned under the weight of their load. They needed grease, but the cart men seemed oblivious of the racket.

If any Indians were about, Andy thought, they would hear the carts before they saw them.

Toward the middle of the afternoon two horsemen showed themselves where the prairie rose up gently into a halfhearted semblance of a hill. Their silhouettes indicated they were Comanche. Andy felt a quickening of pulse, an uncertain mixture of anticipation and anxiety. Martínez made a show of leaving his rifle atop one of the carts. He rode slowly out in the Indians' direction, holding one hand high to indicate he meant no harm. When he reached the halfway point the Comanches wheeled their ponies about and disappeared.

Andy felt disappointed, but Martínez seemed unconcerned on his return. "They will be ready when they are ready."

The vegetation began showing more life, indicating that more rain had fallen than farther to the south. Andy hoped this meant the evening campsite would offer live water. The carts' barrels were down by more than half, which would mean tight rationing if the site proved dry. The oxen had to be considered first, before the men.

Late in the afternoon they passed over a small swell in the prairie, and he saw that they would not be alone at the night's camp. He rough-counted thirty or forty horses loose-herded on the curing grass. A breeze from the north brought the faint odor of burning wood.

He wanted to ride directly to the horse herd and see if Billy's pony might be there. Martínez stopped him with a quick jerk of his head. "Better you stay with the carts. Make not too bold until they have looked us over."

Andy curbed his eagerness and remained beside one of the carts as it approached the camp. Comanches began walking out or in several cases riding their ponies to give the carts a full inspection. They paid less attention to the Mexican cart men than to what they brought with them. At first Andy thought none were going to notice him, but soon he found himself the object of considerable curiosity. One of the warriors pushed so close that Andy was almost nose to nose with him. Andy realized with a start that he had seen the man before. He recognized several of the warriors.

Looking around quickly, he spotted Horse Runner, though the raiding party leader did not notice Andy right away.

"You," a warrior said, poking his finger at Andy, "you are the white Comanche."

That caused Horse Runner to turn around. "Badger Boy!" He hesitated as if he could not believe, then he moved forward to embrace Andy. "You have come back to live among your true people?"

"No, I have come on a quest."

"Quest for what? When we saw you, you were going to give warning to a friend. Did you not find him?"

"I found him. Now there is other trouble. I have come to find a small boy who was taken, a Texan boy. He belongs to my friends." He watched Horse Runner's dark eyes for any sign that the raider had knowledge of Billy.

The eyes betrayed nothing. "I know of no boy."

"He was with an old man. The old man was killed and the boy stolen."

"Not by us." Horse Runner made a sweeping motion toward the other warriors. "We took horses. We did not have the fortune to take scalps." He hastened to add, "You may look among us. You will not find a boy."

Disappointed in not finding Billy, Andy was nevertheless pleased that

Horse Runner's party was not responsible for killing Vince Purdy. He had a friendly feeling toward these warriors. He had been revulsed at the thought of their having another friend's blood on their hands.

Yet his basic problem remained. If this group did not have Billy, who did? Where were they?

"Do you know of other such parties that might have taken the boy?" he asked.

"We have not met any other parties except a few hunters. We saw a few Kiowas who fought the blue-coat reservation soldiers. They had no boy with them." Horse Runner seemed little concerned. "Your friends who lost the boy, they have other children?"

"Just a little girl."

"They should have another boy, then they can forget this one. He is better off with The People. *You* would be better off to stay with The People and not go back to the Texans."

"It is not an easy thing, losing a child and a grandfather. Their hearts are on the ground."

"Many times have *our* hearts been on the ground because of the Texans. I do not find it here . . ." he touched his chest, ". . . to weep for them."

"It is my fault . . . my shame . . . that they lost him." He explained that he had made it a point not to mention to anyone that he had seen Horse Runner's raiders before he reached the Monahan farm. "I feared they would send out men to stop you, and there would be deaths on both sides."

Horse Runner did not grasp the point. "What does it matter that you did not tell them about us? We are not the ones who took the boy."

"But if I had told them there was danger the boy and his grandfather would not have gone out alone."

"The spirits were against them. There was nothing you could do against the spirits."

Andy saw that he could not explain his logic to Horse Runner.

Horse Runner said, "Forget the boy. Stay with us if you would like. Soon we will be in our own camp and celebrate our victories. There will be feasting and dancing and singing."

"It is a matter of honor. I must find him."

Honor was something Horse Runner understood. He said, "If you like, I will go with you. I know most of the camps."

Andy explained in general terms about the agreement with Martínez and the *Comancheros*. "If I find the boy, I have nothing to trade for him. I must stay with the Mexicans."

The raiding party had evidently ransacked at least a couple of homes, for they had picked up such miscellaneous treasures as some cooking pots, a clock, and a couple of hand-sewn quilts of intricate design. These had more appeal to them than to the *Comancheros*, but Martínez was receptive to trading for as many of their stolen horses and mules as they chose to offer. Because horses were precious commodities to the Indians, they were willing to part with only a few. They were happy to trade the mules, which they considered inferior to the horses.

Martínez and the cart men spread out their trading goods for the Indians' inspection. As Andy expected, there were mostly knives, hatchets, beads, blankets, and the like. Negotiations seemed to continue for hours, jovial at first but taking on a more and more serious air as the evening wore on. At a critical stage Martínez uncovered a jug and offered it as a gesture of goodwill.

Andy turned away, wishing it had not happened. He had observed the chaos whiskey could cause in a Comanche camp. But Martínez wisely restricted the gift to a single jug, enough to loosen the Indians' spirits, yet not enough to get them recklessly drunk. Each time the jug was passed around, Martínez made a show of drinking from it. Andy doubted much actually passed his lips, for the trader would want to keep his wits sharp. As the stack of dry wood beside the campfire gradually dwindled, the Indians traded off more of their horses than they intended and settled for fewer of the trade goods.

Andy decided Martínez could skin a prairie chicken without mussing its feathers.

At daylight Martínez took stock of the horses and mules he had acquired. "These I can sell for good money in Taos or Santa Fe. Not bad for an evening of work."

Andy pointed out, "All these are stolen stock. They belong to somebody."

"Yes, they do. To me."

Martínez considered it good policy to move on early while most of the Indians still slept, lest some begin to reconsider their transactions in full sunlight. The extra animals were tied together on long ropes and led rather than herded. Not until they had put a couple of hours behind them did he allow the cart men to stop and fix a simple breakfast.

Andy said, "I thought you had no fear of Indians."

"Not fear. Caution. Indians sometimes change their minds."

"If you didn't cheat them, you wouldn't have to worry."

"Who cheated them? All was done in the open, where everyone could see. I made no one to trade. It was of their own choice."

"With a little help from the whiskey."

Martínez frowned. "Do you want to go with us and find that boy, or not?"

"I've got no choice."

"Then keep eyes open, and ears, but mouth shut."

CHAPTER

FOURTEEN

ndy was reminded how formidable distances could be across the high plains. Movement had always been slow when the pace was set by horses dragging travois loaded down with camp equipment and folded tepee skins. Plodding ox teams made it equally slow now. Much of the time he was hard put to see landmarks. The prairie had a gentle rolling character, the seasoned grass short and near golden in the sun. He sensed that Martínez knew where he was going despite the sameness of the landscape, mile after mile. Now and again Andy saw wheel ruts cut during some long-forgotten rainy spell, but these would quickly disappear. Even more rarely he would see a horseman or two at long distance. They vanished like wraiths.

Toward evening the little caravan reached a small stream. Andy tried in vain to remember if he had been there before. One small watercourse looked much the same as another. They made camp, and before long a half-dozen Kiowas appeared as suddenly as if they had risen up from the ground. Using sign language and a few Kiowa words he knew, Martínez welcomed them to camp.

They sat and smoked around the fire, using it for ceremony but remaining back far enough not to be made uncomfortable by its heat. Andy quickly discerned that the Kiowas had little to trade, but nevertheless Martínez passed out a few cheap gifts, mostly small mirrors and shiny metal figures. One of the Indians had an ancient rifle but explained through motions that the hammer was broken. Martínez spoke in Spanish to one of the cart men, who took the rifle and examined it. Soon he was filing a replacement part from a piece of steel.

Andy wondered at Martínez's show of generosity when he had nothing evident to gain. The *Comanchero* told him he had much to learn if he should ever decide to become a merchant. "Next time they may have something to trade. They will remember us."

The Kiowas stayed to supper. By then the cart man had the rifle ready. He fired it once to demonstrate that it was again serviceable, though it missed its target by at least a foot. Andy saw that the sight was bent.

"Are you goin' to get him to fix that?" he asked Martínez.

The trader shook his head. "If they shot at you, would you want it fixed? They are happy enough that it fires."

"When are you goin' to ask them if they've seen some Comanches with a boy captive?"

"In time. With Indians one does not rush, or have you forgotten?"

Andy decided he had forgotten much. He had become accustomed to Texans' lack of ceremony when taking care of business. Like them, he wanted to get to the red meat first and handle the amenities later.

The Kiowas provided what Andy thought was the perfect opening. They were curious about him, for he was clearly white though he possessed many Comanche characteristics. With sign language Martínez told them that Andy had been stolen as a boy.

Impatiently Andy said, "Now's the time to ask them about Billy."

But the Kiowas moved on to other interests, and the question went unasked. Andy sat chafing, trying to control his frustration. At length he attempted to break into the hand-signal conversation, but the Kiowas ignored him.

Martínez quietly shook his head. "They get suspicious when you push. In time I will give them a little whiskey. It loosens the tongue. Go now, water your horse or something."

Andy forced himself to pull away from the conversation and put his trust in Martínez. But he kept looking back, trying to read the sign language from a distance, picking up only fragments of it. He watched Martínez produce a jug from beneath the stack of goods in one of the carts and pass it among the Indians. From the high level to which they had to tilt it, he knew Martínez had been careful not to give them a full container.

It took only a short time for the Kiowas to fall into a celebratory state. Not long afterward, they began falling to sleep, one by one.

Martínez appeared cold sober. He had made a show of drinking with them, but Andy doubted that much whiskey had gone down his throat. He walked up to Andy, nodding in satisfaction. "They told me they came across some Comanches yesterday, with many horses and mules." He pointed northwestward. "A boy was with them. The Kiowas thought the boy was white. He seemed to be a prisoner."

Andy's spirits lifted. "That'd be Billy for sure."

"Not for sure. Could be some other boy."

Andy dismissed a fleeting uncertainty. "After we've come so far, it's got to be Billy. When are we gettin' started?"

"Daylight."

"We could go a long ways in the dark."

"And get lost. You are like the Texans, too much hurry. If we do find the Comanches, and the boy is with them, do not show much interest. They would ask more ransom."

"I don't care about the price. I just want to get Billy back."

"You must care. What if they ask more than your friends can pay? You do more harm than good."

"I have a knack for that."

"That I have seen for myself."

More than once, Martínez warned Andy not to set his expectations too high. Riding along ahead of the carts, he said, "We may find they have moved on."

"Then we'll follow 'til we catch up."

"Often they divide. We follow one group, we may find that the boy is with another. The Comanche are not *gente de razón*, men of reason. They are not like us, who find a place for ourselves and build our house and plant our fields. They are like the wild animals of the prairie, they travel where it is their pleasure, and when."

Andy realized Martínez was being realistic, trying to build his resistance against disappointment. But he preferred to remain positive.

"Old Preacher Webb often said that when you've got faith enough, your faith will usually be rewarded. So I've got faith, and I'm hangin' on to it whether I really believe it or not."

Martínez shook his head. "I wish I could take you to my priest. There is much he could teach you."

By the middle of the afternoon Andy began seeing horse tracks. A substantial number had been made by iron shoes. These, he reasoned, were from horses recently taken. The tracks left by Billy's pony would probably be smaller than the average. He found several sets of pony tracks but had no way of knowing which, if any, were Billy's.

Martínez warned, "If we do find the boy, show no interest. Make as if you do not know him."

"He'll know *me*. He'll figure I've come to rescue him."

"And you have. But do not let the Comanches know it."

Martínez had been over this ground before. Obviously he did not appraise Andy's intelligence too highly. Andy resented that, but he was in no position to do much about it. He was here at Martínez's sufferance.

He toyed briefly with the notion that he might do better on his own. He recognized it as an idle thought, even a dangerous one. But everything about this mission was dangerous. He had climbed out to the far edge of a bluff that could break off at any time.

Martínez said, "It is not far now. Soon there is water and a good place for camp."

The cart men were not the first to reach it. They came across a horse herd tended by two young warriors. Andy rode close, trying to appear curious rather than seriously interested. One of the warriors, armed only with a bow and arrows so far as Andy could see, rode over to challenge him. Andy spoke a greeting in Comanche. Still suspicious, the young man answered in kind. Andy complimented him on having so many fine horses. The warrior answered with a degree of pride that most had been obtained by honest theft from the Texans.

"Why are you with those Mexicans?" he asked.

"We visit many camps, trading."

"Do you think he would trade for some of these horses, and the mules?"

"On the right terms. Trading is his work."

"He has with him whiskey?"

"You must ask him about that."

All the while he talked, Andy's gaze roamed over the horses. He did not see Billy's pony. Though disappointed, he was not without hope. The pony might be tied in camp. Most warriors kept one or more horses tied near the tepee in case of need. They did not walk when they could ride.

He pulled away to join Martínez and the carts. The encampment was not large, a dozen tepees lined along a small creek, their flap openings facing east so the morning sunrise would bring its light inside. Andy judged that most of the men had been away on a raid and had rejoined families at this prearranged meeting place within the last day or two. He smelled cooking meat and knew it was not buffalo. He had seen a couple of mule carcasses at the edge of camp, stripped of any meat worth eating as well as the hides. Mules were for trading or eating, not for riding.

A small group of Indians ventured out to watch the carts pass. Andy saw no friendliness in their faces.

Martínez moved upstream a little ways from the Comanches. "We camp here," he said. "Let them come to us. We do not wish to seem in a hurry to trade. They will expect too much."

"They didn't look all that glad to see us."

"There is a bad mood in this camp. I can feel it."

Andy guessed that something had gone wrong for the Indians. Perhaps there had been an argument over dividing the spoils, or worse, the raiders had lost a man or two in skirmishes along the way.

Riding past the tepees, Andy had given each a moment's careful scrutiny. "I did not see Billy anywhere. If he is here he must be tied up inside one of the tepees." He wished he could search every one of them.

Martínez seemed to sense his thoughts. "Patience. I said from the first, he may not be here."

"But if he isn't, he has been. I can sense it."

Martínez snorted. "Sense it? You think you can smell him, like a dog?"

"I've got a feelin', that's all."

"Someday you will have a feeling that you are about to be killed, and you will be right. Patience. With patience, all things can be known." Martínez looked back toward the Indian camp. His eyes revealed misgivings.

One of the cart men spoke to him in Spanish. Andy did not understand the words, but he knew the man was concerned about something. Martínez told Andy, "He says we should not stop here at all. But we will look the coward if we go on. You must never let the Comanche think you are coward."

They finished making camp. Martínez looked apprehensively toward the tepees. "Maybe they do not come to trade at all. That might be best."

"But if they don't, how will we find out anything about Billy?"

Martínez gave him no answer.

They had finished a meager supper when three warriors walked into camp. They walked silently around the two carts, peering inside without touching anything, then went to the dwindling campfire and seated themselves on the ground. They did not speak a word. In a short while others appeared, more or less repeating the motions of the first group. Several stared at Andy, evidently trying to figure out who or what he was, but they asked no questions and he offered no answers. The mood was sullen. Andy looked vainly to Martínez for guidance. Whatever the Mexican was thinking, he did not allow it to show in his face. He produced a pipe, stuffed the bowl with tobacco, lighted it, and handed it to the man sitting on the end. Each man took a couple of puffs and passed it on to the next.

They looked no friendlier.

With a combination of Comanche words and sign language, Martínez welcomed the men to camp and asked them what was their pleasure. Andy listened intently. He feared at first that he might have forgotten too much, but he found that he understood the talk. The gist was that most of these men had taken part in a raid that penetrated the Texas settlements, accumulating many horses and mules as well as other booty. They had returned to this place where their families waited. Dissension had broken out regarding division of the spoils, and this group had been left feeling robbed. A larger band had gone on with more than their share. These Comanches wanted to trade the mules and some of the horses.

Martínez replied that trade was his reason for being here. "Bring what you want to sell."

"First," said the man who seemed to be the leader, "you have whiskey?"

Reluctantly Martínez said, "Only a little. Afterward, we drink in celebration of a good trade."

"We drink now." The leader was emphatic.

Andy could sense a wreck coming. Angry at their fellow raiders, these Comanches were willing to take out their frustrations on whoever was handy.

Martínez went to the nearest cart and dug beneath a pile of trade goods. He brought forth a jug, shaking it to judge how full it was. "There is enough here so each can have a drink," he said. "After the trading, another drink."

The jug was passed, but Andy saw that the first who received it were partaking liberally of its contents. It was empty before the last three men had their turn. Quarreling among themselves, they turned on Martínez with a demand for more. Martínez spoke to one of the cart men, who hurriedly brought another jug. Andy could see tension rising in Martínez's face.

He decided this was his chance to look through the camp while the men were engrossed in the whiskey and the negotiations. He slipped away carefully, looking back to see if his leaving had been noticed. He saw no indication that anyone was paying attention to him. Walking down into the camp, he saw only women and a few children, most of them outside.

As he passed each tepee he called softly. "Billy! Are you in there?"

He received no answer. By the time he had walked through the entire camp he was satisfied that the boy was not here. But a nagging feeling persisted: he *had* been.

He approached a middle-aged woman who was cutting thin strips of mule meat to dry. He decided he had nothing to lose by asking outright. "Grandmother, I am looking for my brother. He has about six summers. He stands this high." He indicated Billy's height. "He was taken from my family not long ago. I believe he has been here."

She stared at him as if he had two heads. "You talk like one of The People, but you have the look of a *teibo*."

"I am both," he admitted. "But what of my brother? You have seen him?"

"Such a one was here. Those who cheated us took him and went on." She pointed her chin to the northwest. "He is a Texan boy. He is claimed as a son by one called Fights with Bears."

Andy could remember no one wearing such a name. He might be of a different band than Andy's, or he could have changed his name from something else. It was customary among The People to shed an old name if a new one seemed more appropriate.

"Thank you, Grandmother." He started back to the cart camp, for he had found out what he wanted to know.

He knew from the racket that something had gone badly wrong in his absence. The Indians had emptied the carts in their search for more whiskey. Goods lay scattered and trampled on the ground. Shouting, quarreling warriors wrestled each other for possession of the several jugs they had found. Andy looked for Martínez and found that the cart men had carried him out past the edge of camp. He lay on a blanket. One of his helpers pressed a folded cloth against a wound in Martínez's shoulder. Blood streaked the side of his head.

One of the cart men spoke to Andy in Spanish, but Andy could not understand. Martínez groaned. "I knew we should have gone on."

Andy saw that Martínez had been knifed in the shoulder. He had another wound on the side of his head, probably administered by a club. "I could not stop them," Martínez wheezed. "They wanted the whiskey."

"I could've told you that. It was a mistake, bringin' it in the first place."

"I need no lectures, boy."

Andy said, "I found out about Billy. He was here. That other bunch took him with them. I believe I know where they went."

Martínez was incredulous. "You think we can go after them now?"

"We have to."

"Look. Look what they have done to the camp. The trade goods. They took two of the oxen for beef. And see what they have done to me. I have not the strength to go on."

"But you promised."

"A dead man cannot keep promises, and I am nearly dead. If I live to get back to Anton Chico, I will never go among the Comanches again."

"You're quittin'?"

"What else is to be done? If this time is not the death of me, the next will be."

Andy saw that argument was futile. Clearly, Martínez was in no condition to continue the search. He would be fortunate to get away from here with one cart and perhaps most of the horses and mules for which he had traded earlier. He would be doubly fortunate if his small crew did not have to bury him in some unmarked grave between here and his valley home.

Andy said, "I'm sorry. I had hoped we could get Billy without things comin' to this kind of pass."

"You should give up and come with us, or go home. You see here what can happen."

"I kept my mouth shut when I should've talked, and Billy got taken because of it. I promised myself I'd bring him back or never go home at all."

"You are a fool."

"I don't doubt that. But I'm goin' on by myself."

Martínez gave him a look of despair. "You do not have to be by yourself." He spoke in Spanish. A cart man removed a crucifix and chain from Martínez's neck. Martínez handed it to Andy.

"It has been blessed by a priest in Santa Fe. Wear this and you will not be alone."

"Doesn't look like it helped you much."

"I am alive. I do not ask more of God."

At first light, Andy saddled Long Red and was on his way. The tracks were many and easy to follow.

CHAPTER
FIFTEEN

Rusty Shannon stood on the bottom rung of the corral fence, studying three riders approaching from the north. He recognized James Monahan, Evan Gifford, and Len Tanner. He could not see Andy. He blinked in an effort to sharpen his sight, but still he saw only the three. Dread built a knot in his stomach.

Josie Monahan climbed up beside him. "What you lookin' at?"

"Riders comin'. Your brother James, Evan, and Len."

Her eyes brightened for only a moment, then trouble darkened them again. "What about Billy? And Andy?"

Rusty shook his head.

Josie leaned against him and choked off a small cry of disappointment. She glanced back toward her sister's house. Geneva sat in a rocking chair on the dog run, rocking the baby girl.

Josie said, "She's gone half crazy with worry and grief. At least Evan is comin' back. Maybe that'll help."

Rusty had watched Geneva waste away. He knew she had eaten but little, and he doubted that she had slept much. She clung to the baby as if the girl were the only family left to her. She had drained herself of tears. Now her eyes were dry and hollow and haunted.

Josie said, "I'd better go tell Geneva and Mama."

She seemed reluctant to start. Rusty hugged her for whatever comfort that might give her, then watched her move away toward her sister. He opened the corral gate and waited. He felt no need for a lot of questions. Despair in the dusty, bearded faces told him almost all he needed to know. He asked only, "Andy?"

Tanner's expression was grim. "He wouldn't come back with us. He's still out there somewhere, lookin'."

Geneva hurried out from her cabin, carrying the baby, and ran to meet her husband. He folded both of them into his arms. Rusty heard her cry. Clemmie came from the larger family house with Preacher Webb. She shaded her eyes with her hand a moment, then rushed to embrace her son. Webb trailed, letting her have her moment with James.

Rusty asked Tanner, "Find any trace of the boy?"

"We saw Indian sign, but there was no way to tell if they still had Billy or not."

Rusty's voice turned critical. "I don't see how you could've let Andy stay up there by himself."

"He wasn't by himself." Tanner explained about the *Comancheros* and the deal James had offered to barter the boy's freedom with horses.

Rusty protested, "But Andy's just a boy himself."

"Maybe you ain't paid enough attention to him lately. He don't act like a boy when he's got his mind made up. Said he was goin' to find Billy however long it took."

"You still ought to've stopped him."

"Tell you the truth, I don't think we really wanted to. He feels like it's his fault Billy got taken. Another thing, he can go places the rest of us can't. If anybody's to find Billy, it'll be him."

Rusty's anxiety was not appeased, but he saw it was useless to belabor the point. "Did you see Captain Burmeister anywhere?"

"Not since he turned back."

"He went out again, soon as his men got a little rest, supplies, and some fresh horses. God knows where he is."

"I'm surprised you didn't go with him."

"I don't have the strength to keep up on a hard ride. I'd be a millstone around everybody's neck. And somebody needed to be here besides Preacher Webb and Macy in case some Comanches or Kiowas decided to pay another visit."

Rusty watched Geneva and the baby return to their cabin. Evan had an arm around his wife's shoulders. Rusty ached for all of them. He could imagine the hell Evan had endured in the futile search for his son, the heartbreak he must have suffered in turning back.

Preacher Webb moved up beside Rusty and Tanner. "We prayed mighty hard. Sometimes it takes awhile, but you generally get an answer if you don't give up hope."

From someone else Rusty might have taken that as an empty platitude, but he knew Webb believed with all his soul.

Webb walked back to the family house with Clemmie and James. Rusty watched in silence. Clemmie had taken her father's death hard, but she had never let her back bend. She stood straight and determined.

Knowing it was futile, Rusty climbed onto the fence again and looked northward. Josie reached up and gripped his arm. "I can see in your face what you're thinkin'. Don't. You'd never find Andy. One boy alone, out in hundreds of miles of open prairie."

"A boy who considers himself a man."

Tanner declared, "He *is* a man, I tell you. He's given himself a job that few men would have the guts to try."

"I ought to be up there with him."

"You'd never make it past the first Comanche camp. But he will. He's got enough Indian in him."

Captain Burmeister returned in a couple of days with his little group of frontier guards. He was painfully frustrated, men and horses weary, dried out, and hungry. "It is hopeless," he told Rusty. "Of water there is not enough. It will never be a country for white men, not while we live."

"There is water," Rusty argued. "Otherwise, the Indians couldn't stay."

"But only the Indian knows where it is."

"Tanner was tellin' me about runnin' across some oxcart traders out of New Mexico. Looks like they know how to find water. Someday somebody will start markin' the water holes and the trails. Once it's done, that country won't be a mystery anymore. There won't be anyplace safe for Comanches to hide."

"Someday," Burmeister said. "But it is for now that we must worry. We know so little, and we are so few."

Rusty had been chewing on an idea for several days. "Captain, could you use another man?"

Burmeister's gray mustache lifted in a smile. "As in times past, before the fools on both sides carried us into war?"

"Like then. I realize it's not quite the same as the old-time rangers, and I know I'll be awhile gettin' my full strength back. But I feel like there's things I can do to make myself useful."

"But you have your own home, far from here."

"Not anymore. I've been carpetbagged out of it. I need to stay up in this part of the country for now, but I don't want to keep bein' a burden to the Monahans."

Tanner's mouth sagged open. Rusty had not mentioned the idea to him.

Burmeister turned. "And you, Private Tanner? What of you?"

Tanner grinned. "Why the hell not? When I was a ranger I went hungry half the time, and I never got paid what they promised me. They was the best years of my life."

"I cannot guarantee you will be paid this time. In Austin promises are many, but the well is often dry."

Rusty had one reservation. "Somethin' you ought to know, Captain, before you swear me in. There's a charge against me down home. It's a false charge, but it's on the books just the same."

"Not murder, I hope."

"Nothin' like that. I'm charged with aidin' and abettin' the escape of a criminal. But I never did it. He took one of my horses without me knowin' it. They claim I gave it to him."

"They?"

"Two brothers by the name of Oldham. Durin' the war they hid out in the brush. I had some trouble with them."

"They did not serve in the Confederate Army?"

"Nor the Union Army either. But now they're state police."

Burmeister scowled. "Do not worry about the state police. There are some good men but also some rotten apples. They have no authority over my company."

Rusty's announcement took Josie by surprise. She was dismayed. "Rusty, you can't. You mustn't."

"I can't stay here just doin' nothin'."

"You have a home here as long as you want it."

"It's your home, not mine."

"But it could be your home. You could be one of us."

He took her hands. "The Monahans have been the nearest thing to family that I've had since Daddy Mike and Mother Dora. There's not a family anywhere that I'd rather be a part of."

"I've always hoped that you and me—"

"I know. If I was in a shape for marryin', you're the one I'd ask. But I'd have nothin' to offer you now, not so much as a roof over your head or a plot of ground for a garden. And there's Billy out yonder somewhere, and Andy. I can't be thinkin' of makin' a home 'til that's all settled."

"What do you think you can do?"

"Ride. Watch. Listen. Maybe somewhere out there I'll find somethin' or hear somethin'. I don't know what, and I won't know 'til it happens."

She pressed his hand against her lips. "When the job is done, you know where I'll be."

Burmeister had set up his base camp several miles from the Monahan place. On the way there Rusty was aware that Burmeister watched him with a critical eye. When they reached the camp, the captain asked him, "You are tired?"

Rusty was, but he chose not to acknowledge it. "I'm doin' better than I thought I might."

"We will not push you too hard, not at first."

"I'll tote my share of the load."

"You always did. Always you were a good man on patrol. There was not much you did not see."

"You're wantin' me to go on scout?"

"Tomorrow, and only as far as you feel strong. Take Private Tanner with you. Look for sign of Indians. But do not engage. Come back and report."

"Yes sir." It would feel good to be doing something useful again and not be considered an invalid. "There's nobody I'd rather have with me than Tanner. Even if he does sometimes talk 'til my ears hurt."

The camp reminded him of earlier times, before and during the war when he had served with the rangers in the Fort Belknap country. Burmeister maintained a loose form of military discipline and routine that lent at least some structure to each day. Rusty studied the men, quietly trying to assess their potential. He found that most had escaped Confederate service, a couple of them by going to Mexico, a couple more by serving in the Union Army. One or two he suspected of having been brush men, hiding out from conscription officers. That did not necessarily brand them in his view. James Monahan had done it. On the other hand, so had the Oldham brothers.

Rusty guessed that his first day's ride with Tanner covered about twenty miles, about as much as he could expect while watching the ground for tracks. The last few miles set his shoulder to throbbing and aggravated an old leg pain from his long-ago arrow wound.

Tanner commented, "You're lookin' a little peaked."

"It's your eyes. I'm doin' just fine."

"Well, I'm tired if you're not. I say it's time to make camp. Got to think of the horses."

The ride had not been long enough to tax the horses unduly. Rusty appreciated that Tanner was watching out for his welfare without making an issue of it.

They stopped at a small seep he remembered from scouting trips long ago. The seep fed a narrow creek, its water trailing for a couple of hundred yards before disappearing into the sand. Along the creek's short course a thin band of green grass offered grazing for the horses. Rusty and Tanner staked their mounts with long rawhide reatas that gave the animals considerable freedom to move around.

Tanner watched them. "Just like old times. The horses are gettin' fed better than we are. I can imagine the good supper Clemmie Monahan is servin' tonight."

Rusty chewed hard on a salty strip of dried jerky. "Andy may not have even this much to eat."

"He can get by on lizards and rattlesnakes if he has to. He's that much Comanche."

Rusty shuddered at the thought. "If I had any notion where he's at, any notion at all—"

"You'd go there and lose that red hair before it has a chance to start gettin' gray."

The only horse tracks he and Tanner had seen all day had been remnants of old ones, headed north. They found no sign of recent Indian incursion. Years ago, under the old loose frontier-ranger organization, the men had scouted along established north-south lines a little beyond the settlements, riding until they met scouts coming from counterpart camps. At that point they turned back and re-rode the same line. The system had worked well so long as the frontier companies had manpower enough. Some Indian raids were broken up before they were well started. The system had become less and less effective as the war drew men away from the frontier and the ranger companies.

Rusty knew Captain Burmeister lacked men enough to make the routine work as well as it once had. Intercepting Indians would be as much a matter of luck—of being at the right place at the right time—as of organization.

Tanner said, "This ought to be the job of the United States Army, but them generals don't see Indians as a serious problem."

"They're mostly stayin' back in the settled parts of the state where Indians *aren't* a problem. They spend most of their time lookin' for Confederate conspiracies."

"Well, I've learned one thing for damned sure."

"What's that?"

"Don't ever lose a war. It don't pay."

They were within sight of the camp when one of the scouts rode out to intercept them. His expression indicated that he was not the bearer of good news. He said, "Captain Burmeister wanted me to let you know you've got company waitin' for you."

Rusty asked, "Who is it?"

"Couple of brothers. I don't recall the name. The younger one has just got one arm."

Rusty frowned at Tanner. "The Oldhams. I've wondered how long it would take them to figure out where I'm at." He looked back at the messenger. "Did the captain say what he wants me to do?"

"No, just said he didn't want you ridin' in unawares."

Tanner said, "You take Clyde. I'll take Buddy-Boy. We can put an end to them once and for all."

Rusty realized Tanner was serious. "I don't want us to kill anybody. Remember, they're state police."

"Damned poor recommendation."

The scout said, "There's a third man with them. Deputy of some kind, I think."

The Oldham brothers and the deputy waited outside Burmeister's tent, their stance stiff and expectant. Burmeister and two of his men stood nearby, watching them. Tanner's rifle lay across the pommel of his saddle, ready.

Rusty dismounted, keeping his horse between himself and the Oldhams. He said, "I expected you a lot sooner, Clyde."

"It ain't that we didn't try. You're a hard man to locate."

"Now that you've found me, what do you figure on doin'?"

"We've come to arrest you."

Rusty said, "If you plan on shootin' me in the back again, you've come a long ways on a fool's errand. I'm not goin' with you."

Clyde started to reach into his pocket but stopped abruptly when Tanner swung his rifle around. He swallowed hard. "I'm just goin' after my warrant."

Tanner said, "See that that's all you go after."

Buddy Oldham dropped his hand to the butt of a pistol on his hip but made no effort to draw the weapon. He stared into the muzzle of Tanner's rifle.

Tanner said, "Better raise that hand, Buddy, or this time you're liable to lose more than your arm."

Buddy lifted his hand clear, his eyes flashing anger.

Clyde demanded, "Where's that Indian kid of yours, Shannon?"

None of your damned business, Rusty thought. But he said, "He's not here."

"Probably runnin' with his Comanche friends." Clyde scowled. "When he left down yonder, we followed him. Second or third day out, a bunch of Comanches come swarmin' down on us. I'd swear on a stack of Bibles that boy was with them. He was after our scalps."

Rusty wondered. Andy hadn't told him about that, if it was true.

Tanner said, "Damned shame he didn't get them."

Captain Burmeister reached out for the warrant. "I will read that, if you please."

Clyde hesitated. "I come to serve it on Shannon."

"I am commanding officer here. I will read it first."

Grudgingly Clyde handed it over. Burmeister glanced at the paper. "This judge, his name is not known to me. How am I to know this document is real?"

"It's got the court seal on it."

"Perhaps it is real. Perhaps it is not. You will tell me about the charges against Private Shannon."

Clyde's eyes widened. "*Private* Shannon?"

"He is a member of my company. Therefore he is an officer of the state, as you claim to be. My authority as captain is superior to yours. He will go or not go, as I choose."

Buddy Oldham's face colored. "Authority! You sound like some kind of a Dutchman. Me and my brother don't have to take orders from no immigrant."

Burmeister's mustache twitched in growing anger. "I fought for this country already before you were born. Private Shannon tells me you spent the last war hiding in the brush. You fought for nobody."

Clyde said, "It wasn't our war. We had no stake in either side."

"But now you wear a badge that is too big for you and swear out charges against those from whom you would steal."

"We ain't stole nothin'—"

"You have taken Private Shannon's land, have you not?"

"He owed back taxes. I paid them fair and legal."

Rusty held his tongue. He wanted to refute what Oldham said, but the captain seemed to be doing a good job of it without his interference.

Burmeister said, "Once before you have arrested him, and you shot him in the back."

"He tried to escape."

"So you claim. It is an excuse as old as Pharaoh."

Tanner put in, "If you let them take Rusty, he'll never get halfway home. They'll kill him."

Burmeister nodded. "So we will put the boot on another foot. Mr. Oldham, if it is your will to take him I do not prevent you. But I will send Private Tanner and some of my other men as escort. If you make any move to kill him, any move whatever . . ." He did not finish. He did not have to.

Buddy Oldham's face went crimson. "Don't let them scare you, Clyde."

Clyde looked at Tanner with dread. He said, "They do scare me. It's *us* who wouldn't live to get back. They'd kill us sure as hell."

Burmeister agreed. "Possibly so. But is that not what you planned for Private Shannon?"

Clyde Oldham had the trapped look of an animal hemmed into a corner.

Buddy was too outraged to understand his brother's fear. "Ain't we goin' to take him?" He raised the stump of an arm. "Look what he done. He left me half a man. You swore to me, Clyde. You swore we'd kill him for that."

"Shut up, Buddy. You don't see what we're up against."

"I see you're givin' up after we've rode all this way, after we been chased by Indians and everything. You're fixin' to turn around and leave him."

"Sometimes you get dealt a bad hand. You fold and wait for a better deal." Clyde cut his gaze back to Rusty. "So this time the pot is yours. But the game ain't over."

"It's no game to me, Clyde." Rusty looked regretfully at Buddy. "I never wanted to shoot your brother. He forced it on me."

Clyde did not acknowledge that he had heard. "Thanks for the farm, Shannon. It's a good one."

"Don't be likin' it too much. One way or another I'll get it back."

"Come visit any time. We'll be lookin' for you." Clyde jerked his head at his brother and the deputy. They went to their horses.

Watching them mount, Rusty said, "I didn't expect them to give up that easy."

Tanner said, "They ain't given up. You'll be seein' them again."

Rusty did not want to think about that. "This horse is tired and sweaty. I'm goin' to water him and brush him down." He led the horse to a makeshift corral and pulled the saddle off. He dropped the blanket and bent down to pick it up.

A fence post exploded just above his head. A split second later he heard the loud, flat sound of a rifle.

Tanner shouted, "Get down, Rusty." Tanner steadied his rifle across a fence rail and fired at the retreating Clyde.

Burmeister and his scouts quickly covered Buddy and the deputy with their firearms. Rusty felt points of fire in his face. Clyde's shot had driven splinters into his skin. He reached up and felt the warm stickiness of blood on his fingers.

Bent low in the saddle, Clyde was spurring away, his boots flailing at his horse's ribs, his shirttail standing out behind him. His hat blew off, but he did not slow down.

Tanner watched Clyde's desperate flight with disgust. "Had my sights on him right between the shoulder blades. Gettin' to where I can't shoot worth a damn anymore."

Rusty pulled at a splinter that had pierced his cheek. It burned as if it had been set afire.

Burmeister walked up to Buddy Oldham, his eyes smoldering. "That is some brother you have. He tried to do murder here."

Stubbornly Buddy said, "We got a warrant."

"Take your warrant and go before I get mad. You don't want to see a German get mad. It is a terrible thing, all thunder and lightning."

Buddy glared at the captain, then turned to Rusty, hatred burning in his eyes. He said, "You come south any time you're ready. We'll give you back your farm . . . six feet of it."

Buddy and the deputy left. Watching the deputy dismount to pick up Clyde's lost hat, Tanner said, "Losin' his arm made Buddy mean as poison."

"He's not as dangerous as Clyde."

"Clyde's a coward."

"That's why he's dangerous. He'll get you when you're not lookin'." He reached up and felt his burning cheek.

Burmeister gave Rusty an anxious study. "You bleed. He hit you?"

"Just splinters. They'll come out." Rusty turned to Tanner. "Thanks, Len. If he'd had time for a second shot he'd've killed me sure."

Tanner shrugged, his gaze on Clyde and the deputy, riding away. "That's what I'm paid so high for."

CHAPTER

SIXTEEN

The horse tracks were easy for Andy to follow. This far up in their plains stronghold, the raiders had no reason to try to cover them. Their direction gave him a strong clue about the destination. He remembered a place where his band had camped several times, a location that offered water enough and trees for shade and shelter from the wind.

To look less like a white man he had shed his hat, shirt, and long underwear, keeping only his trousers and the moccasins. The rest he tied behind the cantle. He remembered the time soon after he fell back into Texan hands that his uncle, Jim Pickard, had come to have a look at him. The uncle had rejected him because he considered him a savage beyond redemption.

He ought to get a look at me now, Andy thought.

The camp was where he expected it to be. As before, he approached the horse herd first, looking for Billy's pony or Vince Purdy's mount. And again he was disappointed.

He rode into camp with all the boldness he could muster, trying not to show any sign of his nagging concern that some of Tonkawa Killer's friends might be here. He saw a few faces he remembered, though they stared at him without recognition. He had grown, and his features had matured since he had been with the Texans. The camp people met him with both curiosity and suspicion, for they were not prepared to see a white-skinned young man come among them of his own accord.

He spoke in the Comanche tongue, and their suspicions began to fade. To a man he remembered having ridden with Steals the Ponies he said, "Do you not remember me? Steals the Ponies is my brother. I was known as Badger Boy."

With recognition came a warm welcome. "Come. Come and eat. There is plenty."

Andy was glad to accept. He had eaten little besides a bit of tough jerky since leaving Martínez. His host plied him with questions about his years among the Texans, about the Texans' strange lifeways. Andy tailored his answers to what he thought the man would want to hear. "They are a strange people," he conceded. "But not all their ways are bad."

When the questions began to lag, he offered his own. "Do you know where I might find Steals the Ponies?"

The Comanche said, "He left here yesterday and went north with his family. They joined some others who came back from a raid against the Texans."

Andy's senses sharpened. "A raid?"

"Yes. I went myself. We took many horses."

Andy thought of Vince Purdy. "And scalps?"

"Only one. An old man we found."

"No one else?"

"We took a small boy. Fights with Bears was the leader. He claimed the boy and the horses. I took second coup on the old man, but I got only this." He lifted a watch that hung around his neck on a leather thong along with his medicine bag. Its case looked like silver.

Vince Purdy's! Andy thought.

He reached out. "May I see it?"

His host lifted the thong from around his neck. "It is of little use. It is but a pretty trinket."

Andy clasped the watch with reverence, as if somehow it contained the spirit of Vince Purdy. In his mind's eye he visualized the kind old gentleman, and his throat tightened. This keepsake would mean much to the Monahans if he lived to return it to them.

He saw that it had run down. Evidently its new owner did not know to wind it. He would not have understood the white man's concept of time anyway. Andy started to wind it but changed his mind. He asked, "What will you do with it?"

"I may give it to my wife's father. He is old and becoming foolish. He likes things that shine."

"Would you trade it to me?"

The man's eyes brightened. Comanches enjoyed the challenge of trading. "What do you have to offer?"

Andy knew he did not have much. "A white-man hat. It will keep the sun from your head in summer and snow from your hair in winter."

"Not enough."

"A white-man shirt. It will help protect you when the cold winds blow."

The Indian shook his head. "My father-in-law would not like those. They do not shine."

Andy considered long before offering, "The saddle, then. The white man's saddle is comfortable. It will not rub sores on your legs." He would regret giving it up, but he could ride bareback. He had done it for years with The People.

Nothing about the saddle was fancy. It was plain, its seat slick from long use. Someone had already ridden it for years before Rusty had acquired it for Andy. The Comanche rubbed his hands over it, his eyes shining with delight. He said, "I wanted the old man's saddle, but Fights with Bears would not give it up. We trade."

Andy wondered if the watch would still run, but he did not wind it. Its ticking might give his host second thoughts. He put it around his neck.

He said, "You mentioned a boy." He trembled a little, fearing the answer. "What became of him?"

"Fights with Bears took him north." The Comanche pointed with his chin. "He has not decided whether to keep him to raise as a slave or to kill him. The boy has caused him much trouble. Fights with Bears is not a man of much patience."

Good for Billy, Andy thought. The more fight he showed, the better his chance of surviving. Andy remembered that when he had first been taken he had been subjected to heavy abuse. He realized later that he was being tested for his prospects as a warrior. Had he not kept fighting back, he might have been killed.

He asked, "Was my brother on the raid with you?"

"No. Fights with Bears was the leader. He and Steals the Ponies do not like one another."

Andy was relieved that his brother had not participated in Vince Purdy's killing and Billy's kidnapping. Yet he would have thought no less of him if he had been a party to the incident. The Comanches were simply following the customs of their grandfathers. Raiding enemies was a natural part of their life, like eating, like breathing. It almost took on the aspects of a game, though ofttimes a deadly one. Living with them, Andy had regarded this as normal. Now, having lived away from them, he could no longer accept it without question, not when it took the lives of good people like Vince Purdy and involved the capture of innocent children like Billy Gifford.

Yet, white men of the North and South had fought one another during four long years for reasons he had never quite fathomed. They had killed strangers, people they had never seen before and who had never done them harm. He could not see a great difference between that and the Comanche way.

Impatience set his skin to prickling. He was eager to move on, to find Steals the Ponies. Perhaps his brother could help him in some way to free Billy. "I must go," he said. "The longer I wait, the farther my brother may travel."

His host tried to get him to stay the night. "With families, they move slowly. You could start with the morning's light and catch them before the sun sleeps again."

Andy had another potential problem to consider. He had not seen everyone in this camp, nor had everyone seen him. A friend of Tonkawa Killer might yet recognize him.

He said, "I can ride far before the sun sleeps."

To replace the saddle, Andy obtained a rawhide rope to loop behind his horse's shoulders. He could tuck his knees beneath it to hold him steady should he encounter rough traveling. Except for his trousers, he left his white-man clothing behind in return for the hospitality. With a stick, his host drew a rough map on the ground. He described the site where he thought the group was likely to camp for at least a few days. The description sounded familiar.

"I believe I remember the place," Andy said.

"May friendly spirits ride with you."

The trail was as plain as a white man's wagon road, beaten out not only by horses but by tepee poles lashed together to form travois. Andy could have followed it at a lope and in the dark, but he did not want to push Long Red. He might have to depend upon the horse's stamina if circumstances called for a hard run.

In the middle of the afternoon he came suddenly upon three Comanche hunters on horseback. Two carried deer carcasses in front of them. They reined up and waited for Andy, suspicion strong in their faces. The one not encumbered held a bow with an arrow fitted into its string.

Nervously Andy greeted them in their own language. Like so many others he had encountered, they wanted to know how a white youth knew the words of The People. He explained as briefly as he could. "I have been away from my people a long time. I am looking for them."

He decided against using his brother's name. Should things go badly, he did not want to bring trouble to Steals the Ponies.

The hunters accepted him with reservations. "Ride with us," one said. "We will take you to our camp. Perhaps there you will find your family."

Nearing the encampment, they passed by the horse herd. This time Andy was not disappointed. He recognized Billy's pony and Purdy's horse standing together near the outer edge, like two old acquaintances thrown unwillingly among strangers.

One of the hunters said, "We hope you find what you are looking for."

Andy already had. He saw a woman cooking meat over an open fire in front of a tepee. She was Steals the Ponies's wife. Seeing no other woman with her, he assumed she was still the only one. Two children, a boy and a girl, played nearby.

He approached slowly, not wanting to startle her. She looked up at him without recognition. He said, "Do you not know me?"

Her face was blank. "I do not believe so."

"I am Badger Boy."

She almost turned over the meat pot. She embraced him, then stood back for a better look. "I can see now, but you are much changed. You were a boy. Now you are a man."

"I have come to see my brother."

"He scouts for buffalo. He should be here soon."

The boy and girl had stopped their play to stare at him in curiosity. He asked, "These are yours?"

"Yes. Before winter there will be another." She looked away, then pointed. "He comes. Say nothing. See if he recognizes you."

Andy's heartbeat quickened. The passage of years had not changed the way his brother sat on his horse. Andy could have recognized him from far away. Steals the Ponies did not seem to notice the visitor at first. He dismounted, obviously tired, and tied his horse behind the tepee. He carried his medicine shield inside, for it was a sacred thing to be protected from harm.

Coming back outside, he spoke to his wife. "I am hungry."

"The meat is soon ready. Look. Someone has come to see you."

Steals the Ponies stared blankly a moment, then his eyes brightened and the weariness fell away. "Badger Boy!" He embraced his brother with such strength that Andy almost lost his breath. "But Badger Boy is no longer a fit name. You are not a boy."

"Among the Texans I am known as Andy."

Steals the Ponies spoke the name but found it not to his liking. "It means nothing. We must find you a new name, something better."

His delight began to fade, and concern crowded in. "You should not be here. Have you forgotten why you left us, why you had to go back and live with the Texans?"

"I have not forgotten. I remember the one who was killed." He avoided speaking the name. "I had hoped none of his friends are in this camp."

"They come and they go. One is here. Do you remember Fights with Bears?"

Andy had been hearing the name but could not recall the look of the man. His brother nodded toward the tepee. "We will go inside. We would not want him to see you."

"You believe he would still want me dead?"

"His wives are sisters of the one who was killed."

After entering, Andy waited until his brother sat, leaning against a back rest, then he seated himself.

Steals the Ponies said, "When you left, we agreed you should never come back. Why are you here again?"

"I have come looking for a boy. He is the son of people who have been good to me. I am told he was taken by Fights with Bears. I have come to take him back to his family."

Trouble pinched his brother's eyes. "You have come far and risked your life for nothing. You want too much. Fights with Bears has claimed the boy for his own. He will not give him up."

Andy remembered the proposal James and Evan had made to Martínez. "Perhaps he would trade for horses."

"He already has many horses. If you brought him more he would probably take them, kill you, and keep the boy. He listens to bad spirits, that one."

Andy did not know what else to propose for trade. He did not know how much money the Monahans might have. It was unlikely Fights with Bears had much concept of money's value anyway. Comanches understood goods, something they could hold in their hands, something they could use.

Coins were of value only for ornamentation, and paper money was worth nothing at all.

"What can I do?" he asked.

"Go back to the Texans. You belong among them now. Forget about the boy. Tell them he is dead."

"His family are my friends. They weep for him."

"If they are young they can have other children."

"It would not be the same. Texans love their children just as The People do."

"Fights with Bears would not even talk to you."

"Then I will steal the boy in the night."

Steals the Ponies stared at Andy in disbelief. "Your Texas friends are too far away. He would catch you and kill you. He might be angry enough to kill the boy."

"I have traveled many days to find Billy. Now that I know where he is, I cannot turn away from him."

"You must. Or are you so willing to die for the Texans?"

Andy considered a long time before suggesting, "What if I offered to trade myself for him?"

"Fights with Bears would kill you and keep the boy. Why would you suggest such a foolish thing?"

"Because it is my fault the boy was taken." He explained about his failure to warn of the raiding party he had encountered prior to Billy's capture.

Steals the Ponies was incredulous. "You would trade your life for this boy? It would not be reasonable, even if Fights with Bears were a man of his word and would let the boy go. But of course he will not."

"I will not go back without Billy. I could not face those who have given me a home. I would be ashamed."

"You cannot stay here. There are others besides Fights with Bears who would gladly kill you." Steals the Ponies's expression became grave. "Even if they did not, you would not want to share the future of our people."

"What do you mean by that?"

"I have had a vision. It came to me one night, clear as in daylight. I saw our prairies without buffalo. Where the buffalo should have been, I saw the blue-coat soldiers. They were as many as the buffalo. We were helpless and hungry and cold." He shivered. "They herded us like the white man's cattle to a terrible place where we did not want to go."

"The reservation?"

"I think so. Many of our people are already there. It is the wish of the Texans and the soldiers that we all go there or that we die."

Andy argued, "The bluecoats have done little against The People since the white man's war ended. The Texans cry for help, but the soldiers do not listen."

"They will, and soon. The vision was very strong. For your own good, your place is among the Texans. You do not belong among The People anymore. If Fights with Bears and his friends do not kill you, the soldiers may. They will not see you as a white man. They will see you as one of us."

The bleakness of Steals the Ponies's vision left Andy depressed. He wanted to believe that his brother had simply experienced a bad dream. Yet during his years with the Comanches he had heard many stories about visions that came to pass. The People had strong faith in them. He could not dismiss this one lightly.

He said, "Perhaps the vision was a warning of what *might* happen. Were you not shown a way to avoid it?"

"The soldiers were too many. Their guns were too powerful."

"If the vision was true, there is no future here for Billy either. I must take him back to his own. It is a matter of honor."

Andy's brother sat in silence a long time, his face an expressionless mask. But Andy imagined he could see the mind hard at work behind half-closed eyes. He could sense the internal struggle. At last Steals the Ponies spoke. "You talk of your honor. If I helped you do this thing, I would lose my own honor. I would betray my people."

"Not all the people. Just Fights with Bears. You said you do not like him."

Steals the Ponies went silent again for a time, thinking. Finally he said, "There might be a way, but the spirits must be with you. You could die if they are not."

Eagerly Andy asked, "What is it?"

"I have not thought it all through. We will talk of it later. Now I must move your horse so Fights with Bears will not see him and wonder."

"I do not want to place you in danger. This is a thing I should do by myself."

"Fights with Bears would not kill me, and I would not kill him. We are bound together by the blood of The People. But you are not of our blood, and neither is the boy. He would kill you both. So I will help you."

Steals the Ponies was gone awhile. His wife was in and out of the tepee several times. Andy could sense that she was curious, but she asked no questions. The two children came inside and stared silently at Andy without approaching too closely. He wanted to tell them he was their uncle, but he decided against it. They might tell other children later, and word might find its way to Fights with Bears. He would know that Steals the Ponies was somehow involved in Billy's liberation . . . if it worked.

When his brother returned, Andy asked, "What do we do now?"

"We rest. We wait. We can do nothing until Fights with Bears and his family are asleep."

"Do you know for certain where Billy is?"

"He is in their lodge. They keep him tied because he tries to run away. I wonder about his intelligence. Even if he were to escape and not be found, by himself he would soon starve. The boy does not reason well."

"He has the stubborn will of the Monahans." Andy did not know how to explain the fierce independence of the family who had suffered so much because they stood by their unpopular convictions. He said, "They have much in common with the Comanches."

That was explanation enough for Steals the Ponies. "Sleep now. You will have little time for it later. You have far to travel."

So much was running through Andy's mind that he did not expect to sleep at all. However, when his brother shook his shoulder gently to awaken him, he was surprised to see that it was dark outside.

His brother said, "It will soon be time. You must eat now."

Andy did not feel like eating. He burned with excitement over what was coming. Steals the Ponies said, "You will need strength. Eat."

Andy forced himself to down the leftover meat from the previous evening.

Steals the Ponies said, "I have been to the lodge of Fights with Bears. Not everything is as we would want it to be. One of the children is sick."

"Billy?"

"One of the others. But when a child is sick, its mother does not sleep well. It will be difficult for me to crawl into the lodge without arousing the family."

If caught, Steals the Ponies would be expelled from the band at the very least. He and his family would be outcasts. Andy said, "That is not for you to do. It is for me."

"I am pleased to see that you have much courage. I would be more pleased if I saw that you were also blessed with much judgment."

Andy asked, "Do you know where the boy will be sleeping?"

"I have seen him tied to a lodge pole." Steals the Ponies picked up a stick and drew a circle in the sand to represent the interior of a tepee. He pointed out the front flap, then moved the point of the stick around the perimeter and stabbed it into the ground. "This is where I have seen him. I suspect the other children are placed around him at night to make it difficult for him to escape."

"Once I have freed him, what then?"

"I will have two horses for you. The sorrel on which you came and another for the boy."

"What about his pony?"

"It will not travel fast enough. I have other use for the pony and the tracks it makes."

Andy did not understand. His brother explained, "I will take another horse and lead the pony southward. That is the direction Fights with Bears would expect. I will leave a clear trail. When I have misled him far enough, my trail will disappear. I will circle back to camp while he is still looking for my tracks."

"But south is where I need to go with the boy."

"Not at first. You will ride eastward in the creek where you will not leave a trail. You must travel far before you leave the creek."

"That would put us into the settlements a long way east of where the boy's family lives."

"But east from where Fights with Bears will be looking for you."

Andy could see flaws in his brother's plan, but it was better than anything he had been able to think up. It had all the marks of the trickster, the coyote.

Much depended upon Andy's being able to get the boy out of the tepee without arousing the family. Beyond that, much depended upon being able to fool Fights with Bears.

He said, "I hope he is not very smart."

"He has been in many battles. Not one has he lost."

CHAPTER
SEVENTEEN

The moon provided light enough for Andy to see that the tepee skins were rolled up a foot or so from the bottom to allow fresh air to pass through. He would be able to crawl in where he chose rather than have to enter through the front flap and feel his way around. He looked behind him but could not see Steals the Ponies. He had the comfort of faith that his brother was back there somewhere, holding two pairs of horses.

From inside he could hear loud snoring. He guessed it came from Fights with Bears. That was gratifying. But not so welcome were the sounds of a child's cough and a woman's calming whisper. Andy lay on his stomach at the tepee's edge, listening, his skin prickling with impatience.

He waited until some time had passed since the last cough. He began to drag himself forward slowly, trying to make no sound. Somewhere a dog barked, and he froze. The child whimpered, causing him to wait again, half in and half out of the lodge.

As his eyes adjusted to the interior's poor light, he was able to see the sleepers. The largest he took to be Fights with Bears, lying on his back, snoring again after having lain on his side for a while. Next to him lay one of his wives. Andy sought out the second wife. She lay among the children. He assumed that the sick child was one of hers.

It took him some time to be sure which of the other dark lumps was

Billy. He was not quite in the place Steals the Ponies had indicated in his rough dirt sketch. Billy's hands were tied above his head, a leather thong binding them to a tepee pole. He lay with his feet together. Andy suspected they were also bound.

He began backing out of the tepee but bumped against one of the other children. The child grunted and raised up on one elbow. Andy lay still, barely daring to breathe, until the child settled down and resumed sleep. Then he crawled free of the tepee, backwards, and inched his way around to the pole where Billy was tied.

Billy stirred restlessly. He appeared to be asleep, but Andy knew he could not be comfortable with his hands lashed above his head. If startled, he was likely to cry out and awaken the family. Andy dragged himself inside the tepee just far enough to reach Billy. Gripping his knife in a cold-sweaty hand, he cut the thong attached to the pole. His hands suddenly free, Billy brought them down in reflex and opened his eyes in surprise.

Andy clamped a hand over Billy's mouth before the boy could do more than grunt. Billy stared wildly at him and for a few seconds fought to pull free.

"Shhh," Andy hissed, softly as he could.

Billy calmed. Andy removed the hand and crooked his finger, silently beckoning. He began backing out of the tepee. Hands and feet still tied, Billy wriggled after him.

The sick child coughed and cried out. Instantly its mother was awake, speaking gently. She dipped a cloth into a bowl of water and laid it across the fevered face. Andy froze again and motioned for Billy to do the same.

Fights with Bears gave a loud grunt and pushed himself up on one arm. He demanded, "Can you not keep that girl quiet? I want to sleep."

The child's mother did not take the comment in good grace. She answered with a sharp retort. Andy feared the two would become too angry with one another to go back to sleep. But the man grunted something unintelligible and lay back down. In a few minutes the child became quiet, and its mother stretched out beside it.

Andy feared she was not asleep. She might not sleep the rest of the night. He could not afford to wait too long. After a few minutes he began crawling again, inches at a time. Billy came along after him. It seemed an hour before the boy was out of the tepee. Andy cut the leather thong that bound Billy's hands, then the one that tied his feet.

Billy recognized him in the dim light of the half moon. "Andy!"

Andy shushed him again and beckoned for him to follow. Billy was awkward on his feet. He fell to hands and knees. Being tied had cut his circulation and numbed his arms and legs. Andy lifted the boy up and carried him in the direction where Steals the Ponies would be waiting. Billy clung desperately to his neck.

Andy's brother stood in the edge of the creek, holding four horses. He appeared much relieved. "It took you a long time," he said. "I feared you had entered the wrong lodge."

Billy reacted with fear to Steals the Ponies. Andy whispered, "Don't be afraid. This is my brother."

Billy did not understand that. Andy would explain it to him later, when they were far from here.

Steals the Ponies said, "Put the boy on this horse. He is one of best I have. I hope he can ride without a saddle."

"He can. He will."

Billy recognized his own pony and asked why he could not ride it. That was something else Andy would have to explain later. For the moment he said only, "This is your horse now." He mounted Long Red.

Steals the Ponies swung up onto a third horse. He had a leather rope around the neck of Billy's pony. "Remember," he admonished, "follow the creek eastward. If the spirits are with us, it will be daylight before Fights with Bears knows the boy is gone. I will see that the pony leaves good, clear tracks for him to follow."

Andy felt as if he would choke. The breach between him and The People, already broad, would be irretrievably unbridgeable after this.

He grasped his brother's arm. "You have done a brave thing for me."

"But it is the last thing I can ever do for you. With what you do tonight, you have chosen the white man's road. You are no longer Comanche."

"It is a hard thing to know that I may never see you again."

Steals the Ponies's voice was grave. "Perhaps we will see each other in another world, less troubled than this one. Now go. Do not look back."

Andy did look back, once. He saw Steals the Ponies ride up out of the creek, leading Billy's pony. Moving southward, he was quickly lost from sight.

Billy asked, "Why do we ride in the water?"

"So we don't leave tracks."

"Your brother leaves tracks."

"So they will follow him, not us."

"Are you takin' me home, Andy?"

"That's my intention."

"They killed Granddaddy Vince."

"I know."

"He had a watch. It looked like the one you're wearin' around your neck."

"I'm takin' it home, too. Now, let's don't talk for a while. Let's just ride."

It seemed beyond reason to ride eastward when all his instincts tried to pull him south, but he recognized his brother's wisdom. Fights with Bears would expect the escapees to flee southward. The false trail created by Steals the Ponies would bear him out.

Andy recognized that his brother was running some risk, but he felt that Steals the Ponies was wily enough to avoid being caught. At some point he would see to it that his trail came to an end. He would circle back to camp and be the picture of innocence when Fights with Bears finally returned empty-handed. By that time Andy and Billy should be beyond reach.

Daylight gave Andy his first clear look at the boy. Billy's back showed quirt marks. His face was bruised and swollen.

"Treated you pretty mean, didn't they?" he said.

"They wanted me to cry, and I did, a little. Pretty soon I found out that when I cried they hurt me more, especially that big ugly one. Never could figure out what his name was."

"It'd take you a week to learn his Comanche name. In English you'd call him Fights with Bears."

"He's the one killed Granddaddy Vince. We didn't know where they came from. All at once they were there. After that ugly one killed Grand-daddy, I thought he was fixin' to kill me, too. But he whipped me and tied me to my pony."

"Figured on makin' a slave out of you, or maybe a warrior if you showed enough fight."

"Is that what happened to you?"

Andy searched his memory. "Pretty much. It was a long time ago."

"You didn't have anybody to come after you and take you back?"

"They tried, but they didn't know where I'd be. I had some notion where I might find you."

"I'm glad. I don't want to live with the Indians. I just want to go home to Mama and Daddy."

"That's where I'm takin' you."

The creek gradually narrowed, its flow shallow and sluggish. Andy suspected by midmorning that it had about run its course. After several hours of traveling in a generally easterly direction he thought it should be safe to turn south. Even assuming the unlikely proposition that Fights with Bears had seen through the ploy, Andy figured he and Billy had a long lead.

He came to a bend where gravel had accumulated in times of high water. "Here's where we'll quit the water. We won't leave much of a track."

Billy said, "I'm hungry."

Andy handed over a bit of pemmican his sister-in-law had given him. "It may not taste like your mother's cookin', but the hungrier you are the better it gets."

Riding up out of the creek, Andy stopped for a long look around. He did not expect pursuit, but it would be dangerous to take too much for granted. Billy responded in kind to his concern.

"They after us?"

"I don't see a thing, not a buffalo, not even a prairie chicken."

"I wish we had us a prairie chicken right now."

"Eat what I gave you."

He had to fight down a temptation to run the horses. Instinct told him to put as much distance behind them as possible, but they had a long way to go. It would not be done in a day, or even two. The horses had to be spared if they were to go all the way.

Once Andy saw half a dozen horsemen on the horizon. His pulse raced. He dropped down the side of a low hill and quickly dismounted. "Get down, Billy. Maybe they didn't see us."

"Indians? You think they're after us?"

"Probably a huntin' party, after buffalo. But they might settle for us."

"If they're Comanche, can't you talk to them?"

"They might not be Comanche. And if they are, they may be friends of Fights with Bears."

In a little while the riders were gone. Andy found himself sweating more than the afternoon sun would justify. He said, "Some people claim this country is empty. But they never rode across it hopin' not to see anybody."

At dusk Andy saw the light of a fire directly in his path.

"We'd better wait for night, then go around," he said. "No tellin' who that might be."

Billy asked worriedly, "You think they're lookin' for us?"

"Not likely. But in the dark it's hard to tell who your friends are."

They rested the horses until the stars were out. Andy and Billy passed closely enough to smell the smoke of the campfire and of meat roasting over it. Billy said, "I sure am hungry."

Andy was too, but he had learned long ago to ignore hunger when other considerations pressed harder. "We'll get a-plenty to eat at the Monahan farm."

"That's still a long ways off."

Andy heard laughter from the camp, and a voice raised in a shout. He brought Long Red to a stop and listened. He was almost certain he heard some words in English.

"Billy, those may be white men."

"Let's go see."

"Not too fast. We'll work our way up close and make sure." Andy was uneasy. It did not seem reasonable to encounter white men up here in what was essentially a Comanche stronghold. Perhaps they were soldiers, making an extended scout. Or they could be frontier guards like Captain Burmeister's ranger detachment.

He dismounted and led Long Red but motioned for Billy to stay mounted. Billy's horse was too tall and Billy's legs too short for him to mount without help. They halted fifty yards from the firelight. Listening intently, Andy discerned that the men were indeed speaking English.

By himself he might have moved on, hungry or not. But the boy had had little to eat all day except a bit of pemmican, which he had forced down. "Billy, we're goin' to take a chance. Let me do the talkin'."

He led the two horses to within twenty yards of the fire. He shouted, "Hello the camp!"

Instantly several men jumped away from the campfire's reflected light. Someone shouted back, "Who's out there?"

"Just two of us. We're white."

"Show yourselves, but come in slow."

Andy could not see the weapons aimed at him, but he could feel them. He led the horses as near the fire as they would go. He raised both hands.

A voice demanded from the darkness, "Where's your guns?"

"All I've got is a rifle." He raised it so the speaker could see.

A man emerged from the night, into the flickering light. He carried a pistol aimed at Andy. "You talk white enough, but you both look Indian to me."

Andy said, "There's a reason. We got away from a Comanche camp."

He looked toward meat roasting over the fire. "The boy is awful hungry. That's why we came in."

The man's suspicions were not yet satisfied. "You got names?"

"He's Billy Gifford. Comanches stole him from his folks a little while back. Mine's Andy Pickard. They took me when I wasn't no bigger than he is."

The man lowered the pistol. "Lift the boy down. You-all help yourselves to some buffalo haunch."

Other men emerged from the darkness. Andy saw six altogether. They were a ragged bunch. If there was a comb or a razor in camp, it must have lain undisturbed for days in the bottom of a saddlebag. One man wore what remained of a Union Army coat. Another wore patched Confederate gray trousers. If nothing else, the outfit appeared to be politically neutral.

The one in gray complained, "Jake, we come to trade with the Comanches. They won't take it kindly, us helpin' these runaways."

Andy said, "They don't need to know about it. Me and Billy sure ain't goin' to tell them."

The complainer said, "Indians got ways of knowin' everything. Claim spirits come and whisper the news in their ear."

Andy started to deny it but could not. Despite his years in the white man's world and many earnest sermons by Preacher Webb, he had not become convinced that such spirits did not exist. He was almost certain he had felt their presence in certain sacred places.

Nothing about this place struck him as sacred, however. He said, "I doubt there's any spirits watchin' us here."

Jake said, "We've got nothin' against you boys. But you have to understand, we're out here to try and strike a trade with the Indians. We can't afford to stir them up."

"Then just let us have a little somethin' to eat, please sir, and we'll be on our way. Nobody'll ever know we was here."

The trader considered. "No, you're here, and you'd just as well stay all night with us. No tellin' what you might stumble into out in the dark."

Andy was so intent on eating, and on watching Billy wolf down a big chunk of roast, that he paid little attention to the appearance of the camp. But as his appetite began to be satisfied, he looked around. He realized there were no wagons. A string of pack mules was tied to a rope picket line beyond the firelight. The packs lay on the ground in the middle of camp. From what he could see, they contained mostly bottles and jugs.

Whiskey runners, he realized.

The *Comancheros* had used liquor mainly as a come-along to help them dispose of their trade goods. With these men, liquor was the trade goods.

Jake plied him with questions about himself and Billy. He seemed particularly interested when Andy told him about the offer James and Evan had made to the *Comanchero* about ransoming the boy with horses. The man's eagerness made Andy uneasy. He wished he had not talked so much.

His stomach full, Billy's exhaustion caught up with him. He fell asleep and slumped over onto the ground. From one of the packs Jake brought a blanket and spread it. "The boy's wore out. I expect you are, too. You'd best get yourself some sleep."

Andy was tired, but he was suspicious, too. He lay beside Billy on the blanket but tried to fight off weariness. He could hear several traders huddling with Jake near the fire, talking in low tones. He heard just enough to sharpen his suspicions, then to stir fear.

Jake suggested that they should take the boys home and demand that the Monahan family give them as many horses as had been proposed to the *Comanchero*. The smuggler in gray argued if they took the boys back to the band from whom they had escaped, the Indians should be grateful enough to take the whole cargo of whiskey off their hands at an even higher price in horses.

Jake seemed not to have thought of that. "Adcock, you got a good head on your shoulders."

Andy felt chilled at the thought of going back to Fights with Bears. He doubted that Steals the Ponies, tied down by Comanche tradition, could do much to help him or Billy.

The traders made considerable use of their own merchandise in premature celebration of the profit they were to realize. One finished off a bottle and tossed it into the fire. Almost immediately the bottle exploded with a flash of bright flame.

"You damned fool," Adcock yelled, "you could've put somebody's eye out."

The answer was a rough curse. The two men fell into a violent quarrel until Jake put a stop to it. "No more throwin' bottles into the fire, and no more of this damned fightin'. Else I'll knock somebody in the head."

The two fell back, mumbling dire but empty threats until they descended into a blind stupor.

The other traders were not so besotted that they forgot their plan.

They made their beds in a protective rough circle around Andy and Billy. Andy was sure this was not to guard them from outside danger but to prevent them from escaping. Any desire for sleep fell away as he contemplated the dark prospect of falling into the hostile hands of Fights with Bears.

He had purposely avoided encountering Indians, but a false sense of security had brought him willingly into the camp of white men treacherous enough to sell out him and Billy for a price. He dwelt bitterly on the irony of his bad judgment.

He waited until the sounds of even breathing indicated that the men were asleep. He raised up slowly, intending to make his way to the picket line. He would retrieve his and Billy's horses, then come back for Billy.

Jake spoke roughly, "Better do it in your britches, boy. Out in the dark, somebody's apt to blow a hole in you."

Alarmed, then frustrated, Andy muttered, "Wasn't goin' nowhere."

Billy stirred just enough to turn over on the blanket. Andy lay back down beside him, his stomach knotting with worry. His eyes remained open. He tried to think of a way that might allow him to get Billy out of this camp. If they could just reach their horses, they would not have to worry about saddling up. Neither had a saddle. They had been traveling bareback.

He thought about the explosion of the empty bottle. In the dim light of the smoldering campfire he could see the traders' packs of goods. He wondered what would happen to full whiskey bottles or jugs if they fell into the coals. He had had no experience with liquor. It might burn. On the other hand, like water it might simply put the fire out.

If it did burn, it should cause enough excitement to create a momentary diversion. After all, some people called it fire water.

He crawled to the edge of the blanket to see if he would be challenged as before. He was not. Jake seemed to have gone to sleep. Andy crawled a few inches more and paused, expecting someone to stop him. No one did.

He wriggled up against one of the packs that the men had opened earlier and from which they had imbibed freely. He could barely see, but his probing hands found several jugs. They seemed to be of clay. He got his arms around three of them and carefully crawled back, setting them on the ground within reach of the fire. He returned for more. Before carrying three additional jugs away he uncorked those that remained. The whiskey softly gurgled out onto the canvas.

He waited, listening for an indication that he had disturbed anyone.

Then he placed the jugs in the fire and crawled back to the blanket. He pulled the edge of it up and over himself and Billy as a shield against flying pieces of clay in event the jugs reacted as the bottle had.

A cork blew free with a sound like a small-caliber gunshot. Enough whiskey spouted out behind it to ignite a large bluish flame. The jug exploded with a loud pop, the flames blazing high. One by one the other jugs began to blow.

The camp came awake as if a thunderbolt had struck. Confused men shouted and cursed, trying to scramble away from flames that lighted up the night. Coals and firebrands flew in all directions. One landed on the canvas where Andy had spilled several jugs of whiskey. A second blaze flared up, almost as large as the first.

Andy grabbed Billy, who seemed too groggy to grasp what was happening. For the moment the traders were too involved in trying to escape the fires to pay any attention. He ran for the picket line. There the horses and mules reared and kicked, panicked by the noise and the flashes of fire.

Andy plopped Billy up on top of his horse and freed the reins from the picket rope. He untied his own reins and swung up onto Long Red. He wished he could cut the picket line and free the rest of the horses to run away, but Jake had confiscated his knife as well as his rifle. He had neither the time nor the inclination to try to retrieve them.

"Let's see how fast these horses can run," he said.

Billy was still bewildered. He had no inkling of the danger they had been in. But he followed Andy's lead.

"What started all the fire back there?" he wanted to know.

Andy said, "Maybe lightnin'."

"Shouldn't we ought to stay and help put it out?"

"They got all the help they need." Andy looked at the sky to be sure he was traveling in the right direction. He made a little correction and said, "You're doin' just fine, Billy. First thing you know, you'll be home."

CHAPTER

EIGHTEEN

For two days Captain Burmeister's rangers had followed the whiskey runners. Rusty and Len Tanner rode in front as trackers, though any man in the group could have read the trail as easily. The contrabanders seemed to have had no concern about being followed. They had no reason to suspect that a sharp-eyed settler had tipped the rangers about their passage.

The farmer had lost family members to raiding Indians. He had told Burmeister, "If there hadn't been half a dozen of them I'd've lit into them runners myself. They don't give a damn about the trouble they cause. They'll get some Indians drunk and cheat them. That'll make the Indians mad, and they'll come raidin' honest folks."

Burmeister had promised, "We will stop them if we catch them before they pass out of Texas."

"How will you know where the border line is at?"

Burmeister's gray mustache had wiggled. "We won't."

The settler had ridden along the first day but felt he had to drop out and return to protect his family. "If you catch them," he said, "bring them back to my farm. We'll throw the biggest barbecue you ever seen. And if you're lookin' for a place to hang them runners, I've got a grove of live-oak trees that ain't bein' used for nothin' but shade."

Burmeister had promised to remember the offer.

Tanner was a little bothered. "The thought of hangin' always kind of chokes me up," he told Rusty. "The captain wouldn't really do that, would he?"

Rusty shook his head. "I don't think the law calls for hangin' whiskey smugglers. They'll just get room and board awhile at the state penitentiary."

"Not too much room, I hope, and not much board."

Most of this second day Tanner had said so little that Rusty had begun to be concerned about him. Ordinarily Tanner seldom gave his jaw much rest. If a bird flew in front of him he would speculate for half an hour on what kind it was, what it ate, and what its mating habits were.

Rusty asked him, "You feelin' all right?"

"Nothin' wrong with me. It's you I been worried about."

"Why me?"

"Because you ain't said nothin' about Andy. Yesterday and today I ain't heard you mention his name."

"What can I say that I haven't already said? God only knows where he is or what he's doin'." Rusty bit down on the words and did not finish speaking all of his thought. *If he's not been killed already . . .*

Tanner said, "After we catch up to these runners, maybe me and you ought to take leave and go huntin' him."

"You have any idea how much country we might have to cover? We could ride 'til our whiskers got tangled in our stirrups and still never find him."

Rusty wished Tanner would drop the subject.

But Tanner always had another word, or several. "Better than waitin', wonderin'. Think about it anyway."

Rusty *had* been thinking about it. He simply saw no solution. The two of them, searching aimlessly across an impossibly broad, open land neither of them knew . . . If the Indians didn't get them, hunger and thirst would.

Tanner went into another long, unaccustomed silence. He broke it suddenly. "Looky yonder." He pulled on his reins. "Way up there. Is that buffalo, or is it horses?"

Rusty squinted against the sun's glare on the waving brown grass. "Looks to me like two horses. Can't tell whether they're comin' or goin'."

Tanner studied them a minute. "I believe they're comin' this way. Must be Indians."

"Or a couple of those whiskey runners comin' back." Rusty pulled his horse around. "We better tell the captain."

Burmeister had halted his detail and was waiting. Rusty told him, "We see two horseback riders comin' this way. Our guess is that they're Indians."

"Two of them only?"

"They could be scoutin' for a larger bunch."

Rusty could see momentary conflict in Burmeister's eyes. This mission had been intended to overtake whiskey runners, but stopping incursion by Indian raiders was of greater importance. Burmeister pointed to a shallow ravine carved by runoff water after rare hard rains. "We hide. We wait."

The men followed him.

Rusty and Tanner crawled up over the edge and lay on their bellies so they could see. Rusty caught an occasional glimpse of the riders as they came over a rise, then lost them as they dropped to lower ground. "Still comin' toward us," he said.

Tanner nodded. "Sure look like Indians to me. A little one and a big one." He brought up his rifle but did not aim.

Rusty said, "Let's not be quick to shoot. If they're scoutin', there's no tellin' how far out front they are and how big of a bunch may be followin' after them."

Sweat seeped from beneath Rusty's hatband and ran down to burn his eyes. He wiped away what he could and blinked away the rest. "Does somethin' about that bigger one look familiar to you, Len?"

"He sets his horse like Andy."

Rusty looked again, then gave a glad shout. "It *is* Andy, and he's got Billy with him!" He turned and yelled at the men in the ravine, "It's our boys. Don't anybody shoot."

Rusty scrambled to his feet. The two riders stopped abruptly and seemed about to turn back. Tanner said, "They don't know who we are." He took off his hat and waved it. "Andy! Billy! It's us."

The two riders hesitated a little longer, then seemed satisfied. They set their horses into a long trot. Andy jumped to the ground and ran to throw his arms around Rusty. Tears of relief rolled down his face, leaving tracks in the dust. Tanner reached up, lifted Billy from his horse's back, and hugged him.

"Young'un," he declared, "we was afraid we'd never see you again."

"Andy found me," Billy said. "Where's Mama? Where's Daddy?"

Rusty hugged him when Tanner got through. "They're at home. We'll be takin' you to them."

Both boys were scratched as if they had ridden through brush. Billy was badly sunburned, his lips blistered and swollen. Tanner handed him a canteen. The boy drank so desperately that Tanner had to take the water back from him. "Easy, Billy. Not all at once."

Andy watched Burmeister and the rangers ride up out of the ravine. He turned and glanced worriedly at the trail over which he and Billy had come. "We're bein' chased. Last time I saw them was maybe half an hour ago."

"Comanches?"

"No, whiskey merchants. They figured on tradin' me and Billy back to the Indians for a lot of horses. We got away from them, but they must still figure we're worth somethin'. They've been on our trail."

Burmeister came up in time to hear the last of it. He asked only one question. "How many are they?"

"Six, if none of them got trampled in the excitement."

"There was excitement?"

"I managed to put some of their whiskey jugs into the fire. Caused a hell of a commotion. I never knew the stuff would burn like that."

Burmeister said, "That is good to consider if ever you are tempted to drink it." He turned back to the task at hand.

"You and the boy could help us capture those *verdammten*. Do you object if we make of you bait?"

Andy frowned. "I'll do whatever you want me to, but leave Billy out of it. He's wore out. He's had too many scares already for a boy his age."

Burmeister accepted. "We want them to think you are too tired to go on. When they come close we will move up and . . ." He made a quick motion as if catching a bug in his hand.

Andy said, "I won't have to play at bein' tired. I'm wore to a frazzle."

Rusty felt himself swelling with pride. "Andy, for bringin' Billy back, the Monahans would let you live on their farm the rest of your life and never do a lick of work."

"All I want is for them to forgive me. And then I'd like to forgive myself."

Tanner interrupted. "It's hard to tell through the heat waves, but I think I see somethin' to the north."

Burmeister signaled the rangers to drop back out of sight. Rusty admonished Andy, "Be careful. If they act like they're fixin' to shoot, you scoot down into the ravine."

"They ain't goin' to shoot me. They'd rather sell me and watch a Comanche do it."

Rusty retreated but stayed in a shallow part of the ravine so he could see over the edge. He had checked his rifle a couple of times before he had identified Andy and Billy. He checked it again.

The riders gradually materialized out of the dancing heat. He counted four. Andy had said there were six. That gave the rangers excellent odds.

The longer Rusty watched them, the more his anger built. The idea of their being depraved enough to sell two boys to the Indians . . . he almost hoped they would put up a fight. He felt that he could kill all four without a twinge of conscience.

The riders were two hundred yards away, then one hundred. Rusty whispered, "Andy, come on down from there."

Andy sat hunched as if exhausted, as if he did not care whether he was caught or not. He waited until the men were fifty yards away before he acknowledged them. He stood his ground until they were within twenty yards. Then he put his mount into a hard trot down into the ravine.

Burmeister shouted an order. "Go get them boogers."

The rangers swarmed out of the ravine, encircling the whiskey runners before they had a chance to react. One dressed in Confederate gray foolishly fired at Burmeister but missed. A ranger shot him out of the saddle. The other men raised their hands.

One demanded, "What in the hell is this?"

Burmeister said, "What the hell it is, you are under arrest for running whiskey."

"We got no whiskey on us."

Rusty said, "But you did have. We've got two witnesses that say so."

Andy rode up out of the ravine. He said, "Howdy, Jake. How did you like the fireworks?"

Jake muttered, "You damned hoodoo. I ought to've cut your throat the minute you rode into camp."

"But then you couldn't have sold me to the Indians."

Burmeister said to the smuggler leader, "You were six men. Now you are four. Where are the other two?"

Jake did not answer.

Andy guessed, "They likely stayed to watch what was left of the whiskey while these came after me and Billy."

Tanner dismounted and examined the fallen man. Burmeister leaned from his saddle. "He is dead?"

Tanner nodded. "He showed damned poor judgment for a man who wasn't no better shot."

Andy had no sympathy. "He's the one who first said they ought to trade me and Billy for horses."

Burmeister said, "The weather is warm. He will not keep well." He turned to the smuggler named Jake. "He was your man. You will bury him here."

Jake scowled. "I don't see no shovel."

Burmeister pointed to a bend in the ravine where runoff water had deposited a layer of stones. "Rocks will cover him finely enough."

The burying went slowly because the three smugglers had to carry the stones an armload at a time to the top of the ravine. Their shirts were soon soaked with sweat.

Rusty asked the captain, "Ought we to go back and find them other two?"

"We have these. Indians will get the rest perhaps. Better we get the little boy home to his family."

Tanner agreed. "I want to be there and see the look on his mama's face."

Rusty thought of Geneva's despair and the futility he had felt in any effort to comfort her. The reunion would be a joyous moment for the Monahans. He knew he would stand back and watch in lonely silence. He was not part of the family, not that one or any other.

The afternoon was wearing down when Burmeister judged the grave to be covered well enough. He asked Jake, "Do you wish to say words over your friend?"

Jake's hands were rough and bleeding from handling the stones. He grunted. "Ain't no use. He can't hear them."

Burmeister removed his hat. "But the Lord can, so I will speak to Him." He looked up. "Lord, we send Thy way this day a lowly sinner who lost his way. Thou may send him to Heaven or to Hell, it is for Thee to judge. We are done with him. Amen." He turned. "Let us be gone from this place."

They were a couple of miles from the Monahan farm when James and Macy burst suddenly and unexpectedly from a grove of trees. Half the rangers raised guns before they recognized that the riders presented no threat.

James spurred up, face flushed with excitement. "You found Billy!" He reached out and threw both arms around the surprised boy. His voice was jubilant. "There'll be a big celebration tonight."

Burmeister said, "And time for a bit of prayer, I would hope."

James nodded vigorously. "Preacher Webb will see to that. I swear, it was lookin' like we'd have to bury half the family, startin' with Billy's mama. How'd you-all get him back?"

Rusty said, "Andy found him."

James turned toward Andy. "I reckon it takes an Indian to know where to look. No offense meant."

Rusty said, "The way you came bustin' out of the timber, we could've shot you."

James's excitement diminished. "We didn't know at first but what you-all might be Indians. We been out lookin' for sign."

Burmeister asked, "You have seen Indians?"

"One, for sure. He showed up yesterday evenin', watchin' the houses. We've seen him two or three times, but when we go out lookin' for him we can't find him. We figure he's scoutin' us for a war party."

Andy swallowed hard, his expression grim. "Fights with Bears. He knew where he found Billy. He knew we'd bring him back here. Most likely he's waitin' to try to grab him again."

Rusty doubted. "He ought to know Billy's goin' to be guarded extra heavy. He could steal some other boy a lot easier."

"Fights with Bears had him and lost him. That done hurt to his pride. He doesn't want to settle for some other boy. He wants Billy back."

James declared, "Well, he ain't goin' to get him, not as long as there's a Monahan breathin'."

James seemed for the first time to notice the three prisoners, their hands tied to their saddles.

Tanner explained the circumstances. He said, "Maybe the Comanches would settle for a few scalps instead of Billy. Here's three they can have."

The smuggler Jake reacted with fear. "You wouldn't do that to a white man. Would you?"

Tanner kept a straight face. "You were fixin' to let them have two white boys."

Approaching the corrals, Rusty saw many horses penned there. He assumed that James and the others had gathered as many as they could find and brought them here where they could be kept under guard. He saw several of the Monahans' neighbors gathered at the barn. It appeared that much of the community had come together for mutual protection.

Josie was the first family member to see the procession coming. She stood in front of the main house, shading her eyes. She turned and shouted something, then ran to the house in which Geneva and Evan lived. In a moment Geneva rushed out the door, holding her little girl in her arms. Josie took the girl from her so Geneva could run toward her son.

"Billy! Billy!" she cried.

Billy slid down from his horse. It was a long way to the ground, and he went to his knees. He was instantly on his feet and running to meet his mother.

Dust had gotten into Rusty's eyes and made them burn. He looked away.

In a minute the Monahans were all gathered around Billy. Clemmie hugged him, then he was passed to Josie and Alice and Preacher Webb. The boy's father had been in the corral among the horses. He vaulted over a fence and went running to grab his son.

Face shining with tears, Clemmie walked forward to meet Rusty and Burmeister and the others. "Men," she said, her voice near breaking, "there ain't words enough . . ."

Burmeister bowed without leaving the saddle. "Madam, it is to this young man that all thanks should go." He nodded toward Andy. "He found him and brought him out."

Clemmie looked up. "Get down off of that horse, Andy Pickard." Her tone of voice was commanding.

Sheepishly Andy complied, looking as if he dreaded a whipping. Clemmie threw her arms around him and embraced him so tightly Rusty half expected to hear Andy's ribs crack. For a small woman, she had always been amazingly strong.

"God bless you, Andy," she declared.

He stammered, "I'm . . . I'm sorry about your daddy."

"It was God's doin', not yours or mine. We can't fault the Lord for doin' His will."

Haltingly Andy said, "I got his watch back for you."

He slipped the loop over his head and handed her the silver timepiece. Reverently she pressed it to her cheek. "Bless you, Andy." She cleared her throat and turned toward the larger group of horsemen. "You-all must be tired and thirsty and hungry. Come on up to the house. We'll fix you a celebration supper."

Burmeister dismounted and touched the brim of his hat. "In a while, madam. First we must see to the horses."

Geneva released Billy only long enough for the other family members to hug him again, then she clasped him as if she never intended to let him go. She leaned her head against her husband's shoulder and cried.

Rusty wanted to go to her but could not. Instead, Josie came and put her arms around him. "It's a happy day you've brought us, Rusty."

He found it hard to speak. "It was Andy's doin'."

"Billy told us a little. If it hadn't been for you and the rangers, Andy and Billy might not've gotten home. I don't know how Geneva could've lived. It's a bitter thing to lose family."

"I can imagine."

"You've been a member of this family for a long time, Rusty, whether you've realized it or not. And so will Andy be from now on. It takes more than just blood to make a family. It takes love."

She tiptoed to kiss him on his bewhiskered cheek. Warmth rushed into his face.

He said, "Maybe you shouldn't do that out here in the sight of God and everybody."

"I'll do it again, Rusty Shannon, whenever I want to. But I'll wait 'til you get rid of those whiskers."

Preacher Webb led the family and everyone else within hearing in a prayer of thanksgiving for Billy's deliverance. "Lord, we thank Thee mightily for the deliverance of this child who was lost. And we beseech Thy blessings on the lad who brought him back to us, for in some ways he is also a lost soul, seeking his way."

Andy appeared overwhelmed. Rusty tried to ease his discomfort. "I know you've been blamin' yourself, but nobody else feels that way. You heard what Clemmie said."

"You don't suppose she just said that to make me feel better?"

"Clemmie Monahan never says anything she doesn't mean."

Andy had long since lost his shirt. Josie fetched him one that belonged to James. Bearing patches on the elbows, it draped around him like a tent. The sleeves extended almost to the tips of his fingers. "At least it covers you up decent," she said.

When she was gone Andy rolled the sleeves up past his wrists. Ruefully he said, "I don't guess folks will ever get used to the Indian side of me."

Rusty said, "Main thing is that *you* know who you are."

"But I don't. I felt out of place when I was up there amongst the Comanches. I feel out of place here. Maybe I don't fit anywhere."

Though he was offered any bed in the house, Andy chose to sleep on the ground in the rangers' camp near the barn. Rusty knew he felt suffocated by all the attention from the Monahans and their neighbors who had gathered in anticipation of an Indian raid. The rangers at least did not fawn over him.

Rusty was awakened by a shout of alarm. The sun was just beginning to rise. A night guard shouted again. "Everybody up. Indians comin'!"

Rusty cast off his blanket and grabbed for his boots, the only thing he had taken off the night before. He grasped his rifle and jumped to his feet. The night guard pointed.

In the dawn's rosy glow Rusty saw more than a dozen Comanches standing their horses in a rough line. A single warrior moved out twenty yards in front of the others. He gestured with a bow and shouted words Rusty did not understand. He asked, "Andy, do you know what he's sayin'?"

Andy listened, his face grim. He sucked in a deep breath and slowly let it go. "He's makin' a challenge."

"A challenge?"

"That's Fights with Bears. He's the one who had Billy."

"Well, he's not gettin' him back. Every last man here would die before they take that boy again."

Andy shook his head. "He's not askin' for Billy. He's askin' for me."

"You?"

"I shamed him. I stole Billy right out from under him while he was asleep. It's a matter of pride."

"You ain't goin' out there to him."

Andy picked up the rifle he had recovered from the smugglers. He checked the load. "If I don't they'll charge down on this place."

"We've got men and guns enough to whip them."

"But what'll it cost? I've got people on both sides. I don't want to see anybody dead."

"That Indian wants to see *you* dead."

"Maybe he'll settle for somethin' less." Andy walked toward the lone warrior, the rifle cradled in his arms.

Rusty shouted, "For God's sake come back here."

Andy kept walking. He focused his main attention on Fights with Bears, but he tried to watch the line of Comanches to the rear as well. If they decided to rush him he would have no chance. But Bears was Andy's immediate concern. The rest were likely to take their cue from him. Bears had no firearm that Andy could see. He held a lance and had a bow and a quiver of arrows slung over his shoulder.

Andy had the advantage. His rifle was loaded and cocked. He stopped twenty feet short of the horseman. He felt cold sweat on his forehead and hoped Bears could not see it. He said, "I am the one you asked for."

Bears looked at the rifle. "You have come armed."

"You are armed, too." The lance had a sharp-looking flint point, fashioned for killing buffalo. Bears could drive it all the way through Andy's body if he so chose.

Bears's eyes were fierce. "You stole the boy that belonged to me."

"He never did belong to you. He belongs to his mother and father."

"I won him in battle."

"It was no battle. You killed a helpless old man and took the boy. They had no chance."

"No matter. He was mine. You stole him from me. You owe me something."

"A fight?" Andy raised the muzzle of the rifle an inch. "I could kill you before you could move."

"My warriors would kill you before you drew another breath."

"And there are enough white men at this place to kill them all. Who would be the winner? Not your warriors. Not you or me."

Bears tried to show defiance, but his eyes reflected frustration. "You have a good fighting spirit. I would take you in place of the boy."

"I would never be accepted. I have killed one of The People. I am told that the one who died was a brother to your wives. They would gladly hack me to pieces."

Bears's mouth twisted as he contemplated the impasse. "It is a matter of honor. I must satisfy my honor."

"Perhaps you would like to have my scalp."

That surprised and puzzled the Comanche.

Andy said, "Here, I will give it to you." Laying down his rifle, he drew his knife. He reached up for one of his braids, cut it off and tossed it. Bears almost dropped his lance in grabbing for it. Andy cut off the other and threw it. Bears missed it but picked it up from the ground with the point of his lance.

Andy retrieved his rifle. "You can have a scalp dance over those."

For a moment Bears seemed perplexed. Then he raised the braids high over his head and gave a loud, victorious whoop. The warriors behind him took up the cry. Bears rode slowly forward, lowering the lance.

The rifle felt slick in Andy's sweaty hands. He pointed its muzzle at Bears, his finger on the trigger. One twitch and the Comanche would be dead. The battle would be on.

Bears touched a flat side of the lance point against Andy's arm. Then he wheeled his horse around and set it into a long trot back toward the waiting warriors. As he passed them, shouting and holding the braids 'high, they turned and followed him away.

Andy had held his breath. Lungs burning, he gasped for air and allowed himself to wipe a sleeve across his forehead. The cuff came down over his hand.

Rusty hurried out to his side. "You all right?"

"I'm not bleedin', if that's what you mean."

"I thought he meant to kill you."

"He knew I'd take him with me. He didn't want me *that* bad. So he accepted a piece of my scalp and counted coup. That was enough to patch up his pride."

"He's liable to keep tryin' to get you."

"I doubt it. Him and his wives will make medicine with those braids. They'll try to cast spells and send dark spirits after me. But I think that'll be all of it."

The Indians were quickly fading from sight. Rusty looked relieved. "You afraid of dark spirits?"

"I wish I could say I'm not, but there's still a part of me that wonders."

"Don't worry. We'll sic Preacher Webb onto them."

CHAPTER

NINETEEN

By the next day the neighbors were dispersing back to their own homes, feeling that at least for a time the Indian threat was over. A courier arrived looking for Captain Burmeister. He handed the officer an envelope. "You're hard to find," he said. "Been huntin' you for a week."

"I have been busy for a week, and much more." Burmeister tore the edge from the envelope and unfolded the letter, frowning as he read. Finished, he called his rangers around him. "It is from the governor's office that I have received this. The money is gone. We are to disband."

Tanner commented, "I didn't figure we'd get paid anyhow."

Rusty asked, "What'll you do now, Captain?"

"The letter says there is other work for me. I am to become a judge."

"That's better than ridin' all over hell and gone chasin' Indians and whiskey runners."

"Perhaps." The captain folded the letter and put it in his shirt pocket. "I am no longer so young. But I liked it, to be a ranger again even for just a little while. What will you do, Private Shannon?"

"Go back home. I've some unfinished business there."

"You will be subject to arrest if you go there."

"I'm subject to arrest anywhere. Even here, if the Oldham brothers take a notion to come for me again, or to send somebody. I can't go on forever with a warrant hangin' over my head. I want to get things straightened out, whatever it takes."

Burmeister said, "All I can give you is a wish for good luck. I have not even the money to pay you for the time you have served."

"I knew that when I joined up. It's always been that way with the rangers. One day of side meat and a month of sowbelly."

Burmeister nodded agreement. "If a character witness you need, send for me. I will gladly serve."

Rusty knew Burmeister's record as a Union officer during the war would give his word extra weight in a reconstruction court. Especially if he were a judge. "I'd be much obliged."

Josie grasped both of Rusty's hands when he told her. She said, "You have friends here who would never let the state police take you away. Stay. The government is bound to change sooner or later."

"I can't keep leanin' on my friends. I've got to find some way to settle this. I have to try to get back what's mine."

"I've told you before, it doesn't matter to me whether you have anything or not."

"It matters to me. I've got to set things right."

"Even if it means goin' to jail?"

"Even that."

She leaned her head against his chest. "All right," she said reluctantly. "I'll keep on waitin'."

Holding her hands, he stepped back to look at her. "Josie, you know I get strong feelin's when I'm with you. For a long time I wasn't sure if they were really for you or if they were for somebody else."

"You mean Geneva?"

He did not answer. He did not have to.

She said, "She's got a life of her own, a husband and two little ones. She's out of your reach. But I'm not. I'm here. All you have to do is ask me."

"I know. But I don't have a right to ask you so long as I've got nothin' to offer."

"I don't need anything. I'd live in a tent. I'd live in a dugout if it was with you. It wouldn't bother me."

"It would bother *me*. I couldn't do it."

She looked up at him, eyes glistening. "Then go. Do what you have to. I'll be here whenever you come back."

Something was different about Andy. Rusty puzzled over it a minute, then realized what it was.

"What did you do to your hair?" he asked.

Andy said, "Alice cut it for me. It looked ragged with the braids hacked off."

"You don't look much like a Comanche anymore."

Soberly Andy said, "My brother saw a vision. It told him the old ways are almost gone. He said I have to walk the white man's road whether I want to or not."

"Think you can?"

"He didn't say I'd like it. He said I don't have a choice."

Rusty made a sweeping motion with his arm. "You like this place and the Monahans, don't you?"

"They're good people. But I don't want to stay here while you and Len go back home."

"There's no tellin' what we may run into."

"But it's home—at least the nearest thing to home that I have."

"I may end up in jail."

"Me and Tanner will bust you out."

Rusty smiled. "Aidin' and abettin' a fugitive is what caused all this trouble in the first place."

"So I ought to be gettin' pretty good at it."

Rusty ached to see the farm where he had spent the larger part of his life, but he knew he must defer that visit until he learned how things stood with him and reconstruction law. His first destination, then, was the Tom Blessing farm.

He and Andy and Tanner tried to be vigilant, but their vigilance was compromised by the excitement of nearing home. Consequently they almost ran into an armed band of riders. Just in time they dropped into a dry creek bed and dismounted to avoid being seen.

"Soldiers?" Rusty asked.

Andy's eyesight was the keenest. He said, "No, they ain't wearin' uniforms."

Tanner said, "State police. They got the look of high authority and meanness. Maybe they're huntin' for you, Rusty."

"I wouldn't think so. The Oldhams don't know but what I'm still at the Monahans'. But that bunch is sure on the hunt for somebody."

Tanner grimaced. "I'd hate to be the one they're after. They look serious enough to shoot him on sight."

Rusty added, "Then claim he tried to get away."

The three remained in the creek bed until the posse passed out of sight. Later they cautiously dismounted in timber and watched the Tom Blessing place for a while before showing themselves. No one was working in the fields. The only sign of life Rusty saw was a thin rise of smoke from the cabin's chimney.

He said, "No sign of trouble, and I don't want to stay here 'til dark." He mounted and moved his horse out into the open. Andy and Tanner followed.

A dog announced their coming. Tom Blessing's wife came to the edge of the dog run and held her hand over her eyes. When Rusty hesitated fifty yards out, she shouted, "It's all right. Come on in."

Rusty dismounted and took off his hat. "Kind of spooked us a little, not seein' Tom or Shanty or anybody."

She said, "They're over at Shanty's place. Our boys, too. They're puttin' up a new cabin for him."

"Takin' a chance, aren't they? Some of the hotheads around here will burn it down like before."

"Not likely. Tom and our boys paid a visit to Fowler Gaskin and everybody else they thought might have such notions. Put the fear of God into them. Ain't heard a word out of Fowler since, nor anybody else."

"What about Jeremiah Brackett and his son, Farley?"

"Farley's got himself in real bad trouble. He's run the law ragged tryin' to catch him, so they've been campin' on his daddy's doorstep. The old man's got too much grief on his plate to bedevil Shanty or anybody else."

Rusty and the others watered their horses. He told Mrs. Blessing, "We'll ride on over to Shanty's. I need to talk to Tom."

She warned, "Keep a sharp eye out for the Oldhams and their state police. They came back mighty sore over not bein' able to arrest you. Tom says Buddy's gone a little crazy."

"He always did seem about three aces shy of a full deck. I'll watch out for him."

Shanty's crop of corn had been cut and set up in shocks across the field. His dog came trotting out to meet the visitors. Hearing him bark, Shanty put aside an ax with which he had been trimming a log. He stared a moment until he was sure, then hobbled toward Rusty. Beyond him Rusty could see that the cabin walls were almost finished.

"Mr. Rusty," Shanty shouted, "welcome home. And you, Mr. Tanner, and Andy."

Rusty stepped down and grasped Shanty's hand. "It's good to see you. You been gettin' along all right?"

"Fine as frog hair. I wisht you'd look at the cabin the Blessings are helpin' me build. It'll be bigger than the old one was."

"I'm glad, Shanty."

"It'll feel good to stay at my own place and take care of my own land, just me and my old dog. Hope it don't rain before we get done."

Rusty saw no sign of a rain cloud. "Doesn't appear likely."

Shanty's enthusiasm gave way to concern. "You looked as much dead as alive last time we seen you."

"I've healed up pretty good. Don't have a lot of strength in that shoulder, but it'll get better."

"Them Oldhams don't mean to just wound you in the shoulder next time. They'll aim for your heart."

Tom Blessing strode out to greet Rusty and the others. He still had a crushing handshake. "Been expectin' you," he said, "even though I hoped you wouldn't come. Things have turned off real mean around here."

"I thought they already were."

"They've got worse. The Oldhams and a bunch of state police made a wild sashay after Farley Brackett. He shot one of them dead and wounded two more before he got away."

"I don't suppose Buddy or Clyde were hit."

"No such luck. Now there's hell to pay. Governor Davis is threatenin' martial law."

"Maybe they're too busy to be worryin' about me."

"The Oldhams ain't forgot you. They've added some new charges. Fleein' to avoid prosecution, refusal to submit to arrest. Also attempted murder. They claim you fired on Clyde up at the Monahan place."

Tanner protested, "That was me, not Rusty."

"Doesn't matter. They say it was Rusty, and the carpetbag judge we've got will take their word for it. He's hell on any old rebel that gets brought before his bench."

Rusty said, "I've thought some about givin' myself up. Not to the Oldhams but to the court."

"You'd better get over that notion. The judge would turn you over to the Oldhams anyway. Remember what they did to you the last time."

Rusty rubbed his shoulder. "What can I do?"

"Smart thing would be to quit this part of the country and not show yourself again 'til the government changes. It will, when all the old Texans finally get a chance to vote."

"But Clyde Oldham stole my farm. I want it back."

"Be patient. The land ain't goin' anywhere."

Rusty, Tanner, and Andy pitched in to help with the cabin raising. They finished the walls awhile before sundown. Tom Blessing stepped back to gaze on the work, smiling in satisfaction. "Me and the boys all got our chores to see after before dark. We'll start on the roof in the mornin'."

Shanty bowed to all of them in the subservient manner cultivated during long years of slavery. "I'm much obliged to all of you." He stood beside Rusty as the Blessings rode away. He said, "I ain't got no money, but I've got somethin' better. I've got friends."

Rusty nodded. "That's somethin' you couldn't buy if you had all the money in the world. But I'm afraid you've still got some enemies, too."

"Been a long time since they bothered me. Mr. Tom and his boys put the Indian sign on them, and lately the state police been chasin' them around some, too. They ain't had time to mess with old Shanty." He walked to an outdoor fire pit and stirred the coals until they glowed, then added small pieces of dry wood to coax a flame. "You-all are goin' to stay the night here, ain't you?"

Rusty said, "I'm anxious to take a look at my own place."

Shanty warned, "You'll be safer stayin'. Them police don't mess around here, but the Oldhams'll expect you to show up at your farm sooner or later."

Rusty reconsidered. "We'll impose on your hospitality, then. But it'd be a good idea if we sleep a little ways out yonder, just in case."

Shanty said, "That old dog of mine'll warn you if anybody comes snoopin' around. He don't let nothin' bigger than a rabbit come close without he raises a ruckus."

Andy had told Rusty about the night Fowler Gaskin broke into the smokehouse without arousing the dog. But he said, "He's a good one, all right."

Shanty said, "Hope you-all like catfish. I caught me a big one down in that deep hole."

Tanner grinned. "Sounds like a feast to me."

They sat around the campfire after a supper of catfish and corn bread.

Rusty recounted Andy's rescue of Billy. Shanty enlarged on what Tom Blessing had told about Farley Brackett's scrap with the state police. "They thought they had him, but it was the other way around. Folks say Clyde Oldham turned tail and run like a scalded dog. Buddy stayed 'til he was out of cartridges. Got to give him credit for guts. He's just shy on sense."

Shanty punched at the fire. "Ain't hardly nobody likes the Oldhams except a few people in the courthouse. They help one another steal everything that ain't nailed down tight."

Tanner said, "There'll be a big comeuppance someday."

Eventually Shanty yawned. The day's work had been hard. He said, "Tonight I'm goin' to sleep in my own house."

Tanner pointed out, "It's got no roof yet."

"Don't matter. It's got walls, so I'll be sleepin' indoors."

Rusty was up long before daylight. He roused Andy and Tanner from their blankets. "We don't want to ride up to the farm in broad daylight. Let's go while it's still dark."

He knew where the Oldhams had posted guards in the timber along the river to watch his farm when they had been looking for him before. He thought he might find some of them there, but a careful search turned up no one. He said, "If it was a good place for them to watch from, I reckon it'll do for us. Let's wait here a spell and see if there's any sign of life."

He watched the chimney in particular. If anyone was staying in the cabin, there should soon be smoke. But none appeared.

As the sun came up and spilled strong morning light across the farm, he could see the field and the garden. He winced in disappointment. "There's weeds out there tall as the corn. And that corn ought to've already been cut. It's dryin' up."

Tanner pointed out, "Clyde and Buddy didn't take this place because they wanted to farm it. They took it to spite you."

After an hour he still saw no sign that anyone was in or around the cabin. Andy volunteered, "I'll go see for sure. Nobody's lookin' for me."

Tanner said, "Even if they was, they wouldn't know you. You don't look Indian anymore with your hair cut."

Andy rode up to the cabin, circling it first, then entering. Shortly he reappeared and waved for Rusty and Tanner to come on. He waited for them at the dog run. "Rusty," he said, "you won't like what you see. It's a boar's nest in there."

Rusty knew Tom Blessing had hauled away everything that could be moved so the Oldhams would not get it. Someone had brought in a broken-backed table and a couple of wooden boxes that evidently served in place of chairs. Two iron pots and a tin bucket sat on the cold hearth, smelling of spoiled meat, grease, and congealed beans. Coffee grounds had been spilled across the floor between the hearth and the table. Two tin plates held remnants of the last meal someone had eaten here. A piece of corn bread had molded almost to the color of gray ash.

Tanner said, "Somebody's mother sure didn't teach them much."

Rusty replied, "Looks like the time I was gone to the rangers and Fowler Gaskin moved in. Took lye soap and lots of water to get the stink out."

Andy said, "We can throw all this stuff away and at least sweep out a little." He looked for a broom but did not find one.

Rusty said, "Never mind. It'd just tell the Oldhams that somebody had been here. They'd figure it was me." He felt resentful, remembering how hard Mother Dora had worked to keep the cabin clean. "Let's shut the door behind us and leave things the way they are. I've got a visit to make."

Tanner said, "There ain't nobody left to see."

Rusty did not answer him. He rode to the small rock-fenced plot that served as the Shannon family cemetery. Tanner and Andy trailed. Stepping down from the saddle, Rusty handed the reins to Andy and opened the wooden gate. He stopped before the stone markers and took off his hat. For a long time he stood, staring, remembering.

Andy's voice broke into his consciousness. "Rusty, there's a rider comin' this way. We'd better be movin' down to the timber."

Rusty tried to see him but could not. Andy's eyes were sharper than his own. He hoped they were sharper than those of the oncoming horseman. Turning again to the stones, he said, "Daddy Mike, Mother Dora, they've stole this place from us for now. But I swear to you we'll get it back."

From their place of concealment Rusty and the others watched the horseman ride up to the cabin and draw a bucket of water from the well. After a fast drink he moved on. Andy was the first to identify him. "Farley Brackett."

Tanner said, "He's sure pushin' on them bridle reins."

Andy pointed. "He's got reason. Looky yonder."

Half a dozen horsemen followed along in Brackett's tracks. Rusty asked, "Do they look like soldiers?"

Andy squinted. "State police would be my guess. They're after Farley."

Tanner observed, "Don't look like they're really wantin' to get close to him. They're probably thinkin' about the last time they did it."

Andy said, "The Oldham brothers must be with them. I see a man with just one arm."

Rusty pulled the skin at the corners of his eyes to sharpen his vision. "That's Buddy, all right, and Clyde just behind him."

Tanner said, "Sounds like Clyde. If there's to be any shootin', he'll be behind somebody." He looked down at his rifle but did not reach for it. "I believe I could pick off both of them from here. Nobody would ever know who done it."

Rusty replied, "Somebody else would take up the warrant they put out against me. And I need them alive if I'm ever to get my farm back. Dead men don't sign deeds."

Tanner shrugged. "If Farley had any brains, he'd be halfway to California by now instead of wearin' out posses around here. And that's what you ought to do, Rusty, get away 'til Texas has a new government."

"No tellin' how long that'll be."

They remained hidden in the timber by the river until dusk, then made their way back to Shanty's farm. The dog greeted them two hundred yards from the cabin and barked at them the rest of the way in.

Rusty did not want to cause anxiety to Shanty. He shouted, "It's just us. We're comin' in."

The rising moon revealed that the roof had been added during the day and partially shingled. Rusty felt a fleeting guilt for not having remained here to help with the work.

Shanty emerged from the darkness of the log walls. "You-all come on in. I'll stir up the fire and fix you somethin' to eat."

"We brought venison." Rusty had decided to take a chance and shoot a deer so they would not burden Shanty's food supply. He dismounted and eased the carcass down from Alamo's back.

The dog sniffed eagerly at it. Shanty shooed him away. "You'll get your share by and by. Git!" He carried the deer to a crude bench set beside what would be the front door when the cabin was finished. He fetched a butcher knife and cut a generous portion of backstrap.

He asked Rusty, "Get a look at your farm?"

"Doesn't appear like anybody's done a lick of work. They're lettin' the crops go."

"I know. And after all the sweat we put in plowin' and plantin'. The Lord can't abide slothful ways. He'll sooner or later fix them Oldham boys."

Tanner declared, "But He generally needs some help. That's what I keep tryin' to tell Rusty."

Shanty said, "If the Lord needs help, it'll come. He'll send out a call, and the right man will hear. He's got mysterious ways."

Rusty had been asleep a short time when the dog set up a racket. From out in the darkness someone yelled, "Hello the house!"

Shanty's voice answered from one of the open windows that as yet had no glass. "Who's out yonder?"

"Farley Brackett. All right if I come in?"

"Come ahead. Ain't no police here."

Rusty sensed reluctance in Shanty's voice. Neither Farley nor his father had shown him any respect.

Farley led his horse up to the dying embers of Shanty's outdoor fire. "You got anything a starved-out man could eat? Them state police been houndin' me so bad I ain't et since the day before yesterday."

Rusty said, "There's still some venison."

Farley whirled in surprise, drawing his pistol. "Who in the hell? . . ."

"Rusty Shannon. You don't need the gun."

Farley holstered the weapon. "I come mighty close to shootin' you. Ain't good manners to walk up behind a man in the dark. Bad for the health, too."

"We saw you stop for a drink of water at my place. Saw the posse that was after you."

"They ain't really wantin' to catch me and have an open fight, especially Clyde Oldham. He wants to dry-gulch me where I wouldn't have a chance."

"Why don't you hightail it for Mexico, or maybe Arizona?"

"Been wantin' to, but my pockets are empty. My old daddy has some gettin'-away money waitin' for me, but they keep a guard around his place so that I dassn't try to go in." He turned to Shanty. "That's why I've come to your place. I need a favor from you."

Rusty said crisply, "I don't see where Shanty owes you any favors. You tried once to run him off of his place."

"I have repented my ways."

Shanty asked, "What's the favor?"

"My old daddy works several nig—fellers like you. I don't think the police would take much notice if another one was to show up there. It's hard to tell you people apart. My daddy could give you the money, and you could fetch it here to me. I'd pay you for your trouble."

Shanty said, "Your old daddy don't have no use for the likes of me. How come you think he'd trust me with his money?"

"I'd write a note for you to give him."

Firmly Rusty said, "Shanty, the Oldhams know who you are and where to find you. If they caught on to what you were up to they might damned well kill you. At least they'd see to it that you never got out of jail."

Andy had stood back, listening, saying nothing. Now he spoke. "Shanty don't need to go. I will."

Rusty turned on him. "Why? Why you?"

"Anything to bedevil them Oldhams." He rubbed the quirt mark on his face. It still burned at times. "They owe me."

Rusty argued, "It'd be just as risky for you as for Shanty. They'd grab you by the collar as soon as you showed up."

"But I wouldn't show up, not to where they could see me. I sneaked into a Comanche tepee and got Billy out without wakin' anybody. I ought to be able to slip into the Brackett house without stirrin' up the police."

Rusty disapproved, but he soon saw he was going to lose the argument. He said, "I'll ride with you, then. I want to be close by in case you need help."

"No. You stay here. All of you stay here. This is a job I'd best do by myself, the coyote way."

CHAPTER

TWENTY

ndy could barely make out the house as a thin cloud stole most of the limited light from a quarter moon. Farley Brackett had told him three times, "Don't forget, my old daddy's bedroom is in the southwest corner. If you go into the wrong one my mother or my sister are liable to holler."

Andy had become impatient with the advice. Farley seemed to consider him slow in the head. He suspected that Farley was not especially concerned about Andy's safety. He wanted to get his money as quickly as possible and run.

Farley had said, "I just wisht I could shoot me one more state policeman before I leave. Clyde Oldham would be my pick. Or Buddy if I couldn't get Clyde."

Rusty asked, "What is it you like so much about shootin' police?"

"I don't rightly know. Maybe it's the way they jump when they're hit. Anyway, they're all Yankees at heart. Texas could do with a lot less of them."

Andy stopped a hundred yards out and tied the reins to a tree. He reasoned that the guards would have moved close to the house at dark. Before he put down his full weight he tested each step for twigs that might crack or gravel that might slip underfoot. Shortly he saw a flash of fire as someone lighted a cigarette. Good. He had *that* guard located.

The cloud drifted on, uncovering the moon, though the light remained dim. Andy moved sideways to put more distance between him and the guard he had spotted. He stopped abruptly as he caught a movement and heard a voice.

"Silas, you got any tobacco? I'm plumb out."

The guard he had seen first moved toward the voice. "Yeah, but be careful when you light it. If the captain sees it, we'll all catch hell."

"Reminds me of an officer I had in the army. Mad about somethin' all the time. He's sure got it in for them Oldhams."

"With good reason. We almost had Farley Brackett, 'til Buddy charged in before we was ready and got his horse knocked out from under him. Damn, but that Farley's a crack shot."

"At least Buddy's better than Clyde. Never saw a man who could disappear so quick when he hears a gun go off."

While the two guards continued their conversation, Andy circled around them. He was almost to the back of the house. He worried over a dim patch of moonlight he had to cross before he could reach the porch. He worked along carefully in the shadow of a shed, looked hard in all directions, then passed quickly through the stretch of open ground. He stopped in the darkness of the porch, listening for any indication that someone had seen him. He could still hear faintly the guards' conversation. The only other sound was crickets in the trees.

The back door was open for ventilation, so he need not worry about noisy hinges. Inside the house, he found himself in a hallway that extended all the way to the open front door. He saw the dark outline of a guard sitting on the edge of the front porch.

The floor creaked under his weight, giving him a moment's pause until he saw that the guard was not responding. He decided that nervousness exaggerated his perception of the noise.

Jeremiah Brackett slept in the southwest corner room, Farley had said. The doors to two other bedrooms opened into the hallway. Bethel and Elnora Brackett slept in those, he reasoned. He had no wish to awaken them. Startled, they might cry out and bring the guards running in.

His eyes grew accustomed to the gloom. He could make out a bureau with a mirror on it and a pitcher and bowl. Brackett's bed was pulled up next to the deep window for fresh air. Brackett snored softly.

Andy touched his shoulder and leaned down to whisper in his ear. "Mr. Brackett. Wake up."

The farmer jerked. His snoring ended abruptly with a choking sound. He raised up from his pillow, looking around wildly.

"No noise, Mr. Brackett," Andy whispered. "There's a guard sittin' on your front porch."

"Who are you?" Brackett demanded hoarsely. "If you're here to rob me you've come to a poor place."

"You remember me. I'm Andy Pickard, from over at Rusty Shannon's."

"The Indian boy? What do you want?"

"I've come on an errand for Farley. He says you've saved some gettin'-away money for him."

Brackett seemed to have awakened fully. He swung his legs out of the bed and set his feet on the floor. "How do I know you're doin' this for Farley? How do I know you're not here to take the money and light out with it?"

Andy reached into his shirt pocket. "Got a letter from him to you. He was aimin' to send Shanty, but I've come instead."

"Shanty? That darkey?" The thought seemed to puzzle Brackett. He unfolded the letter but could not read it in the poor light. He reached toward a lamp.

Andy said, "I wouldn't light that. Might cause the guards to come in and see what's goin' on."

Brackett tried holding the letter close to the window but still could not read it. "I'll have to take your word. I reckon if you weren't honest, Shannon wouldn't have put up with you for so long."

He pulled a pair of trousers over his bare legs and half buttoned them. "The money's in the parlor, hidden in the back of a drawer."

"I hope you can get it without rousin' up the guard on the porch."

Brackett's weight made the floor squeak more than it had under Andy. Andy stood in the hallway, his back to the wall beside the parlor door, and watched the guard. The slump of the man's shoulders indicated that he might be asleep, but Andy knew he could not count on that.

He heard the desk drawer slide, wood dragging upon wood. It rattled as Brackett reached inside. Andy heard the drawer being closed again, slowly and carefully.

All the caution went for nothing, because Brackett knocked something off of the desk. It crashed on the floor. Andy's heart leaped.

He heard a woman's startled cry from one of the bedrooms. The guard jumped to his feet, pistol in his hand. Mrs. Brackett came into the hallway, carrying a lighted lamp. Andy desperately signaled for her to blow it out, but it was too late. The guard stood in the front door, eyes wide.

Andy recognized Buddy Oldham.

Jeremiah came out of the parlor. Buddy took a quick glance at him and jumped off of the porch. He turned and fired a wild shot into the hallway. He shouted, "Git him, Clyde. It's Farley Brackett!"

Andy realized that in his confusion Buddy had mistaken the father for the son. Both Oldhams fired again. Elnora Brackett gasped and dropped the lamp. It smashed, spreading kerosene on the floor. Flames hungrily followed the flow.

Clyde Oldham shouted, "We got him. Shoot! Shoot!"

A dozen shots exploded from the darkness, smashing into the walls.

Bethel rushed from her bedroom and gasped in horror. She ran to her mother, twisted on the floor. Andy helped her drag Elnora away from the flames.

Jeremiah hobbled to the door, waving his arms. "Stop firing! You've hit my wife!"

Andy heard the thud of a bullet as it caught Jeremiah in the chest. It was followed by another. The farmer grabbed at the door facing, sighed, and fell, his body sliding down the wall.

Andy lay flat on the floor and motioned for Bethel to do the same. He shouted, "Quit firin'. Farley Brackett's not here."

The firing tapered off, then stopped. The two guards who had been in the backyard rushed into the hallway from the far end. They wasted only a few seconds surveying the situation. One went to the front door and called to his companions, "It's over with. We got two people shot in here."

The other guard trotted into the nearest bedroom and returned with a heavy quilt to spread over the flames. He stomped on the quilt until the fire was snuffed out.

Clyde Oldham entered the hallway, trembling with excitement. "We got him. We got him." Buddy followed, pistol in his hand. It was still smoking.

Andy's fear receded. In its place came outrage. "You sorry son of a bitch, you shot Farley's mother and father. Farley ain't here. He never was."

Buddy argued, "But I saw him."

"You saw Jeremiah, and you killed him."

Clyde recognized Andy for the first time. "You're Rusty Shannon's Indian."

Defiantly Andy said, "I'm nobody's Indian."

Someone found another lamp and lighted it. A policeman of severe countenance motioned for the holder to lower it while he looked first at Jeremiah, then at Elnora. She was still alive and moaning. He gave Clyde Oldham a look of loathing.

"All you did here was kill an old man and wound an old woman. I've had as much of your bungling as I can handle, Clyde. You're off the force."

Clyde demanded, "You're firin' me?"

"Damn right. And take your quick-triggered brother with you. I'll be at the courthouse in the morning to pay you off. Then I never want to see either one of you, ever again."

Buddy argued, "But Captain, I was certain—"

"Git, before I take a notion to shoot you myself."

Bethel knelt and took her mother's hand. Elnora squeezed Bethel's fingers. Her eyelids fluttered open. She turned her head painfully and looked toward her husband. Her voice was barely audible. "Is he—"

"Yes, Mama, he's gone."

Elnora closed her eyes against a flow of tears. "I'm sorry I treated him badly. I wish . . ."

She sobbed softly. Bethel laid her arm across her mother and cried.

The police captain growled, "It was so damned unnecessary." He cut his gaze to Andy. "Who are you? I don't remember I ever saw you before."

"Name's Andy Pickard."

"What were you doing here?"

Under the circumstances, lying came easy. "I was lookin' for a job. They asked me to spend the night."

The captain gave him a critical study. "Do you always sleep with your clothes on?"

"Yes sir, most of the time."

The captain shook his head in disdain. "It'll take forty years for this part of the country to become civilized." He looked down at Bethel. "We'll see what we can do about your mother's wound, then carry her to town. Can you get one of your hands to hitch a team to your wagon?"

A black woman hesitantly entered the front door, her husband close behind her. "Lord God," she cried. She rushed to Bethel's side.

Bethel told the man to fetch a team and hitch up the wagon as the police captain had said.

The captain gave directions as two policemen carried Elnora into her room. He asked Bethel, "About your father . . . you want to bury him here or in town?"

"Here," she murmured. "Here's where he belongs."

The captain turned to his men. "Well, don't just stand there. Get that old man up from the floor. Carry him into that room yonder. The least we can do is to lay him out like a Christian."

Andy followed Bethel into the room where the police had carried her mother. She studied Andy as if she were seeing him for the first time. "What *were* you doin' here?"

He made sure none of the rangers could hear him, then explained his mission for Farley. "Your dad was fetchin' some money for him out of the parlor. It's probably in his pocket."

Bethel's voice went hard. "I almost wish they *would* catch him. It was him and his wild ways that caused all this."

"I heard the war turned him thataway."

"A lot of other men went to war without goin' outlaw. Anyway, it won't do any good to give him the money now. He won't leave 'til he's evened the score for this."

"How many more state police has he got to shoot?"

"Two, at least. The Oldhams." Bethel turned to the black woman. "Flora, I want you to go and bring all the hands. We've got a lot to do. We've got to let our neighbors know."

Andy stopped in the door and stared down the hallway toward the darkness of the front yard. "I dread goin' back and tellin' your brother what happened."

"It's mostly his doin'."

Andy saw a dark figure step up onto the porch and enter the hallway into the lamplight. It was Rusty. Andy met him halfway. "You oughtn't to be here," he said urgently. "There's police all over the place."

"I heard the shootin'."

Andy beckoned Rusty into Elnora's room. He said, "You followed me, didn't you?"

"I just said I wouldn't come with you. I didn't promise not to follow you. Wasn't no tellin' what trouble you might get into." He looked with concern at the wounded woman. "What about her husband?"

Andy shook his head. "Buddy Oldham started the shootin'. He saw the father and thought he was Farley." A worrisome thought struck him. "I hope Farley didn't come with you."

"I convinced him to stay at Shanty's. Told him he might bring danger to his folks." Ruefully Rusty added, "He did that without even bein' here."

Andy told Rusty about the captain firing the Oldhams. "Just the same, they've still got charges against you. Better get away from here before somebody recognizes you."

"We'd better both get away from here."

Andy took Bethel's hand. "You goin' to be all right?"

"It'll be a long time before I'm all right. But if you're askin' whether it's all right for you to go, the answer is yes. I've got good folks here to help me, and there'll be neighbors here in the mornin'."

"I'm sorry about all this. It wouldn't have happened if I hadn't come."

"But you came for Farley. It wasn't your fault. Wasn't anybody's fault but Farley's and the Oldhams'."

"I'll come back when I can and see if I can be any help."

"I'd like that, Andy. You'll be welcome." She clasped his hand tightly, then released it.

Andy felt a glow unlike any he had known before. He said quickly, "We better go, Rusty."

Some of the black laborers had begun coming in so that there was traffic on the front porch and in the hallway. Andy and Rusty departed through the back door into the darkness. No one seemed to pay them any attention, probably assuming they were policemen.

They retrieved their horses and started toward Shanty's. Rusty asked, "Did you get Farley's money?"

"No. There wasn't a chance, once the excitement started. He don't deserve it anyway."

Rusty grimaced. "I was hopin' he'd take it and go west, or down to Mexico. I'm afraid now he'll stay around for a chance at the Oldhams."

Andy said hopefully, "Maybe they'll kill one another, and it'll all be over."

"I've got a problem with that. Clyde Oldham took my farm in his name. He's the only one can sign it back over to me."

"He won't ever do it."

"He might, with my gun barrel stuck in his ear."

The coming sunrise was already lacing the skyline clouds with pink and purple when Andy and Rusty rode up to Shanty's place. The dog announced them. Farley Brackett came out from beneath the shed where he had spent the night. Andy had known he was unlikely to sleep in the cabin under the same roof with Shanty. Farley held a pistol in his hand until he was certain no one had come with Andy and Rusty, and no one had followed.

He demanded, "Where's my money?"

Andy felt like hitting him. "I didn't get it."

Farley's face twisted with anger. "Did that damned old man refuse to give it to you?"

Outrage gave a sharp edge to Andy's voice. "That damned old man died *tryin'* to give it to me."

Farley stood slack-jawed. "Died?"

In as few words as possible, Andy told him what had happened. Farley looked as if he had been shot in the stomach. "How bad is my mother hurt? What about my sister?"

"Your mother is probably on the way to town by now. Your sister wasn't hit."

Shanty had heard most of it. He stood silent, eyes sympathetic for a man who had shown him only contempt.

Farley turned his back, pulling himself together. When he turned again, his face was taut with anger and hatred. "What about them Oldhams? They still at our place?"

Andy said, "The captain fired them. Told them he would pay them off in town."

"Town!" Farley dropped his hand to the butt of his pistol. "Whereabouts in town?"

"I don't know. Courthouse, I guess."

Rusty frowned, motioning for Andy to be quiet. But the bag was already open and the cat let out.

Farley started for the corral, where his horse stood waiting for feed. "Then they'll get paid off twice."

Rusty said, "I wish you hadn't told him. Now he's on his way to kill the Oldhams."

"Wouldn't make any difference whether I told him or not. He'd figure it out."

Rusty swung back into the saddle. "We've got to try and get to town ahead of him. Maybe we can find some way to stop this."

"We might delay it, but I doubt we can stop it short of killin' him ourselves. Bethel said he won't leave here 'til he gets his revenge on Clyde and Buddy. I expect she's right."

Rusty said, "Shanty, see if you can keep Farley here a little longer. Offer him coffee, fix him breakfast . . . anything you can do."

"I'll try, Mr. Rusty, but looks to me like he's got the devil ridin' with him. Watch out he don't kill *you* if you get in his way."

Rusty spurred into a lope. Andy managed to bring Long Red up even.

He said, "He'll know what you're up to. He'll run that horse to death tryin' to beat us to town."

Andy had reason to fear they might run their own horses to death. Rusty kept pushing hard, frequently looking back over his shoulder. Andy looked back too, but could not see Farley.

He said, "Hadn't we better slow down a little? I can feel my horse givin' out."

"He can give out after we've done what we have to."

Andy muttered under his breath, then realized he had been talking Comanche to himself. He understood Rusty's reason for wanting to keep Clyde Oldham alive, but he could not help thinking that the community would be better off without either the Oldhams or Farley Brackett.

The courthouse was new, built of stone, with a cupola and a parapet. The old frame building had served well, but the local reconstruction government had decided that its dignity demanded something better, no matter the cost. The taxpayers were mostly rebels anyway.

Rusty reined up at the low rail fence that surrounded the courthouse square. His horse was lathered and breathing hard. Andy pulled in beside him and tied Long Red to a post. He said, "Maybe you'd better let me go talk to the Oldhams, if I can find them in there. Goin' by what they did last night, they may shoot you and *then* ask what you want."

"No, I want to try and make a bargain with Clyde."

Andy shrugged and followed Rusty up the steps. He had never been inside the new courthouse. Once through the door, he had no idea where the state police office might be. But Rusty knew. He led off down a corridor, Andy on his heels.

Andy remembered the captain from the night before. The officer looked up. He recognized Andy, but he did not seem to know Rusty.

Rusty said, "I'm lookin' for the Oldham brothers."

The captain studied him a moment. "I released them from the service this morning. They are no responsibility of mine."

"But where are they at?"

The captain's eyes narrowed. "Are you some kin of the Bracketts?"

"No, I'm Rusty Shannon. But if I don't find the Oldhams pretty quick, they're fixin' to meet up with a member of the Brackett family."

That got the captain's attention. "You mean Farley?"

"Yes, and if he gets to them first Jeremiah won't be the only man needs buryin'."

The captain said, "The Oldhams were in a surly mood when they left here. I would guess they have gone to one of the liquor establishments around the square to soak their anger in whiskey. What is your interest in them?"

"Clyde Oldham owes me a farm."

"I know about that. And you wish him to remain alive until you get it back?"

"That'd be long enough."

The officer reached for his pistol and belt, hanging on a hat rack beside the door. "I'll take the north side of the square. You take the south. But stand clear if Farley Brackett shows up. He belongs to me."

Rusty and Andy stepped out into the hallway. Rusty stopped so abruptly that Andy bumped into him. A sturdy man with a thick gray mustache came out of an office on the other side. Rusty exclaimed, "Captain Burmeister!"

"Private Shannon. And Andy." The old ranger limped across the hall, his hand outstretched.

The police captain stopped, puzzled. "You know these men, Judge Burmeister?"

"Indeed. Many a long mile Private Shannon and I rode together as rangers. And Andy, he did a remarkable thing."

Rusty was still immobilized by surprise. "You're the new judge here? What happened to the other one?"

"He was a stealer. A little one only, but he did not share with the big stealers in Austin. He was fired. What brings you here?"

"Hopin' to stop a killin'. Maybe two of them. You remember the Oldham brothers?"

Burmeister nodded briskly. "But too well. Who are they about to kill?"

"More likely it'll be the other way around if we can't stop it."

"Then go, by all means. My docket is full already with murders." Judge Burmeister waited until Rusty and Andy were near the door before he called and pointed. "My office is here. Come visit sometime."

The police captain collared one of his deputies to help him. They went out another door.

To Andy's recollection, two whiskey shops stood on the street due south of the courthouse. He was considered underage and had not been allowed inside. He followed Rusty into the first one. A quick look around did not reveal the Oldhams. Rusty glanced anxiously up the street. Andy knew he was looking for Farley.

Rusty said, "Let's try this other one."

He headed for another, which Andy knew by reputation. Its sign marked it as LONE STAR GROCERY, with smaller letters proclaiming that it dealt in the finest of tobacco and spiritous liquors, and a billiard table from St. Louis. It was known as a hangout for off-duty state police and others of Union leanings. Most old Confederates avoided it.

Buddy Oldham sat at a table, a full glass and a half-empty bottle in front of him. Clyde Oldham stood with his back turned. He was haranguing half a dozen listeners with an account of how they had been unjustly dismissed from the state police force because of a natural mistake anyone might have made. "The old man was a die-hard rebel anyway," he declared. "Ought to've been killed years ago, him and Farley, too."

Buddy recognized Rusty and pushed his chair back from the table. He called to his brother. "Clyde."

Clyde was so busy talking that he did not hear the first time. Buddy repeated the call and stood up. "Clyde, looky who just came in."

Clyde turned. He froze a moment, then placed a hand on his pistol. "Rusty Shannon, you are under arrest."

Rusty said, "You've got no authority to arrest anybody. But if you want to try, there's a lot bigger game than me out yonder lookin' for you."

Buddy asked, "And who would that be?"

The startled expression in Clyde's face indicated that he already guessed. He spoke the name fearfully. "Farley Brackett?"

Rusty nodded. "He's on his way. May already be here. I'd advise you boys to go out the back door and not let your shirttails touch you 'til you're in the next county. Maybe two counties over."

Clyde's voice was shaky. "How come you tellin' us?"

"Because I want to keep you alive, at least 'til you sign my farm back to me."

"That'll be a cold day in hell." Clyde jerked his head. "Come on, Buddy." He started for the back door.

Buddy did not follow. Stubbornly he said, "I ain't scared of Farley Brackett. Almost got him a couple of times. Get him now and maybe they'll take us back into the police. Even if they don't, there's a reward on him."

Clyde was halfway to the back door. "I never seen a dead man collect a reward. Come on, Buddy, let's go while we can."

"No. I'm takin' Farley Brackett." Buddy started for the front. Clyde trotted after him and grabbed a handful of Buddy's shirt. Buddy jerked loose and went out the door.

Trembling, Clyde started after him but stopped, still inside the saloon.

"Come on, you men," he called. "Buddy don't stand a chance. You got to help him."

Nobody seemed much inclined to move. Rusty said, "He's your brother. You stop him."

Clyde's hands shook as he surveyed the men in the room, some of them state police. "If we work together we can get Brackett this time. We'll split the reward, even money for everybody."

Nobody moved.

Clyde drew his pistol and shuffled uncertainly out the door. Rusty and Andy followed.

Andy asked Rusty, "Ain't you goin' to stop them?"

Rusty answered gravely, "It's gone out of our hands. The only thing that'll stop Buddy now is a bullet."

Buddy stood in the center of the street, pistol in hand, waiting. Farley was riding toward him. Other men, sensing what was building, hurried out of the way. As Farley dismounted and dropped his reins, Buddy shouted, "Farley Brackett, you are under arrest in the name of the law!"

Brackett did not reply. He walked toward Buddy. Buddy shouted at him to stop, but Farley kept coming. Buddy raised the pistol and fired.

Farley did not even flinch. He drew his revolver and put two shots into Buddy's chest. Buddy buckled forward and fell on his face. He twitched a couple of times and was still.

Clyde made a noise that was almost a scream. The hand that held the pistol shook uncontrollably. He tried to raise the weapon, but he could not lift it. It was as if it weighed a hundred pounds.

Farley strode past Buddy and bore down on Clyde. Clyde cried out, "No!" His whole body was shaking. The pistol fell from his hand, and he sank to his knees.

"For God's sake, don't kill me."

"You wounded my mother. You killed my old daddy," Farley shouted at him. "Now pick up that pistol and die like a man."

Clyde hunched over, sobbing. "Oh God. Don't." He twisted around, trying to find Rusty. "Shannon, help me. Don't let him do it."

Andy did not know whether to pity the man or walk over and spit on him. He looked at Rusty, seeking Rusty's reaction.

Rusty walked forward to stand beside Clyde. "Farley, you've killed Buddy. One ought to be enough. I need Clyde to stay alive."

Farley hesitated, then leveled his pistol almost in Clyde's face. "I need him dead worse than you need him alive."

Rusty stepped between the two men. "I said one is enough. You'd better get on your horse and ride. There's a bunch of state police comin' around the courthouse."

Farley did not appear to believe him until he heard the captain shout. He gave Clyde a poisonous look. "All right, Shannon. But whatever you need him for, you better take care of it quick, because I'll be back."

He ran to his horse. He spurred out between two buildings and was gone. The captain called for his men to get their horses, but it would take them a few minutes.

A few minutes was all Farley Brackett needed.

Rusty reached down and took hold of Clyde's collar. "Get up from there. You're goin' over to the courthouse with me and sign some papers."

Clyde had quit sobbing. He resisted Rusty's strong pull. "I ain't signin' nothin'."

"You will. I know where Farley's goin'. Mess with me and I'll take you to him."

Andy knew that was a bluff, but he kept a straight face. Rusty too, could play the trickster.

Reluctantly Clyde got up onto wobbly legs. "You wouldn't do that. You wouldn't turn a man over to somebody like Farley."

"I will if you don't dot every i and cross every t just like Judge Burmeister tells you."

It took about an hour for the judge to write out the deed and for all parties to sign it. Clyde's signature was shaky but legal. Done, Rusty said, "Judge, after I get the place cleaned up, I'd like you to come out and see it. We'll barbecue a hog."

"That would make me glad, Private Shannon. Glad indeed."

Rusty and Andy escorted Clyde to his horse. Clyde was still in shock, his gaze roaming up and down the street as if he expected Farley Brackett to come charging back any minute. He asked, "What we goin' to do about Buddy?"

Rusty said, "The county will take care of the buryin'. If I was you I'd leave before Farley shows up again and buries *you*. I wouldn't stop runnin' 'til I got to Louisiana. Maybe even Mississippi."

Farley had ridden westward. Clyde reined his horse eastward and put him into a lope. Andy doubted that he would slow down until the horse was exhausted. He said, "I hope we've seen the last of him. And Farley, too."

Rusty said, "You never know."

Up the street a wagon arrived, driven by a black farmhand. Bethel

Brackett sat beside him. Rusty watched them. "Looks like they're headed for the doctor's. I expect they've got Mrs. Brackett in the wagon."

"That's the way I figure it."

Rusty made a thin smile. "That Bethel's a nice-lookin' girl but a little light in weight. Maybe you'd better go see if you can be any help to her."

Andy nodded. "I think I'll do that." He trotted up the street.

Rusty held the deed tightly in his hand. Watching Andy speak to the girl, he was reminded of Josie Monahan. Soon as he caught up doing what was needful around the farm, he would write Josie a letter.

He might even take it to her himself.

EPILOGUE

By the December election of 1873, the disenfranchised Confederate veterans had regained the right to vote. Two to one, they chose Richard Coke over the longtime reconstruction governor, Edmund J. Davis, a basically honest man who had been given too much power for his own good or the good of the people of Texas. Davis for a time rejected the results and maintained that the election was unconstitutional. As the inauguration date approached in January 1874, Davis held out, refusing to relinquish his office. For several days armed groups from both sides jockeyed for position in and around the state capital, threatening but never quite coming to violence.

Barricaded in the capitol building, Davis twice telegraphed President Ulysses S. Grant, begging for military force to keep him in office. Grant refused, advising him to give up the struggle. Davis did, finally, and a new era dawned in Texas.

A new constitution was written, guaranteeing that no governor ever again would have dictatorial powers. The Texas Rangers were reorganized, stronger and more efficient than ever before.